OVER~~TURE~~

BY EMILY DONOHO

Gypsum Moon Publishing

Overturned

This is a work of fiction. Real places, institutions, incidents, and United States Supreme Court cases are mentioned, but the characters are the product of the author's imagination. Any resemblance to actual persons, living or dead, is entirely coincidental.

First paperback edition
published by Gypsum Moon Publishing, March 2022

Cover design © March 2022 by Emily Donoho

ISBN 978-1-8380357-3-0

To James, my partner, for his indefatigable support and computer wizardry, and my parents for believing in my writing. This book has been a long time in the making. I also want to thank my horses, for getting me out of the house occasionally, Aki Smith and Robin Rice for their patience and editing skills, the Writer's Detective Group on Facebook for technical advice, and Joe Garret and Katie Bowen for medical expertise.

Epitaph

If you see in a province the oppression of the poor and the
violation of justice and righteousness, do not be amazed at the
matter, for the high official is watched by a higher, and there are
yet higher ones over them.
--Ecclesiastes 5:8

Who is the third who walks always beside you?
When I count, there are only you and I together
But when I look ahead up the white road
There is always another one walking beside you
Gliding wrapt in a brown mantle, hooded
I do not know whether a man or a woman
—But who is that on the other side of you?
    -- T.S. Eliot, *The Waste Land*

CONTENTS

Part 1

Chapter One

February 2010

A blizzard blew silently against the windshield of the Ford sedan. Individual snowflakes hung against the glass, scurrying at the pane before whirling into a million others. Roads, other cars, and Washington Heights itself dissolved into a sheer white wall. Squinting, searching the white for the edges of the road, Alex Boswell gently eased his car alongside the square low-rises and ornate pre-war brownstones, passing shopfronts busy with mom-and-pop stores, salons, bakeries, car mechanics, Kosher delis, and Dominican restaurants. The neighborhood was vibrant, lively, a dizzying convergence of cultures and community that hadn't yet been eaten away by gentrification. Today, wind and snow dampened its energy. A handful of Dominican street food vendors braved the weather while other Heights residents hurried along the sidewalks or huddled under awnings.

Even in a snowstorm, you can't escape the memories. Twenty years ago, the Heights was the epicenter of the crack epidemic. Dealers on every corner. Shootings every day. The fallout touching everyone, like a plague or malicious wind. Alex saw himself canvassing a nearby building after a drug murder, and one resident of a more law-abiding nature with a sign on his door stating, *Crack next door,* and a hand-drawn arrow pointing at the neighboring apartment. Comic and tragic, all at once. A homicide detective sees both sides.

It occurred to him that he hadn't been in Washington Heights for a DOA in over a year, which would have been unheard of in the early 1990s.

It also occurred to him that his partner, Ray Espinosa, had been complaining for the last ten minutes about his seventeen-year old daughter's boyfriend, and he expected a response.

"Uh, well, who doesn't make stupid decisions about dating at seventeen, or you know, at fifty-two?" Alex turned the car onto West 188th Street.

"Yeah, you sleeping with an ADA last year wasn't clever," noted Ray, with his usual degree of tact.

"Not my best decision." Like most of his relationships. He tapped the brakes, descending the hill. The wheels locked. "Fuck," he growled, tapping harder, but the car fought his requests. It lurched sideways. Alex yanked the wheel into the skid, but the tires skated on sheet ice. Nothing to grip. The back end swung around. They were going to hit something. A curb. Another car. The sedan stopped facing the wrong way on 188th.

"Shit," Ray said.

Alex lost his breath and couldn't speak. He delicately feathered the accelerator with his right foot, guiding the car into a tentative U-turn. *Nothing happened other than an unplanned donut,* he admonished himself. *At least pretend it's not a big deal.* Veins in his head swelled with blood. Sweat felt like a slimy film between his hands and the steering wheel. Dammit, this crap was *not* what he needed on his way to a crime scene. Another car accident in 2002 had opened an abyss. He'd broken down in late '04, winding up with diagnoses of post-traumatic stress disorder and depression. He'd ticked every box in the *DSM-IV:* flashbacks, dissociative experiences, suicidal thoughts. When another vehicle had t-boned the one he was in, it had spun one-hundred-eighty degrees, and Zoë Sheehan, the young assistant district attorney driving it, had been killed.

Snow flurries pelted the car. Bright yellow lights spiraled in his peripheral vision, swirling around the snow. His chest hurt, like a clamp tightening around his heart.

Ray looked at him closely. "This is triggering you."

"No," he panted. "Well, yes, maybe. But it's fine. I'll be fine."

"You can deal with this crime scene?"

"Do I have a choice?"

Detectives and uniforms roamed everywhere, on their phones, on their radios. Once it started, it wasn't like there was a switch in his head where he could turn it off, and yes, his psychiatrist taught him relaxation exercises, but they don't do shit in the middle of a frenetic crime scene.

Just man up and deal. Before he started therapy, wasn't that his trusted *modus operandi*?

He wiped snow out of his eyes, then approached a young patrol officer guarding the boundary between the staging area and the crime scene. Behind him, NYPD tape sealed off the benches and the snowy lawn at the corner of Inwood Hill Park, bordered by Dyckman Street and Payson Avenue. More strips of tape blocked off Payson and the gravel path leading into the park.

"Whaddaya got?" Alex shoved his fingers into his armpits, hiding the trembling, warming his hands.

"I've been sitting on the DOA, Detective. It's bad." The officer's teeth chattered. Snow peppered his dark blue uniform with white flecks that melted into the blue, only to be replaced by more flecks. "You hear?"

"I hear what?" No trash talk from the uniform, a bad sign. Already, he saw news vans parallel parking along Dyckman. Another bad sign.

"DOA's a child," the cop responded. "Six or seven year old girl. Black. She's been left in the park."

"Aw, fuck." His stomach lurched towards his feet. A kid. Not a long-term drug addict or a homeless person or somebody who no one other than Manhattan North Homicide would give a damn about. A kid thrown away and discarded, a true victim, a case that made you feel queasy no matter how seasoned you were. "Where's the path into the scene?" Alex asked, focusing his mind on practicalities. Tangled ropes of crime scene tape, arranged like airport security mazes, marked out no clear paths.

"Uh, Detective Indelicata said it's better to get CSU in there quickly, so it's just kinda keeping civilians out," stuttered the young cop.

As if this wasn't already a shitshow, Alex thought, tasting arid bitterness in his mouth. All it needed was Vito Indelicata.

He spotted the precinct detective, encircled by a herd of blue uniforms and NYPD windbreakers. Vito was sixty-two, the age by which most cops had long since retired, but he radiated vitality and enthusiasm, middle age and three decades of working the streets having left his considerable energy untouched. Vito was the Big Man, brashly Italian, a veteran of the 34th Precinct detective squad, arrogant, extraverted, hardass, everything a TV detective should be but inhabiting the real world, loudly. The brass loved him. They gave him the Medal of Honor in '95. Last year, they gave him the Medal of Valor, right before he published a book about his life in the NYPD and secured interviews on all the talk shows, publicizing it. He lapped up the attention, delighted by seeing his face on television, savoring his opportunity to tell America about 'real' detective work and, mainly, himself.

Alex had read the book. Everyone had read the book. Everyone had wanted to know if they were in it and what Vito said about them.

Alex hadn't actually read it from cover to cover. Rather, he'd borrowed a kindle off a colleague in MNHS, then he'd searched the ebook for his own name. It wasn't exactly *The Wire.*

"Ray, this shit's like science fiction," he had complained to his partner. "Have you read it? *'Alex Boswell arrives on the scene. He's the youngest detective in the Manhattan North Homicide squad, prickly and quirky, a brilliant investigator were he not drowning his brilliance in a bottle of Jack Daniels. He has these deep brown eyes that are like pools of chocolate and these long eyelashes that make him look like he's in a dream, the kind of look that women buy lots of mascara for. As TARU are setting up their surveillance, Boswell is wandering around the parking lot drinking Jack from a bottle until he's sweating whiskey and can barely put a sentence together. The sergeant sends him home. Such a waste of talent, we say.'* Prickly? What the fuck. What's he talking about? None of that's true. I never drank on the job like that, like walking around getting fucked up at a crime scene with a bottle of whiskey. That gets your ass fired, and I was a high functioning alcoholic."

A slight smile had toyed with Ray's mouth. "It's not complete bullshit. He spelled your name right and said you have nice eyes."

And Alex had realized that if Ray, 'Princess Ray' of all people, was telling him he was taking it too seriously, he was probably taking it too seriously. He had lowered his reading glasses and batted his eyelashes at Ray. "Yeah, both of those are true."

On seeing Vito bellowing orders at people as he hurtled towards himself and Ray, Alex thought, of course Vito took digs at him in his fucking book. Should he have expected auspicious treatment? Respect? No chance. He had little patience for Vito and his ego, and he doubted that Vito had much time for him. Thank God for murders in the Heights sinking to around .02 per 100,000. The neighborhood was as safe as it had ever been. Alex hardly worked any cases in the 34th Precinct these days. And with a dozen detectives in the precinct squad and a dozen in MNHS, his odds of not working with Vito were a favorable 24-1.

This time, his horse lost the race. Vito greeted them with an overenthusiastic grin. "Hey, fuckin' hell, they wake up and send Homicide after all. What's up, man?"

"A dead kid in a city park," Alex said flatly. Vito would never know about his illness. Adrenaline clouded his head. It curdled inside his stomach. His heart thudded in double-time. But he had to pull himself together, control the crime scene. The crime scene was already out of control, so busy with officers and police vehicles that it looked as if a blue and white army had invaded.

"Christ, Lex. Haven't seen you in like a *year*," Vito exclaimed. "I got a book published and everything. You know about my book? I even been on TV. I thought you woulda shown up for the launch party. It was a *great* fucking party. Even got strippers. Fuckin' epic." He smiled at the memory of his great party. "I wondered if you was still alive."

Unfortunately, Alex thought, feeling even more sour and irritable. He shoved his hands into his windbreaker pockets, surveying the scene from the edge of the cordon no one else had noticed. Crime Scene techs and detectives traipsed carelessly around the park, the street, kicking the snow and mud into slushy trenches until it looked like the Somme. You keep people on the same paths through the crime scene; you document who has access, minimizing contamination, improving your likelihood of finding admissible evidence. Vito hadn't done that. It was a free-for-all.

Alex released a leaden sigh. On days like this, he believed the entire purpose of his job was detangling other people's disasters. Well, it was what it was. Behind him, Vito was babbling about his book sales. They had a dead child! *Just shut the fuck up,* he thought, but swallowed the words before he said them aloud. Snapping at Vito would make the precinct detective into a bigger pain in the ass. Tuning Vito out, Alex threaded around the airport security maze and approached the DOA. She'd been left underneath the red oak tree beside the children's playground. A sodden bedsheet had been wadded up near her feet.

"Why the fuck does this crime scene look like Midtown on a Friday night?" Alex snarled. "And what's the deal with that motherfucking sheet? Was it on her?"

"Yeah, the first wit I talked to and her friend put it on her, then called the police. They thought they was being respectful," said Vito.

"So someone's moved it before I got here?"

"One of the first officers did," said Vito with a *don't-look-at-me* shrug.

"Oh, my God," groaned Alex. You couldn't expect civilians to know crime scene protocols, but any cop should know not to touch *anything*.

Vito touched his arm. "Be cool, Lex. Just 'cause it's in *Practical Homicide* don't mean we *gotta* do it. It's all good."

"Did you put out a BOLO yet? Contact Missing Persons?"

"I'm getting there, man."

"Clearly," growled Alex as he donned rubber gloves and squatted beside the DOA. If it was in Vernon Geberth's *Practical Homicide Investigation,* the death investigator's bible, you probably should do it. He remembered why he spent years skirting Vito's cases.

Ray cast him a mincing smile, then said, "Indelicata, I want to talk to the witness who found her. Why don't you show me where she is, huh?" Still smiling tightly, Ray tugged Vito away so the man could bloviate somewhere else. He knew Alex liked a quiet dialogue with a crime scene.

Alex sucked in a lung-filling breath. Cold bit at his nostrils. *Forget the woozy white noise. Focus.* The child wore jeans and a New York Knicks hoodie. Methodically, he scanned the girl for injuries. Blood had dried and matted in the black hair. Head wound. He leaned forward, studying the bloody dent in the scalp. Wouldn't know until the autopsy, but it moved to the front of the line as a prospective cause of death. What if it was a sex thing? The thought churned up stronger ripples of nausea.

Gently, he touched the girl's limbs. They were flaccid, pliable.

"You got what you need, Andre?" he asked the assistant Medical Examiner.

Andre Brown, a Black man in his forties, indicated his camera and some sample baggies. "Yeah, we can move her."

Alex pulled up her shirt, noting patches of blue skin with pale splotches on the side, the shoulder, the hip. Maximum lividity. She'd been dead for at least eight to twelve hours. She wasn't in *rigor mortis,* so make that at least twenty-four hours, more if she'd been outside for a while. He scrutinized the head wound again. Head wounds bleed like crazy, but no blood had stained the snow, the damp vegetation, or the sheet, for that matter. The lividity patterns told him she was on her side when she died and had stayed that way long enough for the pattern to become fixed. But she lay face down in the snow. *Fuck,* Alex mouthed inaudibly, his gut fluttery, and he flicked his eyes around the park that he suspected wasn't the primary crime scene.

"She was moved," he said flatly.

"Yep, probably," agreed Brown.

"You see that head wound, Andre?"

"Yep. But gotta get her downtown to know for sure."

"She's outta rigor. Could be at least twenty-four hours."

"Who knows. Or she never went in. She's outside. If she's been outside for a while, it might not have set in, and kids sometimes don't get it, 'cause they don't have the muscle bulk."

"Yeah." Alex knew all this – just his wishful thinking that they could swiftly and efficiently estimate time-of-death.

"People on Everest don't go into rigor, but they're so fucking frozen it looks like rigor."

Alex squinted. Snowflakes caught in his eyelashes. "Everest?"

"Yeah, did you know bodies just stay up there? It's almost impossible to move them. If you climb the popular route, you actually gotta step over this guy they've called 'Green Boots.' Everyone who climbs it steps over him. That's like hundreds of people."

"Sounds like this fucking crime scene."

"I think that would put me off," reflected Brown. "Having to walk over a dead guy on my way up the mountain. I think there's actually more than one 'cause it's super dangerous to get them off the mountain. I mean, that and the slow death of all your cells and pulmonary edema."

"Yeah, I found you can kill plenty of cells by just drinking a lot, and it's cheaper and less like hard work." Alex thought, *see, I'm not humorless.* Vito's characterization of him in his book made him feel weirdly defensive.

He reached into the girl's pockets and fished out three frozen gummy bears, hard as colored rocks. Lightly, he squeezed them in his gloved hand, then he slipped them into an evidence baggie. How long do gummy bears take to freeze? Long enough to fit in with his observations about lividity. There were grass stains on the jeans and another unidentifiable stain on the hoodie. Blood? Something else?

Wind-blown snow lashed at his eyes, and he held his forearm against his face as he creaked to his feet. Pain shot through his thighs and calves. Unhurried, he walked in a spiral around the girl, loosening his muscles, inspecting the ground for signs of disturbance. Crime Scene and half the Detective Bureau had taken care of that, blending the snow and mud into a brown, slushy gruel. Forget lifting any footprints. He removed his little Olympus digital camera from his pocket, then snapped photos of the girl, the park, the surrounding buildings. Sure, he had access to CSU's considerably more professional photos, but he liked having his own. He sketched the scene in his damp notepad, the DOA a stick figure in the middle of the page, and Alex counting his steps to estimate the distance between the girl and a bench, the playground, the oak trees, the spiky iron fence. What buildings have a line of sight on her? The row of walk-ups on the other side of Payson. He wrote down addresses. His hand shook. Anyone who saw would think he was cold.

He sensed Ray's presence at his back and spun around to face his partner.

"I talked to the person who found her." With a queasy look on his face, Ray eyed the DOA as Brown bagged her hands and then signaled his assistant to ready the stretcher.

"Vito said she put the sheet on her."

"Yeah. She lives in that building. Number 49." Ray pointed to one of the five-story sandstone walk-ups.

"She know this kid?" Alex's fingers had turned into lumps of ice.

"Never seen her, she said. Found her like an hour ago, just lying here, called the cops."

"Why the sheet?"

"What Vito told you. She thought it was the respectful thing to do."

"Could she be related?"

"A little old Cuban lady? I doubt it."

Alex glanced at Vito, who was gesticulating to shivering cops like a preacher on a pulpit.

"I don't think she's a suspect," Ray added.

"I wanna call every precinct in the city. Get that damned BOLO out. I don't know why the fuck Vito doesn't do these things immediately. I'm gonna personally kill the cop who moved the sheet." Alex rested his flank against the hood of the nearest squad car.

"I already did," said Ray. "Read him the riot act. We gotta canvass those buildings."

"Yeah."

Ray ran off to organize a canvass, and Alex took a moment to breathe, to loosen the wires squeezing his chest. Distractions interfered with his concentration. Helicopters. Radios. A young assistant district attorney leaping out of a car, demanding, "Alex, what do you think? A child! Jesus, this is gonna be a mess. Do you have kind of ID?"

"No," he said tetchily.

He would live with feeling ill, anxiety like a roadblock in his head, his heart beating into his ribs like a drummer in those metal bands his youngest daughter used to like. So long as he didn't succumb to an intense flashback, or dissociate, he could get by.

They started with the first floor of the walk-up on the corner of Dyckman and Payson. As people answered, Alex studied their faces, asking himself, where were they, on a scale of lying like rugs to genuinely stunned and clueless. Always the latter. "Oh my God, a child?" they exclaimed, if they spoke English. Half the people in the buildings spoke

14

only Spanish, so Ray questioned them while Alex listened to the faint thrum of wind beating against the windows. He picked out the odd Spanish word. *Nada. Lo siento.*

Alex and Ray clambered through all five floors of that building, then they followed the same procedures in the adjacent ones. By the time they'd ascended to the fifth floor of the fourth apartment block along Payson, they'd learned nothing useful, but Alex's knees, back, and the right side of his ribcage were in agony. To his dismay, he would be fifty-three tomorrow, his pains and general age-related deterioration insolently reminding him of that.

What now, he thought. Station officers at the park entrance for the next week. Any city park had regular night visitors – dog walkers, the homeless, kids drinking, addicts, anyone who liked solitude. Maybe someone saw something.

The detectives descended five flights of stairs, Alex concealing his limp. If he looked sore, Ray would flap about it and push him to take up yoga or vitamin supplements. As if that could fix an old gunshot wound! Holding his breath, he stepped out of the warm entryway, and the fangs of wind and snow pierced his face and neck. He cast his gaze over the street, shivering. Dozens of uniformed officers and plainclothes detectives wearing NYPD windbreakers patrolled Dyckman and Payson. Officers manned roadblocks where Dyckman intersected with Broadway and Seaman Avenue, and they taped off the entire corner of Inwood Hill Park. Vito had mobilized half the police department. There were more cops on the street than civilians. This was a problem. The crime scene cleared too fast, the park too crowded with uniforms, assistant MEs, crime scene techs, brass, detectives. Alex had arrived too late to control it. Vito loved redballs. Vito loved the bosses throwing every resource in the department at him, so he could throw it at a case and feel like he was commanding an army. But sometimes, you don't want an army, not immediately, not when you can learn something when the crime scene is still and silent, and you can examine it with calm, rational precision.

Alex's iPhone rang. He looked at it and muttered, "Dammit." It was his commanding officer, so he couldn't duck the call.

"Hello, Alex," said Lieutenant Joanna Gibson. "We've gotten a call from Lenox Hill Hospital." She sounded unruffled, as though giving a weather forecast. "They've had a patient come into their ER with some injuries on her hands and forearms, a broken wrist, claiming she was carjacked, and her daughter was in the car. You'd better go there forthwith."

"Lenox Hill?" he repeated. The Upper East Side. Nowhere near Inwood Hill Park.

"Yes," she confirmed.

"Ten-four, Lieu," he replied, already marching towards his car. He dabbed at snow stuck to his eyelashes. "Ray, Gibson wants us at Lenox Hill Hospital forthwith."

"Upper East Side?" said Ray.

"No, the *other* Lenox Hill Hospital."

Ray ignored his sarcasm. "They got something?"

"Yeah. Someone who says she was carjacked with her kid in the car." Alex wrote Vito a text. *I got a potential lead re mother. Will go downtown and check it out. Let me know if you find anything around here.* He trusted Gibson's instincts. She was still a detective at heart. If Lenox Hill had a real witness, victim, or perp, he wanted to keep Vito as far away as possible, like in Canada or Mexico. But he could not explain to Ray, Gibson, or to anyone else why he didn't trust New York City's most brilliant detective to carry out a tactful, restrained, and lawful interview with a key witness or suspect.

Ray wriggled through the *ad hoc* NYPD parking lot and drove downtown on Lenox. Alex adjusted his weight in the passenger seat and crossed one ankle over his knee. His guts entwined into knots

Meanwhile, his partner resumed complaining about his kid. "They're totally wild at that school. It's these kids she's hanging out with, man. Anna wants to transfer her to St. Margaret's…"

"A Catholic school?" interjected Alex. "You really think that won't be full of *other* kids whose parents shipped them there 'cause they were getting in trouble at a public school? It's an expensive way for her to find even sketchier friends."

"It'll teach her some damned values, some discipline," Ray grumbled, and Alex knew better than to continue arguing.

They parked in a loading bay at Lenox Hill Hospital, squeezing between the five RMPs already there. Missing Persons detectives and half a dozen Administration for Children's Services personnel had beat them to the hospital. The moment the doctors reported a missing child, every authority in the city had been notified. On entering the waiting room, Alex clocked a fat Italian detective with a handlebar mustache. Nick Selvio, a Missing Persons detective, once a colleague from the One-Oh-Three detective squad in the mid-80s.

"Whoa, Boswell." Selvio clasped Alex's hand, then gave him a thump on the back. "Lex. Do they still call you that? Wow. It's been a long time. In all the crime scenes, in all the world…"

"Yeah." When had he last seen Selvio? Was it that rooftop New Year party at his apartment in 1991? It scared him when he noticed the passage of time, twenty years, gone like a fast train. "You here on this alleged carjacking thing?"

"Yes. You look good. Have you lost weight?"

Lost weight? He was almost fifty-three, and his diet was dreadful. "I doubt it. You talk to this woman?" Selvio, he thought, had gained weight.

"I did. It's been a Bureau party here all day. There are a couple Special Victims detectives here somewhere, and Auto Crimes was here. Are you still MNHS? I didn't think we were bringing in Homicide yet."

"Yeah. This might have a connection to a homicide I'm working."

Selvio's eyes flickered down the corridor, then abruptly lowered to his memo pad. "Ah, fuck. Okay. She's called Gemma Lennon. Black. Twenty-eight years old. She's got an address in Inwood, on Isham Street, and said she was carjacked by a Hispanic male on Friday morning on West 186th and Audubon. Her daughter was in the car and is now missing, along with the car. She arrived at the ER here a couple hours ago with a concussion and a broken wrist. Admitted herself. No one was with her. Her daughter is called Suzanne Lennon. She's seven, and she was wearing a Knicks hoodie and jeans."

Isham Street was only a couple blocks away from the park. Alex gulped in a breath. "A Knicks hoodie?"

"Yeah."

"My DOA has a Knicks hoodie and coulda been dead for at least twenty-four hours. ME hasn't nailed it down but that could put it around Friday. Why the hell are we hearing about this on Sunday?"

"Well…" The detectives moved aside as medical staff pushed a gurney through the corridor. "I guess that's why you're here. You'd better talk to her." Selvio led everyone to the alleged victim's room.

Two ACS workers, a young guy and an older woman, were already there, engrossed in an intense conversation with a rail-thin Black woman, who was sitting on the bed, swathed in an oversized hospital gown. She had dark bruises on her right cheekbone and a cast on her right arm.

Selvio waved at the social workers, and they joined the gathering in the hallway.

17

Alex said, "I'm Detective Boswell, this is Detective Espinosa. We're Manhattan North Homicide. We need to talk to her. You got anything you can tell me first?"

Their eyes widened. "Homicide?" said the young guy, awestruck.

"Yeah. She on your radar? Before today, I mean."

"No, she's not."

"No investigations or anything?"

"Nope. Her child allegedly went missing on Friday, but neither she nor anyone else reported it until today. So, we have some concerns about that."

"Well, no shit." Alex eyed the woman through the glass in the door. The headache spiked into his eye sockets, accompanied by shimmering auras and light nausea. The drive downtown hadn't cleared this up. Well, he had to grit his teeth and bear it. He opened the door and said, "Hi, Ms. Lennon. I'm Detective Boswell, and this is Detective Espinosa."

"I already talked to a detective," Lennon said tonelessly.

"Yeah, I know. But we're in a different department and just trying to figure out what happened. We hear you were carjacked? Can you tell us about it?"

"It was on West 186th." That same emotionless tone.

He expected more cooperation and urgency from someone whose kid had been taken in a carjacking. "We're here to help you, but you gotta help us out. Detective Selvio said it was at 186th and Audubon. What happened at 186th and Audubon?"

"This man came up, threw me out of the car. He hit me and threw me out of the car. I landed on the road on my arm. Then he got in and drove away."

"Where did he hit you?"

"I don't know. My head I guess."

"With his fist or did he use some kinda weapon?"

"I don't know. He ripped open the door, and I was overpowered. Just suddenly, I was on the road. And the car... it had gone."

"Do you know if there were any witnesses? Did anyone stop and help you?"

"No one was there," she sniffed. "No one saw."

Nowadays, where in Manhattan was there *no one* in the middle of the day? Letting that slide, Alex moved on with his questions. "Was anyone else in the car?"

"Yes." Her voice slipped to a shaky whisper. "My girl... My girl was in the car."

First, establish that her kid is or isn't the DOA in Inwood Hill Park. If she is, then prod her for more details, canvass 186th and Audubon for any witnesses, put a description of the car on all the wires, run her name through the soup of acronyms. If not, leave it with the precinct detectives, ACS, and Missing Persons; make it not his problem.

"When did this happen?" Ray asked.

"I don't know," Lennon mumbled.

"You told Detective Selvio it was Friday," Ray pointed out.

"Yeah, Friday."

"Why didn't you report it until now?"

She moaned, "I thought it was a nightmare. I thought I would wake up, and it would be over."

Ray and Alex exchanged a look, and Alex asked, "Have you got a picture of her? Like in your wallet or on your phone or something? Anything we can use so people know what she looks like."

"No, he already asked me," she wailed, pointing at Selvio. "I never took pictures."

"Hey, it's okay, it's cool," Ray said in his most reassuring voice, as if comforting one of his children. "Look, we found someone. It's probably not her, but you know, it's better to rule it out. I mean, we gotta know. We gotta know who we found. It's not easy. I'm really sorry, but it's a thing we gotta do. We're gonna show you a photo, okay?"

This was the worst way to ID a vic. The least humane. But Alex slid the Olympus out from underneath the windbreaker and flicked through his crime scene photos until he arrived at a not-too-gory close-up of the DOA's face. Part of him hoped that the kid in Inwood Hill Park wasn't Lennon's kid. When he showed her the camera, she squeaked out a distressed warble and rolled into a ball in the hospital bed.

"Is it...?" Ray began to say.

"Oh," she whispered, her voice so soft that Alex had to strain his ears to hear. "You found...How? I can't... Suzanne... Yes."

Alex put the camera away. "I'm very sorry."

"We're gonna give you a moment, okay?" Ray said. "Then... we're gonna have to ask a few more questions about what happened, and someone from Victim's Services will be here to help you out."

Along with Selvio and the ACS workers, they reconnoitered in the corridor. Alex kept his hands hidden, shoved into the windbreaker pockets and scrunching the fabric around his fingers.

"You think she was really jacked?" Selvio wondered.

Alex shrugged expansively. "Who knows? Why the fuck did she wait two days to tell someone? Your kid is taken in a carjacking, you don't wait, do you? You run screaming to the nearest cop. Unless it's someone you know, like there's a custody dispute or something else fucked up. I guess there are reasons. But we go with the story, we get her talking…" He looked at Ray, and Ray bobbed his head, understanding. So long as Gemma Lennon was a witness or a complainant, they could interview her, but as soon as she became a suspect, they would have to read her the *Miranda* rights or talk her into waiving them, potentially losing out on any semi-legal opportunity to question her.

In a conga line bound to panic any witness, the detectives and ACS filed back into the examination room.

"We are very sorry," Alex repeated. "Is there anything we can do? You sure there's no one you can call?"

"No…" Lennon burrowed her face into the pillow. Then, "My sister…"

"Your sister?"

"Stephanie… She's in Scarsdale. She's head chef at a restaurant. Her husband is a policeman."

"Good. You have your cell? You can get us your sister's number?"

Lennon pointed to the cell phone on the bedside table. Alex chewed on the soft inside of his lip, thinking, the alleged carjacker hadn't stolen the cell phone. He handed it to Lennon, who unlocked it and found her sister's number. "That's her."

Ray wrote the number in his memo book. "Can you tell us any more details about what happened?" he pressed. "We need everything you can remember. Even little things that don't seem important."

"I can't. I told you. I don't remember."

"When he left, which way did he drive?"

"I don't know."

"What did the man look like?"

"He was Hispanic. Like you."

"Right." Ray worked hard to keep his expression impassive, professional. "Was he young? Old? What was he wearing? Did he say anything? Did he have a beard? Glasses? Clean-shaven? Anything."

"I can't *remember*," she cried.

"Could you recognize him if you saw him?"

"I don't know."

"You don't think it was anyone you knew? Would anyone have wanted to hurt you or Suzanne?"

"*No.* I didn't *know* him."

"Is Suzanne's father still involved?" Alex's forehead creased with concern, his lips slightly parted, his hands hidden in the windbreaker, his illness at his heels, the trembling not letting him forget about that.

"He's *dead*. But he's never been around since I was pregnant."

"Does he have relatives?"

"No."

"Is that a road you drive a lot? Would someone know you were gonna be there?"

"*Who* would care about that? No."

"Okay, what were you doing before you got to that intersection? Where were you going?"

"Does it matter?"

Alex shuffled closer to her. "Anything you can tell us about that day helps."

"I just *can't*," she whimpered. "Those other detectives asked me the same thing, but I can't remember."

"What about the car?" Ray asked. "Your car?"

"It's a Honda. A Honda Accord."

"What color?"

"Grey."

Ray smiled. "I have an old Accord. What year's yours?"

"2002."

"Same age as mine. Great car. It's never let me down." Ray tried to put her at ease. "What's the license plate? We can get guys out looking for it."

"MHT-754," she muttered.

Ray scribbled that in the memo pad while Lennon wrapped herself in the hospital sheets, turning her back to them – gone. The three detectives saw the road's end with this interview and caught one another's eyes before retreating.

"She won't be let out for another day or so," Selvio said when they convened in the corridor, liaising with the SVU and Auto Crimes detectives.

"They think her injuries were caused by some sort of blunt force trauma," added the SVU detective.

"You think?" Alex rolled his eyes.

"You haven't changed," commented Selvio. "He's always quick with the sarcasm, isn't he?" he said to Ray.

"Always," agreed Ray with a smile.

"Do the doctors think the injuries are consistent with her story?" Alex asked. He would interview the doctors himself, once he caught up to one.

"Possibly," replied SVU. "If she put her hand out while being thrown onto the ground and hit her head in the struggle. She doesn't have any abrasions, though."

"Like you'd get if you fell onto road," said Alex.

"Yeah."

"Huh." Alex touched his chin as two nurses ran past them. "What about injuries on her head or face?"

"No smoking guns one way or another, I'm afraid," sighed Selvio. "Concussion could be from an assault. Or from a car accident. Or from falling in the shower."

"Lex, aren't you always saying think like a defense lawyer?" Ray said. "Maybe she's lying. Maybe she isn't. Maybe someone she knows wants to blackmail her, and she was afraid to report it. Maybe she just doesn't trust the police, like a lot of people in this city. Maybe someone wanted to steal an eight-year old Accord and didn't know there was a kid in the back."

"Who the hell wants to steal an eight-year old Accord?" Alex smiled bleakly.

"That sensible drug dealer who wants a safe, reliable family station wagon."

"Ya'll will verify your ID?" interrupted SVU, eager to wash a redball out of his hair.

"Yeah," Alex answered, serious again. His iPhone buzzed inside his pocket. His boss? An ADA? Someone else wondering why he hadn't closed the case in half a day?

Fuck, Vito. He wished it had been his boss or an ADA. The precinct detective texted, *What you got?*

Likely ID of DOA. Mother in hospital with concussion. BOLO I'll send out has details, Alex typed back.

I should go to Lenox Hill.

Oh, God no. Alex crushed his tongue between his teeth. Selvio, Auto Crimes, and ACS had already established a police presence with Lennon here at Lenox Hill. They had sent other teams to 186th and Audubon.

She's not compos mentis *enough for further interview,* he wrote. *Missing Persons and Auto Crimes at 186 and Audubon. You should go there.*

The phone rang as he texted. The ME's office.

"Hey, Alex," Dr. Brown said. "Your bosses have lit a fire under my boss' ass – they want the Inwood Hill DOA autopsied like now, so she's at the front of the line."

"Yes, okay," Alex said, thinking, good, an official cause of death and whatever else the autopsy revealed would shift this case forward. It also saved him from running a canvass with Vito. His illness smoldered inside his central nervous system, the past and present merging together, his coping abilities stretched to the limits, and Vito's blustery narcissism pushing him far beyond any limits. His shrink called it 'trigger stacking.'

"Ray, they're gonna cut her open now," he said levelly. "I should go. You wanna head to 186th and Audubon? Meet Vito there and start canvassing for people who saw the car, or who saw Lennon. If her story has a single grain of truth to it, she'll have been staggering around the neighborhood, looking for the subway, a taxi, a bus, you know, some way of getting from there to here."

"Okay." Ray was typing something on his phone. "I'll run you to First, then go back uptown."

Chapter Two

The snow outran the snowplows. Vehicles marched cautiously along faint parallel tracks cutting across the roads. Brooklyn and Queens were invisible in the white shroud, while the Queensboro and Williamsburg bridges had turned into halos of lights strung across the dull, metallic river.

Alex sat in the passenger seat with his heart racing like he was on a crack high. He swore at the NYPD for being too cheap to put winter tires on unmarked sedans. He swore at his malfunctioning brain. His near-miss of a donut on 188th had shaken him. But it damn well shouldn't trigger an uncontrollable episode – like the six weeks of sick leave and then three months of limited duty he'd miraculously survived after he was first diagnosed. Then, he'd severed tendons in his left wrist by punching out a window during a dissociative episode. It took months to heal – and it still ached when he spent hours typing – but he needed those five months to learn some vague control strategies for the flashbacks. He couldn't afford a severe dissociative episode during a warrant entry or a footchase or anything else broadly dangerous.

While he fought PTSD on one side of the ring, he battled depression and medications on the other. There were the meds that screwed with his bowels and gave him petrifying cramps and the shits for weeks. There were the meds that incapacitated him with brain fog, leaving him standing vacantly over a shirt, wondering how to put it on. There were the meds that sent his heartrate skyrocketing, like he'd snorted one line of coke too many. Finally, there was sertraline, which stabilized his volatile mood swings but caused headaches and cloudy tiredness. He lived with the headaches. After six months, his flashbacks and panic attacks were upsetting but not overwhelming, while the psychopharmaceuticals checked his depression. Still, he felt untethered, as if his life had lost all direction. He wasn't handling his own cases, just supporting his colleagues with theirs, like a glorified admin guy. Worryingly, no one in the squad mocked him for sitting on his ass or malingering from full duty.

In fact, no one hurled any abuse whatsoever. What if they preferred him safely off the streets? Would they say that to his face? Although he'd mastered Excel and the antediluvian NYPD software, he was bored and short-tempered. He'd begged Jo Gibson to either take him off limited or transfer him to some post where he would be a permanent house cat. This sort-of-being-a-homicide-detective-but-not-really was driving him mad.

"Do you believe you're safe on the streets?" she'd asked. "And safe around a firearm?"

"Yeah," he had replied earnestly. "All I've done since the end of December is practice techniques for controlling the symptoms."

"You reckon they're controlled?"

"Yeah. Enough. I mean, I still get them sometimes, but it's not as intense."

"What does that mean?"

"It flashes in my head," he replied, setting his jaw as he hunted for words. It was something that the English language had no words for. "But doesn't last long. I don't... switch off... I guess...from reality."

"Right." The lieutenant unwrapped, then rewrapped her bright yellow scarf. She spoke slowly, elongating vowels in her Bronx African-American accent. "This isn't a question I want to ask, but... have you been... suicidal?"

"Not for a while. Not since February."

"That's only like five months ago."

"I really haven't thought about it," he said. "The meds help. I promise they help."

"Okay, we'll try it. But you gotta tell me if you're not handling things. The deal is that if you have any suicidal thoughts, you give me your gun back. Forthwith. And if your partners have concerns, I'm gonna ask that they tell me."

"Does anyone in this squad still trust me?" he'd asked bitterly. "No one's given me shit or said a word about going back."

"I ordered them to not push you. And it's hard for people, you know. Cops, dealing with mental health shit? What do you expect?"

Not a lot. A mentally ill homicide detective? Too much of a stereotype in fiction, but in reality, a good way to lose your gun if someone thought you were a danger to yourself, so you kept it as quiet as you could.

"I said you would do it when you were ready. But you hear me? I can't have you putting yourself or anyone else in danger."

"Got it."

"It will be a shitshow for both of us if something happens," she'd cautioned.

"I know."

"We're both playing fast and loose, Alex," she said in a grave tone. "We probably should have notified Occupational Health."

"I know."

If anyone had concerns, Alex never heard about it. He readjusted to the streets, chronically anxious that his meds were blunting his mind. Did his colleagues see it? He evaluated every eye-roll, quip, or whispered rumor hinting that they believed he'd lost his mental acuity. He worried about his sluggish brain whenever he found himself staring blankly at a file, fretful that some critical piece of evidence had slyly escaped his SSRI-addled brain.

Despite his whacked-out neurotransmitters, he handled his caseload, kept his clearance rate floating around or marginally above average, and his doubts about his capabilities on the job gradually subsided. His colleagues resumed giving him shit, a sure sign that a detective respects you. All the same, he cringed at the change in himself, the irrefutable awareness that the meds slowed his thoughts, and he no longer had the mental dexterity to keep sixteen cases in the air at one time, like he had in the '90s. But 2000s New York had calmed down, surprising everyone by becoming one of the safest big cities in the US. He hadn't been strangled by his own caseload in years.

Moreover, he hadn't hurt himself since late '04. Five years of cognitive-behavioral therapy never quite eliminated the flashbacks and dissociation, but he stayed off modified assignment. A few months ago, he'd started a new therapy called EMDR, where the psychiatrist asked him to move his eyes back and forth while consciously recalling a traumatic event, then rating how he felt about it on a numerical scale. He found it unsettling as hell, but he hadn't suffered a single flashback.

Nonetheless, his shrink had warned him that he was always looking at management rather than cure. Right now, he needed to manage the elevated heart rate and the headache. He jumped out of the car, squinting as the wind whipped snow into his eyes. "I'm gonna walk around the block."

Ray nodded, worried. "Want me to go with you?"

"Nah, I'll see you later. I'll call you after this is done."

Slush seeped into his shoes. Cars crept tentatively along First, and people waddled across the sidewalk, heads down against the beating wind. Alex trudged through the snow to East 29th Street. He fixed his gaze on the Nicholas Scopetta Children's Center, a rust-colored sandstone building with Neo-Gothic arches and cornices curling like ancient scrolls. From there, he tried visualizing his Calm Place, a vast desert in Africa or Australia with no people, no crime, no guns, no death investigations, just endless sky, high mesas, burnt red sand, a maze of red-walled canyons, and no snow. He had to imagine himself in that desert, far away from 29th Street and First Avenue, with wheels and car horns roaring in his ears and exhaust fumes steaming in his nostrils. True, he was never great at these visualizations, but he leaned on a lamp post, his eyes shut, attentive to his chest rising and falling. He grasped at the fulgurating image in his mind, a photo his daughter, who lived in Sydney, had sent him from her travels to Western Australia. Behind his eyelids, he sensed the occasional strange look from passerby. They probably assumed he was drunk or high, but in New York no one cared that much. After a couple minutes – he lacked the patience for more – he opened his eyes and retreated downtown on First, towards Bellevue Hospital Complex. The snow saturated his windbreaker and swirled around the traffic lights.

Ray was predictably parked in the same place, waiting. "You alright?"

"Fine. I'm gonna go in and see if the ME's started."

"You sure you gonna be all right?"

"My heart's not pounding as hard. I'm better off if I just get on with things."

Ray frowned, turning on the car's electrics, but he didn't start it.

"It's under control, Ray." Sometimes, he thought, the labels of PTSD and depression made him feel like he had more control over it; sometimes it made him feel more confused and stressed.

"You sure?"

"Yeah."

"Call me when you're done."

Alex stood for a moment, with snow dusting his hair and shoulders, his eyes lost on the blue Fusion rolling into the glacier of crawling vehicles on First until the traffic swallowed the car. He pushed through the double doors in the building's glass façade and signed his name on the log sheet. The receptionist abruptly switched windows from Facebook to an Excel spreadsheet, mumbling, "Hi, Alex," without shifting her eyes from the screen.

"Alex?" said Brown as he emerged from the examination room. "C'mon. I was just about to start."

Alex clasped his arms over his chest, shuddering at the sight of the bodies on tables, waiting in line for their turn under the knife. They were

27

white, Black, Hispanic, Jewish, Asian, African, Middle-Eastern, young, old, ODs, suicides, heart attacks, and only one common denominator – their deaths were officially unexplained within the jurisdiction of New York County. Most of these people weren't here because of crime. The best way to end up in the ME's office was to die alone. One man was being cut open by another assistant ME, while a gloomy Missing Persons detective rolled the deceased's fingers in black ink.

The stench of decomposition burned Alex's sinuses and throat. A shadow of mortality and loneliness brushed over him, freezing his insides, but he said to the ME, "Jesus, it's like Penn Station in here." Gallows humor brought you some distance between the living and the dead.

"Yeah, first stop on the way to the Hampdens," replied Brown. Then he spoke into his recorder. "I'm Dr. Andre Brown, Assistant Medical Examiner, beginning an autopsy on Jane Doe on February 11th 2010, case number 10-22-19. With me is Detective Alex Boswell from Manhattan North Homicide. Other than the head wound, there are no external injuries. She looks in good health. No superficial indications of sexual trauma or any abuse."

"No evidence she was forcibly restrained?"

"Nothing like that, Alex. But if she struggled with someone, there might be DNA under her fingernails. We'll obviously run it."

If they had an adult vic, Alex would banter with the ME, but neither could bring themselves to say much while autopsying a kid. Brown was the real hard man here, his face composed, professional, and he placed each organ on a scale and moved it to the table with as much emotion as a mechanic disassembling an engine.

When his examination arrived at the head wound, he commented, "It's a blunt force injury, but it's gone deep, like a centimeter deep, from something sharp. Corner of a table, a two-by-four, who knows. Can't really say."

Alex nodded, having come across some inventive weapons in his career, including a live iguana, a leg of lamb, and a frozen chicken.

"We'll take samples from around the wound, see if there are flecks of paint, wood, anything, but you know how it goes... we might not find anything we can identify or trace."

"Media's all over my ass with this case, so with my luck, no chance." Only in crime shows, crime novels and, unfortunately, the minds of jurors, is a detective guaranteed to identify forensic evidence on the victim traceable to an object that the detective will also find, and that the object won't have been cleaned, lost, contaminated.

Brown turned on his circular saw, then seconds later, he revealed the brain, a grey jellied mass. Alex felt blood draining from his head, and he steadied himself using the counter at his back. His stomach, still upset from his panic attack earlier, heaved and twisted, and he fought down the urge to puke. At least his belly was empty. If he'd eaten anything today, it would have come up, and a veteran homicide cop shouldn't be sick in the ME's exam room. Christ, he hated these cases.

After a few minutes of poking and prodding, the ME said, "Huh, well, we have a lot of hemorrhaging around the brain. A lot of swelling and pressure. Could have been over a few days, but we'll have to do more tests to be sure. I'd hazard a guess that if this kid had seen a doctor immediately, there would have been a chance of saving her, though how much or with what kind of brain damage, I can't say."

"We got detectives looking at every hospital in the city," Alex said, rubbing his cheek, hoping his face had some color. The MissPer detective twitched a curious eyebrow at him from across the room, as if he'd seen him go white. "As far as I know, no reports of anyone bringing a child matching her description into one."

"No reports? Jesus. But I could have told you that. I don't see any evidence that she was given any medical attention for this injury."

"You'll write it up as a homicide?"

Brown said, "Yeah. You have anyone who can do a formal ID?"

"The mother's in the hospital."

"You found the mother?"

"Yeah, I think so."

"What's she saying?"

"That her daughter was kidnapped during a carjacking."

"When did she file the report?"

"She didn't. Walked into the hospital with a broken arm and a concussion. Told the docs, and they called ACS and us."

"Right," said Brown, considering the girl.

"She...the mother... has a sister." Alex flipped through his memo book. "We'll bring her in."

Out on First Avenue, Alex bought himself an expresso from a street van, cleansing the rancid morgue taste from his mouth and throat. It would be at least a week or two before toxicology scans and an analysis of stomach contents came through, evidence which can tell a detective a lot about what someone was doing in the twenty-four hours before they died. Now, he had to get his head around this investigation, both the mother-as-perp angle and the carjacker angle, and he thought the ball had been dropped the second Vito and the first officers had allowed half the police department to contaminate the crime scene. How do you recover from that?

Chapter Three

The door squeaked, and Ray walked into the MNHS office, looking cold, with frost lining his scarf. He wilted into his chair and rested his head on a binder. A minute or two passed, and he sat up, kneading his hands into his eyes. "How did the autopsy go?"

"It went." Alex repeated what the ME told him. His throat felt raw from shouting at people all day. "How did things go on 186th?"

"I learned Gemma Lennon works at Yeshiva University—"

"Really? She's as Jewish as you are." Alex smiled with tired wryness.

"In the canteen. And does some tutoring for ESL students. But they said she wasn't at work on Friday. They said that was unusual. Normally, she shows up, doesn't say much, no problems with anyone – you know I asked – but she's patient with the ESL kids."

"Did anyone see her anywhere near there on Friday?"

Ray worked the heel of his hand into his forehead. "Nope. You know Vito. He's got juice. He'll get the Borough Chief to mobilize half the police department, so everything got canvassed and then some, but we got *nada*."

"Huh," breathed Alex, digesting this. Gemma Lennon didn't tell him she worked at Yeshiva, and when he asked if anyone knew she would be on that block, she said no. *Other than your co-workers and students.* The first lie he caught.

While his computer phlegmatically booted up, he strayed to the kitchenette, hunting for coffee. Ray shouted at his back, "Can you get me a cup?"

Then two C team detectives, on their four-by-twelve, pitched into the chorus, "Me too!"

"Does this look like fucking Starbucks?" Alex called back and heard their derisive snorting from the squad room, them knowing he would make the coffee anyway. He caustically added, "And I thought Ray was off coffee."

Ray answered, "I am, but this is a kid, man."

As he waited for coffee to trickle into the pot, Alex realized that he'd eaten nothing since early morning. No time, and he'd felt too queasy anyway. Phone in for a pizza, then make calls to Auto Crimes. If Lennon or someone else had moved her daughter's body in her car, what would they have done with it? Abandon it somewhere. Sell it to a scrapyard and hope someone crushed it into a cube before the police found it. Trade it into a low-end secondhand dealer for cash.

He poured a mug of coffee for himself. Ray and the C team could pour their own – did he look like their barista? Afterwards, he called the local Dominos branch, ordering pizzas. The light, crispy Italian pizza from Nardini's, an Italian joint on West 134th, would be easier on his stomach, but his colleagues were cheap, and Dominos' number was stuck to the wall on a post-it note. Auto Crimes' number, less important, was on the NYPD website.

Someone on a four-by-twelve in Auto Crimes eventually faxed them a list of scrap yards and dealers in the tri-state area. The pizza arrived at the same time. Alex wolfed down the pizza. It steadied his quivery hands but gave him some grumbling cramps. Ray refused to touch it. He was on a diet that didn't include pizza.

"You're not a rabbit," sniggered a C team detective. "You can't live on fucking salad."

"Princess Ray. What kind of New Yorker are you?"

"I'm Puerto Rican."

"Gimme a break. You were born in fucking Queens."

Ray, smiling, told them pizza wasn't good for their hearts or their bowels, so who would have the last laugh in the end.

Most scrapyards answered the phone, scrapyards often keeping unsociable hours. No one said that they'd seen the Honda. They might be lying, given the longstanding connections between organized crime and scrapyards, but the detectives had run out of leads. Where do you go in the middle of the night with nothing to follow? Ray said that sleep and a clearer head tomorrow had a hundred advantages. He also believed that yoga, green tea, and meditation cleared the mind, but he was on point about some things.

Alex grunted, "See ya" to his colleagues as he shut down the computer, glancing at the file one final time. No, nothing for it unless he got some sleep, or someone phoned him with a fresh lead. Avoiding ice and slush, he picked a route along the streets to the subway station. The tracks on West 137th were elevated above the road, and he slid his MetroCard into the turnstile, before climbing onto the platform. He heard the soft hiss of cars passing below the el pillars. One hand on his aching right side, he shifted his weight from foot to foot, staring at the track fading into the darkness. A beam of yellow light splashed across the rails. A 1 train screamed into the station. Alex boarded it, then he dropped onto an orange seat as the train lurched forward. More people filed on at 125th. Mostly Black and Latino, a couple whites, a family of Sikhs. Young. Old. No one making eye contact with anyone in the car. A few more stops passed by, and the train dove underground. At West 86th Street, Alex debarked and walked beside rows of snow-encased ginkgo trees and streetlights to his apartment on West 87th, between Amsterdam and Columbus.

He let himself into the apartment building, a red brick low-rise with spidery fire escape stairs clinging to the facade. The damp cold inside slapped him with an icy backhander. These old buildings froze as soon as the heat went off. Teeth chattering, he cranked up the thermostat, hearing the boiler rumble to life.

His head hurt like someone beating a mallet against his temples. He stripped off his suit, which felt sweaty despite the snow, and then he washed his face with warm water as he gulped down antidepressants and ibuprofen. He curled onto his side, seizing his head in both hands. His insomnia had no sympathy. The panic attack in the morning had given it strength. It didn't care that he'd been on his feet since 0700. For a couple hours he thrashed under his blankets. Finally, he surrendered to it, sitting up with his laptop on his knees, writing a HIPAA request to NYC Health and Hospitals for access to Gemma Lennon's and Suzanne Lennon's medical records. Being law enforcement, he could get those records without a warrant or the patient's consent provided that it pertained to a crime and was limited in scope. If he could not sleep, he might as well do something useful.

Chapter Four

Immediately after roll call, Gibson asked the detectives working the Lennon case for a meeting. Alex and Ray said that they got nothing from the scrapyards. Ray had stalked Gemma on Facebook and Google, but she didn't use social media. Marcus Wheeler had brought Lennon's sister, Stephanie, in for the ID and a cursory interview, and beyond ID-ing Suzanne, she'd refused to cooperate. She was a chef at a high-end restaurant in White Plains, and her husband was a cop with the Westchester PD. She'd told Wheeler to fuck off, directing him to her lawyer when he'd asked her why Gemma hadn't gone to the police after the alleged carjacking. Gemma was vulnerable, Stephanie grudgingly revealed, and she wouldn't go to the police. But she hadn't told Wheeler what she meant by that.

As the detectives started to leave Gibson's office, she said, "Alex, wait here a minute."

He exchanged a look with Ray and Wheeler – Wheeler saying with his eyes that he had no idea, Ray saying that he did – and then they abandoned Alex looking uneasily at his boss, biting his thumbnail, confident that she was going to ask him about his mental health. He had to talk it over with her because she had saved his career, saved him, more than once. When he gave up the drink, she had his back. When his health took a turn for the worse five years ago, she could have had him declared unfit for duty and shipped to a rubber gun squad. Instead, Gibson had contacted the psychiatrist privately, and his treatment remained off-the-books.

"You feeling alright?" she asked. "Ray said—"

"Yeah, I know I wasn't great yesterday. Car did a donut on the ice. I'm amazed we didn't hit anything. I…" Mouth half open, he searched for words. "I guess it was a trigger, like the feeling of the car losing control, and I felt kind of unwell after that."

"You still on your meds?"

"Always. She's got me doing a new thing, and it's helping with the flashbacks."

"That's good. So, when you say 'kind of unwell,' you don't mean a flashback?"

"No, I meant I felt anxious and shaky, and my heart was racing."

"If you're concerned, you'll call her? If you think you're getting worse?"

"Yeah. But I'm not."

"Are you okay today?"

"As much as any day." He held his left hand in his right, running his thumb along the scars. "Better than when I did this."

Gibson moved a stack of paperwork across her desk. "I fucking hope so. I just don't want you to crash and burn."

"Me, neither. It's probably worse for me."

"Just stay on top of it. It's not something to fuck around with. If you can't cope—"

"I'm really fine. I just hate cases with kids."

She pursed her lips. "Everyone does."

Once he'd returned to his desk, he dug around the detritus for his reading glasses. Another sign of impending decrepitude. He had only gotten them a few years ago, a reluctant concession to reality: no longer seeing small print. The detectives said that the glasses made him look old. Fucking ancient, they cackled. The glasses reminded him that he was on the wrong side of fifty, but they also let him read without headaches.

His desk phone trilled. He answered it with a desultory, "Manhattan North Homicide, this is Detective Boswell."

"Hello, Detective. I'm Officer Julio Sanchez. I've been posted at the hospital with Gemma Lennon. I had orders to report to you if there was any change in her status."

"What's happening?"

"They're discharging her today."

"All right. You know when?"

"Maybe in an hour or two."

"Okay, thank you, call me forthwith if anything changes."

"Ten-four."

If Gemma consented to another interview, he would see where that led. He ambled to the kitchenette to brew more coffee. A colleague, Catriona Silver, was using a butter knife to pry the coffee filter out of the top of the machine.

Alex waited with crossed arms, remembering Cat's story about euthanizing her own cat with her police-issued 9mm. "Vet's fucking expensive. According to the NYPD, I'm trained to shoot." A character, people called her, when they were being nice. She was from Williamsburg's Orthodox Jewish community but not Orthodox herself, impatient, opinionated, only 5'1 but easily capable of terrifying male suspects and most cops. She had joined MNHS two years ago, transferring from Computer Crimes, and she'd proven herself as a shrewd, smart investigator, who did things her own way, on her own time. Like most homicide detectives, to some extent.

At this moment, she was thwacking the side of the coffee machine with the knife. "This thing's an ancient piece of shit, Alex. Why don't we get another one?"

"We're in a recession," he said. "I'm not sure violence is the answer."

She gave it another thwack. The filter freed itself. "I think it is."

Alex rested his hip against the counter. Maybe Gemma Lennon would feel more relaxed with a female detective. Maybe not, and Cat wasn't the most relaxing of people to be with, but she was also funny and personable. "This Lennon case is a fucking headache," he commented.

"I saw the headline in the *Post*."

"We gotta interview the mother without the press corps or the entire New York defense bar finding out. Wanna come with me? It'll be fun."

"Sure it will. Mom a suspect?" Cat asked.

Alex tensed his shoulders in a shrug. "I haven't ruled her out."

"She talkin'?"

"Sort of."

"Isn't Ray the secondary on this case?"

"Yeah, I know Ray acts like my mother, but he's actually not a woman." Alex raised an eyebrow as Cat laughed loudly. "I'm thinking she might talk to you more than she'll talk to me or him."

"What, like the sisterhood? A special connection? Next time I got a neurotic Jewish male perp, you're my first port of call." Cat almost snorted out her coffee.

He ignored the backhanded insult. "She's pretty weird and freaked out. Well, really weird. Sometimes female suspects seem better with female cops."

"If she's that freaked, you should bring a dog along. I hear emotional support animals are *the* cutting-edge thing now."

"Yeah, if this doesn't work, I'll see if the K9 Unit'll lend me one." He rinsed a mug in the sink, then drank a mouthful of water. "But come on, Silver, give it a shot with me."

"Maybe she just don't wanna talk."

"Definitely," he said with a tight smile. "But I gotta try."

Cat poured coffee into a plastic travel mug. "Okay, just 'cause you're a mensch. You'll owe me one."

As he gathered his keys, shield, and gun, he furrowed his brows at the phone. If any precinct detective but Vito had caught this case, Alex would call them. After all, MNHS was an assistive squad. It wasn't exclusively Alex's case. But he didn't want Vito within ten blocks of Lennon, and every interaction with the precinct detective gave him a rancid feeling in the pit of his stomach. He felt distant, preoccupied with the past, with things he had never talked about to anyone.

"Alex, you coming?" Cat said with rising impatience. "I haven't got all day."

"Yeah." He scrubbed his palms against both eye sockets, composing his mind again.

Chapter Five

The city plows had cleared the snow, but sooty, grey mountains loomed over the sides of the roads. Where 125th intersected with Park, Alex turned downtown, gunning it for East 77th. The new Fusions replacing the Crown Victorias were nippy and agile. They did zero to sixty in about eight seconds. You could peel off the line at lights and dart around traffic. The old Crown Vics had big V8s but handled like boats.

Cat laughed, "You're one of those guys who seems soft, gentle, and mild mannered, but behind the wheel of a car you're fuckin' *insane.*"

"I don't want to spend the rest of my life in traffic."

"Dude, you live in the wrong city."

They abandoned the car in the hospital loading bay. It took them no time to find Lennon, who was sitting in the front atrium, vacuously gazing at people parading through the revolving door. She wore jeans and a purple blouse. A pair of patrolmen lounged nearby, ostensibly not watching her but watching her. She looked as though she was waiting for someone.

"Hi, Gemma. I'm Detective Boswell," Alex reminded her softly. "This is Detective Silver. How you doing?" Her clothes weren't torn, dirty, or disheveled, like you imagined clothes looking if your complainant had been in a fight with someone.

"Okay," she said emotionlessly.

"It's good they let you out, huh?"

"Yeah."

"I've been in hospitals, more than I'd like. I can never wait to get out."

"Yeah."

"The food sucks."

"Yeah, I guess."

"I can never sleep. It's too damn hot and stuffy, and these beds are awful on my back."

"Yeah."

"Is someone coming to get you?"

"My sister's at work. She works crazy hours. I was gonna take the subway home, but my apartment…" Her voice cracked a little, and her eyes fell to the floor. "It… I can't… You know." She looked at him, stricken. "Without my girl there…"

There was his opening. "If it would help, we can go to the apartment with you—"

"No, I can't *be* in the apartment," she moaned. "We can't go back there. We can't. No way. I can't."

Damn, he thought, there goes Plan A. Talking her into bringing them into the apartment for a warrantless, yet legal search. He had plan B. "Alright, we can take you to the office, on West 133rd, and you can help us. We can talk a little more about what happened, and it might make things easier. Then we can call your sister, or a friend or whoever, and have them pick you up."

"I don't know," Lennon muttered.

"They won't let you stay here." He put his right hand over his heart. "Talking about things helps. I know it's hard. I can't imagine the pain you're in. But it helps us. It will help you too, finding justice, closure. The sooner we know everything, the easier it'll be for us to find him. And you're the only person who saw him."

Cat arched a wry eyebrow at his silver-tongued bullshit.

Glassy-eyed, Lennon fussed around with a bag of medication. "What's your first name?"

"Alex."

"Alex," she echoed, staring past his shoulder. "I saw… On the news… They talked about Suzanne." She choked up as she said her daughter's name. "They said homicide detectives were investigating it."

"Yeah." Alex sat in the chair next to her, resting his left ankle on his right knee. Would she ask him about the cause of Suzanne's death, did she know, would she pretend not to?

"How am I gonna pay these medical bills?" she cried suddenly. "Do you *know* what the co-pay on my insurance is?"

"Yeah, it sucks," Alex replied, painfully familiar with the hardships of battling health insurance companies.

"There may be victim's compensation funds and stuff like that," Cat said. "You gotta get in touch with Victim's Services. We can talk about that in the office."

Lennon filled out some forms at reception, repeating her complaints about insurance, then she followed them through the revolving door, cooperating out of her own free will, which was the important thing. They piloted her to the car. Alex opened the passenger door, and she peered nervously at the radios and electronics on the dash. Then she wormed into the back seat. Voluntarily.

Cat twisted around in the passenger seat. "Who're you texting?"

"Does it matter?" Lennon answered. "I can text, right?"

"Yeah. Of course you can."

Alex cut back to the West Side through the park, funneled under the tunnel formed by trees and stone walls. The detectives softly urged Lennon to talk about her daughter. At first, she refused, repeating, "Suzanne isn't here anymore." But then she mumbled that Suzanne liked going down to the water's edge in Inwood Hill Park and throwing rocks into the river; she liked trains and planes; she used to insist on going to the subway stations or Metro North stations and watching trains come and go; she often got into trouble at school.

"What kinda trouble?" asked Alex, driving one-handed, resting his left elbow on the windowsill.

"Just little kid stuff. Fighting with other kids. Mouthing off to the teacher, bothering other kids, not sitting still in class, not doing her work, you know. I mean, I try, I try with her, but I'm on my own, I have to work, I can't *be* there all the time."

"I once locked a kid in a utility closet for a whole day," reflected Cat.

Acting as though she'd said too much, Lennon fell silent.

In an effort to prompt her, Cat said, "My favorite plane was the F-14. Did Suzanne have a favorite?"

"You're a detective," said Lennon shortly. "It's a man's job."

"Not since the '70s," Cat sniffed, her feminist hackles rising, but at a sharp glance from Alex, she snapped her mouth shut, then rambled about her visits to *The Intrepid*. Her stories about aircraft carriers and fighter jets didn't elicit any further outbursts.

Alex asked if Suzanne liked the playground near Payson Avenue. No response. He played through all the scenarios. Lennon could be in so much shock that she genuinely remembered nothing. She could be guilty but lacking the wherewithal or *cojones* for a believable cover up. She could be innocent but protecting someone she knew.

As Alex parked the car, his iPhone squawked with a text from Ray. *Vito's at the office. Heard you had Lennon. We're putting together photo arrays. He's spending more time telling me a story about you than working. Did you really get blind drunk at a DEA dinner?* with an eye-rolling emoji.

Cool. Just got here. How did Vito know we had Lennon? Alex felt his pulse quickening, his stomach going into free-fall.

Ray responded, *Because everyone knows everything. I know you don't like him, but he is the catching precinct detective.*

He wiped his sweaty palm against his thigh. They ushered Lennon up the stairs, Cat noticing and Lennon oblivious to him swallowing an antacid.

"What are you taking?" Cat hissed in his ear.

"Ranitidine. Calms my stomach down."

"Not Xanax," she said.

"I wish."

He wished he had more than Xanax or Ranitidine when an overweight Black man wearing a suit intercepted them at the Wheel desk, and Lennon collapsed into the man's arms like she'd fainted.

"Chris?" she breathed. "What are you doing here?"

"Your sister called me," the man replied. "Said you were gonna be here."

"Sorry," said the officer at the Wheel, grimacing apologetically at Alex and Cat. "He said he was representing Ms. Lennon."

"You're a lawyer?" Alex demanded. That text she sent in the car probably went to her sister, who phoned a lawyer. Godammit – could nothing go right?

"Chris Dalziel," the lawyer replied, shaking the detectives' hands. "I'm an old family friend, and I'm a medical malpractice attorney, to be honest, but Steph asked me to help out Gemma. Gemma, you know not to say anything, right? You don't *have* to talk to them."

Cat scowled at Alex, mouthing the word *fuck.*

He compressed his lips and eyebrows, conveying that he wasn't thrilled, either. "Why does she need counsel?" he asked the lawyer. "As far as we're concerned, she's a victim, the one person who saw the perpetrator."

"Her sister's just looking out for her," Dalziel responded. "Said she shouldn't be left on her own in a police precinct. What do you want to do, Gemma? I can take you to Steph's, or you can talk to the detectives. I can be with you if you want to talk to them. It's up to you."

"I've talked to them enough," Lennon said, sounding exhausted.

"Gemma," Alex insisted, "We need you. We're most likely to find this guy in the next day or two."

"My daughter's safe now. She doesn't need this," she murmured.

That knocked him back. His suspicions ballooned into an ache that filled his whole body. "I promise, this won't take long. I know it's tough, and we'll support you through it. I promise. Just look at some faces with us, alright?"

"Criminal law isn't really my thing," Dalziel admitted. "But I know they can't keep you here. You only just got out of the hospital, and an awful thing has happened. It's okay if you're not up for this today."

"I'd like to go to Steph's," Lennon whispered.

Alex had no intentions of holding the woman against her, or her sister's, will. Impossible with a lawyer here, the brother-in-law being a cop, and the media attention at Defcon four. But why did her sister call an attorney forthwith? What did Stephanie Lennon know that he should? He stepped aside, scowling as the lawyer escorted Lennon around him and down the stairs.

"Guess she wasn't talking to nobody," Cat said.

Before Alex could speak, Vito whipped through the door and plowed into them like a tornado. "What the fuck? You let her go? Because some malpractice shitbag said he was lawyer?"

"What was I supposed to do?" Alex replied tetchily. "I didn't think forcibly detaining her when she had counsel there was a good idea."

"Me and Espinosa got a photo array of every mope in the Heights that's been picked up by Auto Crime in the last five years. I mean, you still playin' at her bein' a vic, but I know where your head is. I know how you work. I know you. You called her kid's school yet? I assume you've run her through SAFIS and NCIC? ACS? And her sister? You check *her* out? What about the lawyer?"

"Yeah, Vito, we've done that. If you bothered looking at the file, you'd know. And we'll check out the lawyer. Obviously."

"I know you hadda talk with her before that lawyer showed up. You get anything?"

"No."

"We gotta get a fuckin' warrant for her place. You know, I been busy with a lotta shit. You have any idea how much pressure I been under? Any fuckin' idea? Like my brain's been crushed into chip packets, and some shitbird is stomping on it. Fuckin' crushed into little tiny pieces-"

Slightly baffled, Alex remarked, "Overdoing it with the press for the book, huh?"

"Oh, you don't have a fuckin' clue, Alex, but what I'm saying is, I got all this other shit to deal with, and Homicide's not even on the ball with getting a Goddamned search warrant."

"I think we need more before we can get a warrant."

"*You* think you need more," Vito snorted. "We're not talkin' articles of impeachment here. It's a fuckin' search warrant. Look, I'll fuckin' do it. I can get us one by tomorrow."

"No, I think we should be patient." The last thing Alex wanted was a Vito warrant, with more fantasy than *The Lord of the Rings.*

"I'll be patient *today,*" Vito huffed. "But what the fuck are you waiting for?"

"Probable cause, for a start." Alex walked into his cubicle, Vito tailgating him like an angry truck driver.

"We got probable cause. I been lookin' for this jacker in every inch of the Heights. We're running DNA on every fuckin' piece of trash my guys found in the park. I've canvassed every apartment within a ten-block radius. There ain't any fuckin' jacker. Where's your guts, man? You used to have them. What about the kid's father? Where is he in all this?"

"Dead, apparently," sighed Alex.

"Can we verify that?"

"Probably." Alex riffled through his memo pad. "Yeah. Cause of death a heroin OD five years ago. Lived in Newark and died at University Hospital."

"Other relatives?" Vito thrust himself into Alex's personal space.

Alex breathed in the oily scent of pungent cologne. It congealed in his throat and made him feel sick to his stomach. Vito must bathe himself in vats of that stuff.

"She's clearly a fuckin' suspect," sputtered Vito. "Why else would she get her sister to call a lawyer, as like the first Goddamned thing she did?"

"Yeah, possibly, but we might be wrong. There's no record of her with ACS, and the only PC I've got is her delay in reporting her child missing." And his gut feelings and suspicious comments he caught on-the-fly, but those wouldn't hold up in court.

"That's fuckin' PC to me. You get some forensics to stick in there, you got a warrant."

The feeling between them was bitter and unpleasant. Pointedly, Alex spun his chair away from Vito, then he tapped the lawyer's name into Google. There he was: an associate in a medical malpractice firm with an address in Morningside Heights. Alex opened the DCJS window to run the name. No criminal record in New York. He would run him through NCIC and WOLF, checking for convictions in other states and for outstanding warrants, covering his ass, but he didn't expect leads out of that.

"You got *no* fuckin' guts anymore." Acting disappointed, Vito squarely folded his arms.

"Whatever. We gotta watch our backs on this case. Absence of evidence *isn't* evidence you can take to court. If I've made the wrong call, you can call me an idiot. You can tell any reporter you want that I screwed up. You know we gotta push the carjacker story and see if anything falls out."

"I'll give it another day, but you bring Lennon back in for any more questioning, I gotta be there. Hear me?"

"I hear you." Alex desperately needed a fresh strategy for the investigation, but the fight drained from his body. A feeling of cloudy desolation passed through him, a cold blast cracking his bones. He swigged a drink from the tepid coffee on the desk.

Vito's phone suddenly played Sinatra. He turned his back to the homicide detectives, plastering the phone against the side of his face, saying, "Yeah, yeah, gotcha." Then he shot through the door like the building was burning down.

Stunned, Alex fumbled his coffee mug. He caught the eyes of Ray and Cat, who both shrugged testily. If Vito had a TV interviewer or a Hollywood screenwriter on the phone, he would drop the homicide investigation like a hot coal. Whatever – it got him out of the MNHS squad room.

"Well, this was a fuckin' waste of my afternoon," Cat complained.

More people giving him flak. One of those days that made him wonder why he got out of bed. "It didn't go like I wanted it to, either. Jesus, I wasn't expecting her sister to send a lawyer straight off the damned bat."

"Really? I heard Wheeler interviewed the sister, and she said Lennon was 'vulnerable.'"

"We don't know what that means," Ray said. "We're still waiting on some hospital records, but so far, we got nothing suggesting she had—"

"You didn't tell me it was Indelicata's case," Cat interrupted. "Did you see that he didn't even look at me? Like I wasn't in the fuckin' room. You know, he doesn't fuckin' treat female detectives like colleagues, doesn't give them the Goddamned time of day, unless it's to say you'd look better in a mini-skirt."

"He doesn't like me either," Alex said.

"Not the same fuckin' thing. He hasn't said he wants to see you in a mini-skirt."

"Believe me, no one wants to see me in a mini-skirt."

"You're missing the point."

"No, I get it." A pang of guilt at being male, working in a police department with deep undercurrents of misogyny.

"Yeah, sure you do. Doesn't fuckin' matter. This case, it's not my circus, not my monkeys."

"What?"

"I think it's a Polish saying. I got two oxy ODs this week and that assault one DV case, and this CI's left me about ten messages. I'm outta here."

And she was, leaving Alex with the Polish proverb. Words he should pin to his cubicle wall alongside Vernon Geberth's quote reminding him that death investigation was God's work.

"Gibson thinks we should canvass Lennon's building again," Ray said.

"You got any better ideas?"

"No. I've already signed out a car."

Fresh eyes, a fresh canvass could pick up something the first canvasses had missed or overlooked. Cases had broken that way. It was SOP when you had no other leads.

Fucking meds, Alex swore as he buzzed the front door of the sandstone low-rise. He touched his forehead. Pain hammered his temples, and he felt the sweat oozing along his skin. *Just deal.* He scratched at his lower back. It wouldn't last forever. These headaches never did. He buzzed the door again, barking, "Police!" and someone let them into a coldly institutional stairwell. They climbed the stairs, their footsteps hollow and metallic.

"What's with Vito?" Ray asked. "He was in a weird mood from the moment he showed up at our office, and you obviously wanted to interview Lennon without him. You always grate on each other, but it seemed... I dunno... worse today. Are you pissed about the book thing?"

"It's a shitshow of a redball. Crime scene was a dumpster fire from the start. We fuck this up, it's a child homicide, so it's gonna hit the fan. I want to arrest someone for Suzanne's murder. I stopped caring about the book thing." That wasn't entirely true. The book hit him where it hurt, describing him as a raging alcoholic, the only concrete trait he possessed in Vito's literary opus. Will from AA said that you are not the disease, and the disease isn't you. The disease is something that's in you, but it doesn't define everything about you. In Vito's book, Alex wasn't himself; he was the disease, and that bothered him. More than he should let it.

"No kidding. Me too. But what's the beef with you guys? To be honest, he wasn't exactly flattering towards you in that book."

"Vito's main purpose in life is stroking Vito's ego," Alex said tartly. "He doesn't like people who don't do stroking. Don't think he gives any fucks about any vics. Even kids. It's just about him."

"Yeah, no shit, but come on, man, there's obviously more to it than that. Like you slept with his girlfriend or something."

Tiredly, Alex faced his partner. Ray was too shrewd a detective to be pawned off easily. "I didn't, and he's been married for thirty years—"

"Like that would stop *him* from having something on the side," Ray observed scathingly.

"True, it hasn't. His wife's the most long-suffering woman in New York. But we fell out over work stuff. It was the '90s. This city was falling apart, crack was everywhere, and everyone was pushed to the limits."

"What happened at work?"

"The mishegoss lawsuits are made of, Ray, which is why I probably shouldn't say much. We fell out…" Too late, but he tried swallowing the words. Clearing his throat, he growled, "It's gotta do with the wrongful convictions that came out in that *Times* investigation last year. It was all fucked."

"What? Wrongful convictions? Are you being sued?" Ray's voice rose half an octave.

Alex instantly regretted bringing up the miscarriage of justice cases. "Not me personally, to my knowledge, but those guys who were exonerated are filing suit against the department, and I'd rather keep my mouth shut and not be in the middle of it."

"But were they your cases?" Ray's voice floated at that falsetto. "You know that guy who got outta prison, who's been writing in *The Atlantic* about race and criminal justice. What's he called? Serrachia? Is he one of them?"

"I don't read *The Atlantic*." As he said it, he knew he wouldn't get away with dodging the question.

"That's hardly the point, and you know it."

"Yeah, I worked on some of them. I did a little bit of work on that one. We gonna do this canvass, or what?" Alex had a closed, hurt expression, which forced Ray to back off.

They made their way through the building, questioning neighbors who said they saw Gemma and Suzanne in the stairwell on occasion, but they didn't know her, like most people in New York apartment buildings. She never even said superficial hellos in the stairwell. The Dominican neighbors assumed she didn't speak Spanish.

Wearied and footsore, they labored through the entryway door. A treacherous layer of black ice sparkled under the streetlights. Ice crystals glittered on parked cars, lamp posts, newspaper boxes.

"What do you want to do?" Ray queried.

"Been a long fucking day. My head's killing me. Can't think of anything else we can do tonight." Alex massaged his frozen hands together while Ray unlocked the car. The Heights and Harlem seemed like they had gone into hibernation, or a deep freeze. For about ten minutes, they sat in companionable silence, listening to the hissing chatter of the police radio, but nothing much was happening anywhere.

Around West 138th, Ray asked, "Is Vito being sued? Is that why he stormed out of the office like his butt was on fire?"

Obviously, Ray had been thinking about miscarriages of justice and civil litigation for the entirety of the canvass. Alex looked away from his partner. "Maybe. I don't know. I thought he'd picked up a call from Jerry Bruckheimer."

Ray gave him a look, not buying the flippance.

"He's been named in lawsuits before," Alex added. "He's never given a fuck."

"You were the primary MNHS detective. Think they're gonna ask you to testify?"

"I doubt it. They'll settle. The city always settles this shit."

Ray maneuvered the car into the lot behind their building, silently concentrating on the ice, but Alex worried that his partner had started doing his obsessive schtick, extrapolating (not incorrectly) that Alex had made a substantial contribution to the miscarriages of justice. He could almost see the gears turning inside Ray's head.

Avoiding those questions, Alex said, "I'm at the physio again this week."

"For your back?"

"Yeah." The physical therapist who had worked on his wrist following the window incident had helped him regain all function in his hand after severing tendons. She was a genius, and he was in chronic pain from old injuries to his back and his ribs. He saw her once every two weeks. Regular physio didn't touch the permanent knot of pain in his side, but it helped his back.

"That's good," Ray said in bland tone. Normally, he would blather on about yoga and losing weight.

"I think so. I'll see you tomorrow. Subways are only once an hour tonight so I gotta run." Alex shoved his cold hands into his pockets as he

swung uptown towards the 137th Street station. Yeah, he'd contributed –
to things he wished he could forget. If Ray's instincts were right, and the
complainants had sued Vito and the city, Alex prayed for a settlement.
Should the cases go to court, he didn't see how he could stay out of it.
But they never go to court.

Chapter Six

The Honda Accord was found, parked amongst BMWs, Mercedes, and Cadillacs on East 83rd and Third Avenue, between a gym called SoulCycle, where you could ride an exercise bike and practice yoga, and a vegan restaurant called Leaf. The Honda was a beat-up heap: the bumper crumpled, the radiator exposed through gashes in the metal, the left headlight smashed. An Upper East Side resident had called it into the police, complaining that it must be abandoned as it didn't fit in with the general car population, and, more importantly, it was taking up their parking space. That's how you get New Yorkers to assist with criminal investigations – you fuck with their parking.

"Ray, you can get lunch here, for a change." Alex pointed to the vegan restaurant. Nothing worse than a partner who refused to eat food, who made him feel guilty for greasy take-out.

"I'm not vegan anymore. Haven't been for like two months." Ray wrinkled his brows, as if Alex should know this.

"I lose track."

"I'm going lactose-free."

"Oh," sighed Alex. Ray was always trying diets – gluten free, carb free, sugar free, fuck-knows-what free, as though the perfect lifestyle for maximum health, fitness, and living forever awaited his discovery. He earned that squad moniker, "Princess Ray."

"You know, they've been finding more evidence suggesting gut health is totally linked to mental health."

"I think I'd be even more depressed if I couldn't eat cheese," Alex quipped. He dropped to one knee in the slush to inspect the smashed grill.

Ray did what he always did when Alex interrupted one of his health monologues with a wiseass crack, which was ignore it and continue talking. "If you ate better, you might feel better. You have all these microbiomes in your intestines… like bacteria… and they have an effect on your mood, your energy, how much weight you gain or lose, maybe even cancer, everything. There's good ones and bad ones, and what you need to be at your healthiest is the right balance of these things…"

And Alex did what he always did when Ray latched onto a new health fad, which was ignore him. Someone had neatly parallel parked the Accord in a tight space, squashed between an Audi A6 and a Cadillac Escalade, and he surmised from the thigh-high piles of dirty snow around both vehicles that neither had moved since that heavy snowfall. They could run the plates, verify it with the owners.

"These old Accords have airbags, right?" he asked, interrupting Ray, who was espousing the benefits of repopulating the intestines with 'good' bacteria.

"Oh, yeah," Ray answered. "They're super safe cars."

"The ones in this haven't gone off." Some old CDs and candy wrappers had fallen on the seats and into the footwell. A more thorough search would proceed once it arrived at the impound. Alex stepped back from the Accord, then he waved at the police tow truck driver, signaling him to do his thing.

For the last week, Gibson had been fending off journalists, Mayor Bloomberg, and the brass, while the media plastered the internet and newspapers with headlines about carjackings and murdered children. If you believed the hype, you'd think it was 1991 again. The discovery of Lennon's car in the Upper East did little to improve the boss' mood.

"Why the fuck did no one canvass near the hospital?" she snapped at her mortified investigative team. "It's been two weeks. You're damned lucky the perp didn't move it and dump it somewhere. They've had plenty of time."

"Why wouldn't she pick it up?" Wheeler asked. "You know, if she knew where it was."

"A million reasons," Ray said. "Could be too traumatized, upset, guilt-ridden. Or she doesn't want to be seen in a car that she said was stolen."

"How did you think she *got* to the hospital?" Gibson queried.

"Could've walked," Wheeler suggested sheepishly.

"Bus?" offered Alex. They'd tracked Lennon's MetroCard, so they'd already known she hadn't used it anywhere in the subway system that day. "You can pay cash on a bus, and the M101, 102, and 103 stop right in front of the hospital."

"But she clearly didn't use a damned bus, did she?" Gibson said acidly.

Liberated from the uncomfortable meeting, Ray paced in an agitated circle around the squad room, wearing out the floor. "Jesus, she's on a rampage."

"She's never been very patient with fuck-ups," Alex said. "We shoulda canvassed near the hospital."

"Yeah. I can't believe we didn't think about it."

"It's only lost us a few days. Gibson's pissed, but it's not that bad." That panic attack had washed him out. What if he was sicker than he realized?

"A few days that could close this case. Gibson's not wrong. We can't afford to make those mistakes."

"No, I know. We shoulda been more on it. I wasn't feeling well. I need to be more careful when I'm having a bad day. I dunno… Maybe I should up my meds again."

"We all fucked up. You weren't the only person working the case."

"I guess so."

"Vito let everyone and their dog into the crime scene," Ray added.

Alex swallowed the unease and self-doubt rising like bile. But Ray spoke the truth. "Yeah, that fucked it."

They called Highway, the NYPD unit that investigates motor vehicle accidents, but they had no record of the grey Honda being involved in any. Alex wasn't optimistic about that lead panning out: if you suffered a minor fender bender while committing a class A felony, reporting it to the police was unlikely to be a priority. With a new focus for the investigation, he contacted the owners of the Audi and the Cadillac, who hadn't noticed the Accord when they parked, and then he organized a canvass of East 83rd with detectives and patrol officers from the 19th Precinct. They spent several days knocking on every door between East 83rd and East 77th. Most Upper East Siders were friendly and cooperative. People profusely thanked the detectives for their service on 9/11, and Alex reckoned his kidneys had as much of a workout as his legs, drinking his body weight in tea and coffee during that canvass, but no one recognized Lennon or the car.

A week after the discovery of the Accord, forensics identified traces of the black paint the city used on signposts embedded in the crumpled grill. Alex contacted the City Department of Transport, hunting for reports of damaged signs. A 'no parking' sign on West 234th Street and Broadway, in Riverdale, had been knocked over on February 9th. The Department of Transport suspected a car had crashed into it but had no witnesses. These things happened sometimes. Of course, the sign was now replaced, the old one discarded, and no one cared enough about a 'no parking' sign to analyze it for traces of paint belonging to the vehicle that hit it.

In the meantime, SAFIS reported that the only fingerprints in the car belonged to Gemma and her daughter. The lab, unsurprisingly, found no one else's DNA inside the car or on Suzanne herself.

A judge signed a search warrant for Lennon's apartment, but in three weeks, she could have easily cleaned or disposed of any evidence. They could not directly prove that Gemma had put Suzanne in the car two days after killing her, abandoned her body in Inwood Hill Park, crashed the car into a sign in the Bronx, and then parked it near Lenox Hill Hospital before admitting herself. The story played, but Alex would feel more confident with direct evidence, and the District Attorney's office refused to sign off on an arrest warrant without it. None of the powers-that-be wanted to risk arresting the grieving mother when there was still a chance that she didn't do it. If this search warrant hit a dead end, Alex had no backup plan. If they found something useful that led to a clearance, he might be promoted to first grade.

Vito lurked around the entryway to the Isham Street apartment, engrossed with his smart phone. TARU had set up a surveillance op across the road, monitoring the apartment phones. No one answered the door, so they rammed it open. Alex and Ray moved lightly across the threshold together, holding their firearms. They went through the rooms, covering one another's backs, clearing the apartment even though no one expected any violence, or anyone at all. You clear it anyway. Everyone knew stories of cops who got injured or killed because they were blasé about clearing a place where they didn't expect trouble.

As soon as he re-holstered his gun, Alex realized Vito hadn't budged from his perch near the door. "You coming or you futzing with your screen all night?" he said over his shoulder, infuriated at that hairbag. The man was texting people or reading his email while himself, Ray, and the patrol officers risked their asses.

Vito's glare could have made the brickwork bleed. "I was busy. TARU said no one was fuckin' here. I had to deal with some things, and you and Espinosa, you do entries like you're special ops. You don't need my fat ass tagging along."

"Does someone on Grindr?" Alex knew about it because he'd recently worked a case where a vic had met a perp on it.

"Don't be a dick, Alex. You're not as funny as you think." Vito pushed past him.

Alex dawdled for a moment, kneading the back of his neck, surprised that Vito hadn't come back with a snappier rejoinder. His mind flitted to his conversations with Vito about chip packets and Ray about lawsuits.

But like he told Ray, the department usually settled with the plaintiffs and rarely disciplined the officers involved, so Alex doubted that would put Vito off his game. Well, could be anything, like his wife getting fed up with his affairs.

Dust and mold burned his sinuses. He sneezed, blowing his nose. Shaking the sting out of his head, he scanned the kitchen. Dirty plates formed stacks next to the sink, growing colorful ecosystems of mold. A handful of cockroaches lounged in various states of repose near the dishes. Alex noted remnants of eggs and toast. The ME had told him that he'd found partially digested eggs and toast in Suzanne's stomach. Taking two strides to his left brought him into the living room. It had bare, off-white walls with flaking plaster, a 1990s TV, and a moth-eaten, beige sofa speckled with brownish stains. He knelt over the stains. Could be anything. Coffee. Wine. Pasta sauce. Next to the sofa, he saw indentations in the carpet from a table, but no table, and faint stains on the dusty carpet. That could also be coffee or wine, and if it wasn't, forensic methods for aging bloodstains weren't reliable. He took more pictures and sketched a rough schematic.

Next, he surveyed Suzanne's room. A Thomas the Tank Engine duvet lay rumpled on the bed, as if its occupant might return at any moment. Toy Second World War aircraft were piled in a heap on the floor, like a vintage airshow gone wrong. He dug his nails into his sternum, flinching at the sad, emptiness underneath it. Child murders always snap your heart into dozens of pieces. The hardest cases to work. He knelt down beside her school bag, which lay half open beside the WWII planes. Addition and spelling. The latest assignment dated the Wednesday before she was found. Two CSU officers joined him in the bedroom and sprinkled dust onto the desk and the mirror.

One squatted beside Alex and picked up a small airplane. "Boswell, should we bag these?" he asked, gently turning the plane between his thumb and forefinger.

Alex felt a spine-snapping weight pulling him downwards. He didn't know. "Yeah," he said softly. Why not? Bag everything that moved.

Leaving them to their dusting, he wafted into the bathroom. In the medicine cabinet, he found bottles of Flexeril, a muscle relaxant with sedative properties. He'd been prescribed the stuff for his back after the car accident. It had dulled the pain, and the sedative properties would have been a delight if only they hadn't upset his stomach.

"Hey, Lex," said Vito, strolling into the bathroom. He acted cool and professional. They could have a coolly professional relationship.

Sometimes. His gaze slid to the medication in Alex's hand. "What's that for?"

"It's a muscle relaxant," said Alex. "Also makes you completely zotzed."

"Yeah?"

"I've taken it."

"For fun?"

Alex sighed, then sneezed again. The dust was killing his sinuses. "Not really."

"This search ain't gonna get us shit." Vito's lower lip jutted forward. "You shoulda got this warrant *days* ago."

Alex drew the musty air into his lungs. It clogged his throat. Clouds from his own breath floated in front of his eyes. "Well, I don't know." Wincing, he asked himself the same question. First missing the car, then this. Sometimes, he worried he could only be a little crazy for so long before it interfered with his work. He braced himself for the blow from Vito, with his knack for verbally punching him straight in the guts. Today, he deserved it. He felt like he was due for a bad turnaround in his head.

"Whatever," Vito shifted his hefty weight back and forth. "Look, man, I got a thing. I gotta hit the road. You can finish this?"

"Sure." Alex squinted, astounded to not have his competence as a detective disputed.

Vito grunted opprobriously, then shouldered past him, abandoning him in that frigid bathroom. Who was that guy and what had he done to Vito Indelicata? The Vito he knew would not shirk at the opportunity to tell Alex how he could have done this better, that he wasn't the cop he used to be. Vito should have spotted his moment of weakness, like a hyena on a PBS documentary, and lunged for his jugular. Alex dithered, listening to footsteps, to the scuffles of CSU working. The bathroom required another thorough perusal, alone, with a clearer head. He blew his nose again and excavated the cabinets under the sink. Drain-O. Spare toilet paper. Female sanitary products. He ambled into the living room, where Ray was convening with CSU, wrapping it up.

After they'd secured the apartment and advised TARU to keep monitoring the phones, Ray's face greyed out with anxiety as he peered at his phone. "Shit. I gotta get home. Anna says Tia's in trouble with the school *again*. That kid, man… If she gets expelled, she's *going* to that Catholic school. I don't care what it costs."

"I'll deal with the paperwork," Alex said. "Don't worry about it." He knew better than to offer parenting advice. Ray would become defensive, then point out that Alex was hardly present when *his* girls were teenagers. Alex didn't need that pointed out.

Back at the office, he wrote property logs and a 'five summarizing the search. He shut off the computer, at the same time pushing himself to his feet, arching and twisting his body against his sore muscles. A quick visit to his locker to rescue a shirt that needed cleaning and a travel mug, then he rode a 1 train to West 86th, eyes closed but with a cop's awareness of everyone boarding the train. After leaving the subway, he bought a chocolate bar, bread, and cereal at a twenty-four hour bodega. With his groceries pinned to his side, he unlocked the main door and trundled upwards to his fourth-floor apartment. Immediately, he took a quick, hot shower, cleansing himself from sweat and city grunge. Trying to relax, to unclutter his head, he flopped onto the sofa, flicking on the TV for company but mostly, he ignored it. His mind whirred: subpoena Lennon's cell phone and internet data, speak with people at Suzanne's school again, follow up with NYC Hospitals about those medical records that hadn't shown up yet.

The job wouldn't release him, not even for a few hours. Had it ever? Sometimes, it felt like a parasite, like those wasps that take over the body of a spider, eating his organs, staring out of his eye sockets, telling him what to do. He pressed both palms into his gut. Selvio had thought he lost weight. He'd quit the drink in '95 and swam semi-regularly, but he never got rid of it, no matter how much he thought about exercise. When he was unwell, he lost his appetite and about ten pounds, but it always came back. He was only 5'8 but broad-shouldered and barrel-chested, so he carried a little extra weight without it becoming too cumbersome. Remorse over his unhealthy diet and lifestyle melted into regret – losing touch with Selvio. The age of social media hadn't stopped the continental drift of old friendships.

Seeking distractions, he tuned into the TV news, which was reporting on the wars in Iraq and Afghanistan, gloomy and endless. The news shifted from international to local. Some floods upstate, a lost dog in the Catskills that turned up two months later in Yonkers, more delays on the construction of the Second Avenue subway, and then the chirpy blonde news anchor stared raptly through the TV screen, pronouncing, "Between June and September of last year, the convictions of five more prisoners from New York County serving life sentences were vacated by the courts as miscarriages of justice, when new evidence and allegations of police misconduct came to light in a joint investigation by *The New York Times* and the Innocence Project."

Alex's breath got trapped between his lungs and his throat.

The reporter continued in her tinny voice, "ABC7 Eyewitness News has found out that Arjit Gundara, the US Attorney for the Southern District of New York, has convened a federal grand jury to investigate claims that the New York City Police Department has violated the civil rights of these five prisoners."

Oh, fuck. Panic, like a machete, slashed through his guts. He mopped at the sweat beading on his forehead. Ray had a hell of a nose, but not even he had foreseen this. Civil litigation had become the least of anyone's problems, an unimportant footnote. There were cops in the department who'd been sued dozens of times (both deserved and frivolous), and they were still on the job. But federal criminal investigations were light years from civil suits. Indictments, criminal charges, and no one escaping consequences with a six-figure settlement.

Alex folded his legs on the sofa, screwing his eyes closed. How well he remembered feeling sick to his stomach last year, when the *Times* published that Pulitzer-prize winning investigation, proving the innocence of prisoners with decades'-old murder convictions from Manhattan courts, alleging police and prosecutorial misconduct at worst, ineptitude at best. Perhaps there were others – well, undoubtedly – but the reporters and the Innocence Project lawyers had uncovered cases from Washington Heights connected by a singular thread: Vito as the primary precinct detective. The news anchor said their names, but Alex knew two of them without listening. Ernesto Serrachia. Guillermo Quixano. He'd been the MNHS primary on their cases.

Fucking liberal commie bullshit, Vito had texted Alex, when the courts vacated the convictions last summer.

Alex knew it wasn't. He had never answered Vito's text.

"All five of these cases were in the 34th Precinct, which covers Washington Heights and Inwood," the news anchor explained. "They may be the tip of the iceberg. We have been informed that the grand jury is focusing on the detective squad in that precinct, but the United States Attorney's office will not comment on an ongoing investigation."

In the late '80s and early '90s, the city surpassed its own murder rates every year, with more than six homicides per day north of 59th Street alone. Like every cop he knew, Alex did sloppy things if they tipped a case towards viability: prodding a reluctant witness at a line-up, fudging probable cause on a search warrant, believing any junk science, concluding a smudged partial print was good enough. Anything to keep his clearance rate near sixty percent, and it never was. No one really thought about false confessions in those days, either, not until the exoneration of the five men convicted of raping the Central Park Jogger. Everyone thought about confessions and interrogations differently after that.

His hands trembled. He woke up his iPhone, swiping to his contacts and tapping Vito's name.

"Lex, I told you, I ain't got nothin' –" Vito started saying. The man sounded tired.

"A fucking *grand jury?*" Alex exploded. "A federal case? Are you fucking kidding me? When were you gonna tell me? I had to find out from the news, from ABC. Were you just gonna sulk around until I got a subpoena?"

"Yo, man, cool your jets." Vito resumed his cocky, Brooklyn gruffness. "It's no biggie."

"No *'biggie?'* You need me to tell you how grand juries work? They'll hand out subpoenas like candy at Halloween, to anyone, to everyone who was ever involved with those cases, and everyone who even talked to anyone involved with those cases—"

"I know, I know, but it ain't gonna stick. The US Attorney, the Indian guy, wants a Senate seat. He's runnin' on a Democratic ticket. He gotta kiss the asses of all the avocado-eating liberals who hate cops, ya know."

"Vito—"

"Calm the fuck down. Okay? It ain't gonna be a thing. I know that guy wrote some shit in *The Atlantic,* but it don't matter. It's just like a liberal rag. It don't matter. Okay?"

Then Vito hung up, so Alex couldn't yell at him anymore. He dropped the phone onto the sofa. The TV had gone to commercials hawking things that seemed trivial, meaningless, and he flicked it off. His hands vibrated against the remote. His heart propelled hot blood through his arteries. No doubt, the feds were going to subpoena him. If he wanted those investigations to appear less fucked up than he remembered, he would have to perjure himself, like he did fifteen or twenty years ago. And if he perjured himself in front of a federal grand jury, the magnitude of fucked up would increase tenfold.

Part 2

Chapter Seven

January 1987

A bagpiper had planted himself on the square near One Police Plaza, his back to the Brooklyn Bridge and the East River, and he played snappy Scottish marches and wore an NYPD dress uniform. The gold buttons on his chest gleamed brightly in the low winter sun, like stars in a line. Alex wondered why the piper was there and if he ought to know the answer to that. A holiday? Had someone important died? The pipes keened in his ears as he approached the brutalist cube of a building. Too bad the music didn't drown his thoughts – or indeed, his terror, about this meeting. He was a young precinct detective who worked in a rough precinct in Queens; he had a screwed up personal life; and he had no idea why the Chief of Detectives wanted to see him. Not any more than he understood why a piper played tunes next to One Police Plaza. Cops called it the 'Puzzle Palace.' Today, he was puzzled. The Chief of Detectives oversaw five thousand people in the Detective Bureau, thousands of officers far more experienced and important than himself.

He felt sick, sweating profusely even though the Arctic wind streamed off the East River. He fussed with the shield clipped to his belt while making fleeting eye contact with the bored officers on security detail. The door slammed shut behind him, and the pipes grew faint. His lieutenant had said that the Chief of Detectives wanted a meeting. About the Magliozzi case? That started with a homicide, a Mob hit, but it led investigators to a mobster in the Bonano family named Gino Magliozzi, the target of a larger FBI operation. It was Alex's investigation, his wire, and his interrogation that opened fresh investigative avenues for the NYPD's Organized Crime Bureau and the FBI. The last he'd heard, Magliozzi himself had negotiated with the feds for reduced charges in exchange for turning state's on more mobsters. Those guys rolled on each other faster than a soccer ball kicked down the street.

As far as Alex knew, he hadn't violated any department regulations. But what if he'd blindly or stupidly run into trouble? Or an IAB complaint festered? *How could you have done that?* It wasn't like he fudged crime stats, took bribes, or sold cases. Only one guy in his entire eight-year career as a cop had offered, and that mope got charged with bribery.

Three uniformed cops joined him in the elevator, chattering about the Yankees. The team had evidently lost an important game to the Orioles, and the three men were heartbroken. Alex hoped they didn't notice the perspiration at his hairline. As he advanced along a corporately bland hallway, he tried to inhale steady, regular breaths, get oxygen to his brain. But he felt queasy and lightheaded when he knocked on the door leading to a corner office, where the Chief's secretary let him into the front room. She smiled at him, reassuring and avuncular, probably like she did for every schlemiel who ended up here.

"My name is Detective Alex Boswell," he said. "I have an appointment?"

Still smiling, she looked down at the book spread across her desk. "Oh, yes. Just take a seat there. He'll be with you in a minute." She indicated the four chairs along the wall underneath portraits of the current Police Commissioner and past ones, stern, unsmiling faces emerging from dark backgrounds, forever watching over a police department of 40,000 people. Each one bore an expression like being Police Commissioner made you into a miserable son of a bitch.

Alex sat on a faded blue fabric chair and crossed his right leg over his left knee. The phone rang, and the secretary picked up, saying in a metallic voice, "Chief of Detective's office." She prattled in noncommittal platitudes, while Alex gnawed at his fingernails until he pranged nerves. Blood oozed from the wound, so he covered his hand. After ten nerve-wracking minutes, the door opposite her desk opened: Robert Colangelo, the Chief of Detectives, his face instantly recognizable from the ceremony when Alex – and about fifty other cops – made the Bureau, from the news, and from his portrait on the wall of the precinct.

"Detective Boswell?" the Chief said.

His head swirled like he'd inhaled gasoline fumes. He followed Colangelo through the door. The Chief had a large window overlooking the three bridges – Manhattan, Brooklyn, Williamsburg – most of Lower Manhattan, the twin World Trade Center towers like huge monoliths, the grey river, the rows of buildings stacked in jumbled blocks atop steep-sided canyons. Colangelo indicated that Alex should sit. He lowered himself onto a chair, stilling his hands, but they ached and twitched. He folded them over his thigh so the Chief wouldn't see the blood on his right one.

"What can I do for you, Detective?" A beatific smile brightened Colangelo's face. The consummate politician.

Alex looked at him in surprise. What could the Chief of Detectives do for him, a twenty-nine year old precinct detective out in Queens? "Uh, what, sir?" he stammered, his gaze flitting from Colangelo's eyes to the bridges, like arteries connecting the heart of Manhattan to the rest of the body. Cars flowed across the bridges. Like blood, he thought, extending the metaphor, the city a living thing.

"You done good, Boswell, good for the department, good for the city." Colangelo tapped his fingers on the desk, drawing Alex's eyes from the window to the manila folder. His own personnel file. "This Magliozzi case, it's big stuff, eh? A federal task force."

Alex nodded and locked his fingers together.

"And you caught the case. It was your case. And very smartly handled. I look through this file, I see other good stuff. You closed that Curran case earlier this year. Made a hell of a dent in the Westies. It was great work. You closed a couple more homicides. This department isn't just about who you know. It's not all nepotism. It can't be. I want to move away from that. It's about what you can do. You know, I want to recognize young detectives off to a great start in their careers, help 'em out, know what I mean?"

Alex really didn't. Was he about to make second grade, at twenty-nine, or did the Chief mean something else? "Sorry, sir," he squeaked out. "I'm not following."

"You're wanting a transfer out of the Queens precinct, I can help you with that."

"Oh." It was true; Alex had never planned on spending years and years of his life investigating the banal, trivial shit you spend a lot of your time investigating as a precinct detective. Like a man bungee-jumping or shooting speedballs, he got a thrill from his redballs. He'd daydreamed about working high-grade felonies in a specialized squad. It was also true that his heart had always resided in Manhattan. He'd only moved to Queens because his personal life fell apart, and while he sometimes found the courage to face down a perp with a loaded gun, he'd never found the courage to deal with that mess, so he'd fled the scene. And he'd settled comfortably in the 103rd Precinct. Sure, he might have mentioned offhand to a few people that he had ambitions beyond the precinct squad, but he did not mean *at this second.* It would be easy – another couple years working at the One-Oh-Three.

"I understand," said Colangelo, his smile as warm as a fire on a winter's day. "You're playin' the big balls game with these cases. You want more. I get it. You don't wanna go back to shoplifting cases or finding out if someone's boyfriend really hits them or serving notices or figuring out if they were really robbed or just lost something. So… what can I do?"

A moment can pass, then it will be too late. A career case might not land in the One-Oh-Three Precinct for another year, or two or three, and he might not catch it if it did, and the Chief knew his name, his face now. He would forget next week, or tomorrow. Despite that, Alex's mind blanked. Where should he go? What specialized unit?

"I dunno," he said, tongue-tied.

"You like organized crime cases? OCCB's lookin' for people."

Alex touched his lips with his fingers. "I like working homicides—" he caught himself, stumbled over words. "I mean – I'm good on those types of cases. I closed all the homicides I got in the One-Oh-Three."

"You looking at a Homicide squad?"

"Yes, sir, I guess. Manhattan North. Manhattan South. Something like that." Last year, in one of the endless reorganizations of the police department, the Manhattan Homicide Task Force had split into two squads with the island divided at 59th Street: Manhattan North Homicide's bailiwick encompassing everything above 59th, and Manhattan South Homicide covering everything below it. They were meant to be the best of the best, with a reputation for handling complex, sensitive investigations.

"Harlem and Washington Heights are just getting worse," contemplated the Chief. "I haven't seen anything like this crack cocaine that's on the street. Reagan keeps talking about the 'war on drugs' and if it's a war, we sure are losing. Makes you miss the '70s. Liam Corcoran, he's the C/O up there, he's got like three dozen detectives, and they're working flat out."

He wasn't exactly selling the post, but Alex remembered the detectives from Queens Homicide who had worked with him on those murder cases. They probably hadn't thought much of him, a young, inexperienced precinct detective, but they carried a prestige about them, an aura, men who understood life and death in a way few people ever would, almost like they possessed power over death itself.

"I would go there, sir, if an assignment were available," he said.

"It could be," said Colangelo. "I'll make some calls."

"Yes, sir."

The Chief stood up, indicating that Alex should do the same. They shook hands, the Chief saying that someone would be in touch.

Alex felt blood pouring out of his head, but he nodded and met the Chief's eyes. "Thank you, sir."

In an instant, he'd transferred to a prestigious investigative unit, away from his friends in the Queens detective squad, a family when his own rejected him, and while he would not miss the precinct itself, he would miss them. But you have to take these chances when they come. The guys in the squad would understand. Hell, if and when they got an opportunity like this one, they wouldn't turn it down, either.

Chapter Eight

February 1987

Alex woke up lying on his side in the bathtub, his mouth bone dry, his head hurting so much that he wondered if he'd smashed it on something last night. A putrid wave of nausea cascaded through his innards. *Not in the fucking tub.* He dragged himself over the side, sliding onto the floor, then he crawled on his hands and knees to the toilet, where he spewed out the remnants of last night's debauchery as stringy, acidic liquid. *Oh, well, thank fuck I made the john.* His whole body felt sore, every muscle aching. His stomach convulsed again. He hugged the toilet, retching, his throat burning, and he spit acid into the bowl.

It had been a hell of a party. His last as a One-Oh-Three squad detective because in two days, he would be starting his new post in Manhattan North Homicide. It was also his thirtieth. If it's your farewell party-birthday-party extravaganza, you might as well make it spectacular. To hell with the next day!

In fairness, it was easy to say that the night before, and easier to regret. The pain in his head almost made him scream. But he shuffled into the living room, where one of his housemates, an ESU officer called Enrique Ortiz, and a few other refugees from the party hunkered in steamy, hungover darkness. The living room stank, acidly pungent with sweat, cigarette smoke, and booze. Countless empty bottles and cans rolled around on the floor. Cigarette butts peppered the table. Overstuffed trashbags squatted in a slipshod pile near the trashcan.

His One-Oh-Three partner, Fred Symington, commented, "Jesus, Lex, you were *fucked* last night."

So were you, Alex thought. Fred's face was paler than the white walls. A coffee mug quivered in his hand. Alex eyeballed another One-Oh-Three colleague, Nick Selvio, cataleptic on an armchair, hugging a Nesquick bottle. Why? Because they'd been mixing Nesquick with

Jameson. No wonder Alex felt so ill. Things that seem ingenious when drunk out of your mind usually never are when considered in the sober light of day.

"Where the fuck is Jimmy?" he asked.

Mad Jimmy Flynn was a CSU detective who drank more singlehandedly than an entire detective squad, but most of the time, you never knew the difference between him being drunk or sober anyway. His antics were legendary. He regularly walked butt-naked through the kitchen, grinning insolently when housemates shouted at him. He'd written *Alex is a cunt,* in ham, on the window after they'd fallen out about dishes. He'd once used the apartment vacuum cleaner to suction brake fluid out of his car.

"Oh, *shit,*" Ortiz said.

Alex looked at him.

"I put him outside," explained Ortiz.

"It's fucking February. Why the hell did you put him outside?"

"He was pissing in the Goddamned clean laundry basket. *My* fucking clean laundry basket. It ain't clean anymore."

"Somebody should make sure he's alive," said Alex.

"There's the door, Lex." Fred pointed to the door.

Alex oozed onto the stained, threadbare sofa, burrowing his thumbs into the mercury yolk roiling inside his eye sockets. "I didn't throw him outside." When no one said anything or moved after a while, he grumbled, "Someone has to be responsible in this fucking house," and with a tortured groan, he heaved himself to his feet.

One of Ortiz's ESU buddies was prostrate in front of the door like he had tried to get out but hadn't made it. Alex nearly decked it, tripping over the guy's body. As he recovered his balance, his stomach writhed in another paroxysm, and he vomited into the hedge beside the door. Woozily, he got up and shambled around the rowhouse. There was Jimmy, unconscious, lying with his torso in the neighbor's yard and his legs on the sidewalk. The neighbors were out of town this week.

"Come on, pal," Alex said, kneeling beside him. "Jimmy, let's go inside." He grabbed Jimmy by the upper arm, feeling the strain on his back as he realized Jimmy was incapable of standing or walking under his own power. So Alex slung Jimmy's right arm around his neck and shoulder and held him around the waist, the way you're trained when removing people in similar states from the streets. He dragged Jimmy inside the apartment and dumped him on the floor, seconds before his own legs lost function, and he crumpled into a heap of hungover misery on the sofa.

"You want coffee?" Ortiz asked.

"Yeah." Moaning, he buried his face in his hands.

"Oh, Dave is taking your room," Ortiz stated, handing Alex a cup of coffee.

Alex breathed in the aromatic steam rising out of the mug – pungent spices, burnt chocolate. His brain sputtered like a car with a dead starter motor. Oh, yeah, he didn't live here anymore. He had moved to a tiny studio apartment in Chinatown, as much of a hole as this place, but miles closer to his new command and no Jimmy to piss in the laundry when he got drunk. Tentatively, he lapped at the coffee. It recoiled inside his stomach like oil in a hot frying pan. "Who's Dave?"

"That's Dave." Ortiz pointed to the ESU cop passed out against the door.

Alex nodded tiredly and risked another tiny mouthful.

"You remember passing out on the john?" Fred asked.

"Huh?"

Fred sputtered his coffee, laughing. "You went in and didn't come out for a long time. We were pounding on the door and you didn't answer. So, Jimmy and me went out, climbed up to the window, and you were sitting on the john, completely fucked. Jimmy climbed up like fucking Rambo and broke the locks."

This is almost over, Alex thought. Rueful pangs knifed his chest. He shouldn't feel like this, because his new post was a giant step forward for his career. Moreover, he could take it as an opportunity to cast aside all the shit his ex-wife had put him through and become a useful father to his two daughters. She would try to undermine that, because she was a vindictive bitch, but they were his kids too, and he would act more adult-like, step up to the parenting plate. While his move back to Manhattan was spurred by the Chief of Detectives' offer to transfer him to any squad he wanted, he had come to see that he needed a change, for more than his career. No way would he bring his kids to this hole.

Or, for that matter, let them see him in this state, trembling and as pale as a DOA fished from the river. He sniffed in the steam and peered over the rim of his mug at Dave, taking his place here. Dave snored and rolled up against the door. Ortiz shoved him in the ribs with his foot, and Dave moaned but was otherwise oblivious. New York's finest indeed.

"You all right there, Lex?" Fred asked.

"I just feel pretty rough," he answered. *Homicide squad, man,* they had said when he told them about the transfer. *People are dying to get that post!* They were pleased for him – an elite investigative unit, big cases. *You'll make first grade in a year!*

Whatever he said to himself, he felt like his life had moved on too fast. He had been raised in the Jewish community of the Lower East Side, then he floated through a criminal justice degree at CCNY, before joining the NYPD, and after he graduated from the Academy, he walked a beat in the Sixth Precinct, his first posting. Later, he got a post in the Tenth Precinct detective squad, first as a 'white shield,' which means you're an investigator in the squad, but you don't get the coveted gold shield – the rank of detective – until you've done at least eighteen months of that. A steadily climbing career trajectory, the thing so many cops have wet dreams about, yet here he was, conflicted and upset. It made no Goddamned sense.

Amidst party debris – mostly cans, bottles, and pizza boxes – he lay down on the squalid living room carpet, then he rolled onto his side, an ineffective attempt to shift the pain and nausea inside his belly. When that didn't work, he whined, "Do we still have Alka-Seltzer in this place?" The coarse carpet fibers scraped against his cheek.

Fred giggled at the schadenfreude while he offered up a glass of water with a tablet of Alka-Seltzer. Alex propped himself upright on one elbow so he could guzzle the whole glass. He sank to the floor again, knees curled to his chest with his aching head on his forearm.

By 1600 hours, he felt like he'd been hit by a small train, but his digestive system started working again. About an hour beforehand, Fred and Enrique had made breakfast of sorts; he'd succeeded at eating a fried egg and an Eggo waffle. Enrique insisted that fried eggs cured any hangover. Everyone had their pet hangover cures. Most of it was bullshit. There was only time and pathetic promises to never drink again, until you did.

On his way out, Alex opened the cleaning closet, where his now ex-housemates had stowed things he had forgotten: a couple t-shirts, a tie, and a book. He rammed them into a plastic shopping bag, then stood awkwardly by the door, watching Nick Selvio – who had returned to the land of the living – and Ortiz tossing beer cans into a trash bag. Mad Jimmy crawled onto the sofa and fell asleep. Dave threw up in the bathroom. Fred smoked a cigarette.

"Well, I think I'd better go," Alex said. "I have a lot of unpacking to do."

Fred said, "How about I walk you to the subway station?"

"Yeah, that'd be nice."

Ortiz and Selvio shook his hand. They were all cops, tough, streetwise, no lingering on long goodbyes. "Take care, man." Alex and Fred joined the bustling street and walked along Fresh Pond Avenue towards the M subway station, past the butchers, greengrocers, cash converters, and delis; past rowhouses and three and four-story walk-ups with tatty awnings. Ridgewood teemed with that quintessential New York ethnic mix, Black and Hispanic, Jewish and Greek and Italian, Caribbean and Irish.

The subway line in Queens reared above the roads, and the two detectives stopped underneath the el pillars where they crossed Fresh Pond Avenue. A train roared overhead. Alex fished around in his pocket for a subway token, then held it tightly in his hand. Yeah, he was only crossing the East River, not leaving the planet, but he feared that he might not see Fred for a while. They would not have long nights out or the profound connection of working as partners, the way they did now.

"Alex, I meant to tell you, but I guess that party got pretty wild, and I didn't get to it," breathed Fred once the train roared away.

Worried, he looked into Fred's blue eyes. Fred only used the entirety of his first name when he had something significant to say.

"It's good you've got the Homicide squad job," continued Fred carefully. "Really good. Things are gonna have to change for me as well. I'm gonna have to get it together, you see. Be a responsible adult and all that. Gotta rein in some of the late nights and all the crazy shit. 'Cause Celia's pregnant."

"Oh, wow, congratulations." Alex rocked backwards, shocked, but spitting out the boilerplate response. Celia was Fred's long-term girlfriend, who he had promised to marry at some point. From the look in Fred's eyes, Alex read between the lines that the pregnancy wasn't entirely planned, or at least not entirely planned by Fred, but he was happy, he would roll with it.

"So, I'm gonna have to step up," Fred explained. "I'm gonna have to be there for her, for the kid."

Alex nodded, sucking on his lower lip. From where he stood underneath the train tracks, he saw Fred embracing this unexpected reality, his life transforming inexorably, at the very point where Alex had failed with his own daughters, Sarah and Elana. Being there – or not.

Fred grasped his shoulder and held it in a firm grip. "I'll miss you, I'll miss working with you in the squad, man, but you'll only be across the river."

"Yeah, it won't be the same," Alex muttered.

"No, but is anything?"

There didn't seem to be anything left to say. The el pillar trembled under the weight of another train approaching. Alex remarked flaccidly, "See you soon, I hope." He scaled the station's stairs, his feet and his heart turning to lead. People scrabbled around him as if their world might end if they missed that train. Alex didn't care if he missed the train. There would always be another one. Unhurried, he rammed his token through the slot in the turnstiles, arriving on the platform at the same time as the train. Its doors hissed open, and he crossed the gap. His chest felt hollow, like a piece of his heart had been cut away. When the train squealed and pitched forwards, he torqued his pelvis around in his seat to gaze backwards out the window, bidding a silent, mournful farewell to Queens, to the One-Oh-Three Precinct, to his life for the past three years. It had seemed much longer than that. This was something new. It was exciting. Queens was behind him, and he would look forward to it, dammit.

Chapter Nine

Alex resisted his impulse to rip off his nails while his new C/O, Lieutenant Liam Corcoran, read through the day's announcements at roll call and then introduced him to his new squad. The homicide detectives craned their heads around. Their eyes disemboweled him like the ME's scalpel. He felt acutely aware of what he looked like: young, nothing like as slim or fit as he should be, those troubled lines crinkling around soulful brown eyes. Some of these men – and they were all men – had been police officers for longer than he had been alive. They were hard men, schooled in catastrophe, entrusted with pursuing that most egregious of crimes, the theft of human life. They knew the suffering of the streets intimately, facing the reckoning of mortality every day, sudden, cruel, terrible, but in their world, commonplace. They knew everything about interrogations, using informants, surveillance, forensics, pathology, the Penal Law, the twists and turns of Criminal Procedure Law. The light seemed to catch in their eyes, that stark certainty, that confidence born from years devoted to flying a true line between slivers of evidence, weaving narratives around a body on the sidewalk, the contradictions of the CPL, and the tawdry horror of the violence on the city streets. This was the major leagues. If you were good enough, nothing else you would ever do as a cop mattered this much, and if you weren't, within a year or two you would be transferred to another unit or a precinct squad.

Alex trapped his tongue between his molars. *What the hell am I doing here?* he asked himself. *I'm not the detective these men are.*

But here he was. Immediately after roll call, he met with his new boss. Liam Corcoran was well-spoken, for a cop, with a slight Irish affectation. He prattled about his expectations of any death investigator assigned to his elite unit. He described the squad's biggest redballs, ones Alex had read about in the newspaper. The Chambers murder. The Edmund Perry case. Then he digressed, telling Alex about his family, who emigrated to New York from a small town in Donegal called Ardara. Alex could now locate Ardara, because Corcoran had a huge map of Ireland covering half

69

a wall, with his family's hometown on the squiggly northwest coastline marked by a thumbtack and a green and gold flag, the colors of County Donegal's hurling team. Alex also learned that hurling was a sport, not what happens after too much whiskey. On the other wall, half a dozen dead Irish revolutionaries glowered at him from the black backgrounds of their portraits.

"And where are you from?" queried Corcoran.

"The Lower East Side," Alex replied.

"No, I mean, where's your family from? Boswell sounds like a Scottish name. Is it?"

Oh, he thought. Corcoran looking for a fellow Celt. "Uh, no. My great-grandfather was a Russian Jew who fled the pogroms. His last name was Beskryostnov. He was assigned a name that sounded...I guess...American. Couldn't start a new life here with a name no one could pronounce."

"Ah. Yes. The Lower East," Corcoran said haltingly, shifting his weight in his chair and rearranging pens inside a mug.

Alex kicked himself for his smartass mouth and oblique indictment of anti-Semitism here and abroad. Don't go there with the new Catholic boss. Not yet.

"Boswell doesn't sound Jewish, but sure, that makes sense," Corcoran continued. "Lots of Jews on the Lower East. There used to be anyway. And you grew up there? It wasn't as wild as it is now, sure."

"It was different." At times, he felt like a stealth Jew, quietly infiltrating the NYPD ranks of Catholics and WASPs because a century ago, his great-grandfather had desperately assimilated, jettisoning his Russian identity.

"Do you go to a synagogue?"

"Uh, not for a while." His voice caught in his throat. His gaze shifted towards the statues – a diminutive Virgin Mary on the desk and a crucifix affixed to the wall.

"I know Jews believe in God, but there's lots about it I don't quite get," Corcoran said. "But it doesn't matter. It's good to believe in something, so it is. For this job. And sure, God is the same for you as He is for me and all of us. God has put us here, to speak for the dead."

"Yes, sir."

"There will be times when your faith is all you have."

"Yes, sir."

Thankfully, Corcoran steered the conversation back to the escalating violence that went hand-in-hand with crack cocaine, coke combined with water and baking soda into a rock-like freebase form that people smoked instead of snorted. It made cocaine affordable. Unlike powdered coke, you didn't need a chemistry degree to make something that got people high. And unlike heroin, supply wasn't tightly controlled by the Mafia and other organized crime syndicates. Anyone could be a drug dealer, and the police bleakly joked that there were 25,000 crack cottage industries in New York. The high was intense but short-lived, so people took hit after hit, three bucks each, losing themselves to addiction within the blink of an eye. Crack cared little for borders, scourging cities across the country, but Washington Heights was a gateway for cocaine imported from South and Central America. Dealers flooded the place, and the drug trade reigned over the corners. Corcoran could remember the heroin epidemic; he could remember the assassinations of Martin Luther King, Malcolm X, and the Kennedy brothers; he could remember Vietnam War protests and civil rights protests. But crack had precipitated a pandemic of violence, more virulent than heroin or civil unrest or anything he'd seen.

In early 1986, Corcoran had handpicked his initial Manhattan North Homicide squad, guys he'd known for years, some of the best investigators on the job, but in 1987, when the Chief of Detectives called him and said he had a promising young detective who he wanted to send to the squad, Corcoran was happy to take anyone who was breathing. Nonetheless, he stated, he'd examined Alex's personnel file and asked around, learning that Alex had a key role in closing a big multi-agency Mafia case, which meant he had his wits about him and played nice with others. He was thirty, so he lacked the experience Corcoran thought so fundamental in a skilled death investigator, but according to his file and his previous supervisors, he was a sensible cop with good instincts.

"Sure, you'll get the experience here," he told Alex at the end of their meeting. "More than you ever wanted, I'm afraid."

He assigned Alex to the B team (the squad had four teams of detectives, who rotated between shifts), partnering him with Detective Eddie Trenemen, a burly 6'2 African-American cop who had been with the Homicide Task Force before it split into the Manhattan North and South Homicide squads. Trenemen had grown up in West Harlem, then 1969 happened, and like a lot of poor kids, he found himself drafted into the army, shipped to Vietnam. When the war ended, he joined the NYPD. After bouncing around precincts, he'd worked in the Three-Oh precinct squad for a few years before becoming a full-time homicide detective. He wore flawlessly ironed shirts and custom-tailored suits, and he radiated contentment as he wheeled department Crown Victorias around desolate streets and crumbling buildings. "A Black guy and a Jew," he said to Alex, treating systemic inequality and racism with wry humor. "We're the new face of the NYPD! We'll be on the next recruitment brochure." No matter how grisly the crime scene, he never seemed dark or introspective, instead relishing the challenges of inner-city ghettos, those fissures of violence where people needed him, and the work mattered.

Alex immediately liked him. Mostly, he was relieved that Corcoran hadn't assigned him to Mikey Brady or Declan Keohane, two abrasive Irish cops who habitually slung epithets about anyone who wasn't white or Catholic, and who ostensibly hadn't learned anything new since 1965 or worked any harder, even though the murder rate broke every record and three decades of progressive Supreme Court decisions meant a detective had to move cautiously. Now and again, Alex saw glimmers of talent and inspiration when they worked a case, but he generally assumed that their Emerald Society and 100th Precinct connections to Corcoran kept them in the boss' good graces. The old white Irish boys' club. The Chief of D's had told him, 'It's not all nepotism,' but any cop knew a hell of a lot of it was.

The B team also had Martín Vasquez and Bill Ryan. Vasquez was Black, but of Dominican descent, bilingual, low-key and steady in his case work. He was married to a nurse, who would phone the squad room looking for him whenever he worked lots of overtime or the detectives went out drinking. Every man in the squad knew her. The son of immigrants who'd settled in the Heights, Vasquez connected to the people they were policing, and he had siblings, cousins, and in-laws in the neighborhood. He introduced himself as Marty; he was sick of people Anglicizing his name, stressing the *a* instead of the *i*. Ryan, another Irish cop, was oddly well-educated, holding a master's degree in philosophy. With gentle mannerisms, he professed his love for sailing and fishing, and he owned a small sailboat berthed at a marina near his home in the Rockaways. The other two detectives on the B team were Matt Cohen, another Jew, from Canarsie, observant and formal, with a quirky, understated sense of humor, and Sam Rizzo, Italian, also from Brooklyn, an OCCB detective before moving to Homicide, a man known for his limitless collection of colorfully inappropriate stories about sex workers, ex-girlfriends, and Mobsters

Alex quickly earned points by keeping up with Keohane and Brady on the pints and proving himself to be good-humored at taking squad practical jokes, like blown-up condoms and porn on his desk, a dead trout in his locker, and his phone superglued to the receiver. Welcome to the fucking squad. All squads, in some ways, were the same.

During his first set with Eddie, Alex read through paperwork and cleaned up large amounts of admin for Eddie's open investigations. Although he found paperwork less aversive than Eddie did, he felt out of his depth as he got to know his partner's style of working cases. At a crime scene, Eddie not only absorbed physical evidence, but everything and everyone on the periphery. Other detectives might be drawing sketches, staring at a body, or making tasteless jokes, but Eddie would quietly stand back, taking his time, taking in the scene, and then he would suddenly pinpoint something vital that no one else had noticed. His memory was extraordinary. Unlike himself and every cop Alex had ever known, Eddie never brought a notepad to crime scenes. He remembered every detail, every face, every word witnesses said, and he could tell you months later which shootings involved a .38 revolver with hollow points, or whose alibi was a lie, or if a witness in one case had associations to another one, years later. Somehow, he'd escaped the virus that was afflicting big city homicide squads, the who-really-gives-a-shit contagion that infects detectives when they've worked sixty or seventy drug murders, and their hearts sink whenever the length of another victim's criminal history rivals the Talmud. But Eddie never showed symptoms of burnout. He worked every case until all conceivable leads had been exhausted, then he worked it a bit more. Clarity of thought and a warm, honest approach to dealing with people, even the toughest characters, underpinned his whole philosophy of police work.

They went to the uptown precincts, and Eddie introduced Alex to their detective squads; they went to the seediest bars, the ones that saw fights every week; they went to the projects where Eddie said you would find the most trouble, the open-air drug markets, the burned-out buildings, the corners where dealers fought for customers and a simple insult could lead to a drive-by shooting. Within a few weeks, Eddie saw something he liked in his young partner, and Alex was surveilling perps or questioning witnesses unsupervised. Within a month, he was primary detective on his own cases. No one had training wheels for long up here.

Alex learned that Eddie, who was fifty-one, had a wife and two teenage children, a boy and a girl, and they lived in Riverdale, and Eddie's wife, Stella, taught finance at Columbia University's business school. "She's a brilliant lady," Eddie said. "The first Black female professor in the business school!" Alex learned that Eddie had been given the purple heart after serving two military tours in Vietnam. Eddie spoke fondly of his family, of walking a beat in the Bronx, of working as a detective in Harlem, and he didn't speak fondly of Vietnam. "It was hell," he'd said with uncharacteristic bleakness after they'd worked a case where an argument between two Vietnam vets had escalated into fists and baseball bats, and the loser ended up DOA in the Columbia Pres ICU. Alex winced like he'd stepped on a knife, disturbed by his partner's pained reaction. He changed the subject.

He also avoided the subject of his own sordid personal life, although after a month, his colleagues surely had some idea because they were detectives. Still, Alex felt ashamed. Eddie had this Norman Rockwell family thing going on, while he was estranged from his ex-wife, and he hadn't seen his daughters in two years. His ex thought he was an asshole, and he wouldn't disagree. Since starting this post, he'd left her half a dozen answering machine messages, stressing that he'd moved back to Manhattan, and he would like to see the girls. Catherine never returned his calls. While rambling uselessly to her answering machine, he chewed his nails and fingertips to shreds. Blood smeared around his fingers. Furious at her, at himself, he whacked the phone against the receiver, then held his hand under the cold kitchen tap until the frigid water dulled the pain.

That night, Alex and Eddie sat in the car, eating burgers on their laps, watching a perp's apartment. Eddie asked Alex why he had band-aids on the first three fingers of his right hand. This time, Alex drearily unloaded the truth – the saga of his failed marriage, only skipping the part about his affair with a patrolwoman. No good way to explain that. Sure, he had been miserable, the relationship dying like an oxygen-starved fire, the affair a release, but Eddie had a weirdly prim sensitivity, given his line of work, and he would see that as a profound personal failure. It was, but Alex wanted to keep his partner's respect.

"You gotta be tough to be married to a cop," said Eddie, nodding sagely. "Stella's the toughest person I know. But she understands me, and the job. She gets how important it is, you know, especially *this* job, solving murders. But it's hard on people, and some people, they don't understand. They resent all the time it takes. It takes *you*. It's not like teaching college kids about corporate finance. They can never have that part of you, and they have to be cool with that."

"Catherine never understood it."

"But it's also important for kids to have a father," Eddie added in a serious tone. "To know he cares."

"I've said that."

Eddie smiled encouragingly as he chewed on his burger. "Be persistent. Those kids gotta know you love them."

"I'm not sure they do. I walked out. They stayed in the Village."

"I mean, sure, you've made mistakes, you've fucked up. You wouldn't be the first, you know. There's a long line. But she can't legally keep you from them."

"Yeah." Possibly not, but a family lawyer would cost hundreds of dollars.

Once, they had been driving along Amsterdam when Eddie swerved to the curb, observing, "This place is perpy as hell. Look, that guy's gonna try to rob that liquor store," and Alex looked, seeing nothing suspicious, while Eddie radioed in a ten-ten, a possible crime. The guy he'd identified kicked in the store's glass door just as two sector cars arrived. The uniforms arrested him. Alex was amazed. The perp hadn't seemed any sketchier than anyone else on that street.

Even if had thirty more years on the job, he would never end up as streetwise and sharp as Eddie Trenemen.

Chapter Ten

August 1987

Alex, wearing jeans and a grey CCNY t-shirt, paced beside the red brick townhouses on West 11th Street, across the road from PS 41. His gut churned like a washing machine. He'd barely managed to stomach half a bagel at 0600 this morning. He tried to arrange the thoughts in his head like pieces on those outdoor chessboards in a windstorm. With Catherine refusing to respond to any messages, he had come here, where he knew he would find her and the girls. He had now been in Manhattan for six months, yet he hadn't seen his kids. In six months, Catherine could have answered the Goddamned phone.

Using his detective skills, he'd worked out where the girls went to school, and then he'd made up an excuse to leave an eight-by-four early. He felt like a stalker, but what else could he do? Showing up at Catherine's apartment seemed like a more egregious transgression. At least this was somewhat public. Barring orders of protection, a father could wait for his daughters at their school.

A taxi halted at the curb next to an Italian café. He stopped his pacing and folded his arms tightly under his ribs. Somehow, he knew she would be in that car. Yes – Catherine smartly stepped out of the cab. She wore a frilly blue top with a low V-shaped neckline, slim jeans that hugged her butt, and pointy, high-heeled boots. She worked in public relations, fashioning media images and statements for celebrities, politicians, companies, and she'd finely crafted her own look so impeccably that you wanted her running your PR.

Run, disappear around the corner! His heart sped up, and his stomach shriveled into a wiry ball of nausea. Their relationship had been like the 100-year flood, and he had been in the way. No, he couldn't run, because Catherine saw him, and she was striding imperiously towards him, her expression frosty.

"Alex! What the hell are you doing here?" she hissed.

"I wanna see my kids. I've left you like a dozen messages on your machine."

"How did you know they went to this school?"

He breathed hard, like he'd run up a steep hill. "I'm a detective. I can find things out."

"You should leave."

"You can't bitch that I don't give a damn about the girls when you don't answer my calls. You don't have a problem accepting my child support checks every month, but you're not gonna pick up the fucking phone?"

"*You* care so much, you slept with that broad," Catherine snarled.

Okay, that part was his fault, but at that point, Alex hadn't cared anymore, not about Catherine or his marriage. PO Abbey Giancarlo had been cute, interested, and not mad at him. Still.

"It's my legal right to see them," he stated firmly.

"Then get a fucking lawyer."

Anger radiated from her whole being, leaking through his pores like fine, sharp grains under his skin. "I hope I don't have to. I don't need that complication in my life. Neither do you. We've already gone through all that. Wasn't once enough?"

"They don't need a loser like you in their lives." She lowered her voice and looked around nervously, as though afraid other parents might see them.

"They need their father."

"So they learn that you don't give a shit? That you care more about the NYPD and schtupping whatever cute girl cop you have your eyes on than your family?"

What *had* they once seen in each other? That shock raced through his body, the surprise that you had once been in love with someone who hated you so vehemently, but then, it should not surprise him at all since he dealt with those interpersonal dynamics every day at work. Trying to sound calm, rational, he said, "The job takes a lot of time, and it takes a lot outta you. Outta everyone. The shift patterns are crazy. That's just how it is. It wasn't me trying to piss you off. Lots of cops' partners struggle with it for a while."

Nonetheless, he had slept with Abbey Giancarlo.

"The freakin' job," she sneered. "You always blame everything but yourself and talk like you do the most important job in the world. Why do cops say 'the job' all the time? Working at Walmart is a job. Waiting tables is a job. Brain surgery is a job. Everything is a Goddammed job.

It's you who didn't come home at night. It's you who didn't give a shit about the girls when they were little. It's you who slept around. Not 'the job.'"

His eyes felt heavy, falling down to the sidewalk. "I'm trying to do things differently. Like I said in those messages, I'm Homicide now. It won't be like walking a beat or being in a precinct squad."

"Will it really?" She planted her hands on her hips.

He placed a hardened look on his face, but his heart splintered. He didn't know what he could do or say to fix it, or if anything would really change. The long hours, the awkward shift patterns, and the trauma on the streets wouldn't.

The bell from the school broke into their silence, a claxon exploding across the humming West Village traffic. Alex watched the expectant parents lining up near the entrance. A few parents nosily eyed him and Catherine, like bystanders at a crime scene.

"It would be a shock for the girls to see you here," suggested Catherine, her voice a fraction gentler.

"Do they wanna see me?" he asked softly.

She hesitated for a moment. "I don't know."

Like any good cop, he could spot a lie from any distance. The anger rose again, a taste like sour acid in his throat. "Look, Catherine. If you think it would be too much of a scene for them to see me here, I'll go. I'll go right now. But I really wanna see them. I need to. And they need to see me. Please, call me sometime, okay? I don't want this to be a thing with lawyers and all that shit." His voice sounded broken, defeated.

She considered him, their ruined relationship standing before them, an inaccessible, sheer mountainside.

"I'll call you," she said curtly.

The hopeless impotence overpowering, agonizing, he whirled away from PS 41, glancing over his shoulder at the children pouring out of the front doors to their waiting, happy parents. He kept race-walking, striding quickly along 11th, so distracted when he crossed the star-like intersection of Greenwich, 11th, and Seventh that he forgot to look for cars coming from the other side of West 11th, flying at an angle surprising to anyone accustomed to Manhattan's usual grid. A taxi whipping around the corner nearly hit him. The cab honked, the driver mouthing the words *fuck you, asshole*, and Alex looked at the man, shrugging apologetically. *Sorry, pal.* Digging his nails into his palms, he jogged uptown on Seventh until 14th Street, and then he cantered down the subway station stairs.

A 2 train disgorged its arrivals. Alex boarded it, fighting for breath amongst writhing, crushing bodies, and he squeezed onto the last empty seat, curled over his belly as if his appendix had ruptured. The train thundered into Canal Street. He swayed to his feet. The doors were sliding shut, and he leapt onto the platform before he missed his stop.

Instead of wallowing in his lonely apartment, he strayed amongst the crowded streets of Chinatown. The pavement was burgeoning with people, carts, trash, and the air felt viscous with that New York stench, exhaust and urine. On the streets and in the small shops jumbled along the narrow sidewalks, you could buy every kind of food imaginable, and a lot of stuff that was pretty unimaginable as well – exotic fruit, eels, fish, frogs, snakes, chicken feet, pig feet, hearts and livers and brains of God only knew what, dumplings, curries and stews and chow mein. You could be on the streets of Beijing or Shang-Hai. Alex wandered aimlessly amongst the overflowing stalls until his growling stomach and the hectic streets guided him to a fried food cart. The guy manning the cart only spoke Mandarin. Unruffled, Alex gesticulated towards the menu, buying spare-ribs and rice rolls, topped with a spicey sauce. He ate it on the street. He found it less taxing to eat take-out or street food rather than cook for himself.

His apartment was on Mulberry Street, a couple blocks south of the chaotic Canal Street intersection. It wasn't a peaceful or a particularly crime-free block, but the rent was cheap, on the third floor of a five-story walk-up above a laundromat and a noodle place. Often, he smelled the noodles and spices in the apartment.

Once inside, he poured himself a large glass of Jameson. As he stared at the golden liquid, he saw himself stumbling into that West Village apartment after a hair-raising midnight tour, tremulously pouring a whisky, just in time for Catherine to kick him in the teeth. "The girls will see that any time you're stressed or unhappy, you drink. You think I want them to have that as an example? A role model? Jesus fucking Christ." That, and his habit of coming home at strange hours when he worked overtime, finished four-by-twelves, or the guys from the precinct went out drinking, the last commonly following the others. Fred had told him he wouldn't stay out anymore when Celia had her baby. Why hadn't Alex curtailed his post-tour boozing sessions? Too late now.

He tossed back most of the whiskey. It rasped against his throat, heating his insides. He swallowed another mouthful and stared out the window overlooking Mulberry Street. Traffic was stationary, the gridlock like a heap of toy cars and trucks thrown all over the road. Drivers pounded their horns. A thousand windows stared at the streets. Eight million people in this city, and if he winked out of existence, the universe would barely ripple. Loneliness slithered around his heart like a venomous snake. *Don't be so fucking depressed. You're thirty years old and in a Manhattan homicide squad.* There were guys from his graduating class at the Academy still walking a beat, wondering when they would get a transfer to something else, a promotion, or a gold shield.

Staying his hand from pouring another whiskey, he picked up his phone and called Sam Rizzo and Marty Vasquez, the two MNHS detectives most likely to join him for spur-of-the-moment drinks. He wasn't sure if they liked him, but they were always up for the pub, and drinking with colleagues was less depressing than drinking alone. Although he liked Eddie, he saw him as someone to respect the hell out of, not someone to get smashed with. Besides, Eddie responsibly went home to his college professor wife and his kids, never staying out late or getting hammered.

Marty and Sam were predictable, as ever. Alex met them at a bar called the Glendale in the West Village, a Lower Manhattan cop hang-out, faintly lit with smoky overhead lights and small windows squinting at Bleeker Street. Dense wood panels and heavy oak furniture darkly cladded the interior. The owner had decorated the walls with 1920s and '30s advertisements for alcoholic beverages, photos of Marilyn Monroe, Elvis, and Cary Grant, and more black-and-white photos of the city from the same decades. A permanent haze of cigarette smoke blurred your vision well before you drank a single beer.

The detectives sat in an unlit corner booth, chatting about work and squad gossip, until Alex, with four pints in his belly, announced, "My ex-wife is still a horrible bitch. I tried to see my kids today, and she wouldn't fucking let me. When's it gonna be about the girls having their father in their lives and not her being pissed at me?"

Marty and Sam nodded sympathetically. Sam lit a cigarette. By now, the whole squad knew about his disreputable personal history. Late-night stakeouts, long car rides tailing perps, longer nights out drinking, scary warrant entries, the intense connection that arises from facing danger together, from working as a team against man's awful inhumanity to man. There are no more secrets. Hadn't Catherine occasionally bitched that Alex's colleagues knew more about his innermost thoughts and emotions than she did? That allegation was true.

"Okay, I fucked around with a patrolwoman. That's my fault. But it shouldn't be about that anymore. That was years ago. Things were shit between us, and I did it. I'm fucking guilty. And maybe I was emotionally unavailable. She accused me of that, and she was probably right. But now… it's time to move on, isn't it? It should be about the kids. Not how she feels about me. She thinks I… I don't fucking know what she thinks. But fuck her."

Marty and Sam kept at it with the sympathetic nods and grunts.

"There was a time when she wasn't such a bitch," Alex reflected sadly. "When we were students at CCNY together. I guess the job changed things."

The three finished their beers and bought another round. They knew how the job changed relationships. Long nights on duty, overtime, Alex coming home after work, unable to tell her about the things he had seen, and Catherine staying up all night with sick kids because it wasn't like he had any control over his shift patterns. Even if he hadn't slept with Abbey Giancarlo, the relationship would have blown apart. Abbey was a symptom.

Marty observed that his wife was the most patient woman in the world. "But she's got her own life. Her own friends. Her own shit she does. And she works a lot of nights. She's working tonight. It's not like she's sitting up every night waiting for me to get home. That helps. Sometimes."

"Does it help at *all?*" smirked Sam. "She calls at least once a week to bitch that you're in a bar and not home. I've been tempted to say that you're not at the Glendale – you're with your other girlfriend."

Marty laughed dryly. "Please don't. She'll change the locks on the doors."

Sam argued that it was easier to avoid commitment. "I just get some ass whenever I can."

They vacated the Glendale, wandering up the road to the Bitter End because it had a late license. Its walls were plastered in album covers, and its crowd was young and fashionable, women wearing leggings, bearded men wearing plaid. An acoustic band played Dylan covers. A few sets later, the Dylan-tribute band handed the stage to a trio of women singing folk songs in a three-part harmony.

"Eight out of ten for fuckability," commented Rizzo, drawing deeply on a cigarette. "Oh, shit. I can't say that anymore, can I? They got a female detective on the C team now. Can you fucking believe it? What's the world coming to? In the '70s, women were safely in the Policewoman's Bureau. That's gone now. They've started letting them walk beats, get gold shields. Now they're homicide detectives. There's gonna be a woman commissioner if we're not careful."

Jean Allan had transferred to MNHS from Vice last month. As Rizzo said, she worked on the C team, not their team, so luckily for Rizzo (or maybe Allan), he only had to interact with her in passing.

"I heard on the wire that she was a stripper before joining the NYPD," commented Marty flippantly. No one knew if that was true, or if it was a misogynistic rumor that made a female homicide detective seem less threatening.

"She did some undercover work in Vice," Alex said. That, he knew, wasn't a rumor. Allan herself told him about it over a beer one night. She preferred to socialize with the younger detectives, the ones who didn't eye her askance or treat her like a sex object or a secretary. "The L-T's more enlightened than he looks," she had reflected. "You know, I was in Vice 'cause it was the only specialized post a female detective could get. So you could go undercover as a pross. I hated it. But this, this is big step. More than half the people in this squad are chauvinist assholes, but it's still a big step and fuck them. In a few years, they'll be dead or retired."

Anyway, it made her less threatening to Rizzo. "I'll imagine her naked. Maybe I can get her in bed."

Alex poured the remnants of his beer down his throat. "Don't think you're her type." Maybe the brazen chauvinism would die or retire with the old guys.

"What's her type then?"

"Someone who's not a schmuck."

For some reason, Rizzo found this hilarious, and he laughed so hard he couldn't breathe.

"Oh, shit," Alex said, cutting into Sam's hysterics. "It's an eight-by-four tomorrow, isn't it? I'm gonna be fucked." Unsteadily, he squirmed off the bar stool. "I'm gonna hit the road. Before I'm too wasted to remember where I live."

"You taking a cab?" Marty asked, looking considerably more sober than Alex felt. He hadn't pre-gamed the pub with a sizable glass of whiskey.

"It's not far. Just a couple subway stops."

"You can get home?"

"Jesus, Marty, I'm not *that* drunk." He eyeballed Sam, who was wheezing through his giggling fit. "Better make sure *he* gets home."

"He always does," Marty sighed. "You sure you're okay?"

"Yeah." Alex held a smile long enough to reassure Marty that he was perfectly capable of taking the subway, and then he ventured out into the sticky night. He stumbled, not as steady on his feet as he'd hoped. *Fuck,* he swore, dizzily catching himself on a road sign. Panting through his mouth in fast, ragged gasps, he imagined soothing waves calming the dizziness and nausea, then he unwrapped his arm from the sign. Relieved that he hadn't fallen over or puked, he wove through the nightlife to the West 4th Street subway station.

That morning reminded Alex why drinking hard before an eight-by-four was always a mistake. He slumped against a bulkhead on the 4 train as it rattled uptown to East 116th Street. Every bump and lurch of the subway hurt his head and body. He stared at his Styrofoam coffee cup. It quivered like a fallen slinky in his grip. His stomach and guts noisily wrestled with the bagel he'd eaten for breakfast.

The Manhattan North Homicide squad offices were in the 25th Precinct on East 119th Street, a four-story building of grey and beige concrete like a fortress planted on half the block between Lexington and Park. On the first floor, the windows formed a tiny strip squinting along the top edge of a reddish brick wall. Above them, beyond the range at which most people could throw a rock, the concrete lightened to a dusky grey, and the offices had normal-sized windows exposing their occupants to daylight. The station house bustled with the changeover between the night tour and the day tour. Bleary-eyed cops drove into the parking lot, or waddled out of the precinct's front doors, while brighter, day tour ones strode in. They related stories, laughing at sick and twisted things. Perps, picked up on the night tour, shouted abuse in the precinct's "cage."

The noise and chaos pounded spikes into Alex's head. Too hungover for tales of last night's carnage, he hiked up the three flights of rackety metal stairs to the MNHS office, which was comparatively quiet. Eddie was already in – he always arrived at the office five minutes early, a rule, like the law of gravity.

Between scribbling on paperwork and clattering at his typewriter, he took a single, swift glance at Alex's gaunt face. "Heavy night?"

"Met up with Marty and Sam," explained Alex, muddling through his spacey hangover and burning indigestion to make sense out of the paperwork on his desk. Some Aided reports. An OLBS sheet. A 'five from a precinct detective.

The phone rang. Eddie reorganized a file while giving him a gentle smirk.

His hand quivering, Alex picked it up. "Manhattan North Homicide, this is Detective Boswell."

The caller was a precinct detective at the Three-Four with a thick Italian-Brooklyn accent, who identified himself as Vito Indelicata. "You gotta send guys here forthwith," he barked. "We got a dead rabbi in the Heights and every fuckin' reporter in New York and the brass coming in like a Goddamned roach infestation."

Alex bit into his dry tongue. "Sorry? A rabbi? What address?" He had heard stories about Detective Indelicata. The man had something of a reputation for being either the consummate, old-style police detective, the kind of cop where people sighed and said regretfully, 'they don't make 'em like that anymore,' or an asshole, depending on who was telling the stories, but Alex hadn't personally worked with him.

"West 170th and Fort Washington," said the precinct detective, snapping off the words. "There's been reports of shots fired."

"Ten-four," Alex muttered. The detective had hung up. He stifled the moan gurgling in his throat. "Eddie, we gotta go to a shooting at 170th and Fort Washington."

"Who's the vic?"

"A rabbi," sighed Alex.

"Aw, Jesus."

They looked at one another. When the street violence spilled out of the ghettos and the drug corners, it hit the headlines, it frightened people, and the press and politicians went apoplectic. It was, they knew, incredibly racist, a Black or Latino victim on the corners garnering a fraction of the attention and resources as a white one. But neither man thought about that more than he had to. No point: their job was the same, whatever the ethnicity or class of the victim.

"Your case, Alex." Eddie buttoned up his jacket and neatened his tie. "You wanna drive?"

No, thought Alex, but he didn't want Eddie to know the extent of his hangover – although Eddie definitely did know – so he said, "Yeah, sure." He adjusted his own tie, then slung his sport jacket over his shoulders.

They signed out a silver Crown Victoria. Alex extracted it from the parking space in a ponderous five-point turn. Worried about his sluggish reaction time, he drove uptown like a sensible thirty-year old man, foregoing jackrabbit stops and starts at lights. His head swam. Eddie teased him about his driving. Because he was being too careful, or too reckless?

The car could hardly move once they'd arrived at the crime scene. It was mayhem: police tape cordoning off an entire block, more than two dozen police vehicles scattered across the road and parked up on the sidewalks, reporters straining against a line of police at the staging area, bystanders ogling the scene. Alex ditched the Crown Vic in the middle of the road. The homicide detectives clipped their gold shields to their belts. With watchful self-assurance, Eddie wove around the army of cops and reporters. Alex followed, feeling less self-assured but trying to project it anyway. The detectives signed themselves into the scene, then ducked under the tape. They advanced about fifty yards to the DOA, who was encircled by a shoal of CSU, detectives, uniforms. Unnoticed in the chaos, Alex raked his fingers across his pounding forehead as he looked over the victim. Mid-seventies white male, wearing a crisp black suit, a navy blue tie, and a yarmulke. The man had fallen onto his right side. His voluminous, bushy grey beard spilled onto the sidewalk. Blood unfurled into a red expanse across the white shirt, soaking the black coat and the grey hairs of the beard.

"Who the fuck are you?" demanded a heavyset Italian detective, who was commandeering the scene, shouting orders to Patrol, CSU, other detectives, and anyone else in his way. The guy was in his mid-forties, about 6'1, with a broad girth, wide shoulders, his sheer physical presence and loud personality dwarfing everyone who came near him. He did not say who the fuck he was.

But Alex had a damned good guess. He inwardly shied away, peering over his shoulder at Eddie, who'd been waylaid near the edge of the staging area. *Dammit, you're the Homicide primary*, he told himself. He would not be intimidated, not even by a bolshy first grade detective with a storied reputation that ranged beyond the borders of his precinct. He raised his chin and then straightened his spine and shoulders.

"Detective Indelicata," he said. "I'm Detective Boswell, Homicide. Whaddaya got?"

Indelicata considered him, an eyefucking that chilled his entrails. "DOA's called Elam Liebowitz. Rabbi at the B'nai Israel synagogue up by Fort Tryon Park. You Eddie Trenemen's new partner?"

"Yes." Alex unrolled latex gloves over both his hands and squatted beside the DOA. The blossoming bloodstains on the white shirt guided his eye to the wound under the left shoulder blade. Exit wound or entrance wound, he wondered. You can't always tell by looking. There was a story going around Homicide about Matt Cohen being in the ME's office observing an autopsy, an assistant ME demonstrating to some med students that day, and she asked Matt to label a bullet wound as an entrance or exit. The veteran detective got it wrong, to the assistant ME's glee, who pointed out to her students, "See, it's not easy to tell!" Matt had never lived that down.

That all said, Alex considered the relative size and angle of the holes. He hazarded a guess that the vic had been shot from the front.

"How long you been in Homicide?"

"Six months."

"You can't be a day over thirty-two. Corcoran must be getting fuckin' desperate. He'll take anyone!"

Alex continued his study of the bullet holes in the vic's chest and back. Without measuring them, it was hard to say beyond reasonable doubt – and one wouldn't say beyond a reasonable doubt – but they looked round in shape. The slugs had struck him at a ninety-ish degree angle, the shooter most likely standing upright, facing him.

"How old *are* you?" Indelicata queried.

"Thirty."

"Hah. Well, you're young but you can't be that useless then. Eddie and Corcoran don't put up with the useless ones for as long as six months."

Alex asked, "You find any slugs?"

".38 Super hollow points. Two of 'em."

"Who found him?"

"'Shots fired' report from a guy in that bodega there." Indelicata waggled his hand at a bodega. "So... Patrol shows up, eventually. Shots are fired in this fuckin' neighborhood all the time. It's not like there's any fuckin' hurry. But anyways, they get here, and here he is."

Out of habit, Alex reached for the rabbi's pockets, searching for wallet, keys, ID, money, or anything else.

Indelicata interrupted, "We already searched him. Just a driving license. No credit cards. No cash. No keys. Nothing. Nada."

Robbery, thought Alex as he stood up, hating the creaking feeling in his knees. He scanned the block, sketching the scene in his memo book. Indelicata was still giving him that frozen stare.

"You takin' photos?" Indelicata asked gruffly.

"CSU's taking photos."

"You'll want your own. You always want your own. Jesus. Ain't Trenemen teaching you anything?"

Eddie may have said that. But Alex hadn't remembered to buy himself a camera. Blood flooded the capillaries inside his cheeks. *Stay on point! Don't let him throw you.* "You round up any eyewits yet?"

"Picked up everyone who was on the street. They're at the station house now. So far, everyone sayin' they haven't seen shit."

"The Washington Heights mantra," Alex sighed.

"Yeah, that's it. Maybe you ain't as naïve and bewildered as you look. Yo, Trenemen!" he shouted to Eddie. "Your partner, he's green as fuckin' grass but might be real police!"

Eddie grinned and gave a 'thumbs up' sign.

"What about the wits in the bodega?" Alex pretended not to hear the supercilious crap.

"Uh, the shop owner was freaking out and not wanting to leave his shop and sayin' we can't make him. I been organizin' crime scene searches and a canvass of every building on this block and don't have time for that shit. Fuck him. So he's still there."

Alex rubbed circles into his sore forehead. He could do with less pain right now. "You got guys looking for a gun? Shooter coulda dumped it." He eyed up a trash can with garbage spewing out of it like slow-motion vomiting. At least people had tried throwing the trash in the bin, even if the Department of Sanitation had made no effort to clear it.

"What do you think? This ain't my first rodeo, Boswell. Looks like yours, though."

He felt too ill to be patronized. "I'm gonna talk to the guy in the bodega. Then head to your station house and start interviewing witnesses."

"Sounds great, we got things here under control," Indelicata said brightly, before he saw someone and shouted, "Hey, Craig!" while lumbering across the road.

Alex swallowed a yawn. *Get it together,* he snapped at his wallowing brain, then he trotted over to Eddie, who was absorbed in a conversation with CSU. He explained his rough plan, adding, "Indelicata says he's got this," gesturing expansively, meaning the whole crime scene, "under control." Were there any seeds of doubt in his partner's dark eyes? He felt his belief in himself as a death investigator withering. Should he – of all the people here – be running point on a redball crime scene?

"Yeah, that's good, Alex," Eddie answered coolly. "I've just been talking to Mark here. Their rough guess is that the shooter fired from five or six feet away, but the ME's gotta have a better look first. Right now, they got guys all over this block, looking for anything, anything at all." He exchanged a glum look with the CSU cop. "Fucking outdoor homicide. Forensics ain't gonna be worth shit. But Indelicata's got more street sense than most cops you'll ever meet. He'll come up with something."

"He seemed to want to run the crime scene singlehandedly."

"Vito loves the limelight," laughed Eddie. "More cameras, the happier he is."

A larger-than-life character, Alex thought as he strode into the store. One waiting for his own TV show. He squashed himself behind the checkout counter, where two Dominican guys in their fifties sat slouched forward, their faces sweaty and taught. Putting on a gently sympathetic smile, Alex faced the men, but backed up until the sharp edge of a shelf bit into his spine. He let his weight rest on the shelf. "I'm Detective Boswell, from Homicide. Think you can help me out with what happened on the street outside there?"

"I talk to these cops," complained the younger man in heavily accented English. "How many times do I need to say the same thing?"

"Sorry, it's just how it works. I can take a statement here, or we can schlep to the station house. I know you want to stay with your shop. What's your name?"

"Ricardo Alvarez." The man mumbled under his breath in Spanish.

Alex had just enough Spanish to recognize the word "*Policía*" and a few swear words. "This guy was killed in front of your store. We wanna catch the people who did it."

The bodega owner twitched his shoulders diffidently. "Always people getting killed. Always hearing gunshots."

"You hear these gunshots?" Alex asked.

"*Si*," he replied.

"At what time?"

"Don't know. Maybe like… eight-thirty? The dead man, the rabbi, he came into the store, bought milk. Then he went out. Then I hear the gunshots."

"He came into the store?" repeated Alex, his heart picking up speed. "You said he bought milk. He had his wallet?"

"I guess so."

Given the vic had no wallet on him now, Alex wrote that down. "You have a receipt or something that could give me an exact time?"

"He pay in cash. No receipt."

"Was anyone else in the store?"

"*Si*. Two customers."

"When did they leave?"

"They lay on the floor when the shots went off. They didn't leave."

"Where are they now? Still here?"

Alvarez dismissively held out both palms. "*Policía los tomó*."

"At the station house," supplied a beat cop.

On touching his brow, Alex felt a layer of sweat. He unbuttoned his collar, but his tie scrunched against his throat. The heat inside the bodega and the hangover pureed his brain into liquid. "Anyone else?"

"Roberto, my cousin, who helps me in the shop." Alvarez indicated his companion, then spoke to him in Spanish. The other guy bobbed his head like a cab driver's dash-ornament. The shop owner added, "He does not speak English. *No hablas ingles.*"

"No," said Roberto with an apologetic sigh.

"And where was he?"

"Here. He lay on the floor with me behind this counter."

"What happened after the rabbi bought milk?"

"He went out of the store. Then, I hear the shots."

"How long after he left?"

Alvarez gave a prolonged shrug.

"You must have some idea."

"Don't know. Maybe... a couple minutes."

"How many shots did you hear?"

"Two, three," said Alvarez.

Alex looked at Roberto, then wobbled through his appalling, pidgin Spanish. "*Cuantos balazos?*" One of those stock phrases you learn, *how many gunshots?*

"*Dos, tres.*"

"Did you see anybody hanging around? *Viste a alguien aqui?*"

"No," said Roberto.

"You?" Alex fixed a riveting gaze on Ricardo.

"It's... It's a busy block."

"Would you recognize them?"

"Don't know. No. I don't look."

"Could you describe the people you saw?"

"I tell you, I don't look."

"Roberto," Alex turned back to Roberto, then stodgily translated in his head, before venturing, "*Viste a alguien...sospechoso en el calle?*"

"No," said Roberto. "*Todo el mundo es un traficante de drogas.*"

All the world traffics drugs. The most edifying but least useful witness statement he'd ever heard. "Well, we may ask you to come into the precinct to look at a line-up."

"I told you, I didn't see no one," Ricardo insisted.

Alex altered his position, so the pressure from the shelf shifted to a part of his back that hadn't gone numb. "Was Rabbi Liebowitz a regular customer here?"

"No, never seen him before."

"Any of your regulars give anyone trouble?"

"I stay out of people's business. Mind your own business, that's what they say here."

"You never saw anyone hassling people for money or anything?"

"No."

"What about dealers on the corners?"

"No, I don't know them."

"But there are dealers on this corner?"

"There are dealers on all the corners now," wheezed Alvarez sadly. "This used to be a good neighborhood for families. But now…"

"Do you have a gun?"

The shop owner's eyes widened a fraction. "A .22."

"Can I see it?"

The man unlocked a drawer under the till. "This neighborhood, it's dangerous. *Muy peligrosa.* I have to protect myself." He handed Alex a gun, a Walther P22, and his hands were shaking.

Even though the rabbi had been shot with a .38, Alex inspected the weapon. It held two rounds, but there were no signs of it being fired, not at any point in his lifetime given the dust on it and corrosion around the edges of the metal. "You have a permit for this?"

"Yes."

"I'll have to hold onto this gun until we check it and verify that it's legal and wasn't used in any crime."

Alvarez sighed, at once irritated and expecting this, and he swore at the police in Spanish.

His cousin asked, "*Lo devolverás?*"

"Sorry?" said Alex. A word he didn't know.

"He's asking if you'll give it back," said a patrolman.

"Maybe. If his permit checks." Alex bagged the firearm. He could run Alvarez through NCIC, DCJS, and BETA for priors, prints, and a firearms permit. Scraping his parched tongue against his back teeth, he gave the men his card in case they remembered anything else, then he squirmed his way towards the door. As he studied the street, he sifted through that conversation for the bullshit, for the truth, thinking the former outweighed the latter by a considerable amount. The shopkeeper kept that .22 around. He must know which skels made their patch in his neighborhood, who to look out for, and who to not piss off by blabbing to the police.

Eddie was already canvassing, and Alex joined him for a couple hours. The people who reticently responded said they hadn't seen anything, or maybe they heard the shots, but you hear shots all the time on this block. With little left to canvass, Alex caught a ride to the precinct in a Three-Four sector car. From the back seat, he tried reviewing his notes but reading in the moving car reawakened the nausea. One of the young uniforms in the car blabbered about joining the Detective Bureau, complaining about not getting a posting as a 'white shield.' Wholly uninterested, Alex uttered acknowledging noises in his throat. What if he interviewed the bodega owner again, this time in the precinct, or interviewed his cousin with someone who could really speak Spanish, and God help them all if it turned out to be a hate crime, the vic targeted because he was a rabbi.

The witnesses waited in a secure area in the middle of the precinct house, dubbed 'the fishtank.' They wanted to be anywhere else. Several jumped to their feet when Alex appeared – a man who looked in charge, although his suit was rumpled, sweat-stained, and his tie hung loosely around his throat. Nevertheless, he had a gold shield clipped to one hip and a gun clipped to the other.

One man cried, "I know Constitutional law! You can't hold us here without *habeas corpus!*"

Offering a pacifying half-smile, Alex indicated that Mr. *habeas corpus* should accompany him. "We can't hold you," he said agreeably. "But we're just trying to figure out what happened in front of that bodega. Did you see the man get shot?"

"I came after," the witness said bluntly. "He was already dead."

"Did you overhear anything?"

"Heard nothing."

A few more questions ruled out the man as a suspect or a cooperative witness. Alex wrote down the wit's name, age, address, letting him go with the comment, "See, we aren't unlawfully detaining you," and then he interviewed the other witnesses, one at a time. His hangover lingered as a blunt headache. A dozen wits later, he had five descriptions of hearing gunshots, one nebulous description of a Black man with a beard, and another equally as nebulous description of a Latino or mixed-race man without a beard. He sent those two wits to the sketch artist. He sent everyone else home. His throat felt raw and arid. He rested his forehead in his palms, shutting his eyes.

A Three-Four precinct detective called Skegs shoved open the door. "Boswell, Rabbi Liebowitz's wife has just arrived. She's looking for someone who's workin' the case. You got a minute?"

No, he thought, not at all prepared to deal with the victim's wife, but he said, "Yes." His stomach curdled with apprehension. He had to be delicate, empathetic, reconstruct the vic's movements for the last twenty-four hours of his life, and, at the same time, pose the question, is there anyone who might want your husband dead, including you. Where the hell was Indelicata? This was his case.

When he queried Skegs about that, the detective chuckled. "You don't know Vito. He'll work this case harder than anyone, but he's his own man."

"What does that mean?" asked Alex, feeling stupid and naïve.

"He'll... like work the informants, work the *streets,* like old-school, you know? He's notorious for being bad at paperwork, but he says, detective work ain't *about* paperwork."

Alex felt pretty sure it was, but he held his tongue.

Skegs continued, "Vito will disappear, the boss won't even know where he's got to. But when he comes back, he'll have a lead, sometimes a suspect. He knows how to talk to *people.* You gotta respect him."

Wherever Indelicata had got to, it was not the Three-Four station house, so Alex retied his tie and stole paper towels from the bathroom to mop the sweat off his forehead and neck. Calming his breathing, he collected his wits, his scraps of evidence, then he found Liebowitz's wife, Mary, waiting at the Wheel with the desk sergeant. He knew that detectives from the Three-Four had delivered the death notice and asked her a few questions, but she had not provided them with any information at that time. Rigid, like a statue, she sat in a plastic chair next to the desk, clasping a purse with both hands, her knuckles white.

Alex arranged his features into his best disarming-but-serious expression. "I'm Detective Boswell with Homicide. What can I help you with?"

Shaking his hand, Mary Liebowitz said tightly, "The detectives told me I should come here. If I wanted to ask how the investigation was going."

He shepherded her towards an interview room. "Can I get you anything? I can probably find tea or coffee in this precinct."

"No, no thanks. It's okay. I just wanted to know... how it was going."

"We're working on developing leads." A euphemism for 'we haven't found shit.' "If you have any information that you think might help us, anything about your husband..." He filled his lungs with every molecule of air he could breathe in. "These are never easy questions to ask, but we have to ask them, you know. Was he involved in anything, well, that involved people who might wanna hurt him? Like gambling, or did he owe money to a loan shark? That sorta thing."

Her mouth open and closed silently until she croaked, "Elam would never do any of what you're suggesting. You don't think the person who did this was someone who *knew* him, do you?"

"We have to look at every possibility."

"We don't *know* people like that, Detective Boswell," she insisted, her expression hardening.

Alex retreated from that line of questioning. Eddie was much better at this than himself. His partner had a way with people, a soothing manner, the right words, calming the most distressed witness while eliciting information. "Can you tell me what your husband did, normally, on his way to the synagogue. We know he'd gone into the bodega to buy milk."

"Yes, he sometimes stopped at a store on the way if we needed something."

"Did he always stop at that one?"

"He'd go to wherever was convenient. But yes, he had been in that bodega before."

"Did he ever say anything about it?"

"No. It was just a bodega."

"What time did he leave your house?"

"The same time as always. Like eight."

"Did anything seem unusual?"

"No… No… Oh, God… I told him…" Her voice died away as tears dazzled her eyes.

"Told him what?' Alex prompted.

"Are you Jewish?" She careered into a new subject. "The other detective, the Black guy, he said you were Jewish."

"Yeah. What did you tell your husband?"

"Boswell? Where does that come from?"

He suppressed a dismayed sigh. Working with victims' families was the hardest part of the job. "My great-grandfather had a very Russian name and had to change it."

"He was a Russian Jew? He escaped from Russia?"

"Yeah."

"He came here, to New York?"

"Yeah. He stayed in the Lower East."

"Do you go to Temple?"

Oh, God. "No, not really."

Her face fell in disappointment. A non-observant Reformed Jew, the worst thing.

Because he needed her cooperation, he said, "I do this. Isn't that what the Torah teaches? Isn't that what *mitzvah* is? To go out and do good, meaningful things in the world? To seek justice? I solve murders. I give a voice to the dead."

"Yes." Her voice became small, quiet. "Yes. I see that."

"I know I'm useless at Temple, and I can't remember holidays, but this job... It's God's work." That's what Eddie always said.

"Yes. I guess I get that."

"What did you tell Elam?"

"To not go to B'nai Israel. To see if he could move to a synagogue somewhere else. Not one near Fort Tryon. I said the neighborhood is getting really bad, and it wasn't safe." She wiped her tear-stained face with the back of her hand and then reached for his hand. He took it. "But he said it was fine. He said, it was violent, sure, but it was just the gangs and drug dealers shooting each other. He said they don't bother you if you're not a part of their thing. He said I was worrying for no good reason." She met Alex's gaze, her green eyes brimming with wild pain and anger. "But it's not like that, is it?"

"We'll do everything we can to find who did this," he replied, a weak-ass response, but he had nothing comforting or reassuring to say.

"Will you come to shiva?" she asked shortly. "It's tomorrow."

Alex faltered, startled, but detectives often attend victims' funerals, so a brief appearance wouldn't be that unconventional. "Yeah, sure." Cynically, he reckoned that he could suss out Liebowitz's family, friends, acquaintances, and guilt shot through his heart, point-blank, because he shouldn't do work as a shiva guest. But he couldn't stop being a cop.

"Do you know the Kaddish?"

"No, sorry. My Hebrew's terrible." Worse than his Spanish. He finished off his plastic cup of water, feeling it slide down his throat, and he winced as the guilt slugged him in the gut. His relatives were kickboxing in their graves.

"Oh. Well, I'd still like you to come. You're the only Jewish detective...on my husband's...case."

"Okay, I'll be there," he agreed. As he escorted her out of the precinct, he promised to keep her abreast of any breakthroughs, and he helped her into a waiting yellow cab. She must have paid the driver well. Taxi drivers were avoiding Washington Heights nowadays. Thinking the neighborhood *was* getting dangerous, for everyone, he ascended the stairs and then bought a Milky Way from the vending machine that lived in the corridor beside the detective squad room. With witnesses to chase down and photo arrays to arrange, he had no time for a real meal. He crunched the nougat and chocolate between his teeth, pushing his hand into the soft paunch on his belly: thirty, and already overweight. *This is how detectives get fat.* But he continued eating his candy bar. No time for guilt, either.

At the MNHS office, boxes of files had expelled their contents onto Alex's desk and invaded the floor around his feet: files from the DA's office, Parole, and Probation for anyone with priors for agg assault or first-degree robbery who had an address in uptown Manhattan. A stack of ViCAP reports from the FBI had taken over the narrow space around the typewriter. Alex was flipping through every file, seeking similar MOs, weapons, witness IDs, or anything that caught his attention. Although Alex's visit to the shiva house had been unenlightening, Eddie was interviewing people at the synagogue, on the chance it was not a random stick-up job and the rabbi had been killed by someone who knew him, while Vito Indelicata was, as per *his* MO, in some unknown location.

Hours trickled past. Alex's attention roved from the files to other distractions: biting his nails bloody, D team detectives talking on the phone, Sam Rizzo and Marty Vasquez giggling like teenage girls at something that must be immensely funny. Alex slightly rotated his office chair, turning one eye towards their cubicle. He felt unsure of his footing in the social part of the Homicide squad. When they went out drinking after a tour, he felt better about it (or at least too drunk to care), but now he felt separated from squad room banter. They did not dislike him; he held his own in investigations and could take a joke, which meant they were happy enough to have him there, but he got the sense that they didn't know what to make of him because he could not seem to be anything but shy and serious.

His phone burst to life. Another distraction. "Manhattan North Homicide, this is Detective Boswell."

"You one of the detectives working on the Liebowitz case?" asked an unfamiliar male voice. He had a Spanish accent.

"Yes," Alex responded warily. A tip line connected to officers who should screen calls before they forwarded people to Homicide, but Alex had concluded that the screeners were useless hairbags because the calls hadn't stopped. Everyone with a conspiracy theory or an axe to grind thought they knew who killed Liebowitz.

"I know a guy," announced the caller. "He's got a gun, and he's done some stick-ups."

"Sorry, who are you?" *And please don't tell me you think it was Lee Harvey Oswald or the CIA.*

"I'm a guy who knows a guy."

Alex churlishly ground his back teeth. "I need more than that. 'A guy.' Who is this guy?"

"His name's Ernie Serrachia. Dominican guy. Lives around there. He says he popped the dude on 170th."

"Yeah? How do you know him?"

"I just know him. He wants to be a tough guy, a *jefe,* to *own* that block, man." As unexpectedly as he'd called, the tipster hung up.

"Hello? Hello?" Alex said to the dialtone. He smacked the phone down, snapping, "Fuck you too!" which caught the attention of Rizzo and Vasquez, who were not accustomed to their taciturn young colleague getting into fits of rage.

"What's wrong, Lex? *Que pasa?*" Marty asked.

Recently they had started calling him *Lex,* which meant they must have some sort of affection for him and had somehow learned that's what cops had called him ever since he'd walked a beat in the Sixth.

"Another asshole just called with an anonymous tip for the Liebowitz case," Alex complained. "Gave me a name, says this guy bragged he shot someone on 170th. I got nothing else. How do I know this schmuck isn't bullshitting me? It's just been endless."

"Is it William Webster?" giggled Rizzo.

"Who—?" Alex began, but then he recalled that William Webster was the director of the CIA. "Oh. No, it's not anyone in the federal government, for a change."

"Chase it up," Marty said, shrugging. "Then at least you've covered your ass."

Cover your ass, an investigator's, or any police officer's, first priority; covering your boss' ass being the second. A few calls and database searches later, Alex traced the phone call to a payphone in the Bronx, and he discovered an Ernesto Serrachia living at an address on West 168th, with priors for possessing and distributing cocaine, but no violent felonies. Reading between the lines, Alex surmised that Serrachia was a crack addict who funded his habit with some small-time dealing. He asked Marty to round up the two eyewits who purported seeing the shooter, begged detectives and patrol at the 44th Precinct to sniff around the payphone, and then he conscripted Rizzo into accompanying him to Serrachia's apartment.

"This case is so fucked," Alex bitched as he drove uptown. "This poor schmuck gets shot around eight-thirty am, like almost rush hour, but I got nothing. The people who know him say he was a paragon of virtue. No one sees a fucking thing. Ballistics can't trace the slugs. No prints on the cartridge or anywhere. What am I supposed to do?"

"That's the Heights for you."

"And the media's giving me an ulcer."

"Welcome to the big leagues, man. Jesus, watch that red Dodge! Your driving's giving me an ulcer! Eddie said you were a fuckin' maniac."

"It's considered speed." Alex swerved between a Dodge Dart and a Ford Econoline van.

They parked near the building, a scabby low-rise with a rust-eaten fire escape clinging like a black centipede to the façade. Warily, Alex nudged the main door with the side of his forearm. It swung open. Inhaling sharply, he stepped backwards. Rizzo pointed to the broken locks, rusted into twisted, malformed metal. Those hadn't worked for a while. Alex rested one hand on the butt of his gun. He blinked as his pupils adjusted to the gloomy entryway. Discarded crack pipes crunched under his feet. Cockroaches darted across the floor. A shadow scampered along the wall. A rat? They heard the indistinct murmur of voices through the thin walls. They should have brought in Patrol for backup. Too late, just have to be cautious. He met Rizzo's eyes and nodded. The other detective's pudgy face betrayed no fear, but he also had a hand on his gun. Serrachia lived on the sixth floor, so they marched up the dully lit stairs. Around the fourth floor, Alex's heart knocked against his ribcage. On the sixth-floor landing, he stopped to catch his breath. His chest burned like he'd taken a lungful of fire. Rizzo wheezed and coughed like a pneumonia patient, growling, "This year I'm fuckin' giving up the cigarettes."

When his breathing levelled out, Alex proceeded along a murky corridor, then rapped his knuckles against the first door, holding out his shield, so whoever looked through the peephole would see they were the police.

Locks clicked, then the door cracked open. A seventy-something Latina woman peered suspiciously at the detectives. "*Policia?*" she asked dubiously.

"Yes. *Si.*" Alex should have brought Vasquez instead of Rizzo or become more proficient at Spanish himself. "Does Ernie Serrachia live here?"

The woman blinked, baffled.

Alex stumbled through his high school Spanish. *"Ernesto vive aqui?"*

The woman sighed, like she'd been here before, then she impatiently shouted over her shoulder, "Ernesto!" Along with rapid-fire Spanish too dense for Alex to follow. A wiry thirty-year old Dominican man appeared at the door. His pupils were wildly dilated, the jittery, fox-in-headlights stare of a long-term drug user.

"Ernie, you think you can come with us to the station house?" Alex asked, praying this guy spoke English. Somewhere in the room, he heard young children squealing. The older lady shouted at them in Spanish.

"Por que? W-why?" stuttered Serrachia.

"We wanna talk to you about something you might've seen a couple blocks from here."

"I ain't seen nothing," Serrachia responded, his eyes hopping from one detective to the other.

"Well, come in, and we'll talk about it."

Willing but wary, Serrachia shadowed the detectives down the six flights of stairs. He asked in the same stammering tone, "Is this about my case?"

"Your drug case?"

"Y-yes."

"Could be." Homicide was a hell of a way to violate your parole, Alex thought.

They drove to the Three-Four on West 183rd, where Vasquez had arranged a line-up with the eyewitnesses. Before questioning Serrachia, they wanted to see if the eyewits recognized him. An ID would be formidable leverage for an interrogation. Serrachia seemed bewildered by the line-up, but he cooperated. Neither witness identified him. With that strategy a failure, Alex marshaled him into the interrogation room.

First, Alex took Serrachia's details. Over a couple hours, he filibustered, rambling but seeking weak points, touching on the drug trade in the neighborhood, politics, Reagan, the contras in Nicaragua, but the gulf between himself and the suspect felt like the Atlantic. He wasn't getting into this guy's head. He swerved to Serrachia's crack habit, his arrests and prison stints. Serrachia, agitated, his hands in constant motion, offered him some information, like how he thought he once had the chance to join the Dominican Republic's national soccer team but smoked his hopes and health down the crack pipe.

Alex swilled a mouthful of water for his raw throat. He offered a cup to Serrachia. "You know what happened on 170th and Fort Washington?"

Serrachia ignored the water and looked befuddled. "No?"

"We have a witness who says you were there. You know, at the bodega."

"The bodega," echoed Serrachia. "What bodega?"

"The one at 170th and Fort Washington," said Alex, his eyes searching. "You were at that bodega, you needed cash, right?"

"I do… I mean, who doesn't? But I wasn't at the bodega."

"You thought, the rabbi, he wasn't going to put up much of a fight, right? An old guy like that. You point a gun at him, he'll give it straight up."

"A gun? A rabbi?"

Alex knuckled down on the story. "You didn't *mean* to shoot him. I've seen your rap sheet. Talked to your Parole officer. You're not a guy who shoots people. But you're all shaky, your head's messed up, and he doesn't give it up, and you don't know what to do. And the gun goes off. It just goes off. But you didn't *mean* to." He concentrated on every twitch in Serrachia's body, how he responded to the 'out' dangling before him.

"I-I don't know what you're *talking* about. You're thinking I shot the rabbi? I was thinking, you brought me in 'cause I was slinging gear again. I ain't never shot *anybody*."

"Do you know about the rabbi?" Alex moved around the interrogation room and straddled the chair nearest Serrachia.

"You mean, the one in the news?"

"Yeah. So, you know about him."

"'Cause they talk about him in all the papers and on TV." The suspect's eyes popped out of his skull. "I mean, that's what I know. I wasn't *there*. I swear, I wasn't there. You're wanting to string me up for this?"

"I want the truth. What do you know about him? You know, from the news."

"Just what's in the news," Serrachia panted. "He was shot on 170th in the morning, near a bodega."

"With what? What kind of gun?"

"How would I know that?"

"Maybe they said on the TV." They didn't. The police had not released that information to the media in case it compromised the investigation.

"I don't know. I don't remember if they said it. But I don't know."

"What do you remember?"

"From the news?"

"Yeah."

"He was a rabbi at a synagogue in the Heights. Something Israel."

"Anything else?"

"No...*nada.*"

"The name of the bodega?"

"I don't know."

"It's two blocks from your apartment. You don't know its name?"

"Ricardo's? Roberto's? I don't pay attention."

"So, you've been around that bodega."

"Yeah, but not this week."

"Let's say you're not lying." Alex rolled his shoulders back. "Do you know who hangs around that bodega? Gangs? Slingers? Anyone after a fix?"

"I-I know a few people," squeaked Serrachia. "I talk to them sometimes. We help each other out. But they're harmless. They wouldn't commit no murder."

"Who are they? What are their names?"

Serrachia sputtered half dozen names and descriptions: a few Latinos, a white guy, a couple Black guys.

"That's all?" Alex stared at the six names in his memo book.

"Yeah."

"You live there. You don't know the lowlifes on your block?"

"Uh, it's New York, man. Do you know all the people who are on *your* block?"

A reasonable point. Alex knew his neighbors by sight, but he couldn't say anything about them. "And if we were to search your apartment, we wouldn't find a gun?"

"I don't have no gun."

"Did you have a gun?"

"I ain't never had a gun."

"Ernie, you can't help yourself if you lie to me. Like if we find out you were really at the bodega, or you really have a gun, this gets a lot worse for you. But if it was just an accident, you know, you should tell me now, and you might do a lot less time than twenty-five-to-life."

"Twenty-five-to-life? Jesus, I don't want to do *any* time. I didn't do it. I ain't lying, man. I wasn't there."

"So, if you were not at the bodega, where were you on the 5th of August? It was a Friday morning."

"Man, if I say, you'll violate me," muttered Serrachia miserably.

"You don't, I'll violate you with a homicide charge. Someone says you were on West 170th and Fort Washington around eight-thirty am."

"Awww," Serrachia moaned. "I don't know why anyone would say that. Who said that?"

"Doesn't matter. Where were you?"

The man's eyes flicked manically back and forth. "Near here. On the corner of 180th and Broadway."

"Doing what?"

"Uh, sellin'."

"And you got a drug crew as alibi witnesses?" Alex raised an eyebrow.

"No." Serrachia's face lit up. "Cops."

"Cops?" Alex's brows wrinkled together.

"Yeah, I left to go get some empanadas, and next thing I hear, cops are grabbin' everyone on the corner. Those guys we thought were buyers, they were cops. Pretending to buy the shit." He seemed astonished that these things could happen.

Alex swallowed a hard lump in his gullet. "What's the name of the place you got the empanadas?" he asked wearily.

"Las Riojas," said Serrachia. "It's a Dominican take-out on West 195th."

Alex left him fermenting in the interrogation room. For half an hour, his phone calls ran in circles, only to discover that it wasn't an operation run by Narcotics at all, but rather by the Special Narcotics Enforcement Unit, a division of the New York City Housing Police. He slogged through thickets of NYCH bureaucracy until he got through to a lieutenant at SNEU, who did not know who was working where, but assured Alex that he would find out. Because he needed to stay on the premises, Alex sent Rizzo on a mission to Las Riojas, bribing him with booze and ten bucks for a take-out.

"You'll just about owe me a blow job for this one," said Rizzo, but he went.

Alex returned to the antsy suspect in the interrogation room, who repeatedly massaged his hands together and jiggled his leg. Jonesing, Serrachia had resigned himself to parole violations, and he remained unmoved, even by the threat of mandatory minimum prison sentences. *This loser smokes too much crack,* Alex thought, *but he doesn't have the chutzpah to pull off a stick-up.*

You could be surprised at who did, however.

Again, he left Serrachia waiting. The crackhead seemed oddly patient, in his jittery way. He wasn't begging for a lawyer, yet. How long could Alex detain him before he started asking for counsel, or how much more aggressively could he pursue his interrogation without advising Serrachia of his rights? A grey area in the law, and Alex with one foot in a place that wasn't an unlawful interrogation, the other on the side where he plainly had to *Mirandize* the suspect. With Rizzo at the Dominican take-out, Vasquez back at MNHS, and Eddie and Vito elsewhere, he had no one's judgment but his own. Should he phone the DA? No, wait for more information. Don't create a circus around this guy yet. If the Housing police said the alibi checked, he would let Serrachia go. If the Housing police did not confirm the alibi, he would call the DA and read Serrachia his rights. Breaking this case would make his career. He would finally feel like he deserved to be in the Homicide squad.

But the silent phones slackened time itself. Every second ticked past in time to his anxious heartbeat. He nibbled through his nails, then impatiently phoned the Four-Four squad, chasing down updates from their phone booth canvass.

"Your caller was a Hispanic male?" asked the detective.

"Yeah," said Alex irritably.

"The only people anyone saw using that payphone today were two Black females. Sorry."

"Copy that," he replied, hissing, "*Fuck*" as soon as he hung up. Theoretically, they could dust the payphone for prints, but he would never get approval for that. Too many resources for no meaningful gain. There would be hundreds of prints, many with criminal records, and no hope of pinpointing when any individual used that phone.

Rizzo reappeared, first removing his jacket, then lazily stretching his arms. "Traffic was shit but your perp's onto something – excellent empanadas. Really good." He pointedly licked his lips. "Got you outta that blow job."

"I'm happy to hear that. Did they give you anything else?"

"Oh, yeah, they know the guy. Says he's a regular. Comes in, kinda the same time every day. And he was there on August 5th. Same time as always, they says. Like 0840 hours."

This lead felt like another diversion on a highway where every exit led to the wrong place. Restively, Alex resumed mangling his fingertips as he waited for SNEU's call. His gut twisted itself into distracting cramps. He had work he could be doing on other cases, mindboggling amounts of it, but not from the Three-Four station house. Why had he brought Serrachia here? If he'd gone to MNHS, he could detain the suspect for an easy forty-eight hours while he sorted out his paperwork.

An hour later, SNEU called the Three-Four's Wheel desk, and it took ten minutes for them to locate Alex because they didn't recognize his name offhand.

"Oh. Him? Jesus, he's young for MNHS," a cop said, but Alex pretended he hadn't overheard when he grabbed the phone.

"Boswell? What is it you're looking for?" the SNEU lieutenant asked. He sounded like he had better things to do. "Details of a buy-and-bust we conducted last week?"

"I don't need that many details," Alex said. "Were your guys on West 180th and Broadway last Friday? The 5th. Early, like 0800 to 0830."

"Yeah, we were. Made several collars."

"Was there a Dominican guy there called Ernesto Serrachia?"

"Oh, yeah, Ernie," said the cop. "He's always there."

"Was he there on the 5th?"

"Yeah, sure, but we didn't collar him. We'd done recon, seen him, but not seen him with the product. By the time we got our operation underway, Serrachia'd gone, but we'll get that *pendejo* next time."

"When did he leave?"

"Dunno. We made our arrests at around 0845, so he was gone by then. But he'd been there early. Probably seein' if he could beg a couple vials off the slingers he knows. He woulda left before 0840, but not a lot before 0830."

Alex scribbled in his memo pad, noting the lieutenant's name and shield number. He blew out a long sigh and stared morosely at the American flag pinned to the wall. An alibi he couldn't dispute. His first redball in Homicide, and it was a Goddamn whodunit. Would people wonder if he really had what it took to be a homicide detective? A trifecta of intelligence, experience, and sheer bloody-mindedness. He wondered that himself as he trudged down the stairs to the interrogation room, where he let Ernie Serrachia go.

"You're not gonna hold me?" Serrachia asked, surprised. "For violating my parole?"

"No." Alex heard the vexation creeping into his voice. He couldn't care less about a minor narcotics case. "Not this time."

The jittery crackhead scuttled out the door, and Alex ducked into the bathroom and washed his face with cold water. The whole day felt like a waste of time, but he had to write up the DD-5s for all of it. Hell, he gave it his best shot, he reminded himself. Covering his ass. Sometimes, that is all you can do.

Chapter Eleven

October 1987

"It'll go down." Indelicata drew himself upwards, exuding confidence. "I *know* this neighborhood. I been talkin' to my people. It'll go down."

Alex slouched against the dusky brick wall of the Two-Five station house, gazing despondently across East 119th at the pre-Civil War walk-ups, with neo-classical columns and ornate gables of greys and reds, laced with black fire stairs. West on 119th, the elevated Metro North tracks ran underneath a scabrous brick low-rise with severe, staring windows, and further along rose a high-rise project, awkward and startled, as if it had surprised itself by growing higher than everything else in the neighborhood.

Indelicata lit a Cuban cigar. "Don't look so fuckin' miserable, Lex."

"This case is killing me with stress."

"Hey, then don't let it get to you."

"If the vic was some poor junkie killed over a gram of heroin, we woulda shitcanned this by now." Alex massaged the knuckles of his left hand with his right.

"I hear ya, pal," Vito said philosophically. "But he ain't, and that ain't how it plays, huh."

The detectives had come from a task force meeting in the Manhattan North Homicide offices, the ninth circle of hell, which included the Police Commissioner himself, the Manhattan North Operations Chief, the Manhattan North Detective Bureau Chief, representatives from Mayor Koch's office and the Rabbinical Council, a guy from the Anti-Defamation League, their respective bosses, and the Chief of Detectives. Rabbi Liebowitz had been shot in August, and two months later, they had no leads, only one dead end after another. The Jewish community was livid, accusing the NYPD of not trying hard enough, of anti-Semitism.

"Boswell is Jewish," Corcoran had said in the meeting. As if that mattered to anyone.

The detectives had assured everyone that they were developing leads. Bullshit, for sure. People from the neighborhood weren't anti-Semites. Most seemed saddened that the old guy, who had nothing to do with drug trafficking, got caught up in the violence. They just didn't want to end up in the same position. But no one in that meeting possessed the chutzpah to complain about witness protection – or lack thereof – to NYPD top brass. The brass did not want to know about *any* institutional failures.

Vito wielded his cigar with the macho confidence of Bogart's detective in the *Maltese Falcon*. Soothingly, he patted Alex's right shoulder. "Trust me, my CIs, they know what goes on. I got eyes and ears on these streets. They'll come through. Give 'em time."

"I hope so."

Over these last two months, Alex had gotten through Vito's overbearing swagger. Underneath it, Vito loved young detectives, and he loved imparting his knowledge. He had taken Alex under his great, broad wings, saying Alex couldn't be more different in temperament to himself, quiet and cautious, sarcastic and insecure, but he liked the young detective's stubborn, relentless approach to investigations, the way he squeezed evidence out of a stone, and his dark, wry sense of humor. Alex felt as though he was being mentored, becoming a better detective under the guidance of Vito and Eddie. He knew they saw promise in him. A *rabbi* you call it, when a seasoned cop mentors a young one, ironically. Over expensive Scotch last night – Vito's twenty-one year Lagavulin, apparently a gift from a grateful complainant – Vito had imperturbably reassured them that they *would* break this case. Eddie seemed to believe him.

Alex had his doubts, but he kept them well hidden. *These guys know more about death investigation than you ever will,* he reminded himself. The cool fall air nipped at his skin. He rewrapped the scarf around his throat, then frowned at his watch. Six hours to go before the tour ended, and he could lock himself inside a bar. Meetings with NYPD brass made him feel desperate for a drink. So did redballs. So did the mayor and the chiefs when they acted surprised that a street could be full of witnesses who had gone blind and deaf.

"I'd better get back upstairs," he said. "Maybe if I'm lucky, I'll catch a case with some evidence." If he was really lucky, he thought, he would not catch anything. Then he might have breathing space to work on cases he'd neglected because Corcoran demanded he devote all his waking hours to Liebowitz. One redball didn't make those disappear or magically clear themselves.

As he shoved his shoulder into the precinct door, he glanced back at Vito casually smoking his cigar, a man who let the pressure roll off his back like raindrops striking an overcoat. *Don't let it get to you.* Alex wished he could shrug his shoulders and shake it off as effortlessly as Vito.

"Alex, I got some curry from that Indian you like," said Eddie once Alex had puffed up the three flights of stairs. "Figured after that meeting from hell, we could do with something decent in our bellies." He pointed to a leaning tower of Styrofoam boxes.

"Yeah, good. I'm hungry." Alex saw that the C team was also in: Jean Allan, and three of her colleagues, along with Marty and Bill from his own team. The others must be out in the field.

Like they had not eaten for a week, the detectives attacked the food, divvying up pakoras, rice, naan, and about seven curries, Bill and Jean vying over who got the hottest one. While eating a madras, Alex wrote an affidavit, a search warrant for a neglected case. He listened to his colleagues' banter, but a corrosive feeling of isolation and worthlessness locked him inside his own head. Back in the One-Oh-Three, he'd felt like one of the boys, but here, unclimbable walls and wire stood between him and the lighthearted teasing.

"You hear about last night?"

"Yeah, Ryan had his pants off."

"Again?"

"I had to change after that DOA. You know, when they've been there a while, and spurt gases and fluids at you when you turn them over."

"Oh, yeah, you need a reason."

"True – I can always get it from Vasquez when he's passed out on the sofa."

"I'm always ready, babe."

Alex envisaged Bill, after his mishap, wandering around the squad room in his underwear. You can only survive this work if you relish every opportunity to laugh at the comic. Otherwise, it was all too damned tragic.

A full belly fractionally lightened his mood. But not for long. The phone screamed at him, bursting his eardrums as he was soaking up the remnants of curry with a naan. Bill had run into the can for a leak, and Marty was on his phone to someone else. The redball had kept Alex and Eddie off normal rotation for a couple weeks, but that couldn't go on indefinitely. Tepidly, Alex cradled the phone, saying his name. A precinct detective from the Three-Four called Wakowski reported a DOA near Fairview and Fort George. Alex's heart sank like a breeze block in the river. So much for a quiet, intimate evening with his existing caseload. He abandoned the naan and whipped his jacket off the back of his chair.

Just before he ran out the door, he heard Jean comment, "Man, no rest for the weary, huh." Her team wasn't catching today.

"Never," he sighed.

Alex and Eddie parked their Crown Vic behind a radio car, then they scoped out their surroundings, a barren block of pebble-dashed grey low-rises, with graffiti-spattered walls and windows boarded with splintering plywood. Crime scene tape flapped in front of a building with mossy, rotting brickwork.

The first officers had cleared the scene, but people were catcalling and gawking beyond the police lines. The DOA was a twenty-something Hispanic male who had received one gunshot wound to the upper thigh and another to the abdomen. He had bled out, the dark red pools coagulating into small ponds, staining the concrete, running into cracks in the pavement. *Abdominal aorta, or femoral,* Alex thought. As was his way, Eddie turned to the people on the street, while Alex, the precinct detective, and the assistant ME examined the body. Femoral, the ME hazarded, and Alex reckoned he was getting pretty good at this. The man had a red bandana tied around his head and a gold chain draped around his neck.

A high-pitched scream pierced through the police radios and cop talk. Startled, Alex jumped back from the body and craned his neck over his shoulder. He saw a fifty-something Hispanic woman fighting furiously against the officers guarding the perimeter of the crime scene. She looked small, no taller than 5'2, but the male officers panted and struggled to hold her back.

The woman screamed, "My son! *Mi hijo! No puede detenerme.*"

Suddenly alert, Alex dashed over to her and put both his hands on her shoulders. The uniforms slunk out of his way. For a moment, he felt her straining, heaving her feathery weight against his one sixty pounds. He resisted strength that transcended muscle and size. If she kept fighting, he might have let go, but then she sagged into his chest like a punctured balloon. She felt lighter than a child. Gently, he directed her away from the crime scene to the other side of the staging area, saying, "I'm so sorry…"

"Why can't I see my son?"

"I'm sorry," he repeated. "It's a crime scene. We can't let anyone near, not until we've collected all the evidence we can."

"A crime scene," she whispered. "Who are you? You a detective?"

"I'm Detective Alex Boswell. I'm with Manhattan North Homicide."

"Homicide." She choked on the word.

"What's your name?" he said in a soft voice.

"Bettina Perez."

"Okay, Ms. Perez, and your son? What's his name?"

"Sal. Salvador." Tears shone on her cheeks. "An eye for an eye until everyone is blind."

"Sorry, I'm not following." Alex brought her to his Crown Vic and opened the door, letting her sit in the passenger seat. He squatted down, so he was about eye level with her.

"I tried… I tried… to raise him right." She looked into his eyes, her own starred with tears. "But tell me, tell me, how am I supposed to tell him he's gotta go work for three bucks an hour at KFC when he can make thousands of dollars a day on the corners? How am I supposed to tell him that? And all his friends, they're doing the same thing."

Alex had no answers. "You're sure he was slinging?"

"Yeah, yeah," she wept. "He was involved with these people, this gang, and he had cuts and bruises on his hands last week, and I says, what happened, and he says, 'I beat up some guy who'd beat up one of my crew.' I say, you can't be *involved* with these people, you gotta get your life together. What am I *supposed* to do?"

"Do you think these people, this other gang, are the people who did this?"

"I told you." She sounded impatient again. "An eye for an eye. And one of Sal's gang, they'll go out now and shoot someone else's boy. When does it *stop?*"

"If we can find them, we can arrest them," Alex replied lamely. An arrest which would not stop the cycle of carnage at all.

"One of them, he's called Zippy, like these kids, they don't even use their real names. But Zippy, I remember, 'cause Sal said his name, and you remember some wannabe gangster calling himself Zippy. He's got a child too. But he's still selling drugs. He's gonna end up dead or in jail, and his child's gonna grow up without a father. This cycle of violence, of trauma, it's got to stop. It has to." Alex opened his mouth to ask her more questions about Zippy, or where her son sold drugs, but she raced ahead of him. "You gotta go to 190th and Bennett. That's where Sal sometimes stayed, with his girlfriend, this girl named Dora, who... well... I thought…" She dropped her voice, "She's an addict, she uses needles, and she don't look well, she have HIV, I swear, I work in St. Luke's as a healthcare assistant, I know, and I tell Sal, but he doesn't want to know."

Alex wrote scrawling, shorthand notes in his memo book.

"I kicked him out of my house," she continued angrily. "I shouldn't have."

"Because he was selling crack?"

"He was using too. Using something. Said he didn't, but I could see, I know. Told him he couldn't come back 'till he'd cleaned his act up. What kind of mother am I?"

"You do what you can, but sometimes…" The words wedged inside his throat. "We will catch these people. I promise."

"God is on the side of the righteous." She clutched his forearm. Pain glazed her eyes. "He will guide you if you listen. He'll help you find justice for Sal."

"Yeah, ma'am." Alex left Bettina Perez with his card and an assurance that he would speak to her soon, perhaps tomorrow when he knew more, and then he checked in with the search and the canvass that Eddie and precinct detectives had organized, before radioing 1PP to run warrant checks on the apartments overlooking the street. With the crime scene in hand, Alex and Eddie drove to West 190th and Bennett, chasing their only lead.

The moment they set off on foot down 190th, Alex became conscious of the light, flat and grey, and the ominous clouds roiling above the spires and tower blocks. The block felt menacing and sad: boarded-up low-rises, gaping, broken windows, vacant lots of wire and weeds littered with vials, crack pipes, skeletal shopping carts, and garbage. Discarded plastic bags shivered in the wind. Normal city detritus. He saw nothing that justified the dread wrapping wire around his entrails.

"What's up?" asked Eddie.

"Dunno. Got a weird feeling in my gut." He studied the low-rise across the street with its decomposing fire escape and eyeless windows. "Maybe it's just the curry disagreeing with me," he added, holding his hand against his stomach.

"It is very quiet on this street," observed Eddie. The bitter wind hissed around the buildings, and he said, "There's gonna be a storm tonight. I think we're gonna get some sleet."

"You figure?"

"Pressure's dropping."

"Yeah, but it's October 3rd. Seems early for that. It's just gonna rain."
Alex lowered his eyes to his memo book, rereading the address.

That was when the gunfire rang out.

Three shots, *bang, bang, bang.*

Alex threw himself to the ground. Panic and pain in his right side as the noise shattered the stillness. Another three shots ruptured his eardrums. They came from across the road. His whole right side felt heavy, wrong. Something told him the pain was important. He held his ribs, then he looked, gawking. Blood besmeared his fingers, sticky, warm, staggeringly crimson. It was saturating his sport jacket. Shredded red flesh protruded through the tears in the grey cloth. He forgot how to breathe. Metallic adrenaline swamped his tastebuds.

"Eddie!" he gasped. "I think I've been shot." Eddie would know what to do because he was the most levelheaded guy in the New York City Police Department, and he would not be afraid.

But he heard nothing. He wrenched his body around, searching for his partner, who had been a step or two behind him. Eddie, curled on his side. "Eddie!" Alex's throat closed up. Eddie was motionless. Blood pooled on the sidewalk and flowed into small rivers between the pavement slabs. Alex wheezed out a strangled noise as terror throttled him, seizing his breath, his body. His mind blanked, but he drew his gun. Oh, God, oh, God, he had to think. Eddie wasn't conscious. He might already be DOA. Fuck, he was trained for this. He was a New York City cop, and he was trained for this. Fluid boiled inside his chest. Coughing, tasting blood. A lung. They got a lung. You have two lungs, so losing one isn't imminently vital. Next thing, get to a safer place. Behind the engine block of a car. They said it could protect you from bullets. Had they said that in the Academy or in some movie? He crawled on his hands and knees to his partner. Another three shots struck the building above him. A big caliber. An assault rifle. The motherfuckers had a rifle. He fell to his belly on the pavement, paralyzed. *No, you have to move Eddie.* Eddie opened his eyes, staring at him. Terror and pain glazed his brown eyes, but he was alive! His mouth moved; blood bubbled between his lips, trickling down the side of his chin.

"It's all right, Eddie," Alex panted. "It'll be all right, it'll be all right, it'll be all right." He forced his death investigator's eyes to assess Eddie's wound. He'd taken a bullet to the stomach – a gaping hole, shining organs poking through ruined flesh. Probably got the abdominal aorta. He would bleed out. Or die of sepsis or peritonitis. Fuck, fuck, fuck, it was bad. Alex felt himself sinking downwards, losing consciousness. *No, Alex,* he said to himself. *Breathe.* A taste like salted metal filled his mouth. Blood on his tongue, his lips. Oh, yeah, he had a slug in his lung. *Don't look at your side. You have to function. You have to. Don't just sit there.* He wrapped his arms around Eddie's shoulders and lugged the man towards the front wheel of the nearest car, a black Toyota Camry. Eddie weighed almost two hundred pounds, but adrenaline gave Alex superman strength despite his wounds. He heaved his partner against the car's front tire. Eddie's muscles twitched, and he uttered a creaky moan. More blood dribbled out of his mouth. Alex groped around Eddie's blood-soaked waist, searching for the portable radio clipped to his belt. Another shot struck the car window. Whimpering, Alex sprawled across Eddie, hands clasped over the back of his head, protecting Eddie and his own face and neck from flying shards of glass. Eddie's body spasmed with strained breaths. You can't breathe like that for long and survive. Alex pressed the 'transmit' button on the radio, shouting hysterically, "*Ten-thirteen, ten-thirteen, ten-thirteen.* Shots fired at Manhattan North Homicide Unit 325, urgent! 720 West 190th Street! Be advised, I'm shot, perps at the location. Rush a bus! Ten-fifty-four. Ten-fifty-four. *Ten-thirteen!*"

"Ten-four. Units are on the way, K." Every cop on the citywide frequency would hear his desperate ten-thirteen.

Alex tore off his blood-soaked jacket and shoved it into Eddie's stomach, wracking his mind for scraps of first-aid courses from the Academy. *Stop bleeding at all costs.* He heard sirens, at first distant, but closing in. He coughed violently, spitting up more blood. His breath gurgled. Blood covered everything in sight, his hands, the car, the sidewalk, his clothes. His head was floating, spinning. He buried his face against Eddie's shoulder. "I'm sorry, Eddie." He was going to die. He had a punctured lung, and he was going to drown in his own blood and die.

Heavy boots thudded across pavement. Equipment jangled. Two ESU cops were crouching at his side. One held his bloody hand. "What's your name?"

"Alex." All he knew was pain. More pain than he had ever imagined anyone could feel and still be alive.

"What's your birthday?"

"February 12th, 1957."

"Do you know where you are?"

He shut his eyes, expecting to pass out.

"Come on, Alex, stay with us."

"190th Street."

"Who's the president?"

"Reagan."

"Can you feel your feet and legs and wiggle your toes?"

He wiggled his toes. "Yeah."

Yes, he'd been trained to do this. Assess the vic. Is he conscious? Are his mental faculties functioning? Has he sustained a spinal injury? But he only wanted the pain to stop.

The ambulance crew rushed in as soon as ESU let them. In seconds, they'd whisked Eddie onto a bus. The paramedics asked Alex the same questions – his name, his age, the president, his spine. A familiar face appeared amongst the uniforms and EMS guys. Vito Indelicata.

"Fuck, Alex! What have you done to yourself?" exclaimed Indelicata while EMS rolled Alex onto a stretcher and strapped a blood pressure cuff to his arm. They cut off his clothes. Vito leaned over him. "We *got* those assholes. You gonna be okay."

Vito's voice sounded distant, muffled behind walls of pain. Alex coughed up more blood. *Fuck, what if the blood runs out?* A chill spread through his body, like lying naked in a blizzard. He tried breathing but liquid sloshed inside his chest, where the air should be. It hurt, Jesus, it hurt. EMS covered him in blankets and shoved gauze into the wounds. They couldn't give him gas because he had lung injuries, but they jabbed a syringe filled with morphine into a vein in his left arm. Colors changed into a medley of whites and yellows as the world pulled away, the impossible sensation of flying backwards through a tunnel. The ambulance floated through the city like it had wings.

They took them to Columbia Presbyterian on West 168th Street. The morphine wore off, leaving Alex feeling sick, falling out of his tunnel, confused but sensing doctors thrusting tubes between his ribs. And the pain, the pain overwhelmed every sense, every nerve. It was everywhere. Death would be a relief. The only thing that would take away the pain. "Please, stop!" he begged the trauma doctors, who were trying to save his life. "Please, just let me go. Let me die. What are you doing? Just let me go."

The ER staff barked, "Thirty-year old male, he's got a gunshot wound to the right lung and a hemothorax and pneumothorax. Heart rate 140…"

The paneled ceiling above him wheeled like the hospital was attached to a giant ceiling fan. A doctor shouted something about hypovolemic shock. A nurse said, "You need a CT scan and emergency surgery," before giving him a shot of Propofol, which knocked him out completely.

Chapter Twelve

Alex heard squeaking wheels in the corridor outside, then murmuring voices, thudding footsteps. He'd been somewhere else in this hospital but wasn't there now. An aching tightness cut into his right side. His throat hurt, as if he'd scraped it with sandpaper. Unexpectedly, the door groaned on its hinges. A ray of light shot into the dark hospital room. He squinted and raised an arm to his eyes, blocking the light. His arm caught on lines and wires attached to his neck and chest. Groggily, he watched the ECG machine, the green squiggles plunging between peaks and troughs, like his kids' drawing of a mountain range.

"Lex, you awake?" Vito's gruff voice. He had come in with Bill Ryan. The two sat in chairs flanking Alex's bed.

"I guess," Alex murmured, unsure.

"You remember when the doctors woke you up in the ICU after surgery? You been in there for the last four days. You had a breathing tube, and you had an infection after the surgery. They thought you were getting septic."

"Not really." Maybe. A hazy flicker of a memory, a doctor, dark-complexioned, like he was from the Middle East, saying something to him. He'd tried moving his head, but he found tubes hooked into his neck and his nostrils. It slid away from his consciousness when he reached for it. Four days in the ICU with an NG tube and a central line. Probably just as well that he didn't remember.

"Like havin' too much to drink, huh?" A hapless smile crossed Vito's face.

"Yeah." Speaking scraped at his throat. His eyes fell to the wound on his right side. *My God, it's worse than I thought.* The lower half of his ribcage was savaged by a gruesome tangled knot of swollen, inflamed stitches and lacerations, with oozing drains peering shyly out of the gashes. Drains for infection. More drains for removing air and blood from the lung. The sight of it made him feel queasy, and he tugged at the hospital gown, partially hiding it.

"They pulled a lot of shrapnel out of you," Bill said. "We think you got hit by a ricochet. So that's good, because it didn't penetrate with the same velocity as a direct hit, which probably would have been fatal, but bad because it created more than one entrance wound and damage over a wider area. They had to open you up completely to look for all the pieces and stop internal bleeding and then stitch you back together. I think most of the bleeding was in the lungs. A little in your liver. It missed your other organs."

"You lost so much blood they were worried about cardiac arrest, and it could've injured your heart," said Vito. "You had to get a couple transfusions."

Alex glanced at the lines again – fluids, antibiotics, painkillers. He could never give blood at department blood drives again. An absurdly trivial thought, given the circumstances. Eyes lightly closing, he touched his throat. His fingers ran into plastic, the catheter in his jugular, which connected to tubes coiling up into bags of fluid. Inside his body, a tube followed the vein all the way into his heart. *How fucking weird is that?*

Vito, seeing the look on his face, added, "Doc thinks your heart's probably alright. They're monitoring it with that CVC line."

Probably? "Huh. How's Eddie?" he slurred, drugged and overwhelmed.

For a beat, Bill and Vito were silent.

Finally, Bill sighed, "He's been in and out of surgery."

"He likely?"

Another beat. His voice going quiet, Bill said, "Touch and go. They don't know."

"Got his spinal cord," Vito stated gravely. "If he lives, they don't think he's gonna walk again."

"What?" A shock zapped through his spine.

"It's not good."

Fuck, Eddie couldn't be paralyzed. Maybe this was a nightmare. Maybe they'd never set foot on West 190th Street. Maybe he would wake up sweating and scared but unhurt in his apartment.

"Hey, we got the guys," said Vito. "Two fuckin' assholes with an AR-18. Fuck knows where they got it."

"IRA uses them," Bill commented.

"Well, it's the insurgency weapon of choice worldwide," remarked Vito.

"Fuck," wheezed Alex. How did that get on the streets? He quivered at the sensation of ice freezing his spinal cord. "They're sure Eddie's paralyzed?"

"Yeah, the docs are pretty sure," Bill said sadly.

"Those assholes, they saw yous, thought they'd start blastin' away," Vito growled. "Wanted to take out a couple cops. We got 'em dead to rights on attempted murder one. And..." He put a beefy hand on Alex's forearm, and Alex saw abrasions on his knuckles. "We made sure we got 'em good, taught 'em a lesson. You gotta make guys think twice about going after cops. Otherwise, we got no chance out there. No fuckin' chance. It's become a *war* out there."

"These dealers don't care," Bill noted, still sounding sad. "There used to be kind of a sense to it, but now..."

"They were still on the street when ESU got there," Vito continued. "ESU subdued them, we took 'em in."

"Who... Were they perps we'd collared? Or the ones we were looking for?" Pain in his ribcage broke through the barriers of morphine.

"Probably don't know you for shit. You ever run into a pair of shitbirds called Adi Nichol and Kevin West?"

Having never heard those names in his life, Alex shook his head. He winced at the sting in the right side of his throat from the CVC line.

"Yeah, that's what I thought. They said they didn't know you, either. They thought some plainclothes guys would be there. So, they saw you and Eddie, thought, those are them, blasted away. Didn't give a fuck what cops they shot. Street Crime's been hanging around on that block. Busted some of their crew last week. They claimin' they're BLA, but those losers ain't nobody."

"BLA? But Eddie's Black," Alex muttered weakly.

"The only color those assholes see is blue." Bill kneaded the blue-tinged bags under his eyes. "We're going to go, but we'll be by again tomorrow."

Vito, his hand still on Alex's arm, said, "You alright for a short statement first?"

"My throat really hurts, Vito. I didn't see shit anyway." He gently ran his fingers down his windpipe. They bumped over the catheter. From working at the other end of this – interviewing victims in hospitals – he knew that the endotracheal tube they insert in the ICU irritates the throat, but it should feel better in a day or two.

"A short statement," Vito said.

"I can write it."

What did he remember? The gunfire. The pain shattering his mind. Eddie's terrible wound. Vito handed him the memo book, and he painstakingly scribbled a three-sentence paragraph. His arm felt weak, uncoordinated.

A doctor came in, nodding at Vito and Bill before he checked Alex's temperature, blood pressure, the CVC line, and then he held a cold stethoscope against his chest. Pain spurted like a geyser when Alex breathed deeply enough for the doctor to hear his lungs, but the doctor seemed pleased with the vitals, saying in a lilting Arabic accent, "You're actually awake. Good. You probably don't remember me very well."

Foggily, Alex read the nametag pinned on the man's chest. Dr. Faisel Naziri. The Middle-Eastern doctor from his ICU dream. "Sort of," he muttered.

"I operated on you. How do you feel?"

"I dunno," Alex answered.

"You're on a fair bit of morphine, and we kept you sedated in the ICU. You had a temp of 102, but it looks good now. 98.2." Naziri eased the hospital gown aside. "Are you in much pain?"

"Yeah, hurts like a bitch to breathe." Should he swear? "Sorry."

"Okay, we'll raise your dose of pain meds a little." The doctor dabbed at the wound with sterile pads, probing it for swelling or signs of more internal bleeding. That stung through the opiates, like all the morphine in the world couldn't hide the pain.

Alex sank his teeth into his lower lip, trying not to whimper in front of his colleagues. "How long they gonna keep me here?"

"I'm still concerned about infection. We cleaned it out, but gunshot wounds have a high risk of sepsis. We had to insert mesh to stabilize part of the chest wall. That's also an infection risk."

"Come on, what's the damage, doc?" Alex rasped. He had to know.

"We were waiting until you were alert enough to understand." The doctor spoke in the perfectly correct English of someone who'd learned it as a second language, then become fluent without the idiomatic slobbery typical of native speakers. "Two of the fragments transected your right lung, and we had to perform a lung resection to stop significant bleeding from bronchial arteries. Another fragment entered your abdominal cavity and lacerated your liver. The good news is that a transfusion stabilized you, and we were able to staple the injury sites and spare over half of the lung. We will not discharge you until you're mobile, and we feel you're more or less past the risk of complications, like sepsis, or more bleeding." Naziri shrugged regretfully. "I don't know how long

116

that will be. But your temperature and blood pressure are within normal parameters, the lung sounds clearer than it has been, and this is draining. Your bloods aren't showing high infection markers at the moment, which is very positive. I'll be back here tomorrow. The nurses and a pulmonary resident are always on the ward if you have any concerns or need anything. Do you have any questions?"

"No," Alex said, dazed and speechless.

Naziri wrote some notes on the chart. "You might in a few days." Then he departed from the room, heading to his next medical disaster.

Alex shivered. They had spared *over half* his lung. What did that mean? They had removed part of it. "Did you know?" he huskily asked Vito and Bill. "About the lung?"

"Um, yes," Bill responded, sounding uncomfortable. "But we thought it was better for you to hear that from a doctor."

Another deep breath sent molten waves of pain spilling through the morphine. Alex gingerly rolled towards his left side to rest his head on his forearm but got himself tangled in knotted CVC tubes and ECG wires. Bill rearranged the tubes. Slightly panicked, Alex grabbed Bill's hand. The Irish detective reiterated that he would visit tomorrow, then Alex heard the fading thumps of their footsteps retreating, the door clicking shut. Morphine shot down his jugular, into his heart, and it enveloped his brain like sinking into a warm bath.

Part 3

Chapter Thirteen

March 2010

The moment Alex saw Sarah's name flash on his cell, he knew she wanted something. Sarah never called him to say hi, find out how he was, or meet for coffee. His failures at parenting, and he paid for it every time he talked to her.

His gut instincts proved right – she wanted him to schlep to her apartment in Prospect Park, so he could move a Craigslist-acquired washing machine out of her garden and install it in the kitchen. Like most young professionals in New York, Sarah, a nurse in the cardiology department at Roosevelt Hospital, lived in a rented place in the outer boroughs, an old Brooklyn townhouse, once decadent when built in the late-nineteenth century, but now divided into small apartments with secondhand, Craigslist appliances.

"You can hire people to do this," Alex said dryly.

"They cost money, Dad. And this was like a fifty-dollar machine. My sister said you did the whole kitchen in the West 87th Street place yourself. The cabinets and everything. Surely this isn't that difficult, but me and my roommate can't move it. I know it's like a giant step back for feminism, but it needs a man. I'm just asking for your help."

The truth was, he did not have the spine to withstand that. He'd never found a way to make up for his absence during her childhood and their dysfunctional relationship now, but he dragged himself across town on his RDO because he had to try.

The machine sat gauchely in the picturesque, well-tended garden. When Alex and Sarah attempted to lift it, she gave way under the weight, him taking all of it with a sudden spasm of pain in his back. He precariously eased the machine to the ground without damaging it or injuring himself.

Breathless, he said, "You and I are not getting this up the stairs. I'm gonna put my back out if we try. You need *two* men." Being a man who spent half his life knocking on strangers' doors, he immediately started canvassing the block for helpful neighbors, to Sarah's surprise.

"Are you gonna say you're the police?" she asked as he rapped on a door.

"Uh, no. The washing machine hasn't committed any felonies."

They found a friendly male neighbor, a Haitian accountant who spoke more French than English. It took Alex and the Haitian, neither an expert in washing machine removal, about twenty minutes of debate and planning to work out the safest technique for carrying the machine up the stairs without hurting themselves. Once they achieved that, they rocked and wiggled it into the gap underneath the kitchen cabinets, with Sarah, a hand in her mouth, entreating, "Oh, be careful." The washing machine in place, Sarah gave the man a grateful bottle of wine. He said something in French that neither Sarah nor Alex understood, but it sounded appreciative, and then he left.

Alex crawled underneath the cupboard, contorting his body so he could connect the hoses in the back of the thing to the tap. He clenched a flashlight in his teeth and identified the cold water in-pipe and the waste-water hose, the relevant attachment points on the machine, then he wrestled everything into place, finding the screwing-in process arduous and fiddly. Hoses secured, he plugged the machine into a socket.

"Okay," he breathed, taking the flashlight out of his mouth. "If this thing isn't a useless pile of shit, it should work."

"Thanks, Dad."

As he twisted around the cabinets, a sharp twinge fired through his right side. His gunshot wound, reminding him of its presence. It did that when he torqued the mass of scar tissue knitted between his seventh and twelfth ribs, where those 45mm rounds had splintered nerves, costal cartilage, and intercostal muscles. He had lived with the stabbing twinges and dull pain for so long that he barely remembered what it was like to not have chronic pain in his side.

"You all right?" Sarah asked. She'd seen him wince and hesitate.

"Yeah, fine. Just the gunshot wound." Coughing, which hurt his side even more, he pulled himself to his feet. "Turn on the machine and see if it works. If I fucked up the hoses, you'll know when it floods your kitchen."

Sarah looked pensive, indifferent to washing machines and flooding kitchens. "Can't they do *anything* for that wound? It's been causing you trouble for years."

"I'm used to it."

"But there must be something."

"No. I mean, they could go in and scrape out scar tissue, but it's a lot of nerve pain so that probably wouldn't help."

"Oh. Bet your chest x-rays are interesting."

"Yeah, they always get the med students in to look." They did, and he wanted to keep the conversation somewhat light.

"Have they tried steroid injections?"

"No," he said, unable to hold himself back from sounding annoyed. "There's too much scar tissue between my ribs." This stuff was between him and his doctor.

"What about drugs for nerve pain like gabapentin?"

Yes, he'd investigated that, but his doctor was worried about it interacting with his anti-depressants. Clutching his throbbing side, he glared at her, as if his eyes could hurl knives into this conversation and kill it. He couldn't deal with telling her about the anti-depressants. "I get to have these conversations about my health with like five people, who are about five people too many, but I gotta do it. I love you, kiddo, but I really don't want to have them with you, okay?"

"Fine, whatever. Mom says you never really dealt with it," she muttered, sounding hurt. "With the shooting. Like with therapy and stuff."

"Jesus Christ, honey. It was the '80s. The police department wasn't doing therapy." He shaded his eyes with his palm. "Can we talk about something else?"

Sarah blinked back tears. "Dad, I'm... I don't know. Ellie says we should get along better. She emailed me saying she might come out to New York for a couple months next year for a work thing. Like a visiting fellow at NYU or something like that. But she said she won't take the job if she has to come out and deal with family drama. She said you and I need to 'get our shit together and figure it out.'" She framed the last phrase in air quotes with her fingers. "I guess I wanted to talk to you about that. Not just get you to put in the washing machine. I mean, I needed that too, but I also wanted to talk."

Ellie in New York for a few months. Something to look forward to, spending time with the daughter who understood him, the one he understood. She'd moved to Brisbane for her PhD, married an Australian, divorced the Australian (following the family tradition), but stayed in Australia for a lecturing job at the University of New South Wales. Even with Skype, Australia seemed like another planet. He felt a little hurt that she hadn't emailed him, but then, arguing with her sister about their parents' history and which parent was most at fault was something of a pastime for both girls.

"Well, how does Ellie think we should 'figure it out?'" He resigned himself to the pain drilling into his ribs – one of those days where it played up.

"She says I wind you up. She says I should stop saying things that wind you up."

"Well, yeah. That's a good place to start."

"And she says you do that. You get defensive and reactive and sarcastic."

That was true as well. Arching an eyebrow, he said, "Yeah."

"Then I get mad at you."

"You're always mad at me."

"Dad…" She covered her face with both hands. "You don't listen."

"Things always go to shit when you bring up my health or my problems with alcohol or depression or whatever. I get that you're still pissed at me for that, but it's just this thing that I have, and rehashing why it made me a terrible father doesn't do any good."

"You've never called it depression before." She looked straight into his face, surprised.

"Haven't I?" Fuck. He'd surprised himself by saying that aloud.

"No. You just talked about having PTSD after you hurt your hand."

"Well, it woulda been before that," he said sarcastically.

"You know what I mean, Dad. But depression?"

"I guess I'm trying out calling it something else. Seeing how that goes."

"Does that mean you're working stuff out?"

"It means I'm calling it different things. I don't know."

"Are you on medication for it?"

He hesitated. Well, he'd run headlong into this one. No sense in lying. She would know. She was his kid, and she'd inherited that sixth sense. "Yes. For a while now. Zoloft."

"Does it help?"

He studied his black loafers and the dog-eared, grey linoleum on the floor. "Some."

"Any trouble with side-effects?"

"Headaches." He tapped the washing machine's power button. Its LED lights flickered to life. "It turns on."

"I guess you're still seeing a therapist?" Her gaze rolled towards his hands.

He wondered if she was looking at the scars from the window incident, pale fleshy stripes snaking across his left hand. "Yeah, a psychiatrist. The same one I've been seeing since I was diagnosed. I'm always gonna be sick, honey."

"I'm glad you can talk about it. Lots of men don't. Especially cops. I mean, it's good you're dealing—"

"I didn't have a choice," he cut in dryly.

"Yeah, I know. But still... It's a good thing. Repressing this stuff isn't healthy at all. You know I went to see a counsellor in January."

"Oh."

"He told me I'm pissed at you because it's a projection of how I feel about myself. He said I need to accept the choices I made and look ahead. I always kinda blamed you for my shitty relationships, but I guess some of them are on me. I need to stop dating assholes. I also kind of wish I'd gone to med school, but no way did I have the grades."

"Is that also my fault?" He remembered her low grades, her boozy parties, and his ex blaming him – if not for his lousy parenting, then his lousy genes. Sarah rarely spoke to him in those days. During high school and college, she kept him at a distance until 9/11, when the terror that stunned the city and her fear that he'd been one of the cops who died in the Towers brought them together for about a week.

"I mean, no. That's the whole thing I'm trying to get to. And my therapist says maybe I don't really want to go to med school. I'm just always feeling like I'm in Ellie's shadow, and *she's* a doctor, of sorts. She got into the good college, the good PhD program, you guys made me feel like the black sheep—"

"You 'guys?' I never had any issue with you going to SUNY. That was all your mother."

"You were disappointed in me too."

"I was concerned that you were making some stupid choices. But not about colleges or careers."

"I'm just telling you how *I* saw things. Ellie said we don't communicate well—"

"No shit." He folded his arms, clasping both elbows with each hand.

"She says I should start telling you things and not just holding everything inside."

"You tell me where I fucked up all the time."

"Dad...I'm trying..." she protested.

"No. You're doing the same things you always do... Trying to use me and my issues to figure out yours. But seriously, you're only thirty. There are no armies between you and applying to medical school."

"I don't *know* if that's what I want. I'd be hundreds of thousands of dollars in debt for the rest of my life. My therapist thinks I need more self-esteem, and I should stop comparing myself to the cardio-thoracic surgeons on the ward, or my sister. Or you."

"You shouldn't compare yourself to any of those people. Especially me."

"Well, no, but... The media always portrays homicide detectives as super sexy heroes, outsmarting criminal masterminds."

"I've never met a criminal mastermind in my life." Alex hurt his side with his sardonic burst of laughter.

"You're being obtuse and wiseass again."

"Yeah, you're right. Sorry." She was making an effort, sort of, and he should try.

Sarah slumped into the wall, her face fixed in a jaundiced scowl. "Why do we argue about everything? This is what I'm talking about. This isn't the conversation I wanted to have today."

"Well, what conversation did you want?"

"My therapist also said I need to be honest with you and Mom."

"Honest?" Alex said, baffled. "About what?"

"Life."

He raised both eyebrows querulously. Setting her jaw, she slowly rolled up the sleeve on her left arm, then she pointed to four thin, parallel scars on her forearm, each one about six inches long. Alex eyeballed the scars, wrestling with the significance and everything else about this conversation, before he sputtered, "You said you got those from catsitting your friend's cat."

"They weren't from the cat," Sarah whispered hoarsely.

"What?"

Sarah fished dirty dishes out of the sink. "I wish my roommate didn't abandon her crap in the sink like this."

"Where did you get the scars?" insisted Alex.

"When I was in college, I started... uh... cutting myself. I don't know. I was unhappy, and it was a way of dealing with it, I guess. My therapist says it was a way of feeling like I had control over something, and it was like the blood could take away all my bad feelings. I dunno... It's really

123

hard to explain why. It just felt like a thing I had to do. It felt right. It sounds really fucked up, but that's what it felt like. I did the cuts on my arm first but realized the cat story wasn't like a long-term excuse, because I don't have a cat. So, I started cutting my thighs, 'cause it was easier to hide. I did it for years. I was sometimes mad 'cause you and Mom and hadn't noticed. Like I wanted you to notice, but also wanted to hide it."

Alex lost his ability to speak, as if he'd been punched in the throat. He stood stock still, absorbing guilt and shock. He was a detective. Should he have been switched on? Noticed something? No doubt. But he had always suffered a blind spot; she'd pushed him away when she was young, and he'd lost himself in his illness while their troubles broadened inside a supermax prison of dysfunction neither could escape.

"Does your mother know?" he asked softly.

"Yeah. Told her like a week ago."

"How'd she take it?"

"Badly. Broke down in tears and said she'd done a terrible job. But she'd heard you had some mental health stuff—"

"How?" With the girls being adults, he had no further reasons to interact with Catherine.

"Ellie probably said something. I didn't. I thought it was confidential. I guess whales don't require much practice with confidentiality, so she probably has no idea…"

"I think she studies fish and coral reefs, but it doesn't matter." He'd hoped Ellie wouldn't tell her mother, but he wasn't surprised that she did. "That must've made Catherine feel better. She always liked blaming me for everything."

"And you liked blaming her." Sarah said irritably.

"Some kids inherit a million bucks from their parents," he quipped. Sweat stuck to his sides. "You inherited a mental illness."

"That's a way to put it. I guess being a smartass is part of your defense mechanisms."

"So my shrink tells me. Have you stopped?"

"Yes. I stopped a while ago… Like a few months after you hurt your hand. I didn't do anything nearly as serious, but I guess it made me think, you know. Like it wasn't my fault my family was screwed up, and you and Mom had all your issues, and then there was the shooting, and that really messed you up, and I don't think anyone really got that. So… I dunno."

"I'm glad my breakdown was good for something," he said, but the sarcasm felt flaccid.

"I didn't mean it like that."

"I know."

"Well… my therapist thought I should tell you guys."

"Yeah," he said in a choked voice. "Right, kiddo, I'm gonna hit the pool today. Need to go before it closes."

"It's good you're swimming," she said quietly.

"Yeah, well, gotta stay fit enough to run down perps." He tried to smile.

"You know." Her voice trembled. "You can ring me, like if you're around Midtown and you want lunch or something. Ellie really wants us to figure it out. And I want to do better."

"Yeah. So do I." It broke his heart that their relationship swung between stilted, awkward conversations and outright conflict, but he never knew what to do about it. Today, he had come clean about the SSRIs, and she had come clean about the self-harm, a rare moment of candor. Was that a start?

He double-checked the washing machine installation, which seemed copacetic. Then he hugged her, outwardly warm, affectionate, but inside, he flinched, the loneliness cutting deep, like touching someone's hand through shattered glass. Did she feel the same way? Arms crossed, eyes cast onto the pavement, he hiked alongside the Brooklyn condos and townhouses towards the F line subway station in Prospect Park. He passed tidy condos with flower boxes perched atop the freshly painted stoops, a row of upscale boutiques, a French café, a coffee shop, an African hair salon, an Indian restaurant. No wonder rents around Prospect Park had shot up like a rocket. That was this city for you: if you could afford to live somewhere, you probably didn't want to. The city was far safer than his 1990s self could have ever imagined, but at the same time, a thirty-three year old cop had no chance in hell of buying an apartment on the Upper West Side, or in Prospect Park for that matter.

Halfway down the corridor leading to the subway platform, a busker played an Ornette Coleman solo on an alto saxophone. The tune deafened everyone in the echoing acoustics of the tunnel. Alex tossed a dollar bill into the sax player's case. He felt relieved when he could hear live music without flashbacks. It triggered him on sensitive days. That dollar might build karma, stop the next attack, like paying the Mafia for protection inside his head.

His karma held as the subway bounced and shrieked towards Manhattan, even though a mariachi band tested it by boarding at York Street and playing maracas and guitars until East Broadway. Alex transferred from the F to the C at West 4th, riding that to West 23rd, the closest stop to the Chelsea Piers swimming pool. He walked briskly towards the West Side Highway. At every step, he felt like his heart spurted blood from a severed artery. He wanted to fly back to Brooklyn, hug his kid, tell her he was sorry for everything, but face-to-face, he only had sarcastic quips. What the hell was wrong with him?

Once in the locker rooms, he changed into his swim trunks. For a few seconds, he closed his eyes, breathing in the astringent odor of chlorine, listening to the splashes of other swimmers. He jumped into the water, immersing his whole body in a swift dive to the pool floor. Surfacing, he swam aggressive laps, back and forth, as if he could outrun those years framed by sadness and guilt. Instead, one tempest from the past consumed another. Worries about the federal grand jury and wrongful convictions gathered strength, like storms on the sea. He swam harder. Fifteen laps, then twenty. It stayed with him.

Last year, when the spate of NY County miscarriages of justice first appeared in the *Times,* Alex, feeling nervous, had hunted for information. He'd grilled Sam Rizzo, who worked for the Special Narcotics Investigative Unit, based out of an office in One Hogan Place. This made him a useful man for DA's office gossip and more trustworthy than anyone with a vested interest in DA's office politics. Sam was physically in the building, but still employed by the NYPD.

Over drinks a year ago, Rizzo on self-aggrandizing microbrews and Alex on diet coke (beverages neither would have touched in the early '90s), Rizzo told Alex that Cyril Wakefield, the newly-elected New York County DA, had reorganized the whole place. He'd run his campaign on reforming and modernizing criminal justice, and now that he'd taken up his office, he set out to prove his commitment to justice, equality, and ethics. Among other reforms, he created the Conviction Integrity Program, dedicated to investigating post-conviction claims of innocence.

Ostensibly not worried about lawsuits or Manhattan North Homicide's reputation, Rizzo explained that they were primarily examining cases where modern DNA technology could exonerate a defendant (as with the Central Park Jogger), incidents of prosecutorial failure to disclose *Brady* material (not a detective's fault), and cases where the indictment and conviction had been pretty miraculous in the first place, the defendant convicted by weak eyewitnesses, untrustworthy informants, or iffy forensic science (apparently fingerprints, hair, handwriting, to name a few, were not as reliable as Alex had been led to believe over the last two decades). Alex had found his former colleague's composure reassuring. "It's mainly just looking at the DNA stuff," Rizzo had said. "And the fucked up forensics. What were we supposed to do? They said it was *science!*"

Alex swam until he hyperventilated. He had to stop. He grasped the side of the pool, bobbing on the water, mouth open, winded and lightheaded. His side and shoulder muscles burned. But he pushed off the tiles into another lap.

Yesterday, the worse for wear with sleeplessness and stress, he had called Rizzo, hoping to pin him down for more diet coke and microbrews. Rizzo said that he was dating a woman who had two kids from a prior relationship, and between that and work, he had no free time.

"My God, you're being a sensible adult," Alex exclaimed. "When did that happen?"

"I don't know," Rizzo answered, sounding equally as baffled. "But look, Alex, this wrongful convictions thing, it's the US Attorney. You know that's got fuck-all to do with the DA. The Conviction Integrity Program *isn't* prosecuting anyone. That isn't what it does. They just review cases. Get people out of prison. Wakefield's not going after dirty cops. Or any cops. Whatever this federal grand jury's doing, NYDA's office has zero involvement in it."

"But the DA's reviewing old cases? Do you know if they've been subpoenaed?"

"How would I know that? It's a big office, and I'm on a different floor. It's just some lawyers who work in that unit. I don't fuckin' know who they are."

"Have you been subpoenaed?"

He heard Rizzo breathing over the phone. "Yeah. Um, so has Vasquez."

"Fuck. Who else?"

"Uh, Hurley's got a subpoena."

Alex almost dropped the phone. "*Hurley?* Fuck. When was he gonna tell me?"

"I guess he didn't wanna worry you."

"I bet." He gulped in air like he'd been trapped under water. "You saw me do that cursory interview with Ernie Serrachia. What do you think?"

"You did everything right. You checked his story and let the guy walk. It's Indelicata who got him to confess five or six months later. That's on him, not you."

"It was my paperwork, my lead." Guilt crackled inside his throat.

"So fuckin' what? If Vito brings him in and gaslights him while you're recovering from being shot, that ain't got anything to do with you."

Too exhausted and breathless to swim another lap, Alex slithered out of the pool, then immersed himself in the hot tub, warming his tired muscles and his achy ribcage. He listened to the hum of the pool machinery, the resonant voices of people in the warehouse, the ripples of moving water. James, Sam, and Marty couldn't and wouldn't implicate him in any civil rights violations because he'd never told them anything. Still, they should have forewarned him of the grand jury. Like he wouldn't find out?

After ten minutes, the hot tub sickened and overheated him, as if he'd stuck his head inside a steamer. He crawled out and stood in the shower, running it lukewarm so it cooled his internal temperature.

He could give James shit for not warning him about the subpoenas. James had pipe band practice in Lower Manhattan today, closer than his house on Staten Island or his command at Queens Homicide. After five years of working in a Staten Island precinct, James had become antsy, while the department had forgotten why they'd launched him out of MNHS. It affirmed the old truism – once you've been murder police, nothing else you'll ever do matters as much. James, who once told Alex he liked the slow-lane life of a Staten Island precinct detective, woke up one day wondering what the hell he was doing with himself. He heard on FINEST that a couple Queens Homicide guys were retiring, and he asked for a transfer. To the surprise of everyone who remembered the drama and excessive force complaints surrounding his departure from MNHS, he got it without any fuss.

"You a vet?"

Startled, Alex opened his eyes. He flicked off the shower. "Sorry?"

"Are you a vet?" queried the guy in the adjacent shower. He was Black, late-twenties. Muscles rippled along his arms and his six-pack of abs, and he seemed utterly comfortable holding a conversation with a stranger while butt-naked. Then again, you would be if you had a body like that.

"Uh, no," Alex said. He quickly tied his towel around his hips. He did not have a body like that, and the towel covered up most of his belly.

"But that's gotta be from shrapnel."

"What?" He breathed in. "Oh, I'm a police officer." The scars, a bubbling knot of pink and red tissue roughly the size of his hand, tangled over his lower ribs. Like it or not, it caught people's attention; he couldn't count the conversations he'd endured over the years in pool and police locker rooms.

"You were shot in the line?"

"Yeah."

"That's like the shrapnel wounds I saw in Afghanistan."

"Yeah, it was an AR-18." Unlucky, he thought, people randomly bringing up the shooting twice in one day.

"In New York?"

"Washington Heights."

"Insurgents had those in Afghanistan and Iraq."

"It's a popular gun."

"How long ago?"

"'87."

"'87?" The vet sounded surprised.

"Yeah." Alex dried himself, then reached for his grey t-shirt, tugging it over his chest, hiding the wound. The scars always looked pink and inflamed. You wouldn't assume they were twenty-three years old. They could be from 2007, or newer.

"I've come back from Afghanistan. I was shot in Helmand. Shot in the leg. I been honorably discharged from the Army."

Alex imagined a trap door opening underneath his feet. He threw on the rest of his clothes – jeans and a grey John Jay College hoodie he'd acquired while attending a course there on DNA evidence. "That's... I'm sorry to hear that," he said.

"You went back to the police after being shot?" The vet pinned him with a hard stare, cutting into his flesh with tangible intensity and sorrow. Couldn't the guy at least put on a towel?

"Yeah."

"Doing the same things... You're not like an admin guy."

I am, really, he thought, but he said, "No, I'm a detective."

"Like you solve murders?"

That's all anyone thinks detectives do, he thought wearisomely, but it was also what he really did. "Sometimes. I try to."

"Huh. They say my leg's never gonna be right," the vet said miserably.

Alex allowed himself a curious glance at the vet's leg. The left one bore a maze of scars over the knee, and the calf muscles had wasted away until the shin bones pressed against the flesh like sticks.

"You got long term issues?" asked the vet.

"Yes," Alex admitted. His discomfort prickled his skin. "Pain, mainly."

"How do you deal with being in pain every day? I wake up in agony, and think, this is just gonna be my life, forever."

Welcome to my world. Holding fire, Alex shrugged. "You learn to live with it."

"I keep trying to figure out what to do now." Still naked, the man slouched on a bench. "I keep thinking I'm over there, you know."

"It's tough." Lots of vets were coming back from Iraq and Afghanistan with PTSD, the psychic injuries worse than the physical ones. Well, so were his. "You should talk to someone, like a counselor," he added.

"Like therapy?" snorted the vet.

"Yeah, someone who gets trauma."

"Are you in therapy?" The vet skeptically tightened his mouth.

"Yeah." Alex stretched, knuckling the small of his back.

"Don't they just make you talk about your family, your childhood?"

"Usually not."

Affixing a blandly sympathetic smile to his face, Alex scurried out of the warehouse. Halfway across Eleventh Avenue, he anxiously patted his hip for his keys and wallet, afraid he'd been flustered enough to forget. Thank God, he had them. He bought a coffee at one of the many artisan shops on West 23rd. Cuddling the warm cup, he walked to the A train station at West 23rd and Eighth Avenue, keeping his pace measured. He hoped so. Did he look frantic to the people on the street? Well, most New Yorkers appeared frantic, even when strolling out to buy a newspaper, so who would know. His hand shook as he stuffed the MetroCard into the turnstile. Caffeine overdose or his illness? Both. He increased his caffeine intake when he felt unwell. Subduing the trembling, he tensed his hands around the Styrofoam as the train rocketed downtown.

The Emerald Society Pipes and Drums, the NYPD's pipe band, were practicing in James Madison Plaza, a grassy square between St. James Place and Madison Street beneath the hulking, cubic shadow of One Police Plaza. With St. Patrick's Day less than a week away, they wore their full regalia: blue kilts, furry, phallic hats, golden capes like sails draping down their backs. They marched in military-straight lines up and down the park, entertaining the tourists, Wall Street workers, and other bystanders. Alex defied the aroma of a nearby coffee cart – *another* expresso would irritate his stomach. Instead, he sat on a bench at the edge of the square, and he tightly braced his arms across his diaphragm, letting the howling bagpipes and booming drums mask his thoughts and his cravings.

The pipe major cut the noise. Just like that, you could hear traffic, airplanes, seagulls. He said something to the band, and they tumbled out of formation, swirling into little groups and wandering around the park.

James Hurley had seen Alex when they'd marched past him. Accompanied by two other pipers, he hurried over to Alex's bench.

130

"Lex, you come down here to listen?"

"Yeah, and to talk to you."

A flicker of worry passed through James' pale blue eyes, bleakly funny because it was hard to take James seriously, dressed like that. He shifted the pipes around under his arm. "Uh, sure, what's up? They're giving us like twenty minutes. But hey, have you had a look at Vito's book?"

"Unfortunately."

"Did you see what he wrote about me?"

Alex had been so dismayed by what Vito wrote about him that he hadn't seen it. "No. Didn't read the whole thing."

"You ain't missing anything. He's not winning a Pulitzer." His face alight with that devilish grin, James fished his phone out of his sporran, then ran his fingers across the screen, reading, '*Detective James Hurley exudes Irish sexual magnetism. When he enters the interrogation room, I can see the female witness undressing him with her eyes. Black, white, Indian, Latina. They all do. To be the one who gets to ravish him, who gets to undress that alabaster Celtic body and feel those rippling muscles and that throbbing member—* '"

Laughter overtook his reading. The other piper moaned, "Oh, God, Hurley's reading that crap *again*. Someone's gotta ban that book."

"Throw it on a fuckin' bonfire," his friend sniggered. "Alabaster?"

Alex readjusted his spine and hips. The metal bench was digging into his lower back. "So, in this book, I'm chugging entire bottles of whiskey at crime scenes, and you're good in bed."

"Hey, I'm *great* in bed."

"It wasn't like that. I wasn't getting wasted in the middle of a tour. That's not what it was. It's just like the stereotype of what people think alcoholism is, but that's not—"

"Of course it's shit. He's writing knuckleheaded trash. But let's face it, I am great in bed." James wouldn't let him spiral wherever he was spiraling.

"Yeah, that goes without saying, babe."

"You schlep down here to bitch about the book?" James made a thumbs up gesture at the other pipers and waved them off. Before leaving, one slid a finger across his throat, a warning of what would happen to James if he failed to return to practice in twenty minutes.

"No," Alex answered. "But he made me look like a fucking hot mess in that book. If people know who I am from that... It's not good."

"People might just know who you are. You've worked some big cases. Your face sometimes shows up on the news."

"I can only hope," Alex said doubtfully.

James sat down next to him. They watched traffic pouring across the bridge, curling around the ramps. For a few minutes, they said nothing. They didn't need to. There are some friends whose love is a trust so deep, so bound in shared experience, that it continues where it left off no matter how infrequently you see one another, with no need for small talk or space-filling conversation. There were the usual police partner things, but there were other things that they held close to their chests. Like after Alex's December '04 breakdown, the flashbacks and dissociative episodes ran wild before the meds kicked in and he attained some tenuous control skills. He would fall out of his own body, leaving it lying on the floor. Where did his mind go? Holding his partner's internal organs inside his body with his blood-soaked jacket. Lying on a stretcher with bullets in his chest as ER docs pumped blood back into his body. Crawling out of a brutally smashed car and looking into the young ADA's lifeless eyes. When he came back to his body, he couldn't handle life – leaving the apartment, cleaning, or eating. As he cycled through dark spells of illness, James would move onto his sofa, camping out there until Alex was well enough to take care of himself. All winter, Alex felt so sick, so drained, like he could sleep forever, and he studied his kitchen knives, pills, and his old revolver that no longer had ammo. Even killing himself demanded energy and aforethought. He had neither. But James dragged him outside for walks, got some food into him, talked him through the coping techniques. If James hadn't looked after him, he would have been admitted into hospital, no doubt losing his job because you can cover up a lot, but you can't cover up a psychiatric admission. Recovery wasn't linear, but later that year, or some time into the next one, therapy and meds reduced the severity of the episodes. It had been a few years since James had last stayed at his place, forcing ice cream down his throat.

Hell, he could have fucked up the pool vet's day by telling him those stories. *Medication and years of therapy, buddy. Hope you can afford both.* He barely could, and New York City detectives were relatively well-paid.

James had removed his furry hat. It sat beside him like a weird-looking pet. He rested the pipes on his lap, absently worrying at the golden tassels wrapped around the drones. "You never drag your ass to pipe band practice unless there's something bothering you."

Alex sucked in a deep breath, then took a shallow one. "I heard you got a subpoena from a federal grand jury. The one investigating wrongful convictions on those old cases."

"Aw, dammit. How'd you hear?"

"I'm a detective. I hear things. Why didn't you tell me?"

James massaged his cheeks. "Fucking Rizzo. He has a big mouth. Because... I don't know... It would worry you, and you would do this."

"Do you have a lawyer?"

"I don't need a fuckin' lawyer."

Alex shoved his hands into the kangaroo pocket of his hoodie. "You should get a fucking lawyer. At least talk to your union rep."

"Have you got a subpoena?"

"Not yet. But the last one to get a subpoena is the rotten egg. I was the MNHS primary on a couple of those cases. Ryan was MNHS primary on two, and I think Jay McAllister, you know, from the A team, had another. The grand jury aren't gonna indict two dead guys, are they? So, they're probably after me and Indelicata. When are you testifying?"

"Early next week."

"What are you gonna tell them?"

"Dammit, Lex, we thought those guys were *guilty,* didn't we? It's not like they were choir boys before we picked them up."

"But they didn't commit the murders we said they did, either."

"So they say."

"I hear Serrachia wrote a pretty good article in *The Atlantic* about being compelled to confess." Curious and a little self-destructive, Alex had gone to *The Atlantic's* website and read the feature. Prison had somehow turned that strung-out crackhead into a loquacious writer, who had alluded to their cursory interview in September of '87, but without mentioning Alex by name. Alex had felt faintly grateful towards the guy, although from Serrachia's point of view, Alex had merely been some cop who interviewed him, briefly and inconsequentially, then sent him home. Either way, it was an indictment of the system, but not Alex personally.

"So? Neither of us was there when Indelicata interrogated him. You were on medical leave, and I'd been in the squad for about a week."

"I know. What are you gonna tell the grand jury?"

"What's there to tell them? The evidence pointed to guilt. We thought we had the right guy. The cases were shit, but we thought we had the perp. We didn't have DNA. What were we gonna do?"

"What about Vito? You know he hustled. You gonna say that?"

"Man. We all hustled. And we thought Vito was a damned good detective. Well, *they* did. *They* gave him the Medal of Honor and the Medal of Valor and enough fuckin' other awards to be more decorated than fuckin' Katherine Hepburn. You know how much he got outta that book deal?"

"No."

"Me neither. But I bet it's a fuck-ton more than you and I make in a year. He was on every TV show known to man. If you didn't know him, you'd think he wasn't an asshole. Which is kind of fucked up. I saw him when he went on the *Daily Show*. He was *funny*. I swear to God, they're gonna make a fuckin' miniseries based on that piece of trash. So... who the fuck are we to argue with the man who's like the consummate NYPD detective, huh?"

"You always thought he was full of shit."

"Well, yeah, and so did you. After a while anyway. But we don't gotta *tell* anyone that we thought he was the biggest cockwomble in the Bureau. He said he had evidence, we believed him. The best detective in the whole fuckin' NYPD. You're gonna believe him, right? Besides, you got anything on him that ain't hearsay? I don't."

Alex did. That was the problem. And those prosecutors knew something. There had to be more to the grand jury than a fishing expedition or a PR campaign. But James had a subpoena, so breathing a word, congealing his friend's ephemeral hearsay into admissible evidence, would land them both in worlds of pain. All he said was, "Cockwomble?"

James laughed with unflappable resolve and shoved the pipes under his right arm, playing at the tuning slides on the drones. "Yeah, it's good, isn't it? Shit. I gotta go back to getting my ass kicked." He gestured towards where the pipe band reassembled their formation. "You take care of yourself. They still got you medicated?"

"Yeah. I don't see how I'm ever getting off that shit. But you know I'm always going through phases of fine and phases of not so fine."

"Where are you now?"

Alex shrugged, not knowing himself.

"Once this St. Patrick's Day clusterfuckery is over, we should go out for non-alcoholic drinks after practice. Pipe major will relax for about five minutes until he gets it into his fuckin' head that he wants us to compete at the Worlds in Glasgow in August. You gonna watch us in the parade?"

"The 17th? I'm on an eight-by-four."

"Tell Gibson you've found an Irish ancestor," James smirked.

"Yeah, I'll tell her about all those Irish Jews."

134

James straightened out his kilt, then he walked away, smacking the bag under his arm, the pipes squealing and humming as he tuned his drones. Even after ten years of working in different squads, Alex missed their partnership. Warmth he felt in James' presence leeched out of his body, leaving him with a bitter frost in his heart. He half-closed his eyes so the park blurred under his eyelashes. The drums kicked off into a cantering beat, a snappy rattle shaking the wires buried in his chest. The pipers played a jig that James called 'The Bonawe Highlanders.' Alex knitted his fingers together inside his hoodie and listened to the tunes for a while.

Chapter Fourteen

Slivers of light from the streetlamps shone like halos around the blackout curtains. Alex rolled away from the light, onto his stomach, and he felt the strain in the small of his back. He turned onto his right side. Sheets bunched against his skin. He cut off the circulation in his arm. Then he flopped onto his left side. His mind felt like the Kentucky Derby. *What would that grand jury find* running to the outside of *Who would talk. Who else knew what happened* taking the lead, but *Why the hell had Sarah self-harmed as a student* coming up fast on the inside. *How had he been so blind* was charging through an opening in the field. But he'd Googled it. *If people wanted to hide it, they did* galloped nose to nose with *he'd never been the father she deserved.* He raised himself on an elbow, sipping at his water. Dammit, he needed the horse race in his head to cross the finish line and let him sleep. Tomorrow, he had a session with his shrink, then a four-by-twelve.

Around 0200, those horses were still circling the track. *Fuck you all,* he said to them, surrendering to his insomnia and padding into the living room. He curled up on the sofa, channel-surfing past animated porn (what was the point?), a right-wing talk show host, the shopping channel, finally settling on a *Law and Order* rerun, the only tolerable thing on TV. If only death investigation was that easy! It always was in the mythical 27th Precinct. You never saw Lennie Briscoe standing over his fourteenth straight drug murder, silently suffering, bargaining with an apathetic God for a scrap of physical evidence, for one lousy witness swearing blind that they had no knowledge whatsoever of anything. And there was always a twist at the end, so no one ended up wrongfully convicted. The *Law and Order* episode concluded, but Alex felt both sad and unsettled. He scrolled through the numbers on his iPhone until he found the one he wanted, an ER nurse called Rachel with whom he had two one-night stands. He had met her late one night in Columbia Pres as he waited for a shooting vic to either live or die (he lived). They shared a dark, sick sense of humor and a history of dysfunctional relationships. The antidepressants killed his sex drive – a side-effect he hadn't revealed to Sarah – but miraculously, everything worked with Rachel the first time, while the second time nothing worked. However, she smoked too much weed to care. Third time, who knows.

A short, stilted conversation led to him catching a subway to her place in Brooklyn Heights. The 2 train creaked along the tracks, but then hissed to a stop in a tunnel after the Wall Street station, somewhere under the East River. The lights flickered. The engine fell silent. The passengers, half a dozen or so, shifted in their seats. The lights flickered again. Years of MTA underfunding meant that breakdowns should be a routine hassle, like cockroaches and traffic jams. Every New Yorker knew that. Alex stared through the window at the dark concrete outside. The lights failed, plunging the train into pitch black murk. His fellow passengers turned on their phone flashlights. He heard gunfire, sirens, paramedics screeching breathless questions. *Can you move your toes?* Yes, he could. He tasted blood.

A white flash, like lightning. Lights flipped, and he could see. The advertisements on the ceiling. The orange seats. The multicolored spaghetti of the subway map. That other place, a shadowy street with blood and the sirens, wasn't real. The train vibrated, groaned, then crept forward. Other passengers clapped and cheered. Alex held his head with both hands, breathing fast. Why was this happening to him, again? The flashback had caught him by surprise. At least it was transitory, unlike the ones that paralyzed him on the floor for hours. But with all the time and money he had spent on a therapist for the last five years, the calming techniques should help more. It wasn't like his health insurance paid for it, God no. He couldn't risk NYPD Medical Services getting wind, and it was arguably a pre-existing condition anyway.

The train labored into Brooklyn, and he left it at Borough Hall. Municipal buildings inhabited the blocks above the station – City Hall, the Kings County DA's office, courthouses, other government offices – so no one was here at four in the morning. The silence disconcerted him. No New Yorker likes an eerie, vacant subway station, no more than they like empty streets. He rested his back against a pillar, sweating like the station was a sauna. Press on to Rachel's? Or catch the next 2 train going the other way? What if it broke down again under the river?

His feet carried him above ground. He walked along Court Street, towards Atlantic Avenue, where Rachel lived. At 0430, the street seemed ghostly, the shops shuttered, a glittering layer of frost decorating the bare trees, a few people maundering through the cold. That pastel early morning light brushed the sky with greying streaks. He shivered uncontrollably. *What the hell am I doing*, he asked himself, too broken for the emptiness of a casual relationship. A car rumbled behind him. When he turned to look, he saw a taxi. He thrust his hand horizontally towards the road, and the taxi obligingly pulled to the curb. Saying, "Manhattan. West 87th, between Amsterdam and Columbus," he sank onto the leather seat, and gloom soaked through his gut like caustic oil. The taxi driver took off like a fighter jet for Manhattan.

From the back of the cab, Alex texted Rachel, *Not feeling so great. Think I'm going to stay home tonight.* Thank God for text messaging, he thought, a way of communicating when you didn't feel like talking to anyone.

Ok. Up to you, Rachel wrote back. They didn't have the kind of relationship where she cared if he flaked out.

The taxi ride cost Alex thirty-five bucks, which stung, but he'd lost faith in the MTA. And the cab delivered him to his bed. His eyes watered. He dug his thumbnail into the scarred tendons in his wrist. Underneath, his pulse throbbed. He grappled with visualizing his Calm Place, that desert far from Brooklyn, where there were no casually unsatisfying relationships and no subways.

He slept fitfully, for two hours at most, then he lay in bed long past first light, upset by last night's flashback and his attempt at meaningless sex. Both were evidence of his illness re-emerging. But this morning, it stayed submerged; no flashbacks, mechanical failures, or even weirdos on the train hounding him on the subway ride to Dr. Theresa Gillard's Chelsea office. Then, on the corner of 25th and Seventh, he encountered a busker vamping on an electric guitar. *It's all going wrong.* The power chords stabbed into his heart. *Beat, damn you,* he thought, tapping his chest. It was beating, fast. Quickly, he gathered his wits and jogged past the busker, afraid he would trigger an attack.

When he got to the psychiatrist's office, he said, "It's starting again."

"What do you mean?" she asked.

"The flashbacks," and he told her about having one last night on the 2.

"I'm not surprised," she said placidly. "I don't think we've addressed all of the trauma that you haven't processed. I think we've peeled back some layers. I know we've talked a lot about the shooting in 1987, and the fact that you experienced PTSD symptoms related to that for a long time."

"I talked about it yesterday. Twice. My daughter mentioned it, and a military vet at the pool asked me about the scars."

"Did you? Was it upsetting?"

"Talking to Sarah is usually upsetting," he said.

"Those relationships can be tough. It will be a slow process."

"The rest of my life?"

"She has a lot of pain. So do you. It's slow. But I think we should maybe start addressing the shooting with EMDR and see how it goes."

"A magic bullet?"

"It's never so simple, Alex." Gillard put forth a warm smile, as if empathy and her laser pointer *could* be magic bullets if he tried hard enough. Then she ran him through his deep breathing exercises before she directed his attention to the laser pointer and asked him about the shooting. Not details of what happened, but how he felt about it; the terror, the despair as he gave up seconds before ESU arrived, the pain that drove him to crazily beg the ER staff to stop treating him and then to scream for morphine during those weeks on the ward.

Although he wasn't hungry, Alex swung by the deli on West 135th and Broadway, buying a bagel with cream cheese. The coffee menu tempted him, and he succumbed to his third cup. His blood felt as if it had turned into viscous liquid. Coffee might dilute it. Inopportunely, he'd planned on driving up to Scarsdale in a last-ditch effort to cajole Gemma Lennon into consenting to an interview. Far from the ideal day for therapy or a weird, insomnia-riddled night, but the timing between his EMDR appointments and the rest of his life was rarely ideal. Anyway, he would not survive the day on an empty stomach, so he ate the bagel without enthusiasm.

At roll call, the detectives summarized their progress on open cases. Gibson made a few inconsequential announcements, a few jokes, and then her tone changed – humorless, grave. "The Chief of D's is concerned about Detective Indelicata and this grand jury, and he doesn't want the Lennon investigation compromised in any way. I'm not in the loop with what's happening to Indelicata – I think he's temporarily suspended – but the orders I've got are that we're to take full control over the Lennon investigation."

Alex almost spit out a mouthful of coffee. That meant the Chief of Detectives was having some kind of heart attack. That meant the federal investigation scared the hell out of him. Vito, their celebrity detective, off the case. Suspended! Vito, who got away with everything, suspended. The world *was* changing. No wonder Vito had been in such a thunderous mood at Lennon's apartment.

Gibson looked at him. "Alex, that means, you're the primary on it, okay? Everything's going through you, Ray, and me. Everything."

He nodded, rattled.

"You gonna bring in Gemma Lennon today?" Gibson asked.

"Yes," said Ray. "Gonna try anyway."

"What've we got on her?"

Alex drew his breath in sharp. His head felt as if he'd stuck it inside a box of Semtex. Beyond the white noise screaming in his ears, he heard Ray outlining their weak case against Lennon. What if they were wrong? The system had been wrong so many times. No one had seen Lennon crash into the sign in Riverdale or carry her daughter into the park.

"There are no traces of anything matching the pattern injury on Suzanne. Lab ID'd MDF particles at the injury site," Ray was saying. "But what isn't made out of MDF? Cheap furniture. Construction materials. I think her mother got rid of a table, but I can't prove it."

"You gotta find something else," Gibson insisted. "You don't have her at the scene. You know she's out there, like mentally, and her lawyer could argue she was just too traumatized to report the jacking after it happened and probably call an expert. And he could say that the jacker wore gloves and a Tyvek suit... We're under a lot of scrutiny, guys. We need to be fair and completely thorough. You got her medical records, right?"

"Yeah," Ray answered. "They say she was hospitalized after a suicide attempt at sixteen but no further records of her being treated for a mental illness or anything else."

"What about Suzanne's records?"

"Nothing. Normal kid stuff. The 'flu. An ear infection. Nothing weird."

"When you talk to her, be careful. *If* she's guilty, we need everything we do to be totally above board."

"Ten-four." Alex sniffed in a harsh breath. He visualized himself sweeping his brain matter across the floor. The lieutenant shared some of his concerns. More than she let on, but not as many as she should. If she knew the extent of his involvement with the 34th Precinct miscarriage of justice cases, she would not be coolly signing paperwork as she sent them out of her office.

Cat appeared at his elbow. Smiling wryly, she handed Alex a cup of coffee from the shop on West 135th. "You look like you could use this."

"Yeah, thanks." Shit, his frazzled state must be obvious, but he was bewildered, suspicious, and he inspected the lid for tampering, damaging it being a classic Homicide prank. No evidence of it. He ventured a tentative sip. Unsullied black coffee, the way he liked it. Cat was notorious for not bringing coffee to people, for snapping at colleagues, *Do I look like a fucking delivery service?* Vito suspended, Cat offering genuine coffee. Had sleep deprivation and a PTSD relapse made him delusional?

"I owe you this," she said.

Alex narrowed his eyes. "What?"

"Remember? The bet? Wheeler's online dating. I said he's gonna see the girl he saw last week, and you said he's gonna be on a date with someone else by Tuesday. I said I'd get you coffee if you were right. I'm a woman of my word."

Oh, yeah. That happened. Insomnia, stress, and therapy interfered with his short-term memory of inconsequential office mishegoss. "I told you," he said, covering up his lapse. "Who's he seeing now?"

"Some girl who's trying to figure out how to make us all drive electric cars."

"That's a job?"

"Apparently."

"Huh." Alex felt like he had fine dust in his eyes.

Ray caught up to them, so they immediately changed the subject to work. He took a dim view of adolescent hijinks like betting on a colleague's sex life.

"Who's driving?" Ray asked.

"You." Alex poured the coffee down his throat, although he'd hit peak coffee at the previous cup. "I didn't sleep last night and saw Gillard before work today."

Ray frowned, concerned. "Right. More of that rapid-eye movement stuff?"

"Yeah."

"You holding up okay?"

"I'm just tired." He said nothing pertaining to his aborted attempt at hooking up with Rachel or the resurgence of his flashbacks. For Ray, the former would be evidence of his moral and personal failings, while the latter would worry him. Alex would never hear the end of either.

They drove across the Henry Hudson Bridge, a glittering white arc curving over the Spuyten Duyvil, the confluence of the Harlem River and the Hudson, the Harlem snaking around the top end of Manhattan, the Hudson a vast expanse of silver-grey water, blending into the hazy purples and greens of the Palisades on the far side. They got mired down in traffic on the Hudson Parkway, where Alex spaced out, drifting to some other place, a sporadic conversation with Sarah about mental health, or was it the Two-Five Precinct, MNHS's old office, losing track of exonerating evidence, pursuing convictions at any cost, questioning who knew what, and when did they know it, always interspersed with crackling ten codes.

Something prodded him in the ribs.

"Hey, Lex, wake up," Ray said.

Disoriented, he blinked cobwebs out of his eyes. The car was stationary. They were on a residential street with two-story condos, each one with a mown lawn, flowerpots, and iron gates.

"You passed out near Riverdale," said Ray.

"Yeah, well, like I said, I didn't sleep last night."

"You up for this?"

"I'll be fine." Alex rubbed his face, yawning, pressure popping in his ears. "I probably wouldn't know what to do with myself if I slept well."

"Cut down on some of your meds and lose weight?" suggested Ray.

Like an old couple having the same spat for the thousandth time, Alex flicked his eyes at his partner in a prickly glare, while Ray responded with a nonchalant shrug. They hopped out of the car and knocked on the door.

Gemma Lennon answered, her expression confused. "Oh. You."

From the back of the condo, they heard her sister yelling, "Is it the damn police?"

"Gemma, we came by to see if you're alright, and we wanna talk more about what happened," Alex said.

"Okay," she said tonelessly.

No resistance. No need for bullshit (and he'd prepared plenty). Not what he expected.

Not what Ray expected either, given the bewildered look on his face, but he regained his professionalism and led a placid Gemma towards the car.

As Ray and Gemma descended the stoop, Stephanie Lennon charged through the door. She cornered Alex against the porch railings. "She needs a lawyer."

"That's up to her."

"I think she needs a lawyer."

"It's not your call."

Stephanie ran down the stairs, darting between Gemma and the car, grasping her sister's hands. "Gemma, you have rights. I'll call Chris, okay. You don't have to go with them."

"Don't I?" she said. "God sent them here."

"Gemma, the New York Police Department sent them here."

Gemma pulled away from her sister and planted herself beside the police car.

Covering his ass, Alex said, "Gemma, your sister's right. You can have a lawyer. You wanna phone that guy who came to the office last time? Or anyone? It's up to you."

"No, it's fine," she responded in a wispy voice.

Stephanie stared at Alex and Ray, fury warping her features. "She's not in her right mind."

Alex's gaze flicked to Gemma, who sedately crawled into the back of the Fusion. She seemed sane enough to him – not a delusional, raving lunatic. That was the criteria that mattered, from a legal standpoint. While they drove into Manhattan, he occasionally twisted his neck to peer at the suspect in the backseat. She fretted at her zipper, and her face steamed up with tears and emotion. He shut his eyes, feeling his ribcage rising, falling, a slight ache in his gunshot wound, the car's vibrations in his bones. Ray was taking the scenic route to West 133rd, wheeling off the Hudson Parkway onto Riverside Drive, then turning up the hill onto Payson. The spindly branches of oak trees in Inwood Hill Park rose into view.

"Why are we going *this* way?" Lennon whimpered.

"The phone says there's a crash further along… on the Hudson Parkway," Alex lied amiably.

They crossed Dyckman, rolling alongside the park until Ray found a parking space, not far from where a group of Latino teenage boys kicked a soccer ball back and forth on the muddy pitch beside the playground. The neighborhood had created a shrine for Suzanne around the red oak tree. It had looked better a couple weeks ago, before snow and sleet had wilted the flowers, although some Samaritan had added fresh ones. Scruffy, damp stuffed animals and toy trains tussled in a wearied orgy in the center of the ring of flowers. Jesus and the Virgin Mary stood shoulder to shoulder, their colors melting into one another like watercolor.

"What's this?" Lennon demanded, pressing her face against the window.

"The people from the neighborhood made it for Suzanne," Alex said. "Wanna stop and look?"

"Why?" she whispered.

"To show respect." His heart fluttered, over-caffeinated.

"Yeah," Ray added. "People who never even met your daughter, they care about her. *We* care about her. Wanna get out and see what they made?"

"No, I can't," she wept. "This place... What a terrible place for her to be, but they made it into something beautiful."

"Did you bring her here, Gemma?" Alex asked. "The park is green in the summer. There's always kids playing soccer or baseball. It's close to your apartment, and the city's made a great playground, haven't they?" He waved towards the blue slides and jungle bars. A few children hurled themselves down the slides, squealing with delight. The parents passively looked on, chatting and smoking cigarettes. "Is that what you were thinking?"

"Nothing lasts, does it? Before you know it, they want to smoke weed behind the trees. They don't want to play on the swings anymore."

"Yeah, things always change. People change. But your memory, well, that lasts. Do you remember bringing Suzanne here?" *Careful,* he thought, brushing against the line between interrogating a suspect and interviewing a witness.

"I can't," she murmured. "Please, go. Please."

They drove onwards. Eschewing a serious conversation with a delicate suspect in the car, Alex and Ray chatted quietly to one another about movies.

"My kids are obsessed with *How to Train Your Dragon,*" Ray commented. "You seen it?"

"No. The last thing I saw was *The Men Who Stare at Goats.*"

"I heard that was good. But not what I want to take the kids to."

"Tia's seventeen. She'd be fine. She'd like it."

"She's not allowed R-rated movies."

Alex resisted rolling his eyes and sarcasm, never quite agreeing with his partner's Chinook helicopter approach to parenting. Somewhere between himself and Ray, someone wasn't setting up their kids for a lifetime of therapy.

Once they'd let themselves into the MNHS office – which looked municipally nondescript; nothing like a precinct house – Alex and Ray herded a dazed Gemma into an interrogation room. It was windowless and sparse but for the one-way mirror, with austere breeze block walls and a thick steel table bolted to the floor, the whole place carrying a doleful weight that made you want to leave the room forthwith and have a beer to recover. When people came in here, they knew they had hit rock bottom.

144

They settled Lennon at the table, and Ray went out to watch through the one-way until he was needed. Alex asked if she wanted tea or coffee or a soda, his standard warm-up with a suspect. She shook her head. "You sure?" he asked as he retrieved a digital video camera. Getting a confession on video, so the potential jury could see and hear it, was paramount. As was a recording proving that he had not coerced her in any way. They didn't videotape many interrogations in the '90s.

She stared at him as if she'd never heard of a vending machine.

Grimacing contritely, Alex set up the camera in front of the one-way. "Gemma, there will be a lot of questions, but if your story is on video, it will help you. So, I'm gonna start this, then we can talk, okay?"

"Yeah," she muttered, stooping over the table like a broken doll.

He pressed 'record,' and then in a formal voice, for the prosecutor, for the jury and the judge, he stated, "This is Detective Second Grade Alex Boswell, Manhattan North Homicide, and I'm with Detective Second Grade Rafael Espinosa, also Manhattan North Homicide, and this is an interview with Gemma Lennon, a twenty-eight year old Black female, of 2443 Isham Street in case 10-34-6, Suzanne Lennon. Gemma, you're aware you can end this interview and leave at any time?"

She blearily moved her head in acknowledgement.

"You have to say it. It's better for the recording."

"Oh. Yes."

"You're not here under any duress?"

"No."

"You're willing to talk to me without your lawyer present?"

"Yes."

"You know, we've been talking to your neighbors and people at Suzanne's school and her friends, and I have to say, it sounds like she was a tough kid." Making himself comfortable for the long haul, Alex rocked back in the chair, crossing his ankles, resting both hands over his belly. The monologue was his favored interrogation technique. You make the suspect sit there and shut up while you ramble about justice, about right and wrong or about nonsense, or tell some story that shows how much you understand them. Your strategy depends on your reading of the suspect.

"Yeah," whispered Lennon.

"And you were on your own with her. Her dad's a junkie. He's in prison, then dead from an OD. So, there you were, all on your own, working your ass off. Two damn jobs. That's how expensive it is to live in this city these days. Fucking crazy. You're doing your best. And sometimes, your best is never good enough. I understand that. I get it. I've been there too." He paused with a slight quiver in his lower lip. "I have two kids, two daughters. They're both adults now. One's a nurse here in New York, and the other is a marine biologist out in Australia. So, I guess they've done alright, but when they were growing up, I was so lost in my own fucked up world. I was hardly there for them. They were born around the time I joined the police, and neither me nor my ex-wife knew how *hard* the job would be, and after I graduated from the Academy and was on my first beat, working nights, overtime, whatever, I was barely in the apartment. All the stuff you have to do with babies, stay up all night, doctor's visits, my ex had to do on her own. She was pissed at me, pissed at the girls. Think she had – what do you call it? Postpartum depression? And I just ran away from it. I'd be out on duty, then after, we'd hit the bars. That was the early 1980s, the city was going nuts. Not as nuts as it got ten years later, but it was going that way. I'd come home from work, and I could not deal with being a father. It feels terrible, saying that, but it's the truth. I had addicts, drunks, perps, victims, colleagues, my boss, screaming at me for eight or nine or sometimes even twelve or more hours, then I'd come home, and my daughters would be crying, my ex would be angry. I gotta say, I didn't handle it well. I was young, I had kids way too young, like at nineteen, and you shouldn't say that your kids are mistakes, and they're not, but the older one wasn't intentional, you know. The younger one, well, my ex wanted her, like having another baby would fix something in our lives. It didn't. And I coulda done a lot better, but I didn't." He sighed, sickened by his admissions, his self-loathing, but he was betting all of Rockefeller Center that he could manipulate Lennon with his sordid story. His did not end in murder, but that wasn't the point. The point is to show the suspect that you get them; you've fucked up, and you're coming clean. In the atmosphere of the confessional, they might come clean too.

Ray glided through the door but withdrew into the background, letting Alex do his thing.

Alex collected his thoughts, breathing in so she heard his inhalation, then he plunged onwards. "When the girls were little, my ex finally decided that she'd had enough and divorced me. Then after the divorce, I made another mistake, as far as the girls were concerned. I ran away. Got outta Manhattan and worked at a precinct in Queens. I saw them maybe like once or twice in the three years I was in Queens. God, if that. Then in the late '80s, I got this post, here in Manhattan, and sometimes I tried to crawl back into their lives, and I couldn't. It was too damned late. I'd blown it. And I still can't. My kid who's still in New York hardly talks to me. And the one in Australia… well, it's Australia, isn't it? So… You can't go back. You can't erase what you've done. You can only ask for forgiveness." His gaze wandered to Ray, who stood near the door, hands behind his back, his face as impassive as the weatherman's. "And I feel guilty about that. Every day. But I see all that. I see it now. Like twenty years later. But when those kids are little, and all you want to do is get away 'cause you're tired and you have a headache… But they're demanding things from you. They don't give a shit that you're tired and have a headache. I never found a way – I fucked up, and no… it's no surprise that my ex thinks I'm an asshole. But it's all hindsight, and all I could think about at the time was how I felt *at that moment,* and I was stressed, I was overwhelmed." He exhaled everything from his lungs. "I didn't know what to do."

"I'm really tired," Lennon murmured. "Can I go?"

"I know you are. But just listen for a little longer, okay?"

"Then I can go?"

"Yeah, you'll be outta here." *One way or another*, he thought. "But you gotta listen to me. I get it. That's what I'm trying to tell you. Sometimes, you feel like you're not enough, you can't do enough, when life and everything else is crashing down on your head. When it's more than you can handle. You know that feeling?"

"Yeah," she whispered.

He half-shut his eyes, tensed his fingers. "There was one time… the older one crashed her bike and broke her arm and had to get surgery, pins put in it. I got the call, so I went to the hospital, and her mom was already there, with the guy she was dating at the time, and so was the younger one. I go into the hospital room, and there's my oldest kid, her arm in a cast, and my ex's boyfriend holding her other hand. Like *I* shoulda been. I was so pissed. I just felt this rage. At myself, mostly. I stormed outta that room, and there was my twelve-year old in the corridor, like freaking out. Everyone was in the hospital room with her sister, who had just come outta surgery, and there she was, all alone. She reached out for me, tried to take my hand, but I was so pissed off that I didn't care. I saw it, but I walked right past. Turned around and left. I felt sick to my stomach about it, but I still did it. I fucked up but good. You ask, how can you do that to your kid, when you love them, and I don't know the answer. She's like thirty now, and she doesn't really believe I love her. I tell her I do, but why should she believe me? I've spent years asking for forgiveness."

"Have they forgiven you?" murmured Lennon.

147

"I don't know. I've told them about what I saw on the streets, the things that does to your head. I mean, those are excuses, and you can't really excuse it, but I admitted I fucked up, they didn't deserve it. It was me, not them. I told them the God's-honest-truth, I opened myself up. I wasn't there for them when they were little, but I can only try to be there for them *now*. It's all I can do."

"You can pray," she said, cupping her hands over her nose and mouth.

"Yeah, but you can't keep lying. You gotta tell the truth. To me. To yourself." Alex unclasped his hands from his belly and leaned towards her, thinking, *I have just given you all of it. Everything. You have to come clean now, you bitch.* "You're her mother. You know, she's gone, you can't ask for *her* forgiveness, but you can ask for forgiveness, for justice." He caught Ray's eyes. He'd yanked his heart out, thrown it on the table, and he needed a breather.

Like a teammate catching a pass, Ray swooped in from the shadows. "You're right, God can forgive you, Gemma," he said quietly, taking the other chair across from the suspect. Alex relied on Ray to pull the God card, Ray Catholic enough to do it with conviction. "But you gotta tell the truth. God can't help you if you keep lying." He put his right hand over her left one. "You gotta be truthful to God. He will forgive all our sins, he will open his arms to us, but you gotta say, you gotta be honest, like Detective Boswell was. God loves you, he wants to forgive you. He loves you just like you love your daughter. But you have to do *your* part."

"God loves me," she repeated.

"Yeah. He does. No matter what you did. You know that. But you know you have to be straight with him."

"I didn't do it," Lennon sniffed as tears spilled from her eyes. "I would never have hurt her."

Ray grasped both her hands in his. "You can tell us, Gemma. We know you wouldn't have hurt her. But you gotta tell us what happened."

"I left her."

"Where did you leave her?"

"In the apartment. Alone in the apartment. I swear, I was just going out for a little while. And I know she was *seven* and all, but she'd been having a tantrum. She had them sometimes. And it was too much. I... I just walked out, and she screamed at me, 'Mommy!' but I went out of the apartment. I came back, of course I came back, and when I walked into the living room..." Her head fell to the table, sobs shaking her shoulders.

"You walked into the living room," prompted Ray.

"Yes, I did. She was lying under the table, and there was blood everywhere. She had a big cut on her head. Like she'd hit it on the corner of the table. I tried to revive her, but she was gone."

"You didn't call 911?" Ray asked softly. "How did you know she was gone?"

"I'm her *mom,*" she cried. "I *know.* I panicked. I was afraid. I didn't know what to do. It was like, it wasn't even me doing these things. I wrapped her up and cleaned her face, so she looked, you know, angelic. She was an angel now. No, I didn't call 911. She didn't need the police or an ambulance because she had become an angel. I took her to my car, and I was going to drive to the hospital, but... Suzanne liked to play in Inwood Hill Park. We'd walk there from the apartment. She liked the slides and things. And there were some kids there, and, like you said, they were always playing soccer, you know, in that grassy bit next to the playground. Suzanne would sometimes play with them. They were older kids, but they always let her join the games. I took her there. To the tree. The big oak tree. You know it's been there for hundreds of years? Hundreds!"

"Yeah, it's an old tree," said Ray.

"That won't change. It's been there long before us, and we're all gonna die, but that damn oak tree's gonna be there."

"It will," said Ray solemnly. "You took Suzanne to the tree?"

"I was afraid – if I went to the hospital, there would be questions, and cops, and I just wanted to leave her in *peace.*"

Alex felt his heart, *thud, thud, thud.* "You took her to the park – to the oak tree – on Saturday night?"

"Yeah."

"When did you find her injured?"

"I don't *know.* It's all a blur. I can't remember."

"Okay. She went to school on Wednesday. I saw her assignments, and the school told me she was there on Wednesday, but you gave her a sick note for Thursday and Friday."

"Yeah, yeah," Lennon moaned into her hands.

"You said she had a tantrum. Was it Thursday or Friday?"

"Friday."

"Okay. And you said she hit her head on a table. We didn't find a table in your apartment. What happened to it?" Alex steadfastly held her gaze.

"I took it out," she said, her voice losing all affect.

"Like, where?" Ray gently urged.

"I couldn't bear to look at it," she whispered. "I got rid of it. I put it outside. Friday's the day they collect all the trash, you know, so I left it on the curb."

"What kind of table was it?" Ray asked.

"I don't know. Just one I bought from the Salvation Army."

"Do you know what it was made out of?"

"*No,*" she cried. "It was just a cheap, used one. It cost me twenty bucks."

The detectives exchanged a swift glance, pain on their faces. That secondhand table was buried under weeks of garbage in a city landfill, gone forever.

"You're doing great." Ray stretched his lips into a shallow smile. "Tell us about Friday and Saturday night."

"She was on the sofa. I thought she'd wake up. She was lying there like she was asleep. Peaceful. Really peaceful. The devil was out of her. He was finally out. She would wake up, and it would be alright. I begged the Lord to wake her, but she was gone. Just gone. I thought she would wake up."

"So, between Friday night and Saturday night, she was in your apartment, and you were waiting for her to wake up?" said Ray.

Shuddering, Lennon nodded. Tears dripped along her cheeks. "Waiting and praying."

"'The devil was out of her?'" Alex repeated, sharing another look with his partner. *Oh, shit*, he thought, remembering what her sister said about her 'not being in her right mind.' Blink an eye, and you're wondering if you've walked straight into a 40.15, not guilty by reason of insanity.

"The devil was in her, then he was gone."

"How do you get the devil out?"

"He just came out. I walked out of the house. He was there. Then I went back in, and he was gone."

"Sometimes, you have to beat the devil out," Ray said.

Alex warned Ray with his eyes to be careful.

"He came out himself. But he took Suzanne with him." She whimpered as if wounded. "I didn't want him to *take* her. That isn't what I wanted. I didn't want him to take my baby. But he took her. I prayed. I had her in the house, and I prayed for her to come back, but God said, you can't have her, the devil came out but she's with me now. She's an angel, and we're not good enough, none of us are good enough to have angels with us. So, God had to take her. I know she's with God now. She's one of his angels. She's safer in Heaven than she ever will be here on Earth."

150

Alex thought he should direct the conversation away from the devil and angels. "You took her to the park on Saturday night. How'd you get there?"

"The car."

"It's close to your apartment."

"I couldn't *carry* her myself. She was too strong for me, too heavy. I tried to carry her, but I couldn't."

"You used the car. Then what?"

"I put her where she would be safe," she wept. "I put her between the playground and the big tree. It was dark. There was no one there. It was peaceful. It was just like she was asleep. There were angels in that park. They came down to see her."

"You left her with the angels?"

"Yeah. They told me they would look out for her."

"What happened after you left her?"

"I got back in the car. I drove away from my baby. I drove away and left her with the angels. I knew she was safe, I knew it, but I... I wasn't watching, I was driving crazy, like I was drunk or something. I wasn't watching. I drove over the river. There's roadworks on that bit of Broadway. And I was going through them, and it was dark, and I tried to go round some cones and hit a sign. I got out and saw the front of the car had a big dent and a light was smashed. I'd done something to my arm, but I didn't really feel it, you know. I was gonna go home and like, take an overdose of muscle relaxants. I could join Suzanne in Heaven, but then, God doesn't let you come to Heaven if you've taken your own life. If I did that, I'd have spent an eternity in Hell and never seen her again. Never. I went to the hospital."

"Gemma." Alex's tone was gentle, but serious. "You understand at this point, we are going to have to advise you of your rights." They had sprinted headlong across the line between witness and suspect. If he'd been playing it safe, he would have *Mirandized* her thirty minutes ago, but when the story is flowing like a river in spate, you do not want to throw a dam in the middle at that moment.

Her hands fell from her face. She stared at him, wide-eyed. "You mean... Like Olivia Benson. Like on *Law and Order?*"

"Yes. Like on *Law and Order.* We are going to have to charge you, you see, because of the story you told about the carjacker, but if you continue to tell the truth about how you found Suzanne, the DA will downgrade it." Possibly not, but Alex said it to soften the homicide charge. "Do you understand that you have the right to remain silent, and anything you say can and will be used against you in a court of law?"

Lennon nodded, and her pupils dilated into blank, glassy slates.

"And do you understand that you have the right to an attorney, and if you cannot afford one, one will be provided at no cost?"

She nodded again. But he felt a wire pulling around his guts like a snare – his nagging doubts about her competency. Oh, well, the lawyers would have to duke it out. He slid a *Miranda* waiver across the table. "This says that we've advised you of your rights." She signed it. Sometimes, it still amazed him when people cooperated and signed those things. You would think anyone who had seen *Law and Order* or any of the array of crime shows populating television would know to shut up and ask for counsel the moment the police brought them anywhere. Astoundingly, people talked anyway, and most of them were legally competent. Alex had a theory that a guilty person, burdened with the weight of his or her misdeeds, aches for the opportunity to confess, to unburden themselves, and a good interrogator finds the weak point in the perp's defenses that allows the truth to spill out.

Ray said, "Pray with me. Pray for God's forgiveness." He held her hands again, muttering a quiet prayer. Alex heard snatches of Latin. Both Ray and Lennon bowed their heads, Lennon drowning in floods of tears.

Then the detectives offered Lennon space to collect herself, and they silently withdrew, opening the door to Gibson, Cat, Marcus, and two A team detectives gathered around the one-way. "The master," the young A team detective said, touching his elbow. *I'm something, but I don't know about that.* Alex rested his back against the wall. He dug his fingertips into his sandy eyelids. Telling his own story had worked, but it left him feeling vaporous, thin and vulnerable, without anything stable in himself. Whatever – a good strategy was a good strategy. And he hadn't risked a false confession. He hadn't threatened her, lied about evidence that didn't exist, spent hours confusing her, or even offered her an 'out.' He'd simply told a true story about his own life. No defense lawyer could play that video and argue otherwise.

Ray patted his shoulder blades. "Well, we got her. Jesus. I sometimes can't..." He shook his head with disgust and befuddlement. "It's gonna go to a 40.15, isn't it?"

"It might," said Gibson. "When I was C/O in the 17th, we had a case where a guy murdered his wife because he thought she'd been abducted and replaced by aliens. He's probably still in Kirby."

Meanwhile, in the interrogation room, Gemma lay her head on the table and fell asleep. The blissful sleep of the guilty.

"I've talked to an ADA," continued Gibson. "They still wanna charge her with murder two, endangering the welfare of a child, and obstruction."

Not taking your injured kid to the hospital fell within the purview of the manslaughter statute, but every detective outside of that interrogation room wondered if she was responsible for her daughter's fatal injury. Did she really leave the apartment, only to come back and find Suzanne wounded? Alex had trouble believing that, but he had no evidence one way or another. Like Gibson and Ray said, it seemed primed for an insanity plea, the woman having oscillated from demonic possession to *Law and Order* in the space of minutes.

He stretched his back, wincing at ribs crunching in his right side. Pain from his old wound got worse when he was tired. But he shouldered open the door. "Gemma," he said.

She did not raise her head.

"Gemma," he repeated, lightly brushing her forearm. "Is everything you're telling us the truth?"

"Yes," she said hoarsely.

"Okay, Gemma, I'm going to have to put you under arrest. Please stand up, alright?"

Before Alex read out any of the charges, she cried, "You can't! You can't!" She launched past him, flinging herself at Ray, who caught her by wrapping an arm around her waist, pinning her against his chest, but while he was fit – he'd run the New York Marathon in four hours – she was possessed by something far stronger and hurled them both backwards against the wall. Alex leapt to his partner's assistance. Ray had been winded, but he fought her to the floor while Alex pulled her arms around her back. Together, the detectives subdued her just as their colleagues stormed in. They tried to be gentle, but she kicked and clawed, fighting like her life depended on it. She ignored their entreaties to calm down. They cuffed her, but she lashed out with her high heels, catching Alex's left ankle with a stinging blow. He hopped on one foot as half a dozen detectives wrestled Lennon upright, then bundled her into the corridor.

"We can't take her to Central Booking in this state," Alex panted. "Fuck," he swore, unable to weight his left foot. "Call a fucking bus. A 9.41." Someone rang EMS, while Lennon rocked back and forth, unresponsive to any questions from paramedics or cops. The ambulance carted her away, Alex called the DA's office, and everyone hoped that she could be processed and arraigned sooner rather than later. But that required assisting counsel and understanding the nature of the proceedings against her, and today, both seemed like a longshot.

The phones exploded as Alex iced and elevated his leg on a spare office chair. He answered a few press calls with, "I cannot comment on an ongoing investigation," rerouting reporters to the NYPD spokesperson. He handled calls he couldn't reroute from a deputy commissioner, someone in the DA's office, the Chief of Detectives himself, the Deputy Inspector at the Three-Four. He explained that yes, she had been advised of her rights; yes, she had confessed on video; yes, she currently appeared to be a danger to herself and others; yes, it would be nice if she could be arraigned tomorrow. His side and his ankle throbbed, his insides seethed, but the screaming phones, the hounding reporters, and the imperious bosses would tear their pound of flesh off his body before the tour ended.

Part 4

Chapter Fifteen

October 1987

A nurse pushing a cart stuffed with meal trays appeared at the door of Alex's hospital room. *Oh, fuck no,* he thought. His digestive tract nosedived into a queasy barrel-roll. The nurse maneuvered her cart through the door. Arduously, he half-lifted himself on an elbow. "It's okay," he rasped. "I'm not hungry."

"You probably won't have much of an appetite for a little while," the nurse drawled in a Harlem accent as she checked his blood pressure and temperature. "But you need to eat. Your body needs food to heal."

"I think I need more pain meds," he said drearily.

"I'll speak to the charge nurse," she replied. "But please, eat a little. It really is important."

Grudgingly, he pecked at the food; a bland, rubbery chicken breast, soggy rice, and overcooked, floppy vegetables – unappetizing if he was healthy. When he couldn't swallow any more of it, he lay on his back, eyes closed, resting but not sleeping because the wound burned like an oil fire, ruthless, unquenchable. Merely breathing stirred up swells of blinding pain. A basic, life sustaining bodily function, and it pierced his chest like jagged lathes, sharpened points reaching towards his heart.

Dr. Naziri had said he was lucky to be alive. *Depends on your interpretation of luck.* Alex's didn't include taking a bullet. He envisaged his injuries on an autopsied victim. How would he write the report? Bullets shredding intercostal muscles and shattering the cartilage connecting the lower five ribs. One cutting into the liver, striking a rib, leaving pieces floating in his abdominal cavity but by some miracle, missing the stomach, intestines, and pancreas. Two big pieces of shrapnel lacerating the right lung, then piercing the first layer of the pericardium, the protective sack around the heart, and another large fragment landing a couple millimeters shy of the descending aorta, just nicking the arterial wall. If that had punctured or if the one near the heart had gone a little further, Alex would have been dead before EMS arrived on the scene.

Naziri had fished out the fragments of lead. He'd cauterized bleeding in the liver and stapled the lacerations in the lung. The lower lobe had suffered the heaviest damage, those bronchial arteries irreparable, and the surgeon had removed it. Losing a third of his lung saved Alex's life. Otherwise, he would have bled to death. For ten days after his ICU discharge, Alex had the CVC line in his throat monitoring his heart and administering antibiotics, painkillers, and, potentially, another transfusion. He had tubes buried in his chest, draining blood and fluid. He'd sobbed with relief when they removed some of the drains, extracted the CVC from his jugular, then let him take a shower.

Every day, nurses and a physical therapist asked him to practice breathing exercises, and they made him stretch his thoracic muscles. "You can't breathe shallowly," they said, however much it hurt not to. More than once, he'd wept in front of the physical therapist. They ordered him to walk around the ward, at least once per day. If he stayed in bed, he risked deep vein thrombosis, which could also kill him. He was constantly out of breath, too weak to stand for more than five minutes, and his fatigue was a cumbrous, static weight, but he slogged through his rehab and reluctantly nibbled at the hospital food. He would do anything to get out of this hospital or, for that matter, take a piss or a shower without agonizing pain, on the verge of passing out.

As he had been shot in the line, he received a steady stream of visitors, frequently people who he didn't want to see under the best of circumstances. Someone from Mayor Koch's office. A deputy police commissioner. The douchebag Deputy Inspector of the Two-Five. The Borough Chief for Manhattan. The Chief of Detectives himself. A few journalists. He wanted to be left alone, but they came anyway to congratulate him for being alive, offer condolences, and tell him how wonderfully he had served the people of New York. By walking along a street and getting shot? Yeah, right. Sometimes, Stella Trenemen visited, reporting that Eddie had been transferred to New York Presbyterian in Morningside Heights and was having yet more surgery, the doctors in a drag-out fight to control internal bleeding and infection. Bettina Perez arrived with a bouquet of flowers. "I'm praying to God for no revenge, for no more violence, but I don't know if He's listening. I know you got shot looking for the boys who shot my son. Lord, I'm sorry. I'm so sorry.

The shootings. The death. It's too much. But God has been looking out for you."

Sure, that's why I'm here with half a lung and my partner's paralyzed, Alex thought, but he smiled anyway, preferring her genuine sympathy over the tiresome, canned compassion of Mayor Koch's peons and NYPD brass.

MNHS detectives stopped by nearly every day, even ones he had limited patience for, like Brady and Keohane. Corcoran and Vito visited regularly, the latter always saying in an overexcited tone, "How ya doin', kid? You're looking *great,*" while Corcoran, like a Belfast grandfather, said, "How are you, lad? You have a wee bit more color in your face." Reliably, Vito told Alex funny stories, about cases, about the job, like being called to Prospect Park in his beat cop days because a couple had reported a baby abandoned in a canvass bag. It turned out that the weakly-moving creature in the bag was a live chicken. Alex floated in fuzzy darkness, lost between opiates and pain, sporadically listening but often not. He knew he looked anything but great: he was waxen and sick, his face colorless, and he had exhausted, sunken lines around his eyes. Every night, he woke up in paralyzing agony and beseeched the night shift staff for more morphine. Most of the time, they complied.

Despite the visitors, days were indistinguishable from one another. The routines of wound care, physical therapy, nauseating meals, and hobbling to the bathroom had become stagnant, unremitting, as if he was living the same day, over and over again. After enough morphine, he could almost convince himself that he'd woken up in a dystopian science fiction show where the whole universe had crumpled into the corridors of Columbia Presbyterian's thoracic unit, or that he had in fact died in the shooting, and his soul was trapped in some miserable purgatory, reliving the same shitty day for an eternity.

He spent hours catnapping, too exhausted for rehab exercises, but resting wasn't any easier with knives spearing into his ribs and every muscle in his body knotting and cramping. Some days, his pain grew so intense that he sobbed, certain that a bullet rupturing his aorta would have done him a favor. Today was one, but they'd jacked up the morphine, and it helped him give less fucks. The pain was there but skulking at a distance.

He heard his name. A familiar voice. One so close to his heart. He opened his eyes, stunned, because Fred Symington stood uncomfortably at the foot of his bed.

"Lex, you leave the squad for nine months and look what happens." Fred forced out a smile.

Alex hadn't seen Fred since leaving the One-Oh-Three. "This is what it takes to get you to Manhattan?"

"Yeah, well. How you holding up?"

"Been better."

"I can imagine. What's the damage?"

"My right side's torn to shreds. They had to put some mesh in there. And hack out part of the lung." He sniffed in a shallow breath, wincing. Oh, he could weep, but not with Fred here.

"Fuck. A lot of lung?"

"Some. The lower lobe. There was a lot of bleeding."

"Will it heal okay?"

"Yeah, they say it should unless I get septic again. Then I'm very fucked. But they have me on every antibiotic in the world, and they've taken out the central line." He touched the bandage on the side of his neck, where they'd stitched up the holes.

Fred sat down, folding his right leg over his left. Worry shrouded his face. "Lucky, I guess."

"Not really. Lucky woulda been not getting shot."

"Well, true. But unluckier would have been ending up dead."

Or paralyzed, Alex thought bleakly, *fighting for my life, like Eddie.*

"I heard on the wire you were shot with an assault rifle? Jesus."

"Yeah."

"And your partner's still in critical condition? Paralyzed?"

"Yeah."

"Fuck. Permanently?"

"That's what his wife tells me the doctors think." Alex had no idea how many times he'd repeated this conversation. Too many. "How's Celia and the baby?"

"They're good. Lotta work. Late nights. At least he's started sleeping now, sort of. We're moving to a bigger house in Bay Side."

"Bigger?"

"Might have another kid in a few years."

"Ah, that's good. Bay Side's practically in Long Island."

"It's got good schools."

"It's far from things."

"From here, yeah. But it's closer to the beach, and it's nice out there. This place is turning into a shithole. I've thought about applying to the Nassau County PD. It would be quieter."

"Yeah, but you'd be back on patrol for a few years. I doubt they'd put you into a detective squad straightaway. How's the squad?"

"Same as ever. Well, Selvio's trying to transfer to TARU. You know he was always kind of a geek. If I stay with the NYPD, I'm thinking of looking for a specialized unit myself. I can barely figure out the microwave, so probably not TARU. I dunno... like Major Case, maybe. Jamaica's just getting worse, and I've got a kid to think about. This..." Frowning, he gestured towards Alex and the hospital room. "Kind of brought it home. How dangerous things are getting."

"Yeah." Alex scratched near the IV in his forearm. "What about Jimmy and Ortiz? Do you hear from them?"

"Ortiz is still doing his ESU thing. You know he's too much of an adrenaline junkie for anything else. But he's moved outta that shitty apartment. I heard IA's looking at Jimmy."

"For what?"

"Being a prick. Word on the street is that he exposed himself to a female detective. She wasn't impressed."

"Jesus. He was always gonna get his ass in trouble for doing something stupid." Alex's eyes involuntarily fluttered closed. He lost the thread of the conversation, like something light and invisible slipping from his hand. "I'm sorry, Fred. I'm so fucked. I'm on enough morphine to supply every junkie in uptown Manhattan. I can barely stay awake."

"You took a bullet."

"I'll walk you to the door of the ward. They want me as mobile as possible, and I haven't done very much today."

Pain shot through his ribs, straight past the morphine, as he swung his feet to the floor and unsteadily eased himself upright with the aid of the wall and the bed. Fred looked upset. Dragging the IV stand, Alex shuffled towards the main door, with Fred walking beside him at his funereal pace.

Fred grasped Alex's shoulder. "You'll call me when you're outta here?"

"Yeah, I'll let you know."

Despondent, Alex watched Fred walking down the long corridor, then he inched back to his room, shuffling past the nurse's station.

The charge nurse commented, "Hey, good to see you up and about a little. How you feeling?"

"Not great," he admitted. "It hurts like hell."

"How are your bowels?" she asked.

"Fine," he sighed. The nurses loved asking him about his bowel function, and he looked forward to never having a conversation about that again.

It dismayed him that hobbling ten yards between the ward entrance and his room and back would knock him out for hours, until nightfall. Then he would wake up feeling groggy, exhausted, yet desperate for a shower. His side burned and pounded. That never stopped. He should ask for more morphine. They were pretty liberal with it because he risked pneumonia if he didn't fill his lungs with enough air. Pain would always be with him, and the wound was gruesome, a swollen mass of stitches and bright red flesh, oozing fluids and blood, demanding constant care to fight infection, and oh God, if only he could time travel and not walk along that street in that moment. Or heal faster so he could get the hell out of this purgatory. Or drop dead from complications. Any of those would do.

Around three weeks after Fred's visit, Dr. Naziri sent him down to have an echocardiogram and CT scan. "I want to check your heart function again and also check the lung for any further bleeding," the doctor explained. "But your last blood tests don't show any further signs of infection, so if your lung looks good, I think we can discharge you in a few days."

What if it's not good, Alex thought queasily, his eyes locking on the echo screen as the technician pressed the probe into his chest. The lung was slowly knitting back together, after a fashion, but if his heart was still injured, he would be stuck here longer. Or living with a cardiac impairment for the rest of his life, on a million drugs and a house cat in the NYPD if he stayed with the department at all. The indistinct, oscillating images on the monitor meant nothing to him, but Naziri and the cardiologist, a Nigerian guy called Dr. Adisa, visibly relaxed, grinning, jauntily pointing out the heart's structures like professors giving an anatomy lesson. An aortic valve here, a right atrium there. Alex stared at his left ventricle and released the breath he'd been holding. The images on the screen shivered. Breathing in, he nodded as the cardiologist said more medical things. A crushing weight rolled off his chest, leaving him with a sense of relief that felt like light and air. He'd dodged that bullet – well, he didn't dodge anything, but he'd survived major thoracic trauma with no long-term damage to his heart.

The nurses showed him how to change the bandage, and he convinced them he could manage it himself. Peeling strips of gauze off his skin, dabbing the wound with an antiseptic solution on a cotton ball that stung like he'd annoyed a wasp nest, then taping fresh gauze over his side. It needed changing every day. All being well, Naziri said, the remaining drains should come out in another week or two.

Chapter Sixteen

His sister Helen flew out from Denver, and his parents took a train from Duchess County. They'd been told he would need help once he was released from the hospital. Discharged straight into the fangs of family dynamics. But the hospital wouldn't let him out otherwise. "You live alone," they'd said. "We can't let you go home unless there's someone there." He'd sought Helen's assistance, pleading with her to fly here so he could go home, but he dreaded having his mother breathing down his neck. When she showed up at Columbia Pres, he tried dissuading her, assuring her that Helen could handle it, but she refused to be stopped. He couldn't really convince her that he was mostly independent while lying in a hospital bed with IVs in his arms or taking over ten minutes to hobble to the bathroom for a piss.

It was as bad as he imagined it to be. Within three days of their arrival in his apartment, his mother had complained about the neighborhood ("I can't *believe* you're living here. This street smells like trash"), the demographics of the neighborhood ("All these Chinese people. There are no Jews here"), his apartment ("It's so small. Doesn't the police department pay you enough so you can live in a better place than this?"), his job ("It's dangerous. Look what happened to you. This wouldn't have happened if you'd become a doctor"), and his decision to resume doing it once he healed ("Why can't you be sensible and do something safer? You could go back to school"). The mutilated lung left him constantly breathless, and his mother's fusillade of complaints and relentless harassment choked him until he couldn't breathe at all.

Four days after his discharge, he limped towards the kitchen alcove, disinterested in any kind of food but still under doctor's orders to eat, even if his stomach didn't feel up to it.

His mother leapt for his throat. "Alex, why aren't you in bed? You need to rest. If you asked, someone would bring you something to eat."

Bracing himself against the sofa, staying on his feet taxing enough without being yelled at, he groaned, "The doctors said I *shouldn't* lie in bed all the time. They said I *need* to be up as much as I can."

His father, forever taciturn and sardonic, observed, "You're moving faster than yesterday."

"I'm just trying to help and all I get is flak," his mother said acidly.

"You hovering over me and trying to tie me to the damn bed *isn't* helping," Alex snapped.

"Your mother's just worried about you," his father said, without shifting from the chair. He was overweight, with stents in his arteries, along with a triple bypass, and he tended to stay put on sofas and Laz-e-Boy chairs. His doctors had probably told him not to be so sedentary, either, but Alex sure as hell wasn't wading into that argument.

"I don't know why I bother," his mother sighed bitterly. "I schlep all the way into the city for you, and you know what the pollution here does to my asthma. And I get no appreciation. You just kvetch. You're probably tired and in pain, but your attitude is disappointing."

He was tired and in pain, and if he had more energy and less pain, he would have thrown the sandwiches on the table at the wall. Tears welled behind his eyes: of anger, of frustration with his body for not working, with his parents for not getting it, of terrible emotions that escaped his control, wordless but explosive in his chest. Instead of crying, he pecked at a turkey sandwich, but his interest in food had dropped from queasy absence to an elemental nonexistence. He retreated to the bed, curling his body into a tight ball, his head buried under the covers. Hiding as well as anyone can in a studio apartment.

That night, after his parents cabbed it back to their Midtown hotel, he looked imploringly at Helen, who was camping on the sofa. "You gotta help me," he begged. "You gotta get Mom outta here. She's driving me completely fucking crazy, and I can't deal."

Helen, a social worker, nodded in that social worker way, overtly empathetic and listening. "Yeah, I gotcha." She was the only one of the three siblings who got along with their mother. Their other sister, Ruth, was finishing law school in Vermont; she hadn't been on speaking terms with their mother for the last two years. "To be fair, Alex," Helen added. "Mom kind of makes one good point. Even in this city, most doctors and lawyers go through life without getting shot. They also make more money."

"Yeah," Alex replied. "I know. But you're not gonna change my mind."

"Didn't think so, but just putting it out there."

Alex never knew what Helen said, but the next day, his parents were on a MetroNorth train to Duchess County. Thank God. He owed Helen big time. But even with his mother out of his hair, he felt like an abstraction, trapped in the apartment, losing his independence, relying on Helen to clean, cook, and shop. On bad days, she had to help him change the bandages. Nights were torture: an unrelenting fire raging inside the wound, a hungry inferno burning without end. He could only lie on his left side and woke up in anguish at any movement. What little fitness he'd once possessed had vanished like snow in a heatwave. He could not even traverse the damned studio apartment, from the bed to the bathroom, without terrible pain and with more fatigue than he'd ever known.

At the same time, every day of convalescence made him antsier, bored of looking at the nicotine-tinged walls, the brown shag carpet, the chipped yellow linoleum. Although his side felt as though it was being stabbed by a white-hot poker, he rallied his strength, and then he limped onto the landing. From there, he squinted down the stairwell. You could see straight to the ground floor, three dizzying, spiraling layers of balconies and stairways. He felt flushed, his brain wobbling inside his skull. But he would conquer those three flights of stairs, dammit. Hobbling and almost falling on his face, he survived the expedition to the ground floor, but climbing back up felt like ascending Everest. He hyperventilated until he was lightheaded. His heart thrashed against his aching breastbone. At the third-floor landing, his legs buckled, and he collapsed against the door. Pain flared, blistering, and then nauseating. Something warm and wet stuck to his skin. *Oh, motherfucker*, he gasped. Blood seeped through the stitches, dying his hoodie red.

Helen flung open the door. "Jesus, Al." She helped him into bed, compressing the wound with a towel while threatening to call EMS if the bleeding didn't stop in the next twenty minutes. Blood soaked most of a bath towel, but it stopped, and she didn't chastise him for doing too much, although he knew she was thinking it.

"Give it another week before you try the stairs again," she suggested as she handed him a clean t-shirt.

The next day, Alex awoke in so much pain that he almost fainted when his bladder forced him to his feet. Spots of fresh blood stained his t-shirt. After shuffling out of the can, he knelt against the bed, resting his forehead on the mattress. Ice drilled into his internal organs. Groaning, he hugged the duvet as uncontrollable shivers juddered his insides.

"Alex?" queried Helen, looking worried. "You're white as a sheet."

He whispered, "I think I gotta go to the hospital."

She placed her palm over his forehead. "My God, you're on fire."

"But I'm freezing," he muttered.

Helen recruited Bill Ryan to drive them to Columbia Pres. While Bill navigated his Lincoln through traffic, Alex cried, "I wish I'd died in the shooting." This would never end. The pain would always be with him. The docs had promised that his injuries would eventually heal well enough for him to live a relatively normal life, but he wasn't buying it.

"They'll give you some nice drugs in the hospital, and you'll feel a lot better," Bill said, speaking in the placating tone he used when promising suspects deals with the DA they were never going to get.

Bill and Helen held him upright, one on each arm, and they carried him into the ER. He almost passed out. He saw colored lights, severed limbs, and bodies with their guts hanging out, but Bill and Helen said that he was hallucinating. Someone got a hold of Dr. Naziri, who had him promptly transferred to the pulmonary ward.

"You did what? Three flights of stairs in a walk-up? Unaided?" Naziri sounded unimpressed. Not least because Alex was running a fever of 102 degrees. He sent Alex for x-rays, replaced a drain, then restitched the tear in the wound, warning him that he'd developed an infection and partially ripped open an artery. The infection had been brewing for days. The hallucinations were symptoms of septic shock. Without mincing words, Naziri said that Alex shouldn't overdo it. And he should pay more attention to his body. Yes, he would get better, but it would take time. If he reinjured his healing insides, he would need another major surgery, potentially setting his recovery back by months. Groggy from morphine and fever, Alex promised the surgeon that he wouldn't push himself so hard. They kept him on the ward for three nights, attached to an IV drip dispensing antibiotics and opiates. Finally, the fever broke. When Bill and Helen rolled him out to the car in a wheelchair, he felt brittle, like rusty, flaking metal, and he could sleep for weeks, if only the pain would take its talons out of his side and let him.

Bill assisted him with the ascent up the apartment's stairs, then he dragged in a hefty box of books – philosophy, history, and a few classic novels. "You'll find something to give your mind a workout, so you can rest your body."

Alex prodded at the contents of the box. Nietzsche. Kant. Foucault. *Middlemarch. Crime and Punishment.* It didn't get better. God forbid Bill should read mindless trash. But his other colleagues had sent him a box-full of VHS tapes, and he'd already watched the handful of decent movies. The rest were porn and shoot-em-up action films. *You dicks*, he'd thought vexatiously. He didn't want to see that shit, any of it. He settled on David Halberstam's *The Best and The Brightest*. The seven-hundred page treatise on the Vietnam War seemed like the lightest reading there. And Bill was right – it gave him something else to think about, keeping him occupied for days.

To his astonishment, Catherine called and said she wanted to bring the girls over to his apartment. He had only seen them five or six times since he'd confronted her outside the school, and he was suspicious that she deliberately tied them up with other activities on days he had RDOs. Anyway, Catherine explained that the day after the shooting, the morning news had been on the TV while the girls ate breakfast, and the NY1 reporter had declared that two policemen had been shot last night in Washington Heights. Catherine admitted that she had not, at first, paid much attention, that being the sort of news you expected from Washington Heights, but then Ellie screamed. Catherine ran into the other room in a panic, thinking Ellie had hurt herself or someone was breaking in through the window. Eleven-year old Ellie shrieked, "Daddy's been shot!"

"No, sweetie," Catherine had said automatically. "There are lots of policemen in New York."

"It is Daddy," Ellie cried. The reporter on the TV announced the names of the two victims and said that they were in critical condition. Families were meant to be notified before journalists released the names of victims, but somehow, the distance between Alex and Catherine over the years got in the way of that happening.

Catherine, unexpectedly, treated him a bit better than the roaches in the laundry room. They had a civilized conversation. She apologized for not visiting him in the hospital but feared it would be too traumatic for the girls. They could stay for a night. Helen was there, and Catherine had always liked Helen. Better than him. He had no 'kid things' at his place, so when they came, they stocked it with a few games and toys. The stuffed animals, plastic horses, and board games cluttered his floor and overtook the dining table, bringing a flicker of warmth and color to the dismal place. Sarah dedicated her attention to the plastic horses and playing card games with Helen, while Ellie glued herself to Alex's side, determined to help him with anything he needed. Should she order pizza? Did he want a cup of coffee? A newspaper? When he slept for a little while, exhausted after a battle with the stairs and then a chapter of *The Best and the Brightest*, she sat beside him on the bed, reading *Watership Down*.

"Daddy, will you get better?" she asked.

"I'm getting better," he replied. "I made it to the second-floor landing." He had defeated those damn stairs – some of them – without bleeding or hallucinating, but he wouldn't traumatize his daughter with too much gore.

"How long?"

"I don't know, honey."

"Does it still hurt a lot?"

"Yeah."

"Can I see it?"

He roughly cleared his throat. "I'm not sure you want to. It's not nice."

"I want to," she insisted.

"Like you won't have enough to tell your therapist when you're thirty?"

"What?" She scrunched her brows together.

"Nevermind." She could handle *Watership Down,* he figured, and he eased his back against the headboard, delicately pushing up his t-shirt so she could see the wound. Well, the surgical scar on his chest. The gunshot wound itself was hidden underneath a broad, white bandage.

Seemingly unfazed, she said, "It looks like it hurts. Can anything make it better?"

"Time and rest. There's no magic thing they can do that would make it heal faster."

"It would be really cool if there was." She smiled a little.

"Yeah, no shit." No shit indeed. His pain management was not working very well. They had finally cut his opiates, which meant he relied on ibuprofen, acetaminophen, and now that he was also off the antibiotics, supplementing it with alcohol.

Every day, when he changed the bandages, he stared at his wound, a plethoric raised knot of crisscrossing sutures and seeping drains, slightly bigger than his palm. Like the MEs do, Naziri had performed a sternotomy, sawing his breastbone in half, splitting open the ribcage and abdomen. After patching up the mess the slugs had made of his insides, the surgeon re-attached the two halves of the sternum with steel wires. Alex suffered an incessant, throbbing ache inside his chest. Like lava, it melted into the hotter fires corroding his wounded ribs. That thought again: the countless times spent watching autopsies, a witness to the havoc bullets wreak on the body. Now it was his organs, not ones belonging to some poor schmuck on the ME's table. It would always give him pain and some degree of reduced lung function. A reminder of the violence, for the rest of his life. He taped a new bandage to his side, then cleaned the incisions on his chest and abdomen. Concealing it for now. He scrunched up the old bandage and threw it into the trash.

Two months out of the hospital found Alex recovering enough strength to cook on his own, climb the stairs without collapsing or bleeding (although it took him about ten minutes), and even limp sluggishly to the corner shop. Since he wasn't fit enough for the wonders of New York public transport, Bill chauffeured him to Columbia Pres for more scans. Naziri seemed enthused by the results. A few days later, he listened to Alex's lung, then yanked out the drains, a sickening sensation that made Alex almost faint as they slid through his ribs. Smiling like he'd found lost treasure, the surgeon deftly sewed in a few more stitches, sealing the holes in his flesh.

Convinced that her brother was safe from sepsis and functional enough to take care of himself, Helen flew back to Denver. The Vietnamese guy who owned the corner bodega at Bayard Street recognized Alex, both as a local and from the news about the cop shooting, and he refused to let him pay for groceries. If the bag was heavy, he sent his son to help Alex carry it back to the apartment. By ten weeks or so, Alex had regained enough mobility and stamina to travel further than the shops on the same block as his apartment, but his lung capacity and cardio remained hopeless. Any stairs or uphill pressed his heart into pumping so hard it felt close to bursting. He always ran out of air and fell to his knees, panting desperately, scared, waiting for his heart find its rhythm and his lungs to resume working. The physical therapist who visited once per week never appeared concerned. "Healing takes time," she said. Despite her reassurances, he found it maddening, at times breaking down in tears with pain and frustration because his broken body wouldn't climb more than three flights of stairs. Before the shooting, he'd taken his body for granted – it worked perfectly despite being slightly overweight – but now he couldn't anymore. It would never be the same, never as fit or as strong.

He lived in fits and starts, dreams and frustrations, with the constant roar of traffic and sirens in the little apartment. The place was austere and cheerless. A serviceable sofa and armchair. An out-of-sorts dining table. The dusty, brown shag carpet and yellow lino. At least his appetite had reappeared, and to prove he wasn't useless, he cooked for himself and the girls when they visited. He had some modest cooking skills, rarely used in his lazy years of surviving on take-out and street food. He knew how to make a quiche, pizza, pasta sauce, or a stew from scratch, and he could grill steak and burgers until they were faultlessly medium-rare. Ellie liked to fret over him. "If you need a break, Dad, I can stir the sauce." Yes, he needed one. The wound devoured his strength; he struggled to stay on his feet for more than half an hour. He handed the kitchen to Ellie, defeated by a ragu. All of it seemed beyond Sarah, who played with her horses and stuffed animals and sometimes whined about wanting to go back to her mother's.

Winter persisted, a bitter New York winter with driving sleet, but Alex began feeling a touch more optimistic about police work and returning to it. He was bored, missing the guys in the squad and the heady rush of investigations that fires up the entire central nervous system. Visits from his colleagues broke up the tedium, although when he saw them, he yearned for the job, and his chest ached from more than the surgery when they told him stories about their cases. At the same time, he couldn't subdue his anxiety about facing the dangers of the streets again. It had taken up permanent residence inside his head. Still, he *wanted* his health and his old life back, even though he had nightmares about gunfire and occasionally thought he heard it outside. He hadn't suffered any more sepsis-induced hallucinations, but the severed limbs and blood and guts troubled his dreams. On a few occasions, Ellie woke him up in the middle of the night, because he'd called for help in his sleep. He'd never talked in his sleep before. Most nights, he woke himself up, gasping convulsively, soaked in cold sweat. He washed his sheets every few days.

When he felt well enough to ride the subway as far as Morningside Heights, he travelled to New York Pres, finally visiting Eddie. He willed his feet to step on board that train. It scared him when he heard those reports from Stella and his colleagues on Eddie's prognosis. He would live, but he would never walk again. He would need a stoma bag for the rest of his life. Alex tightened his fingers around the subway pole until his hand hurt. The pole felt slippery with his sweat. Apprehension fizzed inside his gut, tying it into tight cramps. As if he hadn't spent his career dealing with horrific injuries! In October, he'd been a few millimeters away from death. Down to nothing more than the randomness of bullet trajectories, here he was, on his feet, weeks away from going back to the job, while Eddie was permanently disabled.

He crossed underneath the venerable Georgian buildings of Columbia University, then shouldered through the hospital's revolving door. Stella had told him the ward, and any homicide detective should know his way around his local hospitals. The convoluted maze seemed longer than he remembered. The antiseptic hospital smell stuck to the back of his throat. His wound bounded in time to his pulse, hurting more with every beat.

Eventually, he found Eddie in a private room with views over the university quadrangle's classical architecture, surrounded by a blocky cityscape of six and seven story Harlem walk-ups. The delicate, lopsided spires of St. John the Divine floated above the walk-ups.

Alex's heart accelerated like it had started a drag-race. "Hi, Eddie," he rasped. Eddie had lost an alarming amount of weight, the outline under the sheets wraithlike, skeletal, his cheeks hollowed out, the crinkled lines under his eyes forming fissures in his skin. A central line emerged from his collarbone like an alien, with lumens spilling out from the shoulder like tentacles. An ECG machine bleeped. Stella sat beside him, grading her students' exams.

Delighted, Eddie beamed, "Hey. Alex. Good to see you! Stella's been saying, you would come soon."

"Yeah, well, how are you doing?" What a stupid question – other than having lost the use of his legs and his large intestine, Eddie was fine.

"I'm still alive," said Eddie. "And they been saying I'm likely to be for the foreseeable future, which is a lot better than what they were saying a few months ago."

"Yeah." Alex glanced over at Stella, who indicated he should take the chair on the other side of Eddie.

"Everyone in the squad has been around. They practically live here. They said you took a ricochet to your chest. Nearly got your heart but just missed."

"Yeah. My right lung's been fucked. Now I have less of it."

"They said that too. But you got here. How you doing?"

"All right. I guess. Recovering. I was never that fit and now I'm worse. But I've been seeing more of my girls. My ex decided me nearly getting killed was a reason to start talking to me again."

"You know what they say about clouds and silver linings. You still off work?"

"Yeah. Until they take the stitches out, and I pass a medical."

"That's good. That's good." Eddie's eyes flickered shut. "When I came to, after the first surgery, first thing I thought was you'd been killed, or you were a sorry mess, like me. I can't tell you how it warmed my heart to hear that you'd make a one hundred percent recovery—"

"I wouldn't go that far," Alex interrupted. "They think I'm always gonna have issues with it."

"Hey, at least your intestines are in one piece. There's a lot to be said for shitting and pissing normally," Eddie cackled.

Not seeing the funny, Alex stared at him, lips frozen into an anxious grimace. Stella seemed deeply engrossed in the exam on her knees.

"Hey, I've had a great career," Eddie grinned. "I coulda done with having it a few more years, but it's been great. It's been fun. And they got the sons of bitches who did it. Indelicata's been in, said they've been charged with attempted murder one. Did he tell you?"

"You gonna tell him about Florida, Eddie?" Stella interjected, raising her eyes from her grading.

"Yeah, Florida. Stella's been offered a job as a professor at the University of Florida. Tenure track n' everything. So, when I can travel again, we're gonna go down there."

"You're moving to Florida?" Alex said numbly.

"We are." Eddie sounded thrilled. "New York winters are gonna get hard for me. New York's gonna be too hard. Every building in this city has stairs, and I'm gonna be stuck in a wheelchair. Could do with being some place warm. And we're looking at a little house on the beach near Miami. The Atlantic Ocean, right there."

"So it gets blown away in the next hurricane?"

Eddie's face split into an even wider grin, and he laughed. "Oh, Alex. You can always be relied on for your sunny optimism!"

"I'm realistic."

"It'll be a while anyway," Stella said. "They're not letting Eddie out of this place for some time yet."

"I think I'm gonna start writing." Eddie held up his hands, wriggling his fingers. "I can't walk but I can still type."

"Writing what?" Alex touched his lips. They felt dry and cracked.

"Novels. Like crime novels. You know, like Joseph Wambaugh. He's an ex-cop."

"There aren't many crime novels from the perspective of a Black detective," added Stella. "It's a very white genre."

"Less so when I get mine published," Eddie said jauntily. "People wanna read about what we do."

"Yeah, I guess that's a thing," said Alex in a gravelly voice, not processing anything. He was absorbed by the CVC line and a sign on the wall reminding staff that this was a high dependency spinal unit.

Eddie laughed heartily, as though he wasn't paralyzed in the high dependency unit. "I mean, not *really* what we do. You gotta make it exciting, like with gunfights and car chases and running after serial killers or guys who wanna kill the president."

"Getting shot was pretty exciting," Alex remarked flatly.

"The last thing I remember is talking about the weather."

Alex wished that was all he remembered. He moved his eyes from Eddie to Stella. Eddie joked, acting sanguine, but Stella seemed both sad and resolute, her back to a wall, facing something huge and dark and frightening.

"What if the detective's wife turned out to be a KGB spy?" asked Eddie.

"What?" said Alex.

"For my book. You think that could work?"

"Oh." He drew in a shivery breath. His nostrils flared at the sting of disinfectant. "Yeah, I guess if the Russians gave a fuck about crack dealers shooting each other in Washington Heights."

"You're the most pragmatic man I know. Almost as pragmatic as Stella!"

Stella wrote a large 'C' on someone's paper and shook her head.

A nurse bustled into the room to draw blood, and Alex muttered a pained, awkward farewell, with Eddie easily tired out, unable to see visitors for very long, but he assured Alex that he was improving every day. Alex felt like he'd been electrocuted. By his partner's condition. By the news of his move to Florida.

He sniffed back the tears as he limped through the wide glass doors. Several escaped and crept down his cheeks. A crane working on a nearby high-rise clashed one steel beam into another. *Gunshots!* Alex jumped. The sirens of every squad car in the city screamed towards him. He saw the white panels on the ambulance. He tasted tangy blood and fear. Pain in his side nearly forced him to his knees.

Panicky, he cast his eyes around the street. There was a bar, not far from the uptown subway entrance. The Morningside Bar and Grill. He changed his course, crossing West 116th, then he threw his weight into the green lacquered door. A few old men read newspapers over beer and cigarettes. Somewhere, he heard a siren. He licked his lips, tasting blood. But it came from biting his lip, not his lung. He inhaled musty scents – leather, wood, spicy cigarette smoke. Blinking, he leaned unsteadily on the bar, ordering a shot of Jameson. The bartender must think he was already drunk. Deftly, he threw back the whiskey. It tingled on its way down. Heat dispersed from his stomach to his limbs, cauterizing the boiling pain inside his arteries. He swallowed another three shots.

"Rough day, huh?" grunted the bartender.

"Yeah." His tight-lipped expression dissuaded the bartender from asking more questions.

He paid up, then tipsily wandered onto 116th. Dusk had fallen, the city lights rising, Morningside Heights alive with that disjointed mixture of ghetto and students. His brain floated inside his skull, unmoored from thoughts, emotions, the city itself. Dazed, he watched the street, feeling insignificant, a speck amongst eight million other specks. Shaking his head like sand had fallen into his eyes, he jogged down the stairs into the 116th Street station. His eyes watered, and he held his ribs while boarding a 2 train.

When he arrived at his apartment on Mulberry Street, he reared back in surprise. Catherine and the girls were waiting impatiently in front of the noodle place. It came back to him: the conversation from a week ago when he'd promised he would take them tonight, as she had a date. Shit, she was furious, and he was in trouble. His heart crashed through the pavement as she bore down upon him, snarling and spitting.

"Where have you been? You were supposed to be here half an hour ago."

"Sorry, I was seeing Eddie at New York Pres. The subways were delayed." Why the hell did he say that? It might be true, as subway delays were a viable excuse for being late, but this time it wasn't, and she knew it.

"Bullshit," she hissed. "You're drunk. You've been out drinking."

"I haven't," he protested.

"You know, I thought your near-death experience would have turned you into a mature, responsible adult. I thought, this is the kind of thing that changes people."

"I fucked up, I lost track of time, but I'm here now, okay?"

Sarah and Ellie, upset by the hostility, started crying.

"I'm not letting you have them when you've been drinking and lying to me."

"Catherine," he pled. "Can we go inside and not have a domestic on the street?" If they went in, he could talk sense into her, the girls could play with the toys they had up there, she would see that they were happy and that he could be trusted.

"We're not having anything on the street. I'm taking them home." She shoved past him, searching for a cab with its light on.

"Catherine," he entreated as she waved at an oncoming taxi.

Ellie grabbed his hand, holding it so tightly she cut off his circulation, and she huddled against his flank, while Sarah seemed uncertain as to which parent she wanted to ally herself with. A taxi plowed to a halt at the curb, and Catherine yanked open the back door, irately beckoning the

173

girls to get inside. Sarah made her decision, leaping onto the leather seat. Sobbing, Ellie clung to Alex.

"You're upsetting her," Catherine snarled.

"*I'm* upsetting her? You're the one who's just hailed a cab."

"'Cause of your behavior. Ellie, come *on.*"

Ellie cuddled closer to Alex's hip. Her mother grasped her other hand and jerked her away from him. She screeched, attracting the attention of everyone on Mulberry Street. The vendors selling shellfish and spices across the street; the young Chinese guys who had just bought noodles; the two Black ladies in hijabs and African robes, pushing prams; the Chinese woman with three quiet children, who looked relieved this one wasn't hers; the two long-legged male sex workers on a cigarette break. They all stopped what they were doing.

"I wanna stay with Daddy," Ellie wailed as Catherine hustled her into the cab.

Alex stood planted on the curb, numb, helpless. He felt like he'd been hit in the head with a bag of nails. Catherine whacked the door shut, then the taxi swerved into the raucous stream of traffic. The bystanders resumed their business, shrugging off the drama in that New Yorker way. Furious, his blood simmering, Alex stalked into the apartment. Dammit, they had been getting along. Why had he gone to that bar and spaced out her date? Because he was upset. Because fucking it up was inevitable, a tessellated pattern destined to continue forever, like perps with rap sheets a mile long who can't stop doing the things that got them put away the first ten times.

He flopped onto the edge of his bed and stared at the dilapidated kitchen squashed against a corner. A cockroach stared back at him, antennae inquisitively twitching. He stood up, and the roach shot under the cabinets. Exhaling through gritted teeth, he grabbed the Glenmorangie from the counter, a whisky he meant to open when he celebrated something. *Fuck it. What's to celebrate,* he thought mirthlessly. He twisted the cap off, then swigged it straight from the bottle. Without letting go of the whisky, he collapsed onto the bed, spread-eagled on his back. The wound punished him. Each wobbling breath spurred ever-strengthening assaults. Images played in his mind, a continuous loop like a tape stuck in the VCR: Catherine raging, Ellie crying for him, Eddie wasting away under the hospital sheets, Stella holding that frozen anguish. Growing thicker, pain infused his head with a nauseating mist, as if the air he breathed had turned foul. He gazed hopelessly at the ceiling, eyes glued to the dark green splotches in the corner above the kitchen. The plaster sagged where droplets of water gathered until they swelled enough to fall to the floor. Another thing in this shuttle crash of an evening. The odds of his landlord fixing it were about a million-to-one. He squeezed his waterlogged eyes shut, then propped himself on an elbow to glug another mouthful of Glenmorangie, the only solution to his misery.

Chapter Seventeen

Afraid he would pass out or puke, Alex kept his eyes resolutely closed as he felt Dr. Naziri prodding at his wound, cutting through the stitches. After the initial sharp shot of local anesthetic, Alex lost sensation in his right side. The pain retracted its claws. It was like a part of his body no longer belonged to him. He didn't want it back. Speaking in professional euphemisms, Naziri said the damage to the skin and muscle had been too catastrophic for unproblematic healing. While the surgical scars on his chest had healed into smooth, thin lines, the scars from the wound itself had become reddened, swollen lumps, often itching or burning, and Alex had to apply moisturizer daily, or the itching drove him to madness.

Underneath the scars, it refused to fully heal. On cold, damp days, his side ached. The ribs always felt stiff and painful first thing in the morning. If he torqued his upper body, ran up a flight of stairs, or chased public transport, the pain hammered him like a Mafia back-alley beating, and it took him an appallingly long time to catch his breath. Full lung function following his pulmonary resection was unlikely to ever return. Apparently, that meant he should avoid marathons and Himalayan peaks, which he'd spent the last thirty-one years avoiding anyway. Inside, he had only two-thirds of his right lung, permanent damage to muscles and costal cartilage which sparked muscle spasms and nerve pain, and fibrous adhesions woven around the chest wall and the lower five floating ribs. His chest x-rays entertained the entire staff of the thoracic unit.

Nevertheless, he could grit his teeth and tolerate his sore ribcage. He could conceal his limp when he needed to, although it hurt like hell when he did. The perps that could outrun him now were probably the ones that would have outrun him before the shooting. A few days after Naziri extracted the stitches, Alex visited NYPD Medical Services for a physical. The doctor was confident that his complications wouldn't hinder him as a detective and declared him fit for active duty.

Five months, he thought. *Jesus. Feels like ten years. A lifetime.* The last time he wore a suit and clipped a shield to his belt seemed like it had been in another life entirely. Fuck, was he ready for this? For the last couple months, he'd dreamed about it, hoped for it, bargained for it, but now his heart raced, and his stomach felt like a ball of razor wire. As he rode the 6 train uptown, he cringed at his ashen reflection flickering across the subway windows.

The squad greeted him like a returning hero. A rambunctious herd of detectives surrounded him, effusively clapping him on the back, shaking his hand. Blood poured through the veins in his cheeks. He had walked down the wrong street at the wrong time. Not remotely heroic. But he smiled when he discovered his phone superglued to the receiver. Then Rizzo handed him a gift, a small box covered in silver wrapping paper. Suspicious, he opened it. A phallic vibrator. Someone else had drawn a penis in chalk on the back of his office chair.

Suddenly, out of nowhere, Vito hurled into him, thumping him between the shoulder blades, knocking the wind out of him with his enthusiasm. "How fuckin' great to see you! Couldn't fuckin' wait to get back to chasin' the bad guys, huh? Back to rollin' in the dirt!" Playfully, he boxed at Alex, like a fat, Italian Muhammed Ali.

Protective of his wound, Alex warded off the blows with his right forearm. "Vito, it's still sore."

Laughing heartily, Vito held up his palms. "Okay, okay. It's just so great you're back. So fuckin' great. We gotta get a drink some time. Catch up. I meant to visit you at your place, but you know, with the job, the wife, the kids, it just gets crazy. I gotta see where Brady's at with a case, but we'll get a drink and catch up soon."

"Sure," Alex answered, catching a couple breaths as Vito bounded away.

When he stopped by his locker, he discovered that someone had attached frilly red French lace to his bulletproof vest. A Marty Vasquez special. You could sometimes recognize the perp of a prank by its style. He made a half-assed attempt to yank off the lace, but it was stitched on, and he decided to make that a problem for the future.

His euphoria abruptly diminished as soon as he saw his desk. His heart buckled like a building being demolished. Months' worth of work had accumulated, along with an extensive collection of porn magazines, both gay and straight. He massaged his fingers into his left temple with one hand as he shoveled magazines onto the floor with his other arm.

His colleagues had redistributed as many of his and Eddie's cases as they could. The easy ones. Cases where they had made a collar or identified a perp. Cases already bound over that the DA wanted worked

177

more. The rest remained untouched, for the most part. As Alex grappled with cases that had been out of his mind for almost five months, working out what (if anything) the squad did with them, or what he'd done in that other lifetime, an unfamiliar detective approached his cubicle. The man was about his age – early thirties – with a striking Irish complexion of pale skin, black hair, and radiantly blue eyes.

"I'm James Hurley," the detective stated, grinning like a game show announcer. He snatched Alex's hand in his, giving it a firm shake. "Transferred here about three weeks ago. I've heard a lot about you."

"Oh." Alex swallowed the boulder lodging in his throat. Eddie wasn't coming back. However hard it might be, Corcoran would have brought in someone else. You can't leave a hole in the squad.

"I was in Street Crime," Hurley explained. A plainclothes unit mainly devoted to getting illegal guns off the street, but with a reputation for unsympathetic policing. "Wanted to do something else. They said, after the 190th Street shooting, Homicide needs personnel. *They* wanted me to do something else. But hey, they got me interviewing wits and doing follow-up things with some of these." Still smiling, he patted the tower of files on Alex's desk.

Alex was wondering why *they,* whoever they might be, wanted Hurley to do something that wasn't Street Crime when Corcoran surfaced from his office and motioned for him. He glanced at Hurley out of the corner of his eye, then advanced into the office to sit underneath the L-T's gloomy shrine to Irish Republicanism. He hadn't missed it. By now, he knew that most of those men had been executed in 1916 after a failed uprising.

"How are you feeling?" Corcoran asked.

"I'm happy I'm here." Corcoran wasn't someone with whom he shared how he really felt. Thrilled to be back, but at the same time worried, his moods darker, more distractible, like something had sheared off inside him.

"Are you in much pain still?" queried the lieutenant.

Yes, hurts like a fucking bitch, Alex thought, but his boss didn't need to know. The NYPD doctor had said he could carry out his duties. That should be enough. "A little," he replied. "But nothing I can't deal with."

"Aye, that's good. Well, I'm pleased you're back. It's terrible about Eddie, isn't it? Just awful. The man was a great cop."

"One of the best."

"We were struggling, being short two detectives. So, they sent us James Hurley, who I see you've met? Feisty but talented, they said. He was in Street Crime."

Alex nodded, wondering about Hurley.

"Good. You're going to be partnered with him for now, alright? See how you get on."

Alex continued bobbing his head. "Yes, sir."

"Now… Liebowitz. Vasquez and Ryan took over from our end, but it's really been Indelicata's show. Sure, you know what he's like with a redball in his teeth. It's been a mess, the Orthodox community's been all over the mayor and the commissioner, but we finally have good news, thank God. It went down, so it did. Indelicata's just made an arrest. The name of the suspect has not yet been released."

"Huh," Alex said in surprise. "Who did it?"

"A fellow called Ernesto Serrachia."

Alex blinked and scratched his cheek. "That schlemiel of a crack dealer?"

"Sure, you did a cursory interview of him?"

"Yes, he gave me an alibi." He sucked in a sharp breath. "I thought it checked. Those statements and 'fives are in the file."

"The narc cop and the Dominican take-away employee?"

"Yes, sir."

"They're not certain of the timing. That SNEU unit regularly works that corner, and they can't say for certain if Serrachia was there that day or another one. He said it's a bustling corner – loads of crackheads looking to get a fix, so it's all a wee bit chaotic. You know what eyewits are like."

Alex could only agree – a witness certain of time, direction, or anything else in one interview might be completely unclear on it at the next. Memory is fallible and malleable. But he'd conducted those interviews. He'd believed the witnesses and wrote off Serrachia as a suspect. Left to him, the case would be open. No wonder everyone worshipped the pavement Vito walked on, the real-life incarnation of Columbo or Sherlock Holmes.

Corcoran said, "Don't worry about the wits. Indelicata got a confession."

"He confessed?" repeated Alex stupidly.

"Aye."

"How the hell…" Alex started to say, his insecurity growing as he wondered if he shared so much as a fraction of Vito's instincts, or

Eddie's. Was he really prepared for a return to full duty? Even with sick leave and convalescence, he hadn't felt well rested for months: chronic pain, his body adjusting to the injuries, too many nights of sleep interrupted by nightmares, and now he had to leap in headfirst where he and Eddie had left it, but without Eddie.

"Hey, there isn't anyone in the Bureau who can get a confession like Indelicata," Corcoran reassured him, smiling mildly. "He'd found an eyewit, sure, a prostitute with the street moniker of Loretta, who said she saw the whole thing. Once he confronted Serrachia with that, Serrachia folded."

"Thank God the case is down." The only response that came to mind.

Corcoran said that he didn't have to catch new cases for the next couple tours, then dismissed him. He was mortified with himself for making the wrong call about Serrachia. Doubtful of his skills and instincts, he fell into his cubicle, raking his fingers against his chest, feeling the ridges of the sternotomy wires. They would be there forever. Here he was, and he had to appear as tough as they expected him to be.

But buried under the case files and porn, he found a collection of 'get well' cards, from victims and their families. Incredible, he thought, people gave a damn, even though he'd briefly touched their lives under terrible circumstances. That brought a slight smile to his face, along with upswelling emotions. As they reviewed Alex's cases, Hurley had Alex laughing at his stories: one about peeing in his friend's shampoo bottles at a drunk party; another about building a giant snow penis on the square near 1PP, then being caught and issued a command discipline because his partner in Street Crime could run faster. He told Alex about his family – growing up in Boston until he was sixteen, then his mother moving him and his sisters to New York after his douchebag father, an airline pilot, ran away with a flight attendant. Hurley enriched the story with dry laughter, enjoying the gallows humor in his own screwed up history.

Yeah, this partnership will work, Alex thought. James Hurley couldn't have been more different than Eddie in his temperament or his approach to life, yet Alex immediately recognized that they shared a quality, an electrical process, where they made contact at one point, contact at another point, and the molecules between the two points straightened themselves out. It straightened *him* out; he felt better just by being in their presence.

At the end of that day's tour, Hurley walked out of the bathroom wearing a kilt woven with blue and orange plaid and a dark blue jacket. His socks stopped below his bare knees, and his laces were tied into an elaborate knot snaking around his ankles. What prank was this? Even the new guy was in on it.

"You dress like a Scotsman for some kinky sex club?" Alex asked.

"Nah, I wish." Hurley cracked up like he was in the Comedy Cellar. "It would be more fun. I play in the Emerald Society Pipes and Drums, and we got a dress rehearsal this evening. See." He reached under his desk, where a big black case had been sitting, unnoticed. After hoisting it onto the desk, he snapped open the latches to reveal a jumbled set of shiny black bagpipes. "The only thing getting the blow jobs are these babies."

Hurley extricated the pipes from their case like he was picking up a newborn. He shoved the bag under his armpit and pursed his lips around the blowpipe. His cheeks puffed up as he filled the bag with air, then a high-pitched squeal deafened everyone. The ear-splitting skirling pulsed in Alex's cracked breastbone, vibrating the wires. Vasquez held his hand against ear and laughed. Ryan and Cohen looked unfazed, like people played bagpipes in the squad room every day. Keohane mouthed, *You fucker*. Several detectives from other teams swore, covering their ears. Hurley played about sixteen bars of a tune, before DI Crawford, the Two-Five deputy inspector, burst through the door.

"Those fucking things are *not* an indoor instrument!"

There was no time for Alex to worry about Liebowitz, Serrachia, or ruminate over Indelicata's superior skills in the interrogation room. He worked a few tours where he chased witnesses and paperwork for his open cases, and other detectives conscripted him into a canvass here, an interview there. His convalescence ended when ten minutes before the end of a four-by-twelve, he caught a case, a Black female DOA behind a dumpster on West 138th Street.

Alex squatted over the body, learning what he could from a visual inspection. Grotesque shadows of buildings, cars, and NYPD personnel contorted around his flashlight, Crime Scene's lights, and a sallow streetlight. The work came back to him as easily as breathing. Easier, because his eyes and brain were undamaged. "I think she's been dumped here. Or moved. Look at the PML. Blood's pooled on her stomach and thighs, but she's lying on her back." Burns had peeled the skin on her fingertips – injuries from holding crack pipes, too high to care about the heat. She wore a stringy crop top and blue lace underwear. No sign of her pants. No obvious deadly wounds, either. OD'd? Suffocated? Alex shone the flashlight into her eyes and noted the tiny red pinpricks. Petechial hemorrhaging. The telltale sign of strangulation. It was going to come back from the ME as a murder.

"She'll be out fucking everything that moves, if it'll give her crack," James observed.

"You think she's a pross?" asked Alex.

"Obviously," said James. "You're clearly not spending enough of your time enjoying the best the streets have to offer."

"Do this long enough, you'll learn not to assume anything."

"I can assume she was smoking a hell of a lot of crack."

"Fair. But she could be an unlucky addict who ran into the wrong people."

By 0330, they had completed a spiral search of the crime scene and collected some grungy, damp clothes, which were housing a few spiders. Might have belonged to the vic. Or the perp. Or neither. The lab might throw the detectives a lead if hair or other samples matched something, or someone. Pessimistic but holding out for any straw, they canvassed the closest building with a line of sight on the DOA, turning up nothing. They approached the next low-rise, across 138th, and their portable exploded with cops screaming, *ten-thirteen. Shots fired. Rush a bus.*

Alex and James froze, staring one another. Alex heard blood roaring in his ears. It raced from his heart. He dropped to his knees as if shot, to the surprise of James, the precinct detective, and the uniforms. Gunfire crackled. Where? Who was shooting? Pain swirled into a firestorm that tore through his side. He gulped for air, but none touched his lungs. Trembling, he rolled into a fetal position on the wet sidewalk, face buried in his forearms. Soft moans escaped his throat.

"Lex. Hey. Alex." James squatted down beside him, grabbing his shoulder. "Fuck, man. Get yourself together. It's alright. It's not here. It's in Queens. 107th Avenue and Inwood is in Queens."

Alex half-unfolded himself, then looked into James' bewildered blue eyes. His partner looked confused, yet unafraid. No one was shooting. Not on this block, at any rate. But Alex knew where 107th Avenue and Inwood was. The 103rd Precinct. Oh, God, it could be Fred, Ortiz, Selvio, any number of people he knew.

"What the fuck is wrong?" James asked.

A powerful coughing spasm racked his body. He wiped the back of his hand against his mouth, expecting stringy blood. But there wasn't any – just clear saliva. "I used to work in the One-Oh-Three."

"Come on, this ground probably has needles somewhere. Get up." James grasped his bicep and elbow. Before Alex could resist, the Irish detective had hoisted him to his feet.

The Three-Oh precinct detective and uniforms eyeballed him like he'd lost his mind.

"What do you wanna do?" asked James.

Alex's hands shook so violently he could barely hold a pen, but he said, "Let's finish this canvass."

"You sure? It's late. No one's gonna be happy to see us."

"Well, we can't help that poor schmuck in Jamaica, so we gotta do something." Alex spoke with more fervor in himself than he expected. It took James aback.

"Uh, okay," he responded.

Their canvass until 0400 hours yielded no leads regarding the identity of the DOA, nor any pointing to whoever left her on the street. No one said they knew her. No one had seen anything. No one was pleased to see cops at their door at a ridiculous hour. The detectives gave up and numbly drove to the Two-Five, where James fired off some cursory 'fives and a '61. Alex quivered over the typewriter. The DD-5 form blurred, then spun as if he'd flushed it in a toilet. Alarmed, he rolled his chair backwards on its wheels. The spinning slowed, but he felt like he needed to empty his stomach.

"You wanna come back to mine? I've got a sofa, and it's almost a better neighborhood," James said uneasily.

"No, it isn't. You've got the Lucchese family as neighbors." Warm fluid trickled down his side, like when he'd torn his stitches on the stairs. Panic spiked his heart. He untied his tie and ripped off his jacket.

"I think I'm bleeding," he said.

"How?"

Alex threw his shirt onto the floor. Blood and yellow pus *must* be oozing out of the wound. It had split open when he heard the shots, or the radio call. It had to be!

"Seems okay to me," said James. "Looks like it did when I saw it in the locker room the other day."

In disbelief, Alex touched his side. There was no blood. The scars looked as healed as they'd been that morning – every morning – when he got dressed, the knotted puffy, red flesh snarled over the ribcage that was becoming a normal part of his body.

"Does it hurt?" asked James

"Yeah, it fucking hurts."

"Man, you've probably overdone it. You've been running up and down stairs canvassing for hours. Put your fuckin' shirt back on. Jesus, that ten-thirteen has done your head in."

The warm, seeping fluid on his side had been sweat. The pain came from the broken cartilage, damaged nerves, and muscle spasms, like it always did. James was right. On all counts. He overdid the physical exercise and hearing the ten-thirteen brought him back to his own. But he wasn't anywhere near 107th and Inwood. It wasn't him this time.

"James, please don't tell anyone about this," he entreated. "Especially not anyone in the squad."

Instead of teasing him, James nodded, his face pale and serious. "I won't. Don't worry about it. Let's at least see who the ten-thirteen is. Just so you know."

Through the fog of panic and pain, Alex could feel the trust, the warmth, like electricity running across the space separating his body from James', the telepathic link that sometimes happens between police partners. Barely breathing, they listened to the office's police radio. The citywide frequency was alight; people yelling at one another in ten codes, the dispatcher struggling to get it under control. The cop had been taken to the hospital, and he had died in surgery.

Alex recognized the vic's ID as a patrol unit rather than a detective squad or a specialized unit. "He's a patrolman."

"You know any beat cops there still?"

"Not well anymore."

"That's as good as you're gonna do until morning."

Alex found no solace in the realization that the victim was unlikely to be someone he knew. It didn't matter. The victim was like him, a cop shot in the line. The man had suffered that terrifying moment of knowing he'd been hit, of bleeding out on the street, of an ER trauma team shouting medical things, shoving tubes into veins and down the throat. He begged them to stop, to let him die. *Dammit, I'm not there*, he told himself. He was here, on a street lathered with slush that glistened under the streetlights, a precinct parking lot crammed with blue and white cars, then a long subway ride full of rowdy drunk people to Chinatown.

Even at 0500 hours, Mulberry Street was hopping. Alex wended around a street party and ignored open air drug deals on the route to his apartment. Worried about the wound, he examined it again in the bright lights of his bathroom. The scars were closed. Hurting, but closed. He kneaded moisturizer into the lumps, then he swallowed four ibuprofens, along with a throatful of whisky. Although he saw the smoky morning light outside, he stayed awake and showered with the temperature cranked up as hot as he could tolerate. When the water suddenly turned cold, he swore, slamming the handle into the 'off' position. You'd think in 1988, they would have mastered hot water systems. He pulled on a fresh pair of boxers. Doors crashed, voices rose in a heated domestic – the neighbors arguing in the stairwell. A siren howled down Mulberry Street. People on the street outside shouted at each other in Mandarin. He shut the windows, but cheap single glazing didn't do a whole lot. Giving up on silence, he lay down on his left side and heard the thudding bass from a neighbor's apartment, like a heartbeat through the walls. He smelled the pungent spices of the noodle place on the ground floor. Oh, he was at his wits' end. With all of it. Time to fucking move.

Chapter Eighteen

The victim on West 138th disappeared under fresh cases steamrolling in, another lost soul of the city vanishing into crime statistics, and the Manhattan North Homicide squad careening from one crime scene to the next, without a chance to breathe or write DD-5s for one case before they found themselves standing over another body. New York seemed broken, sagging its shoulders under a recession and its rising crime rates, while the spate of police shootings reaffirmed law enforcement's fear that the city was on a high-speed train to hell. First Alex and Eddie, then the patrolman from the One-Oh-Three. His name was Ed Byrne, and he had been alone, sitting in his RMP guarding a witness in a drug case, when four men ambushed him. After Byrne's death, the NYPD flooded the streets with Tactical Narcotics Teams, who aggressively pursued drug trafficking with buy-and-busts and countless arrests, a frontal assault on the dealers. Even though he'd been zotzed on morphine, Alex recalled Vito saying *it's a fuckin' war out there*, and he feared that Vito might be right. At the same time, city homicides proliferated as fast as crack and illegal guns, and the homicide detectives wondered if the TNTs were pissing hopelessly into the wind.

The seasons still changed, the summer's humidity soon smothering the city, the murder rate rising with the temperature. People always seemed more homicidal during heatwaves. With pain and fatigue as his steadfast companions, Alex dedicated every scrap of his depleting energy to his multiplying caseload. The old part of his life where he didn't suffer an inescapable ache in his ribs dwindled into a dim memory, and he felt as though he'd lost sight of what it had been like to feel well in himself, his insides intact. Mostly, it was a heavy, dull pain, but anything like a footchase, a tussle with a perp, or a six-story walk-up left him in petrifying agony.

The work became relentless and labyrinthine. A drive-by shooting, a domestic fueled by alcohol or crack, an overly-heated card game, a family argument over unwillingness to share drug profits, retaliatory gang shootings, botched robberies, the 98-degree motiveless murder. The vics could be perps, the perps could be vics, a turntable of violence and vengeance that made Alex dizzy (every detective in the squad had at least one case where the victim turned out to be wanted for another murder). He could not hide his eyes from a truth that plagued every big city in America: homicide in the inner-cities was largely ignored, the public and the criminal justice system indifferent. While the state could be draconian when it came to arresting people for possessing small amounts of narcotics, it responded phlegmatically to violence, to injury and death in the New York slums. Alex, injured himself, felt cripplingly encumbered under an onerous caseload and sparse resources from his department for investigating inner-city homicides. Cases he might have cleared had he more time and manpower got cold because he had too little. On the squad white board where they tracked clearances, Alex's name accrued more red ink – uncleared cases. Same as everyone else's.

Finally, the sultry inferno eased off the city, the sky becoming greyer, the air colder, the gloomy winter half-light settling like a haze across Manhattan. It was then that Nichol and West, the two men who shot Alex and Eddie, went on trial for attempted first-degree murder. The first chair ADA was John Carbone, a white-haired veteran and courtroom showman on the cusp of retirement – this was his last trial – who kept a rubber broadsword in his office and cut notches in the blade for every conviction. He was the first Black man to head an NYDA trial bureau. The second chair was Simon McNally, a young Irish prosecutor from Chicago proving himself as a rising star in the NYDA office, feisty, aggressive, dogged.

The prosecutors radiated confidence. ESU had caught the perps red-handed, carrying an Armalite AR-18, which ballistics had matched to the slugs pulled out of Eddie and collected from the street (the bullets in Alex had been too fragmented for identification). The perps had confessed to the Three-Four detective squad, brazenly claiming that the shooting was political, fighting oppression and injustice. They apparently got the rifle from some guy who was running guns to the IRA.

The case captured the attention of the whole city, and the judge issued a sequestration order, which meant witnesses were prohibited from hearing other witnesses. Alex would never hear Eddie's testimony. Eddie had flown back to New York to testify, or really, to roll into the courtroom in his wheelchair and tug the jury's heartstrings, as he remembered nothing. The night he landed, he met the MNHS detectives and –

seemingly – the entirety of the NYPD at the Glendale. Cops from all over the city crammed into the bar to see Eddie.

Amidst the pandemonium, Alex squeezed in a few quiet words with his old partner. Eddie was jovial and lighthearted, his eyes twinkling as he gushed, "You look good, Alex. You've even lost a little weight. I'm so happy you're back to being murder police. You've got the mind for it."

Do you have the nightmares? Alex thought as he smiled over his pint, but he couldn't bring those words to his lips, not here, and Eddie, the center of attention in the Glendale, seemed so damned upbeat for a guy with a severed spinal cord, brightly telling everyone, "I'm writing a book!"

On the outskirts of the party, Alex pushed his shoulder blades against a wall as he nursed his beer. His side seethed with a tireless, slow-burning fire. The party heaved around him in sweaty chaos, but he was adrift, floating away from it like a ship with dead engines. A crowd of older cops mobbed Eddie. Familiar faces – Keohane, Brady, Vasquez – flashed into view amidst the pack, then disappeared.

A hand on his elbow startled him. He jerked his head around.

Stella stood at his side, looking brittle, as if she would crumble under a breath of wind, yet incongruously stoic, like a rock that had withstood the Ice Age. "Hi, Alex. Are *you* holding up okay?"

He wavered on a knife edge – on one side the truth, on the other, acting tough because he was a New York City detective. "I dunno… It's not the same as it was, you know, before. Everything feels different, but …" His lower lip trembled, his words dissolving.

Nodding, Stella touched his shoulder. "You won't be the same."

"Is Eddie?"

"God no," she sighed. "I'm still trying to figure out who he is."

Before Alex could respond, Eddie called for his wife, and Stella met Alex's eyes with a weak smile, another squeeze on the shoulder, then she forged a path through the heaving wall of bodies.

A tsunami of tears burst through his levies. A torrent of emotions – pain, terror, loss, others he couldn't name. Oh fuck, he'd better not lose it in a bar full of cops. *What the hell is wrong with you,* he snarled at himself. He sniffed back the fluid flooding his nasal passages. It stung, and he blew his nose on a napkin. Breathlessly, he chugged the rest of his beer. Eyes lowered towards the floor, he slunk around the tables and the sweaty, drunk cops, then he was out on Bleecker Street. His colleagues weren't sober enough to catch his hasty exit. But he was far too sober, so he made his way to a place called Bar 169, a quirky, unpretentious establishment on the border of Chinatown and the Lower East Side, decorated with fake palm trees and a leopard-print pool table. Conversation and upbeat '80s pop music buzzed at a tolerable level. No one knew that he was a cop, or that he'd been shot. He knocked back a whisky, chalked up a cue, then he handily won a couple pool games. Pool slowed his breathing, lowered his heartrate. His whole world narrowed into that leopard-print expanse and the simple interactions of inertia and gravity. A few people gathered around the table, watching his precise bank shots with awe. Someone bought him a drink. He played another game but felt his concentration and coordination ebbing. At last, weariness and alcohol won, and he handed off his cue to a waiting player, then meandered home through the nightlife along Grand Street.

A few days into the trial, Carbone and McNally called him to the stand. The courtroom had become a sea of blue uniforms and dark suits, with half the cops in New York filling the gallery. Friendly faces – MNHS, detectives from the Tenth, from the Manhattan North precinct squads, Nick Selvio and Enrique Ortiz from the One-Oh-Three, and cops he'd never met in his life but who showed up out of solidarity. His heart spasmed in rapid, percussive beats. If he broke down on the stand, all these cops would see.

McNally led him through the direct examination – Alex telling the judge and jury what happened, or as much as he could piece together. He fought through choking smoke for the steady, professional manner he possessed in any case where he testified as an investigator. The ADA asked him about his injuries, his five months on medical leave, his long-term complications. As he spoke, he visualized his blood vessels relaxing, easing back into ordinary flow. *Pretend you're talking about someone else.* When McNally exhibited the blown-up images from his CT scan and graphic photos of his wounds, taken immediately after he came out of theater, he tried to steady his breathing, but blood slammed into roadblocks barricading his brain and his gut. Already, the court had heard Dr. Naziri describing the path of each bullet with clinical detail, the surgeon assessing the likelihood of surviving such injuries. But Alex was the kicker, a living and, miraculously, still breathing victim. With the judge's permission and the defense lawyer's objection, Alex removed his shirt to show his scars to the jury. They flinched. The police officers in the gallery shifted and looked at one another uncomfortably.

McNally smiled, his steely grey eyes hinting at warmth. "Thank you, Detective Boswell," and he sat down.

"Any questions for this witness, Mr. Burnett?" queried the judge.

"No, Your Honor," replied the defense attorney.

The prosecutors had predicted that. Beating up on a cop wounded in the line wouldn't play well to the jury. Whatever advantage Burnett might gain by highlighting that Alex and Eddie had never seen the perps – which they'd acknowledged on direct anyway – would be easily outweighed by looking like an asshole.

"The witness is excused," said the judge. "Thank you, Detective Boswell."

Alex stepped down to a rising cheer from the assembled cops, which the judge curtly silenced with a sharp word. He glanced at West and Nichol. They were staring blankly forwards. *Fucking pricks*, he thought. His eyes flicked over the jury. Five whites, four Blacks, two Latinos, and one Asian guy. Juries usually deliberate along amorphous lines of race, class, indifference, and very rarely, justice. Would they buy McNally and Carbone's case-in-chief? Or would they sympathize with the defendants? Anyone who was a victim of police brutality might. The prosecutors had given Alex a peek at their closing arguments, which first restated the strength of their case, stressing the jury's solemn duty to reach their verdict based on facts alone, then it wove in a 'thin blue line' narrative, avowing that an attack on police officers was an attack on all New Yorkers. Did anyone in this city believe that anymore? Those twelve jurors, for their part, looked ashen and stunned, and one had even cried, so maybe. For today.

Out in the corridor, Corcoran, Vasquez, Indelicata and other sequestered cops had been hovering near the double doors, and when Alex emerged from the trial part, they sprang to their feet. James, who wasn't sequestered, ran out of the courtroom behind Alex, ramming his shoulder through the doors before they swung shut.

"Alex, how did it go?"

"Did they cross you?"

"How'd the jury react?"

"What did the perps do?"

"I wish I coulda been in there."

"James, how'd he do?"

Alex felt his blood pooling in his feet. "It went okay. I think. He didn't cross-examine me. McNally and Carbone said he wouldn't." He looked at James. "Do you think it went okay?"

"You did fuckin' great," James said. "You fuckin' nailed it."

"What did you think of the jury?"

James patted him on the shoulder. "They were crying like they were watching the end of *Cinema Paradiso*. *I* was practically crying. Juror number three looked like she hates cops, but she was crying. You got them."

The corridor chorus responded with, "Fuckin' fantastic."

"Good to hear."

"Those shitbirds better get attempted murder one."

Marty and Vito asked Alex another wearisome string of questions, keen for the rerun of his testimony, and he snapped, "Do I look like the court reporter? I need a beer."

Yes, beer was the answer to every heartache or traumatizing court appearance. A small herd of detectives and uniforms raced across Lower Manhattan to the Glendale. They settled in, burning through a few rounds, although it was 1400 hours, which meant the cops on four-by-twelves disappeared quickly and sheepishly, fearing C/Ds if caught, and then the ones with family obligations trickled out shortly thereafter. Even James ran away before 1700 hours, apologizing profusely, but he had a date with an ER nurse. Saved from bullshitting his own excuse, Alex thanked the gods of James' sex life and police shift work. His guts cramped, like they'd frozen, and the beer bubbled without getting through. A molten knife twisted inside his wound. He had his own double date with a hot water bottle and painkillers.

"Is it serious?" Alex asked, covering for himself by feigning interest in James' sex life.

"Definitely not," laughed James. "She's just divorced some guy. It's definitely rebound sex. But she's *gorgeous*. She's from Ghana."

Alex left James to his Ghanaian nurse and rode the 4 train a few stops into Chinatown. The entire day had unnerved him. He paced his tiny floor. He combed through his testimony, second-guessing. What if it hadn't been enough? What if the jury acquitted? And what if they convicted? The damned thing would still be there to be reckoned with. It wouldn't repair his broken body. But you punish murderers with twenty-five-to-life, and that supposedly restores balance to the universe in a cosmic way: justice in its Biblical glory.

Alex asked himself, *Why am I even thinking about this shit?*

Anxious to think about something else, he called Catherine's number, and thank God, Ellie answered the phone. "Are you okay, Dad?"

"Yeah," he said in a winded voice. His old psychic wounds felt like a safe harbor, easy and familiar. "Just wanted to hear from you. I miss you but haven't had a lotta days off."

"I miss you too. Is the trial okay? It's been on the news."

"Yeah, it's okay."

"I wanted to go to the courthouse, but Mom said no. Said I was too young."

"For once, I agree with her." His kids were the last people he'd wanted in that courtroom.

"The news said you testified today."

"Yeah. I did."

"Was it okay?"

"It was fine," he said in his steadiest voice. "I testify in court a lot. It's part of my job."

"But isn't that usually about bad things that happened to other people?"

Jesus, she was a smart kid. "Yes," he acknowledged.

"When will the trial be over?"

"I don't know," he sighed. "Next week, maybe."

"I hope the jury says they're guilty," she said in a somber tone. "They did it and should be punished. Then you'll feel better. I was scared. You know, when it happened."

"Yeah, I hope so too," he replied, emotions fissuring through his voice. His heartrate was rising, fast and loud. He pivoted to a new subject, asking Ellie about school – normal, civilian questions. She liked most of her teachers. She hated her PE class. She had to write a report on tree species in Central Park. Then he asked, "Is your sister around? Can I talk to her?"

"Oh, God. She's grounded," Ellie said. "Mom says she's not allowed to use the phone until Sunday."

"What?" The Israel-Palestine peace process had nothing on his endless merry-go-round with Catherine, or Catherine's equally-as-interminable battles with Sarah. "What did Sarah do?"

"Like a tantrum. Broke a plate. Mom was trying to make her do homework or clean her room or something, and they got into a fight."

"Gotcha. Okay, yeah, I'll talk to her later. I'll try to see you guys soon. Gotta sort something out with your mother. Maybe next week on my days off."

"She's taking us up to see Grandma in Buffalo next week."

"Oh." Alex felt his throat constricting. "Then maybe after that. I gotta go, but I love you."

"I love you, Dad."

Oh, he envied Ellie's uncorrupted faith in retributive justice, a guilty verdict that could erase all this pain and trauma. He stiffly limped to the kitchen alcove and microwaved a leftover chow mein, padding out the beer in his stomach. He'd been too nervous to eat breakfast or lunch. After he'd eaten, he plunged his hand into Bill's box of books, which lived under the table. Bill hadn't retrieved it yet. Without looking, he grabbed one. *Crime and Punishment.* Some dreary Russians torturing themselves over the same shit. Very apt.

A week after his testimony, the trial finally ended, and following three long hours of deliberations, the jury returned a guilty verdict. Two counts of attempted first-degree murder, all lesser included offenses, and one count of possessing an illegal firearm. Elated cops took McNally and Carbone out for drinks, bar-hopping from a place called Amicus Brew near 100 Centre Street, then to a few bars around SoHo and the Village. By the time they got to the Glendale, Alex could barely stand. People had been plying him with alcohol since Amicus Brew. Conversations sounded indistinct in his ears. James poured water down his throat. Indelicata, roaring at the top of his lungs, gave a blow-by-blow account of the latest match between Mike Tyson and Evander Holyfield, knocking over a beer with enthusiastic pantomime boxing motions. McNally regaled a few detectives with a story about spending an unplanned night on a mountain in the French Alps and getting so hypothermic that he thought he was in Florida. The detectives seemed amused, but James was gripping Alex by the arm and chaperoning him out of the bar. Alex threw up into a gingko tree on Bleecker Street, after which he felt a little less drunk. "I can go back in," he panted.

"No way, dude," laughed James. "You're way too fucked. You'll end up sleeping in a bush somewhere. Walk it off a bit, huh?" Alex had too much alcohol in him to argue or to remember the way home himself, so he let James guide him along Spring Street and Canal Street, through the lively crowds of drunk people, parties, drug deals, clubs with their lines outside, the high-octane buzzing of New York nightlife. Alex tried swerving into a couple bars, but James steered him onwards. When he saw the inside of his apartment, the energy drained from his body. The ceiling gyrated. James made him sit up and drink another pint of water. Once he'd convinced himself that Alex wasn't going to asphyxiate on his own puke, he let him pass out in the safety of his bed. But James never got back to Hell's Kitchen. He fell asleep on Alex's sofa, cuddling the vacuum cleaner.

Chapter Nineteen

In the weeks after the trial, Alex tried negotiating a ceasefire with Catherine, but the peace talks fell apart on an evening where he had agreed to take the girls but caught a homicide in Harlem – a twelve-year old boy – during the last fifteen minutes of an eight-by-four. No one cared about clocking out when they had a child victim. Alex and James ignored the end of the tour, working the case flat-out, long past sunset. As the sky darkened, Alex took a breather in his search of the crime scene to call Catherine on a payphone and tell her that he would not be home tonight. Catherine thought that now was a good time to tell him that it would be impossible to share the girls over Christmas, because they were going to her mother's place in Buffalo, and it was such a schlep to get there, and she had assumed he would be working anyway, wouldn't he?

"I was gonna get the time off," Alex started to argue, not convinced himself because the Emerald Society guys generally got those days off.

"I've already finalized these plans with my family," Catherine announced. "They're all gonna be there. You're doing your thing, where you just won't commit or set time aside, then act all hurt when I make plans. You know, we're adults, and adults can make plans…"

"Catherine, I do the best I can, but if my boss tells me I gotta work, or something happens, that's how it is. It's the way the job is."

"Yes," she said in the wearied tone of someone who has heard every excuse. "When you put work ahead of your family."

"Do you understand what work *is?*" he demanded. "Someone else's family has lost their son, their twelve-year old son, and now I gotta find out who did it. And the longer that takes me, the more unlikely it gets that I ever will. So, I need to work this case now. It's not like I'm sitting in an office on Wall Street figuring out how to make some CEO richer. Jesus Christ."

"Alex, my family will be upset if I change plans," Catherine responded. She hung up before he could squeeze in another word.

"I can't believe that woman," Alex said bitterly, and he stormed past James towards the cordoned-off crime scene, where uniforms outside the staging area had grabbed a handful of witnesses. He stopped before he got to the police lines, his face in his hands.

"Let's talk to some of these wits," James said.

"She's never understood that sometimes, I don't have a *choice*," Alex complained. "She thinks it's all about her, or me avoiding responsibility. But a twelve-year old gets shot on the street, I have to investigate it, and dammit, if it takes seventy-two straight fucking hours of work, that's what it takes."

"Fucking right," James said agreeably.

Alex scrubbed at his nose and eyes with his palm, then he approached the softest-looking witnesses, a small group of sulky teenagers. "I'm Detective Boswell. This kid…" he waved towards the evidence cones on the other side of the crime scene tape, obscured by CSU cops and two precinct detectives. The victim had been transported downtown about an hour ago. "Any of you know who he is?"

Blank stares and silence.

"Anyone hear the shots?"

Still, silence.

Alex sighed, thinking, *it's gonna be a long fucking evening.* "Come on. You're hanging out on this block, you hear the shots, you look, right? You look to see where the shooter is, so you know which way to run."

A tall, gangly teen bobbled his head, and Alex caught his eye. "You saw something?"

"On the other side of the street," the kid muttered.

"What did you see?"

"I don't gotta say."

How would Eddie play this, Alex thought. The man had a way with witnesses here. But he possessed a quality, an acumen, that Alex could never have himself. He was too white, too Jewish. He had to find his own way now. "You're right, you don't gotta say anything," he told the wit. "But that kid – he's like twelve. He's not a hardass gang member. He's fucking twelve. They're gunning down twelve-year olds now. You're not gonna tell me you're all right with that. That your mother would be all right with that."

They herded the witness away from his friends, and after dancing around questions for ten minutes, the teen cagily revealed that he knew both the victim and the perp. The latter's family had loose associations with the Crips. There was a longstanding feud. "They better not know this came from me," the witness grumbled. He looked a bit queasy. You would if you thought some guys from the Crips wanted you to unsee what you'd seen.

"They won't," Alex promised.

Over several days, the detectives tracked down and interviewed the feuding families. They ran the names through CARS, NCIC, and DCJS, and the computer relayed a multitude of gun charges, drug charges, and assault charges. The prints on the cartridges had a hit in SAFIS.

Probable cause! A case coming together. Thinking they should head to Vegas with luck like this, Alex and James wrote up a warrant application. A judge and an ADA signed off, and they drove to the apartment, accompanied by ESU's Warrants Squad. The men geared up in their bulletproof vests and checked over their firearms. Alex winced as he adjusted the vest. Tight Kevlar hurt his side, but it was more comfortable than another bullet in his chest.

ESU busted down the door with their ram and charged into the apartment. A brawny teenager lunged for a window, and James sprang on him as he struggled with the latches. They crashed to the ground. The perp bucked James into a wall, squirming free, only for Alex and an ESU cop to tackle him. Alex grabbed the perp's arm, cranking it behind his back so any further struggle caused immense discomfort to his shoulder. The teen stopped thrashing, and Alex slapped the cuffs on him while panting out the *Miranda* warning through the shooting pains in his ribs. Winded, he threw the perp at an ESU officer, then he bowed against the wall. Pain greyed out his vision. James covered for him, focusing everyone's attention on a search-pursuant-to-arrest and dragging the perps into squad cars.

Well-acquainted with the criminal justice system, the perps demanded their lawyers immediately. The tac team searched the apartment, finding thousands of dollars' worth of cocaine, stashed beside an arsenal of firearms. They sent the guns to ballistics and ran the perps through line-ups, where another eyewit from the street identified the teenager and two of his friends. That would make the DA happy. Whatever happened down the line, Alex had a clearance, plus he'd gotten a pile of guns and coke off the street. Yet he felt ill, like he'd eaten something rancid, and he played pool long after his colleagues had left the bar. The kid he'd arrested on a homicide charge was only sixteen. One ruined life following another. Well, you couldn't let the fucked up shit out there rot your insides. Every streetwise cop knew that. He bought another glass of whisky, then he fired the cue ball into the racked balls, sinking two on the break.

Come December '88, Alex was primary on seven open homicide investigations, and he was secondary on half a dozen more. Enough to make him think he should start a drug dealer arbitration service: helping people solve corner disputes without killing one another. Meanwhile, he bounced between court appearances for pretrial hearings in a robbery-homicide case, where a crackhead had killed his cousin and stolen his TV and stereo to fence for drug money; and another case that had come to trial, a dispute in a basement numbers game that ended in a fatal stabbing, with Simon McNally as lead counsel for the prosecution. His performance in Alex and Eddie's attempted murder trial had gained him a promotion and prosecuting more homicides as first-chair.

On Christmas day, Alex and Marty manned the office, hoping the people of uptown Manhattan would get into the Christmas spirit by not committing violent crimes. They ate a microwave dinner, and Marty, whose in-laws were visiting, mourned the Dominican feast he was missing because he wasn't home. Alex wasn't missing anything by not being home, but he acknowledged that the microwavable chicken breast was more depressing than hospital food. By 1600 hours, they'd responded to a 'shots fired' call on West 76th, then arrested an Upper West Side man for the attempted murder of his wife. The perp had written a murder-suicide note before trying to shoot her, but she'd wrestled the gun away from him.

"Holidays suck," stated Marty.

"Yeah, I can't wait until January," said Alex.

On New Year, the B team had an RDO. They spent most of the day drinking, and when Alex woke up on Rizzo's living room floor, it was 1989.

The first week of January saw Alex back in court, testifying in the numbers game trial that had been adjourned until after the holidays. The case ended with a guilty verdict. It wasn't an easy win for McNally: every witness with a rap sheet, and the murder weapon probably in the river. To celebrate, the detectives drank with the ADA, who proved his mountaineering prowess by gracefully ascending a gas station on Twelfth Avenue. Alex watched him with his own feet firmly on the sidewalk, but Mikey Brady attempted to follow McNally and fell into a bay of shopping carts. The noise got people's attention, so they ran away before anyone called the police. They did not want to be explaining themselves to the boss.

That morning, Alex crawled into work so hungover that he spent roll call huddling in the bathroom, kneeling against a toilet as his stomach heaved. The B team was up catching cases today, and no one else was near a phone when he got a call, a DOA on West 150th Street. Win one trial, pick up a fresh homicide: the fucked up rhythm of life and death in this place. At the crime scene, uniforms led him to a forty-something Latina woman with two bullet holes in her torso. While Ronnie Huska, the catching precinct detective, examined the DOA with an assistant ME, Alex queasily perambulated in a half-hearted spiral search, scanning the asphalt for evidence, until he had to run out of the secure area. He hid behind a dumpster. Every muscle in his body ached with the twisting sickness. Vomiting hurt his right side. He squatted on the ground, wheezing, spitting up acid.

"You get gang raped last night?" teased James, who appeared around the other side of the dumpster. James had ditched the post-trial celebrations early, but not because he had any more sense. Rather, he was working his way through the medical profession and had a date with a doctor.

"Feels like it." Alex retraced his path into the crime scene. He swam through nauseating treacle. "You get a full medical by your doctor?" The vic's skirt had a jagged tear down the middle. Sexual assault? The angles of the wounds and blood spatter intimated that the shooter had stood in front of her. They found a .38 caliber slug on the asphalt, burrowed into a pile of plastic bags, syringes, and burnt cardboard boxes. No witnesses. Were there ever?

James smirked. "Yeah. Examined everything."

"I got to see Brady fall off a gas station roof. Fucking idiot, but a poor second to getting laid." Alex had not been in a relationship since he joined MNHS; only a couple dates with a CSU detective last fall that went as far as some mediocre sex but nothing more. After being shot, he shied away from serious relationships. He had no idea why one thing had anything to do with the other, but there it was: an active aversion to intimacy because he felt as though something unnamable and incomprehensible had broken inside his body.

"Why the hell was Brady on a gas station roof?" asked James.

"McNally climbed onto it, and Brady was too drunk to remember that McNally's a rock climber, and he's an overweight New York City detective who thinks the Fort George Hill is the fucking Matterhorn."

"Fuckin' amazing. I feel like I missed out."

"You didn't."

Huska found them. "Vic's called Maria De La Corte. Lives on the 300 block of 155th, according to the cards in her wallet. She's got a green card. She's from Mexico."

"Give us your poor, your tired, your hungry, and we'll give them a three-dollar baggie of crack and a case number," sighed James.

They canvassed the apartment blocks with a sight line on the victim, rounding up a dozen annoyed witnesses, who swore on every bible in New York that they had not seen a thing. Two said they heard a shot, but they gave different times. The detectives canvassed Maria De La Corte's building, a narrow low-rise two blocks from the crime scene, and they escorted her husband into the Three-Four Precinct. He was upset. He was also a suspect because family members always are, especially when Patrol has reports of responding to domestic calls at the address. Too nauseous to think straight, Alex veered into the station house bathroom and threw up the coffee he'd drank twenty minutes ago. He rinsed his mouth with cold water, swallowing a tiny amount. Keeping some of it down would help. His eyes were baggy, bloodshot. His face mirrored the color of the grey breeze block walls. *Why the fuck did I drink so much last night?* Well, he had to pay for his sins, first by acting as though he hadn't puked his guts up when he questioned this guy.

Mauricio De La Corte had a limited grasp of English, and Alex, James, and Huska had an equally as limited grasp of Spanish. Huska conscripted a Puerto Rican colleague, Detective Felipe Morales, to translate. De La Corte, in any case, looked dismayed, insisting that he had no idea what happened to his wife or who would want her dead. He added that he had never used a gun in his life.

This was going nowhere.

"You believe him?" Alex asked Morales when they all stepped outside for fresher air. He still felt ill. Throwing up hadn't settled his stomach.

Morales shrugged. "Not really."

"He a piece of shit?"

"Probably."

"Did you try the paraffin thing?" Paraffin tests detected nitrates on a person's hands, deposited when they fired a gun. Unfortunately, they were useless in court because lots of other things leave the same residue, but it was a handy interrogation trick, because perps didn't know that.

"Yeah, it didn't work," Morales said, disappointed.

"We got enough to hold him?"

"No."

They let De La Corte go and asked Patrol to send a sector car around his apartment, keeping eyes on him while they searched for evidence implicating him or someone else. Patrol would cooperate for a few days, but they could not be counted on for more than that, not unless someone higher up the foodchain thought the case worthy of more resources. Unlikely. The justice system was unequal, some victims deemed worthier than others through nothing more than an accident of race, class, geography. Alex winced as he studied the grisly crime scene Polaroids. Sorrow slit through his sternum like a surgeon's knife. Somewhere – maybe in Mexico – somebody cared about her. She was a person with a life, dreams, hopes, sorrows. You could not let yourself forget that.

The autopsy came back with evidence of strangulation, and a tox scan showed traces of nicotine. De La Corte's acquaintances reported that Maria had been trying to leave Mauricio, but they didn't know why. When Alex, Huska, and Marty went around for their third canvass of the building, they discovered that Mauricio had vanished. A neighbor told Marty in Spanish that Mauricio had gone back to Mexico. Too sad to be in New York without his wife. Alex believed the story as much as he believed in alien abductions, but it didn't matter; suspect or not, Mauricio was in the wind, and Maria De La Corte was a statistic, another casualty of the callous city.

By March, everyone agreed that 1989 was shaping up worse than '88, the homicide rate surpassing last year's. Every time Alex looked at the white board, at his name alongside cases, at the numbers scrawled in black and (mostly) red Sharpie, he felt beaten down. Dispirited, he rested his elbows on the desk, and he frowned at his sullen typewriter and the 'five clasped in its ugly teeth. The desk was a crime scene, the paperwork in piles only surmountable by knowing when he last saw something, deducing how deep it might be buried. He moved a coffee cup out of the way of his elbow so he could type. Unwittingly, he glanced inside. A thin layer of mold floated on the remnants of the coffee. How long had that been there? It demoralized him even more, but he lacked the energy to do anything about it.

On the 'five, he wrote that he'd reviewed SAFIS reports on prints from a gun Street Crime had confiscated, hoping for a connection to a fatal armed robbery of a stash house. To no one's surprise, the perp's (or his associates') fingerprints weren't on it. On his next 'five, he wrote that the forensic polynologist had found leaves and pollen from plants which did not grow in Inwood Hill Park. Someone had probably brought the vic there, post-humously. A dump job. No crime scene to work. Alex found himself staring vacantly at the biology experiment developing inside the coffee cup. He hadn't thrown the cup into the trash. Just moved it to one side. Why? He breathed deeply. The justice system seemed like a rusty old car he was forever repairing with cable ties and duct tape, and the thing fell apart no matter how hard he tried. But he was a hardboiled street cop, not a man weakened by suppurating wounds, drowning under his caseload. That would be career suicide. Resolutely, he gathered his cable ties and duct tape like a determined workman. He slogged onwards with forbearance and bleak cynicism. When he sensed those things slipping, he anesthetized the pains in his chest with whisky.

Chapter Twenty

In April, a white female jogger, an investment banker, was viciously beaten and raped in Central Park. The A team caught the case, working alongside Central Park Precinct detectives, and they picked up a group of Black and Latino teenagers who had, allegedly, been rampaging through the park, harassing joggers and cyclists. As if they'd taken the crack on the streets, the press, the politicians, the DAs, and the NYPD brass erupted into a maddened frenzy, with words like "wolfpack" and "wilding" splashed across the papers and bandied around police precincts and the DA's office. Within days of the attack, five teenagers, interrogated by Manhattan North Homicide and precinct detectives, confessed to the rape.

The case dominated every front page and headlined every news show. A bloviating real estate mogul called Donald Trump took out an $85,000 advertising campaign in the New York daily newspapers, demanding the death penalty. Activists protested in front of 100 Centre Street and at the Two-Four station house, declaring that the confessions were coerced, the distorted outcomes of a racist justice system. Counter-protesters screaming for 'law and order' ringed precincts and courthouses with more encampments. The press binged on the hysteria, and reporters were everywhere. A homicide detective couldn't cross the street without reporters mobbing him, even if he had nothing to do with that investigation.

Then, with racial tensions like a live wire, Alex, James, and Vito Indelicata caught a shooting in a nightclub on West 157th Street. The vic was a twenty-five year old bartender who'd been laundering his friends' drug money. Sector cars were tied up with other calls, but Vito was edgy, impatient, and he insisted that waiting around for backup would squander precious time. Besides, he *knew* these people. He'd even attended the birthday of the club owner's kid. That was a reasonable point – Vito spent more time than most detectives nurturing his relationship with the neighborhood.

The three men entered the darkened club with its thudding bass beats and blinding strobe lights. Swiftly, they identified three street players, frisking them for guns, making two collars. Alex's skin prickled, as if sparks singed the hairs on his arms. Hostility, like the heat of an explosive wildfire scorching across hillsides. The detectives were investigating the murder of a Black guy, but Alex doubted that anyone in this club cared. They cared even less that Vito happened to be pals with the club owner. As Alex cuffed a man who'd been packing an illegal Glock, he shivered at the hatred, brutal, uncloaked, inexorable. They hated him because people who looked like him and wore his uniform were catalysts of oppression and brutality; they hated him before he walked into the nightclub, and they hated him more now, and they would carry their hatred malignantly, like a pampered treasure, long after this night ended, and they went home to their families.

On the street outside, a preacher clambered onto the hood of a car and cried out to the men milling around the club doors, exhorting them to remember the five young boys falsely accused of the Central Park rape, and to remember Michael Stewart, the man killed in police custody in '83. The mob pinned all their hatred of the system onto the three detectives, closing in. Both hands out, Alex reversed until his back pressed against Vito and James. James' pale face looked waxen. Vito puffed out his chest, and he warned the crowd that the department would crush them with armored cars and riot officers. He wasn't helping. *We're on your side,* Alex wanted to scream. *Like hell you are,* the eyes in the crowd retorted. High-pitched pops rattled inside his skull. Panic shot through his chest like a .45mm round.

"Fuck, some asshole's shooting," he hissed frantically in James' ear.

"Not *yet,*" James growled back.

The shots weren't real. He couldn't tell what was real anymore. Vito was swearing like an eerie ogre in a dream, incapable of feeling fear. Metal glinted on people's hips. They were carrying. Everyone carried around here. Alex begged the universe for his life, like he had on West 190th Street. His heart flailed. His side hurt. He touched his own gun, but it wouldn't save him. It might set off a riot. The crowd was armed and outnumbered them. They needed backup, yesterday. Why had he listened to Vito scorning it? Why had he believed that? He couldn't keep the panic out of his voice as he radioed in a breathless ten-thirteen.

The mob swirled closer. Vito seized one guy by the front of his jacket, pushing him backwards into a parked car. The man smacked into the car with a jarring concussion that rattled Alex's bones and stopped his heart.

Anger surged through the mob, sucking Alex's insides out in a great, enervating sniff that left him floating fleshless, eyes closed with his hand on his gun. Sweat gushed down his neck in torrents. But his eardrums clanged with the clarion wailing of sirens, thousands of sirens. The cavalry arrived, a dozen squad cars charging down 157th Street, then summarily dispersing the crowd. No one had fired a shot. It had only been five minutes.

"That went fuckin' sideways quickly," gasped James after they'd convinced Patrol that they were unhurt. He sneered at Vito, "'Don't need no fuckin' backup?' Jesus. Where'd that get us? Near-as-dammit to a fuckin' riot or dead."

Vito upturned both his palms and puckered his lips in indignant innocence. "Hey, people are buyin' the propaganda about the Central Park thing. What can I say?"

"What propaganda?"

"That we arrested those boys just 'cause of their race. It's bullshit. We arrested them 'cause they did it."

Alex backed towards his Crown Vic. The pulse in his throat beat against his tie. He loosened the knot. Did Vito, ESU, and Patrol see his nerves? His chest felt tight; he couldn't breathe, and his skin stung with hot pinpricks. The pain seemed impervious to everything; writing DD-5s, rinsing his face and neck in the bathroom sink, ripping fleshy strips from his fingers until they bled.

When their tour ended, the three shaken detectives did the only thing they could – they went to a bar, a divey uptown cop joint called Dirty Seven's on West 172nd. Vito shotgunned a pint in thirty seconds. "People are getting *uppity,*" he kvetched. "Rampaging through Central Park. Raping women. Attacking cops. What's fuckin' next? This is what happens with guys like Koch as mayor."

"Guys like Koch?" responded Alex as he finished off an entire glass of whisky in one swallow. "Jews?"

Vito exploded into a great belly laugh. "I don't mean Jews like you, Lex," and he kept up the laughter without explaining what sort of Jews he meant.

"Everybody's chasing highs and chasing cash. That's what's makin' people crazy," grunted James. "You've seen the crack lines. Plenty of white people from Long Island, New Jersey, Connecticut, wherever, buying this shit. And the people here are just fuckin' capitalists, playing the market. It's like crack Wall Street. Same fuckin' difference. And what else have they got? You seen many other jobs up here that pay decent money?" He looked unnaturally pale, even for an Irish guy, and he was offering an unnaturally sober analysis of the crack epidemic.

"Yeah," snapped Vito. "The NYPD."

James just laughed at him.

Determined to be as drunk as possible, Alex threw back Scotch until it gummed up his memories of the incident on 157th, 190th Street, and his mental processing in general. But James firmly held his elbow, grumbling about ditching 'that arrogant lunatic,' and he was leading Alex out the door. Once outside, James swore, "We're not gonna get a fuckin' cab in this neighborhood, are we?"

"Gypsy cabs?" Alex slurred.

"If I can find a non-fuckin' sketch one."

"I got a number…" Alex dropped his wallet on the sidewalk, but then amidst his drunken fumbling, unearthed the card for a cab driver who lived in the Heights. Alex had solved the murder of the driver's brother a couple years ago. They reeled into a phone booth, somehow found a quarter, punched in the number – which marvelously still worked – and within five minutes, the cabbie had swept them off the street and was hauling ass downtown. The driver made sociable small talk, asking after Alex's daughters. Alex dimly recalled that the cabbie had a teenaged son. Yes, he lived with his mother in the Dominican Republic. The cabbie had sent him away. The Heights was too dangerous. Too many guns, drugs, and trigger-happy cops. The DR wasn't that safe, either, but it was safer.

"Don't want him slinging, arrested, or dead," sighed the cabbie.

"Sorry," Alex said as the cab stopped on Mulberry Street. "That sucks."

"It's okay. Ten bucks. That's half price for you. For what you did for our family."

There were some tatters of community remaining in this city.

After West 157th Street, Alex's nights got worse, ricocheting from vivid dreams, tormented by violence, to interminable insomnia, which was almost preferable to waking up in cold sweats, his heart pounding. Usually, he tuned out the city's omnipresent inequalities because he had to stay sane, but this time, the cold bite of reality swallowed his denial. Maria De La Corte (among many others) had been raped, left for dead, and he had about four patrol officers for his canvass of West 150th Street, while dozens of officers and detectives had roamed Central Park after the jogger was attacked. You labor eternally in anonymity over shot-to-shit drug traffickers and bludgeoned immigrants, and then you get the case that makes it plain who runs New York City and what they want from their police department.

Fuck all of it, he said to himself. No one had been injured on 157th Street, and the Jogger case had nothing to do with him. Why was he thinking about near-misses or sun-sized redballs, which he needed like another hole in his lung? His actual problem was a defense lawyer arguing that the police had conducted an unlawful search, a warrant based on insufficient evidence. Alex had found the vic's stereo in the aforesaid search, and he'd established probable cause with an informant, who said that the perp had tried fencing him the stereo and TV. The CI had bought the TV. The vic's girlfriend had sent Alex a card expressing her gratitude for the hard work of Manhattan North Homicide – him in particular – on the case. Things like that were like oxygen and kept him going.

Unfortunately, the Jogger case ratcheted up the pressure on everyone, especially the supervisors. Corcoran started pulling in detectives with clearance rates under sixty percent for one-on-one 'come to Jesus' meetings. No one likes being read the riot act by the boss, thinking the next stop is out on your ass, a precinct detective in Brooklyn. The detectives put their heads down and hustled. Their boss had made it clear that he didn't give a damn about weak cases. Crystal clear, Alex realized, when he balked at collaring a guy after a Two-Six precinct detective had written up an arrest warrant application based on labwork reporting that the perp had type A blood, along with a million other New Yorkers, and a line-up where the precinct detective had practically pointed to the suspect.

Corcoran said tersely, "What's the problem, Boswell? You have evidence and a warrant."

"He might not be the guy, sir," Alex muttered in a worried voice. His throat withered around the words.

"That's for the courts to sort out, isn't it? That's what they're for."

Alex opened but then closed his mouth. Why bother arguing that the evidence didn't support the arrest when the precinct detective, the Two-Six supervisor, and an ADA said that it did? The boss, who'd been in a mood for weeks, would crucify him with C/Ds for insubordination. A collar was a collar.

A month or so after the Jogger case arrests, Corcoran had to visit his family in Ireland. Consequently, he sent Alex, James, and Bill to a Detective's Endowment Association dinner in his stead. Bill enjoyed these events, relishing the opportunity to schmooze with the brass and union heavies, who he could usually impress with his erudite knowledge of history and philosophy. For their part, Alex and James thought of it as punishment. Their collective clearance rate was dipping, and Corcoran had ordered them to attend the DEA shindig immediately after castigating them about not clearing cases. Neither could imagine anything more tedious than sitting through a formal, self-aggrandizing dinner. James suggested going in drag, and Bill grumpily vetoed.

As expected, the dinner dragged on like a prison sentence. Alex and James played a wine-drinking game with two detectives from Brooklyn North Robbery, who didn't want to be there, either, while Bill pretended that he didn't know them. One of the robbery detectives, Ignacy Kaminski, was a Polish Jew who could reminisce with Alex about growing up on the Lower East Side, while the other, Ruann Harland, was one of the few Black women to have the gold shield and work in a specialized squad. Every time someone pontificating on stage said a Bureau buzzword from a list the four detectives had constructed, they took a drink. Every time someone said the NYPD had "the greatest detectives in the world," they took two drinks. They got drunk very fast.

While the four of them burned through the wine bottles, the president of the DEA rambled through a speech praising the detectives who closed the Jogger case, and Vito Indelicata, who had the highest clearance rate of anyone in the Bureau. He awarded Vito with Detective of the Month.

"That's gonna make the son of a bitch more unbearable," Harland muttered, grimacing like she'd eaten something rotten.

"He's a fuckin' maniac," agreed James, no longer giggling about sex jokes. "Almost got us fuckin' killed."

Like he'd won a Grammy, Vito officiously soliloquized about how much he loved the job, the department, and his brothers in blue, the greatest detectives in the world.

Alex, James, Kaminski, and Harland took two long drinks.

"Don't give a shit about the sisters, except as pussy," murmured Harland sourly. "But we got nothing else."

"Don't think he means it that way," Alex said. Sure, Vito had an ego the size of a planet, and he'd made a reckless call on 157th Street, but you had to admire his genius as a detective. If Alex possessed half of Vito's street smarts, he would not be at this nauseatingly overindulgent dinner.

Harland raised a skeptical eyebrow. "You ever been alone with him in a car?"

"Well, yeah. Lotsa times."

"I guess you wouldn't have to worry about him suddenly reaching down your pants."

"What?" He blinked, confused, and feeling quite drunk. The slabs of roast beef weren't soaking up the wine in his stomach.

"Nevermind." Harland plunged the corkscrew into a fresh bottle of wine.

During the post-dinner reception, Alex muddled through a conversation with Vito, so legless he could scarcely put sentences together. Vito laughed at him. "Boswell, you're a piece of fuckin' work. I love you."

Meanwhile, James stripped down to his boxers, and Bill escorted him into a taxi. Alex's head was spinning. He propped himself against the hotel's glass door and watched James topple into the cab, then surprisingly, Ruann swept him up by the elbow, towing him towards the curb. She waved down another taxi.

Alex opened his eyes, blinking at a strange ceiling. It was pristine and white instead of speckled with mold and shaded yellow with nicotine. The walls were in the wrong place. *Oh, fuck, what have I done?* Drank far too much. His head and stomach whined about his lousy decisions. Arizona-desert heat scorched through his veins. His body ached from dehydration, and his mouth and throat felt scratchy and dry, like he'd swallowed a tumbleweed. More astonishingly, Ruann was spooning him, her stomach and breasts feeling lusciously soft and warm, pressing against his back, and her fingers gently tracing the scars on his right side. This must be her apartment. She didn't live in a dilapidated closet, but rather a quaint one-bed in Flatbush that smelled clean and fresh. His memory had drowned in the booze. How the hell had he ended up in Brooklyn? Did they have sex? He might have had a very drunk conversation with Vito before he left the hotel.

"You were one of the detectives who got shot in October '87," Ruann whispered into his back. "That's a serious wound."

"Yeah, I was a mess," he muttered.

"Looks like the wounds people get in combat. Is it sore?"

"Yeah, sometimes." His consciousness brushed against an indistinct memory – James being mostly naked and Bill being annoyed, complaining about "fucking reprobates." Ruann's hand followed the scar where it crossed his abdomen. Those feathery fingers crawled up to his chest, to his throat, then stroked downwards along the middle of his stomach to his groin. He felt tingling and warmth where she touched his skin, but he wasn't particularly interested in sex. What was wrong with him? An intelligent, beautiful woman seemed turned on, even pleased that he'd come back to her apartment while wasted. And he had no arousal whatsoever.

Uncannily, she stilled her hand, repositioning her body against his and resting her head over his heart. She would hear it thumping fast. Without moving from his chest, she murmured something about having a lot of fun at an otherwise tedious DEA dinner, adding, "Gotta play 'buzzword bingo' at every dull meeting."

How he wished he didn't feel upset and hungover! Making an excuse about why he needed to leave, he got up, at first sitting on the edge of the bed, trying to remember where his keys and firearm had gone, then consciously shutting out the achy stiffness in his side so he wouldn't limp in front of Ruann. His head felt like it had been stuffed with wool. He dressed himself in his rumpled, odorous suit. With more apologies, he scuttled out the door. She acted cool, but worryingly knowing. Like most women. "You know where I live," she said as he descended the stoop. An odious mass, gelatinous and nauseating, thunked inside his skull. His throat was parched. When he encountered a bodega, he ran inside, buying a bottle of water. Godammit, he should ask Ruann out, like a normal person. She was smart, funny, sarcastic, the sort of woman who understood him, being a cop herself. And he'd bolted from her apartment without asking for her phone number! A part of him wanted to hunt it down, call her, go for a real date with dinner and ridiculous cocktails at an overpriced Midtown restaurant, but he feared his weird lack of sexual interest would doom it from the start.

Then Alex suffered an unlucky losing streak: the unsolved De La Corte case heralded a series of whodunits, and his clearance rate sank further. Afraid of another rebuke from his boss, he pursued one of the more promising cases, a DV homicide in the Three-Two where circumstantial evidence and an unlawful traffic stop pointed to a suspect, and he knew that he had a witness or two if he pressured them enough. He bolstered their testimony with a weak-as-shit partial print on a window and a weaker fiber match from clothing worn by half the population of New York, and he made his case without the baseball bat seized in the aforesaid traffic stop. Two days after a judge signed the arrest warrant, Alex collared the perp. The DA could unravel the farkakte mess they found at the Criminal Court arraignment. One name changed from red to black on the white board. That didn't solve his problems, but it helped. A homicide detective lives or dies by his clearance rate.

Chapter Twenty-One

Several months ago, Alex had watched scores of Berliners on TV tearing down the Berlin Wall. The sight stunned him, the divide between East and West Germany one of those immutable facts of geopolitics, at least in his memory, and now it wasn't. The 1980s had ended with Koch leaving Gracie Mansion, a corruption scandal causing him to lose the Democratic nomination to David Dinkins, who in turn beat an aggressive US Attorney, Rudy Giuliani, in the election. Alex mainly worried about how politics might affect him personally, so the mayoral elections concerned him more than the end of the Cold War or anything else. You don't know what any new mayor and his Police Commissioner are going to do to the police department.

Not a lot changed after Dinkins took office, but the winter stuck around forever, as if the city itself saw no point in accommodating spring. On a bitterly cold afternoon in late March, Alex and James started the four-by-twelve with a crime scene in the basement of a building on West 166th, one of those anorexic places squashed between larger structures. It was derelict, a squat for homeless and addicts, and no one cared enough to restore it or move the dope fiends out. Two queasy-looking uniforms, a white man and a Black woman, idled close to the building. The man said, "It's fuckin' *bad*, pal," when the homicide detectives arrived. They looked at him, thinking, he's a rookie, what does he know.

"Were you the first officers?" Alex asked.

The patrolwoman replied, "I was. A dog walker called it in. The dog thought it smelled pretty good and got loose. It ran into this place."

"I guess the dog likes 'em marinated," said the patrolman. "And aged. Like good steak. Just think about sirloin."

His partner scrunched her face in disgust.

"Was it really a dog walker or some dealer taking their pitbull to guard their stash?" Alex asked dryly, glancing around, thinking, even if you lived on this block, why would you walk your dog near this place?

"Looked like a pit cross," said the patrolwoman with a shrug. "But that's all anyone has around here."

"No fuckin' shit," grumbled James. "We noticed." Matt Cohen was on medical leave after a pitbull bit him in the leg during an apartment entry. It had been guarding a substantial stash of cocaine. Dogs were becoming more popular than .38s. They were meaner.

"You have a path into the scene?" queried Alex.

The patrolwoman indicated the crime scene tape delineating a narrow trail through the chossy bricks and rubble strewn around the remains of a door. Alex asked the officers a few more questions about how they initially secured the scene, then he reviewed their memo books, satisfying himself that their entries were complete, accurate. The chain-of-evidence started the moment the first officers showed up. How many cases had Alex seen lost because the sequence of events had been broken by careless or incomplete entries? He assumed that Vito had only asked the officers some superficial questions – if he'd bothered at all. Vito expended no energy on chain-of-evidence and somehow got away with it.

Like a detective from a 1930s crime movie, Vito shadowed the doorway, lounging against chewed-up plywood and scuffed bricks. He wore a knee-length overcoat, and a fat cigar hung out of the side of his mouth. "You got cigars?" he said in a grim tone. "This one ain't been fresh for a long time." James bummed a cigar off Vito, while Alex dabbed Vick's Vap-o-rub around the edges of his nostrils. The menthol stung the membranes inside his nose.

He gulped down a mouthful of whisky from the flask stowed in his pocket. Hair of the dog, combating the light hangover while fortifying his nerves for whatever grisly, decomposing mess awaited. Hesitantly, he followed James through the broken doorway, stepping over rotting joists and planks, and then down a creaky flight of stairs draped with cobwebs. Trip, and you would impale yourself on a nail. The lights were long since dead, and Crime Scene had set up their own.

"Christ on a bike, this dude's been here since fuckin' last month," James gasped, clenching his cigar between his teeth. "Thank fuck it's not summer. Fuckin' marinated and aged, alright."

"Fuck," Alex wheezed, spreading his fingers over his face as his breakfast threatened to crawl up his throat.

The grinning, decomposing DOA was a Latino male, approximately in his twenties, and the basement was once a shooting gallery but probably hadn't been since this guy gave up his mortal coil here. Junkies and crackheads had their limits. Nonetheless, vials and dusty old crack pipes had been scattered around the floor. Fetid mattresses lay heaped against the wall, and rats had eaten holes in the foam. Alex eyeballed the four grimy vials at his feet, then he documented their position in his sketch. Evidence? He lowered himself into a squat and snapped a photo with his pocket Kodak. The vials had identical red caps with prison bars embossed across the top.

"Twenty-Five-to-Life," Vito said with a knowing smile.

"Cute. A dealer who believes in truth in advertising," Alex quipped.

"I know who's sellin' these babies. It's that gang from the corner of One-Eight-Eight and St. Nick's. An offshoot of the Gheri Curls. They been trying to expand, pick up the trade here in the 160s. It's like a Goddamned corporate merger."

"I doubt anyone's fired up here for a while." Alex coughed, disturbing the toxic liquid in his guts. Acid scalded his throat.

At the same time, James, who'd been examining the body with an assistant ME called Jane Schneider, announced, "He's been shot in the head and his leg's broken. Open fracture. That must've fuckin' hurt. Inflicted pre or post mortem?"

"No clue until we get him in and look at the blood vessels," sighed Schneider.

"It's fuckin' grim but I don't *think* there's an exit wound, so bullet's probably still in there. That'd be good news, huh? Looks like he might have ligature marks on the wrist, although in his state, who can fuckin' tell." No one said anything as James continued his investigation. "Shit. He's still got his wallet. No cash in it. Blockbuster card, though. Wonder why no one took that."

"It's not really a home movie kinda crowd here, is it?" Alex said flatly.

"Hah. True." James read the card. "His name's Jose Medina, or Blockbuster thinks it is. How long do you reckon he's been dead, based on the decomp?"

"Roughly three or four weeks if he was outside the whole time. Maybe closer to two if he was kept warm," replied the ME, shrugging ambivalently.

Alex felt as though the steel wires inside his chest had snapped. A classic whodunit – a DOA decomposing in a shooting gallery, utterly perfect because any witnesses had mutated their brains into receptacles for heroin and crack, and forensics looked like an absurd longshot, a fat Shetland pony winning the Preakness.

"Corcoran's gonna transfer me 'cause I keep getting shitbag cases I can't solve," he complained.

"Maybe the entomologists'll have some idea of time of death," James reflected. "No one else is gonna have a fuckin' clue. This guy's like Times Square for maggots."

"We got lucky with the Blockbuster card," stated Vito confidently. "It's gonna go down. We got his name without fucking around with dentals or prints. If he's got anything to do with the vials, it'll go down. I *know* this gang. C'mon, Lex. Take a ride with me, and we'll go talk to some wits."

"We gotta process this scene and canvass the block," Alex argued, applying more Vick's to his nose. The sweet, sickly smell of death embedded itself inside his nostrils. It polluted his mouth, saturating the lining of his throat and his esophagus. "I haven't even got my head around it or talked to the dog walker, or whatever he is, who called it in."

"Hurley's got it, don't you?"

"Sure, whatever," James responded, squatting on the floor and recoiling. "Oh, man. A human shit. Nice. Exhibit A, right here."

"See, he's got it." Vito cut off Alex's protests by ushering him up the stairs, through the nail-spiked rubble, pushing him into the passenger seat of the grey Crown Vic, and then starting the car. He grinned with boyish joy as he cranked up the volume on a country music station. Willie Nelson deafened them as they breezed past austere low-rises and gaudy pre-war townhouses to St. Nicholas Avenue. The salsa music on someone's boombox shook the air outside of the car. People sat on stoops, schmoozing, smoking, drinking out of paper bags. Around 188th, Vito slowed the car, craning his neck from side to side, as though searching for someone.

"What the hell are we doing?" Alex twisted the volume knob. His eardrums felt like they were bleeding.

"My people know *everything* that goes down in this neighborhood," Vito replied.

"'Your people?'" Alex snorted.

"I got eyes and ears, Lex. Trust me?"

"We haven't even verified the ID or cause of death or anything."

"Lex, you need this case down. So do I. Believe me, I got ways. You trust me?"

"Yeah." Did he, after the proto-riot on West 157th Street?

"You know, this job ain't about following a bunch of set protocols and procedures and hope, miraculously, they turn up evidence. Sometimes, you gotta think *laterally*. Like outside the box. You hear me?"

"We're not even sure who he is. I've barely looked at the scene. Fuck knows if the Blockbuster card has his real name. We haven't run him-"

"If he's a player, people will *know* who he is."

The older detective drove with strength and purpose. Undeniably, he had one of the best clearance rates of any detective in uptown Manhattan. Alex trapped the soft flesh on his lip between his front teeth. If Vito swept him along and closed a stone whodunit with whatever investigative magic he wielded, then it might save his ass.

"Jesus, you smell like a fuckin' mint factory," Vito commented, sniffing. "You ever thought about usin' cigars?"

"They give me a sore throat."

"That's very Jewish, isn't it?" said Vito in a mischievous voice.

"Huh?" Alex wrinkled his eyes, missing the connection.

"You're always bitching about some kinda ache or pain. That's what Jews do, isn't it?"

"Fuck's sake, Vito. I *was* shot in the chest," Alex snapped, puffing like he'd taken a fist to the gut. He should be running his crime scene. James could run it as well as anyone, but the case started there. Not here. Suddenly, he detested Vito for hauling him twenty blocks uptown, and he detested himself for acquiescing. Whatever Vito said, they weren't investigating anything while driving alongside low-rises with oval holes through which bricks showed, pipes stapled to old stonework, and decaying sidewalks that made you feel like you walked over a body.

They circled the block. A shiny Crown Vic screamed 'cop' to everyone who saw it, so the slingers and their crews withdrew into the alleys and apartments. Noticing something, Vito punched the brakes and jerked the car to the curb. Alex felt his stomach lurch. His nostrils burned from the Vick's.

Vito stuck his head out of the car window. "Hey, Loretta."

He made eye contact with a petite Black woman, who tossed a wary glanced over her shoulder, then scampered into their back seat.

"Detective Vito, you can't come here like this. People will see," she said.

"It's fine, it's fine," Vito replied. "You gotta help me with something."

Alex wrenched his body around, fighting the seatbelt cutting into his belly. He eyed the woman behind him. Mid-thirties, with short hair and layers of glossy make-up buffering widened, haunted eyes. An addict, as hollow as a dead tree. *Loretta.* Where had he heard that moniker before? Almost three years ago, returning to work after being shot, Corcoran telling him that Vito had found an eyewitness for the Serrachia case, a prostitute called 'Loretta.' What the hell were they doing here? What would a crackhead hooker know about the inner workings of someone's drug crew, or a body decomposing in a shooting gallery on West 166ᵗʰ?

"I can help you if you help me," she said.

Vito replied amicably, "You know I always will."

"What do you wanna know?"

"Jose Medina. You know him? Lex, hand her this."

A Polaroid photo of the dead man's face. Unconvinced, Alex handed it to their quivery passenger.

The prostitute scanned the photo, not in the least bit bothered that Medina looked very dead. "Yeah, Jose. He's on this corner. 188ᵗʰ and St. Nick's. He's with Los Esqueletos. Well, he was."

"That's what the gang – that Gheri Curls offshoot – who's operating on the next corner is calling themselves," Vito explained to Alex. Then to Loretta he said, "As you can see, he ain't feelin' so hot. Shot in the head. You know about that?"

"Should I?" she said.

"Yeah. I think so, Lo. Anyone taking care of business? It's a hit. Definitely a hit. Anyone big?"

Definitely? Alex gagged on the word, silenced by a look from Vito. They'd examined the body for all of five minutes! It wasn't *definitely* anything.

Vacant lots surrounded by rusty wire and staring windows slid alongside the car as Vito orbited the block, tapping his fingers to the music on the radio. Loretta seemed to contemplate the lyrics, which lamented a missing girl, or a truck, or both. When the song ended and asinine talk radio resumed, she said, "You want someone big?"

"I want whatever you gotta tell me," Vito answered, winking.

"I got you." Loretta paused and ducked her head as a dark-colored Buick Park Avenue swooshed around their car.

"No one can see in the back, honey," Vito said. "The windows are tinted. It's a police car."

"Yes, of course they are." She nervously touched up her lipstick. "Guillermo Quixano."

Vito sniffed, then dramatically exhaled. "That son of a bitch? You sure, Lo?"

"Oh, yeah."

"Lex, he's like a big-time dealer in this neighborhood. I think he's got direct connections to the Colombian and Dominican traffickers down south. You've heard of him."

Alex shook his head. He was too busy dealing with the bodies piling up at the bottom of the drug trade to give a shit about the people at the top, unless he could link them to any of those bodies. They were usually too smart for that.

"Narc have been after him for months, years, but he's good. Slippery."

"He shot him himself," Loretta said with more confidence. The Buick hadn't come back. "I saw it. On 188th and Wadsworth. I was waitin' for a client. Anyway, they had a fight, like yellin' and all, then Guillermo pulls out this big gun and bam. Jose just falls over."

"That's great, Loretta, that's great. 188th and Wadsworth?"

"Yeah."

They drove uptown for about five blocks. Vito stopped the car on a quiet block, between a bakery and a laundromat, then he awkwardly contorted his large frame to reach for something under the driver's seat. Freeing it necessitated determined wiggling. A little breathless, he handed Loretta a small brown paper bag. She snatched it from his hand and reached inside, scooping out a plastic baggie filled with pale grey rocks.

"This shit good?" she asked. "Where'd it come from?"

"You know I'm not gonna tell you that, honey," Vito said. "But trust me, it's good."

Crack. Vito had just handed a witness crack. In a police car. Alex felt like he'd stuck his hand into a fuse box. Familiar blocks, familiar types of people had become surreal, unfamiliar and disturbing. Stress congealed the blood around his bowels. Yeah, Vito played by his own rules, with a flippant disregard for the Patrol Guide, *Practical Homicide Investigation,* and most police SOPs, a lovable rogue, the cowboy detective of every TV trope, but this was something else. This approached Knapp Commission-level shit.

"You gotta be prepared to come to the precinct, make a statement," Vito told Loretta.

"I gotta feed my kids," she said. Underneath the layers of glossy eye makeup, she looked worn out. "And trickin's more and more dangerous. The pimps are worse. The johns are worse. There's AIDS. I got to figure out something. You payin'?"

"Yeah, sweetheart. Don't I always? But you also gotta say that in court, to an ADA, you hear."

She sighed, as if she'd forgotten the small print, only to be reminded of it. "I guess that's the deal."

"That's the deal. We good?"

216

"We good. Can I go?" She radiated the anxiety of an addict desperate to fire up.

"Of course!" Vito held out both palms, and she flitted out of the car, slamming the door. For a beat, Vito intently watched her as she darted around the corner. "See, Lex, it's down!"

"Why the fuck are you running around with crack in the car?" Alex squawked in a strangled voice. "Giving it to witnesses! You realize you could be in serious shit." He didn't want to know where or how Vito got the drugs. He'd heard rumors about drug-running schemes and corruption in the 30th Precinct, but like everyone else, he tacitly avoided knowing too much.

"It ain't felony weight, and it don't matter. How am I gonna get in shit? Not unless you say something, which you ain't gonna do, right?"

No, he wasn't going to report Vito to his supervisors or to IA. The precinct detective had too much juice, too many political connections, and Alex had no evidence but his own word. Snitching would bite him in the ass. "How the hell can you believe her?" He slumped against the door, feeling his lungs deflating like a blown tire.

"She's good. She always comes through for me. And when have I ever let you down? You know we're a team."

"You fed her information and bribed her with crack and money. She'd fucking say anything. Name anybody you wanted. I mean, what are the chances she *saw* this guy shoot our vic. Give me a break. I mean, you said he's a serious dealer, a player. You don't think he'd hire a guy? What dealer who knows how to not get caught is gonna be stupid enough to shoot someone in front of witnesses like that? Or leave a video rental card that can ID the body? That doesn't scream 'professional job,' does it?"

Vito's eyeballs rolled backwards. "*A*-lex," he breathed out. "Come on. Chill, man. Your informants talk to you outta the goodness of their hearts?"

Obviously not. He gave them twenty or thirty bucks or a deal with the DA any time they gave him information.

"You ain't usin' Upper West Side dentists, I imagine. You know what CIs are gonna do with the money you give 'em. Me, I like bein' straight. Makes them play straight. I know what they want, they know what I want. Everyone's happy."

There was a certain amount of truth to that. Instead of arguing, Alex observed flatly, "You'll need more than an informant with a bad crack habit."

"Duh. But we got a name. A lead. And we know Medina hung around Los Esqueletos." Vito turned downtown, back to the crime scene at West 166th. "Don't worry about it. I got this, Lex," he grinned as he dropped Alex off beside sagging strands of crime scene tape.

They left West 166th behind, Alex and James chasing the murder into the night, working the case the way they wanted to work it. James had canvassed the block around 166th. Not one soul knew about the body in a shooting gallery. "Like there's a surprise," James sighed. He'd run Medina's name through CARS, NCIC, and DCJS, discovering a novel of a rap sheet, convictions for everything from criminal nuisance, possession, loitering, to public lewdness. James being James, he'd contacted the arresting officer on the public lewdness case. Apparently, Medina had whipped it out on the subway, showing off to a friend who accused him of having a small penis. Medina wanted to prove it wasn't.

"What a guy," Alex said.

The detectives drove to the address given on Medina's criminal history, 417 West 189th, and they banged on doors, searching for slivers of civic responsibility, a wisp of cooperation. They found neither. If Loretta's statement contained even a scrap of truth, that Medina crossed a dealer, and the dealer made a point that he was a force to be reckoned with, the people on that block weren't going to risk their necks.

With nothing resembling a witness, they returned to the paper trail. The DOA's prints had a hit in SAFIS, corroborating the Blockbuster card, and they spent several days tracking down the contacts on Medina's old OLBS sheets. His mother had left New York, moving to Philly, while he had a brother serving time for crack dealing and a sister teaching high school math in Albany. Neither the mother nor the sister wanted anything to do with him, nor were they too sorry he was dead. The brother, Carlos Medina, was incarcerated in Sing Sing. They arranged a prison visit.

The night before their road trip upstate, Alex received a call at his apartment. Ruann Harland. As soon as she identified herself, blood rushed to his coronary artery, and he almost dropped the phone. He had never expected to hear from her again.

"Why didn't you call me?" she asked. "I kept thinking about you."

"I dunno. I didn't have your number." God, what a pathetic excuse.

"You're a detective. You can get my number. I got yours easy enough."

"I didn't wanna be a jerk or act like a stalker."

"Well, you're a gentleman." Her voice sounded droll. "What are you doing tonight?"

As he was doing nothing, she drove to Chinatown. He felt self-conscious about his cooking, insisting, "I can grill a burger. That's it," and they went out to dinner in a restaurant underneath a Persian rug shop, where the food could have been from Beijing, and they were the only non-Asian people in the room. Afterwards, they returned to his place. He liked her. They shared a sense of humor, bleak and sardonic, and he laughed until his side hurt when she reminded him of James stripping at that DEA dinner. Yet he felt like a frayed rope, stretched until he was one strand away from breaking down. His breathing was strained. His pulse thumped in his ears. The occasional siren outside sounded like the sirens on 190th Street. But Ruann kissed the side of his neck and worked her way over his collarbones, across his chest. These moods came sometimes, like a fog in the night, and he preferred to be unconscious, but with Ruann here, he could not hide underneath the covers or the bottle, so he rode through it, relatively sober. The sex was more memorable than last time, but his body went through the motions. Ruann drifted off with her head on his belly, and he lay awake for hours watching time creep past on the bedside clock. His muscles ached with the effort of keeping them still.

When the detectives set off for Ossining the next morning, Alex felt spacey and nauseated. His sleep-deprived body was unprepared for the interstate and James' driving. The Irish detective barreled along I-87, aiming to beat his previous record of forty-five minutes. While James wove through Westchester traffic like a lunatic, Alex floated through half-asleep dreams. Ruann seemed really into him but seeking something beyond friends-with-benefits. That scared the hell out of him. A serious relationship! Was he ready? He wrenched his cloudy eyes open, woozily reading the signs on the highway to orient himself.

Sing Sing overlooked the Hudson, that vast expanse of grey water dotted with small green islands and boats, and the hazy, forested hills of New Jersey marching along the banks on the other side. They parked under the prison's hulking concrete walls crowned with fangs of razor wire and the watchtowers with sheer sides and black, staring eyes jutting out above the walls. Since no one who could afford otherwise lived near a maximum-security prison, the neighborhood surrounding the place was a mournful trailer park, rammed with tatty mobile homes and lines of ramshackle houses with weedy, overgrown lawns.

The detectives passed through layers of security. Doors clanged and moaned, a noise like dying cattle. The guards, solemn and humorless, stripped Alex and James with their eyes.

James whispered, "You can smell the gang rape in the air."

"Yeah." Whenever he visited a prison, Alex always felt as if some spirit of evil vigilance lurked beyond the gates.

They met Carlos Medina in the visitor's room, where the detectives sat on one side of a glass wall, and Medina leered at them from the other side with an expression somewhere between contempt and indifference. A guard hovered menacingly nearby.

"Your brother, Jose, he's dead," Alex said. No need to waste energy building rapport with this guy. He'd been willing to meet two detectives without his lawyer present, which meant he was either bored or talkative, and it wasn't like he had anywhere to go.

Medina released a world-weary sigh. His hard-man façade crumbled. "There's a surprise."

"Why do you say that?"

"Damn him." Medina inhaled brusquely. Pain sparked across his dark brown eyes. Just as swiftly, he composed himself. "Jose was stupid. Couldn't handle himself. Wanted to be a big shot, but you gotta be smart to be a big shot."

"What does that mean?"

"He wasn't smart."

"In what way wasn't he smart?" Alex rolled up his shirtsleeves to his elbows and folded both his hands on the table.

"He was always trying to push people around, show off, had all these schemes, like bullshit get-rich-quick schemes, said he never had enough money, but, you know, stupid-like, no Goddamned sense. He was never gonna get rich."

"You know anything about these 'schemes?'"

"They were bullshit. Fantasy. Like stealing a painting from the Met and holding it ransom. Selling fraudulent insurance to people. Pretending to be a corrupt DEA agent and scamming Colombian traffickers out of millions. He had crazy ideas from watching too many movies. He wasn't gonna *actually* do any of that."

"But he sold drugs." Alex archly moved one eyebrow.

"Anyone can sell drugs," Medina said scathingly. "Don't have to be a genius to get your hands on some gear in Washington Heights, but you gotta have *some* street smarts to make money at it and not get killed."

"Show off." James scratched his chin. "You know, he was convicted of public lewdness for whipping out his dick on a B train 'cause some dude was making, uh, pejorative comments regarding its size."

Medina showed the whites of his eyes, a cynical tide rolling across his face. "I didn't know, but it sounds like something Jose would do."

"Does getting himself hit by pissing off a dealer sound like something he would do?" Alex prodded.

"Yeah, I said."

"Any dealers in particular?"

Medina thrust his bottom lip forward. "I been in *here* for the past two years, man. How am I supposed to know?"

"Who did he hang out with before you came here?"

"Nobody that matters. They all dead or in prison. He'd have a new crew now."

"You don't know who he coulda pissed off?"

"Not a clue, Detective."

"He ever talk to you?"

"No. Haven't heard from him since I been inside. Didn't talk much outside, either. Not about business anyway."

"Do you know a hooker calling herself Loretta?" Alex asked, fishing. "Someone who Jose might've hung around?"

"I wish I knew some hookers in here," snorted Medina. "But no, I said, I don't know who he hung with."

"Not even street names or maybe the name of a gang? Los Esqueletos? Do you know them?"

The prisoner tightened his eyes and tipped his upper body towards the glass. His guard scowled at him. "Los Esqueletos? If he was with them, *no one's* gonna talk unless they've got a death wish."

"We can put you in protective custody."

"The fuck you can. It would have to be protective custody in another *state*. Like Arizona. But man. If I could help you and get outta here sooner, you don't think I would? I been studying here. When I get out, I'm going to school. Learning a trade. But, listen. I got a great George Bush impression." Putting on an exaggerated white Texan accent, Medina nasally drawled, "I'm President of the United States, and I'm not going to eat any more broccoli."

A dead end. Either Medina knew nothing, or he knew he would be dead if he said anything. After the guards escorted them out of the prison, the detectives tiredly unlocked their car, then ate the sandwiches they'd bought at a gas station *en route*.

"Dammit," growled James, wiping mayonnaise off his lips. "If we were casting for *Saturday Night Live,* that guy would be useful. Who the hell is Loretta?"

"Oh, just some CI of Vito's," Alex answered dismissively, swallowing the last bites of his roast beef.

On their return to the MNHS office, Alex called two of his own CIs and other people named on Medina's OLBS sheets, begging for 'word on the street' about the murder or any intel on Jose Medina. His contacts had bupkes. The case struck an impervious wall, another whodunit but for Vito's dubious informant.

As he re-organized Medina's file, the phone uttered a shrill ring. Hopeful, he lunged for it, pleading with all his heart for it to be the ME or another informant with some evidence.

"Hi, Alex," said Ruann.

Taken by surprise, he shuddered at the jolt inside his chest. Both his hands quivered, sweating, and he wiped his left one against his leg. It hadn't gone *that* well last night, had it?

It plainly had, because Ruann wanted to see him again. He said he was too tired to schlep to Flatbush, so she took a cab to Chinatown and cooked a lasagna on his scruffy 1970s stove, all the while teasing him about his hopeless kitchen. One pot, one frying pan, a half-melted spatula, half a dozen forks and knives. "Roommate?" she asked, pointing at the roach skittering down the wall.

"I've been trying to get rid of them," he muttered in a sheepish tone.

"The saddest bach pad in the world," she laughed. She kissed him on the cheek as she said it, which made it less insulting, then she talked to him for a while about work – clearing a serial bank robbery case that had something to do with the Russian Mob. Inexplicably, that led into another story about a hiking trip upstate.

Although he pretended to listen, he got lost within a miasma of other worries. After three years, he thought he knew Vito, but he sensed a shift in their relationship, a line crossed, a glimpse of a dark shadow. Maybe he still knew Vito, and the shadow only existed in his head, tangling with his sensibilities, his ethics, while in the wider world of criminal justice, no one gave a shit. Surely Vito wasn't selling or using the drugs himself. He had given his CI less than 500mg, a class A misdemeanor. Vito had made a valid point when he said all cops pay CIs, and they're probably going to buy drugs or gamble or do something that was unsavory or illegal. And his gut instincts were formidable, better than Alex's. It would have taken Alex days of methodical investigation to conclusively connect Medina to those crack vials and Los Esqueletos. Vito just knew.

"I might be outta Homicide," he said. It had jumped into his head.

"You're a great detective. I doubt it." Ruann squeezed his forearm.

"My clearance rate sucks. Ever since the Jogger case, my L-T's coming down on detectives who can't clear cases. I just caught one that's gonna screw me over. DOA in a basement shooting gallery. And he'd been there for a while. Like fuck is there gonna be any evidence."

"Bad luck isn't like a disciplinary infraction. They can't downgrade you or punish you 'cause you get a string of whodunits. You know it doesn't work like that."

Ruann was kneading the sinew where his neck met his shoulder, squishing knots against the bone. She dug into the achy trigger points bunched around his lower back and pelvis, then lightly worked the sensitive skin on his scar, pushing at the broken tissue underneath, which hurt, and he bit into his tongue and tightened his muscles. Endorphins flooded his body, tingling along his spine, out to his limbs. He shouldn't tell her that he feared a serious relationship. This felt too good. If he had any sense, he would keep his mouth shut and see where it went.

Chapter Twenty-Two

At 0200 hours, Alex plodded up the stairs in the Canal Street subway station. He limped a little, the wound biting. At department physicals, entries with ESU, or anywhere else that mattered, he could look fit and sound. Anywhere colleagues might judge him. They couldn't know how much it hurt. But here, late at night, off duty and tired, he dragged his right leg to lessen the pain in his side.

He inhaled that familiar subway cocktail, a nightclub toilet with overtones of diesel. Near the top of the stairs, something moved. Alex slowed his ascent, narrowing his eyes at the murky tunnel. *Other people use the subway at 0200, not just me,* he thought ruefully. More footsteps, and a figure sprang out of the shadows. It hurtled towards him. His heart seized up. His police-trained eyes registered a white male, around 5'10. The son of a bitch brandished a boxcutter. Alex spun half-round and leapt sideways. His hand darted towards his gun, but the perp swung the blade towards his neck. He ducked, at the same time lunging for the man's arm. The perp hadn't expected that; he seemed stunned when Alex caught him, freezing, eyes widening. Alex used all his weight to torque the man's elbow, so the fingers released, and the boxcutter clattered onto the stairs. The perp howled, writhing with the super-human strength of someone jacked up on a lot of cocaine. He smashed Alex's mouth with his fist. Alex staggered, seeing lights, tasting blood. For a moment, he lost his grip. The assailant twisted free and raced up the stairs. Gasping, Alex ran after him, drawing his Ruger, yelling, "Police, stop!" But the perp, fitter and faster and on more stimulants, vanished around the corner.

No point in a footchase. Even without the holes in his side, he would never catch that shitbird. His overtaxed lungs burned at every breath, but he kicked his brain into gear. He rammed the gun into its holster, then yanked on latex gloves. Luckily, he always had a pair stashed somewhere. He retrieved the boxcutter and loped up the remaining stairs. The street was swarming with people, happily oblivious to the altercation underground. An attempted mugging? A lone white guy, young, walking with a limp, slightly overweight – yeah, he looked like a soft target. He bumped his mouth with the back of his hand. Blood trickled from a cut on the inside of his upper lip. It hurt like he'd cracked a tooth. He hoped not. Cold and shaky, the shock kicking in, he tottered towards his apartment, then he scrambled to safety inside. His right arm felt stiff and damp. Interesting. He expected the throbbing in his side, but his arm was novel. He looked at it and saw blood spurting from a four-inch wound in his shoulder. "Godammit," he sputtered. The man had stabbed him in the struggle, but adrenaline had made him insensate to pain. *This fucking city. This fucking neighborhood.* To think he occasionally let Catherine bring the girls to this shithole! He spread his fingers over his chest, feeling his heart while he called the Fifth Precinct station house and reported a ten-twenty-four W, an assault with a weapon.

His vague civic duty done, he checked himself over in the bathroom. His lip was swollen, but it had stopped bleeding. Pain sliced through his right shoulder. And his side hurt like he had a scythe hooked under his ribs. He tried staunching the shoulder wound with paper towels, burning through a quarter of a roll, all he had, so he switched to toilet paper, which soaked through faster, disintegrating into bloody shreds. Should he call Ruann? Fuck that. She would be upset and schlep here from Flatbush, even at the unconstitutional hour. But he felt too shaken for intimacy. Whisky and sleep, in that order – all he wanted.

A knock rattled the door. He startled, leaping to his feet. A hand on his gun, he squinted through the peephole and saw two patrolmen at the door, a middle-aged Black cop and a twenty-something Asian cop. Oh, shit, he had called them. He let them in. Their tags identified them as PO Karim and PO Chin. They knew who Alex was because Chin said, "Detective Boswell," and shook his hand, seemingly in awe of him, one of the most elite investigators in New York. But he wasn't feeling very elite. His arm and side hurt, his adrenaline had ebbed into exhaustion, and he'd been the victim of an attempted mugging, like a million other schmucks in this city who weren't homicide detectives.

"You didn't try to detain him?" asked Karim after Alex had described the incident.

Alex sighed deeply. "With what? Duct tape? I don't keep cuffs on me when I'm off-duty. It all happened in seconds. I drew my service weapon, but he ran away."

"What do you think he wanted?"

"I dunno. My wallet?"

"Okay. We need to take photos of your injuries. You know, on the off-chance someone finds him and the DA presses assault charges."

Nodding in weary consent, Alex let them photograph his puffed-up lip with their Polaroid. He stripped off his jacket and shirt, presenting the wound on his shoulder.

Their eyes bugged out of their skulls, and they sucked in audible inhalations. Fretfully, he glanced at the wound. Blood dribbled from its torn, fleshy lips, like a stream in a drought. *Jesus, it's not that bad,* he thought. Just a cut through the first layer or two of muscle.

"That's a hell of a scar," commented Karim.

They weren't looking at his shoulder. Alex acted nonchalant, but blood warmed his cheeks. His hand mechanically covered the old wound. "Gunshot. It's from a few years ago."

"What happened?"

"My partner and I were shot by a couple skels when we were walking down the street in the Heights."

"Oh." Chin's mouth fell open. "A couple homicide detectives were shot in '87. That was you."

"Yeah." Everyone knew about the shooting.

"I remember hearing your partner was paralyzed."

"Yeah."

"God, that's fucking terrible. This city, huh?"

"Yeah," Alex said impatiently. It wasn't something he wanted to remember, or be reminded of, certainly not when some asshole had attacked him in the subway station. Hiding his limp, he recovered his blood-stained shirt and handed the patrolmen the boxcutter, wrapped in cellophane.

"You sure you're all right?" Chin asked. "Your hands…"

Alex frowned at his hands, which shook with a tremor too violent and obvious to hide. "I'm fine. It's just adrenaline."

The two officers returned to their beat. Feeling chills embedding themselves inside his bones, Alex locked his door, double-checking it, then he broke an ice cube free from the tray in his freezer and pushed it into his lip. His shoulder had stiffened; even small movements hurt. He distracted himself with the pile of mail: a credit card bill, a DEA newsletter, a letter from the DEA health insurance company. The doctors wanted him in for yearly CT scans and x-rays of his lung, and the insurance company objected to paying for it. *Fuck you too*, he thought, fed up with fighting these people, and he opened the newsletter instead. He read a blurb declaring that Vito Indelicata had been named DEA welfare officer for Manhattan North. Vito? Welfare officer? Then he heard a cracking noise, followed by a loud thump that pulsed through the walls like an earthquake. It cut the power to his heart. Blinking rapidly, he palmed his chest. He shoved his other hand against his forehead and pushed his fingers through his hair. Part of his ceiling now sat next to the sink, the dust rising around a moldy pile of ragged, damp plasterboard and rubble. Above him, beams and electrical wires exposed themselves like a ribcage with a terrible wound.

"Who the *fuck* did I piss off?" he cried to the empty apartment. "You've got to be fucking kidding. What the fuck am I supposed to do about this at four in the Goddamned morning?"

That malevolent, vengeful Old Testament God he'd never believed in seemed to have it in for him. He filled a tumbler from the Jameson bottle and downed all of it, along with a couple ibuprofens. Chest heaving, he fell into the bed, uncaring of plaster flakes clinging to his hair and clothes. He felt woozy, like he'd been hit in the head, and the tiny apartment spun when he shut his eyes. *Please, don't spin,* he insisted, afraid it would make him puke.

Over the next week, Alex crammed all of his possessions into a rented van and stored things with any friend who had space. As he lived in New York, he had no chance of finding an affordable apartment, at the spur of the moment, in a place that wasn't a hole. But he had to escape this apartment. His pulse jumped into overdrive when he walked from the Canal Street subway. He sweated every movement in his peripheral vision. He was hypervigilant to every sound. He heard the gunshots more often. His insomnia became a monster that sat on his chest every night, breathing its sour breath into his face. The shoulder wound was deeper than he'd first believed, but he gritted his teeth and ate painkillers. And capping off very real injury with an insult, his apartment had a hole in the ceiling the size of a VW Beetle. The landlord told him to pay for the repairs, but he refused, ending his tenancy by posting his keys. Let that motherfucker come after him for leaving before the lease ended. He knew plenty of lawyers.

Most of his stuff ended up spread through the Homicide squad, while a few extraneous things moved in with an Academy buddy and a friend from the Tenth squad. He'd asked Fred Symington for help and felt a sharp sting inside his chest when Fred apologized: no way, because Celia was pregnant with their second kid, and Fred was working his ass off, hoping for a transfer into a specialized squad. Fred raising a family and buying an apartment – adult things, while Alex hadn't moved on from the dysfunction of his twenties, like living in one rented slum after another. Mostly, he imposed on James, sleeping on James' sofa in his Hell's Kitchen one-bed across the street from a sex shop and a self-storage place, a five-minute walk from a strip where you could find a prostitute and borrow money from the Mafia loan shark next door.

Like he'd anticipated, Ruann freaked out when he told her about the mugging. He had to explain his puffy lip, his injured shoulder, and his sudden relocation to James' living room somehow. She rebuked him for not calling her that night and for his impulsive decision to vacate the Mulberry Street apartment. She seemed upset, querying, "What does this relationship mean to you?" Because he hadn't asked for her help with moving or with finding a new place to live. Apparently, that meant he wasn't serious about the relationship. Well, he wasn't, but she was still reading too much into his lousy life management skills. Nonetheless, she offered to cook dinner at her place. Although pain crackled like broken power lines through his side and right arm, he schlepped to Brooklyn, using the subway. He couldn't afford to stay off that horse. While Ruann cooked, he sat on the sofa, sucking on a cold beer, feeling guilty for upsetting her and wishing he had gone to the pub with James and Marty, who were watching a football game. Alex didn't like football but at least that would be fun and drunk. This was neither.

They started dinner in silence. Ruann prodded the marinated chicken around her plate. After a while, she observed, "You said this is the first real food you've had in a week?"

"Yeah. I don't even have a kitchen anymore."

"What? Doesn't James?"

"In a manner of speaking."

"What does that mean?"

"He's got a microwave and a hot plate. The oven worked last year, but it doesn't now. The fridge is also dead." He cleared tightness from his throat as he sipped at the Budweiser.

"Why doesn't James get a guy in to fix it? Or buy a new fucking fridge?"

"His landlord's an asshole and doesn't like spending money, and James can't be fucked chasing it up."

"I know ovens are a pain, but you can get a secondhand fridge for like thirty bucks."

"James lives mostly on take-out anyway." If you knew James, you wouldn't use logic or common sense to question his lifestyle.

"Jesus Christ," Ruann sighed. "One of the city's top investigative units, living worse than students."

"Hey, at least the ceiling hasn't fallen in."

"You had a leak there for months!" She sounded exasperated. "Why didn't you follow up with your landlord?"

Like he gave a damn, Alex thought, rolling his eyes, which seemed to annoy her. The city let landlords get away with maintenance that was just shy of murder.

Ruann was watching him awkwardly handling the fork with his left hand. "You should see a doctor about your shoulder."

"What are they gonna do?" he replied, chewing on the last mouthful of chicken. The lump slid down his throat. ERs transported him back in time to the shooting. When working, he could take refuge in a different place in his head, but if he went as a patient, he had nowhere to run. "It wasn't that deep. I've been taking ibuprofen."

"It could be infected."

"It's fine."

"What about your side? You've been limping more. You always limp when you're tired, or when it's bothering you more than you can cover up."

Fuck, so she'd noticed. That meant other people had as well. "That is what it is," he snapped angrily. "I've got my boss giving me crap about my clearance rate again, now you—"

"Maybe if you didn't sleep on James Hurley's sofa and took better care of yourself, you'd be in a better headspace to clear cases."

"Oh, give me a fucking break, Ruann. If the homicide rate in this city wasn't in double figures every week, I'd be in a 'better headspace.' But I *am* tired. I don't need you telling me what to do. It's like talking to my mother. I'm gonna go back to James' tonight." His breathing felt quick, flustered, and he searched the sofa for his keys, wallet, and raincoat.

"Alex, wait. I'm sorry." Ruann jumped towards him and grabbed his elbow. "I know you're stressed. But calm down. Okay? I didn't mean to upset you."

"I'm not upset," he lied. "I just need some space."

"You're being reactive. You are upset. You're burned out. I hear you. Have you ever thought about transferring to a different unit?"

He stared without blinking, and a deep furrow creased his forehead. "Transferring? No. Why the fuck would I do that? Homicide needs, *needs,* experienced death investigators, and I'm getting there, maybe... I dunno. I'm exhausted and beat up. And you're right. My side's not been good. I shouldn't have come out tonight. It's been a shitty week."

"Alex, I know. I'm sorry. Please, don't storm out like this. I have wine. Just… sit down and let's have a glass of wine."

"My head's in the wrong place. *I'm* sorry." Pain whipped him forwards; he unlocked the deadbolt, then jogged down the stoop as Ruann blinked back tears, the whites of her eyes turning red. Fuck it, he had committed to leaving now. Rain fell in his eyes and soaked his legs and shoulders. A voice in his head urged him to turn around and not act like a douchebag, but he limped onwards until he boarded a Manhattan-bound B train. What was wrong with him? When had running away ever salvaged a floundering relationship? Ruann wasn't like him – she was organized and meticulous and thoughtful with making decisions, but she cared about him, and she had a point. Clearly, he ate like shit, he should lose twenty pounds, and he had moved onto his friend's sofa.

Once he'd let himself into James' place, he peeled off his wet clothes, threw on a t-shirt and boxers, and then he curled up on the couch, where anger, sorrow, and shame, like a vengeful street gang, plunged knives into his body. He sank into an unsettled, light sleep. Not for long – the door creaked and slammed, followed by James' footsteps whumping across the wooden floor. Alex writhed onto his other side, facing the back of the couch.

"What the fuck are you doing here?" asked James, drunkenly stumbling into the living room. "I thought you'd be getting laid at Ruann's."

Without opening his eyes, Alex muttered into the cushion, "We had a kind of a fight…"

"You had a fight and came back here? That's a hell of a fight."

"Yeah."

"About what?"

"I don't really know."

"Hah. You know the *best* way to make up after a fight is to have sex."

James' relationship advice was suspect when he was sober. "That's never worked for me."

"Have you *really* tried?"

"Yes. I got a kid out of it," Alex snapped. "I need sleep."

"You'll have a clearer head in the morning," James said. "At least you'll be less of a grumpy twat." He offered a small, crooked smile, then padded into his bedroom, while Alex shoved the pillow against the sting in his eyes. He heard the whirring of traffic on West 50th, the hissing throb of his own pulse, the pattering of rain on the windows. Something sharp dug into his lower back. Sleep cruelly played with his exhausted brain, teasing him, like the cat he wished James owned to deal with the mice in this place.

The next day, he rode the subway to Flatbush after work, buying a twenty-dollar bottle of wine along the way. He apologized for losing his temper and leaving. Ruann apologized for giving him a hard time.

"I'm just so shit at organizing my life, and my head's been—" he started.

"Doesn't matter." She ripped open the buttons on his shirt, and her tongue plunged down his throat, as if she shared James' make-up sex theory.

His anxious musings ended there; he was living in the moment, and nothing else mattered. No tangential thoughts, no doubts, no pain, just her body against his, her hands and lips exploring him, his nerves afire, and her silky, smooth skin warm under his fingers.

Afterwards, Ruann massaged the knots around his scapula and said he could move into her place if he wanted. *What?* Abruptly, he stood up and scurried into the bathroom. He leaned on the sink, aware of his heartbeat. His eyes wandered to the array of make-up, perfumes, hair products, like an army of little soldiers marching along the shelf. A passing thought – why do women think they need all this shit? *Living together!* He hadn't shared an apartment with any partner since Catherine, and that had gone badly, starting its downhill plummet when he moved into that place in the Village just before Ellie was born. Dismayed, but with no insight, he splashed water over his face.

"Flatbush is too far from work," he said when he returned to the bed. The lamest excuse in the world. Lots of Manhattan cops lived in the outer boroughs and further afield, like Yonkers. So, he added, "You know I'm not good at mornings. I'm gonna be fucked waking up early enough to travel in from Brooklyn for an eight-by-four." That was true, although really, moving in would take the relationship about a hundred miles further than he wanted.

"Bill Ryan makes into your office from the Rockaways."

"He's gotten through *War and Peace* on his commute," Alex snorted.

"Okay," she said, stroking his chest hair. "It's just something to think about."

His mouth and shoulder healed within a few weeks, and then they went on dates; dinners at restaurants a step above greasy Jersey diners; a night at the cinema on West 66th and Amsterdam watching a subtitled French film, which Ruann enjoyed and Alex found mind-numbing; a trip to watch the horse racing at Belmont, which he appreciated more than she did. "This is the whitest sport, ever," she commented. No shit, he thought, feeling like he was in a crash course on race in America, an interracial couple attracting prickly, askance eyefucking from random racegoers and awkward coldness from the guy serving drinks at the racetrack bar. When Alex mentioned that to Ruann, she laughed dryly and said, "Yup. Now you know how I feel when I go into Bloomingdale's."

Sometimes, every cell in his body ached for her presence; he relished the warm glow suffusing through his insides, missing it on nights he slept alone. At other times, they argued. She loved exercise, either the gym or running, and he did not. She fastidiously organized her life, and he did not. She was politically engaged and read the news obsessively, and he did not. She had dreams of a house in Westchester with a yard, children, the middle-class American dream, and he did not. One day, Alex had to sit down, have *the* conversation. He was an emotionally flighty thirty-three year old workaholic, with an ex-wife and two pre-teen daughters. Ruann deserved better than him, a conclusion he reached in the last furlong of the fifth race at Belmont. But he dreaded that adult conversation piled atop work, the stress of being homeless, and the gaping holes in his clearance rate.

On his RDOs, Alex hunted for apartments and reaffirmed what every New Yorker knows: the only thing worse than your current slum landlord is every other slum landlord. His back was killing him because James' sofa suffered from flaccid cushions and broken springs. He longed for his own space, not a damned living room where James left dishes, his clothes, and boxes of condoms on the furniture. Worse, the Hell's Kitchen apartment had no bathroom door (James had nailed up a bedsheet), leaking pipes, a mouse colony, and the sketchy neighborhood made your hair stand on end. Alex worked in neighborhoods where you had to be on your toes, but he was sick of living in them.

Finally, Matt Cohen took pity on him, offering him the spare room in his apartment on Spring Street in SoHo for a nominal rent. A proper bedroom with a real bed and no condoms on the sofa. However, Matt and his partner Karen kept strictly kosher, and Alex had to abide by the rules. That meant foregoing all pork products unless he was out, as its mere presence might contaminate the kitchen, and paying close attention to the classification of dishes as 'milk' or 'meat,' never mixing the two on a shelf. All of that would be tolerable – many things were for cheap rent in SoHo – but Karen kept the apartment meticulously clean and flew into a rage if you so much as left a cushion out of place. You could do surgery on the kitchen floor. Alex had witnessed her washing the outside of the trashcan, disinfecting the broom, and arranging the Tupperware cupboard like an art installation at the Met.

It left a hole in his heart where pepperoni pizza and bacon used to be, and whenever he found himself unwillingly scrubbing something stupid, like skirting boards, he missed James' horizontal attitude towards cleaning.

It had upsides, though: the bed spared his back from more pain, the kitchen appliances worked, and Catherine warmed towards leaving the girls with him. The place wasn't a shithole, for a change, and she hoped some of Matt and Karen's Conservative Jewish practice would rub off on the kids or better yet, rub off on Alex. Although she tried to raise them as observant Jews, compelling their attendance at Temple and Hebrew school had become a weekly trial, compounded by Alex's laissez-faire attitude towards any kind of synagogue attendance. He hadn't gone to Shabbat since he was seventeen.

"It's part of their heritage. Our heritage. Yours too," Catherine said, exasperated, after she'd asked him to take Ellie on a Friday night. His ex had a date, which made him feel lousy for not spending more nights with Ruann, and Sarah had gone to a sleepover with friends.

"It's up to them," Alex answered. "If they wanna go, I'll take them." A safe thing to say, because they would happily use him as an excuse to not go. "But Ellie can stay with me that night. No problem." See, he had his uses. Especially when the Friday in question happened to be an eight-by-four, the next day an RDO, and Ruann was working a four-by-twelve at the Robbery squad. Another thing he didn't feel ready for – introducing Ruann to his daughters. If the relationship fell apart, he would have to explain it to them. They were young – let them believe in the saccharine version of romance and love they saw in the movies. Anyway, he liked having Ellie on her own. When the girls were together, they fought, and he found it exhausting to constantly break up their squabbles, while Sarah was hard work, acting defiant and obstinate most of the time. He got less attitude from perps.

After he collected Ellie at her school, she asked him if they could go to the movies and watch *Dances with Wolves*. Surprised, he said, "That's not a kids' movie."

"I *know*. I don't like kids' movies. They're just kinda lame. Everyone says it's really good. Mom won't let me see it. I promise if we go, I won't tell her."

He chewed on his lower lip, thinking. She was fourteen. At fourteen, he had been riding the subway all over the city, seeing any movie he wanted, provided the theater let him in. For all her neuroses, his mother had allowed Alex and his sisters a loose rein. They went to *Dances with Wolves*. Ellie wept at the deaths of Kevin Costner's horse and the wolf, more so than at the demise of any human in the movie. Alex thought his job was depressing – he saw too much death at work – so he shouldn't allow himself to watch downbeat movies where most of the characters died. Since they both needed cheering up, he indulged her with a stop at a late-night ice cream place on Spring Street where they ate midnight sundaes. As a nightcap, Ellie ordered a hot chocolate, and he ordered a coffee spiked with Kahlua. Only in New York. The Kahlua-laced coffee warmed his belly, and he felt a little less empty and sad.

"You tell your mother I let you have ice cream at midnight, she'll kill me," he warned as they strolled towards Matt's, weaving through the SoHo street life.

Ellie pressed her lips together and pantomimed a zipper with her thumb and forefinger. "Not a word, Dad. Cross my heart."

Chapter Twenty-Three

The Monday his next set started, Alex received a call from his mother in Duchess County. His father had collapsed, a heart attack, his second one in two years. It did not look good. While he dug through clutter under his bed for clothes and train timetables, his mother rang again. His father had not made it. Stunned, Alex called in sick to work, hailed a cab to Grand Central, then jumped on the next Metro North to Brewster. His sister, Ruth, who had driven down from Vermont, picked him up at the train station. That fast. You blink, and he's gone. He'd always gotten along with his dad, better than with his mother. His dad was taciturn, but when he said something, it mattered and was usually funny and droll. He'd worked his way up from sewing clothes in a textile factory in Newark to managing the factory. Every hassle or setback in his life, including two previous heart attacks, streamed around him like he was a rock in a river, untouched by floods or draught. Alex never saw his parents much, but he knew they were tending their garden or walking their dog in a small village near Brewster called Wingdale, the way he knew the sun rose in the morning but never thought about it. In spite of his job, Alex didn't know what happened when people died. Once his father had been there, planting wild bergamot and hyacinths, and then he was nothing more than synapses and electricity in Alex's head, frail and light, broken, changing, and he could not touch it.

It was Jewish tradition to bury the dead within twenty-four hours, a tradition that accounted for bodies decomposing in the desert sun but didn't account for family and friends spread all over the world, from Berlin to Denver. Alex and Ruth spent those three days in Brewster dealing with death certificates and paperwork, desperately persuading their mother to postpone the funeral, which would give people a chance to buy plane tickets. "No one can afford a last-minute flight from Berlin," Ruth argued. "And you know Dad's brother and his kids gotta be there." Grudgingly, their mother conceded. "God will forgive you," Ruth assured her. "I think he has better things to worry about."

"But what happens to your father?" she demanded.

"They'll keep him on ice," Alex said, calm and knowing.

The day Alex got back to the city, he bar-hopped through Greenwich Village with a few cops he knew from his days in the Tenth. The other detectives went home. His heart cracked open, letting molten pain flood into the fissures. Fuck, he wanted to weep. But he couldn't – not in a cop bar. A homeless guy screamed at George Bush, two tall transvestites made out against the side of the building, and a man in cowboy boots walked his pet ferret on a leash, but the Village characters had retreated to one place, and he'd become entrapped in another, an icy black hole that froze his nerves. Eyes cast down to the wet pavement and litter at his feet, he trudged towards the Washington Square subway station on West 4th, but the blue lights of a bar called the A Train, beside the uptown subway entrance, drew him across the road, like a moth to a halogen light.

He shoved open the door, ordered a Bud, and then stared vacantly at a Yankees game on TV for about ten minutes. Baseball bored the shit out of him. Why was he watching it? The bar had a pool table, and he ambled over to it, quarters clenched under his sweaty, curled fingers. Four NYU students were playing doubles. Alex effortlessly beat the students, and just as easily, he trounced two Village hippies and two flamboyantly-dressed gay guys. Mist blanketed his vision. His throat was closing until he couldn't swallow. He stumbled through the door and stared at other people's faces in angry discontent, then he turned into the wind and broke into a run. Sixth Avenue, Houston Street, Varick Street, names as familiar as his own hands, a map printed in his head: down a busy street, past the dark alleys and heaving, laughing bars and the shuttered store fronts, feet wet from puddles, blindly pounding through the rain until he couldn't breathe anymore, his right side on fire, but his body chilled to the bone and panting against the door of Matt's brownstone, the keys awkward in his hands.

His eyes stung. He dialed Ruann, punching at the blurry numbers on the phone. When she picked up, he said, "I'm sorry, Ruann. We want different things. It's not working."

"Alex, what?" she said.

"It's not working," he repeated. "You need someone better."

"It's like three am. You're drunk. Why don't we talk about this later?"

"No," he protested. "I need to do this now."

"Why all this self-destructive behavior, Alex?"

"It's who I am. I can't drag you into this. I'm sorry." He ended the call. Unconsciousness took him like a great dark wing, sweeping him away from his pain until morning.

Listless, his eyes puffed up and achy, he ate breakfast with Matt, desultorily picking his way through a bowl of cornflakes.

"You had a *lot* to drink last night," observed Matt.

"So what?" He paused after each bite.

"I mean, with your father, you could take the rest of the week off. They let you take more than a couple days for bereavement leave."

"Then I'd have *more* time to get wasted," Alex shot back, but his voiced wavered. "I could drink all day. It's not gonna change anything. Work gives me something to do."

Hearing Karen's footsteps in the hallway, he fled into his room and disrobed from his sweatpants and t-shirt. The tears flooded his eyes. He drove his head in his pillow, shaking under labored gasps as the cotton grew damp. His emotions were a runaway horse, unstoppable, uncontrollable. So much for being a stoic, hard police officer. But he sniffed the pain back into his sinuses and put on a suit.

Had he broken up with Ruann last night? For the whole subway ride to the Two-Five, he sleepily interrogated the blank space in his memory. But oh, yes, he had, because he discovered a message from her on his work answering machine. "Alex, I know you're upset about your dad, but we need to talk. Please call me." They definitely did not need to talk. Having drunkenly ended that relationship, he felt relieved, the weight lifting from his shoulders. More guilt – why didn't he want what everyone else wanted? Love, a safe place, the warmth of human touch, someone to wrap him in their arms. No, he had looked that in the eye and thrust it away, preferring his freedom to the chains of a relationship.

He listened to his other messages: the Night Watch had bequeathed him a murder, a thirty-foot smear of blood on the ground floor of an East Harlem high-rise project on East 132nd Street, and the Guatemalan man who had left the blood clinging to life at St. Luke's Hospital. Gunshot to the neck. By the time Alex and James signed out a Crown Vic, the man was dead, and neither Night Watch nor the Two-Five squad had any suspects. Any dying declarations, they asked the Two-Five precinct detective who had gone to the hospital at the start of his tour. Clearly not. They drove to East 132nd and worked the hell out of the neighborhood, banging on doors of every apartment, bringing in witnesses from the street, from the high-rise where the vic had been shot, and from all the neighboring low-rises. No one admitted to knowing him. No one admitted to hearing a shot. The crackhead who found the body claimed he'd just found the body. It happens. Then why was he in the apartment? Because it had an open-door policy – any junkie or crackhead who needed a place to relax and fire up could walk straight in. The pool of suspects seemed endless, the forensics hopeless, because, as the witnesses said, every addict within five blocks knew about 2300 East 132nd, and the place was awash in bodily fluids and fingerprints.

As soon as fingerprints ID'd the vic as Juan Pablo Rodriguez (luckily, in the SAFIS system for some drug charges), Alex and James drove to his family's apartment in the Bronx, an unkempt low-rise in Fordham Heights on a block that looked like Dresden after the war. The turgid cocktail of cigarettes, weed, garbage, and stale urine pricked their nostrils. The apartment itself seemed smaller than James' place, but inhabited by seven people. Alex gave his spiel to the vic's cousins – how sorry he was for their loss, how much he would appreciate any information about Juan Pablo, how important it was that he solve the case and find justice for Juan Pablo. They stared at him as he talked, zotzed on crack or obsessing over their next fix, their blank faces telling him that the MNHS phones wouldn't be lighting up for this one. Crack short-circuited people's capacity give a fuck, even about their own families. As the detectives turned to leave the low-rise, one of the cousins followed them.

Alex and James spun around. Please, Alex thought, tell us about the drugs he was firing, the drugs he was dealing, the money he owed, the people who owed money to him, the women he was sleeping with, the men he was sleeping with, the ones he wasn't sleeping with, the beef he had with someone, the one where he swore that he would get even.

The cousin said haltingly, "You mean to say, Juan Pablo's dead?"

"Yeah, he's dead. That's what we've been talking about. Took a bullet to the throat," Alex said, touching his own throat.

The cousin looked dumbfounded. "Wow."

"Anything else you wanted to tell us?"

"Not really."

It was the kind of case Alex liked to work. Not high profile. Not the cases on crime shows or in crime novels. It was the kind of case that didn't matter to anyone. Not to the family, not to his boss, not to the politicians or the people of New York. Regrettably, it was probably unsolvable, and it mattered to his clearance rate. A more unscrupulous detective like Keohane might find a way to shitcan it or pin it on the nearest skel with a couple gun charges to his name, but Alex played straight, giving any vic as much time as he had.

Why would a man who started his day with an open case file answer the phone four hours later, sign out a Crown Vic, then drive to a sleazy, roach-infested hotel adjacent to the West 175th Street A train station? Another message from Ruann. "Alex, please call me. I know you're busy at work, but please." Alex had every reason to let Bill or Marty or Brady or Keohane take the call, but he'd seized the phone after the first ring. He squatted over the DOA, an overweight white male, the owner of the roach-infested hotel, who had no obvious trauma on his body, and he was sixty-seven years old, smoking and drinking, the prime candidate for a heart attack or a stroke. Alex knew cause of death was none of those things because of lividity, the man's blood congealing into wine-colored patches with pallid white spots on his back where the weight of his body crushed blood vessels, but he lay crumpled on his side – evidence someone had moved him – and the fact that his 1980 Pontiac Grand Am was missing. What more does a homicide detective need to know? Alex eased himself onto his belly and wriggled under the bed. The sour stench of the carpet and dust balls the size of rats nurtured his hangover and kicked his allergies into gear, but he soldiered through his discomfort to extricate an extensive collection of handcuffs, cat'o'nine tails, and strap-on dildos.

"These could be fun," he said, swishing the cat'o'nine tails.

"Didn't know you was into that, Boswell," sniggered the precinct detective.

They pulled a drinking glass from the bedside table for prints. CSU dusted the sink, the TV, and the toilet. They collected fibers, swabbing the bed, the chairs, the nightstand, and they bagged the kinky sex toys. Alex sent out a BOLO describing the Pontiac.

James, raising a dildo roughly the size of a horse penis above his head, pronounced, "We are the finest detectives in the world. New York City homicide detectives. The murder police. The elite of the elite. The best of the best. Countless TV shows, movies, and stories are made about us. From *NYPD Blue* to *The French Connection* to *Die Hard.* We are at once fearless street cops and genius investigators…"

"Shut up, Hurley," said the patrol sergeant. "You're giving me an erection."

James threw the dildo at him. "Well, luckily I've got just the thing for that."

The neighbors told the detectives that they saw a steady stream of young men wandering to and from the hotel. The hotel employees – the lady who ran the front desk and the cleaning crew – knew about their boss' penchant for young men (and sometimes women). They suspected that the owner was running a brothel, but he'd paid them enough keep quiet. It turned out that Vice did too but had not yet caught him with someone who was inarguably under eighteen, and they were sitting on him, waiting for an opportune moment to wring him for information about a wider sex trafficking ring. The Vice detective called it a 'public service murder' as he forwarded Alex his surveillance tapes and DD-5s. A cleaner told Alex that he'd seen a young male slipping into the owner's room not long before he died, white, thin, pallid, like a crackhead or an AIDS victim. Most likely a sex worker, because the staff figured they were all sex workers. *A case with legs,* Alex thought.

The case broke two days later, when AntiCrime cops from the Five-Two Precinct in the Bronx phoned Alex to say that they'd pulled over a white kid driving the Pontiac described on his BOLO. The phone made Alex nervous every time it rang. He was ducking Ruann's calls. *It's not you; it's me.* God, what a useless cliché. Well, he had murders to work.

With James cracking jokes about the benefits of a career change, from a cop to a male hooker, they drove across the river to the Five-Two. The kid collared by AntiCrime asserted that he had never been in Manhattan and a friend had gifted him the car. Yeah, right. His alibi checked, unfortunately, but he still had the car. He knew something. The detectives ramped up the intensity of their questioning until he gave up the name of the guy who sold him the car, a nineteen-year old male pross. The kid said he usually worked the corner of Grand Concourse and East 182nd, where the D line subway provided a steady stream of johns.

As promised, the suspect loitered near the subway station, underweight, pasty-faced, his eye sockets sunken, looking a damned sight older than nineteen. The detectives picked him up. They tossed him, finding two vials of crack, three pills, and a joint. The hotel cleaner ID'd him in a line-up. Detained in the Two-Five's interrogation room, the hooker claimed he knew nothing about the hotel or its owner. In fact, he had never left the Bronx. Alex didn't believe a word. He rambled about forensics, spinning out a lengthy soliloquy describing how hairs collected from the hotel room could be used to ID anyone in the city (not easily, but that was neither here nor there). James, aiming for his Oscar, blubbered about his cousin dying of AIDS. The perp began to crumble. Harsh lighting gleamed off the sweat coating his face as he confessed that the hotel owner was a regular client. He'd gone to the hotel, a normal call, but then the client had a seizure while they were having sex, and the perp panicked. No john had ever dropped dead on him before.

"So, you took his car?" Alex raised an eyebrow.

"Yeah, *he* wasn't gonna need it anymore, was he?"

Alex loved perp logic. He loved it even more when he'd watched the autopsy and seen with his own eyes that the vic had not, in fact, died of natural causes, but rather manual asphyxiation. The detectives completed the statement and left the room. Needing authorization for an arrest warrant, they phoned a hassled ADA, who had about six hundred defendants to juggle and didn't care about this one, and then a judge. While waiting for the judge's signature, they watched through the one-way as the perp frowned cluelessly at the mirror, smoothing out his blonde hair and adjusting his baggy shorts. Then they re-entered the interrogation room, placing him under arrest for felony murder.

Clearing a case made Alex feel slightly better, at least about himself as a detective. The Guatemalan on East 132nd might still be in red, but he'd put this one down. On some days, he might be worth his gold shield.

After booking the perp at Central, Alex and James returned to the office, only to be intercepted at the door by a wild-eyed Marty. He panted, "Lex, I tried to stop her, but that woman is a force of nature."

"What?" Alex narrowed his eyes. His mood faltered and crashed like a helicopter with engine failure.

"Detective Harland," Marty said in a low, urgent voice.

"Oh, fuck." It came out as more of a breath than words. "Shit."

"Guess you gotta deal with this one after all," said Marty.

The whole squad knew he'd broken up with Ruann while wasted at 0300. They knew he had been avoiding her calls for three days. They had even fielded some calls for him. They also asked, "What the hell is wrong with you?" She was smart, beautiful, a great cop, on the cusp of making first grade. Alex said he was too much of a trainwreck for her. She deserved someone who had their shit together. Someone with less baggage than JFK Airport. They understood what he meant. The Homicide squad had no respect for privacy, not their own or anyone else's. The job – unearthing people's darkest and weirdest secrets – didn't lend itself to that. They knew if they bothered hiding things from one another, it would only escalate their colleagues' aspirations to uncover them, and they knew, as perfectly as detectives would know, that Alex's talents at managing death investigations had never extended to his personal life.

Ruann waited at his desk amidst the bomb site of take-out boxes, old coffee cups, and files. Seeing her there, Alex felt painful knots twisting in his intestinal tract. He licked his dry lips, then nervously approached the desk.

"Hi, Ruann."

"How can you work like this? My God." Her face was stony, her arms folded stiffly across her chest.

He responded with an uncomfortable shrug. "I just do."

"Is an interview room free?"

"Yeah." His colleagues watched. Those nosey bastards would shove their ears against the door. Oh, well.

He let her into an interview room, and with a curt "I'll be right back," he scuttled into the bathroom for a piss and a hit from his flask. Evan Williams? Jameson? Who knows? It churned inside his stomach. What was he going to say? He tried to plan out an opening line, but his mind blanked; he had no strategy, no insight, and he met his reflection's gaze in the mirror. Those dark brown eyes with their worried lines looked sorrowful and tired.

He procrastinated by washing his face, retying his tie, and then futzing with the vending machine, buying a pack of M&Ms, although he felt too queasy to eat them now. Out of options, he returned to the interview room.

"What's going on, Alex?" Ruann said.

"I dunno." He chewed on his thumbnail, unable to contain his bad habit. "I'm just not happy."

"About your father?"

"Yeah, obviously, but I wasn't happy before."

"With me? With us?"

"Yeah."

"What? I thought... You never said anything. I thought you were serious about this relationship."

"It didn't feel... right... I guess." Dozens of words in English for break-ups, and he couldn't find any of them.

"What do you mean by that?"

"I don't know."

"Wouldn't it have been better to talk about why, then maybe we could figure out what we could do about it together?"

"That isn't what I wanted."

"What *do* you want, Alex?"

Not to be having this conversation. "Not... what you want," he said, his tongue swollen, him falling over it. "You want a serious relationship. I don't. I'm not there. I've never been there since we started going out. guess I thought... I thought I might... But I'm not ready, and I just feel sick about it, like I'm stringing you along."

"Why don't you want that? We can keep it more casual."

"No, we can't. You can't go backwards. It's already got more intense than I wanted. I dunno... I'm not feeling like it's a good thing for me to have right now."

"You need someone to talk to," stated Ruann, now speaking firmly. "This unit isn't good for you. I'm not sure working homicides for a long time is good for anyone. Some police departments rotate people off homicide squads."

"I talk to them. And I'm fine." He pointed to the wall, where he imagined the homicide detectives were eavesdropping.

"Yeah, I know what cops talk about. It's not... You're burning out. I can see it."

"You said that before. But I'm not." He half-opened his mouth in a grimace. The work *was* hard, but dammit, he was doing the greatest public service anyone could do in this police department.

She scrutinized him as if he'd become transparent, and she saw every one of his organs. "Right. You don't think you're having some post-traumatic stress stuff from being shot, and that's what this is really about? I know your wound gives you more pain than you let on. Or your father? Have you talked to anybody about him? Or are you just trying to do this macho toughing-it-out thing?"

"Jesus," he breathed, sitting back, thumbnail in his teeth. His heart felt like a jackhammer. "I thought you were a robbery detective, not a shrink."

"Well," she said.

"No, I don't know. I don't... You ask my kids, ask my ex-wife, ask PO Abbey Giancarlo, who I cheated on my ex-wife with... they'll tell you I've been fucked up way before that happened." She touched something; the nightmares, the way he heard gunfire that wasn't there, his weird reaction to the Ed Byrne shooting.

"You got some pain deep inside you, some trauma, some need for self-destruction, and I really wish I could help you. I dunno... Maybe you're right. Maybe you need someone else, or you need more time to work out what you need to work out, or maybe you'll crash and burn, and maybe it's on me too. Like when I was a kid, and the cat brought in half-dead birds and mice, and I'd catch them, thinking I could save them. I keep doing that with guys. Finding the fucked up ones, thinking I can put them back together." She was a tough robbery detective, but a tear gathered in the corner of one eye and streaked down her dark cheek. Quickly, she wiped it away.

"You're great, Ruann. Your career's going somewhere. You'll get some kinda promotion if you clear those Russian Mob cases. You gotta do better. You gotta find the ones who aren't fucked up. Maybe stop dating cops, for a start."

"You sure this is what you want? I'll work on things with you. Help you work stuff out."

He shielded his face with his hands, and his breath enveloped his cheeks and eyelids. "Yeah, no. It's what I want. I'm sorry. This is too much, just too much for me to cope with. I can't tell you why. It just… is."

"Okay, Alex." She was streetwise enough to know when a discussion had reached an endpoint, when nothing said now would change anything. "I guess I'll see you around."

"Yeah," he muttered into the table, his head on his forearms. "See you."

The door groaned on its hinges, and she disappeared, out of the squad room and out of his life. He lingered in the interview room, his lungs laboring, his head spinning with countless terrible life choices. Breaking up with Ruann joined the crowded but unfillable box.

His colleagues allowed him space until he had lingered for too long, and then James wedged the door open with his foot, saying, "Lex, come on. We'll go out and drink that hotel murder down."

"I got 'fives and an OLBS for that I have to do," he gasped, his voice hoarse. "And log the shit we took off the perp."

"You do your 'fives, and we'll go out."

"Yeah." Alex followed James to their cubicles. He slid a 'five into his typewriter. Someone had left a porn magazine on his desk, with a sticky note, *This will cheer you up, love Marty.* Marty had sketched rough cat'o'nine tails on his note. You couldn't expect too much empathy from the Homicide squad. Any flash of affection was soon tempered by teasing and practical jokes. Alex opened the case file for the hotel owner and flipped to the perp's written statement. He typed his name, the date, the case number, and his command into the boxes on the 'five. His eyes roved to the case file next to it, the Guatemalan crackhead. If he could solve *that,* he wouldn't feel so hopeless, a stone whodunit compensating for his grief and the pain of a break-up. It would take some luck to put that down, and he wasn't feeling like he had much of it. He swallowed a furtive mouthful of whisky from his flask.

The following week flew past like an express train. Dealing with the funeral, arguing with his mother, his own heartache avalanched in the landslide of things he had to manage. Ruth was now an estate lawyer in Vermont, and Helen was still a social worker in Colorado. Alex and Ruth fell out with their mother over their father's will, over Alex continuing to work the streets after he'd been shot, and mainly, over Alex's and Ruth's refusal to do readings in Hebrew at the funeral because neither understood a word of it. Helen went to Temple and remained observant, but her younger siblings had let tradition fade from their lives.

"I sent both of you to Hebrew school," their mother said with capacious despair.

Yes, but Alex remembered nothing of the lessons, only sneaking into an alley behind the synagogue and smoking cigarettes with Josh Goldenblatt. His first and last real stint with smoking. Ruth said she spent Hebrew lessons mired in pre-teen angst over a kid called Larry Rosenstein, but the love remained forever unrequited because Larry liked another girl in the class.

"Larry Rosenstein?" Helen's face crumpled in disgust. "Ew."

Ruth feigned confusion and hurt. "What?"

"He was always pulling boogers out of his nose and wiping them under the desk, and I suspect eating them."

The siblings giggled, and Alex wondered what Josh Goldenblatt had done with his life.

The next day, while Alex cleaned dishes from breakfast, their mother exposed another crisis. "Alex, you're not going to give your reading sounding like that, are you?"

"Like what?" he said, although he had some idea.

"The way you talk," she explained irritably. "The New York City cop thing. Can't you sound more… refined? Just this once. The people here, my friends, they're not all from the city. They won't be used to it. You will sound like you're in a Scorsese movie."

"Oh, my God," he moaned. He shoved a plate into the drying rack. "It's just how I talk." *Tawk.* Jesus, she was after him about his fucking accent? Of all the insane things that didn't matter, that probably mattered the least. He'd never moderated the Lower East Side working class dialect, the dropped 'r's,' the diphthongs on words like *coffee*, the hard 'th's' sounding like 'd's.' His parents clung to a neurosis about it, a belief that a broad regional accent made you sound underwhelmingly cultured and worse, uneducated. Although he pretended that it didn't bother him, he was a little hurt that his mother had asked him to change his accent.

As if his mother wasn't causing him enough misery, Alex skirmished with Catherine over bringing the girls up to Brewster for the funeral. Catherine complained that they had a trip arranged with their friends, and they would be profoundly disappointed if they could not go. Unbelievable – it was their grandfather's funeral. Like he did with perps, uncooperative witnesses, or incompetent uniforms and precinct detectives, he obdurately stood his ground, refusing to accept excuses or equivocation. It got him what he wanted, for now, but that always backfired on him eventually.

Both wearing black dresses, Ellie and Sarah sat with him in the front row of the synagogue. Helen, his mother, and the rabbi read passages from the Torah in Hebrew. Alex, Ruth, and half a dozen other Philistines read in English, Alex speaking in his normal accent. He hated public speaking, the whole service stressful enough without thinking consciously about how he pronounced vowels or adding 'r's' to words when he naturally dropped them. The funeral ended with Hebrew prayers and the cantor singing a keening *Kel Maleh Rachamim*. The girls fidgeted, and Alex felt bored and guilty – for his boredom at the funeral and for being a lapsed, cynical Jew. In his mild, uncomplaining way, his father had always been a touch disappointed that Alex and Ruth had drifted away from Temple.

They returned to his mother's house to sit shiva. She had beseeched her three children to sit for every minute of the seven days, but only Helen had volunteered. Alex and Ruth conceded to three days. It was all Alex reckoned he could take of prayers, of the unceasing stream of guests, of sitting around doing nothing, of neither showering nor shaving. But he knew his father would have appreciated his half-assed effort to observe the tradition.

During shiva, Sarah and Ellie kept close to Alex and his sisters. They didn't know anyone there and found the whole thing unnerving. As did Alex, not knowing many of his parents' friends from Duchess County, either, while they seemed disappointed that he couldn't recite the Kaddish but enthralled with his job, soliciting his views about cases in the news, or the trashy murder mystery they were reading, and when it got too much, he would shoot his sisters a desperate look, *save me now,* and they would dive in and divert the shiva guest.

"It's your own fault, Al," Helen teased. "If you were an accountant, no one would care."

"Mom and Dad would have preferred that," he said.

"Could be worse," Ruth observed wryly. "If you were a brain surgeon, Mom would be setting you up with every eligible Jewish woman in the Tri-State area. I swear, she's had guys lined up for me ever since I finished law school."

"Good ones?" he asked.

"No!"

"I think Dad respected what you do," Helen reflected. "Mom will always think it's too blue-collar."

"Yeah. Can you fucking believe it? She wanted me to sound less, I guess, New York, when I was speaking up there." *New Yawk.* Helen and Ruth – whose respective years in Colorado and Vermont dissipated their own accents – laughed, but they believed it.

God, he wanted to bury his unease and sorrow in the wine, which seemed plentiful, but he had to behave when he was supervising the girls. He drank as much as he thought he sensibly could and lived with the rest. The girls kept him somewhat occupied, with Sarah kvetching about how bored she was (she could take a number) and trying to antagonize her sister, while Ellie peppered him with questions about Judaism, shiva, and her grandfather, and by the third day, she was onto politics, at one point asking what he thought about gun control because she had to write a paper on it for school (he thought he would have a smaller caseload if there were fewer guns).

"Can I quote you as 'NYPD homicide detective Alex Boswell?'"

"That probably sounds better than quoting me as 'Dad.'"

Distracted from gun control by Sarah throwing a paper airplane at her, she flung a wadded-up napkin and a potato knish at her sister. Alex asked if they wanted to take it outside. His quiet, heartfelt sarcasm shut the fight down. How rare, he thought, spending four days with both girls. It made him sad that it had to be here.

In those weeks after the funeral, Catherine, pissed that she had lost a fight with him, curtailed his time with the girls, and in his usual manner, he let her get away with it. He never knew how to combat it without stoking a bigger fire. When Catherine reluctantly asked him to fetch Sarah from a dance class on the West Side, Sarah's resentment flared, only seeing her mother's point of view, on him if nothing else.

"Mom says you don't bother and think the police are more important."

"Let's talk and grab a bite to eat. Go to that Italian on Mercer Street you like?" His gunshot wound pulsed, aglow with flashes of pain. His painkillers and alcohol lived in Matt's apartment. That could wait.

Sarah sighed, her shoulders heaving with all the preteen drama she could muster. "I'm hanging out with friends tonight. They're coming to Mom's."

"Oh. Maybe another time."

"Yeah, you always say that, but it never happens."

"That's not completely true." He hailed a taxi. Sitting in the back seat, he picked at his nails, at a loss for how to explain himself and the job to an eleven-year old.

"It's mostly true," quibbled Sarah. "You didn't come to the school play or the dance recital."

"I know, I'm sorry. I was at work. You know, when someone's been shot, been killed, I have to figure out who did it. Like the cops on TV. I don't have a choice."

Unsympathetic, she huffed, "See."

Giving up, he thought, *this kid should apply to law school.*

The cab stopped at Catherine's place in the West Village, and they both got out. Like an ESU team executing a warrant, Sarah streaked into the building, whacking the door shut behind her. "Sarah, let's talk—" Alex said, but he was speaking to the door. The pain sharpened, and he squeezed his fingers against his ribs. Where they should curve downwards in a smooth ridge, he felt uneven lumps, twisted knots of scar tissue and smashed-up cartilage. He limped down Fifth Avenue and cut diagonally through Washington Square Park, passing the students, stoners, and dope fiends lounging indolently on the grass; the homeless huddling on benches in tattered sleeping bags; the old men playing chess. Long ago, when he'd walked a beat here, Alex had become passable at chess because he had a CI who would only meet him at those chess boards and pass on information while thrashing him. The Sixth Precinct – where his relationship with Catherine started unravelling. His chest felt constricted, like he breathed in something mushy, but the city pollution had never clouded his lungs with this painful, viscous haze.

Chapter Twenty-Four

Media coverage exploded like a field full of landmines as Ernesto Serrachia went on trial for the murder of Elam Liebowitz. As with Bernie Goetz and the Central Park Jogger, the case symbolized everything wrong with the city. The drugs, the crime, the deterioration, and the headlines in *The Daily News, The New York Post*, and every other rag presumed Serrachia guilty before opening arguments.

A battalion of reporters blockaded the sidewalk around the Criminal Courts Building and spilled into Centre Street. Rain poured from the slate grey sky, but the journalists were undaunted. Although uniformed police kept a tight space free at the door, the reporters had formed a gauntlet before the main stairway, which anyone entering or exiting the Criminal Courts had to pass through.

Alex shielded his eyes against the eager flashes of cameras. The roar from the reporters muffled out individual questions. Rain pelted his face, mingling with the sweat on his forehead. The inside of the Criminal Courts was comparatively serene. He marveled that so much noise could be reduced to silence by double-glazing. All sound, gone. He settled on a bench that hurt his lower back in the municipally dull room next door to the trial part, where he waited alongside other law enforcement witnesses, the four patrol officers who had been the first on the scene, and two CSU detectives. Eddie's testimony had already been read out. He was too ill to fly to New York, and no one had objected because he wasn't material to the case against Serrachia. The patrolmen testified first, then the clerk called Alex.

As Alex stretched his stiff right side and legs, a CSU detective complained, "We'll be here all day. And probably tomorrow. I think they're calling Indelicata after you."

"He's not here," Alex noted.

The CSU cop irritably jerked her eyes sideways. Vito did whatever the hell he wanted, which wasn't wait for hours in 100 Centre Street when he could show up at a trial five minutes after he should have been cited for contempt.

Leon Mitchell, the prosecutor, first established the foundation, routine questions about Alex's experience in the NYPD and with homicide investigations. Next, Mitchell solicited ponderous testimony about the Liebowitz investigation. Securing the crime scene, searching it, canvassing the streets, interviewing dozens of witnesses, observing the autopsy, receiving an anonymous tip. The defense attorney objected. The prosecutor tried finagling it in, but the defense countered that the state had failed to ID the anonymous tipster, so how could the accused cross-examine him? While the lawyers argued, Alex downed the complimentary water. He glanced at Serrachia. The defendant's features had frozen into an expression of muddled perplexity, like he'd woken up in this courtroom after a heavy night and had no idea how he got here.

Mitchell rephrased, "So, did you receive a phone call regarding this case?"

"Yes," Alex said.

"What did the caller say?"

"The caller implicated Serrachia in the crime and said he lived nearby."

"Then what did you do?"

"I tried finding the caller by tracing the call. I couldn't ID him, but I confirmed that Serrachia did in fact live nearby, and I ran a background check on him."

"What do you mean by a background check?"

Alex disentangled the state and federal databases – DCJS, NCIC, and ViCAP, the FBI's unit responsible for investigating serial crimes, which tracks and analyzes data about homicides and sexual assaults across the country and alerts you to similar crimes committed somewhere else.

"And then what?"

"I got an address for Serrachia, and I went to his apartment on West 168th Street."

"Is that all standard procedure?"

"Yeah, it is." He drank more water and felt it sliding into his stomach.

"Even though you couldn't identify the caller?"

"Yeah. We were chasing every lead we got."

"Did you tell Detective Indelicata about Mr. Serrachia?"

"Not directly, but I filed a DD-5," Alex said carefully.

"Was he involved with this particular interview?"

"No."

"Were you accompanied by any other colleagues?"

"Yes. Detective Sam Rizzo, also with Manhattan North Homicide."

"What happened after you went to Mr. Serrachia's apartment?"

"I brought him to the 34th Precinct house and interviewed him."

"What did you talk about?"

"I got his life story, then I asked him where he was on August 5th, 1987. He said he wasn't at the crime scene and that he didn't do it."

"Did he say where he was?"

"He said he was selling crack on West 180th Street."

"Did you believe him?"

"Well, at the time," Alex responded warily. The prosecutor eyeballed him with a warning look. Don't answer a question you haven't been asked, the first rule of testifying, and Mitchell had not asked him about the SNEU cop or the Dominican take-out server.

"Did you detain him after your interview?"

"No."

"Remind us, how long had you been in Homicide at that point?" asked Mitchell, surprising him with a question totally unrelated to that cursory interview.

"Five or six months."

"Five or six months. That's not very long, for a death investigator. When you later heard that Detective Indelicata had found eyewitnesses, did you revise your opinion as to Mr. Serrachia's guilt?"

"Yes."

"Thank you, Detective Boswell." The direct examination abruptly concluded, like the prosecutor had driven a truck into a wall.

Alex hadn't felt so unbalanced and confused in court since he'd testified as a rookie in the early '80s. Before he could piece his thoughts together, the defense lawyer loudly cleared his throat and rose for his cross. The lawyer would ask him about the alibi witnesses. Why hadn't Mitchell inoculated the jury on direct? That stuff should be part of discovery – legally, it had to be. But the prosecutor hadn't prepped him on it (or much else), and he had no strategy for handling those questions. Mitchell was an odd guy, slippery, unpredictable, and he had little respect for the exclusionary rule, the Fourth Amendment, the Fifth Amendment, and a number of other constitutional protections afforded to criminal defendants. Mitchell wanted to be a police officer, one in the 1930s, years before the Warren Court and civil rights. He once admitted to Alex that he thought the people who lived in the inner-cities must be predisposed towards crime and drug use. Otherwise, they would be going to law school instead of slinging crack. Alex had been taken aback, thinking,

This motherfucker has no clue. Most police officers loved the prosecutor, but Alex got an uncomfortable feeling inside his gut whenever he worked with him. The guy was a fucking snake.

"When you went to my client's apartment, did you have any evidence against him, other than this completely unverifiable phone call?" asked the defense lawyer.

"No."

"And you said you traced the call?"

"Yeah."

"Remind us how?"

"I traced it to a phone booth in the Bronx, in the 44th Precinct, and detectives from that precinct canvassed the area."

"Yeah. The Bronx. And did you ever find out who made it?"

"No."

"You have said that the caller who provided this 'tip' was male and spoke with a Spanish accent?"

"Yeah."

"According to your DD-5, written on the 8th of September, 1987, you said that the 44th Precinct detectives reported two Black females using the payphone in question around the time of the call. Is that right?"

"I believe so."

"You believe so? That's what you wrote on a DD-5 dated 8th September, 1987." The lawyer turned to the stenographer. "Let the record reflect that I am showing the witness Exhibit 124, a DD-5, signed Detective A. Boswell, dated the 8th of September, 1987. You wrote, 'Det. McBryde of 44th Precinct Squad informed me that two Black females were observed using the payphone at 7869 Grand Concourse between 1400 hours and 1600 hours.'"

"Yes," said Alex, trying to sound calm, not sighing as he said it.

"No males?"

"No." *Calm,* he repeated to himself.

"This caller could have been anyone. You had no way of knowing who he was or whether or not he was providing you truthful information?"

"No."

"And did you ever find a murder weapon?"

"No."

"In your interview with my client on the 8th of September, did he say he shot Mr. Liebowitz?"

"He denied it."

"How long did you interview him for?"

"Four hours."

"Four hours. Wherein he denied being anywhere near that bodega on that day?"

"Yes."

"Wherein he denied any involvement in or knowledge of this terribly tragic crime?"

"Yes."

"And you believed him?"

Mitchell's face hardened into stone. His icy blue eyes shackled Alex inside a cell, plain truth on one side, equivocal perjury on the other. And at that moment, Vito, the jury's TV detective, sauntered into the gallery, then ensconced his bulk behind the prosecution table. Alex flicked his gaze from Mitchell to Vito. Vito winked.

"I had no evidence he was lying," Alex said.

"That means you believed him?"

"It means I didn't have enough evidence to hold him," Alex squirmed.

"You're saying, during your whole four-hour interview, you never found anything that gave you probable cause to arrest him?"

"Yeah."

"So, you let him leave the precinct?"

"Yes."

"And afterwards, did you find any evidence to support arresting him?"

"No."

"You dismissed the lead entirely?"

"I guess."

"None of your paperwork after the 8th of September mentions Mr. Serrachia again, Detective. That surely means you discounted him as a suspect?"

"I was keeping an open mind."

"Not that open. You did not follow up this particular lead after September 8th, did you?"

"No, but lots of people were working the case."

"Like Detective Indelicata?"

"Yeah, he was the primary."

"That means he was in charge of the whole investigation?"

Alex nodded and took another swig of water, wetting his throat. "Yeah."

"He saw your paperwork, took it upon himself to investigate Mr. Serrachia further?"

"I guess so."

"When Detective Indelicata made that decision and then interrogated my client, were you there?"

"No, I wasn't."

"Where were you?"

"At home on medical leave." His blood pressure shot upwards; he felt it pounding through the big arteries in his chest.

"For what?"

"For line of duty injuries. I was shot."

"When?"

"October 3rd, '87."

"What was the nature of your injuries?"

Relevance, Alex thought, glancing at Mitchell. The prosecutor compressed his lips. "Uh, I took a bullet to the right side of my ribcage."

"Sorry to hear that, Detective. You were seriously injured?"

"Yeah."

"Significant blood loss and major thoracic trauma, wasn't it?"

"Yes." *Stop this,* Alex wanted to scream at Mitchell, but the man was motionless, his face calculating.

"You lost part of your right lung?"

"Yeah." How did the lawyer know that?

"You're very lucky to be here."

"So they tell me."

"How long were you on leave for?"

"Five months."

"Right. Five months from October. So, you were very much out of commission and have no idea how long Detective Indelicata interviewed my client, or what he said?"

"No." Alex held his breath.

"You were on leave when he found the two alleged eyewitnesses?"

"Yes, I was."

"Did he speak to you about my client while you were on leave?"

"No. I wasn't in a state to talk about work."

"Understandable. What you're saying, is all the evidence the state is presenting against my client, it's stuff you've only heard about secondhand?"

"Yeah."

"Not directly?"

"No."

"I'm finished with this witness, Your Honor."

Mitchell passed on the redirect, and his thin lips conveyed smug satisfaction.

Stunned, Alex climbed down from the stand. Why had Mitchell let the defense attorney run with that? The shooting had nothing to do with Serrachia's case! And how the hell had *he* escaped without being grilled alive about evidence that had everything to do with it, like those alibi witnesses? God knows, the defense bar had its share of useless lawyers, but even the most incompetent lawyer had survived law school and passed the New York Bar exam, which meant they ought to be bright enough to figure out that witnesses who gave a detective a credible alibi created plenty of reasonable doubt, even if they changed their story later. And under *Brady v. Maryland,* the prosecution should have turned over those exculpatory witness statements and 'fives.

Should have. How far would Vito and Mitchell go? Sweat tickled his ribs. He limped down the mottled hallway, his wound alive, throbbing. A pair of journalists eyeballed him, and he darted into the bathroom before they made an approach. One followed, and Alex threw him a withering glare across the urinals. His fury could have melted a rock. The journalist took a leak, then scuttled out the door without speaking. He knew an uncooperative source when he saw one. Alex zipped up his fly. As if he could cleanse himself, he splashed water over his eyes and cheeks until it dribbled down his neck. The water cooled his skin, but it couldn't untie the knots in his stomach. He dried his face. He re-tied his tie for no reason. Then he slipped past the journalists, slinking into the trial part, and he sat down near the door, worrying at his lips. Over drinks a few months ago, Alex had asked Vito how he got Serrachia to confess, and Vito had smiled, his hand between Alex's shoulder blades. "I can get in their heads. But you know, it comes from your gut. In there." He'd swatted Alex's belly with the back of his other hand. "You just gotta feel it." Whatever the fuck that meant.

Now the precinct detective looked bright and dapper on the witness stand. Wearing a pinstripe three-piece suit and a metallic magenta tie, he stood out, a beacon of color lighting up the dreary courtroom. He rocked indolently towards the back of the witness stand, eyes alight, smiling easily, like he owned the joint.

Mitchell's second chair, Padraig Whelan, asked Vito about the crime scene, at first boring the jury because Vito reiterated testimony they'd heard from other cops. Whelan loved Reagan and the Mets, and he was unashamedly using the DA's office as a stepping-stone to a Wall Street firm or political run. He had a clipped, efficient questioning style that moved the testimony along. Juries didn't find him boring, but they didn't find him particularly likable, either. Within an hour, he'd arrived at Vito's eyewitnesses. Both Alex and the jury pricked their ears.

Vito testified that he had ferreted out two wits who reported seeing a man, apparently ID'd as Serrachia, accost the rabbi and then shoot him when he refused to hand over his wallet. Did anyone find the proceeds of the robbery or the weapon in Serrachia's apartment? No, Vito said, but Serrachia probably spent the money on crack and threw everything else in the river.

One of the witnesses was that prostitute, Loretta, whose real name was Elizabeth Weltmayer. Funny how she seemed to have a habit of witnessing murders. Months ago, when they finally set a trial date, Alex had read Vito's 'fives and witness statements. They were exasperating. *I could write a clearer report after ten pints.* Vito hadn't established where the witnesses stood, their lines of sight, their personal interests, or criminal histories. Nonetheless, he got away with possessing crack, bribing witnesses, then doing a lazy-ass job corroborating their statements. One would think the latter would safely cover up the former, but neither Vito's supervisors, the DAs, nor Internal Affairs seemed concerned. Although Alex felt sick and uncomfortable with his knowledge of how Vito handled CIs, he was swamped under too many open cases to bother following it up, and besides, no third grade detective in his right mind would double-check or quarrel with the investigative integrity of a first grader.

Smiling confidently, Vito told the court about bringing Serrachia into the station house, chatting about sports, the 1986 World Cup, Serrachia's delight at Argentina's win against Germany in the final, Vito admiring Maradona as the best soccer player of his generation, Serrachia divulging that he was once a promising soccer player before screwing up his life with crack, and from there, Serrachia confessing to shooting Liebowitz. *Too fucking easy*, Alex thought. Then again, he had no idea who played who in a World Cup final in '86. He had never connected with the perp, not enough.

The defense attorney stood up. "Your colleague, Detective Boswell, just testified that he initially dismissed my client as a suspect. Is that true?"

"Yeah, he did, but he's not got a lot of experience," Vito answered dismissively.

"You're saying he made the wrong call?" said the lawyer.

"He didn't push the suspect hard enough. But *he* didn't have two eyewitnesses who saw your client do it."

"Did you ever ask yourself if Detective Boswell made the right call?"

"I had two eyewitnesses and a confession."

"But Detective Boswell is in Manhattan North Homicide, isn't he? That's like an elite homicide investigation unit."

Vito shrugged. "You get those posts knowing the right people. I been on the streets longer. I know the people in my precinct."

"Did you know my client?"

"Not before this case, no."

"You're saying Detective Boswell lacks experience?"

Vito's gaze darted unapologetically towards Alex. "He'd only been in the Homicide squad six months at the time, but I'm sayin', I had information he didn't. He wasn't around for most of the investigation due to the line of duty injuries he received in October."

"When did he come back to work?"

"Like around February."

"And you interrogated my client on January 28th?"

"That's about right."

"Let's go to the interrogation. You talked to my client for eight hours, didn't you?"

"Yeah, maybe something like that."

"Eight hours, without food, rest, bathroom breaks?"

"That's what he's saying?" snorted Vito.

"Yes, Detective."

"That ain't true."

"Which part isn't true?"

"He wanted to use the bathroom, we let him. He wanted a sandwich, I brought him one."

"But you interrogated him for eight hours? Without counsel?"

"Yeah. He said he didn't want a lawyer."

"You talked about sports, became his friend, his confidant, manipulated him, is that right?"

"I got him to want to tell me the truth."

Alex glanced down at his watch. Anxiety broke through the riverbanks, bringing nausea and more sweat. He quivered at the thought of being here when court adjourned, with journalists poised to attack him and Vito slapping him on the back, that meaningless gesture of masculine friendship compensating for calling Alex incompetent on the stand. While the defense lawyer harangued Vito about physical evidence, Alex quietly rose to his feet, then he sloped out of the courtroom. Bearded Orthodox Jews in yarmulkes and black suits loitered by the door. They eyed him questioningly. Thank God he knew this building like his own neighborhood, and he threaded a back route through the corridors that led him to the parking garage, a close escape from press and nosey bystanders.

As soon as he was outside, he merged into the suited herd scurrying through Foley Square, heads bowed against the rain. Droplets clung to his eyelashes, and he pawed at his eyes with his sleeve. He gave a wide berth to reporters who hadn't made it into the Criminal Courts and a small, wet cluster of protesters, who chanted and waved signs accusing the NYPD of persecuting minorities. Protests had been busier and more vociferous a month ago, when they tried three of the kids charged with the Central Park rape. The protesters must be losing as much energy for this as Alex was.

He walked to the Chambers Street entrance for the 4, 5, 6 line and trotted unevenly down the stairs, favoring his right side. Street cacophony vanished. The PA announced that there was a twenty-minute delay on the line. Exhaling harshly, several times, he slouched against a wall coated with colorful graffiti; three-dimensional letters hinting of English words, stars and flames, a skull with bulging eyes rising above a yin-yang symbol that swirled like a Dali painting into a whirlpool below. You did not see so much graffiti in the subways now, the MTA having cracked down on subway writers with the view that the graffiti on the trains and in the stations embodied the mayhem and violence. Superficial bullshit, Alex thought. Getting rid of it wasn't making the city any less violent.

Case in point: James, in the office, writing a new homicide supplemental report and updating an OLBS sheet for a perp they had collared last week. The guy used a two-by-four from a nearby construction site to bludgeon someone whom he'd thought had stolen his cocaine. The only thing he had going for him was his honesty: he admitted without any preamble that he'd done it, and the motherfucker deserved it.

Alex glanced at the report over James' shoulder. "Why the fuck can't drug dealers solve their disputes with angry memos and meetings like everyone else?"

James laughed as he finished typing. "How did the trial go?"

"I guess my testimony went all right. The cross wasn't as hard as I thought it was gonna be."

"The defense lawyer didn't sodomize you with a tire iron?"

"No, he was gentle and loving. But Vito Indelicata called me an idiot, so I still need a drink. You almost done with that?"

"The only person who Vito thinks isn't an idiot is Vito." James removed his report from the typewriter, placed the main copy into the file, then left a carbon copy in Corcoran's mailbox.

The phone rang. Overjoyed that they weren't catching cases, they skipped out the door, while two A team detectives collected their windbreakers and car keys. James drove them south to a Midtown East cop bar called the Blackthorn Tavern. He had a blue 1986 Mustang he'd acquired six months ago from a police auction. The vehicle impound people owed him a favor from his Street Crime Unit days, so against NYPD rules, they had sold the car to James for a fraction of its worth. His right foot glued to the floor, James screeched down Park Avenue, weaving in sickening lurches around any vehicle going slower than his.

Once settled at the bar, they downed a few beers and exchanged war stories with three detectives from the Midtown North Precinct and Manhattan South Homicide. Alex's head felt clouded. The jovial MSHS detective slapped him between the shoulder blades. James declared it time to shift to the next venue, so they tripped down Madison until they came to another bar, called O'Neill's. Half a dozen musicians huddled in a corner with the furtive intensity of an illegal numbers game. But they were playing Irish music, not numbers. The detectives bought drinks, and James, who knew the musicians, borrowed a whistle and joined the session for a few tunes. Alex sat on the outskirts. The jigs and reels drew him in until he fell into a tide race of notes, too fast to fight, an eddying current sweeping away thoughts about Serrachia's trial, his open cases, Catherine ducking his calls, his father, the panic and the gunshots waking him in the middle of the night, the pain in his side. So many things to not think about.

While waiting at the bar for another round, he caught sight of a pool table on the far side of the session. He placed a beer under James' nose and put a hand on his shoulder. "I'll just be there." Pointing to the pool table. James was mid-tune, the whistle in his mouth, so he raised both eyebrows in acknowledgment without missing a note.

Hoping he wasn't too wrecked to play, Alex placed his twenty-five cents on the table, challenging the winner of the previous game, a mid-sixties white guy in an expensive suit. Alex's best game might have been two or three pints ago. Nonetheless, he beat the old guy, then he played the man's younger colleague, beating him too. Next, he dispatched two twenty-something Black guys with frizzy Afros, followed by a paunchy white guy sporting overdone hair gel. After that, no one wanted to play him, which was okay because with his eyes losing focus, he doubted he would continue winning.

He returned to the session. As he tipsily settled into a chair near the musicians, James appeared beside him, balancing a shot in each hand. "Tequila."

"Oh, Jesus," Alex said. "I'm already fucked."

"Don't be a pussy," James said and knocked his back.

Alex sighed, but he drank the liquor. At James' urging, they endured a second round of tequila shots. *That was stupid*, Alex thought, as the second shot thrust him beyond that line, from pleasantly drunk to nauseously wasted.

James clutched Alex's arm. "Let's go back to mine."

Yes, back to James'. Stumbling drunkenly into Matt's late at night would land him balls deep in Karen's fury, or Matt warning him that more cops die from suicide and alcoholism than line of duty injuries. It was like being sixteen.

James fished the car keys out of his pocket.

"James, you're way too hammered to drive," Alex protested. "Why don't we just hail a cab?"

James squinted at the keys. "Nah, s'all right," he slurred.

"No, come on, we'll look for a cab." Nausea crashed through his belly in a sudden, awful wave. Losing his balance, he fell onto one knee and threw up against the side of a closed bank.

"Classy." James said, his hand on Alex's back. "You all right?"

"Yeah, enough." His mouth tasted rancid, but he rebalanced himself underneath the Bank of America sign and then planted his feet on the curb, intently watching the street for an empty cab. When one eventually appeared, he held his arm out. The car pulled to the curb. Pretending they weren't wholly legless, Alex and James clambered into the back seat, and the West Indian driver gave them a thorough eyefuck before veering onto the road and flooring it. Alex latched his eyes onto the skyscrapers, fixed points that never moved; otherwise, the car's swaying would trigger another round of vomiting.

Two weeks after Alex testified in Serrachia's trial, the detectives gathered around the small television in the squad room, awaiting the verdict. The NY1 reporter stood in the middle of Foley Square, interviewing an Orthodox rabbi about what this verdict meant for the

Orthodox community, filling airtime while awaiting news from the courtroom.

Worries over his situation at Matt and Karen's apartment engrossed Alex's attention while he half-watched the TV and wrote a 'five. Karen ran a SoHo gallery. "She's an intense person," Matt would say. Well, she was something. Any time she spoke to Alex, she sounded prickly and cross, even by New York standards. His skin crawled, and his blood pressure worried his doctor. Matt had let him move in, but Karen acted annoyed, like he was an imposition. He'd asked Matt if Karen had a problem with him, and his colleague gently laughed, "Oh, Lex, don't worry about it." Fine, but he still had to share the space. When he was in the apartment, he tiptoed around her, keeping his forays into communal areas limited to the times she wasn't there. He ate out any time he felt a craving for a pizza or bacon, which wasn't healthy for his heart or his bank balance. As he couldn't live like this much longer without losing his mind, he conducted daily searches of property advertisements. Most rentals he could afford in Manhattan were holes, but with some of his inheritance coming in from his father, he thought, maybe, maybe he could stump up a deposit for buying an apartment. No more slum landlords, bacon insults stuck to the windows, or pain in the ass housemates. He would be a 'homeowner,' like a real adult.

"We have word that the jury has reached their verdict." The reporter on the TV broke into Alex's musings. "The jury has found Ernesto Serrachia guilty on all counts of the indictment…" The sentence disappeared under the noise of detectives hollering and whooping. Several clapped Alex on the back. Others clinked celebratory coffee mugs. A career case, one that might help him make grade, eventually, yet he felt more surprised than elated. Everywhere he looked, he saw reasonable doubt. But that was juries. Unpredictable.

Someone turned off the TV, the buzz subsided as people got back to work, and then Alex's phone rang.

"Lex," gushed Vito excitedly. "Don't know if you seen the news, but we fuckin' hit a home run!"

"Yeah, sure," Alex replied, without enthusiasm in his voice.

"Why you gotta be so fuckin' down all the time? We won."

Sure, they won, but the trial and the conviction felt like dipping a coffee mug into the Hudson, pretending it had some impact on the water volume in the river.

Chapter Twenty-Five

After a couple months of looking at places he did not like or could not realistically afford, Alex felt like giving up on Manhattan. Real estate here was a minefield, and Hunters Point, or Williamsburg, or Greenpoint wouldn't be unlivable. They were only just across the East River. Thinking, *this is fucking pointless*, he viewed an apartment on West 87th, between Amsterdam and Columbus, but he promised himself he would look at those places in Brooklyn and the Bronx next week. He didn't expect to ever find an affordable apartment on the Upper West Side. This one was a four-story low-rise constructed of unadorned red bricks with a fire escape painted to match the façade, a little incongruous at the end of a block largely occupied by ostentatious Queen Anne style townhouses, with their bay windows, sculpted cornices, and stone buttresses.

Alex and the real estate guy climbed up the stairs, through the barren, exposed concrete. The real estate guy unlocked a door on the fourth floor. They entered a narrow hallway leading to a cramped living room that connected to a galley kitchen. Stains and a thick quilt of dog hair obscured the carpet. "It's a bit of a project," said the real estate guy when Alex squatted on his haunches, forensically examining one of the stains. On the other side of the hall, he found a bathroom door holding a tacky, dusty stained-glass window. Mold and schmutz stained the tiles, while the grouting had deteriorated into brown sludge, but when he turned on the shower, it produced hot water. Fucking luxury compared to some places he'd lived. Then he followed the real estate guy into the bedroom. "It needs some work, but you can see the potential," the man said, sounding sheepish. More dog hair and grotty carpet, and the closet door hung precariously by one hinge, but the room would fit a queen-sized bed if you had no interest in floor space, and a double if you did. The large window faced south, catching the sun.

"How many dogs did these people have?" Alex asked, sneezing as dust and dog hair stung his sinuses.

"Some," said the real estate guy.

The place needed a fresh coat of paint, the kitchen cabinets replaced, dire green wallpaper removed, the bathroom retiled, and, above all, a new carpet, but Alex liked it more than everything he had seen. He wrote a check for a painful amount of cash, putting a deposit on it, and he signed his life away at the bank, arranging the mortgage. Never had he been so thrilled by the prospect of grilling bacon in his own kitchen.

During these last few months, he'd been tailing James to his Irish music sessions. He had yet to develop James' infinite enthusiasm for jigs and reels, but he found them tolerable, and indeed, preferable over Karen's censorious glares and spikey personality. How did Matt put up with her? He never kvetched about her neuroses. "Oh, she's just a bit quirky," he would say with affection. *One way to put it,* Alex thought vexatiously after Karen chastised him for not cleaning a plate before he went to work at 0700. Matt's view was that Alex should have cleaned the damned plate.

On an evening following an eight-by-four, Alex harbored a lager and a whisky side-by-side in Mona's, a brick dive bar on Avenue B. The Lower East Side had changed since he was a kid here in the 1960s, the Jews, the Poles, the Ukrainians moving elsewhere, while the next wave of immigrants, from China, South Asia, and Central and South America, moved in. Clubs, bars, a mosque, or a housing project might have a faint Star of David hiding in the woodwork, or a dusty mezuzah clinging to a doorframe, ghosts of the Jews who once lived here. Street gangs sold drugs and violence menaced the slums, yet artists, asylum seekers, counter-culture diehards, and anyone else living on society's fringes gathered here, where the neighborhood was still too weird and lawless to have attracted the developers. They squatted in the abandoned buildings, rubbing shoulders with the new immigrants and the dealers, and everyone kind of got along in the chaotic Lower East Side way they always had.

A fiddle player kicked off a set of reels. Her playing seemed to fly, so quick and light, the tune bouncy, danceable. Alex found himself tapping his foot. He stopped thinking about Karen and Lower East Side history, and he turned his head towards the fiddler. Fiery red hair tumbled down her back, tangling like she was too carefree to style it. She wore a tie-dye tunic with diaphanous sleeves that fluttered as she bowed the fiddle.

"Charlotte, what're those tunes?" James asked once the set finished.

Charlotte, thought Alex, the name imprinting in his head.

"I think the first one's called McFadden's Handsome Daughter, the second one's the Flooded Road to Glenties. Third one, I don't know," she responded.

A few sets of tunes later, the detectives went to the can for a piss. Once finished, Alex casually commented, "Who's the fiddle player? The redhead. Charlotte?"

James grinned as he washed his hands. "Yeah, she's a fuckin' great fiddler. She's cute, isn't she?"

"Yeah."

James' grin widened. "You back in the game?"

"I'm always in the game."

"You're *never* in the game. You're always hung up on how pissed off you are at your ex-wife, and women don't think that's a turn-on, you'll be surprised to know. *You* ended things with Ruann 'cause she wanted commitment, and you got all freaked out."

"I'm not," Alex protested, although he knew James was right.

"I'll introduce you to Charlotte. Try something for me, huh? Not a word about your ex."

"All right," Alex said with an eye-roll.

Most of the musicians took a breather between tunes, scattering to the bar, the toilet, or out for a cigarette. Ever the opportunist, James grabbed Charlotte's hand and led her to Alex's table.

"This is Alex," James said. "He's also a homicide detective."

Charlotte eyed him up as if he was some endangered species, then she sat down at his table with her G-and-T. He told her a few stories about the job; chasing perps in a squad-car when he was a patrolman and investigating high-profile homicide cases. She seemed intrigued. It sounded like a TV show. Brimming with bubbly energy, she said that she was trying to write a novel, and she lived with a friend on Sullivan Street in a one bed-apartment divided into three rooms with sheets and a curtain rail. She had started a degree in classics at NYU but moved to Edinburgh for a year abroad, finished her degree at Edinburgh University, then stayed in Scotland until her visa ran out. She eschewed the whole bourgeoise idea of "a career," instead dreaming of buying a van and living in it, working on the land, playing tunes, writing books. He found her hippy dippy attitude towards life charming, almost endearing, like traveling to another country, one far more interesting and vivacious than your own. So unlike Ruann, or any other cop.

The morning sun stabbed into his eyes. It slowly brought him back to consciousness. He lay sprawled on a futon, wearing only his boxers, staring at a yellow ceiling, yellow walls, and a teal sheet covered in spiraling mandala, dangling from the ceiling. Karen would have a stroke if someone painted a wall any color that wasn't eggshell-white. Stray, hazy details from the night oozed through his brain. Meeting Charlotte at the session, fast-talking their way into a club, laughing about how much they both hated clubs, then staggering into her apartment and fumbling through mediocre sex because they were both too drunk. Her roommates probably heard everything.

Charlotte had wrapped herself around his body and nestled her head against his chest.

"What's this?" she asked, touching his lower ribs.

"My ribcage," he suggested, not awake.

"I mean these scars."

His attention on it now, he sniffed in a deep breath while rolling over. He felt a twinge, like a hot blade stabbing his side. "Oh. I was shot a few years ago." He said it more nonchalantly than it deserved. "Be careful. It's tender."

"*Shot?* Jesus. Like with a gun?" In her world, people only got shot on TV. Her hand jumped from his wound to the middle of his stomach.

"Yes." He bit his tongue before letting loose a mordant, *No, with a bow and arrow.* She was pretty, and he'd made it this far. *Watch your mouth. Don't ruin your chances now,* he warned himself.

"By who?" she asked, wide-eyed.

Breathing out through his teeth, he answered, "Some guys who wanted to shoot cops. I was in the wrong place."

"Did you shoot them back?"

"No." For a few seconds, he tuned into the pain. He shut his eyes against the gunfire, against memories of bleeding on the street.

"Why not?"

"They got me first."

"Were you badly hurt?"

"Enough, I guess. I mean, they had to cut out like a third of my lung." Talking about the shooting made it harder to bundle the pain into his out-of-the-way corner.

"Fuck." She paused, mentally working her way around that. "So, you're missing part of your lung?"

"Yeah."

"That sounds really bad. It looks like it was bad."

"It was a big gun. I almost arrested from blood loss."

"Arrested?" She looked confused.

A homicide detective had an easy familiarity with the medical jargon surrounding violent death and injury. "Yeah, like my heart almost stopped." Grimacing, he shifted onto his other side and let his arm fall across her chest and shoulders. "It's a nice morning. We shouldn't talk about that."

"We could talk about something else."

"Or nothing." There were no more words. The sun shone through threadbare curtains, casting a smoky light through the room. How was it that snow melts, that spring comes, that dawn whitens behind the New York skyline? One kiss, and nothing else. They trembled and turned towards one another, open with desire, and he was in her, so high he never wanted to come down, and they came together, a cartwheel fall, spinning, tumbling, interlocked.

As he dressed himself, she asked for his phone number. Surprised, yet not surprised, he wrote it on a notebook. She pressed herself against his side, and he breathed in her scent, spring flowers, a grassy meadow, those sweetened candles on her windowsill. Sparks leapt along his spine, shooting through his limbs. He held her one more time before letting himself out of the apartment, buoyed by the lightness in his belly.

"I'll call," she said, following him down to the sidewalk.

Before the year ended, Alex had moved out of Matt's apartment, packing James' Mustang and Bill's Lincoln with everything he owned. He would always remember receiving the keys from the lawyer, an object he marveled at for some time. One key for the entryway on West 87th, tree-lined and so peaceful that he could forget the violence ripping the streets asunder only a few miles north, and the other key for the apartment itself, a Yale lock affixed to an oak door, the wood weathered and darkened by almost a century of tenants. Catherine bitched at him for not buying a two-bed, with a room for the girls to stay in, but they hardly stayed at his anyway, and what civil servant can afford a two-bed on the Upper West Side? Yes, he could have bought a bigger place in Queens. Hell, he could have bought a mansion in Bed-Stuy. Then Catherine would have bitched about it being too far away, or too dangerous. Whatever — this was his place now. Every wall, door, counter, all of it, except for the building itself. And *he* was delighted with it. *Who cares what my ex thinks?* He hadn't since the early '80s. He introduced Charlotte to the little apartment after he'd furnished it and made it habitable. As giddy as punch-drunk teenagers, they sanctified the bed and the sofa. *His* bed and sofa.

"You could have like three people living in an apartment this size," she observed sleepily, cuddling into the ribs on his unhurt side. "Imagine, if people really *used* urban space. There would be no homelessness."

"Huh," he snorted. She had some strange ideas, sweet and rose-tinted, as if there were easy solutions to problems like violence and homelessness. But he kept his cynicism at bay. It upset her when he got too dark.

"What?" Charlotte asked.

"Just thinking about work."

"Do you ever think about anything else?" she said, gently teasing.

"You." He pulled her against his chest and kissed her.

A few days later, he brought the girls along to see the place.

Sarah slouched on the sofa, her thumbs frenetically working at a handheld video game, while Ellie explored the apartment, commenting, "It's cute, but it's not very big. These kitchen cabinets are falling apart."

"No, it's not. But it's mine. I'm gonna fix the kitchen at some point." It was a hole, but it was his hole.

"You mean, you'll get someone to fix it. Mom always she'll fix things, but she means pay someone to do it."

"No, I'll do it myself. I can put cabinets in. Dad taught me." He winced. The memory stung like acid on a wound. "Wanna take a walk and check out the neighborhood?"

"Okay," said Ellie. "Can we get cake? My friend Jen says the best cake shop is on the Upper West Side." She giggled. "Mom says the apartment is too small, but even *she* likes the Upper West Side."

"Well, it's like Mecca for New York Jews," he responded dryly.

"What?" asked Ellie, not getting his humor.

"Nevermind. Let's go out."

"No. I'm staying," snapped Sarah, staring harshly at her game.

Alex sighed. "Sarah, it's a nice day. You're not gonna sit in here playing with that thing all afternoon."

"Why not?"

He crossed his arms over his chest, confronting pre-teen intransigence and her fundamentally philosophical query. "Because… I told you you're not."

"So?"

Pursing his lips into a thin smile, he knelt down beside her. "Kiddo, in the real world, people tell you that you gotta do things you don't wanna do, and you gotta do them. So, come on." He stood and took her hand.

"The real world sucks," she complained.

"No kidding," he replied, fully in agreement.

Sullenly, she threw the videogame onto the sofa. They left the apartment and moseyed along Amsterdam. The city glittered in the winter sun. Last night's snow shimmered like white jewels adorning the trees, cars, and buildings. The three found a café where they ate cake, and then Alex led the girls into Central Park, three long blocks away from his place, and Sarah forgot her surly mood when she stroked a mounted police horse.

"Why aren't you a mounted cop?" she asked, rubbing the horse's silky brown neck and shoulder.

"'Cause I ended up being a detective," Alex answered. "And I don't know how to ride."

"This would be better," she announced. "You could learn to ride."

The mounted officer smiled, amused. "There you have it, huh."

They crossed the bridge near the duck pond. The girls threw rocks into the pond, giggling when the rocks punched holes in the ice and competing over who could throw a rock the farthest.

"Bet you can't throw a rock as far as me, Dad," said Sarah.

Alex dug one out of the snow, his fingers hurting from the cold, but he flung it as hard as he could. It burst through the ice in a shower of light and spray. Then he picked up a flat rock, aiming for a patch of water where the ice had melted, and he flicked it like a frisbee. It skittered across the water before disappearing into the slate grey ripples. The girls laughed, clapping.

"That's awesome. Show me how to do that," said Ellie.

Even though he lost all feeling in his hands, he spent about half an hour showing them how to skip rocks. How you select an appropriate rock, the right way to flick your wrist and your elbow so it spins as you release it. One of those life skills a father should teach.

Having successfully skimmed a couple rocks, Ellie paused her hunt for another flat one and looked at him, her expression tight-lipped and serious. "Dad, can we spend Christmas here?"

"Yeah, please," added Sarah. "Mom makes us do it with Grandma, and she's really weird."

"And boring," Ellie agreed. "All she does is talk about her medical problems and how much she hates her neighbors." They meant Catherine's mother, the crazy old matriarch of Catherine's large family, who Alex had always found weird and who had always kvetched about her medical problems and her neighbors.

Alex raised his eyes towards the cathedral towers and spires of the Eldorado and San Remo. His heart shriveled. "I gotta work."

Their faces crumpled in disappointment. "You're always working."

"I have to catch bad guys, like Joe Friday." He hoped simplifying the world to the bad guys and good guys they saw on television convinced them that he, at least, was one of the latter, even if it meant he could not spend the holidays with them.

"Come on, Dad." Ellie snaked her eyes in that exaggerated teenage way. "You always say your job isn't like the cops on TV."

Ain't that the truth, Alex thought. "Okay, then I'll tell you like you're an adult. My boss told me I gotta work that week, so I gotta work that week. That's how it goes. We're Jews. What do we care about Christmas?"

"Mom says it's about the family getting together," argued Sarah.

"We do that on Passover." Another holiday he never took off work, along with Hanukah and the High Holy days. "Anyway, your mother hates me, and your grandmother hates me even more, so the family never gets together."

The girls couldn't argue with that.

On a late December morning, the first light of the sun hid behind grey clouds and greyer skyscrapers, the flat darkness weighing down on the shoulders of anyone awake before sunrise. Alex shaved and dressed himself in his suit, more annoyed than usual about working because unlike most years, he had a girlfriend. But Charlotte lathered him with kisses and nuzzled the side of his neck, reassuring him that she did not mind him working through Christmas. It was a bullshit holiday anyway, she explained. A long time ago, it had celebrated the solstice, the longest night, but it had been subjugated to the neoliberal, consumerist monstrosity of capitalism that would destroy the planet. Besides, she would be out late, playing a gig for a group of Irish expats at a hotel in Midtown, the proceeds of which were allegedly not going to the IRA. But Charlotte was more incensed that she had to play *Fairy Tale of New York* and *Galway Girl* instead of her beloved jigs and reels. Whatever the reasons, Alex felt relieved that she put up with his antisocial hours. She kissed him again. The thrill sang through every nerve in his body, and he thrust his tongue into her mouth. Her body arched gloriously against his as she wrapped her arms around his middle. Higher than any dope fiend, bouncing on his toes, he tied his tie, held her one more time, and then he strode to the subway on West 86th and Broadway, feeling hyper and giddy despite the long tour ahead of him.

While the city celebrated peace on earth and goodwill to men, Alex, James, and Matt attended an autoerotic suicide, followed by a DOA who had tried and failed to jump from one rooftop to another, a DV assault with a firearm that left the vic alive but in critical condition, and, alongside an SVU detective, they interviewed an agg assault victim at Columbia Pres who had nearly died from a broomstick being pushed up his rectum. He sheepishly said that he'd consented to rough sex, but he had soft, rubber dildos in mind. Between calls, they acquired a life-size cardboard Santa cut-out, drew bullet holes in it with the red and black Sharpies, then positioned it in the middle of the squad room floor, surrounded by evidence cones. Alex and James wanted to buy a nativity scene and do a multiple, but Matt, the voice of reason, warned, "Our boss is the most Irish Catholic guy in the most Irish Catholic police department outside of Dublin. Think about it. Is that a good idea?" Reluctantly they decided it wasn't, not if they wanted to keep their jobs, so they settled for Santa.

Released from the long, busy tour, Alex and James propped up a bar for a few unwinding beers before going home. When she finished her gig, Charlotte hopped on an uptown 1 train and met Alex at West 87th Street. She threw her arms around him like they'd been separated for ten years, and then she caressed his lips, his throat, his collarbones.

"Lex, I've been doing a lot of meditating," she murmured into his shoulder. "It's really good. Got me through *Fairy Tale of New York.* I think you should try it with me."

She was the only girlfriend who called him that. It was a cop moniker, but Charlotte heard James and others calling him *Lex,* and she liked it. She had asked him how he got it, and he told her about his first partner on his beat in the Sixth, Cal Konenburg, with his aversion towards shouting at you in two syllables when he could shout in one. Neither Alex's first nor his last name suited Cal Konenburg's style, so he dropped the *A*. It stuck, which Alex didn't mind because it was a pretty inoffensive way to abbreviate his name.

Meditation? Probably a waste of time but he played along, sitting on the floor cross-legged, facing her while she talked about centering yourself. She told him to lace his hands together over his diaphragm, to expand his stomach outwards when he inhaled, to clear his mind of all emotions, to concentrate on a single flame and the feeling of breathing. But he looked at the splotchy, lumpy plaster on the living room wall where he'd torn off that green wallpaper and thought about repainting it. He felt twitchy, bored, desperate for another drink. The pain in his right side tugged at his attention. A siren wailed down Amsterdam. A dog barked. A driver on West 87th honked their horn. The downstairs neighbors played music with a heavy beat. He couldn't handle going into his own head. He craved her touch, her breath on his skin.

"Charlotte, this isn't doing anything for me," he complained after ten minutes. "I'm going into rigor. I can't clear my head. I never can. I'm balls deep in cases. I've got a million fucking things I think I need to do. I'm sitting here, and I can't stop thinking about it, and the more we sit, and you talk to me about deep breathing and feeling my soul or whatever, the more I think about all those fucking cases and whatever else. My brain doesn't turn off."

She laughed, a sound like a waterfall, then she crawled over to him and slithered against his body, pushing him onto his back. Her hands inched sexily along his chest, up to his throat. Her soft lips pressed into his mouth, and his insides vibrated as a thousand tiny needles fired through his spine.

"Okay, okay," she giggled. "You're like a tumbleweed. Always rolling."

"Sure," he said.

"In all the tumbling in your head, you'll come up with the great insight that solves the cases, like Sam Spade."

"Uh, I wish it worked like that, but it usually doesn't. All I'm really achieving on a good day is death investigation SOP. And I still gotta paint this place and do something about the kitchen because all the cabinets are fucked. Sam Spade probably doesn't do DIY."

"You're multi-talented. You can solve murders and fix cabinets. Bet Sam Spade *can't* do that." Her fingers glided to the middle of his chest, then down the line of hair to his belly, to his groin, electrifying every nerve they touched. She flung her legs over his hips. "Well, what about sex and maybe watching crappy television? Would that clear your mind?"

"Sounds like a better idea."

A week later, Alex combined a belated house-warming party with a New Year party. He rounded up officers from his own squad and the Manhattan North precincts. Nick Selvio, from the One-Oh-Three, heard about the new apartment on the wire, and he called Alex, promising to show his face at the party. Alex wasn't bothered that Selvio had more or less invited himself, but he felt a little hurt that Fred hadn't also invited himself. More worryingly, Fred seemed elusive. Multiple calls to the One-Oh-Three squad room later, Alex finally reached him. He was no longer in possession of Fred's home number now that his ex-partner lived in Bay Side. Why the hell hadn't Fred given him the number? Why hadn't he asked for it?

Sounding dismayed, Fred sighed, "I'm sorry, Lex. I'm happy for you, like it's so great you've bought a place. So great. But I'm completely swamped with the kids. Celia really needs me home."

"Come out for an hour," Alex said, a pleading note in his voice. "I haven't seen you since…the shooting. Since you came to the hospital."

"I know, it's shit. But I really can't. It's not just an hour. It will take me an hour to *get* to the Upper West Side."

"You can't take a night off?"

"No, Alex, it doesn't work like that, but that's not something you would understand, would you?"

Something changed in Fred's tone. "What?" Alex croaked, sickened by his painful memories of pathetically blown priorities.

"You seeing your kids much?"

"They're with their mother in Buffalo, like every damn Hanukah and Christmas and New Year. You're really going there, Fred?" He was conscious of blood leaving his internal organs, the sensation of his digestive tract immobilizing.

"Well, I'm just saying, I've got to put the kids and Celia ahead of things, you know." Fred's tone became uncomfortable. "Look, man, I gotta run. See you 'round." The phone line went dead.

Alex held his face in his hands and willed his heart to pump some blood back into his gut. Whatever partnership he once had with Fred melted into nothing, leaving him with a knife in the belly. Fred was a different person. Alex wondered if he himself was. But he was having a party all the same. On New Year's Eve, he christened his apartment, filling it with cops, their partners, and Charlotte, who was captivated by these policemen and women, with their cynical pragmatism and bleak, gallows humor that seemed alluring and dangerous, the antithesis of her Village hippy circles.

An hour before midnight, Alex cornered Selvio in the kitchen. "I think Fred's mad at me," he said in a quiet voice.

"He got turned down from Major Case," replied Selvio with a shrug. "He was really upset when you got shot, but I think he was a bit pissed at you, you know, 'cause you got the transfer to Homicide outta nowhere, and he's been working his ass off and hasn't made grade or been transferred."

"I worked *my* ass off on those organized crime cases," snapped Alex bitterly. "Why is this my fault? The department does what it does, and sometimes it's fucking arbitrary as hell."

"I'm not saying it makes sense. It's just Fred being kinda difficult. To be honest, he hasn't been out drinking with anyone for a couple years. He had another kid and stopped doing anything fun. I wouldn't take it personally."

"Yeah." How the hell else should he take it? Beer slid down his throat the wrong way. Tickling heat cut through his chest; he coughed harshly, then tried soothing it with another mouthful, finishing the can.

"Don't breathe in the beer," Selvio advised. "Is your colleague, Detective Allan, single?"

Alex snorted. "Yeah, but if she thinks you're prowling around, she'll chop your balls off."

Chuckling, Selvio sauntered away to get his balls chopped off. Alex cracked open a fresh beer and drained it. God, he wished he didn't feel like shit and appreciated the party more. Nothing in the last week had gone well. Yesterday, he'd wrestled with an uncooperative perp. Today, he was paying for it, living with an ulcerating burn in his ribs that neither the beer nor the company numbed.

"What's wrong?" Charlotte joined him in the kitchen and nuzzled his neck and his cheek.

"My gunshot wound hurts tonight. More than normal." He suppressed the impulse to bitch about Fred. What could he say, or how was he supposed to get his head around Selvio's report? Everyone knew transferring to elite units depended on politics and luck as much as hard work and talent. How could Fred resent him for that?

"Have you taken anything for it?"

"Ibuprofen."

"Western medicine doesn't have *all* the answers."

Oh, fuck, she was going to do something weird, but he checked his caustic objections. It would be weird but harmless, and she took this stuff seriously. Charlotte rummaged through the kitchen, collecting salt, cumin, cloves, ginger, and then she boiled water. She poured the spices into the water and dropped a tea towel into the pan. A few minutes later, she fished it out with a fork. "Put that against the scar."

"Really?"

"It won't make it worse, will it?"

"Probably not." He squashed the hot tea towel into his side, flinching and grunting as it burned his skin, but he squeezed it, holding it there until it cooled. It drew out some of the pain. Enough, so he could breathe without tears in his eyes. *Yes, heat, you idiot.* A hot water bottle would have worked just as well. But he hugged Charlotte. She thrust her tongue into his mouth. Her hands glided under his shirt, and his skin sizzled at her touch. Yeah, let her think the ginger and salt cocktail worked. "I gotta use the can," he murmured into her ear. "Back in a sec."

Someone was in the john. He lounged beside the door, watching two precinct detectives from the Two-Three squad munch through the Doritos on the coffee table. Then Bill Ryan squeezed out of the bathroom and tottered towards the sofa. He grinned drunkenly. "Great party, Lex. You alright?"

"Yeah," Alex answered.

"I've got to tell you… I got this fucking crazy message. Some nutcase saying they know who killed Elam Liebowitz, and it wasn't Ernie Serrachia. Can you fucking believe it? Guy's been tried and convicted. What more do people want?"

"What nutcase?" Alex asked, sounding more sober and serious than he'd intended. Completely repressing his niggling doubts about that defendant would require a significant amount of alcohol. *Why is this weighing on you,* he argued with his conscience. *Don't be so neurotic.* It wasn't his problem. Other than trial prep, he hadn't touched the case since October, '87, so what did he know? The evidence against Serrachia could have been better than it looked. Bill and Marty had worked it after the shooting, and they'd never panicked or quizzed him about those exculpatory witness statements.

"Oh, it doesn't matter," Bill replied flippantly. "Where the hell did I put my beer?" And he wandered off in search of his beer.

Alex necked the rest of his beer, then he fetched another one from a nearby case. He planned on getting fantastically wrecked. Alcohol would vanquish Serrachia, his wound, Eddie, Fred, his father, and everything else. At least for tonight. "Fuck 1990," he said to the Two-Three detectives on the sofa and clanked his beer can against theirs.

Fifteen minutes or so before midnight, Alex had only achieved marginal tipsiness, mainly because he got diverted into a make-out session with Charlotte in the bathroom when people destroyed a bottle of Smirnoff. Nonetheless, it seemed perfectly reasonable that James was opening a window, in December, and then jumping onto the fire escape stairs.

"You coming?" James asked. "It's your apartment."

Alex straddled the windowsill and shimmied onto the airy staircase, weaving with a touch of vertigo. Grinning manically, James bounded upwards, and Alex yelled, "What the hell are you doing?" But he ran after him, gripping the rough, weather-beaten railings. Behind him, he heard the groans and rattles of several others crawling through the window. The stairs stopped about four feet below the roof.

"Maybe you can't get to the roof," Alex said. His side ached, Charlotte's remedy wearing off. His head whirled with the yawning exposure.

"Nah, I think we can." James clambered onto the railings, using gaps between bricks as handholds for balance, like a rock climber. He got his arms on the roof ledge and disappeared over the side.

"Is it all right?" Alex called nervously.

James' head and shoulders appeared against the pale sky. "Yeah, it's fuckin' fantastic up here! Come on. Once you stand up on that railing, it's not that high, and you got this huge ledge, and it's a piece of cake."

Alex stepped onto the bottom rail while digging his fingers into the narrow gap between a drainpipe and the bricks. Adrenaline seared through his system as he crouched with his knees against the top rail. The nothingness below reached out for him. His hands ached from his death grip on the drainpipe.

"Just stand," said James. "Then you'll be fine."

He steeled his nerves, like he would when busting down a door, and slowly straightened his knees. The roof ledge greeted him like a long-lost lover, and he threw his arms around it, taking in heavy, relieved lungfuls of air, before thrutching himself over, swinging his legs and rolling onto the roof.

"Fun, eh?" said James.

"Is it all right?" called Charlotte from the stairs.

"Yeah, come up here," Alex called back.

Cautiously, she scaled the railings and grasped the drainpipe, and with more confidence, she hoisted herself up and over onto the roof. "That's cool," she said, pressing herself against Alex's side. "Are your ribs better?"

"A little." He held her close.

The city lights sparkled in a wheeling galaxy; the Hudson murky and black to the west, New Jersey's hazy glow beyond it. Closer, the four and five-story walk-ups were punctuated by the taller West Side skyscrapers, the medieval towers of the Eldorado, the San Remo, the Ansonia, leading the eye towards the Midtown skyline in the south, the Chrysler Building's silvery Art Deco arches, the Met Life Building's blocky outline, the Empire State Building's illuminated steps and glowing pinnacle, the Pan Am Building's white peak. The city blazed away, a dense, glittering wall of spires and pulsing ribbons of lights floating on the dark water.

Marty and Bill appeared at the edge of the parapet and flopped onto the roof. James announced, "My God, we need more booze!" He straddled the parapet like a horse, then he flung his other leg over, vanishing behind the wall. About a dozen other cops struggled with the ascent, laughing anxiously, but climbing up there was now a matter of pride and no one wanting to look scared. James' head popped above the parapet. Bill leaned over and hucked two boxes of beer, Charlotte's fiddle, and James' bagpipes onto the roof.

"Fuck Fred, he's the one who's missing out," Selvio whispered to Alex as he settled himself on the roof.

"Yeah, he is." Alex felt a lump catching in his windpipe. He opened a lively beer and slurped down the foam before it exploded. "Any luck with Jean?"

"Hah," barked Selvio. "You were right."

Someone queried the wisdom of drinking up here, which prompted Jean Allan to tell a story about a DOA call from her beat cop days, the vic splattered on the pavement because he'd been wasted and toppled from the roof of a twelve-story building. Marty recounted that when he'd visited Eddie Trenemen at New York Pres, more than half the other patients in the spinal unit were there because they'd fallen off fire escapes, roofs, or window ledges while drunk or high. At five-to-midnight, Charlotte tuned her fiddle and James assembled his bagpipes, his cheeks puffing out, the drones humming like a low-flying plane. James and Charlotte launched into a strathspey – it bounced from their instruments, steady, cadenced – then they cranked up a gear into a fast set of reels, and forty blocks to the south, the glittering ball fell in Times Square, while fireworks above Brooklyn and across the river in New Jersey splintered the sky, shrouding it with billowing smoke. Marty launched a couple fireworks he'd confiscated from a perp, and a patrol sergeant from the Two-Eight opened a bottle of champagne. They toasted to the arrival of 1991, to one another, and James and Charlotte played more reels as the smoke cleared from the sky, with passing aircraft flying overhead like slow moving stars, the low clouds glowing softly from the New York light pollution, and no one on that rooftop worried about the precipitous storm approaching their city.

Part 5

Chapter Twenty-Six

April 2010

Farah al-Sanneh, the chief of Trial Bureau 50, assigned herself as lead prosecutor on the Lennon case. She'd been promoted three months ago, after her then-supervisor, Simon McNally, had a legendary altercation with Wakefield over the new DA's policy of encouraging his ADAs to turn over discovery earlier than the letter of New York law required (which was pretty much the last minute). McNally was on an indefinite climbing trip in the Alps. That told everyone what they needed to know. As did the promotion of Farah, an Iraqi-American ADA who embodied the stereotype of the big city prosecutor, woeful in her demeanor and forever sprinting through 100 Centre Street with a briefcase overstuffed with motions, affidavits, and answers to motions. Everyone described her as cautious and thorough, never cutting a corner, remarkably mindful of the Constitution and ethics. She prepped diligently for trials, her closing arguments were skillful but sometimes lacked passion, and she would fight hard for a case but showed thin patience for lazy police work. God help the cop whose warrantless search got evidence excluded.

Her expropriation of this case filled Alex's stomach with nervy butterflies, but not because she was a scrupulous attorney who could be tough with cops. Far worse – he had slept with her last year, and they hadn't worked a case together since. She had just broken up with an FBI agent, and he was single, lonely, and in her office working late. No one else was on that floor. In the evening twilight, suddenly, they were kissing, her tongue in his mouth, her hands under his shirt, and seconds later, they had removed one another's clothes. The feeling of her hands sliding against his skin was intoxicating. The heat inside his chest when she took him was like lightning crackling through his nervous system.

They'd laughed at their transgression – office sex! Fun, elicit, a secret that breathed life and excitement into the relationship. He knew he was 'rebound guy,' but he suppressed that for three months.

Until the day he'd been sleeping through those blue-tinged hours before dawn, dimly aware of Farah's hand on his flank.

"Where do you see this going?" she murmured.

That woke him up. "What do you mean?"

"Do you actually want to… I don't know… go out? Make this a real thing. Not just a spend some nights together thing? What are they calling it these days? Fuck buddies. That's a shit label for something really complicated."

He twisted onto his back. Her bronze hand lingered on his belly, rising and falling as he breathed. "I don't know. My track record with 'real things' sucks. I'll freak out and fuck it up. I thought this worked. Doesn't matter what you call it. We don't have to call it anything. Fuck labels."

"It's not working for me. It was fun, at first, being sneaky like teenagers when we're middle-aged adults. But now… I don't know. I feel like we're treading water. I think we should end this before it goes further and drives me crazy with where it isn't going. I mean, sex is okay, and it's not your fault that you're on all those drugs, and it doesn't work that often. You obviously need to be on those drugs."

Oh, shit. His mouth dried out, and he sat up straight in the bed. Farah was bringing *that* up. Anti-depressants killed his sex drive. And she knew about them. She'd discovered the Zoloft in his bathroom while searching for an aspirin. The meds had surprised her – he'd forgotten to hide them – and he'd panicked, begging her to keep her mouth shut. "You know what cops are like."

"It's not anything to be ashamed of," she'd said. "But I get it. The police department is full of macho pricks."

She'd kept her word. She was honest to a fault. But that didn't fix their sex life. "I can do the casual sex thing…" She let the sentence fade away, then breathed in audibly. "I know we don't always get that, and sometimes, I think, I'm forty-eight and basically single, and a part of me wants stability, you know, and to actually be *with* someone. Plus, it's not really ideal that we work together. I don't think my boss would be happy if he found out. Or yours."

"You could transfer to Rackets or something," he said. "Then it wouldn't matter."

"Or you could," she replied.

Complicated indeed. Amidst her waffle, he understood, but he wasn't up for a serious relationship, and as she said, it would be tricky given they worked together. No one was really going to transfer. SSRI side-effects notwithstanding, he didn't feel that way about Farah. He would not move heaven and earth for her, nor would she move it for him. If he was being honest with himself, he would say he hadn't felt that way about anyone since Charlotte Anderson. The handful of girlfriends he'd slept with since Charlotte hadn't been people he would chase through an airport. If Farah wanted serious commitment or a reliable sexual partner, he couldn't offer either one. Still, he suffered a touch of heartsickness and frustration. The SSRIs fucked with everything, especially casual sex. He toyed with throwing them down the toilet. Because suicidal thoughts and debilitating depression would solve his problems? Did he want to go back there? No, the damned things kept his illness in check, not completely level or sane but closer to both, and he had to live with the lousy side-effects.

Working a case with Farah after her promotion was inevitable – one hot redball, the sort of case where a Trial Bureau chief takes the reins, and he had to deal with unresolved tension and sorrow wrapped in a tight band around his heart.

Criminal justice, however, cares little for personal drama. The system grinds on. A grand jury indicted Gemma Lennon for second-degree murder and endangering the welfare of a child, and then she was arraigned in Supreme Court. "Doped up to her Goddamned eyeballs at the arraignment," Farah reflected when Alex met her afterwards. She spritzed cleaning spray onto her glasses. "The judge had to ask her to repeat herself more than once. And she's not using Legal Aid or her malpractice pal anymore. Her sister's hired Marie Adams to represent her."

"Adams? Great." Alex hissed out a throaty breath. He shifted his weight and crossed his left knee over his right one. Adams used to work in the DA's office. Three years ago, she crossed the aisle to the more lucrative world of criminal defense, and she was one of the sharpest defense attorneys downtown, known for representing ostensibly sympathetic defendants and wringing jurors' hearts. He added, "I guess she thinks her client's competent to stand trial."

"Well, she hasn't filed a 730 motion. If she thought she could win it, I'm sure she would."

They were in Farah's office, the prosecutor playing the confession video on her computer. Cringing, Alex listened to snippets of himself describing his lousy parenting. Why hadn't he used some other story? Or bullshitted one?

His eyes wandered to the window. The ADA's office faced the Financial District, overlooking the scaffolding and cranes surrounding the site where the World Trade Center once stood, and a new shining tower rose above the wreckage. The half-light of a cloudy, wet day cast a grey haze through the windows. Like that first time. He had an achy memory of the warmth, the tingling pleasure consuming his body, Farah unbuttoning his shirt, breathing into his neck, his bare skin warm and sweating against hers. It shimmered in his thoughts like an indistinct mirage, water in the desert, distant and improbable.

Today, Farah acted aloof and professional, the consummate trial lawyer. Unmoved by his monologue, she fast-forwarded to Lennon's machinations about the devil.

"Okay, she's got some weird ideas. But weird ideas aren't the same thing as legal insanity or extreme emotional disturbance," she said.

"Yeah, I know." He moved his eyes away from Ground Zero. Did Farah look out that window at the scaffolding, the long shadow of 9/11, and think about this country invading and bombing the hell out of her home country? During their fling, they'd talked about depression and anxiety, but they'd never talked about the war or politics. Then again, it wasn't like people asked for his thoughts on the Holocaust, just because he was Jewish – that would be weird – so it seemed weird and confusing, *thinking* that he should have asked her about the war, merely because her parents had emigrated from Iraq long before Saddam Hussein came into power.

"Adams has already asked if I will accept a 40.15 plea." Farah reminded him that he wasn't thinking about the case at all. "I said no. I don't think she fits the criteria. Her reaction to your story tells me she can understand consequences, generally. She also said to you that she didn't want cops and doctors to be questioning her. And she stuck to the carjacker story until this interrogation. She lied to medical staff, you, Missing Persons, other cops. That tells me she understood and appreciated the consequences of her actions, and she knew it was wrong."

Before this meeting, Alex had gone to an appointment with Gillard. The psychiatrist had asked him to recount the 1987 shooting and emotions or discomfort in his body – and there was plenty of that – associated with it. He had watched her laser flitting from left to right while thinking about his emotions and his painful ribs, then he'd concentrated on relaxing, zoning out, attentive to any spontaneous thought or feeling. Following a session, you were meant to unwind, not attend a meeting in the DA's office with an ex about a murder case.

"Alex? Did you hear what I said? You've spoken to her more than anyone else in LE."

"Oh." His head felt sore and fuzzy. "She was pretty out of it, to be honest, but yeah, she stuck to the story."

"'Out of it?'"

"Kind of spaced out and disengaged." Like how he felt right now.

"I guess her lawyer could argue that the carjacker was some sort of delusion."

"She could argue anything."

"You've been through Lennon's medical records." Farah flipped through the file. "One hospitalization. When she was sixteen?"

"Yeah." While Gillard had decompressed him with her meditation exercises, some of it came back on the subway ride to Foley Square. A little bit of anxiety, a sharp pain in his right side he couldn't block out.

"Did you find any more information about that?"

"No, patient confidentiality," he answered.

"Right. And she was a minor. So that's probably out. Until she started ranting about the devil in your interview, she gave you no other indications of a delusional system or any kind of hallucinations?"

"No."

"What about the people she worked with at Yeshiva? They say anything useful?"

"No."

"Maybe they should be re-interviewed. The only family she has is her sister, Stephanie?"

"Yeah."

"But she's not cooperative?"

"God no. But she said Gemma 'wasn't in her right mind.'"

"And she's a trained psychiatrist, right?" Farah tilted an eyebrow.

"She's a chef," Alex said.

"I know. And ACS, they have nothing? No reports from her school or anything like that?"

"No."

She doodled a 3D cube on a notepad. "You all right, Alex?"

"I'm just not feeling that well today." It seemed sensible to avoid personal stuff, like telling her that he had come here straight from therapy. Whatever feelings he had for her would not advance his shaky mental health or the case.

"Like mentally or are you coming down with something? There's a nasty cold going around."

"Mentally," he admitted wearily.

"Okay, you have to take care of yourself. We'll keep this short today. You found no evidence Lennon was on any medication?"

"Only thing I found in her apartment was muscle relaxants."

"Yeah, I read that in your 'fives. It's a bit weird."

Alex puffed out a noticeably tired breath. "I dunno. I've looked at so many medicine cabinets that I don't know what's weird or normal anymore."

That elicited a tiny smile, like when she found his quips funny. "We should re-interview Lennon's co-workers and those teachers. And maybe the brother-in-law if her sister won't cooperate? You might be able to reach out to him, 'cause, you know, he's a cop."

"Maybe," Alex said doubtfully. The brother-in-law was firmly screwed under the sister's thumb. He doubted that any kind of police fraternal connection would unscrew him.

"Right. Okay. That's where we're at. Take it easy today, and we'll meet soon. Definitely before we turn over discovery."

Leaving things unsaid might be wise, but wisdom had never defined his approach to relationships. He hesitated before leaving her office, loosening his tie, scratching the back of his head with his left hand. His heartbeat flapped in his ears. "You wanna talk about, you know, last year?"

Farah's expression stayed impassive, but she stopped doodling. "Alex, I don't see the point. It happened, and it didn't work. I think it's better for both of us to just focus on the case."

"Yeah." Of course, she had washed it off her fingers. He should do the same.

It was a long subway ride uptown to the office, and he missed roll call. Straightaway, he commandeered the interview room sofa so he could read documents while lying down. It wasn't subtle, and Ray rushed in, asking if he was all right. The whole office must be questioning his mental health.

"I'm just reviewing the murder book," Alex said.

"On the sofa?" queried Ray.

"My back's playing up," Alex lied.

"Farah al-Sanneh's the riding DA, isn't she?" Ray asked.

"Yup."

"That's awkward," Ray said in a disapproving tone. He had starkly Catholic views about casual sex.

"It's not a thing," Alex grumbled. "She's over it."

"Are you?" Ray arched both eyebrows.

"Yeah." After the break-up, his panic attacks returned, triggered by loud noises like subway buskers and construction. He'd felt as if he'd caused so many people grief; their lives would be easier without him. Dangerous thoughts that traversed a precarious ledge. One wrong step, you don't survive the landing. Ray and Gibson had been worried, and Alex imagined their late-night phone calls, panicking over his deteriorating health. If he hadn't been crushed by his depression, too enervated to think or plan anything, he would have been worried. His shrink had raised his SSRI dose until he felt queasy and cloudy, but less suicidal.

"You look tired and pale," Ray observed.

"That's just my face." Alex deflected with sarcasm. "I told Farah I'd review this."

After saying, "If you need anything, shout," Ray closed the door.

Unable to relax or focus, Alex skimmed the news on his phone for ten minutes, only reading headlines, then he reread Suzanne's medical history, but nothing suggested her mother suffered Munchausen's-by-proxy or abused her in any way. He skimmed through the statements her teachers had given him. Somewhere amidst those witness statements, his eyes fluttered shut on their own accord.

When he woke up, half an hour had disappeared. *What the fuck?* He should have been reviewing the case! His headache had reinvented itself as a dull heaviness inside his skull, rather than a hammering pain. His colleagues had let him sleep in peace. There were no phone camera photos of detectives pretending to give him fellatio, no weird stuff overrunning his desk, and not a single random object balanced on his body. Were they treading lightly around him again? Oh, he hoped not! He felt crazier than his diagnoses when they treated him like fragile glass. Feeling bleary, he crossed the squad room to brew a pot of coffee. Flashbacks drained him and fanned his depression like a hot wind blowing through a forest fire. Gillard wanted another session next week; she'd said that he might dip in and out of relapses. For a while. For the rest of his life.

Chapter Twenty-Seven

"Wheeler, you're a piece of shit."

Marcus looked up from a *New Yorker* magazine. Cat Silver was on a rampage, and nothing good could come from that.

"What the hell are you doing reading that up-its-own-rectum-intellectual bourgeoisie crap, Wheeler?" she demanded. "At work!"

"You went to an upstate wine-tasting on your last RDO," protested Marcus. "You don't got a leg to stand on, giving me shit about the *New Yorker*. And you just used the word 'bourgeoisie.' Bet you can't even spell it."

"You're not standing on any legs. You're sitting on your ass. Why aren't you out there working Eugene Solomon?"

A drug dealer found dead seven months ago in the driver's seat of his Range Rover. No witnesses. No physical evidence. "And do what? There's nothing to work."

One cubicle over, Alex browsed through the murder book for one of last year's cases, a double homicide on its way to trial in a month, unless the defendant pled out or moved for a continuance. He tried his damndest to tune out his colleagues, which became impossible when Cat said, "You wanna taste *this*?" and she straddled Marcus, with her crotch in his face.

He screamed, "Ooooooh," in mock hysteria.

His wails abruptly ceased when the sound of heavy footsteps vibrated along the floor. Two strange men in expensive, dark suits spoke to Cat, who had climbed off Marcus' lap with remarkable aplomb. The men had badges pinned to their chests. FBI. Cat shrugged apologetically, waving a finger in Alex's direction. "Gimme a dollar," she said to Marcus.

"A dollar! Why?"

"So I don't plaster your Facebook page with more photos of naked men."

"That was you? You hacked into my Facebook? My Mom reads that."

"Yup. Your passwords suck."

The FBI agents marched across the squad room towards Alex's cubicle.

"Detective Boswell?"

"Uh, yes?" He swallowed, but there was no saliva in his mouth to wet his throat. Had an investigation stumbled into a DEA/FBI/ATF/who-knows-what-alphabet-soup operation? These things happened. In New York, you can't walk three blocks without tripping over another agency's investigation. You collar some shitbag, then your supervisor tells you, no, you can't touch that guy. He's crucial to someone else's case. A case closed, a report sealed, and you rarely found out the reason why. You probably didn't want to know.

The FBI agents served him a white sliver of paper folded into thirds. A subpoena. His heart stalled, like the clutch failed. Fuck, *now* he wished the agents had come here to tell him to keep his hands off some perp or other because they were critical to a federal undercover op. The usual New York criminal justice mishegoss.

His fingers lost coordination as he clumsily unfolded the subpoena. It only supplied his name and a time he had to appear at the Federal District Court for the Southern District of New York, five days from now. He gnawed at his lower lip. What could he tell that grand jury and not kiss his career goodbye?

"This is a shakedown," Marcus whined from the other side of the cubicle.

"Yup," Cat said cheerfully, shaking her head. "You shouldn't use your dog's name as your password."

"Why are you always fucking with me?" asked Marcus.

I'm gonna need a lawyer, Alex thought. A proactive thing to do, more useful than waiting for the train to hit him like he was tied to the tracks. And not a DEA union lawyer, but a real criminal defense lawyer, one who knew their way around the federal court system. He skimmed through his phone contacts, searching the names for a good lawyer who wasn't working on any of his open cases or cases bound over for trial.

"Lex, what are you doing?" Ray's head appeared around the edge of his cubicle. "What's that?"

The subpoena sat in plain view, on top of last year's double homicide.

"You've got a subpoena?" Ray frowned as he shrugged off his jacket. "*Federal* court? For the thing with Vito?"

"Yeah." Alex released a shaking sigh.

"Fuck," Ray said.

"Yeah."

Ray fell heavily onto a chair and swiveled it, staring at him with the laser-eyed look he'd given hundreds of perps.

"We didn't have the technology," Alex said quickly. Fear crawled up his gullet. "DNA was pretty damned limited – it wasn't even a thing until the mid-nineties – so we were building cases based on whatever we had. Sometimes – or a lot of the time – informants lie if they think it's gonna solve their own legal problems, and eyewits suck. They always fucking suck. Or lie. Or both. And we had no time for lots of follow-up interviews and recanvasses, and the bosses were going nuts. If you weren't clearing homicides, Liam Corcoran would nail your balls up on the squad room white board. So, we cleared homicides."

"Yeah," said Ray in an uncertain tone. Ten years younger, Ray had narrowly missed the worst years of the crack epidemic, and he'd put in a few years at OCCB before transferring to Manhattan North Homicide, the former a unit where federal and state money flowed like the Hudson, every investigation was well organized and cautious, everything planned, the cases built so conscientiously that they were architecturally sound enough to withstand whatever bomb a Mob defense lawyer on a six-figure retainer dropped on them.

"What are you gonna do?" Ray asked.

"I dunno. Find a lawyer, for a start."

"What do you think they want?"

"To indict me for violating people's civil rights? For obstruction of justice? I don't know."

"Did you?" pushed Ray.

"I did some things that I shouldn't have." Alex played with his iPhone. "What about Shakima DeSilva? She used to be a cop."

"What?" said Ray.

"I gotta get counsel."

"She's good."

"Yeah."

"But why do you need a high-caliber defense lawyer? Your union reps are free. DeSilva sure isn't. What the hell went on?"

"Lots went on, and I know too much."

"Alex—"

"I can't tell you anything," Alex snapped. "Then you can get subpoenaed. Don't you get it? The more I talk, the more people get subpoenaed. They'll probably send you one anyway if they're after me, but if you don't know anything, you can't testify or perjure yourself trying to save my ass."

"Stop freaking out. Just phone the lawyer if you think it's that serious. She'll know the score. You're doing trial prep? Can I see the murder book?"

Alex threw the binder at Ray, and then he called the Midtown law firm, the guilt of what he had or hadn't done years ago engulfing him, the act of phoning a defense attorney one step towards admitting that the clusterfucks were on his shoulders too. He felt his stomach backflipping as he spoke to the lawyer's secretary, and it turned faster when she put him on hold to transfer the call to the lawyer.

Alex's quiet streak after the Lennon investigation broke late that night: a shooting in the Two-Five Precinct on East 130th. The precinct detective reported that EMS had taken the victim to Roosevelt Hospital. Alex knew he would not leave the streets until long after midnight, so he told Ray to go home. His partner had his wife and three kids, and he had a two-day old Indian take-out. First, he grabbed a one-dollar coffee at a diner, then he drove to the crime scene on East 130th and Madison. Whirling police car lights vaulted off buildings in coruscating reds and blues. He climbed out of the car, clipped his shield to his belt, and after contemplating the scene for a minute or two, he rounded up the precinct detective, a young Black cop who he'd never seen before. The guy must be new to the precinct squad.

"I'm Detective Boswell from Homicide," Alex said.

The young detective said, "Detective Joe Furness. It's good to meet you. You're a legend."

"Yeah, well." Alex felt relieved that the strobe lights of RMPs and the tepid orange glow of streetlights concealed the blush spreading across his cheeks. What had young detectives heard about him? He folded his arms under his ribcage. "Whaddaya got?"

"Thirty year old Hispanic male, Esteban Moreno, shot three times, once in the leg and twice in the abdomen," reported Furness. "He was walking down this street with a friend. Friend is over there. White. Twenty-seven. His driver's license says he's called Derek Brickl." He pointed to a fat white guy puking against the side of a grey low-rise, accompanied by two uniforms and Mia Grossi, a detective Alex had known for years.

"Nice," Alex said. "What happened to him?"

"Totally wankered," said Furness.

"'Wankered?' That's a new one. You talked to him yet?"

"I heard it in a British movie. Anyway, we were waiting for him to attain some level of *compos mentis*. But he's so fucked I doubt he'll remember a damned thing. He can barely remember his name."

Alex watched Grossi and the patrolmen half-carry the man into the squad car, and the patrolmen complained, afraid he would puke in their car. But the detective got the long straw. "When did you start working with Grossi?" Alex asked idly. "She's a good cop."

"Couple months ago," Furness answered. "Just after making the Bureau." He pursed his lips into a thin, nervous line. "This is my first homicide. You know, as a detective."

"Ah," grunted Alex, who had seen dozens of young precinct detectives with their first homicide, as a detective. "Witnesses?"

"Um, well, wits we've interviewed so far say they saw a guy with a beard, maybe, run up, shoot our vic, then run away. Oh, and vic's a local small-time dealer. Mostly cocaine, oxy, weed, whatever you want. We ran his name. He's been picked up twice, once here for possession with intent, another time in Brownsville. I spoke to the arresting officer in Brooklyn, who said it was on an assault charge. Physically throwing a junkie out of an apartment he owns."

"Does he live in Brownsville?"

"No, he rents that out. His address is here in Harlem."

"You know the disposition of those charges?"

"Pled out to assault three. Probation, promised not to do it again."

The young detective was on the ball, for his first homicide. Alex smiled at him. Immediately, he wondered why a dealer would rent out an apartment in one of the roughest parts of Brooklyn. Cleaning his dirty money? But he should keep an open mind. People do strange things for legit reasons, sometimes. Next, he interviewed the first officer, an old Irish patrolman who had responded to the aided call, and he scanned the man's memo book. The officer rambled about the 'good old days,' whenever those were. The '80s and '90s? They hadn't been good. Anything but. Alex scribbled notes and observations in his own memo book, whatever came into his head that could matter later. He measured distances and snapped photos of the 9mm shell casings, the shining, maroon lake of blood, the evidence cones, the townhouses along 130th, the bystanders rubbernecking beyond the staging area. Since Furness and Grossi had the canvass in hand, Alex drove to the Roosevelt in case the vic survived, or at least survived long enough to say who shot him. Anxiety fluttered inside his chest when he parked near the hospital. Sarah worked at the Roosevelt, but in cardiology. He hadn't called her since their unsettling conversation at her apartment. A douchebag move, after everything she'd told him. Of course, he'd meant to, but he always had the thought when he was at work or driving, and he didn't know if he should act normal – really, dysfunctional – or act in some other way, and he had no idea what that was. Besides, she hadn't called him, either. She had a phone.

He trotted through the automatic front doors and flashed tin at the receptionist. "My name's Detective Alex Boswell. I'm here following up on Esteban Moreno."

"Esteban Moreno," repeated the receptionist.

"Yeah, gunshot victim. Thirty year old Hispanic male."

"Let me get the charge nurse when I can," said the receptionist. "It's been a busy night."

Every seat was taken, so he leaned against the wall to wait, lightly closing his eyes, folding his hands behind his lower back.

"Dad? You all right? What are you doing here? Is there something wrong?"

He snapped open his eyes and abruptly realigned his spine. There was Sarah, swaddled in green scrubs, peering into his face. She held a clipboard under one arm, and her curly hair was rammed under a pale green cap.

"If there's something going on, you should call me," she grumbled irritably.

"No, sweetie," he said, recovering. "I'm waiting on a shooting vic."

"Oh... work."

"Yeah. What else?" He hooked his thumbs on his belt.

"I don't know. Your heart, your liver, your wound—"

"My health's fine. It's better than the guy I'm waiting to hear word on." He had no intentions of admitting that his side hurt as much as it did, or that he was having stomach pain again, or that his flashbacks had reappeared. She would act like a health care professional, but more cop-like than any actual doctor, interrogating him on the scripts, the dosages, the symptoms. He couldn't deal with it, not when he had a good old-fashioned drug murder to work, or ever.

Another nurse appeared, Black, her face serious, hassled. "Are you the detective who's here for Esteban Moreno?" she asked brusquely.

"Yeah, how is he?" said Alex, smoothing out his voice, pretending he hadn't been startled and wasn't upset.

Sarah hugged her clipboard and took a few steps back, but she lingered, rubbernecking her father's grisly job.

"ADASTW," said the ER nurse.

"What?" said Alex.

"Arrived Dead And Stayed That Way."

Mordant laughter gurgled in his throat. *Cops and ER nurses are sick as fuck.* The most likely person for a cop to have an affair with was an ER nurse, and he'd slept with a few. "Anybody come in with him? Is there anyone I should interview?"

"Nope."

"Can I talk to the ER consultant who worked on him?"

"At some point. He's in the OR now. Won't be out for six or eight hours."

"Okay. You got his clothes and anything else he had?"

The nurse knew the routine. Swift and efficient, she handed him a clear plastic bag containing Moreno's clothes and personal items, and he signed off on the chain-of-custody paperwork. He would drop these at Property tonight, with the directive to send them on to the lab forthwith.

With no one to interview here, he could either return to the Two-Five and see if he'd been blessed with any witnesses, or he could go home and pick it up from Furness and Grossi in the morning. The deceased would be sent to the ME's office and autopsied tomorrow. The 24/24 rule: you are most likely to break a case in the first twenty-four hours by figuring out what the vic did with their last twenty-four hours. So he decided on East Harlem. A Harlem drug murder was the kind of case he liked, the kind that got the attention of no one, the kind he could work industriously, the way he wanted to work it, and no supervisors or politicians breathing over his shoulder. Moreover, if he went home, he had to confront the two-headed monster of his insomnia and his illness.

"Who was he?" asked Sarah, after the ER nurse had raced off to her next living patient.

"Some guy from East Harlem," Alex scanned the bloodstained clothes in the plastic bag. "Allegedly dealing coke and oxy and other stuff."

Sarah looked worried. "So, he's in the drug trade?"

"It's good money, but anyone you piss off is more likely to shoot you than write an angry email."

"Um, okay." Sarah's eyes flicked back and forth, unconvinced by his deadpan. "I got that from *Breaking Bad.*"

A pang sparked inside his chest. Once again, he'd shoved his foot down his own throat.

"I thought you might phone me," she said in a low voice.

"I…" he stumbled. "Things caught up with me. I was working that case with the woman who killed her kid in the Heights. Redballs like that just take over my life." *And a grand jury investigation and having a PTSD relapse.* He clenched his jaw, swallowing words, tasting bile.

"It's just what you do, Dad," Sarah sighed. "Ray has three kids, and he somehow deals."

"Ray has a color-coded calendar," Alex retorted, but it was also true.

"It's not the work, or the case, or whatever you tell yourself. It's you. It's who you are. My therapist says I've got to accept you for who you are. I mean, Ellie always has. You're not gonna change. You were never going to be that father who coached the soccer team, were you?"

"Really? Now's a shit time to have this conversation." He hated himself for the strident edge in his voice. Softening his tone, he added, "I got this case to work. I gotta go interview some junkies and crackheads. Have to see if I can figure out who shot this guy. Maybe I'll close it before daylight."

"Yeah, you're right. It's a shit time. And I have patients. I'm sorry."

He gave her a light hug. She tensed against him, but then tentatively returned his affection.

"You could call or text me," he said in a low voice.

"Why's it always on me to put the effort in?"

"Oh, Sarah," he groaned. "It's not."

"We're arguing again," she said with wearied wryness.

"Yeah. Let's not. Go see your patients. We'll talk later, okay?"

"Okay."

She checked her phone and her pager, then scurried through the doors sign-posting cardiology. Slowly, it dawned on him that he'd been holding the plastic evidence bag stuffed with Moreno's bloody clothes for that entire awkward conversation. How fucked up. As fucked up as everything else in his life. He jogged through hospital's revolving door. Dammit, he did try. He poured his heart and soul into reconciliation, but she seemed to disbelieve that he bothered at all. Inside the car, he rammed his shoulder blades against the driver's seat. His heart pumped wildly but wasn't powering his lungs. *Breathe*, he told himself. The Calm Place. His desert with endless skies and sandstone mesas. But he had another vision: Esteban Moreno strapped to a gurney in the back of an ambulance, bleeding out while paramedics fought hopelessly to save his life.

His next stop was Property, where he signed in the vic's clothes. Traffic was light in these fading hours of the morning: within half an hour, he'd traveled from One Police Plaza in Lower Manhattan to East 119th Street.

Whenever he visited the Two-Five, MNHS's premises until 1996, he felt like he'd returned to an old house he'd once lived in, the musty smells and cracked grey breeze block walls unchanged, like he'd never left. He had interrogated hundreds of perps in this place. Hundreds of case files, hundreds of witnesses, hundreds of DD-5s, hundreds of gruesome wounds – so many that the names and faces lost meaning, and those deprived of life and those deprived of liberty melted into a singular depressing image. Had the forensics been as fictional as the ones on *CSI?* Had the witnesses lied or misremembered? Had any perp falsely confessed? Had he been too shortsighted, overworked, and incurious to notice? His colleagues who interrogated the Central Park Five honest-to-God believed those were true confessions; look how that went.

"Boswell? You wanted to look over these notes and sketches?" Furness had planted a file in his hand.

Keep your head screwed on. He felt annoyed at the station house for sitting on this block, an unchanging concrete structure that distracted him with his past misjudgments, but he smiled appreciatively at the young detective.

"The Homicide squad used to be in this building, didn't it?" commented Furness unhelpfully.

Damn you. Work the case! "Yeah. It did." He quaffed another mouthful of coffee from his Styrofoam cup, and he read the notes Furness, Grossi, and the first officers had taken at the crime scene. The coffee whipped up acid in his gut. But he pushed himself past his discomfort, questioning the ambulance crew and some of the more cooperative witnesses. It was 0200 – far too late for squandering precious energy with uncooperative ones. Half a dozen interviews later, he'd learned that Moreno lived in his East 118th Street apartment with his ex-girlfriend – a twenty-five year old waitress called Yolanda Villanueva – and, bizarrely, Villanueva's current boyfriend, a guy called Sulaman Ejua. Moreno and Villanueva co-owned the apartment.

"Why?" Alex asked. He could hardly get through a phone call with his ex-wife.

"Sulaman and I couldn't afford the mortgage. Esteban also needed a place to live and offered to help out."

"After you broke up?"

She nodded, shrugging glibly.

"I guess you guys had a pretty amicable break-up."

"Not really. He'd been sleeping around. I was pissed."

The shit you see out here sometimes, thought Alex.

Villanueva explained that Moreno owned and rented out another apartment in Brownsville (like Furness had said), and he had an ongoing saga with the owner of the adjacent building, a Russian guy named Milo Sikorsky. Moreno had been regularly phoning Sikorsky, yelling, cursing, frothing at the mouth, threatening him with everything from breaking his legs to calling the cops. Perhaps not a great move, given Sikorsky's line of work. Villanueva showed Alex the place on Google Streetview, with Moreno's apartment as run-down and dilapidated as most buildings on that street, while Sikorsky's townhouse stood out, freshly painted, with a couple late-model BMWs parked outside. Sikorsky was nearly on a first-name basis with Brooklyn Narcotics.

"I don't think Esteban's business was going well," she speculated. "He always complained about money, talking about losing all of it, maybe having to sell that property."

"He was dealing coke and oxy," Alex said. "How do you not make money?"

"Suck at business? He had a legit landscaping business before, and that went bust. He thought there's more of a market for drugs in this city than landscaping."

"He wouldn't be wrong," Alex responded drolly.

"He also thought the federal government was after him."

"He was slinging cocaine. I'm sure someone was."

"The CIA," she emphasized.

"Oh. Probably not them." He buried a yawn into the back of his wrist.

"He was pretty paranoid. He figured 9/11 was an inside job, and they're microchipping us with vaccines."

"Was he involved in any of these conspiracy theory internet groups?"

"I don't know."

Alex would know once he'd accessed Moreno's internet history. Confident that he'd achieved something, he filled out overtime paperwork and signed off for the night. Either himself or Furness would get a warrant for those Brownsville apartments tomorrow, and ESU would organize a tac-plan for visiting the Russian dealer. Those crazy bastards loved that shit. They could have it. Getting shot once in his life was enough.

He stumbled into his apartment at 0430 hours. His right side throbbed, as if the wound wanted to rip itself out. He blasted himself with the shower, washing off the sweat, the city grime, the crime scene. Hot water poured over his body. It cascaded down his chest, his belly, his legs, that relaxing instant where a shower feels like it cleanses everything. After drying himself, he swallowed his meds, washing them down with a glass of tonic water. These damned drugs were simultaneously ruining and saving his life, he thought. With grudging acceptance – the ruining seemed less important than the saving – he returned the bottle to the cabinet and buried himself in bed.

Sleep evaded his tired body as he listened to the wind tinkering with the roof slates. His mind feverishly darted around his surprise encounter with Sarah – endless repeats, like *Law and Order* on cable, cycling between what he actually said and what he should have said, not just in the hospital but everywhere. It spiraled towards the federal grand jury and his next step on that drug murder. On nights like this, he missed the booze, the half-bottle of whisky that knocked him out, even if the trade-off was feeling like shit the next morning.

Chapter Twenty-Eight

Alex and Ray hunkered inside a van with ESU, watching Milo Sikorsky's apartment on Pitkin Avenue. The ESU officers fell silent, each man perfectly still, coiled, like leopards poised to pounce. Alex stopped breathing, then started when his chest hurt. The Kevlar vest compressed his gunshot wound, the pain in his ribs worsening as he sat here. He counted his breaths. One. Two. Three. Holding another breath, he glanced at the ESU cops, afraid they'd seen his nerves. They certainly would if he passed out. Counting and breathing, he folded his arms anxiously over the Kevlar. Four. Five. Six.

The 'go' order crackled over the radio. ESU sprang out of the van and charged into the apartment. His gun drawn, Alex scrambled after them. He'd barely made it through the door when he saw that ESU had pinned Sikorsky and three other Russians face down on the floor. The perps looked surprised and annoyed. They hauled them into the Two-Five's interrogation room, and they looked even more confused. Alex empathized; he felt as though heavy sediment clogged up his head. He didn't have the heart for a nine-hour interrogation or talking to these skels at all, but he took their details, going through the motions until a raccoon-eyed detective from Brooklyn North Narcotics steamed into the Two-Five, bitching that Alex shouldn't have picked up Sikorsky. Apparently, the Russian was an informant in a bigger operation.

"I'm just after information in a homicide case," Alex squished his tired, scratchy eyeballs with his fingers.

"He's got nothing to do with that," argued the Narc detective.

"How the hell do you know?"

"Whatever. You ain't talking to him."

"I'll do a cursory interview, and we'll see."

The next thing, the detective's captain called the station house and told Alex to leave Sikorsky alone. Alex couldn't blow off orders from a captain, so he grudgingly released the Russians. Someone would bust his balls for allowing Narc to steal his perp, but it was 0200, and he'd swam into the net of another unit's bureaucracy. On the other hand, he had no further reasons to linger around this building tonight. For now, he could escape his burdensome memories.

At home, he paced on the internet, skipping around websites without reading. Every bone and sinew in his body felt utterly spent, but he wasn't sleepy. One could be tired, flat-out exhausted, yet that brought sleep no closer, an inhospitable state that seemed improbable to people who didn't have insomnia. His skin felt clammy, his brain wired. He fired off a text to Sarah. *Sorry, you're right. I'm bad at communicating.* It had the curt dryness of a DD-5 instead of the florid emotionality of a Victorian novel. Sarah would prefer the latter. She would have preferred him to be a different person, a man who wasn't ill and who hadn't made so many stupid choices when he was young.

The iPhone bleated with a fresh text. At 0300? *On night shift,* Sarah wrote. *You were obviously working, and I shouldn't have given you shit. Work was stressful, and it was not a good time. We'll talk later.*

Okay. Love you, he typed back, then his stomach clenched as he anticipated a response. The phone held its repose, cold and silent. It wasn't a communication device that linked you to everything in your life; it was a tiny box made of glass and plastic, meaningless but mocking him with broken dreams.

Unable to quiet his jangling nerves, he stayed up until 0530 writing a warrant application for any documents and financial records relating to Moreno's Brownsville apartment. Furness and Grossi had gone into that place with another tac team but found nothing, just some puzzled Sudanese tenants who said they'd left Sudan to get away from shit like police breaking down their door in the middle of the night.

Only four hours later, Alex tiredly pulled off his reading glasses. Words looked blurry whether he had them on or not. He breathed in the dust permeating the archives room of the NYDA office, then he was coughing into a wasteland of trial transcripts and witness lists from cases Vito had investigated in the early-to-mid 1990s. They ranged from robberies, drug cases, larcenies, B and Es, to assaults, sex crimes, and homicides. Alex scoured witness lists for Elizabeth 'Loretta' Weltmayer, Vito's CI who either had an uncanny knack for watching murders and robberies, or more likely, Vito had bribed her to be an eyewitness whenever a case was falling short in the evidence department. Out of fifty-odd cases, Weltmayer had testified in a dozen. That raised the hairs on the back of his neck. Yeah, the city had a violence problem, but this witness had seen an unusual amount of it, even for early '90s Washington Heights. In each case, she chose the perp from a photo array or said she knew them from the streets. Every time, she asserted that she happened to be firing up at the perfect viewpoint for seeing them commit the offense in question. *No one's memory for faces is that good,* Alex thought cynically, least of all an addict who spent most days on more drugs than Kurt Cobain.

Those were the cases that went to trial. Hundreds more had been pled out, but Alex had no stomach for sifting through those. A handful of other witnesses popped up repeatedly in otherwise unrelated cases, but Alex had no time nor stomach for dealing with that, either. Someone should, but not him. Not his circus. *What a fucking mess,* he thought, worried about cans of worms that would eat holes in the whole justice system.

He sniffed, staring with dreary eyes at the dusty manila folders obscuring the table. If he knew anything about prosecutors, it was that they didn't put key witnesses or potential defendants before the grand jury unless they had some idea of what they might say or had evidence to impeach them on the stand if they lied. He knew James had testified. He knew Sam Rizzo and Marty Vasquez had testified. Who else had the US Attorney scared up? Who gave him the confidence to finally subpoena Alex? Weltmayer? Alex had been sitting in the car when she'd told Vito that she'd seen Guillermo Quixano shoot Jose Medina. She could testify that both detectives were involved. And Alex couldn't prove a negative. He couldn't prove that he didn't know that Vito was planning on stitching up Quixano. He couldn't prove that he didn't know about the baggie of crack under the driver's seat.

The dust was challenging his respiratory system. It would leave him coughing and sneezing for weeks. Fed up with transcripts and this health hazard of a room, he deserted the archives, descending to the eighth floor, where he borrowed a computer from an ex-Manhattan South Homicide detective who worked in the DA's office as an investigator. Alex pulled Weltmayer's OLBS sheets and rap sheets. They told him names and addresses belonging to her next of kin, her associates, and her arrest locations. Assorted arrests for prostitution, loitering, and drug possession. Usually, the charges got dismissed. Sometimes, they didn't. He should not be trying to locate her, but the grand jury scared him. Learning who might be on their witness list was something of tenuous value and legality, but it was something.

Weltmayer's last arrest was in 2005. Prostitution and loitering charges, so she wouldn't still be incarcerated. He ground his teeth into his left thumbnail. That meant she had either got her shit together (unlikely), died (more likely), or left the state (less likely than dead but more likely than cleaned up). Blood oozed from his thumb. He typed her name into Facebook. A few Elizabeth Weltmayers, but not her. So what? Lots of people weren't on Facebook. Her mother's number on the latest OLBS sheet connected him to a young, clueless couple in Brooklyn. He opened the department's reverse telephone search website and ran the mother's name. Frances Weltmayer wasn't that common. There were three in New York City.

"This is Detective Boswell with the NYPD. I'm looking for Elizabeth Weltmayer's mother, Frances?" he inquired on his second call.

"Oh, God, what's happening now?" mumbled the woman on the other end of the line. "Has someone *else* said she's their biological mother and wants money? Jesus Christ. I ain't got no money."

"Uh, no," he said, confused, intrigued. "I'm just doing some follow up stuff on an old case. She'd testified in court—"

The woman laughed, but she sounded bitter and sarcastic. "Sorry, Detective. She won't be able to help you unless you know how to commune with the dead. She died of AIDS in 2006."

Fuck, he wanted to breathe, but stayed professional on the phone. "Oh, I'm very sorry to hear that. Sorry for bothering you."

He never would find out how many children she had bequeathed to the New York City Administration for Children's Services, or what she might have said about Vito or himself. Neither would the US Attorney. The grand jury remained a black hole, sucking him in. Pain filled his chest cavity, and his eyes burned with hot liquid, blurring the words on the computer. Swearing at allergies, he wiped his cheek with his wrist. He had never asked the detectives who worked the Jogger case how they felt after the Central Park Five were exonerated. Did they lose sleep? Did they replay every interrogation in their minds and wonder who else could have falsely confessed? Or did they deny that the confessions were coerced in the first place? Those detectives had been retired for years, and even if Alex hadn't lost touch, that wasn't a conversation you could casually start over a few beers, or sodas. He looked back at twenty-three years of interrogating murder suspects, himself one of the best interrogators in MNHS, empathetic, manipulative, slightly anxious and off-balance. Suspects connected with him. People would tell him anything. Would he swear in court that he'd never once made someone confess to something they hadn't done? God, he couldn't swear to it. How do you know? You think so, you hope so, but you shine your flashlight, and it's dark. He smothered his forehead with both hands. This was worse. This was

298

deliberate. Vito knowingly and willfully manufactured evidence against those defendants, and Alex watched him do it, terrified of what Vito could do to him, so he stayed silent. No one likes a whistleblower, and everyone likes a cop who makes arrests.

"Hey, Boswell."

Hearing his name, he collided with reality: the investigator's room at the DA's office.

Sal Altera, the retired Manhattan South Homicide detective, said, "You wanna cannoli?"

"What?"

"I got cannolis from that place on Houston Street. You know the one."

Alex didn't. "Nah, thanks. I had something to eat before I got here. You're looking good, like a few more isn't gonna make a hell of a lot of difference anyway." Altera had an ample gut on him.

"I'm spreading the love. And the calories. Best cannolis in Manhattan. You're not gonna say no."

Reluctantly, Alex joined the investigators gathered around the cannolis. He ate one, although he had no appetite. The investigators laughed at Altera's stories from his MSHS days. A red-hot pain skewered through Alex's stomach. He was sweating, running out of air. He muttered, "Thanks for the computer. See you," then he dashed into a nearby bathroom. Dizzy with pain, he disinterred antacids from his pocket with the hungry desperation of a jonesing junkie. Scooping handfuls of water from the sinks, he gulped down his drugs, then he hid in a stall with his forehead braced against the cold metal door, pleading with his gut to settle. The meds soothed the searing heat, enough to function. He bolted from the DA's office, as if he'd robbed the place. What enlightenment had he expected to find in twenty-year old case files? Now, the plan seemed crazy.

But he did what he had always done during a mental health crisis: he worked a case. He drove to East Harlem for a daylight canvass of Esteban Moreno's neighbors and friends. One witness related that Moreno planned on moving out of Yolanda Villanueva's place. Only last week, Moreno had sent the wit a text complaining that his ex-girlfriend was sleeping with the lodger, and the atmosphere inside the apartment had become unbearable.

Alex furrowed both brows. "What? The lodger? That's a different person than the boyfriend?"

"Yeah, it's a three-bed apartment, so it was Esteban, Yolanda and Sully... That's her boyfriend... He's a Black dude. But he's not like, a New York Black dude. Came from South Africa—"

"Yeah, he's from Johannesburg. We've spoken to him," interjected Alex, gently moving the witness' statement forward.

"This other guy rents the spare room. He's Puerto Rican. They're definitely not the same dude. I'd swear on a bible that she's cheating on Sully with the Puerto Rican dude."

"You got a name for this 'dude?'"

"Yeah, I think he's called Jorge Ruiz."

"Okay," Alex said. The vic lived in his own *telenovela:* everyone he knew had a motive. "You got anything else on Ruiz? Do you know if Moreno was pissed at him?"

"No. I've never met him," the witness answered apologetically.

Alex mentally outlined search warrants for everyone's phone and emails. Back at the office, he half-heartedly nibbled at a Milky Way while calling Villanueva and Ejua. He got their voicemails. "This is Detective Alex Boswell with the police," he said in that friendly, professional monotone he used for leaving messages. "There's a few more things I wanna talk about with you, so can you call me back as soon as you can? Thanks." He recited his office number and email address, then he started writing a request to Verizon for a cell phone tower dump, a list of any cell phone connected to the towers near the crime scene. Defense lawyers and the ACLU complained, but so far, no court had stopped law enforcement from doing it. The computer screen shimmered out of his focus, like he had something wrong with his eyes.

Ray patted his shoulder. "Man, you gotta get some rest. It's like eleven-thirty anyway. Take off early, huh? That will keep until tomorrow."

"I'm meeting with my lawyer tomorrow," Alex said bleakly.

"Then get some sleep, please. I'll finish it. You've been falling apart all day. You know you're not functioning, and not sleeping is going to make you sicker." Ray gave Alex his coat and his keys, and he resolutely took him by the upper arm, guiding him through the main door, onto Broadway. He would have marched his partner to the subway station, like a perp, had Alex not relented and agreed to go home.

Once there, he doused himself with a five-minute shower, feeling momentarily better as hot water poured over his body. Would he sleep tonight? God knows, he needed it. For once, sleep came – he was *that* tired – but it plunged him into unsettled, vivid nightmares that kept waking him up, evaporating from his memory but leaving him lying in fear and sweat, hearing his drumming heart.

When Alex shaved, he thought the face in the mirror looked straight out of the 4am Port Authority bus terminal. Like anyone in the police department, he would be unsurprised if he had to meet his union rep over a spurious complaint or disciplinary action, but he'd never envisioned meeting a criminal defense attorney while facing federal criminal charges. Shaving didn't erase the sagging strain from his eyes. Suit and tie? Might as well look like a homicide detective. He chose a plain grey suit, one he would wear to work rather than court. He nibbled queasily at a few cornflakes, then he dragged himself down the stairs. He felt like he was moving a body. His own. Clumsily, he fumbled the Metrocard into the turnstile at West 86th. With every subway stop, his guts scrunched into nauseating spasms. At Columbus Circle, he limped underneath cranes, tarps, and scaffolding, the endless redevelopment project, until he stood before an airy modern skyscraper with a façade of glass, reflecting the grey sky.

The elevator shot him up to Aybara-Halewood on the 23rd floor, a spacious law office enlivened with abstract modern paintings and formless sculptures. Kima DeSilva, a partner, had a corner office that could consume Alex's living room. He glanced at the names on the files covering her desk. Defendants who had been exonerated last year.

"Hi, Alex." The lawyer, a fifty-two year old Black woman from Baltimore, wore a blouse splashed with bright yellows and reds. Bracelets and shiny rings adorned both hands, and her hair was braided into long, black corn rows falling down to the small of her back. She'd been a dancer, then a cop, and she still looked like she could outrun men half her age.

"Beats a precinct," he observed. "This why you quit being a cop?" He'd encountered her on the job, when she'd walked a beat in the Two-Eight, and after she passed the bar, she'd defended a few people he had arrested.

"Well, that, and I was fed up with putting half the Black male population of New York in prison for non-violent drug offenses," Kima replied. "And my wife and I wanted a baby, but she said she wouldn't if I was out on the streets risking my ass."

Alex glanced at the photos on the desk: a young girl with corn rows like Kima, smiling, in the company of Kima and another Black woman, and newer photos of the same girl, now a teenager in a red evening gown, playing the violin.

"That's our daughter, Janel," Kima said proudly. "She's fifteen now."

"Fifteen?" said Alex. "When were you in the Two-Eight?"

She laughed. "Sixteen years ago, Alex. I been doing this for way longer than I worked as a cop!"

Fuck, he couldn't keep track of time anymore. He clasped one hand with the other behind his back.

"She loves the violin more than anything. You know she's in the New York Youth Philharmonic. Gonna apply for Julliard when she's a senior. I wasn't good enough to be a professional dancer, to work on Broadway, but Janel… She's got something special." The lawyer turned serious and hard. "Okay. Right. Take a seat."

He did, crossing his legs and balling his hands into fists so he couldn't bite or tear at his sore fingers.

"First thing, if I represent you, you gotta be honest with me. About everything you did, everything you saw. I can't adequately defend clients who don't tell me the truth. And I ain't short of clients. I don't have time for bullshit ones."

"I hear you."

"Second thing, don't talk to people about this investigation. Every single person you speak with about it, that's someone who can get a subpoena, who can testify against you. The only person you ever talk to about this is me, get it? Not your boss, not Ray Espinosa, not your friends or family. Just me."

"Ten-four."

"I've been looking at these cases since you phoned me. Not just your initial investigations, but the ones run by the *Times* and the Innocence Project. I have to say, they are a mess."

He stabbed a thumb into his radial artery, feeling his fibrillating pulse.

"Alright, let's get to it. Serrachia." She scrolled through something on her computer. "You conducted a cursory interview of Serrachia in which he gave you two alibi witnesses, right?"

"Yeah."

"You followed that up and confirmed the alibi?"

"Yeah. Or so I thought."

"Then a few months later, Indelicata re-interviewed those witnesses, and they changed their story, said that they didn't remember when or if they saw Serrachia on that corner on the 5th of August."

"That's right. That's what I heard."

"Alex, are you aware that the statements you took were never in the DA's office file and never turned over to the defense?"

"I didn't know until the trial," he stressed. "After I took the statements, I didn't have much to do with the case. I was… shot at the start of October '87 and off work until February '88. They collared Serrachia right before I came back."

"I know. The Innocence Project used a Freedom of Information request to get old police files. That's how they found them. Someone buried those statements but weren't smart enough to destroy them. I looked at the trial transcripts, and the defense *never* called those witnesses, and he didn't cross you on those statements. You must have found that surprising."

"Yeah. But the prosecutor never prepped me on it."

"Leon Mitchell?"

"Yeah."

"Well, there's a surprise," Kima observed derisively. "Mitchell. What a sleazebag. Your statements disappear before the prosecution hands over discovery, the defense never knows they exist, and Mitchell clearly doesn't think you will be crossed on it. So why bother prepping you? He was probably in on it. Too bad he's dead. There's someone who should be indicted." She reshuffled the files on her desk. "You had nothing to do with Serrachia's interrogation, which is good. But were you aware Indelicata was bribing his 'eyewitnesses' with money and crack?"

"You were a cop… A while ago, but you gotta remember. You know you give CIs money or some perks." He shouldn't be defending Vito to the woman who had to defend him.

Her eyes sparked like metal striking a road. "Yes, some perks, but do most cops use the same witnesses in multiple cases? In a city of eight million people? Did you know Indelicata was doing that?"

"I do now. But I wasn't there when he interviewed those alleged eyewitnesses in the Serrachia case. I was still on medical leave. And a lot of the other ones they testified in weren't mine. They weren't even homicides."

"What do you mean?"

"I looked at old trial transcripts," he admitted. "That sex worker, Elizabeth Weltmayer, testified in more than one case Vito worked on. I thought the US Attorney might call her as a witness."

"Yes, 'Loretta.' She's dead," said Kima.

"I know."

The lawyer raised both eyebrows. They had both done their homework. "She showed up in at least two totally unconnected cases, and you didn't find it strange."

"I did, but what was I gonna do? It should be up to the defense lawyer to go after the credibility of prosecution witnesses."

"Yes, I went to law school," she said with a droll smile, unfazed by his defensiveness. "They may have taught us that. I'm laying out the federal government's case here. You were aware of some fundamental problems with the evidence in these cases, and you kept your mouth shut."

"There were problems with the evidence in half the fucking cases we cleared. The bosses were losing their shit over low homicide clearance rates, so we put schlocky cases together. Vito took it further than that-"

"That's why we're here."

"—but we were all doing it. I mean, I never used a drop piece or buried exonerating evidence or anything like that, but I couldn't count the cases I cleared with weak fingerprint matches or pushing a witness with a photo array or line-up, maybe more than I should have."

"And interrogating people until they confessed?"

"Yeah." Alex gouged his fingertips into his eye sockets. "But I never wanted anyone to confess falsely, dammit. What's the fucking point?"

"That's an environment where miscarriages of justice happen, for sure," said Kima. "But that's not what this grand jury is interested in. Truth is, mistakes you've made because you're overworked or under-resourced or under pressure to raise clearances don't equate to criminal liability." She gazed directly into his eyes, her own more intense than the sun. "But other things do. You ducked my question about Indelicata bribing eyewitnesses. I said, you need to be honest. If the US Attorney knows more than I do, I can't defend you."

Discomfited, he pulled away from her magnetic stare and riveted his eyes on the window. Two pigeons squabbled on the window ledge, then flew off. She had him dead to rights. "I was in the car with him. And he gave Loretta crack. Pulled a small baggie of it out of a paper bag that was under the driver's seat. It wasn't a lot. Less than 500mg." He felt himself shaking. The inside of his mouth tasted caustic, like he'd eaten charcoal.

"Not enough for felony possession. Huh. In exchange for what? Do you know?"

"Yeah. For saying she watched Guillermo Quixano shoot Jose Medina."

"You know where he got it?"

"No idea."

"He just pulled it out from under the seat? Like jumper cables?"

"Yeah." Alex pushed at the blockage in his throat.

"Did he offer Weltmayer anything else?"

"He said he'd pay her to give a statement to the DA and testify."

"That's it?"

"It's all I remember."

"No other snippets of conversation coming to mind?"

"No," he said wearily. Kima was putting him through his courtroom paces. "She took off once she said what Indelicata wanted to hear."

She leaned across her desk. "At what point did you realize she was the same eyewitness who'd testified against Serrachia?"

"Immediately," he exhaled. "Indelicata used her moniker, and I recognized it."

"When did this happen?"

"The day we found Jose Medina's body. I hadn't finished my search of the crime scene, and Indelicata sorta twisted my arm into going with him... To talk to people, he said. I left James Hurley and the other precinct detective to finish processing the scene."

"How did he twist your arm?"

"It's just who he is. He tells people to do things, and they fucking do them."

"Even you?"

"In those days, yeah."

"Did Hurley find anything at the crime scene?"

"The guy had been decomposing in that shooting gallery for weeks," Alex recalled, speaking wryly. "Not even James has that kind of luck."

"Okay. We'll come back to that, but we gotta talk a bit more about the Liebowitz case. You ever come across a guy called Kevin Schiller?"

Biting the squidgy inside of his cheek, Alex started shaking his head, but then froze. "Well, not until last year when they alleged he shot Liebowitz, and I guess proved it with a DNA match."

"You never heard of him before that? Were you aware that his wife called the 34th Precinct and tipped off the detective squad? In 1990?"

"They deposed me about that in the lawsuit, but no, I never got the tip." Schiller was a career stick-up artist, a regular around those blocks who'd died of a speedball OD in 1990-something. Schiller's ex-wife, Maureen, allegedly phoned the police to implicate her husband in Liebowitz's murder. Apparently, no one followed it up. Alex never heard the name until last year when he read about it, and later, a lawyer asked him about it in a deposition.

"She also says she phoned MNHS." Kima spoke solemnly. "Left messages. But no one ever answered."

Alex lowered his gaze to his fingers, which were speckled with dried blood. "She didn't leave messages with me."

"Then who got the messages? Who took over the case after you and Trenemen were shot?"

His throat crinkled like dried leaves. "Bill Ryan and Marty Vasquez."

"You know, Maureen Schiller never appeared as a witness in the original case file. Not a 'five or statement to be found. Vasquez and Ryan never said anything to you?"

"No." He shied away from Kima's disbelieving stare. "Yes. Ryan said something. When we were really wasted at a party. He said he was getting crazy calls about Liebowitz, months after the trial. That's it. We got crazy calls about that case all the time. We'd just ignore half of them. You remember what the Three-Four was like? The whole city. Fucking mishegoss, chaos. And with a redball like that, there's always shitloads of people trying to get the reward, calling you with bogus conspiracies or whatever. Stuff easily gets lost." Or ignored. God knows he'd worked dozens of cases where Vito, a suspect in his sights, certain in his gut that he had the right man, would not 'waste time,' as he said, following up alternate leads. 'It's bullshit,' he once said while they worked a case many years ago, when Alex still thought of him as something of a mentor. 'Bureaucratic bullshit. If I'm right, I'm *right.* They don't want detectives to follow their *gut* anymore.' Here, he had slapped his rather substantial one. 'They want us to be good little bureaucrats, file our paperwork, cover our butts, but that's not what the job *is.* It's not how you be a detective.'

It was his instinct to defend his fellow cops without blinking; turning on them, even in the confines of attorney-client privilege, felt like turning on his own flesh-and-blood.

"What are you thinking, Alex?" Kima asked.

What is the truth? He'd promised her the truth. "Vito got tunnel vision about suspects. Once he thought he was putting a case down, it went down. He wouldn't fuck around with alternative leads or going after anything exonerating."

"What about Vasquez and Ryan?"

"They were good cops," he snapped, feeling sensitive. "If they buried it, it's just 'cause it got lost in the mayhem." Had Marty already told the grand jury about the tip? Had he even known about it? Had Bill drunkenly mentioned it offhand to Alex, but otherwise deleted the message and kept his mouth glued shut because re-opening the Liebowitz case amid '90s mishegoss would have been a mammoth clusterfuck? Bill had been shrewd and cautious, sharply attuned to politics, patriotic and protective of the squad and the police department. Better to let sleeping defendants lie (even if they didn't do it).

"How do you know that if they never talked to you about it?" asked Kima. "When sober."

Fucking word-twisting lawyers, he thought intemperately. "I know *them,*" he said angrily. "I'm guessing."

"Don't 'guess' in front of the grand jury," Kima advised. "Tell them truth – that Ryan mentioned it to you in a bar."

"It was a house party, actually."

"Okay, a party."

"Isn't that hearsay?"

"It's admissible in a federal grand jury proceeding. And Ryan can't testify himself—"

"Yeah, he dies on 9/11, a Goddamned hero, and when this shit rolls down the hill, *he's* the one who gets nailed?" Alex spluttered, losing control over his breathing, panting, like during his panic attacks.

"Keep focus," Kima said mildly. "I don't know what the US Attorney has. But I need to know everything you know."

"Yeah." He counted out seconds as he inhaled, that go-to exercise for containing fight-or-flight reactions.

"What about you? Did you blow off tips?"

"No, not if they looked legit."

"Legit?" Kima echoed, angling her head prosecutorially.

"You know a case like that makes every nutbar crawl outta the woodwork. We had people saying it was the CIA, the Black Panthers, and that old favorite, the Jews..."

"Do you know if the information Ryan received was 'legit?'"

"No idea. I don't even know if he was talking about Schiller. Never said the name. Coulda been anyone. It was just the bullshit people say at a party."

"Did Vasquez ever say anything to you about it?"

Alex shifted his pelvis around in the chair. "No. He wouldn't." If Marty so much as suspected anything hinky, he would keep it close to his chest.

"You know not to contact him about this now, right?" Kima drawled out the vowels of the word *right,* so it wasn't a question anymore. Her dark brown eyes hardened. "The FBI could get a warrant or a court order for your emails or phone records, and if it even *appears* as if you're colluding to obstruct justice and trying to get your story straight—"

"Yeah, I get it," he interrupted querulously. "I know how it works." Emailing Marty had crossed his mind, but the lawyer's warning chilled the air like a northerly wind. If the feds got their hands on any emails that so much as hinted at covering up the cover up, shit's creek would flood into the Hudson.

"Okay, good. But you're also aware that Serrachia isn't your biggest problem?"

"Yeah." He dropped his chin to his chest and tensed his forearm against his sore stomach.

"I need you to tell me everything you know about Guillermo Quixano. Everything. The US Attorney has got Quixano himself testifying to that grand jury. He's got people who were witnesses in that case. He's got people who should have been witnesses in that case but were overlooked. Now, he's got you. So, you need to be dead straight with me. You surely don't need me to tell you that if Indelicata is charged, and you did something to help him, you can be held criminally liable. I need to know what you know and what you did. Hear me?"

"Yeah." A court had overturned Quixano's conviction last year. The man was free, pissed off, and testifying to the grand jury. Unconcerned by the bleeding, Alex peeled a flap of skin from the self-inflicted gouges next to his thumbnail. His mind flitted away from the Midtown law office, with its garish abstract art, its air fresheners and fresh flowers, and he re-entered another world, bleak, greyed out, with grids of crumbling streets overrun by crack cocaine and violence.

Part 6

Chapter Twenty-Nine

April 1992

On an amiably temperate April evening, Alex rode shotgun in Vito's Crown Vic. They were cruising along West 155th through a block party bubbling on the streets. Boomboxes perched on cars pounded salsa music into the night. Young people were smoking, dancing, drinking, playing street soccer, and sometimes sullenly eyefucking the Ford as the detectives drifted by. Two white guys in a late-model grey sedan – obviously cops.

As they toured the neighborhood, Vito gestured towards various people, narrating, "I collared *him* for agg assault, and he's dealing, and he's a great guy, he's walked on a manslaughter charge, he's just done five years for B and E, I picked him up for indecent exposure," and so on. Frequently, he halted the car, then rolled down the window, shouting, "Yo, my man! How's it goin'?"

The person would approach the car and clasp hands with Vito through the window. "Hey, Detective Vit-o. I'm good, man. How's you?"

"Great, *Bueno,*" Vito answered with effusive sincerity. "Streets are hoppin' tonight! It's a great night to be out."

The night proceeded more or less like that – for a couple hours. Alex thought about Corcoran handing his ass to him yesterday. Another week, another riot act about his clearance rate. How many more lives did he have, he wondered, before Corcoran launched him out of the unit. Ryan and Vasquez had reassured Alex that Corcoran was merely blowing off steam.

"You're a great investigator," Bill had said warmly. "And nobody's better at interrogations."

"I dunno." Alex had chugged his pint. "I have a lot of red next to my name."

"Next month, that could be someone else," Bill replied.

"It's been me forever. Corcoran might use me as a warning."

"Nah, he can't let you go. He's been yelling at everyone. Yelled at Marty for not arresting that guy last week, even though the evidence we had would've never held up, and the fella probably didn't do it."

"He's been yelling at everyone who isn't Irish," Marty had interjected acidly. "He also got pissed at me for not cleaning old grounds out of the coffee pot. It's fucking Brady. *He* never cleans it. This job…"

Alex told himself that Bill must know something he didn't. Maybe he had some kind of Irish cop affinity with their boss. But it wasn't just the lieutenant's 'come to Jesus' meeting. All his life, he'd been working towards something, this one thing: CCNY, the Academy, the gold shield, then the Homicide squad – the voice for the voiceless, like he'd told Mary Liebowitz – but now his ribs seemed held in a bone-crushing vice, and he confronted metastasizing apprehension that he wasn't keeping up with the job. He dealt with that anxiety the only way he knew: coating it with several glasses of Johnnie Walker.

Right now, as Vito's ride-along buddy, he wasn't doing anything to change the red to black. Vito had pronounced that he'd found a lead on the Jose Medina case and coaxed Alex into joining him on this escapade, while James stayed in the office, chasing witnesses and reexamining paperwork on fresher cases.

"What are we doing here?" Alex fidgeted with his watch. The twitching second hand felt like it pricked his skin with each tick. So far, this was two hours of his life he would never see again. "You even sure Quixano shot Medina? It's two years and like a thousand drug homicides later. Case is cold as shit."

"I got one eyewit, you saw," Vito replied querulously. "Loretta's good. And those other ones will come around. Trust me. Quixano's a big-time slinger. He's like the Sal Boca of uptown Manhattan. The next El Feo. He's like *the man* on these blocks now. The OG. People, they're gonna remember."

"We had a line-up. More than one. No one ID'd him."

"That's on *you.* You did the line-up. You gotta hold their hands." Vito sounded impatient, like a man explaining alternate-side-of-the-street parking to a tourist. "Give 'em a hint. Help 'em out. They need another shot at it, you give it to 'em. As many as it takes."

"What? I'm pretty sure that's not how it works."

"Lex, you gotta play a long game. Listen to your gut."

"My gut? How you gonna explain *that* to the DA?"

"I'm not."

"It's gotta be in discovery."

"It doesn't."

"But *Brady, Rosario—*"

"Screw the courts, Lex. You think *any* judge has a fuckin' clue what goes on out here?"

"No," Alex said, agreeing for the sake of an easier life.

"How's your clearance rate anyway?"

Alex imagined a wormhole opening under the passenger seat, sucking him into a faraway galaxy. His lips parted with a slight tremor.

"Yeah, that's what you get from followin' the rules. Rules don't apply out here. You gotta trust me, man."

Oh, he longed for his squad room, for his paperwork. If only he'd stayed with James – or sent James out because this was the sort of stupid shit he liked. Unfortunately, Vito had asked for him, not James or anyone else, so here he was, a nervous wreck with dwindling patience.

Vito abruptly jerked the sedan to the curb. He'd spotted some people hanging around a shuttered shop, drinking and smoking. A sunny smile on his face, he hopped out of the car. Alex barked, "Vito!" but Vito barreled towards the young men. There was no backup anywhere, and Vito hadn't taken the portable. Alarmed, Alex snatched it from the center console and shoved it into his belt. It occurred to him that the shooting in '87 made him more nervous than he used to be, more nervous than Vito was. The corner reeked of weed. Stoners weren't dangerous, but jonesing junkies and crackheads might smash your skull if it helped them score. And the dealers would put a bullet between your ribs. His eyes on the people partying, he tensed his right hand against his hip, close to his gun, and he trailed after Vito, who had enthusiastically greeted half a dozen guys and scored a couple cans of beer. Vito offered him one, and Alex guardedly accepted it with a smile not reaching his eyes. The city ordinance prohibiting public drinking and the NYPD regulation forbidding drinking on duty strayed off the precinct detective's radar. True, Alex slipped in sneaky hits from his flask, but he tried to be subtle. Vito wasn't subtle about anything.

Vito swigged his beer. He had enough Spanish to exchange, "*Como estás? Muy bien, estupendo,*" with acquaintances who didn't speak English. He clapped a few people on the shoulders or forearms, then swaggered back to the car. He drove off with gusto before Alex clipped his seatbelt. Immediately, Vito hit the brakes, swapping a few more enthusiastic *holas* through the window.

"You gotta get to *know* the neighborhood," Vito told Alex in a supercilious tone. "You gotta know the people. There's good people here. I know, lotsa cops think this place is full of Black people, Latinos, poor people, shootin' each other and smokin' crack and livin' off welfare checks, and yeah, some are those things, but most of 'em are good people with bad luck, a bad start, no hope, living in a shithole, just trying to get by. You know, you gotta be a role model to the kids, keep 'em in school, tell 'em, outside of the ghetto, is a whole wide world."

Alex nodded in agreement, thinking Vito had a weird combination of narcissism and compassion, bravado, racism, and nuanced understanding.

"So, you never answered my question," Alex said.

"And which one was that?"

"What the hell are we doing?"

"Lex, just be cool."

Be cool with what, Alex thought, and he ground his back teeth until his jaw ached. He wasn't some rookie who needed to learn how a veteran worked the streets; he was a homicide detective, with too many homicides that needed attention. His fault, his practice of diligently answering the office phone. Someone had to when Keohane, Brady, and Rizzo industriously engrossed themselves in essential tasks, like Pavlov's dogs hearing a bell. Those hairbags dodged pulling their weight, and if Corcoran knew about the discrepancies amongst the B team, he never gave any indication that he cared.

"Ah," Vito exclaimed. He veered towards the curb, slamming on the brakes with a jolt that threw Alex into the seatbelt. Vito flung open his door. "C'mon, Lex." The older detective marched towards a skinny Latino man huddled under a tatty awning that was attached to a building cladded by worn brickwork and heavy wire screening the windows. The man wore a faded bandana around his head and a threadbare, green t-shirt. A stained, tattered denim backpack, with one strap half-attached, hung over his right shoulder.

"Yo, Turbo, my man," Vito gushed. "How you been?"

"Oh, man, Detective Vito. Not good. Not good. I been sick, real sick." The man had that unmistakable sunken, underweight frame, typical of long-term drug users. His bloodshot eyes looked hunted, mistrustful. His fingertips were blackened with singe marks from crack pipes. He wrapped his skeletal fingers around Vito's meaty forearm. "I got what you wanted, but you better help me," he entreated.

"You know that's what I do," Vito replied, grinning. "I promised, didn't I? Take a ride with us, eh?"

At the word *us,* Turbo's eyes darted towards Alex. "You said it was just you," he yelped. "*He* better not be a Narc."

"Detective Boswell's cool. He's Homicide," Vito said as he purposefully clasped Turbo by the arm and piloted him towards the car.

Turbo pitched into the backseat of the Crown Vic, and the detectives wiggled into their places in the front seats. The crackhead stank – body odor and the grime of the streets. Alex's nostrils flared. He breathed through his mouth and watched the people outside the car: a couple drinking from a paper bag on the stoop of a brownstone; a woman stumbling out of a laundromat with a basket too big for her to carry; two teens juggling a soccer ball; five or six more young people passing a joint around.

"You got it, Turbo?" Vito asked.

"Yeah, 'course. I been in Los Esqueletos for months. He trusts me. No one else looks at me. They ain't bothered. You keep your head down, do what you're told, no one bothers you."

"Ain't that the truth," Vito acknowledged. "Let's see it."

Turbo's hand plunged into the beat-up backpack. He fished out a crumpled plastic shopping bag. His hands fluttering like a leaf in the wind, he passed it to Vito. "Took some getting, but I got it. They ever find out, I'm a dead man."

Smirking like he'd won a longshot gamble, Vito slid his latex gloves over his hands. He unwrapped the bag and drew out a silver Colt M1991A. Under the pale gleam of the streetlamps, it glinted, as if bejeweled. He checked for rounds in the chamber, then the safety.

Alex's heart missed about five beats. "What the fuck?"

"Guillermo Quixano's gun," pronounced Vito. "Turbo's quite the pickpocket!"

"How the fuck—" Alex started to say but then clamped his teeth together as protestations lodged in his throat. No chain-of-custody, no direct evidence connecting that gun to Quixano, only hearsay from a crackhead.

Wearing that gimlet-eyed grin, Vito handed Turbo a wad of cash, then he drove around the block to a shadowy, deserted alley devoid of streetlamps and witnesses, so no one saw Turbo leaping away from the car, scampering off, making a beeline for the nearest corner with his windfall. *That guy is loyal to whoever gives him crack, or money for crack*, Alex thought distastefully. And he didn't care who it was. Alex would believe the sky was green before he believed that Guillermo Quixano had used that gun to shoot anyone.

"We take this baby to ballistics," Vito announced as he whacked the car into drive, peeling towards the Henry Hudson Parkway.

"Your informant's prints will be all over it. I doubt Quixano's will be."

"Yeah, so what? Look, you gotta spin the 'fives. I'm not sayin' it's a bad thing that he just gave me the gun like this, 'cause it isn't, but it's gonna be better if you say he showed us the stash house where he found the gun. And he knew it was Quixano's 'cause it was Quixano's stash house, and he had a silver Colt. Everyone seen Quixano with the silver Colt. Everyone."

"Why the fuck would Quixano leave an expensive gun like that unattended in a stash house? Two years later? What kind of bullshit story is that? No one's gonna buy that. It proves nothing. Even if it *was* in a stash house, two hundred people could've had access to it if it was under a floorboard or wherever." Hot steam hissed through his veins. Unable to look at Vito, he shifted his eyes upwards towards the cables and soaring tower of the George Washington Bridge. They flew underneath its steel skeleton.

"I dunno. 'Cause he did. 'Cause it's been two years and he didn't think anyone would care anymore. 'Cause he got cocky. That's what I'm gonna write. We say different things, we got a problem, right?"

"Where did your CI really find that gun?"

"I said, don't worry about it." Vito drummed his palms against the wheel. "Remember, you used to trust me. What's happened? What's this shit?"

"He didn't pull it out of a fucking hat."

"Just cool your jets. It don't matter, okay."

Alex heaved a pained sigh.

"I'm tryin' to *help* you, Lex." Vito insisted, as if Alex was a difficult child. "We need this case down."

Quixano was definitely a drug dealer, one with his own little empire on his corners. If he didn't commit this murder, he probably committed another one. If he went down for it, that would dent the drug trade around West 188th, at least for five minutes until some other guy moved in on Quixano's turf. Yet Alex felt his stomach going to hell.

"Hey, how's the place?"

"What?" Alex startled at the *non sequitur*.

"Your apartment. I bet it beats Hurley's sofa or living with Cohen's neurotic-as-fuck girlfriend. Sorry I couldn't make your New Year

314

shindigs. I hear they're epic but ya know, the wife's family always does a big thing every year."

"Oh. It's great."

"You still with that hippy girl from the Village?"

"Yeah."

"What's she called again?"

"Charlotte." Alex studied his fingers. He'd chewed his nails past the quick, and they were dark with slivers of dried blood.

"Two years, huh? That's a hell of a long relationship for you." Vito playfully punched him in the shoulder with the hand not on the wheel.

"Yeah." It was, but he wasn't in the mood to talk about his personal life. He grasped his shoulder, rubbing out the aches. Vito's fist was rock-hard.

Downtown, they left the gun with the property clerk. Vito made a show of filling out the chain-of-custody paperwork, signing his name with a flourish, like it was the Declaration of Independence. He drove Alex back to the Two-Five, saying, "Great work, that was great work tonight. Fun, wasn't it?"

Not the word that came to Alex's mind. "What are the chances the lab results will match?" he remarked cynically, his elbow braced on the roof of the car.

"Don't be so fuckin' down all the time. That's your biggest fuckin' problem." Vito rolled up the window, turned on the engine, and zoomed towards his own precinct.

Alex stood alone under the deepening shadows thrown by the Two-Five's sheer concrete walls. He indulged himself with a long drink from his flask, finding some solace in the warm whisky traveling down to his stomach, heating up his insides. A second swig from the flask – *careful, not too much*, he thought, hastily screwing the cap on the flask – then he trudged up the precinct's stairs, opening the MNHS door in time for a water balloon, shaped like a cock-and-balls, to smack him in the sore shoulder. James had stolen them from a crime scene because he thought they were funny and the previous owner was too dead to notice. Unamused and wet, Alex palmed his shoulder and glared at his colleagues. Cold water dribbled down his arm and his chest.

"You'd think I just interrupted you jerking off," James cackled. "The look on your face!"

Alex pressed his lips into a bemused half-smile, reminding himself to laugh at the comic. Sometimes, it was the only way to get through the day.

***

Although Alex had a pile of open cases to worry about, reservations about Turbo and the silver Colt performed spin cycles inside his guts. He affirmed his suspicions with background investigation he had no time for, but he couldn't get that bizarre evening out of his head. Turbo was really Luca Martinez, a crackhead who sometimes worked for the Dominican drug crews, but usually stole and fenced stuff to fund his pharmaceutical habits. He'd been picked up a year ago on larceny charges but no conviction. Charges dismissed. The detective on that larceny case? Vito Indelicata.

Alex's unease rocketed upwards like the space shuttle when he received a waffling ballistics analysis. The lab could not conclusively match the silver Colt to the bullet extracted from Jose Medina's head. In his mind, the case remained a whodunit, like a thousand other drug murders. He distrusted Vito's informants, and his own CI, who knew the blocks around 188th and St. Nick's, told him that Guillermo Quixano was the rare slinger who tried to keep his crew on this side of civilized. Quixano, the CI explained, felt as frustrated with the violence of the drug trade as the police. Why can't it work like a normal business, he had once complained. Making a better product than our rivals instead of shooting them. There's going to be demand whatever the police do; after all, getting high transcends race, socioeconomics, culture, and history. "You agree, he's got a point," the CI said. "But hey, all this feudal shit keeps *you* employed, right?" Alex dipped his chin in a tiny nod. That was one way to look at it.

Still, the streets can force the hand of the most conscientious dealer. The CI admitted that if Quixano thought his own life or the lives of his crew were in danger, he would "do what needed doing, you get me." Alex got him.

He'd met his CI atop a fifteen-story building with malfunctioning elevators, so he'd ascended hundreds of stairs. The wound on his side pulsed between heavy aches and shooting pain. He limped up the Two-Five's stairway, stopping in his tracks whenever he saw someone so they wouldn't catch him limping. Safely in his cubicle, he swilled water and ibuprofen. His phone screeched. A metallic, recorded female voice asked if he would accept a call from Sing Sing Correctional Facility. Carlos Medina, still in prison, using precious telephone privileges.

"I hear you looking into Jose's case again," Medina said bluntly.

Alex wondered where the hell Medina got his information. "Yeah, we're working on some leads."

316

"It's been two years, man," complained Medina. "Two fuckin' years. You ain't charging anyone 'cause he's a drug dealer. And I'm a drug dealer. Like you people give a fuck."

"That's got nothing to do with it," Alex said. Except it had a lot to do with it. The department was never going to detail dozens of officers to investigate a dead crack slinger rotting in a derelict basement, a guy who no one even reported missing. Alex added, "If we can charge someone, we will. You ever hear of a man called Guillermo Quixano?"

"No. That someone who knew Jose?"

"Maybe. We're looking into it."

"Did he kill him?"

"I don't know. Like I said, we're looking into it."

"You seriously looking?" Medina asked skeptically.

"Yeah. It's what I do."

Medina uttered a disbelieving grunt, before either a guard or another prisoner forced him to hang up. Why did Vito like Quixano for this case? God knows. You couldn't always explain Vito. Alex winced as he crimped his fingertips into the lumps around his tenth rib, then he held his hand over his face, breathing in. Lavender. Charlotte was on an essential oils schtick this month; she'd insisted on rubbing lavender oil into his wound. It made no difference, but it gave her the satisfaction of doing something.

Medina's murder book poked out, buried within a stack of other mostly cold cases. If only Alex had infinite time and resources for every victim here. The older detectives reminisced about the days of the domestic grounder and ninety-percent clearance rates, but they'd become a distant memory before Alex attained his gold shield. In 1992, it seemed like no one had time for anything but picking up bodies. It left him bone tired, his heart atrophying, but all he could do for victims' families was feign hopefulness. Streetwise guys like Carlos Medina knew he was full of shit.

Within seventy-two hours, a triple homicide in the 23rd Precinct threw MNHS into pandemonium. One of the vics was Archibald Huang, a prominent Chinese-American criminal lawyer and gay rights activist, shot in a drive-by along with his client and a bystander. The lawyer and the client died, while the bystander was critically injured. Alex caught the case, thinking how unlucky, the primary on a high-octane redball, an 'oh, shit' case overshadowing everything else.

He worked every inch of the crime scene, interviewing more than fifty witnesses, sending out BOLOs describing the alleged getaway car, screaming at idiot cops to stop contaminating evidence. *Don't touch things! Don't walk in that grass! Just get the fuck out!* Some hours later, James took over the crime scene, freeing Alex to transport evidence to Property, then watch the vics autopsied downtown. Past exhausted, Alex stumbled into the MNHS office, sweaty, desperate to change into a fresher suit. His clothes stank of decomposition and formaldehyde. His right side spasmed, in agony after a whirlwind tour – no sleep, no space to breathe, and twelve hours of overtime.

He bypassed the squad room, hobbling to the lockers, but Corcoran, his face grey with stress, cornered him.

"I'm looking at the board, Boswell," he said. "Mayor Dinkins is upset. He is saying we need more homicides cleared. We're not clearing these, we're basically giving it carte blanche for it to be the Wild West uptown."

"I'm fifty-three percent, sir," Alex said, throwing in the 'sir' as an afterthought to make up for the insolent tone. "I'm doing everything I can." Someone up the NYPD food chain had kicked Corcoran's ass about the lawyer, and now Corcoran was kicking his.

"What about that dealer on West 166th? Medina. I thought you had a suspect."

"Yeah, I dunno."

"Who is it again?"

"A slinger called Guillermo Quixano, but I don't—"

"Why don't you close it? Narc has been after that fella for years, sure. Don't you have a witness?"

Woozy from pain, hunger, and sleep deprivation, Alex swayed towards the wall, biting into his lower lip to stop another yawn. "I don't think she's much of a witness. She's one of Indelicata's CIs. I think he pays her to testify in his cases. And that other eyewit didn't pick him out of a line-up until Vito put him through like three times. The ID's not good, sir. I think it'll have problems in court."

"So Indelicata likes him for it." Corcoran ignored the multiple line-ups and his theory about Vito's CI.

"Yes," Alex admitted. "But there's a problem with the gun. The ballistics were inconclusive, and there were no prints on it."

"Get Indelicata back into it. He'll know how to close it."

"Yes, sir."

Corcoran played a statistics game. The case would be cleared, and he didn't care if a grand jury issued a no bill, or a judge dismissed it, or an ADA *nolle prossed* it. Latter misadventures in the criminal justice system did not factor into a squad's clearance rate. He ordered, "Sort it out with

Indelicata, then make the collar. Where are you for leads on the Huang shooting?"

"We have some wits with the sketch artist at the Two-Three," Alex answered tiredly. Rarely did that work, but the bosses ordered the investigators to do it anyway, so they had a sketch to show journalists. "The Two-Three detectives are looking for the getaway car. James is contacting Parole and Probation about people who might be disgruntled clients or had a beef with the client who was shot. The guy did a lot of activism for the gay community and AIDS advocacy, so I'm gonna see if any religious yahoos were sending him hate mail."

"Good. Keep me in the loop,"

"Yes, sir," Alex promised.

Stung by the boss' rebuke, Alex pressed onwards to the lockers, where he stripped off all his clothes. The gunshot wound had become a fiery ball of pain, like smoldering coals wedged under his ribs. With utmost care, he prodded the scars, as if he could draw out the heat with his fingers. But touching it hurt more. He threw a couple ibuprofens down his throat, then changed into a different suit, creased, but not smelling like the ME's examination room.

The fresher suit didn't help him feel any less schvitzik. Swept up in a terrible darkness eclipsing his whole sky – this case, his boss, his wound, the police department, the ceaseless tit-for-tat violence that kept him running from one crime scene to another – he wilted over his desk, clasping his face with both palms. For several minutes, he breathed forcefully into his hands, his eyelids quivering against his fingertips. Like those fugacious spring thunderstorms, the worst of the torrential darkness passed, and he resignedly shunted a stack of statements from the Huang shooting out of his way. Moving as if his arm was broken, he picked up the phone. He lowered his eyelids again.

"Hey, Lex, you gonna make second grade with that triple if you can put it down," Vito said by way of hello. "I'm watchin' it on the news now."

"We'll see," Alex countered doubtfully, not sharing Vito's optimism about the case being a grounder, making grade, or much else. "Look, Vito, my boss wants that Medina thing cleared. But you saw the ballistics report. I don't know what to do about that." *Other than look for other suspects. No chance in a two-year old drug murder.*

"Let's go to the lab and figure it out."

"Schlep downtown? I'm fucking swamped here. I can't remember the last time I managed to even eat." Alex didn't want to 'figure it out.' He didn't want to know what that even meant.

"You said your boss wants you to close the case. You got half the squad working on the gay lawyer. You haven't eaten? How about we get some food in your belly on the way?"

Regrettably, Corcoran had given him orders. Whatever Vito's game plan might be, Alex had a gut feeling he wouldn't like it, so before meeting the precinct detective and schlepping to the other end of the city, he anesthetized himself with more whisky than he should drink when he had to drive, but to hell with it. The bullshit part of criminal justice was easier to handle when you were a little tipsy. It also made the throbbing in his side a bit more bearable.

A hot dog from a street van revived him, so he wasn't completely dead on his feet, but when he got to the lab, he wasn't feeling anywhere near tipsy enough. Fulsome and smiling, Vito joshed around with John Levi, the pasty-faced lab analyst. Alex worried at his fingernails and his memo book. Levi laughed at Vito's jokes. Then Vito slung his arm around Levi's shoulders, saying blithely, "Ya know that silver Colt we sent you a few weeks ago. The M1991A."

"Yeah, I think so."

"You said the slugs didn't match the firearm?"

Levi stared at him. Alex stared at the floor.

Fidgeting with his glasses, Levi replied, "Uh, I believe I said that I couldn't conclusively determine a match one way or another."

"Yeah, yeah, so you're not discounting the possibility that it *might* match. There's a chance, a good chance, that it did. You're not saying there was one hundred percent no match."

"Well." Levi whistled a drawn-out breath. "We can never be one hundred percent sure of anything. It's not totally, uh, objective. There's a lot of interpretation."

"You mean, it can be interpreted differently." Vito seemed so earnest, the science of ballistics the most interesting thing in the world.

"Yeah, I guess," Levi answered warily. "Like looking at the rifling, the striations and marks, it's not like there's a computer program. I mean, sometimes it's totally obvious, but you, the analyst, have to make sense out of what you see. And obviously the bullets will be damaged when they enter the body and bounce off things, so it's rarely perfect."

"No firearm ever has a one hundred percent match?"

"Usually not, especially if we're analyzing bullets that have hit something, like bone."

"But you look at the rifling, and you decide that it's enough, like a big enough percentage to say, that's the gun that fired this slug?"

"Yeah."

"And this gun, it could be seen differently."

Alex felt himself sweating under his shirt. The hot dog had filled the hole in his stomach, but now his gut writhed in protest.

"Um, the bullet was pretty mangled, so it's hard to say," Levi mumbled.

"But it could be. I mean, you get mangled slugs all the time, right? You're good at making sense outta that shit. You didn't come out and say, no way in hell could this have been the gun."

"True, we didn't."

"And we find a gun, we find a slug, we bring them to you, it must mean there's other evidence connecting those things, right? There were *some* similarities in the rifling and striations?"

"There were some, yes. But lots of weapons—"

"So, in the big picture, you could say those similarities make it likely that gun fired that bullet."

"I guess. There's a certain probability that there could be a match but as I said, hard to say with any certainty, you know, given the damage on the bullet."

"Big picture, John. Come on. What's the big picture?"

"Uh, I can look at the images again. But I don't know. You know my supervisor has to sign off on any report…"

"I'm good pals with him, okay. He's been to my kids' christenings. Don't worry about that."

"Uh, okay…"

"Look, man, it's a huge favor. I'll take you out for a drink, put in a good word with the Commissioner. You help close a murder case. Get a bad guy off the streets. How about that? Like television. Like *Hawaii Five-O*. Like *NYPD Blue*. You think there's a chance that this slug matched this Colt, there's *enough* similarities in the rifling, you gotta come out and say it."

The forensics analyst fretted at his glasses again, but what power could a socially awkward lab nerd muster against Vito? He nodded as Vito spoke, agreeing. He would write a new ballistics report, and Vito smiled, his eyes twinkling, the analyst's best friend in the world.

When Alex and Vito left the lab, Alex demanded, "What the fuck was that?"

"It's the bottom of the ninth. Makin' sure we got our bases covered."

"What? The report said the slug didn't match."

Vito grinned like he had no cares in the world. "The report said the slug *might* not have matched. But it might've."

321

"What if it *isn't* the gun? Juries believe anyone in a white coat."

"Yeah, they do. And it's the gun, trust me. Sometimes, you just gotta get the science on the side of the facts, you know."

This was absurd. "What about the other report?"

"What other report? I didn't see no other report."

Alex sucked on his lip, staring at a huddled camp of ramshackle tents and tarps flapping in a vacant lot. The city's homeless problem was getting worse. Everything was getting worse. Had Vito really told an analyst to rewrite his report, so ambiguous science looked definite? Did he just admit that he would snap his fingers and magically erase the first report? If Alex had descended into a nightmare, he would wake up about now.

He dumped Vito at the Three-Four and then sat in Broadway traffic, trapped behind a bus driver having an altercation with a traffic cop and a Chevy Cavalier. Horns penetrated the hazy pollution. The Cavalier driver and bus driver made obscene gestures at one another. The traffic cop pipped his siren. No, he wasn't in a nightmare. He was wide awake, stuck in this gridlocked lunacy. By now, he knew that it wasn't worth warning Vito that the first report should go into discovery, just as he knew that no one would bother if it didn't. The man stayed out of trouble and cleared cases, not through thoughtful, meticulous investigation, but rather by bulldozing headlong through any obstacle, building such a colossal reputation as the greatest force of nature in the NYPD that his bosses, colleagues, and ADAs simply shook their heads. "That's Vito." He got through shit by virtue of being Vito.

Chapter Thirty

A heatwave arrived in mid-May, and the detectives of Manhattan North Homicide knew the murder rate would rise. Summertime and the living is easy, crooned Gershwin, but he never had to work murders in uptown Manhattan, where the heat steamed out of the sidewalks in a critical mass, becoming its own reason, its own motive. The detectives worked at one hundred miles an hour, slapping band-aids on a city bleeding from all its arteries. Sometimes, the victim would be Archie Huang or Rabbi Liebowitz or the Central Park Jogger, someone who mattered to the world beyond the inner-city, a redball drawing attention, and the rest of the country and city might turn an eye towards the violence, and the Police Commissioner and Chief of Detectives might send extra resources to the squad. Most of the time, the squad slogged through investigations under-resourced, unremarked on. Washington Heights, home of the misdemeanor homicide.

They had watched South Central Los Angeles explode into riots at the end of April, after a jury acquitted the four LAPD officers who beat up Rodney King. Every man and woman in the Homicide squad felt a tremor in their gut. For days, South Central LA burned. It took the army to subdue the unrest. South Central LA was the Washington Heights, the Bed-Stuy or East New York of California, a neighborhood beset by poverty, ravaged by crack, with a relationship between civilians and police like a high-tensile wire. Alex could easily foresee police officers here beating up or shooting civilians (they had), but one day, it would trigger something – then the neighborhood would explode as though someone had buried dynamite under the streets. New York race relations were already on edge. Crown Heights had blown up last year, when the motorcade of an Orthodox Jewish leader struck two Guyanese children, and racial tensions in the neighborhood between Blacks and Jews combusted into the murder of a twenty-nine year old Jewish student and three days of rioting.

The Huang case remaining a whodunit accelerated his plummeting morale. Corcoran harangued him about it every week. The press bayed at his heels. A drive-by in broad daylight should be a grounder, but it wasn't. *Why should anyone make my life easier?* he thought. And this week, he was deeply under the weather with a lung-rattling virus. His joints ached like his bones ground against sharp glass, and his sinuses burned like a brush fire. Yeah, his doctor had warned him that a respiratory infection could lead to pneumonia because of the damage to his right lung, but he couldn't afford sick days. Who has time for that? Not him, not with a caseload he needed a scorecard to keep straight, the press breathing down his neck, and Corcoran busting his balls about Archie Huang.

Hot fluid bubbled inside his chest. Breathing hurt like an arsonist had torched his lungs. The chesty coughs were agonizing. But he painstakingly reviewed Huang's file, excavating through accumulating drifts of paperwork – rap sheets from clients and anti-gay religious fundamentalists, crime scene photos, old DD-5s. While examining the photos, he noticed a bearded man in the gawking crowd on the edge of the scene. It got his attention because the same man appeared in a stack of mugshots – the lawyer's clients. The guy had half a dozen aliases, almost one for every felony, but on his most recent case, he called himself Thomas Rinn. He had recently finished an eighteen-month sentence on a grand theft auto charge, but he had a criminal history spanning the Penal Code, from larceny to gun possession to assault. When a precinct detective had questioned him at the Two-Three station house, he'd claimed that he had an alibi, and the overworked precinct detective hadn't really followed it up. Now Alex followed it up by interviewing the alibi witness. It took him two hours to punch holes in her story, using phone records and her inability to keep her lies straight. She confessed that Rinn told her to say she was with him, promising her sex in return.

"He must be good in bed," Alex said acidly.

"It's the only thing he's good at," replied the witness.

One bit of evidence. Perp deliberately lied about his alibi, plus he'd been stupid enough to hang around the crime scene and get caught on camera. Alex identified the co-defendant from the grand theft auto case, out on parole for a different grand theft auto case. A parole officer sent Alex to the co-defendant's halfway house, and Alex brought him to the Two-Five. The car thief cooperated – playing ball with police investigations was a requirement of his parole. Thank God, Alex thought, too sick for an unruly witness. His lymph nodes felt like golf balls in his throat, and he had a foul, metallic taste in his mouth.

"You should see a doctor," said the car thief. "You sound like you got a lung infection. You should be on antibiotics for that."

"What, you a doctor?" Alex asked hoarsely.

"I done a medical degree. NYU."

"Then why the fuck are you here?" Alex waved at the discolored breeze block walls.

"How do you think I *afforded* med school, man? Didn't want to get into slinging, and school's expensive. Two Cadillacs, that's one year of tuition. I paid for all med school with cars."

"Mazel tov," wheezed Alex. "You didn't think that a record was, you know, a barrier to you working as a doctor?"

"Getting caught wasn't part of the plan."

No matter how many years Alex was on the job, people still astounded him.

In any case, the car thief didn't want to be violated, so he explained, "I only stole one or two cars with Tom. He carried a gun and was prepared to get, like, violent if something didn't go right. But man, I ain't into that shit. I just wanna get the car, clean, safe. No one gets hurt. If it ain't gonna go right, it ain't gonna go right. You leave it. There are lots of cars out there."

"Archie Huang represented you on your case. How did that go?"

The car thief threw back his head, laughing. "Not well, given we did eighteen months each. I mean, that was like a plea bargain. Tom, he wanted a trial. He was *pissed* about Huang pleading it out. But they had us dead to rights. I mean, we did it, didn't we? We weren't gonna win no trial."

"And you said he carried a gun?"

"He *always* had a gun."

Alex coughed again and rested his hand over his aching breastbone, worried that coughing loosened the sternotomy wires. The bone had fused back together, but they said the surgery to remove the wires wasn't worth the risk of general anesthesia or opening up his chest. And his insurance company wouldn't pay for anything that elective. "He say anything to you about wanting to hurt his lawyer?"

"We ain't talked since we got outta prison. But he was mad as hell at Archie when we went in, sayin', that motherfucker has it coming, and like I said, he liked using his gun if he was mad."

"'That motherfucker has it coming,'" Alex repeated.

"Yeah, man, pretty much what he said."

It sounded like probable cause. Alex fluffed up a SAFIS report, a four-point fingerprint match on the steering wheel of the getaway car. It might be mutilated in court, but still, with the crime scene photo, the car thief's statement, and the lying alibi witness, Alex threw together his affidavit. Simon McNally ran with it, although they both knew the case was a weak sister. They convinced a judge to sign an arrest warrant. If Alex cleared this case, Corcoran and the brass would get off his back, and he would be a step closer to second grade. He could do with the money, and he needed the breathing space.

Once authorized, Alex, James, and a dozen patrol officers surrounded the sketchy hand carwash on East 122nd where Thomas Rinn worked. The perp spotted the police cars and shot through the back door of the carwash, sprinting along Madison. The cops ran after him. At Marcus Garvey Park, Rinn whirled to face the police. His right hand was down the back of his pants. They skidded to a halt with their guns drawn. Alex stared at the perp down the barrel of his Ruger. His heart raced. His shooting came to mind. Ed Byrne came to mind. The hell that would break loose if he shot this asshole came to mind. Rinn, thankfully, reconsidered his situation. Raising both hands, he dropped onto the asphalt, lying flat on his belly while they frisked him and slapped the cuffs on his wrists. He was packing a Colt King Cobra.

The cops stuffed Rinn into the back of an RMP, reading him *Miranda*. Alex dropped onto the curb, head down between his knees, feeling sick. Every muscle in his body quivered. His forehead sizzled to the touch. His joints felt like jelly. "You better drive," he wheezed.

James drove downtown and processed the perp at Central Booking while Alex waited in the car, coughing his guts up.

"My mother swore by whisky for curing a 'flu," James said when he returned to the car.

That night, Alex, James, McNally, and the precinct detectives celebrated putting the case down with drinks in the Glendale. It turned out that Irish mothers were wrong: whiskey didn't cure the 'flu, and Alex coughed his lungs to shreds on the subway ride to the Upper West. Unruffled by the late hour, Charlotte met him there. Smiling tenderly, she cuddled his chest, kissed his lips and throat, and then she brewed a sour-tasting concoction. She promised it would alleviate the cough and fever. It upset his stomach, but he crumpled into bed, shivering, too tired, sore, and ill for complaining.

He ran into a building on East 122nd Street, chasing an armed perp. Eddie was with him. They were trapped in a building. They heard thundering footsteps. Someone banged against a door. It wasn't Harlem, but it was. He tried returning fire through the door. His hand was paralyzed. Then it was gone, a bloody stump. Shocked, he stumbled backwards. The Ruger Service Six misfired. The perp fired his weapon, but Alex was outside his own body, watching himself and Eddie while the bullets flew, and he couldn't move a single limb.

His eyes snapped open, and his heart shuddered. He glued his eyes to the carved ceiling skirting boards in the West 87th Street apartment. When he touched his forehead and then his belly, he felt a sticky, warm layer of sweat. The sheets were soaked in it.

"You were moaning and calling for help," Charlotte said. "It woke me up. Are you okay?"

"Yeah. Just a nightmare."

"Want another lemon drink?"

"No. That didn't agree with me."

"Is it bothering your stomach? I forget, it's so sensitive!"

"Yeah." He'd never thought of it that way, but James never complained of nausea or cramps when he was stressed, so perhaps it was.

"I have some tea that will be good for that fever. It should be gentler on your tummy."

"It's alright. Just a long day, and I feel like shit." He didn't tell her about chasing an armed perp. There were things he never talked about with her. Gruesome aspects of the job. Sickening depravity. Near-death experiences. Things she was better off not knowing.

"No, you should have it." She gave him a light kiss on his cheek, then hopped out of bed, and he heard her in the kitchen. He sat up and drew his knees to his chest, the nightmare stuck in his mind, his heart beating out a heavy rhythm. Charlotte didn't know about the chronic nightmares, either. He lacked the words to explain how vivid they were, how his nervous system responded as if he was in physical danger, how he would wake up terrified, unsure of where dreams ended, and reality started.

Charlotte returned, cradling a mug of sweetened, fruity tea, which he drank too quickly to taste. Then he curled around himself under the sheets and felt Charlotte wriggling against his back, burying her face in his neck and shoulder. His cough kicked steel spikes into his chest. He restlessly slid around the fringes of a troubled sleep for a couple hours, far less than he needed.

Spaced out with illness and exhaustion, he started the eight-by-four by writing 'fives, supplemental reports, and charging documents for yesterday's footchase and arrest. He tossed cold and 'flu medication down his throat like M&Ms. It worked as well as Charlotte's damned tea.

The phone screamed.

Bill and Marty were downstairs interrogating a perp, Rizzo and Cohen were in the field somewhere, and Keohane and Brady were pointedly ignoring it. Wheezing, Alex answered, "Manhattan North Homicide, this is Detective Boswell."

A DOA in an apartment on Haven Avenue in Washington Heights. He rattled car keys as he limped through the office, coughing. Pale mucous sputtered up from his lungs, bringing a salty taste to his throat and mouth. Hoarsely, he snapped at Brady, "God forbid, you pick up the phone sometimes."

"Eh," Brady said.

The first officers let Alex and James into the apartment, a small studio bathed in a grotesque, violet light, reeking of death. Everyone in the room looked sick. They stood over the DOA, female, Black, stabbed three times and disemboweled, the apartment ransacked, the TV and jewelry missing. But no evidence of forced entry. The perp was probably someone who knew her. A relative, an acquaintance. Fuck, no one deserved this. Alex winced and folded his arms over his belly, trying to steady his wobbly innards. Clothes rubbing against his skin felt like a thousand tiny spikes. They perforated his joints, his bones. The apartment boiled, beyond one hundred degrees. He raised his eyes towards James and the precinct detective, who'd both gone white. "It never fucking ends, does it?"

"No shit." Even James looked tired, and James was one of the most inexhaustible people Alex knew.

Ellie visited West 87th Street once Alex got past the worst of his illness. Recovering his health had required a hefty course of antibiotics. The car thief had been right about the lung infection. That guy would be better served by med school than prison, but the carceral state was the carceral state. In any case, Alex hadn't seen either of the girls in a month. While he'd been sick, he'd sequestered himself, but Sarah refused to talk to him at all. This time, he deserved her wrath. Six months ago, when Ellie broke her arm falling off her bike and went into the hospital, Alex had been so pissed off at Catherine's boyfriend for showing up before he did, holding Ellie's hand after the surgery – the job of her father, dammit – that he'd stormed out of the hospital, leaving Sarah alone in the waiting room while Catherine and the boyfriend comforted her sister. Stupid and irrational and emotional, his most recent parental felony, and God knows, Sarah handed down life sentences.

Now that he felt better – only combating a lingering cough and the usual spasming pain from his wound – he was delighted to have Ellie for a night. She worked on homework, then asked Charlotte about Seattle and her four years abroad in Scotland. Distant lands of mountains, lakes, and medieval cities must seem like science fiction to a kid from New York. Alex had never taken the girls when he visited his sister Helen in Colorado. Looking dreamy, Ellie said that she would like to live in a place like that, surrounded by craggy mountains, lakes, wilderness. But first, she had to pass this biology final, so she continued reading her textbook.

The homework finished, she announced, "I'm going out to see Hannah and Laura." Two friends who lived near Lincoln Center.

"It's late, Ellie," Alex objected, thinking if he let her go, her mother would kill him.

"It's fine. Mom lets me go all the time."

That was a load of crap. "How you gonna get there?" A coughing convulsion interrupted his questions. He couldn't shake this fucking cough or get rid of the wheezing in the right side of his chest that sounded like James' bagpipes when the bag deflated.

"Subway."

"The subway's not safe."

She rolled her eyes skyward. "Dad, don't be lame."

"I know what goes on. I'm not letting you on it at night."

Charlotte kissed his cheek. "Lex, what if we give her cab money. And enough to get back here."

Ellie's face brightened. "Please, Daddy."

Desperate to not fall out with her, he doled out a crumpled twenty-dollar bill, with the caveat of her promising to be back by midnight. Thinking he'd won the parenting thing, he called her a taxi. But after she'd gallivanted to Lincoln Center, he stayed up, tense, waiting for the sound of footsteps on the stairs. Every noise in the building made him still his breathing and concentrate on listening. Oh, what if something happened? His job meant he could imagine the worst possibilities, a flicking rolodex of every murder, rape, or mugging that ever happened between here and Lincoln Center. It aggravated the tickling heat in his lungs. He wheezed and hacked, holding his right side.

Charlotte massaged his shoulders. "You're too stressed. She'll be fine. It's the Upper West Side."

"Her mother's nuts, but she's not wrong when she says this city is more fucked up than it used to be." He tore a bloody sliver of flesh from his left thumb.

As promised, Ellie returned at five past midnight and went straight to bed. He could breathe, freed from his worst-case scenarios. After a quick nip of whisky, he coasted towards sleep with Charlotte's head on his chest. Listening to her breathing and the air conditioner humming, he felt warmed by a transcendent glow of well-being, the unusual feeling of having his shit together. He had a girlfriend who loved him, and one of his kids didn't hate him.

That feeling lasted until he brought Ellie back to Catherine, who had somehow learned that she'd gone out with friends and no adult. The woman had more CIs than he did.

"That's so *dangerous* and irresponsible," she blustered. "You of all people should know how dangerous the city is."

"She took a cab, she came home when I told her to. It was from West 87th to West 66th. It's a safe neighborhood." He channeled Charlotte's assuredness rather than his own worries. For some inexplicable reason, he had foolishly succumbed to his sixteen-year old's entreaty when he knew the city's dangers too well, just as he knew his ex would rip his head off.

"Is there such a thing as a safe neighborhood? That jogger thought *she* was in a safe neighborhood!"

"Don't buy into the media hype. The park at night has never been *that* safe."

"You're unbelievable."

"I ran all over this city as a kid."

"It's different. There's so much more crime. You ran around the Lower East Side. Around the Bowery! Delancey Street! You wouldn't let the kids do that, would you? I need to be able to trust you, but you never think anything through."

To his dismay, she restricted Ellie's visits. Several times, Ellie called him, tearful, missing him, but he told her to work it out with her mother, which in hindsight was a stupid thing to say because it should not be up to a teenager to figure this shit out. It should be up to him, but it seemed insurmountable. Nothing he could say would make Catherine see him as a better person, and nothing he could do would compel her to answer his phone calls. If he wanted a court to enforce his parental rights, he should have brought his case to Family Court years ago, when he was too adrift in his own head to fight for custody. Like every time he fell out anew with Catherine, he drank more and worked his cases harder.

At least he had Charlotte. The squad teased him mercilessly about his hippy girlfriend, but to him, she was like fresh air, an antidote to the darkness of the streets. Someone who walked in the light and dealt with the living. She loved her music. She laughed at the foibles of fellow New Yorkers. She didn't see the worst in people. She found the trees and glens in Central Park enchanting, full of small delights – birds, insects, squirrels, flowers. They would lie on the grass gazing at bubbling summer clouds, while she rambled dreamily about writing the great novel, traveling, living in a van. Sometimes, she talked about auras, about connecting with spirits. She was learning some energy healing thing, which he pretended to take seriously when she rested both palms against his abdomen and asked if he could feel anything. Well, yes. His nerves tingling at her touch.

"Does your wound feel better?"

"No," he admitted cautiously, afraid he would upset her, but the wound felt as sore as ever.

"Oh, well, maybe I'm not advanced enough," she sighed.

"No one can do much about that," he reassured her. It sounded impracticable and, quite frankly, batshit crazy, but he acted patient and halfheartedly interested because she passionately believed in this stuff.

Moreover, she never kvetched when he drank a lot. She remained upbeat and loving when his moods and stress overrode his sex drive. She didn't ask too many questions when he lay awake with his heart thudding. She never complained when work overtook life, and he cancelled a date or apologized and ran away with little warning. He'd developed some appreciation for Irish music. It made more sense than energy healing. When he wasn't working or out drinking with his colleagues, he tagged along to her sessions and gigs. Often, he would come across James playing the whistle in the sessions. The tunes had emotional resonance yet no actual meaning, a torrent of notes drowning out his thoughts, especially if he had a few beers in him. Charlotte would ramble about achieving mental stillness with meditation and yoga, but Alex looked for unremitting noise – Irish dance tunes rising and falling like rapids in a river.

Around the middle of June, he went out for drinks with Charlotte and some of her music friends at the Bitter End. He nursed a Miller Lite, half-listening to conversations unsullied by crime and violence. Things normal people talk about. There was something pathological about being a cop.

Two of Charlotte's friends told stories about their recent trip playing music in Ireland, while Neil, a flute player from Glasgow, regaled everyone with anecdotes about wild nights out drinking something called Buckfast, a fortified wine, fifteen percent alcohol laced with caffeine. It was either amazing or a terrible idea.

"Aye, so ah was walkin' doon Sauchiehall Street, and ah was fuckin' pished and that was me, doon to me knickers, and would you fuckin' believe it, the polis, nabbin' me. Spent the nicht next tae a couple o' wee junkies, off their heids. Ya ken what I'm talkin' about? Pure fuckin' pish, mate."

Alex couldn't follow, too distracted to parse out the Glaswegian. Something felt off. Charlotte had a million-mile stare, acting as distant as that street in Glasgow, not laying a hand on his thigh or arm or participating in the conversation. She'd lived in Scotland. She should say something. But she intensely stirred her gin and tonic with a straw until it formed little whirlpools. Worried, Alex shot her quizzical glances, an attempt to psychically communicate, *What the hell is wrong.* Had he done something? Probably.

The guitarist playing the gig fingerpicked a couple reels.

"Neil, are those the Andy McGann tunes you played in Mona's last week?" The first words Charlotte had said to anyone since they bought drinks.

"Aye," said Neil.

"Huh." Charlotte resumed playing with her G-and-T.

Fuck, this was going to be a long night. Her stony silence exploded like a ton of C4 under his heart. Alex paced between the bar and the bathroom, consumed three pints in an hour, and chewed his nails bloody.

Angrily, Charlotte swatted at his left hand. "Stop *doing* that," she hissed through clenched teeth. "Why do you do that all the time? Your fingers are a fucking *mess.*"

Because it was a compulsion that he had little control over. Because the tighter apprehension and panic seized him, the less control he had. Each time he struck a nerve, he sparked a small endorphin rush, a feeble tap slowing the flooding anxiety, if only for a second.

Charlotte wrote something on a napkin, then placed it in his palm. Alex unfurled the napkin. It read, *I'm pregnant. We need to talk.*

He thought he'd been kicked in the stomach. Sinking his teeth into the inside of his lip, he met her steely stare and rose from the table, motioning for her to follow him outside. He gazed down Bleecker Street, but he did not see the lines of glowing signs, the people laughing and smoking by the doors of the neighboring gay bar, the ruddy stone walk-ups, or the flamboyant Village nightlife. His brain and eyes had become unglued from one another.

Charlotte brushed against him. For a moment, he thought she would be upset, reaching out to him for comfort, reassuring him that they were in this – whatever it was – together. When he turned to face her, he saw cold fury blazing in her blue eyes. Her mouth was quivering.

"Fuck you, Alex!"

"Charlotte, what happened?"

"You know when the fucking condom broke? That's what happened."

"I told you to get the morning after pill," he argued. "But you said it would be okay."

That made her more hysterical. "You don't get to tell me what fucking chemicals I put in my body!"

"You said you were at the wrong time in your cycle. You said you could time it." He felt defensive. Why should this be all his fault?

"Stop sounding like such a fucking cop. You don't know anything."

"Well, not unless you tell me. What are we gonna do?"

"Fuck you!"

"That was the trouble." Sarcasm wouldn't save him, but it was his only defense.

"I'm going to get this terminated. And you're gonna pay for it."

"Am I?"

"Abso-fucking-lutely. You're responsible for this! I know what detectives make. You can fucking afford it."

"You coulda been on the pill. I also have a mortgage."

"Again with the pills. Why is it my responsibility to fuck up my body with all these hormones when you could have put on three condoms and wrapped your dick up in duct tape? Or got a fucking vasectomy! Fuck you! And fuck your mortgage and your job working for the man and your whole capitalist middle class bullshit."

"Because I don't stay on a futon? I don't think that's what Marx meant." He wasn't helping himself.

"Well, it doesn't get more bourgeoisie than the Upper West Side," she sneered.

"I was mainly going for the low crime rates."

"You don't even see it."

"See what?" He broke eye contact with her, glancing at the people strolling along the street and lounging beside the gay bar, acting oblivious to their argument but clearly listening. Free street entertainment.

"The racism. The fucking institutional racism. By 'low crime rates' you mean 'white.'"

"No, I mean low crime rates. Look at the stats. And I get to see places with high crime rates every day. I don't wanna live there." How the hell did they get here? What did this have to do with their relationship or a positive pregnancy test?

"It's got *everything* to do with race," Charlotte seethed. "Redlining. Funding schools and social programs. This shitty 'war on drugs.' The way *you* police it. Open your Goddamned eyes. Think for a minute. And don't think like a fucking cop."

"Why don't we go back to mine and continue this over a bottle of wine," he offered.

She almost stomped down the sidewalk with an enraged 'fuck you,' but stopped herself mid-spin. "That health clinic on East 2nd and the Bowery," she spat breathlessly. "You know it?"

No, but he could find it.

"You'll meet me there. In front of it. Tomorrow. Give me three hundred bucks in cash."

"Do you want me to go in with you?"

She looked at him like he'd offered to dance naked in the middle of the Bowery. "The fuck I do. You give me the money, then get the hell out of my life."

"Charlotte, we can talk."

"I'm done. You give me the money before I go into the clinic."

"It will look like a drug deal."

"Fuck you," she said again. Then she whirled away and ran along Bleecker.

He felt like he'd been shot, point blank in the heart. Another failed relationship to add to the collection, he thought bleakly. No matter how hard he tried, he would always be alone. He flicked his eyes up at the wooden sign for the Bitter End. Hell no. Instead, he walked four blocks east on Bleecker to the Glendale, to the comfort and safety of a cop bar. But the smarting sting of rejection stayed at his side. Everyone in the bar was wrapped up in their own conversations and social lives, and he felt invisible. The city had always been indifferent. Wasn't that how he liked it? Being alone with his pain? He ordered a Bud and a Jameson, first chugging the beer, then chasing it with the whiskey. Numbing himself with all the booze he could handle, he did it again, and again, until the bartender cut him off.

"Where do you live?" asked the bartender.

Like he could remember. Matt's apartment? That studio in Chinatown? Alcohol blended with blood in his veins. He rested his head on his folded forearms but felt sick as soon as he shut his eyes. The bartender shook him by the shoulder. "Come on, pal." He looked at Alex's shield, his NYPD ID card, his driver's license. Sighing, he firmly removed Alex from the bar stool and half-carried him out the door. "New York's finest. For Christ's sake. Wouldn't do this for a civilian," he said gruffly, waiving his arm at a taxi. Alex found himself flung onto the back seat, hearing the words, "127 West 87th. Make sure he gets inside." Where was 127 West 87th?

The morning before the four-by-twelve started, Alex rode the subway to the East Village. He had no memory of last night's cab ride. Somehow, he had made it inside his apartment but passed out on the living room floor. Now he suffered the consequences: the feeling of being hit by a train while someone drove railroad spikes into his skull. He hadn't eaten breakfast, only nursing himself through half a cup of coffee before the nausea came. The rocking, bouncing subway had him feeling seasick. He held one hand against his stomach, and with the other, he fingered the three hundred dollars of cash in his pocket. After a night's sleep, perhaps she'd changed her mind about leaving him. So clearly, he imagined her holding him, giving him those thrilling kisses, apologizing for being upset and emotional last night, and promising more, if not safer, sex. He would apologize for being horrendously hungover.

Life never goes how you imagine. Conversations planned in your head unravel in the real world. Charlotte's face looked as cold and grey as the Central Park lakes in winter. Furtively, like it was a drug deal, he gave her the money.

"Thanks," she said flatly.

Awkward silence but for the hum of traffic fell across them.

"Is that it?" He chewed on his tongue.

Her expression remained icy and flat. "Yeah. That's it. I'm sorry."

"I didn't think—" he began.

"I'm leaving New York after this. I'm sick of the city. You can't be free here. You can't find yourself. How can you? I mean, so many people come here looking for themselves, but it's the wrong place. Totally the wrong place. It's the center of capitalist greed and inequality, with Wall Street and people living in these ostentatious penthouse apartments worth millions of dollars on the Upper East Side, and then, the worst poverty. Homelessness everywhere. People on the street with nothing but violence and drugs. You know what neoliberalism's really doing? It's causing all these social, economic, and ecological disasters. The free-market fucks everyone but the rich and the profiteers, who are picking off our bones. And telling us it's for our own Goddamned good. Or that it's our fault. If Clinton wins the election in November, it's not gonna make any difference. They're all neoliberals. And this city, it's the center of it. The Financial District. The investment bankers and hedge funds. It's all bullshit. I thought I could find myself here once. Like after I left Edinburgh, I thought New York would be real, authentic. It's not like Edinburgh doesn't have problems too, like lots of heroin…"

"It takes junkies to make a city 'authentic?'" he asked laconically.

"You don't get it. You will never get it. I thought you might, like being a cop would give you perspective, but that was naïve of me." She uttered a short, bitter laugh. "It doesn't. It hardens your heart. It just makes you cynical and cold and slightly racist. And, well, I don't know what I wanted. I don't know what I thought I would find in New York. Or in you. The energy is bad. Everywhere in this city, it's bad. There are no good spirits here. I can't deal anymore. I get this done, walk out of the clinic, I'm gone."

"Where are you going?"

Charlotte shrugged. Her eyes skated away from his.

"You gonna buy a van?"

"Yeah, a van. I'll go west. Maybe I'll go back to Seattle. Or like, Alaska. Live in the wilderness. I don't know. I need to figure my life out. And it isn't gonna be in New York with an alcoholic police detective."

"I don't drink that much," he protested, thinking, it had come around to his personal failings again.

"You do, Alex. You don't know what to do with all your pain. There's no peace in you." She spun around and opened the clinic doors, then she disappeared behind the distorted glass reflections of cars and the rosy sandstone low-rise across the road.

His pulse whooshed in his ears. He ran towards the Bleecker Street subway station, but a payphone stood in his way. An electrifying temptation came over him. Rebounding, re-examining his bad decisions, he dialed Ruann Harland's number. *What the hell are you doing,* he asked himself, but before he could ditch the phone in its cradle, Ruann's voice queried, "Hello?"

"Hey, Ruann. It's Alex."

"Alex?" she repeated, as if she knew more than one.

"Boswell," he added, stupidly committing himself now.

"Oh! Fuck. Hi. How are you?"

"Okay. Wanna meet for a drink?"

"I'm sorry, Alex," she replied in a gentle tone. "I've just got no spare time at the moment. I'm working my ass off on this complex, long-term investigation. I can't tell you much about it, I'm sorry, but if it goes well, I have a shot at making first grade and being transferred to the Intelligence Bureau."

"Intelligence?" he said skeptically. "Don't they just put details on visiting foreign politicians?"

Ruann laughed, a joyful sound strangling his heart. "I think with global terrorism on the rise, it's gonna be a big thing in a few years, with serious investigations, working with the FBI, the CIA. This city's a target, Alex. A lot of the cutting-edge intelligence stuff is gonna have to happen here."

They exchanged a few more platitudes before he heavily clunked the phone into its cradle. A part of him was relieved, the other part hurt. Hadn't he broken up with her? Instead of looking for another one-night stand or rebound, he should take a break from relationships. Until when? Until he got his act together? He swigged his flask, letting whisky fall down his throat, hearing Charlotte calling him an 'alcoholic police detective.' Fuck that – he *was* in control. He leaned on the subway station railings, like he'd ingested one too many. People squeezed around him, ignoring his unsteadiness. The drunk, high, or confused were par for the course on the subway. Break-ups were par for the course everywhere. But the city and his caseload had no patience for heartbreak. He uncurled his spine and cantered briskly over the stairs, descending into the stagnant, hot tunnel.

At work, he gazed blankly at the paperwork consuming his desk, 'fives and the OLBS sheet he'd written for Thomas Rinn, buried under 'fives and the case file for the robbery-homicide on Haven Avenue, with rap sheets from half a dozen potential suspects, a tox report, and an autopsy report with bloody pictures. He felt nauseated and dizzy with his hangover, up to his eyeballs in the nothingness of people's lives, of his life, the meaningless plans, the drugs, the deceptions, all adding up to a stain on the sidewalk. And like his relationship with Charlotte, gone in an instant.

"What's up with you?" asked James.

Massaging his forehead, Alex told him about last night.

"Neil said you both disappeared from the Bitter End. He thought something weird was up. At least you ain't shooting blanks. That's real ghetto street cred, Lex, knocking the girls up! That like ups yours from zero to a thousand. You could have a baby momma."

"I already have two kids and an ex who hates my guts. I kinda figured I wasn't 'shooting blanks.'" He framed it in air quotes.

"Jesus, man, didn't you use a condom?"

"I'm not stupid. Of course I did."

"So how did it get fucked up?"

"Yeah, well, there was a time when it broke. I said, she should go and see a pharmacist for a morning after pill, and she said it was fine, she wasn't in the right place in her cycle or whatever, you know, to get pregnant, and those pills fuck with her. I don't understand women's bodies. How was I supposed to know that was bullshit?"

James' mouth twisted into a caustic smile. "It's *your* fault, but if you made her get a pill, you'd have been an asshole. You can't win. But let me tell you, the other thing Neil said, is that Charlotte's got her own shit... She'll be totally into someone, then she just goes completely nuts and disappears. Did you know Neil went out with her for like two days?"

"No."

"He said she was too crazy. 'Aye, she's aff her nut.' And that's from a guy who got arrested running naked through Glasgow. I said, well, that'll work... Alex finally met someone as crazy as he is."

"Thanks, James," Alex said tonelessly. He bleakly prodded the binder for the Haven Avenue robbery-homicide, as if more evidence would spill out of the file. No more likely than him finding a stable relationship.

The desk phone rang: a shooting in the Heights, on 194th and Broadway. With a weary look at James and aches in his knees, Alex winched himself to his feet. No one ever seemed to resolve their disputes with a gun in any useful or long-term way, but they never gave up trying, making him work for his paycheck.

Their DOA had tattoos from the Wild Cowboys, a prominent Dominican gang, but they couldn't ID him. The witnesses were sullen, uncooperative, and lying themselves blind. They collected some 9mm Luger slugs, some casings, and CSU lifted some fresh footprints. They asked the Three-Four patrol sergeant to pick up guys from the DOA's gang and anyone who had a beef with them. The detectives returned to their office: nothing to do now but write up a '61, 'fives, and crime scene reports for 'John Doe,' and wait for SAFIS to run his fingerprints. When the gang members came in, they could try to leverage something out of them. Maybe one didn't want his ass sent back to prison on a violation.

Maybe one would end up in a jam some day and want to get himself out from under a rock.

Although he had no leads to pursue on any of his whodunits, Alex stayed late writing a search warrant affidavit, then he killed time by squinting at photos of the dead guy's tattoos and calling ConEd, hunting for names of people paying electricity bills on Haven Avenue. At 0200, the Wheel officer kicked him out of the office, passing on a bitchy memo from the DI, a warning that Alex wouldn't get overtime pay for tonight. Alex made his slow way to the Upper West when the night was fresh and too damned long. Fucking tragic, he thought, catching so much overtime when he was with Charlotte, yet none now that she'd ended it. The silence of his apartment fiercely assailed him, as if loneliness and desolation had bought lethal weapons from the local arms dealer and ambushed him at the door. He slugged the Evan Williams until his stomach couldn't take anymore. But he lay in bed, awake, yearning for oblivion while his heart ran laps of Central Park. If willpower alone could compel Charlotte to pick up her phone and call him, his phone would be ringing. It never did.

The next day, Alex interviewed none of the Wild Cowboys. He received a summons to the grand jury room at 100 Centre Street to testify about Guillermo Quixano. *What a clusterfuck,* he thought, annoyed by the case and his sour discontent. The troubles with it would not align in size order. There were too many. He scratched at a *Times* crossword, but the clues eluded his febrile brain. The downtown 6 train bounced and shrieked. Commuters squashed themselves into the hot car. A man dressed as a knight squeezed himself and his sofa into the train. The sofa banged against Alex's knees. Yeah, Medina had worked in Quixano's crew, but the ballistics were basically fiction, the eyewitnesses made Richard Nixon look reliable, and they had nothing else. *This shouldn't go before the grand jury*, Alex thought, *But what am I gonna do.* These decisions were not his. The crossword wasn't his, either. It refused to yield its secrets. Cramps shot through his left leg; he'd folded it under himself to avoid the sofa, torquing it in a way his hip didn't really turn. Hopping lame and holding his sore hip, he disembarked from the train at Chambers Street.

Leon Mitchell restricted his initial questions to the crime scene itself. Afterwards, he grilled Alex with queries about the autopsy. The grand jury paled. Well, he had their attention. Then the lawyer nudged him into narrowly corroborating Elizabeth Weltmayer, aka 'Loretta,' telling Vito that she had witnessed the murder, and hearing Luca Martinez, aka 'Turbo,' affirm that the Colt M1991A belonged to Quixano. Alex kept his doubts and the truth to himself, yet he scuttled like a thief around outright perjury because the prosecutor elegantly stepped over problematic questions. Plainly, Vito and Mitchell talked. In his head, Alex played out their conversation – Vito grumbling that Boswell was 'real police,' maybe, but don't ask too much.

The case was a piece of shit, but the grand jury, fed up with drug dealers running the city corners, indicted the defendant anyway. Before Quixano could be picked up, Alex learned through one of his CIs that he had gone to St. Louis. Coincidence? The CI shrugged, both palms out. He asserted that Quixano would come back, regardless of the bench warrant with his name on it, and besides, the case wasn't hot enough for the department to justify paying a couple detectives to fly to Missouri.

Chapter Thirty-One

Within a month, Alex was primary on four more homicides: a vic in a domestic stabbed in the groin and bleeding out; the shooting of a white guy from Long Island who'd been buying crack on West 173rd and Amsterdam; one prostitute killing another over a couple vials of crack and then firing up at the crime scene; a man shot playing Russian Roulette with his buddies in an East 88th Street townhouse. Whenever Alex watched a crime thriller on TV, the perps were criminal masterminds. Yeah, right, he thought. Not the ones he arrested. Not the ones sticking a single round into a revolver, rotating the cylinder while holding the gun to their heads, passing it around, pulling the trigger, and consequently removing themselves or their friends from the gene pool.

He was secondary on five more cases, one a child homicide that upset James – even James – so much that he broke down in tears at the scene. An infant sexually assaulted, then flung into a dumpster like she was garbage. While James smeared tears across his face, Alex felt his pulse pounding but not pushing any blood through his arteries. A young patrolman took one look at the victim and passed out. As sick as Alex felt, he believed a homicide detective had to show some mettle, so he composed himself, remaining upright and not vomiting, barely. James attacked the case with every ounce of his considerable energy, putting it down within a week. They found photos that they wished they'd never seen, and James collared the baby's uncle, punching him in the face, knocking out two teeth as he wrestled the son of a bitch into the cuffs. That motherfucker wouldn't file an excessive force complaint. No one would care, and he knew it.

If only every case could be closed in a week. The alleged gang shooting on 194th and Broadway, 173rd Street, and Haven Avenue joined Alex's growing whodunit collection. His desk had vanished under a mountain of files, binders, paperwork, capped with a cairn of old coffee cups. Occasionally, he thought about dealing with it, but he let it

341

deteriorate, long after his colleagues had barricaded the cubicle with crime scene tape.

On his days off, he tried connecting with his daughters but usually wound up in a bar with James, Marty, and other colleagues. When he stayed home, Charlotte's absence felt like a burned-out crater in his ribcage. West 87th Street had become grimly saturnine, the loneliness tangible, like a housemate who never leaves the sofa. Only the girls, on the rare occasions they showed up, imbued it with fleeting glimpses of light and life. Although Catherine had started speaking to him again, Sarah maintained radio silence, while Ellie sporadically visited, but she was swamped with college applications and internships. She was stressed, distracted by her applications to competitive colleges, which had her grappling with college essays and SATs.

Alex self-deprecatingly suggested, "You could write your essay about what an asshole I was, and how it made you into a stronger person."

"Dad," she groaned. "I'll figure it out. Lots of kids at school have divorced parents who hate each other. It hardly makes me unique."

That wasn't the customary indictment of his parenting that he expected from his kids. *Mazel tov. No worse than everyone else.* It was almost a compliment.

He opted for bribery. He couldn't do much about college essays or SATs, but if Ellie came around, he promised, he would teach her to drive. Sure, he didn't have a car, but he would figure out something. Anything. Charlotte had left him with a wound as penetrating as any gunshot, and it had gone septic.

Of course, James tried to help, pointing out women in bars who might be single, always with a lewd chat-up line at the ready.

"Like chat-up lines to strangers ever work for anyone in real life," Alex jadedly remarked while they drank at an Upper West Side bar called the Four Provinces. "I think that only works on TV."

"Hey, I've done it."

Alex raised a cynical eyebrow. "Yeah, you were undercover, and she was a hooker. Not the same thing."

"You're not after a wife, for fuck's sake. You find someone who wants the same thing as you. An easy fuck. No emotional crap. No strings."

"I don't know if that's what I want. That's what you do." James always had a few flings on the go.

"It's less drama," James said with an insolent smile.

"Bullshit. Remember that girl…what was she called? Susan? You ended things 'cause she wanted to get serious, and she showed up at your apartment at like 3am when I was living there. You'd gone out watching football or some sport thing with Marty, and she was crying on the street, and I had to borrow your car and give her a lift to Penn 'cause I felt sorry for her, and your neighborhood is really sketchy."

"Hah, yeah, that did happen," sniggered James.

"There's always fucking drama. Has Charlotte been to any sessions?"

"No, don't think she's in New York. That's my point. You're way too hung up on her. You seriously gotta get laid, dude."

Uninterested in curing his broken heart with casual sex, Alex asked, "Do your Irish music friends know where she's gone?"

"West. I heard something about California or Oregon. You gonna stand outside her window with a boombox or something?"

"Outside of John Cusack movies, that's a disorderly conduct charge, isn't it?" Alex breathed out in a loud puff of air, as if he could expel pain with his lungs. There were forty-nine states she could be in, and what difference would it make if he knew which one?

In any event, Ellie took him up on the driving lessons, encouraged by James' offer to let them borrow the Mustang. He said, "Every kid should learn to drive a muscle car with a five-liter V8 and 200 horsepower. It'll make a real driver outta her." Using an empty police parking lot, Alex showed her the basics of stopping and starting, then he spent the next few lessons teaching her clutch control in ponderous, stalling loops through the West 80s.

When she gained control over the clutch and maneuvered the car through Upper West Side traffic with confidence, they went to the Cross-Bronx Expressway and then changed to the Bruckner at the spaghetti interchange in Throg's Neck. There, he taught her what she really needed to know, things he'd learned in advanced driving at the Academy: how to corner at speed, how to anticipate the behavior of other drivers, how to overtake by diving into gaps and judging closing speed, how to negotiate baffling interstate junctions. They raced along the sinuous highway while Alex explained how you estimate the angle of a bend and the speed at which you can drive into it.

Around rush hour, traffic on the Bruckner rolled to a grinding halt. Ellie asked, "Why did you break up with Charlotte? I liked her. I thought you were good together."

Pain rose to the surface, a scalding geyser inside his chest. "I... I did... I do like her. But she broke up with me." Was this a conversation he wanted to have with his teenage daughter? Certainly not the part about broken condoms and abortions.

"Why?"

"I dunno… She said she was sick of New York. Wanted to leave."

"Was it 'cause you're working all the time, like with Mom?'"

"No, I don't think so. She said she didn't want to be in the city anymore. Sometimes, things don't work out." The truth, but not all of it.

"Yeah, she talked a lot about Seattle. It sounds nice. You could have gone out west."

"What am I gonna do out west?"

"I don't know. Whatever detectives do out there. There must be some crime."

"Doesn't matter if there's crime. She didn't wanna be with me anymore."

"Your work colleagues called her a 'communist hippy.' They're a tough crowd. Maybe she didn't like the conservative cop outlook."

"Oh, those guys are always full of shit," Alex sighed, surprised by how much he missed his colleagues ribbing him about Charlotte. Even that. "She wanted me to be someone I wasn't."

"Like into her New Age schtick?"

"Something like that."

"I guess that sucks. Mom broke up with that guy she was seeing last month." She let out a dismayed sigh and nosed into the inside lane. "How do you make a relationship work?"

He tilted his head back, lips tight against his teeth. "I'm fucked if I know, kiddo. You want the exit for Manhattan and the RFK Bridge. No... The *other* lane. That guy'll let you in if you make him."

They were crossing Randall's Island, which confused Ellie with its tangled mess of bridges and causeways, then they circled around to FDR and followed it into Midtown, where they dropped the car off at James' and grabbed dinner at a greasy diner. Ellie loved greasy diners, in part because Catherine banned them like class A drugs. Afterwards, they rode the subway uptown to the West 80s. Alex wrestled with the sofa bed in his living room. The rusty springs stuck, and he tried forcing them free. He yelped – hot pain, sharp metal slicing through the soft skin below his thumb. His phone called out. *Now? Fucking work,* he thought, holding his bleeding hand to his chest. Or Charlotte, changing her mind about him and the city. It was work: the Warrants Squad. His suspect in a three-year old homicide had been found in Brooklyn. The Warrants Squad had been tailing the guy, and they were preparing to arrest him tonight.

Couldn't work leave him alone for one Goddamned night? He told the Warrants Squad sergeant that he wasn't available. Someone else from

Homicide could deal. If it went wrong, they might call him again. He considered unplugging the phone.

"You're staying in?" Ellie asked once he'd hung up. Her rich brown eyes – the same color as his – widened with concern.

He nodded, and Ellie turned on the TV. His hand was still bleeding, so he swiveled into the bathroom. The cut under his thumb stung as he held his hand under the cold tap. Blood swirled amidst the water; it dripped onto white porcelain, painting it red. Wincing, muttering, "Fuck," he stuck a band-aid over the wound. When he re-entered the living room, he saw a sweaty Bruce Willis on the TV, shoulder muscles bulging out of a white wife-beater, shooting bad guys, who toppled over easily, dying bloodlessly, the way no one who is shot ever does.

"What's this?" he asked.

"*Die Hard 2,*" Ellie answered in the peevish tone of all sixteen-year olds who think their parents are slow. "It's about an NYPD detective."

"Kids on the street, thinking blowing each other away is how you solve your problems. And this is the shit that's on the TV, making it look easy," he snapped. Bruce, with no backup in sight, was in a firefight, ducking behind the check-in counter of an airport, firing round after round.

Ellie shrugged indifferently. "It's just a movie, Dad."

Fearing an argument over something stupid, he swallowed the lump blocking his throat. Let her watch her damn movie. Bruce's gunfight looked sexy, exciting. Alex felt his heart beating, a shadow winging over him. Being shot couldn't be further from sexy or exciting, but he had never talked about it with the girls. The shadow was unfurling, racing hotly through his veins, catalyzing tremors in his limbs. His kid couldn't see him like this. He shut the bedroom door, then he rescued the *Times* crossword from the floor. He scribbled at it until his heartrate neared resting speed.

No longer hearing gunfire from his living room, he swung his legs off the bed and got to his feet. His ribs felt stiff at first, then nerve pain set them afire. The reality of being shot. He held his left hand against the old wound as he limped through the door. Ellie was kneeling by a tatty wooden shelf, riffling through his small tape collection, mostly 1970s and '80s rock and some '50s jazz, until she found one that stood out.

"What's this? The Tannahill Weavers? Album's called 'The Land of Light.' I like that."

A knife sliced between his ribs. He felt cold and broken. "Oh, that's Charlotte's. She must've left it here. It's Scottish music. Like fiddles and bagpipes and some songs."

"I liked her music."

"Me too," he sighed wistfully.

"Can I listen to it?"

"Sure." Dammit, he should have given that tape to James, but he was an NYPD detective; he could withstand some fiddles and pipes.

Ellie plugged in the tape, and they listened to a few tracks, neither speaking. He reached for the stop button, but Ellie waved him away from the tape player, before sprawling across the sofa bed, extracting a copy of *Catcher in the Rye* from her backpack.

When she saw him looking quizzically at her book, she said, "Summer reading for school."

"That's a good book."

"Yeah, I dunno, I think it's boring," she answered doubtfully. "His writing style's pretty weird. But I want an A in English next year. Are you seeing the fireworks on the Fourth?"

"Depends on work. Are you going?"

"Doesn't it always? I'm going with Lucy and Jen."

He recoiled at her sarcasm. "Cool. Don't forget to turn off the tape player before you go to bed. Thing's fucked. It'll eat the tape if you leave it on."

With that, he bid her goodnight, leaving her listening to Charlotte's tape. The faint squawks of pipes and fiddles pierced through the door. He showered, then lay on his sheets, only wearing his boxers. The apartment felt like the Louisiana Delta, and he wrestled open his window. His air conditioner misbehaved, but the nearest cooling breeze was in Nova Scotia. He should fix the A/C, again, or buy a new one. No fresh air came through, just the sounds of traffic and sirens, clear and close. His overheated thoughts wheeled like seagulls attacking a dumpster, first to his cases, then to Charlotte, somewhere out west, then to wondering what the Night Watch would bring him in the morning. Like cats bringing you a dead pigeon or mouse. His wound seared like molten fire that wanted to rip him to pieces. At the start of the day, he'd woken up two hours before his alarm, twisting around in the bed, but the pain followed him wherever he rolled. He'd been shot five years ago, and this was as healed as his body would get – constant pain and lung function worse than an asthmatic's. Not many thirty-five year old cops lived with severe, chronic pain.

A shot rang out. He tensed, feeling his heart thump. He was lying in puddles of sweat. Another noise came, a sound like a bag of spanners in a washing machine. The air conditioner, complaining. The loud bang had been the downstairs neighbor slamming their door. What was wrong with his brain? Rather than think about it, he steeled himself against pain, carefully wobbling to his feet, then he tiptoed through the living room. Ellie didn't stir. In the kitchen's hazy darkness, he poured himself a generous helping of Jameson and shook three ibuprofens out of the bottle. He carried the glass and pills back to his room. Loathing his wound, he busied himself with skimming the *Times* while the alcohol circulated through his bloodstream, finally hitting enough major organ systems to knock him into unconsciousness.

That morning, he gave Ellie taxi fare to get to her mother's place in the Village. Catherine threatened to slit his throat if he let the girls use the subway alone. Whatever he said, she refused to buy his assurances that the subways were fine during the day, for the most part, except where they weren't. She liked to remind him of Bernie Goetz. It could have been anyone, she said. At least Bernie had a gun.

"His victims didn't," Alex retorted.

"Does it matter? You more than anyone should know what those sorts of people are like."

"Jesus, Catherine, you trying to join the fucking Klan?" His tongue got ahead of him.

"I'm not racist," she said, furious. "I'm just saying how it is. *You* were attacked in a station. With a boxcutter!"

"Once," he emphasized. "At two in the morning."

"You remember my neighbor, Debbie Markowitz? She was mugged on an A train near 14th Street. Lost two teeth and had her face smashed in. Had to get dentures."

"Yeah, shit happens," he conceded. "But you're more likely to get in a traffic accident than mugged on the subway."

"In New York? I doubt that. My friend Howard, you know, with the hip replacement, had a knife pulled on him on an R train when he asked some guy to move a bag off an empty seat."

Yes, she had a point. The subway could be crazy. "The girls know to move to a different car if there's anyone weird. And to choose busy cars."

"Whatever, I don't want them on it."

Running late, Alex rode the subway himself to West 125th, then he transferred to an M100 bus across town. Near Lenox, he got off the bus and walked through East Harlem's anarchic checkerboard of demolition and rehabilitation, south to East 119th. *What asshole invented suits and ties,* he thought, glancing at the sweat stains under his armpits. The worst clothing for the heat.

347

Like he'd predicted, Night Watch had brought a pigeon, a DOA on East 98th and Park.

"We going to East 98th?" he asked James.

"No, Rizzo and Cohen went. Corcoran just did his Spanish Inquisition thing about those homicides we got nowhere on, my two in the Three-Two Precinct, and your gang shooting on 194th, the 173rd Street crackhead, and that robbery-homicide on Haven. Then I wrote a 'five on the Haven Avenue one. Which said anyone in the fuckin' Heights could have done it 'cause the idiot neighbor always left the main door unlocked so her boyfriend could get in."

Alex slackly melted into the chair. His head ached as much as his side. He reproached himself for not being careful about that whiskey last night, liberally pouring Jameson into a pint glass, paying no attention to how much he poured. Enough. Too much.

"Boss is just PMS-ing," James said. "He'll get over himself."

"We got anything new on those cases?" Alex put his money on '*no*.'

"One is Bronx Homicide's problem. He was on *their* side of the fucking bridge –"

"I've been saying that, but they don't want him."

"Lucky us, Chief of D's is trying to make Manhattan look better for tourists, so he agrees." James forced his features into a weary grin. "Why do cops on TV always have cock-size competitions *for* jurisdiction? Who does that?"

"Dunno. People with more time on their hands. He's probably a suicide anyway, so they'll clear it in a minute. Haven Avenue's a stone-fucking-whodunit."

"Yup. She can take a number and get in line."

"What, are we the DMV now?"

When Marty wafted past his desk, Alex asked him about last night's warrant. Marty looked harried and exhausted. He said there had been shots fired, the perp taking a bullet in the leg, an ESU cop taking one in the arm. It was unlike Marty to sound so subdued and miserable. The Dominican detective wandered back to his cubicle, grumbling to himself about quitting the job. That warrant must have been a mess.

The day wore on, muggy and broiling. The sweltering heat ground their morale under a remorseless heel. No one developed new leads or dug up fresh evidence. More busy work – covering their asses on paper, checking out perps who had outstanding warrants, phoning parole officers to see who was having a hard time toeing the line, hunting down delayed labwork. Their poorly air-conditioned building turned into a sauna.

Tacky, miasmatic air clung to their sinuses, their lungs, their limbs, and sweat dripped off their bodies even though they had rolled up their sleeves and removed their ties. The second their tour ended, they fled downtown to the Glendale, thirsty for cold beers. Village residents set the mood for the Fourth with anticipatory fireworks crackling like gunfire over the townhouses. The hair on the back of his neck stirred, and Alex wiped sweat off his forehead, raising his eyes towards the Glendale's gold-tipped Copperplate letters on its pub sign. With James at his elbow, he limped into the darkened bar. "A Bud," he grunted curtly, and he chugged the ice-cold beer as fast as he could pour it down his throat.

The following day, torrid humidity relented to torrential rain. Shoulders hunched against the deluge, Alex and James traipsed towards the car after an evening spent canvassing parking garages and apartments in the investigation of the 173rd Street homicide. They had interviewed two teenage girls, who'd been terrified that someone would see them talking to cops. Even so, the girls confided that they'd witnessed the shooting *and* caught sight of the getaway car. A silver Ford Escort. Looking for silver Ford Escorts breathed some life into the case, but they had to find the right Ford Escort in a city of over a million vehicles, sifting through DMV records, then questioning Escort owners. After a few hours of schlepping in and out of apartments, the rain had saturated Alex's suit. Water clung to his eyelashes, soaked his hair. He rolled up his sleeves, letting it pelt his bare forearms. It felt like a lukewarm shower.

James cranked the car, and the big V8 convulsed to life. The radio crackled on the citywide channel. An officer from the Three-Four calling out a ten-thirteen at 505 West 162nd Street.

Instantly, James flipped on the lights and sirens, then he threw the car into drive, spinning the wheels when he mashed his foot down. Alex announced over the radio that Manhattan North Homicide Unit 3471 was responding to the call. He held on for dear life as James slalomed through traffic on Broadway, the accelerator pedal pinned to the floor, his hand pounding the horn, hydroplaning though every puddle. They listened to the chaotic radio chatter. An officer having an altercation with a perp, shots fired, by who?

Sirens howling, they screeched onto the 500 block of West 162nd. Parking was impossible, the street packed with blue and white RMPs. They abandoned the car in the middle of the road. With every cop in New York here, Alex thought, the situation must be under control. But they drew their guns and ran towards the building. They sprang up a short flight of steps and burst into the lobby, but then sat back on their heels, confronting an overweight male Latino DOA with a bullet wound in his gut. The detectives looked at one another. Alex saw sweat beading on James' forehead and staining his shirt around his collar. A plainclothes officer, bearded, young, white, huddled on a step, underneath a scrum of other cops. He was covered in blood from his neck to his waist.

Alex's chest heaved, but his lungs felt paralyzed. His heart thudded like people's feet in Irish music sessions. Breathing or not, he had to shift gears, from the adrenaline of responding to a ten-thirteen to his day job – working through the aftermath of a shooting. His hands sweated into the butt of his Ruger, and he shoved the slimy gun into its holster. Meanwhile, the plainclothes officer's colleagues and a paramedic bundled him out of the building, towards a bus. Alex made a note that someone from Homicide needed to interview him. Like now.

"Hey, I know him," James panted. "Michael O'Keefe. He's a great cop. Part of Local Motion." 'Local Motion' was the eponym of the AntiCrime unit that patrolled these blocks, harrying dealers and addicts. They had a reputation, for either inspired police work tackling the Washington Heights crack trade, or aggressively hassling local residents, depending on your point of view.

Dozens of cops and more paramedics thundered around the lobby like spooked cattle trapped in a corral. No one had contained or cordoned off the scene. A police shooting! Why hadn't someone done that? "The fuck we're gonna find any forensic evidence now," Alex muttered in James' ear. Everything had been contaminated, disturbed. The detectives announced themselves as Homicide, which most people there knew already, but it made everyone back off from the body for about half a minute.

"Anyone know who the fuck this guy is?" James demanded.

"I think he's called Kiko Garcia," replied an officer. "Local guy. Lives on the block."

Garcia's hands were outstretched in front of him, and a .38 Smith and Wesson, greasy with blood, lay beside him. He didn't look like a dealer or someone who would shoot a cop, Alex thought, just a kid from a sad neighborhood. His throat was withering with desert dryness. Clearing it, he knelt over the body. One gunshot to Garcia's abdomen, with the powder burns like grey halos around the holes in his clothing. Another shot in the back, but with no powder burns. He'd been shot once at extremely close range, another time further away. Who knows in what order? After documenting the body's position, the detectives tipped him sideways. They noted one bullet wound on the right side of the back and a second wound near the armpit. The bloody slugs were underneath his body, the .38 semi-wadcutters you expected from an NYPD service revolver. The other .38, the Smith and Wesson, still had a round in the chamber. With utmost care, Alex unloaded and bagged the weapon.

"You get a statement from the AntiCrime guys before they left?" he asked the first officer. If it was a bad shooting, the Local Motion cops now had plenty of time to straighten their story.

"Yeah, kinda," said the cop. "O'Keefe was a mess, sitting there outta breath and holding a gun. He kept muttering about this shitbird hitting him in the throat and trying to take his gun, and he was holding his throat, like he'd been hurt. His partners said he'd been dragged into this building fighting with a dealer, and they heard him screaming for help on the radio."

"That's it?"

"Sorry, Boswell. They were all in a state."

"But the partners didn't see anything?"

"No, they arrived after us."

"How the hell did that happen? Why was O'Keefe on his own?"

The cop gave a slow shrug. "I think they said it was part of a plan to flush out a slinger, but it didn't go right."

"No shit," Alex breathed, feeling his pulse spurting forward.

Nothing inflames a neighborhood like a police shooting. Amped up civilians and the press descended on 505 West 162nd Street, amassing at the perimeter of the staging area. Cops mustered witnesses for transport to the Three-Four station house, but a building resident saw Alex and James with their gold shields, and she evaded the round-up in the chaos.

She touched Alex's elbow. "You a detective? I saw, you just been lookin' at Kiko."

He nodded, scribbling the witness' details. She'd lived in this building since she emigrated from the Dominican Republic in 1982.

"Kiko wouldn't hurt no one," she wailed when he asked what she knew. Tears streaked her face. "You detectives gotta know that. You gotta. That officer, he just attack him, he beat him with his radio, over and over, then he just shot him!"

"Did Kiko have a weapon?" queried Alex.

"No, no. He don't have no gun."

"A gun was found."

"It was *planted.*"

"Where were you when you saw this fight?"

"Here. In the lobby. The officer, he come in after Kiko, chasing him, then he beat him."

"Did he identify himself as a police officer?"

"I don't *know*. I didn't hear nothing like that."

Another witness, an older Dominican woman, had joined her friend, weeping, then hugging her. She told Alex that Kiko had dallied in the drug trade but didn't have it in him to work full time for the slingers. He sold clothes on the street, looked after his mother, and helped out with the neighborhood kids. *An all-round mensch,* Alex thought, unsure he believed it.

"I *know* Michael," James said emphatically after Alex had scrawled the second witness' statement in his memo book. "I don't think he'd have shot a man unless he *had* to. He's good people."

"Gun could be a drop piece." Alex wanted to look at the case from all angles, even the worst ones.

"That's not Michael," argued James. "He's hard-as-shit but he plays fair, you know."

By the time the detectives departed from West 162nd, Alex felt like he'd driven into a whiteout, with no picture, no sense of what went down in that building, no useful feelings in his gut, while James swore with his hand over his heart that O'Keefe was a good cop who would have only used lethal force in self-defense. He testily shook his head, exasperated at his partner for acting so reticent to believe a fellow officer. "*You* were shot, for fuck's sake. You should know what it's like."

"Those guys definitely wanted us dead," Alex replied, annoyed that James brought up his shooting. The wound ached underneath the itching scar. "I don't think there was much doubt when the only casualties were me and Eddie. I'm not making a call on this one yet. I don't know."

"Maybe this mope wanted O'Keefe dead."

"Maybe. But how many times do people fuck this up, shoot someone unarmed?"

"You *gotta* give the cop the benefit of the doubt."

"Do I?" Alex's stomach foamed with acid and unease. He felt an ominous chill in his bones. He chewed on his nails until blood trickled from his fingers. James gave him a pulverizing look out of the corner of his eye, sighing, "Jesus" under his breath when Alex asked him to dig out the band-aids from the glove compartment.

There would be no Fourth of July celebrations for Manhattan North Homicide. Corcoran ordered every detective to drop everything and assist in the investigation of the O'Keefe shooting. Anyone on an RDO found themselves hauled into work. Alex had plans to meet Sarah for a Fourth of July dinner, the first time he would have seen her in months, but instead, he made that excruciating phone call.

"I have to work late, honey," he said, his voice saddened. "I'm so sorry. My boss said I don't have a choice."

"You prefer the police over me," Sarah snarled, then she hung up.

He held his palm against his belly, feeling a hard fist punching through his bowels. But he couldn't change his reality or his hours.

James, Vito Indelicata, and IA interviewed O'Keefe and the other Local Motion cops, while Alex and Marty joined the epic canvass operation on West 162nd. Alex imagined his partner safely installed in an interview room, agreeing with O'Keefe, Indelicata, and IA guys about the crack trade, the unquenchable violence, the city's appalling deterioration. Meanwhile, himself, Marty, and everyone else canvassing faced bitter, naked hostility. People here already thought of the police as an occupying force. Now with one of their own shot by a cop, they treated anyone from the NYPD as the enemy, even Marty, with his Dominican-accented Spanish and friendly chat about people's hometowns in the DR. But the detectives mainlined coffee, caffeinating their weariness and frustration, and through sheer perseverance, they picked up that the local Dominican dealers didn't do business in the building where Garcia and O'Keefe had their altercation. Too many of them had grown up there or had friends who did. They had too much respect for their families. Still, that didn't stop them from using the lobby to conceal a stash or hide from the police.

"I don't like this," Alex commented, sipping coffee in the car. His over-caffeinated heart beat out an irregular rhythm. They watched scores of people lining up on the sidewalk outside 505, paying their respects at a makeshift shrine dedicated to Garcia. Votive candles, crosses, and small statues of saints tumbled from the building's front steps, towards the sidewalk. People had tied more crosses and bouquets to the railings.

"Don't like what?" asked Marty.

"The neighborhood. It feels…" Alex shut his eyes for a moment, searching for words. "Like the wheels are about to come off. I dunno… You think this is what South Central LA felt like before the King riots?"

"The wheels *are* off, Lex," Marty said, grief choking his voice. "Crack's fucked this place up. I mean, we were poor, growing up here, but it wasn't like this. There was more community. Now the community's just…" He lost his words, swallowing biliously. "Young people growing up without parents 'cause their parents are addicts, or in prison, or dead. Kids can't play soccer on the street or walk safely to school. Sleeping in bathtubs in case a stray bullet comes through the window. Infrastructure's gone to shit. Like no one cares anymore. You see the crack lines in plain sight, going around the block. You can't get away from the drug trade. It's everywhere. It's a mess. Sometimes, I can't figure out what we're trying to do anymore. What are we stopping? Who are we protecting?"

"I don't know." Alex's feet felt raw, and his right side hurt after tireless hours of canvassing. "But we're not gonna find anything else here tonight."

On the car radio, the news played a clip of Mayor Dinkins at a press conference. He reassured the Dominican community that he was on their side and offered his condolences to the Garcia family.

"We know where he's at, before the investigation's over," Marty snorted. "What's the point of even looking for facts? It's all politics. Does anyone care about what actually happened?"

"I don't think it's gonna matter," Alex said softly, crumpling his brows in his nervous manner as he stared at the people milling around the shrine. Dinkins wouldn't mollify them. City Hall was a thousand miles away.

"It's not. Let's get outta here and grab a drink."

That sounded sensible, a drink in the relative peace of Harlem or the Upper West. Alex turned on the car, and no one noticed the unmarked Ford gliding out of Washington Heights.

At nightfall, Alex's troubled premonitions came to fruition: angry citizens of Washington Heights rushed into the streets, chanting for justice, setting anything flammable on fire, looting stores, overturning cars. Like South Central LA in April, the inevitable had arrived in Manhattan. The beleaguered 34th Precinct called for reinforcements.

The next morning, the air itself inside the Two-Five felt strangling, steeped in fear. Radios howled with frantic ten codes. Central lost control over the noise on the radio frequencies. Several guys in the Two-Five detective squad had already changed out of their suits. They bitched that they didn't fit into their uniforms anymore.

"You Homicide guys too," said Crawford, the deputy inspector. "They want everyone on riot detail."

"I haven't worn the bag for years," Alex complained. Not his street uniform. Sometimes, he wore his dress blues for funerals.

"We're not trained in riot control," said Marty. "Do we look like ESU?"

"Too fucking bad. You argue, I'm giving all of you C/Ds."

Alex's dark blue uniform was rumpled and musty from years of hanging unused in his locker. It squeezed his belly and his shoulders. *Did this ever fit me*, he wondered. It didn't now – he'd put on weight around his gut and muscle across his chest since he last wore the damned thing.

The DI herded everyone into armored vans; Patrol, MNHS, the Two-Five detective squad, every man's face stony and grim as they squeezed onto the rock-hard bench seats. Sliding doors crashed shut, then the vehicles rattled uptown. The bulletproof windows were too small to see through. *Like prison vans, or human traffickers',* Alex thought, filled with dread that was colder than the fiercest ice storm. Some uniforms acted weirdly excited, saying, "Let's get out there and show those motherfuckers!" The men from the Two-Five detective squad complained about the mayor and liberals. Marty and Bill grumbled about Vietnam. Matt murmured a prayer in Hebrew. Keohane and Brady cheerfully reassured everyone they'd been on riot details before – race riots in the '60s. James and Sam mumbled nervous jokes about liking the way their colleagues looked in uniform. Alex stayed silent, feeling sick to his stomach.

The van crossed into Washington Heights. They heard faint chanting outside, then louder clunks as heavy objects smashed against the vehicle's armored flanks. Crawford barked over the radio that he'd arrived with more personnel, before he faced the men in the van, yelling in a drill sergeant voice, "Everyone, move out!" Alex remembered that Crawford had been a captain in Vietnam. The DI seemed eager for a return to battle, a change from the routines of normal civilian policing.

The van door opened, like the gates of hell. Bottles, rocks, and other movable objects sailed through the air. Hundreds of enraged residents marched through the streets, shouting, "Justice! Killer cop," in rhythmic English and Spanish. Every trash can in sight was on fire. Cars were on fire. A sofa was on fire. Broken glass crunched underfoot.

"Holy fucking shit, everything's on fire," someone said.

"It's as bad as Crown Heights last year," someone else said.

Twenty or thirty young men wielding bottles, two-by-fours, and rebars charged towards the van. Cops smashed their nightsticks into the protesters and blasted them with tear gas. A trigger-happy cop launched his canister at some protesters but missed, catching Alex in the line of fire. Alex lost his footing, then lost his vision, and he fell onto one knee. His face and throat stung like wasps diving into his eyes and nasal passages. His right side screamed like he'd torn open his wound. The wasps invaded his respiratory tract. Tears streamed down his cheeks. James, faring better, took his arm, but then something exploded. The two homicide detectives crashed to the asphalt together. Alex scraped his other knee on the tarmac. His ears were ringing, and white lights were flashing in his eyes.

"Holy fuck," James shouted. "Some fucknugget threw a fuckin' M-80!" Another firework sailed overhead, detonating well behind them.

Cops pushed the protesters uptown on Broadway. The air blackened with smoke and tear gas. Barrages of bottles hurtled into the ground, bursting into glass shrapnel. Alex drove his palms into the fires blooming behind his eye sockets. Pain searing his hand, his head, his chest. An ear-splitting crack rocketed, vibrating through his skull, his breastbone. Gunfire! He saw Eddie sprawled on the sidewalk, drenched in blood.

"Eddie!" he gasped.

"Who the fuck is Eddie?" James said.

What kind of question was that? More shots rang out, the high-pitched report of an assault rifle. He was hit. He would die on this street.

"Oh. Eddie. Right. Fuckin' hell. Come on, Lex." James seized him by the elbow.

"I've been shot." A reddish film blurred his vision. But it wasn't Eddie on the ground. It wasn't Alex's blood, either. It was a protester, struck in the head with a nightstick. Two friends tried to staunch the bleeding.

"No, you haven't. We got other problems, but that ain't one right now."

"What's wrong with my eyes?"

"Yeah, you're having one of your episodes. And that motherfucking fuckwit of a cop who didn't pay attention to where he was fuckin' throwing CS is what's wrong with your eyes. 'Friendly fire.' What a dick. Got me too, just not as bad. But your hand's bleeding like a bitch. We gotta go inside." Wheezing audibly, James dragged Alex towards the precinct. The buildings gleamed orange and red. A river of fire cascaded down the hill on 183rd Street, and flames lapped at the station house. Protesters, hit with CS, cried and knelt on the ground. Two guys stepped out of a larger crowd, hurling glass bottles, bricks, and scrap metal. One cop swung his nightstick at a bottle thrower, landing several heavy blows on the guy, who fell, unconscious.

"What are you cocksuckers doing?" bellowed Crawford, seeing Alex, James, and a dozen other cops retreating towards the station house.

"My partner's cut himself and been fuckin' CS'd in his face!" James shouted back.

"Grow a pair!" barked the deputy inspector. "Get back out there! You retreat, these assholes will think they *own* the streets!"

Their escape cut off, they found themselves before the Mounted Unit and officers in dark riot gear, faceless under their helmets. Aggressive officers on 183rd surged towards protesters; God help anyone they caught – he received a beating that made you question the rule of law. Blood gleamed on the asphalt. Three protesters tackled a cop who was savagely thrashing an injured friend. A handful of less committed protesters scattered, disappearing down alleys or through doorways. More committed ones retaliated with rocks and bottles. The mounted officers charged their horses at the bottle throwers, more than a dozen livid young men calling the police "pigs," "motherfuckers," "assholes," "Nazis." The protesters ran under a nearby awning but sustained their onslaught of rocks, metal, glass bottles.

Alex moved away from the projectiles and clutched his nightstick. The handle was slick with his blood. At each breath, caustic particles of CS inflicted fresh burns in his lungs. Another fusillade of flying bottles forced them further down 183rd, further from the shelter of the station house. Suddenly, James screamed, staggering into Alex's side, knocking him off-balance. Blood gushed from James' temple in a crimson torrent, running down his face. He crumpled to his knees. Alex threw himself over his partner, shielding him from a protester, who saw he'd taken out a cop and sprang forward. A heavy blow struck him across the lower back. Hot pain exploded like a grenade inside his spine, and he fell beside James, sprawling onto the asphalt, then instinctively curling around his right side. He heard a scuffle, nightsticks thudding against flesh, grunts, swearing, then someone grabbed him under his armpit.

Marty panted, "Fuck, I found you guys."

Bill had his arm around James, who cradled his head while blood bubbled between his fingers, matting his black hair. "Hurley needs a bus!" Bill cried as he towed James away.

Alex's head spun like he'd necked ten pints. White and yellow lights blotted his vision. The riot was far away. His back was on fire. His knees felt unstable, and he drunkenly pitched into a newspaper box.

"Shit, man, you alright?" Marty gasped, holding him up with a hand under his arm. "That *pendejo* hit you in the back with a fucking two-by-four."

"What are you lazy-ass detective motherfuckers doing? You think you're better than us?" someone yelled.

The fires inside his back and side raged, then burned out, turning numb and cold. Chills ran through his bones and muscles. How was he this cold? It was New York in July, and he shouldn't be cold. Shock. Like being shot. Was he having another episode? *Please, stay with reality. Not this. Not again. Please, not this.* Marty yanked him forward. "Alex!" he

357

cried, which tethered him to reality. Marty's whole body – all six-foot of it – slammed into his, so they both hit the pavement as rocks and bottles bounced off the concrete. Alex smashed his left elbow. A steel shod hoof slammed into the asphalt, brushing his shoulder. He saw the dark belly of a horse, the front hooves dangling over his face, and the horse pivoted on its hindquarters and crashed down with its feet inches from his head. Sparks skittered from its steel shoes. The rider yelled something at the detectives.

"Jesus fucking Christ," yelped Marty, adding some Spanish swear words. He scrabbled to his feet, then hefted Alex upright by his elbow and waist once the mounted officer moved his horse away.

"What the fuck are we doing here?" Alex coughed, and he dizzily clung to Marty's broad shoulder.

"Getting the shit kicked out of us," said Marty. "How's your breathing?"

"Fucked. Chest feels full of CS."

"The smoke won't be helping. Fuck knows what they're burning but it's nasty."

Marty led him towards the outskirts of the riot, cutting down a narrow alley, then dodging around pre-war townhouses on the next block. They came across a mid-sixties Dominican woman administering first-aid to injured protesters on the stoop of a haggard townhouse. About a dozen people, most nursing wounds, fixed their eyes on the detectives. Those glares could have shattered stone.

Marty muttered under his breath, "Christ, this is like villages in Vietnam."

"We should go," Alex wheezed.

Palms out, showing he was unarmed, Marty approached the stoop, speaking urgently to the woman in Spanish. She gave them a harsh eyefuck, worthy of the most badass corner boy, but then she bandaged Alex's palm and handed him an asthma inhaler and a bucket full of cold water, ordering, "*Limpia tus ojos.*"

He sucked on the inhaler in deep, rasping breaths, then splashed water into his eyes. The woman added something, but his Spanish failed him.

"She says you'll have to take off your clothes 'cause the tear gas will be on everything," Marty translated. "But not here. Obviously. And baking soda will help your eyes, but she doesn't have any left."

"Yeah, I know. *Gracias,*" he said gratefully. His lungs hurt, but the inhaler had opened his swollen airways a little.

They departed from the Good Samaritan's stoop, watchfully picking their way around fires, violent scuffles, and plumes of tear gas. Marty seemed unsure of their route or destination. Meanwhile, the entire street was spinning like a merry-go-round, and Alex kept a hand on Marty's shoulder to steady himself.

"I don't feel so good," he breathed. The simmering nausea in his belly boiled over. He couldn't settle it, despite his deliberate breaths and visualizing calm oceans and glassy lakes.

Marty swore in Spanish and steered him onto the next block, looking for any shelter. They found a small barricade of empty squad cars, parked on 186th. "Sit down for a minute," Marty said, his hand on the white hood of a car.

Alex retched; his knees buckled, and he crumpled onto the asphalt beside the car's front wheel, landing in a puddle. Water soaked through the dark cotton. Fuck this uniform. It was covered in CS gas, smoke, blood, and now stagnant, oily water.

"You'd think with the crack industry in this place, it'd be easier to find baking soda," Marty quipped, but the worry in his voice belied the wiseass.

"Were we really getting help on some random person's stoop?" Alex asked, wondering if he'd hallucinated.

"Yeah," answered Marty.

"Someone you knew?"

"No. Can you breathe?"

"Sort of. My throat's swollen. And my lungs are bad enough without CS."

They hid there, shielded from protesters and commanding officers, until the sun fell behind New Jersey.

Fires overran Washington Heights, and the oncoming darkness emboldened the protesters. The captains finally pulled exhausted cops back to the station house. They'd deployed fresh reinforcements. Alex watched James and a dozen other injured cops and protesters loading into ambulances, and he was peripherally aware of Marty arguing that he should join them in the bus.

"He's got a back injury, some bad cuts, and took a heavy hit of CS, sir," stated Marty. "He's been sick."

"He gets a whiff of CS and wants to go on the fuckin' bus?" sneered the DI. "Jesus. They don't make detectives like they used to."

"They don't make commanding officers like they used to," Marty grumbled under his breath.

"You *will* get a C/D for insubordination. That's vacation days docked, Detective," barked Crawford.

Marty shrugged.

Along with everyone else who wasn't injured enough for the ministrations of Columbia Pres, Alex tottered into the armored van. He wanted to gag, to double over. But he'd puked up everything in his stomach while hiding behind those police cars, so he shouldn't be sick on the van. The sliding door thudded shut, and the diesel engine uttered its deep-throated growl. Whenever the van bucked through a pothole, sharp pains shot through his back. Tears oozed along his cheeks. Brady and a uniform superciliously asked if he was crying, and he snapped, "I got CS in my face. Fuck off." Miraculously, he held himself together on the van, but his face had turned grey, and his eyes were hot and swollen. Bill and Marty stopped him from taking the subway, although he insisted that he could manage. No, he was going home in Bill's car, and that was that. At least they didn't chaperone him into the building.

Safely inside his apartment, he stripped off his uniform, leaving it in a crumpled heap like a dead thing in the corner of the bathroom. He threw himself into the shower to rinse tear gas from his body and hair. His head swam like his brain steeped in toxic fumes. He folded himself up on the bathtub floor, scrunching his eyes shut, and he drew choking breaths while the water fell across his body. Scalding pain from swollen alveoli mapped out his lungs. After thirty minutes, he eased his aching limbs over the edge of the tub. *Baking soda,* he reminded himself. Like the woman at that townhouse said. With gritted teeth, he soaked a washcloth in icy water, coated it with baking soda, then he draped it over his scorched eyes. Lying on his back like that, he drifted into dreams filled with fire, broken bottles, M-80s, and tear gas. More than once, adrenaline electrified his muscles, jolting him awake. After a few restless hours, he reached the limbo between consciousness and dreams, the narrow space where you know you're dreaming but can't save yourself from it. He reminded himself that he was in bed, the riot half an island away. He heard distant gunfire. His heart missed a beat. Real gunshots, or in his head?

Alex hobbled into the Two-Five around 0810, starting an eight-by-four ten minutes late, like a normal day. Only James would be off work for a couple weeks with a concussion. The riots hadn't stopped, either, now coming into their third day. Nobody liked 'normal' in the Heights, but now they missed it.

Pissed, Corcoran reassigned Jean Allan from the C team to work with Alex, taking up James' slack. He complained, "Give me strength. Now *we're* short staffed because they didn't have enough riot officers."

Some of the B team detectives could not control their latent misogyny around a female investigator. Brady leered, smarmily asking Jean to bring him coffee, along with an observation about what her pants suit might be hiding, and she shot him a look colder than dry ice. Rizzo and Keohane had never spent so much time in the office doing paperwork. Or pretending they were.

While Jean crossed the squad room with a file under her arm, on a mission to the photocopier, Keohane called, "Hey, Allan, when you gonna do a strip tease for us?"

The stripper rumor hadn't abated for five years. Jean herself thought of it as a long-running, funny joke and hadn't dispelled it. *You have to laugh at these things, or you'll go mad,* she'd once told Alex.

"You ain't good lookin' enough, Declan," she said disdainfully. "Cut back on the donuts and you might get lucky." She started the photocopier, then swore and untangled a paper jam.

The phone rang, and the detectives paused, staring at it. Time doesn't stand still in this city, not even with a redball cop shooting and a riot.

"Careful, Declan," Jean said. "If you answer that phone, you might hurt yourself."

"Fuck you," Keohane muttered as he grabbed the phone.

Alex blocked out the office banter. His eyes stung, and his back and left flank hurt like he had stab wounds reaching something deep inside his abdomen. How novel, a change from his *right* side hurting. Well, that bothered him too. Lethargically, he pecked at the typewriter, writing a 'five summarizing his last interview with a Ford Escort owner in the 173rd Street case. He typed out two sentences, but his bladder distracted him, and he staggered into the men's room for a piss. His urine had a pink tinge. That meant one thing. Internal bleeding. His blood pressure threw itself off a cliff. The building rolled sideways as he lurched into the corridor.

"Lex, what's up? You're fuckin' *white,*" Jean said.

"I'm not feeling great," he admitted.

She put a hand on his shoulder and guided him onto a chair.

"I'm pissing blood," he added.

"What? Fuck." Jean yanked his shirt free from his belt. "Those bruises look *bad,* man. Around your kidneys. Why didn't they put you on a bus with Hurley? Fucking useless assholes. These people…" She touched the

left side below his ribcage. Lights spilled across his vision, bathing the squad room in white and yellow fog.

"Jean, I can't see," he whispered.

Her face taught with worry, she loosened his tie and his belt, at the same time telling him to lie on the floor with his feet propped on a chair, and then she told Corcoran that she was taking him to the hospital.

"Oh, for the love of all that is holy," Corcoran growled. "I'm hemorrhaging personnel."

"I think Boswell has an internal hemorrhage, sir. He doesn't look good and says he has blood in his urine."

"What did they think they were going to accomplish, sending my people to the riots? And the mayor, he's got Garcia's family at Gracie Mansion while I've got men going to the ER."

"Yes, sir, it sucks," said Jean agreeably. "But I'm still taking him to the ER."

Corcoran looked down at Alex. "Why is he on the floor?"

"He was getting shocky."

"Jesus, he's white."

"You think," Jean said.

Alex had never heard his boss swear so much.

Then Jean helped him off the floor and bundled him into her Corolla. She drove uptown towards Columbia Pres with the police radio hissing out calls. Warnings of where not to go. West 168th, Columbia's uptown campus with its medical center, remained safely riot-free. Even the rioters had the sense to leave the hospital alone. Supporting him by the elbow, Jean steered him into the ER, where he lay across three plastic seats. Hard ridges gouged into his shoulder and side, but he felt too weak to sit up. The room spun like a propeller. When he shut his eyes, the room fell like the propeller had frozen. Jean distracted him with funny stories from her days as a Vice detective.

Nausea reared up in an overpowering wave. "I'm gonna be sick," Alex puffed, interrupting an anecdote.

"Okay, it's okay," said Jean as she slung his arm around her shoulders. Without hesitation, she conveyed him into the men's bathroom and helped him to his knees in a stall, then calmly stayed at his side while he was sick. A few guys at the urinals eyeballed Jean askance, but she paid them no mind.

He stopped vomiting. Through gulps of water, he begged her to put him out of his misery with her service weapon. Instead, she chirpily told him more stories about pretending to be a prostitute in Vice undercover ops.

Two hours later, he lay on his back in the scanner while the donut-shaped ring around his body whirred softly. The technician's professional voice, miked into the room, advised him to relax and breathe evenly. Yeah, right. CT scans of his lungs had been a regular feature of his life since the shooting, but this time he *knew* one of his organs was bleeding. He closed his eyes, terrified that he would end up under the knife. Wasn't his body broken enough? Couldn't he catch a break?

The scans showed a minor bleed in his left kidney. Painful, but not life-threatening. Following the CT, they x-rayed his lumbar spine and ribcage. The x-rays were clean. No fractures, but the medical staff goggled at the images of his ribs and lung on the right side and worked themselves into a frenzy. He was so tired, and he almost broke down in tears, begging them to find his records, which proved those were five-year old injuries. Yes, even the broken costal cartilage. Otherwise, they would keep him here overnight for scans, tests, observation. Dammit, his surgeon worked in *this* hospital, but bureaucracy could be inscrutable. Jean, being less emotional, found the right person to yell at, and she got the records released, which settled everybody down.

Concerned about infections, the doctor prescribed him antibiotics and cleansed the wound on his hand. Too late for stitches, so the doctor rebandaged it. On discharge, he advised Alex to drink lots of water and rest until he felt better. The kidney would heal on its own, provided he gave it time and rest. Jean drove him to his apartment, relating more Vice stories, all the way from 168th to 87th. The West Side Highway had never seemed this long. Women and James thought they could sort out every problem with constant chatter. But interrupting her anecdotes demanded energy, and Alex had none. As much as he sweated time off work and losing precious momentum on his cases, he wanted a hot bath and his bed even more.

Chapter Thirty-Two

As two invalids, Alex and James limped into the Bitter End. Alex imagined Charlotte returning to the city. If she did, she would go there. But she wasn't there. To contain his disappointment, he reminded himself of the last things she said – her rant about New York City, about him. She was someone who followed her feelings, more than most people. She wouldn't be back. The bar was full of strangers, and the folk singer finger-picked a guitar, crooning Irish and Scottish ballads about men who murdered cheating wives, women who murdered cheating husbands, siblings who murdered one another for no reason, and one man, from somewhere called Fyvie in Scotland, who murdered his sister because she had slept with a servant. It was too much like work.

James reflected, "See, whenever the fuck these were written, people were no different."

"No shit." No escape from the job, not even in a folk music bar. Staring at the door, Alex picked at the bandage on his left palm and willed Charlotte to walk in from Bleecker Street. It was 1992 – they should have known better. Him to use a better condom, her to take the damn pills. The pregnancy was an excuse – he'd paid for the abortion, he hadn't objected, but she'd stuck a knife into the relationship anyway. It was the job. It was him. It was the darkness in him, how he found desperation even in peace and love. *You don't know what to do with all your pain.* Those words wormed their way into his mind. Charlotte wanted him to be everything, a cynical New York City homicide cop with sordid stories of the streets, but once she got over the novelty, she wanted him to be a guy who embraced spirituality and Celtic mysticism. He would never be that guy. He couldn't walk in the light.

They wandered to the bar, jostling through the crowd.

"Don't think you're meant to drink with a concussion," Alex said, leaning on the bar, feeling his aches and pains. More than he could count.

James raised an eyebrow. "Don't think you're meant to drink with a fucked kidney."

They both bought Bud, with Laphroaig as a chaser.

"We shoulda gone to the Glendale," Alex said.

"Then we'd have to talk to fuckin' cops. I can't be fucked. At least you know you won't find any here. Even with the murder ballads."

Now that James mentioned it, Alex realized he had no stomach for dealing with cops – people who would rant about O'Keefe or the mayor, or who would ask him about the riot or tell an epic story about how they took some perp down. Injuries on his spine, ribs, and kidney shelled his body like enemy bombers, the pain a constant, screaming buzz inside his head. He felt disenchanted and troubled, wearied of police work, of crime, of the city, but at the same time, bored out of his skull by not dealing with any of it for the past nine days. He'd been hurt in the riot over a week ago. This was the first night he felt well enough to leave the West 80s. A fleeting thought passed him by: if he walked out of the job, he would have time for his daughters, for relationships, but when he tried to imagine some purpose to his life that wasn't death investigation, he drew a blank. *Once you've done that, what else are you going to do that matters?* He swallowed the Laphroaig, wincing at the peaty acidity scalding his throat and stomach. Like drinking a peatbog. This stuff should cure something.

Smiling in a spacey manner, James leaned into Alex's shoulder. "Lex, tell me, would you rather screw a model, or have a bitchin' robot suit. Those are your choices."

"What?" Alex squinted at his partner.

"A robot suit or fucking a model."

"Oh." He thought about it for a minute. "A robot suit if it gave you powers, like flying or teleporting."

"Fuck that. Doesn't even need powers. Just needs to clean itself and you never have to do laundry again, and it lasts forever. The model, she'll dump your ass on the street. But fuck it, if you have a robot suit, who fuckin' cares?"

"Yeah, I guess I'd rather have the robot suit if it saves me from the roaches in my building's laundry room."

"Obviously." James ordered another two glasses of whisky. "There's always another model but only one robot suit."

Alex drew his lips into a pained half-smile. "I'm not sure there are *any* models. You ever slept with a model?"

"They're lining up at my door." James grinned, breathing out sharply through his nose. "I saw a *Law and Order* episode where a model was killed, and the detectives interviewed all her model friends, it was fuckin' great, and I thought, why the fuck does that never happen to us?"

"'Cause we're not on TV? Speaking of work, I'm gonna go back in tomorrow."

"Is that a good idea?"

"Probably not, but I'm going nuts just hanging around my apartment."

"They're not signing me off as medically fit until they're sure this concussion's healed and take the stitches out." James rubbed the side of his head. "I'm still getting the worst headaches I've ever got in my fuckin' life. Worse than the worst hangover you can imagine."

"Yeah, you don't wanna end up more brain damaged than you already are. But I got a shitshow of a caseload that's not gonna improve with age, and I'll be okay. I'm off the antibiotics, and my kidney feels better. The rest of it's just bruising, and my ribs hurt. But they always do, so that doesn't count."

"Coulda done with robot suits at that motherfucking riot," James lamented.

"Ones that teleport us somewhere, like Paris."

"Or teleport Crawford. That guy's such a fuckin' douchebag."

"Him and half this department. I wasn't sure who was gonna kill me first – protesters or cops. Nearly got trampled by a horse after I got CS'd." Alex didn't tell James that since he'd been on sick leave, he had been working through bottles of whisky, sometimes watching the TV, or crawling through the window to sit on the fire escape, breathing in New York's steamy approximation of fresh air. On some nights, he wondered if he was overdoing it with the drinking alone. Yeah, he always drank a bit, but he'd let it run too far, and his liver wouldn't cope if he didn't rein it in.

The day after, when he returned from his medical leave, he only had a couple hours to tame his feral paperwork and case files. He paced circuits around the squad room because the toothy police-issued office chair hurt his back. Soon enough, Corcoran sent him and Jean uptown to interview more witnesses in the O'Keefe case. Triage, Alex thought. A cop-shooting takes priority over everything, the pinnacle of 'oh shit' cases. Robert Morgenthau, the District Attorney, had announced that he was convening a grand jury to investigate the shooting, and he wanted the city's best investigators gathering evidence. As if the AntiCrime units would admit to a homicide detective that drop pieces in questionable shootings were SOP. They probably were, but who would confess?

Washington Heights was subdued in the aftermath of the riots, like a forest after a wildfire, somber and smoldering. Nonetheless, business-as-usual had resumed: drug touts and runners patrolling the corners, addicts walking around like zombies looking for a fix, law-abiding citizens trying to avoid the roughest corners. Alex and Jean interviewed Garcia's relatives, his acquaintances, and a dealer collared by Street Crime. The dealer was almost too helpful. "Pissing all over us and calling it rain," Jean said. But Alex ran him through his weak shit one more time. He knew the DA would plea bargain with any scumbag willing to testify before that grand jury.

Three days into it, Alex and Jean had one of Garcia's sisters in the MNHS interview room. The sister trembled under bone-wracking sobs, saying that Garcia used to willingly give ten bucks to anyone who needed food.

Marty knocked on the door. "Lex, you have a phone call. US Marshals."

Why the hell would US Marshals ask for him? Confused, he left Jean with the sister, who was sniveling into handfuls of Kleenex. He grabbed the phone. "Detective Boswell."

"This is Deputy Smith with the US Marshals Service," drawled the soft male voice. "I have in custody at LaGuardia Airport Guillermo Quixano. Picked him up on a bench warrant. We've got a 'wanted' card with your name on it as primary investigator. We don't want to hold him all night."

"Quixano. Ten-four," Alex grunted. Like every other run-of-the-mill drug homicide, the case had slipped from his mind, overshadowed by the O'Keefe case, his injuries, the riots. Quixano, who he didn't like at all for this murder, but a grand jury did, and he had fled to St. Louis. Maybe Vito's instincts were right; maybe Quixano was guilty; maybe it was worth getting him off the streets one way or another because he was responsible for a lot of the crack distribution around the West 180s.

Alex poked his head into the interview room. "I gotta deal with a perp who's been picked up at the airport."

"He can't keep?" Jean asked. "Boss ain't gonna be happy. He don't want single detectives interviewing people on this one."

"The Marshals don't wanna keep him. I'll send Marty in to cover for me."

He promised Marty a few beers in exchange for interviewing the witness with Jean. Then he snagged a car and ran out the door before Corcoran noticed. Well, he was following orders. Corcoran had gotten on his case about collaring Quixano.

"I knew he'd come back," Vito said brightly when Alex collected him at the Three-Four station house *en route* to LaGuardia. "Let's nail this son of a bitch. Show everyone we can still put murderers away. Show everyone we're still in *control* of this place." He spat out the word 'control,' as if the riot had been an affront to him, personally.

They waited in stationary traffic on the Grand Central Parkway. Alex shifted his pelvis in the seat, but no matter how he positioned himself, it felt like an axe was chopping his ribcage in half. Fuck, he needed out of this car, but traffic pinned them on the highway. Roadworks? Accident? He listened to the police radio but heard no reports of any accidents on the Grand Central.

"What's with all this fucking traffic?" he kvetched.

"We're not *in* traffic," Vito said. "We *are* traffic."

Alex glared at him. "My back's fucking killing me."

"What's wrong with it?"

"Got hurt in the riot."

"What?" Vito shot him a swift look, surprised. "You were on a detail?"

"Me and all of MNHS," Alex sighed, arching his bruised spine. "Weren't you?" Surely every detective uptown had been pulled into riot detail?

"You kidding me? I told 'em, no way was I gonna get the shit kicked outta me." Vito patted his bulging belly. "And I ain't fittin' into the bag anyway."

"Huh." Alex marveled at Vito's juice. Even when Manhattan North Homicide, arguably one of the most elite investigative squads in the NYPD, had to go on riot detail, Vito had talked his way out of it. Incredible.

Ahead, parading cones forced three lanes of traffic into one lane. Cars wrestled for space, with ones in the soon-to-be-closed lanes charging ahead, and ones in the open lane almost touching the rear bumpers of cars ahead of them, as if they owned the damned road. Did none of these fuckwits understand how a zipper merge is better for everyone?

An hour later, Alex parked in a bay designated for law enforcement. As he staggered onto the tarmac, various body parts screeched in pain. Not just his side, for a change. Planes took off and landed, and the roaring, whining engines shook his eardrums. He held his fingers against an ear. Security glanced at their shields and IDs, then escorted them into the most desolate of airport outbuildings, the holding cells. Neither the airport personnel nor Vito commented on his uneven gait.

Detained in a cell, Guillermo Quixano slumped on a bench, elbows on his knees. Intricate tattoos of thorns and dragons laced both his forearms. He wore jeans and a solid blue t-shirt. The dragons' heads stared from the back of each hand. Quixano was only in his forties, but the lines around his eyes and grey flecks in his black hair added ten years to his face.

"You bailing out the *ocean*," he commented in a New York accent, lightly inflected with Spanish vowels.

"No shit," Alex concurred. "One fucking drop at a time."

"You ain't gonna stop the drugs in this city arresting me," Quixano observed as Alex gestured for him to get to his feet. "It's way bigger than me."

"You're under arrest for the murder of Jose Medina," Alex intoned while snapping the bracelets on Quixano's wrists. "You have the right to remain silent. Anything you say can and will be used against you in a court of law. You have the right to an attorney. If you cannot afford one, one will be provided at no charge."

"You arresting me for Jose's murder? Jesus Christ." Quixano inhaled. Alex felt the man's body tremble. "Fuckin' NYPD, man."

"Fuckin' slingers gonna learn they don't run things in this city," Vito growled. The detectives shoved Quixano towards the door, the Marshals accompanying them to the car.

"I want a lawyer," said Quixano placidly as the detectives secured him in the back seat.

Knowing his rights, he availed himself of the Fifth Amendment, saying nothing further for the ride through Queens. Alex planned on taking him straight to Central, booking him, then throwing this schlocky case at the DA. It wouldn't be his problem anymore. Let the courts diffuse his doubts and his self-reproach. The system was bigger than one detective.

Vito said, "Nah, let's take him to the station house."

"Why? He's already asked for counsel."

"Whatever. Did you hear him? I didn't. They gonna believe two detectives or a crack dealer?"

Vito being Vito. Alex squashed the objections rising in his throat: any confession would be inadmissible; you can't interrogate someone after they've unambiguously requested a lawyer. *Who's gonna know?* Well, he knew, but he had always felt outshined by Vito, forever a rookie accompanying a hardboiled veteran. His gut scrunched with uneasiness, but fatigue and pain poured through him like a monstrous waterfall. Wordlessly, he drove to the Three-Four station house.

Quixano, for his part, had low expectations of the police. He would have been more surprised if the detectives had respected his Constitutional rights. Showing the same wearied forbearance that Alex had seen in the airport, he leaned back in the interrogation room chair, his doleful eyes floating towards the ceiling.

"You want anything? Coffee? Something from the vending machine?" Alex asked.

"No, thanks," Quixano answered amicably.

"You sure?"

"Yup."

"You obviously knew Jose Medina." Alex got straight to the point. He'd already abased himself, blowing off the Sixth Amendment and *Miranda, Gideon,* and the New York state constitution, Article 1, section 6, because his whole body hurt like he'd suffered the worst beating of his life. Was that why he'd deferred to Vito like a fucking sycophant? Where were his guts? His principles? Not here, whatever the reason. And everyone deferred to Vito, even the ADAs.

If cared at all for this interrogation, he would work on establishing rapport with the perp, on building a strong connection that would break down the man's defenses. He knew that Quixano's parents had emigrated from the Dominican Republic. He knew that Quixano had grown up in the Heights projects. He knew about a few juvenile drug offenses, and he knew that Quixano had upped his game, avoiding narcotics arrests as he ascended the drug crew hierarchy. He knew that Quixano was married, with three kids, and his wife had a semi-legit job as a receptionist in a bookie's. He knew that Quixano liked cooking, baseball, and fishing. So much material, yet he couldn't be bothered getting into Quixano's head.

"I'm not talking about Medina," said Quixano.

"He worked for you?" Alex asked.

Quixano shrugged.

"He did work for you."

An equivocal look crossed Quixano's face.

"What did he do?"

"I'm not talking about him, man."

Vito splayed his enormous hands on the table. He leaned forward and said in a belligerent tone, "We got your gun, pal. That silver Colt."

"I don't have a silver Colt."

".45mm. That's a big fuckin' gun. Shows you the big fuckin' man."

"Overkill," Quixano remarked ambivalently. "I wouldn't have that."

"We got your fingerprints on that gun," Vito stated.

Quixano's prints were not on the gun. Lying about forensic evidence you didn't have was a standard interrogation technique, one Alex had used countless times, but he felt every artery in his body constricting, his blood pounding.

"It ain't my gun," Quixano insisted.

"Then why the fuck are your prints on it?"

"Maybe they ain't my prints."

For three hours, they circled, Quixano holding his immutable ground. He did not budge when Vito declared that he had eyewitnesses. He remained unimpressed by the made-up forensics. The third hour of interrogation withered away, and Alex's forbearance died with it, the mangled remains eradicated by Quixano's heavy-lidded non-reaction, his refusal to confess or give an alibi or offer some story exonerating himself. Alex sniffed in a measured breath through his nostrils. He glanced at Vito. Frustration bloomed on the precinct detective's blotchy face. His wide forehead gleamed with sweat. This was a Goddamned exercise in futility, Alex thought, and Corcoran wanted him working the O'Keefe case, not spending an entire afternoon interrogating a drug dealer who had knocked off another dealer. *End this unlawful interrogation now,* he said to himself. It was pointless anyway. With the grand jury indictment, the burden of proof had shifted to the DA, and the grand jury had indicted without the accused's confession. Arguably, that meant the DA already had enough evidence to proceed with criminal charges.

"What's with you people?" snarled Vito, spittle flying from his lips. "You think you can do whatever the fuck you want? You think the law don't apply to you?"

"'You people?' You've already decided that someone who looks like me committed this murder," Quixano said in a level voice. "You probably decided that before he even got to your Medical Examiner."

"Are you calling me a *racist*?" Vito roared.

Quixano blithely shrugged. "If the shoe fits."

Vito leapt upwards like he had a missile strapped to his ass. He hammered his fist against the table.

It rattled Alex's breastbone. He jumped. His tongue tasted bitter. The suspect flinched.

"And I still didn't shoot him," said Quixano, unmoved.

"I told you to stop fucking lying, you worthless piece of shit!" Vito grappled with Quixano, his bulk overpowering the man as he forcefully hauled him to his feet.

Quixano protested, "Whoa. I asked for a lawyer! I have rights!" He stiffened his body, pulling away in defiance. Vito slugged him in the jaw.

He reeled into the wall with a grunt of pain. "This is excessive force," he panted.

"Excessive?" Vito sneered. He slammed Quixano's head against the cinder blocks, twice, hard. A stomach-wrenching cracking noise shook the walls. Quixano cried out as his legs buckled, and he hit the concrete with a thud. He wrapped himself into a fetal ball on the floor, grasping his head with both hands. Alex saw blood seeping between the man's fingers.

In shock, Alex shouted, "Vito! What the fuck are you *doing*?" You could lie, yell, cry, anything to manipulate a suspect, but Jesus Christ, you could not pummel the shit out of them.

Eyes blazing, Vito rounded on him. "Let's go out for a minute and give this son of a bitch a chance to think about what he wants to tell us." He booted Quixano in the ribs.

Quixano groaned but lay still.

"You hear that, you asshole? Your last fucking chance."

The detectives stepped into the dim corridor outside. As soon as the door rattled shut, Alex snapped, "Vito, you can't use physical force –"

To his great surprise, Vito grabbed him by both shoulders, then hurled him against the breeze blocks. A groan escaped his throat. Pain, like a lit pipe bomb, detonated inside his back and ripped through his ribcage. Vito's red face thrust forwards, inches from his. The man's heavyset hands jabbed hard into the brachial plexus, the bundle of nerves between his shoulders and chest. Blistering nerve pains shot along his arms, from his shoulders down to his fingers. He could barely breathe.

"You don't tell me what to do with my prisoners in my interrogation room," snarled Vito.

Alex smelled the acrid cigar on Vito's breath. It steamed against his face. He hissed, "They're not *your* prisoners. You –"

"You better keep your mouth shut, Alex. You get it? My interrogation room, my prisoners, and I make the fuckin' rules."

"Vito—" Alex's throat closed, like he was choking on tear gas again.

"You say a word, one fuckin' word, I'm gonna tell the bosses that you been drinking on the job."

"What?"

"Everybody knows you gotta fuckin' problem. I say, I seen you sneaking off to your bottle of whisky, your flask in your pocket, what are they gonna do? I say you been drunk, you gotta problem. What are they gonna do? You know that detective who accidentally shot his partner in the Bronx 'cause he was fuckin' hammered? They're on a *roll* now. And

I know you're havin' trouble with clearances. And hell, what if it ain't just the drink. I say, he's got other problems. Bigger ones. He's abusing alcohol, maybe he's abusing other substances. Maybe the K9s find half a ki in your locker, huh? Where does that leave you?"

Alex felt the corridor itself shattering like a dropped glass. His entire sense of himself, the job, his relationships in it, splintering into a million pieces. A man he saw as a friend of sorts, a mentor, a loyal colleague, assaulting a suspect, shoving *him* against a wall. Threatening him! If his boss or any C/O caught him drinking while on duty, especially after the incident with those Bronx detectives, he would be looking at command disciplines, an IA investigation, losing his post or his gold shield. If someone flaked him with cocaine in his locker, he would be looking at the Penal Code and the end of his career.

But Godammit, Vito was gunning to imprison a man on a twenty-five-to-life sentence, a man who might well be innocent. So what if Quixano slung coke? If he was going to be put away, it should be for something he did.

"How can you be so sure he shot Medina?" Alex wheezed. "Your evidence sucks. None of it passes the sniff test."

"Haven't you learned *anything*?" Vito spluttered. His left hand dropped away from Alex's shoulder, towards his firearm.

Alex gasped, but before he could think or react, Vito was driving the butt of the gun into his right side, ramming it under the last ribs, straight into the depths of his old wound. Agony cleaved through every vein in his body. Pain like a vat of boiling oil eating into his skin, boring down to the bone. A scream rose inside his throat, but he held it down to a low grunt.

"I'm gonna go back in there." Vito flicked his eyes towards the one-way. On the other side, Quixano vomited onto the floor under the table, then he crawled to the chair. His face glistened with blood. "What a fuckin' mess," growled Vito. "You with me on this, Lex?"

Alex was in too much pain to speak. Tears welled behind his eyes. The gun ground deeper into his side, wrenching the scarred lower ribs outwards. Something inside him whimpered. He wasn't sure if Vito heard.

"I think he'll talk now. See? I know it ain't what the rules say, and all those fuckin' 1960s Supreme Court cases sayin' these people got certain rights or whatever, but the rules was made up by a bunch of judges and state congressmen. You think *any* of those people have ever interrogated a perp in their lives? What the fuck do they know? Tellin' us how to do our jobs." Vito now sounded friendly, conciliatory.

He let go of Alex's shoulders and holstered his gun. Alex collapsed onto the floor with a groan, holding his side. The wound was alight with white, hot fire. Each breath squeezed out tears. His hands had gone numb, and his chest, arms, and shoulders tingled.

Vito insisted, "You get what I'm sayin'? You better not even tell Hurley. Nobody. It's just between you and me."

"Gotcha," Alex said miserably between labored breaths.

Smiling with the slimy sincerity of a used car salesman, Vito touched his shoulder. "Come back in. Let's finish this up."

Alex's heart fell out of his chest. Everything felt wrong. His insides writhed, and his legs refused his brain's demands. But Vito reached under his left armpit and pulled him to his feet. The dazzling pain of the sudden movement forced more salty water from his eyes. *Why can't I be strong enough?* His resolve foundered, defeated, broken like his body, and he hobbled through the interrogation room's steel door. Quixano glumly eyeballed him. Blood caked the side of the suspect's face and soaked his hair. Hopeless resignation glazed his eyes. Like Alex, he too had no more strength for combating Vito's irresistible force.

"So, you gonna tell us about shooting Jose Medina?" Vito asked. He shoved lined paper across the table, towards Quixano.

"I'd like to see my kids again," muttered Quixano.

"Well, you'd better fuckin' start by owning up," Vito said.

"I've told you the truth," insisted Quixano in a shaken voice.

Without warning, Vito kicked him sharply in the knee. He grunted, doubling over.

"This gets a lot worse if you don't start talkin'," Vito warned.

As if he'd turned to stone, Quixano froze, hunkered around his knees.

Vito smashed his fist into the table. "You want your right eye to match the left one? You want another dent in your skull? Fuckin' talk."

Alex felt sick with a paralyzing nausea. He breathed consciously, lightly, but if he twitched any other muscle, he would puke.

"Yeah, I shot him," Quixano mumbled, dabbing at the blood oozing from his head.

"Don't telling the truth feel good, Guillermo?"

Quixano gave him a look, a flash of anger, but overpowered by futility.

"Write it down."

Slowly, Quixano scrawled words on the page. He spent five minutes worrying at it, then he pushed the paper across the table.

Alex read the rough cursive. *I shot Jose Medina because he was stealing product from our stash for his personal use. I walked up to him on 180th Street and shot him in the head with my Colt then moved the body.*

It didn't explain why Medina's body remained undiscovered for so long, or how he got to the shooting gallery on West 166th, or why he had a broken leg and ligature injuries on his wrists, or anything else Alex could corroborate. Unsteadily, he stood up. "I gotta go to the john." Vito lifted his shoulders in a dismissive shrug, which Alex hardly noticed as he scooted through the door. He pushed his pain out of his way so he could escape as fast as he could walk, but he felt weak and sick, close to fainting. Hidden in a men's room stall, he knelt over a toilet, seizing the sides of the bowl. Queasiness heaved inside his stomach. He retched until he'd emptied it of every meal he'd ever eaten. The stinging buzz in his hands and forearms strengthened, like a million ants burrowing into his flesh, and he rocked backwards against the stall door, massaging his hands together. His tenth rib slid against the ninth, crunching. It should not move like that.

Only one thing was clear. He had to get the fuck out of this place. The station house seemed more pernicious than the riot, a crevasse tainted with malice, violence, corruption. Cast into a blinding darkness, he half-ran through the building. Sweat beaded on his forehead, and his face had whitened. Precinct personnel didn't seem to notice. They were so oblivious that one young precinct detective said, "Oh, Boswell, I've got this case. I was wondering if you had any ideas..." And Alex shot the guy a wild look that sent him scurrying in the opposite direction. Pain slashed his ribcage apart, the old gunshot wound a disc of dry ice, and the newer one a bar of fire across it. Fighting vertigo, he flung himself into his car. So what if he wasn't feeling safe to drive? For all he cared, he could hit the crash barriers at sixty miles per hour. He almost hit a taxi. The cab's sudden appearance at an intersection surprised him. Even though his mind hadn't been on the road – and the cab had the right-of-way – he hit the horn, his instinctive New Yorker reaction. The cab driver, not knowing he was a police car, gave him the finger out the window.

Then in his own office, he immersed himself in writing DD-5s for the O'Keefe case. The phone rang as he clattered away at the typewriter. A precinct detective from the Nineteenth reporting a shooting, the vic in the hospital. *Can't people stop fucking shooting each other, for one Goddamned day.* He rounded up Jean from gossiping in the kitchenette with Marty, Sam, and Bill.

"What's wrong?" she asked. "You're limping again. Like you can barely walk."

"My old wound's playing up," he replied, his voice rough, unable to conceal the pseudo-lie or the pain. "It has bad days."

Jean looked doubtful, but she didn't pursue it further.

They headed for Columbia Pres, where they found the ER residents cracking open the vic's chest, a last-ditch attempt to massage his heart back to life. Homicide detectives not being strangers to the medical aspects of violent death, Alex and Jean knew ninety-seven percent of such efforts fail, and this guy wasn't in the lucky three percent. With it now a murder, they drove to the Nineteenth station house, where they interviewed half a dozen witnesses, then they drove to a low-rise on East 101st, where they arrested the perp, who'd bragged to the wits that he did it because the vic slapped his sister around. After booking him, they wrote '61s, 'fives, and a charging sheet. Alex got a cleared case to his name in six hours, with overtime pay to boot, which should have made him feel better.

Instead, he jetted away from the office, ignoring his colleagues' post-tour drinking plans. "Lex? You up for the pub?" Rizzo yelled at his back. They would wonder why he wasn't. He flagged down an M116 bus, which traversed Harlem and dumped him in Morningside Heights, above the 1,2,3 line. How the fuck did Eddie Trenemen work murders in this place for fifteen years without feeling ill, burning out? Alex had removed a gun from the perp's apartment in his search-pursuant-to-arrest, but there would be another in its place by the end of the week. What was the point? Could you really hammer the city's insurmountable social problems out of existence with heavy-handed policing? It was like whack-a-mole. They shot straight back up.

He forged his way through the crowds at the West 86th Street subway station, leaping up the first few steps, but sickness washed over him, more powerfully than it had before. It knocked him to the ground like a physical blow. He cried out, barely noticing when he hit the stairs. Winded, he sat on his knees, clutching his side. People gathered around. They looked so concerned. So worried. They cared. *You wouldn't care about me if you knew what I've done.* Warding off any assistance, he stumbled to his feet, labored up the remaining stairs, then limped along Broadway and West 87th, forcing his body into every agonizing step. He breathed in a tangy scent, his own sweat. Keys quivered in his hands. His apartment seemed lonely and irksome, demanding adult tasks like paying the superintendent fees, re-grouting the shower, fixing the moody A/C. *Where does anyone find energy for this shit?* He threw off his jacket and shoes, then dove for the Glenlivet. Telling himself to harden up, he rubbed his eyes with his sleeve, but warm, salty tears defied his pleas, trickling down his cheeks. His side was burning up, a new, hotter flame flushing through him with every beat of his heart, like he'd been shot a second time. A broken rib? Internal bleeding? Bruised liver? He looked at his phone, longing to tell James, tell anyone. Never had he felt so desolate and betrayed, the pain surpassing any break-up. But he wholeheartedly believed Vito's threats. The man had meant every word. Despair flowed through his veins like icy water, and he chugged Glenlivet from the bottle until the room gyrated, and the bottle was two-thirds empty.

Part 7

Chapter Thirty-Three

April 2010

It was one of those times where Alex questioned his decision to quit drinking. Sure, he would be dead by now if he had kept at it, but then that would be a relief in its own way. He would not be in a small meeting room in the United States Courthouse for the Southern District of New York before they called him to the grand jury. As he waited, he felt as though someone was boring holes through his stomach. He waffled between staying still or moving. An ulcer flaring, and he should get it looked at, but that seemed like a metaphor for how he felt about this grand jury: having his insides examined as unpleasantly as possible.

Two days ago, he had told Kima DeSilva things he had never told anyone in his life. Attorney-client privilege had provided him with a space where he could cut those secrets free, passing them on to someone else. Briefly, he'd felt light inside. He understood why people confessed to priests, or detectives.

"Okay," she had said imperturbably, like she'd heard similar stories before. "We need to meet with the US Attorney and ask for immunity."

"*Immunity?* What can they charge me with? The statute of limitations ran out on everything years ago."

"It sure did, but they're gonna argue that perjuring yourself in court and then keeping your mouth shut for twenty years about these abuses of power and miscarriages of justice while those guys did time amounts to a conspiracy to obstruct justice and deprive the complainants of their civil rights under color of law. USC Title 18, section 242. As of last year, those guys were still incarcerated, which makes the conspiracy ongoing. God knows if a district court judge is gonna buy that, but if one does, you get charged with obstruction of justice, perjury, violating civil rights, and whatever else they stick in there."

He'd licked his cracking lips. He'd stared out the window overlooking Central Park South. Cars whirled through the Columbus Circle roundabout. People bubbled around the vertiginous marble and granite monument at its center, where Christopher Columbus stood high on his pedestal, overlooking traffic jams.

"You get immunity from the AUSA," Kima continued. "Then you tell them what they want to know. Do you know who else in the Three-Four squad might've been in on these cover-ups?"

"No idea. You think Vito trusted me that much?" He blew out a contemptuous breath.

"What about the informant who gave him Quixano's alleged gun? What else do you know about him?"

Alex scrunched his brows, shaking his head. "Just what I told you." He'd run Luca Martinez, or Turbo, through DCJS last week, but the system had no record of him after 1999. He'd trawled New York State Department of Health for death records, to no avail. "I did a half-assed search. I could look harder. He could've left the state. I didn't run him through NCIC."

"Don't be stupid, Alex. This isn't a bad cop movie. I'll get one of my PIs on it. The feds are after Vito Indelicata. They know he's the main perpetrator. *He's* their guy. He's gotten away with ignoring the Constitution and people's civil rights for three decades. They gotta prove it in court, but they know."

Alex whispered, "So what? How am I gonna testify against Vito? I do that, I'm a snitch. Doesn't matter what he did to me, or to the defendants. You were a cop. You gotta know that."

"You can't lie to the grand jury and say it didn't happen. I know this AUSA, Victor Sullivan. He's good. He's fishing, but he knows what he can catch. You lie to him, it's perjury."

"I can plead the Fifth."

"You can do that. But I wouldn't advise it. If Sullivan can corroborate any allegation Quixano or Serrachia or any of these complainants makes, you still get charged. Maybe we fight it out in court, and the judge decides the conspiracy charge doesn't get the prosecutors around the statute of limitations. Maybe he or she decides it does. But either way, you think your career is in trouble if Indelicata thinks you're a snitch, imagine how it's gonna be if you're a defendant in federal court. Even if the charges don't stick, Jo Gibson's gonna haul your ass off the Homicide squad. She'd have no choice."

He had bowed his head, massaging the bridge of his nose, caught between whirlpools and sea monsters. If only he could hit a stopwatch or a rewind button on time itself. And go where? Back to where poor Elam Liebowitz was gunned down in broad daylight, and young Alex Boswell found himself awestruck by Indelicata. He would warn his thirty-year old self to keep his distance. Vito paid little attention to detectives like James, who had never treated him like God's gift to criminal investigation.

But time only goes one way, and he waited for the prosecutor to call him. Down the hall, a door slammed. An electric shock zapped his heart. Although his lawyer had advised him to exchange cooperation for immunity, he decided that he would take the Fifth if asked about anything incriminating. Yeah, Vito had violated the complainants' civil rights 'under color of law,' the legalese understatement of the decade, but testifying against him felt like violating a sacred code.

The clerk of the court brought him into the grand jury room. Twenty-three citizens sitting in the pews, the prosecutor standing at a podium like a conductor, and the witness facing the grand jury. Alex had testified before countless grand juries, because the state of New York requires a grand jury indictment in any Supreme Court felony case, but God, never at the sharp end of criminal justice. As he took the oath, he adjusted his tie. His fingers curled against the tremors in his hands.

Victor Sullivan, the AUSA, was tall, blonde, and athletic, like he should be on a Scandinavian running team. He smiled broadly, warm, almost welcoming. Alex distrusted him immediately. There was nothing warm or welcoming about this.

"Good of you to join us, Detective," the prosecutor drawled, as if Alex had a choice in the matter. "Now, please state your name, rank, and shield number for the record."

Alex intoned, "Alex Boswell, Detective Second Grade, Manhattan North Homicide, Shield number 8652."

"How old are you?"

"Fifty-three."

After interminable questions covering the length and breadth of Alex's career, the AUSA asked, "Can you explain to these fine ladies and gentlemen what a specialized investigative unit like Manhattan North Homicide does?"

"We cover everything in Manhattan north of 59th Street, and we assist precinct detectives with and contribute resources to investigating homicides and first-degree assault cases involving a firearm."

"Thanks for that," said Sullivan in a voice like an NPR radio presenter, inviting you to relax and listen. "Okay, Detective, let's go back to the summer of 1987. I know it was a long time ago. You were one of the officers investigating the shooting of a man, a rabbi, called Elam Liebowitz. Is that right?"

"Yes," Alex said.

It flooded back to him: the long hours of canvassing, hundreds of witness interviews, the epidemic of hysteria from the mayor's office, the media, and the brass. Under the prosecutor's crisp questioning, he told the jury about his cursory interview with Ernesto Serrachia. He disclosed how and why he'd written off the man as a suspect.

"Then Mr. Serrachia became... what will we say... the prime suspect, didn't he?"

"I guess so."

Sullivan cocked his head to the side. "You guess so?"

"I wasn't involved in those decisions."

"Why not?"

"I was shot in the line of duty on October 3rd. I was on medical leave for over five months and off the investigation." Without thinking, he pressed his hand against the old wound, then caught himself and changed the movement to straightening his tie.

"I'm sorry to hear that. But you were aware that Detective Indelicata considered Mr. Serrachia to be a suspect?"

"Not while I was on sick leave."

"But you were made aware of it?"

"Only when I came back to work, and Lieutenant Corcoran told me."

"When was that?"

"February, '88."

"Did anybody talk to you about the case while you were on medical leave?"

"No."

"Would Detective Indelicata have been aware of what those witnesses and Mr. Serrachia himself told you?"

"Presumably. I filed the witness statements and DD-5s – reports – for the interviews."

"Did you talk to Detective Indelicata directly about those interviews, either before, during, or after your medical leave?"

381

"No."

"Did you talk to anyone else about them?"

"Yeah. But before the shooting."

"Not after?"

"No. I had other things on my mind." He couldn't hold the sarcasm down.

"Who did you talk to?"

"My colleagues, Detective Sam Rizzo and Detective Eddie Trenemen."

"Anyone else?"

"Not that I recall."

"What did you say to Detective Rizzo and Detective Trenemen?"

Alex shut his eyes for half a second. "Just said I had another damned dead end. Something like that." Was it? How the hell could he remember every conversation from twenty years ago?

"Did you tell them that you considered Mr. Serrachia a suspect?"

"I don't remember."

"Do you know if Detective Rizzo or Detective Trenemen spoke to Detective Indelicata about Mr. Serrachia?"

"No, I don't."

"Did you know that Detective Indelicata found and spoke to your two alibi witnesses?"

"Not until I returned from medical leave."

"But he knew who they were, before you were shot?"

"Anybody who read the file would know who they were," Alex sighed. No one who wasn't completely mad or deeply undercover would go out of their way to hide witness' identities from colleagues.

"How did you learn that Detective Indelicata spoke to the witnesses?"

"Lieutenant Corcoran informed me he did."

"Were you aware that they apparently *changed* their testimony after speaking with Detective Indelicata?"

"I'm aware they changed their testimony. I couldn't say when." Alex could play these games as well as any lawyer.

"If you look at this, you'll see the statements they gave to you."

Alex slipped on his reading glasses and glanced over the witness statements he had written twenty-three years ago. Then Sullivan handed him more documents, statements the same witnesses had made to Vito. The first ones unequivocally placed Serrachia on West 180th and then at the Dominican take-out, accounting for his whereabouts around the time of the murder. But in their second statements to Vito, the take-out employee averred that he didn't remember serving Serrachia, while the cop declared that his team hadn't seen Serrachia on the corner when his squad busted that drug crew. Not on August 5th, 1987, at any rate.

"So, they obviously altered their testimony, right?"

"Yeah."

"You'd agree those are contradictory statements? Yours and Detective Indelicata's."

"Yeah."

"Any idea why?"

"No." What had Vito said to those witnesses? Had he threatened them? Bribed them? Jovially twisted words, talking them into so many circles that they no longer knew uptown from downtown? Alex had been so young and naïve then, and Vito, his 'rabbi,' had come to the hospital with him, staying by his side after he was shot.

"Could you take an educated guess?"

"Not really. You know witnesses can just change their testimony for no reason. Happens all the time."

Sullivan's thin lips twisted into a small, dry smile. People were people; witnesses probably panicked and reneged or forgot as often in federal criminal court as they did in New York courts. "During Mr. Serrachia's trial, were you cross-examined about your witness statements from September 9th?"

"No."

"Did that surprise you?"

"Yeah."

"Were you aware they were not in the DA's case file or in discovery?"

"I wasn't working the case anymore. I don't know what was in discovery."

"But the case file?"

"I don't know what was in the file after October 3rd."

"You never looked at it when you came back to work?"

"No. I was still recovering and had a lot of other cases I was working."

"Okay, Detective. You ever hear of a guy called Kevin Schiller?"

"Not until last year when the case was reopened."

"No one contacted you with a tip about him?"

"No."

"Did you know his wife, Maureen Schiller, contacted Detective Indelicata in 1990?"

"I didn't at the time."

"She also says she contacted the Manhattan North Homicide squad after Mr. Serrachia's 1990 trial. Did you know about that?"

"She didn't reach out to me." Alex felt himself breathing rapidly.

"Yes, of course, because as you said, you were taken off the case after you were injured. But she reached out to the MNHS detective who took over the investigation, didn't she? Bill Ryan?"

"So I hear."

"You were friends with Detective Ryan?"

"Yeah."

"Did he ever tell you he'd received information about the Liebowitz case?"

Alex considered lying through his teeth to protect Bill's reputation, saving his old friend from a post-humous dragging across coals. But what if the prosecutor had scared up a witness who knew what Bill had told Alex? Kima had warned him against prevarication. It was an offhand comment at a drunk party. It would not get him indicted for anything, and they couldn't subpoena Bill, much less indict him.

"Yeah," he said, the pain roughening his voice.

"What did he tell you?"

"He mentioned it at a New Year party. Just said someone left him a message. They said Serrachia didn't kill Liebowitz. Some 'nutcase.' I think that's the word he used."

"Is that all he said?"

"Yeah."

"Some nutcase?"

"Yeah."

"Do you know if Detective Ryan or anyone else followed it up?"

"No idea."

"You weren't concerned?"

"I was pretty intoxicated. So was he."

"Sure. But did you ask Detective Ryan about this tip on any subsequent date?"

"No."

"Why not?"

"It was just a throwaway comment at a drunk party. I didn't think about it."

"You didn't think about it all?"

"No."

"What about Detective Ryan's partner? Martín Vasquez. Is it possible he could have known about it?"

"I've never talked to Detective Vasquez about the Serrachia case."

"But is it possible he had the same information as Detective Ryan?"

"I don't know."

"They were partners. They were presumably working the case together after you and Detective Trenemen got shot?"

"I don't know."

"Is it likely that Detective Vasquez also got the tip?"

"I don't know. You'd have to ask him."

"You're saying Detective Ryan told you and not him? His partner?"

"I said, Ryan was drunk. I don't even know if he meant Maureen Schiller's tip. It was a high-profile case. We were getting lots of people phoning in with all kinds of stuff. Theories from Jimmy Hoffa to Shergar. Coulda been anything. I don't know what he told Vasquez."

"Okay. Did you know Maureen Schiller contacted Detective Indelicata again in 1996?"

Alex swallowed angrily, imperceptibly (he hoped) stiffening his shoulders. "No."

"Would Detective Indelicata have told you about a tip like that?"

"No." A pall of unease and aversion adhered to their relationship, Alex's trust and affection destroyed the moment Vito threw him against that wall, and Vito possessing some awareness that he had gone too far, but unable to recognize his own culpability. His ego was far too colossal for that. He'd probably told himself (and everyone else) that Alex was unreasonable and difficult.

"It was, as you say, a high-profile case, during some of the most violent years this city has known, and you needed a suspect. Rabbi Liebowitz was shot in August '87, and by January '88, the police had nothing, right?"

"We were under a lot of pressure," Alex admitted.

"And Ernesto Serrachia, poor, Dominican, addicted to crack cocaine, no one was going to argue with that, were they? He *looked* like a perpetrator. He was the right sort of person to pin this on, wasn't he?"

"I wanted to get the *right* person. I discounted him as a suspect."

"But you didn't say anything when Mr. Serrachia was tried and convicted?"

"No."

"Why?"

"I guess I trusted Indelicata, and the system." His hands were in his lap, out of the grand jury's sight, and he peeled at the skin around his nails until it bled.

"We've heard from other witnesses that Detective Indelicata was like a mentor to you."

I wonder who told him that. Alex cleared gunk from his throat. "Yeah, I guess you could say that."

"You were close to him?"

"For a little while."

"Close enough for him to tell you about manipulating the witnesses."

"No. He never talked to me about those witnesses."

"But you were close?"

"He played cards close to his chest. Kept his people, his informants, away from us. He told people what he thought they needed to know. I didn't need to know that."

"But you protected him?"

"I what?" Alex twitched his brows and rubbed at his receding hairline.

"You were aware that the witnesses changed their testimony, right?"

"Yeah."

"And you never said a word?"

"About what?"

"The witness statements that seemingly disappeared. You never said a word about them, did you?"

"Why would I bother?" Alex exhaled through his teeth. "No one would've listened."

"And you said nothing after Mr. Serrachia was exonerated in 2009, right?"

"He was exonerated. They didn't need me to overturn his conviction."

"Okay," said Sullivan. "Let's move on, shall we?"

It only gets worse from here, thought Alex, caught under a surge of powerless misery.

"In March of 1990, you investigated the murder of a Dominican man from Washington Heights named Jose Medina, is that right?"

"Yeah."

Perfectly cooperative, he answered the prosecutor's questions about the first stages of the investigation, bouncing between the case file and his memory, his details so meticulous and stuffed with police jargon that the jury looked like they were going into rigor.

"You interviewed a couple witnesses with Detective Indelicata. One was a prostitute called 'Loretta.' Her real name was Elizabeth Weltmayer. Is that right?"

The questions felt like heavy rain. "Yes."

"Where did you interview her? The precinct?"

"No, Indelicata's car."

"Inside the car? That doesn't sound like SOP."

386

"It isn't, but Indelicata never gave a damn about SOP." Alex sunk his incisors into the flesh inside his lower lip.

"Am I right to assume she told you that she saw – she ID'd – Guillermo Quixano, who was known to the Narcotics squad and the 34th Precinct squad, shoot Mr. Medina?"

"Yes, that's what she said."

"Was Mr. Quixano a person-of-interest to you before you met Ms. Weltmayer?"

"No."

"Did you personally know of Mr. Quixano and any narcotics trafficking he may have been involved in?"

"No." Alex gulped down a mouthful of water. "But Indelicata did."

"You're saying his name had never been flagged by *your* investigation, prior to your encounter with Ms. Weltmayer?"

"No, it hadn't."

"What about other homicide cases? Has he ever shown up?"

"Not to my knowledge."

"Can you remember any details from your conversation with the aforementioned witness in the car on March 20th? Did Detective Indelicata prompt Ms. Weltmayer in any way?"

"It was twenty years ago. I don't remember." Alex remembered more than he wanted.

"Did Detective Indelicata give Ms. Weltmayer anything in exchange for her cooperation?"

"She was a confidential informant. Everyone gives CIs something."

"Answer the question, Detective."

"Yeah, he gave her money. But that's SOP." His heart contracted as they edged past the line between what he would testify about and what he was afraid to say.

"He gave her money," echoed Sullivan. "Why?"

"I said, it's SOP. CIs put themselves at risk. Drug dealers take a dim view of people who rat on them. They're only gonna give you information if there's something in it for them."

"Do you think she was going to use this money to buy crack cocaine?"

"She was an addict, so I assume that's what she used it for. But CIs aren't exactly upstanding citizens—"

"Detective, did you find her credible?"

Alex squirmed, afraid to perjure himself and say yes, but where would it lead if he said no? "Not really, but that's why you always try to corroborate a CI."

387

"Did you ever corroborate her?"

"No."

"Did anyone – the DA, your supervisors – ask you to?"

"No."

"Did you find that odd? Just completely trusting an informant, a crack addict, who as you say, should always be corroborated."

"Yeah, I guess."

"Were you aware that she also was one of the eyewitnesses in the Serrachia case?"

"I was aware."

"An eyewitness that Detective Indelicata found?"

"Yeah."

"That's a hell of a coincidence, isn't it? Did you wonder about that?"

"I thought it was a hell of a coincidence. Weirder things happen in Washington Heights."

"You had more concerns about it than that. You were asking after her last week, weren't you?"

Alex couldn't keep the stunned expression off his face. How did the AUSA find out? Informants in the DA's office? Or a phone tap on *him?* With the counterterrorism legislation and FISA, it was easier than ever before for the government to monitor your phone or email. "Yeah."

"Why would you do that?"

Alex felt his heart convulsing. "I respectfully decline to answer the questions on the grounds that I'm being compelled to be a witness against myself."

The jurors glanced at one another, their faces puzzled.

If he revealed that he'd found a dozen or so cases where Weltmayer testified, the ones where he believed that Vito had bribed her to perjure herself and claim eyewitness seats to the event, then he would be firing the gun at Vito, but at himself, too. Because the next question was, if you suspected this, why did you not report it to Internal Affairs, to the DA, or to the New York Attorney General? Then you have your conspiracy charge.

Sullivan, unperturbed, bobbed his head. "Fair enough." He picked up a hefty file, one of the many occupying the table beside him. "You know what this is?" Smiling politely, he handed Alex the folder.

Alex read the label on the file. His stomach plunged into thin air. "My medical records." *They subpoenaed this? How?* He almost yelped the word, *"Fuck,"* at once dumbfounded and daunted by the awesome power of a federal grand jury to subpoena whatever they wanted. Everything was in that. The alcoholism, hospitalization, rehab, PTSD, depression, the antidepressants he had been taking since 2005, covered up by himself, his boss, and his squad, so no one would challenge his competency, and he would not lose his gun. The damned grand jury had it. Why? To make him look too crazy and unstable to be on the job? To make him look dishonest, for concealing his mental illness? So many possibilities, and none of them good.

"I'd like to speak to my attorney," he croaked. Defense lawyers were not allowed in the grand jury room, but a witness had the right to consult with his or her attorney at any point. Kima could contest the admissibility of his records. At the very least, she would advise him again to ask for immunity and turn state's witness, but he needed to buy time.

Sullivan's smile went from smugly polite to placating, as if he was the most reasonable guy in the courthouse. "Yes, well, I think it's starting to get late, and it is Friday. Why don't we leave it here and pick it up again when we reconvene on Wednesday?"

The jurors looked livelier than they had been all day. This was interesting, more than a parade of witnesses droning on about the minutiae of death investigation. It had drama. Far too much.

Panic stung Alex's eyes like tear gas as he scurried out of the federal courthouse and ran along Centre Street, to the City Hall subway station. His tripped, his foot twisting, and fangs plunged into his ankle. He fell against the turnstiles, searching for his Metrocard with shaking fingers. More than anything, he needed a drink, the one thing he was not meant to have. Had Homer Simpson, that modern guru, called alcohol "the cause and solution to all of life's problems?" That should be written on his gravestone.

On the 7 train crossing from Hudson Yards to Times Square, he felt motion sick as the train bucked across the tracks. Lights flashed. Wheels and suspension shrieked, as if the steel itself was ripping apart. Most of the lines had upgraded their trains, but the 7 clung onto the '80s deathtraps, like a time-travel carnival ride. *Times Square-42nd Street*. He dashed to the next platform, chilled to his bones but sweating.

Once home, he curled up on the sofa, his laptop balanced on his thighs. Frantically, he hammered out a letter of resignation to Gibson. Each sentence felt like cutting his own flesh with a penknife. What would he do without the job? Write a book, a screenplay, consult for the movies? Isn't that what retired homicide detectives do? Private detective work? Investigating philandering husbands and wives – that would make him suicidal again through sheer tedium. Travel – visit Elana in Australia.

Maybe stay there for a while. Ellie would love that. With no hope for the future, he finished the letter, printed it, then sealed it inside an envelope.

.

Chapter Thirty-Four

Superficially, life looked normal and routine. Alex had to read the cell phone tower dump Verizon had sent him. He also had to read the financials for Moreno's apartments, and he wasn't great at numbers, so he hated making sense out of financials. The forensic accountants had translated it into English, but not even the NYPD's best and brightest could make him better at math. Gemma Lennon's lawyer had filed a 250.10 notice with the court, a notice of intent to proffer psychiatric evidence in connection with an Extreme Emotional Disturbance defense.

He reread his notes from his interviews with Lennon. Farah had asked him to produce evidence that she *was* rational, but, quite frankly, she wasn't. Fog rolled through his head, and he lost track of which documents he was reading, finding himself staring at Vernon Geberth's words: *Death investigation constitutes a heavy responsibility, and as such, let no person deter you from the truth and your own personal commitment to see that justice is done... Remember, we work for God.* He'd pinned the quote to the side of his cubicle.

After roll call, he asked Gibson for a meeting.

"What's up?" she asked. "How was your testimony yesterday?"

He handed her the letter.

She ripped it open, then stared at it in silence for two or three minutes. Finally, she said, "That good, huh?"

"Yeah."

"Also, what the fuck?" She dropped the letter on the desk and unwound her orange scarf.

"I think I'm gonna be a liability, ma'am," he explained sadly. "For you and for the squad."

"In what way?"

"Lots of ways."

She studied his face with an unwavering gaze. "I'm not accepting this. This isn't you. This is your illness. This is you not thinking straight. What the hell have those federal prosecutors found?"

"My lawyer says I should keep my mouth shut."

"I'm ordering you to tell me. It affects you. It affects the squad. I gotta know the scale of shit we're in. Look, I know they're going after Vito Indelicata." She crushed the letter in her fist. "Now, I'm thinking you got something on Vito, something that isn't hearsay. I mean, everyone in the Bureau has hearsay about Vito, but that ain't gonna convict him of shit. So... you gotta tell me why you think you're a 'liability.'"

Where to start? "They've subpoenaed my medical records. All of them."

"So, what? Everyone and their dog knows you been in rehab."

"Everyone and their dog doesn't know I've been diagnosed with PTSD and depression, and I've been on meds for it since 2005."

"And? The department's got policies now. It's not the '80s. You can't discriminate against people for mental health issues."

"Bullshit." A headache rapped against his forehead. "Don't you see the line of questioning? 'Lieutenant, did you know that Detective Boswell had a mental health condition that made him a danger to himself and others? Did you know he was suicidal? Did you know he injured himself by putting his hand through a stained-glass window? Are you aware that he was still suffering from symptoms of post-traumatic stress disorder and depression after he returned to work and continues to suffer them to this day? Are you monitoring this? Are you trained to monitor this? No, you're trained as a law enforcement officer.'"

Gibson looked unconvinced. Her dark brown eyes hardly moved during his monologue. "Again, so what? Neither you nor I are under any legal obligation to disclose anything about your mental health. And for what it's worth, I sent you to one of the best damn psychiatrists in the city, who's been monitoring this for the last five years. You're getting yourself wound up over a lot of nothing."

"It won't be nothing. You *know* I'll have to be examined by Occupational Health. They give me enough hassle about my gunshot wound. And I'm getting flashbacks again." He hated his condition. It would nail his balls to a wall someday.

"Does Gillard know about the flashbacks?"

"Yeah. We're working on it."

"Okay. You're up and down but haven't hurt yourself again. Right?"

"Yeah, but they ask me about it, along with the alcoholism and all that crap, I look like I'm too nuts to be on the job, and I covered it up."

"What does the US Attorney really want? You think he actually cares that you have depression and PTSD? I doubt it. He's using it to rattle your cage."

"He's rattled it," Alex admitted, his shoulders slumping.

"I see that. What do you have on Indelicata?"

He rested his chin on his hands and stared bleakly at her.

"Tell me."

"You could be subpoenaed."

"I don't care. Tell me. That's an order."

His lawyer said he shouldn't, but he had been a cop for thirty years, and when your lieutenant orders you to do something, you do it. So, he did. Gibson listened closely, absorbing every word. Her eyes widened a fraction. Like when he told his lawyer (without the protective shield of attorney-client privilege), he felt the lightness growing, gaining power, buzzing around his nerves, something trapped for almost two decades spreading its wings.

"*Jesus*," Gibson exclaimed when he finished. "What does your lawyer think?"

"She thinks I should ask the prosecutor for immunity and tell them all of it." He spoke wearily, the airy feeling collapsing under the weight of the mess he was in.

"Well, yeah."

"I took the Fifth when the AUSA started asking me about it yesterday."

"Why would you do that? Make a deal and tell them what happened."

"Rat him out?"

"You think he deserves your loyalty? Alex! You walked out of there with a broken rib!"

"Probably broken," he muttered. "I never got it checked."

"My God, assholes like Indelicata get away with this shit for years. I'm sick of cops who treat the people we're policing like animals. That's not what this city needs. He's knowingly made innocent people do twenty years for murders they didn't commit. He does whatever the hell he wants with no regard for anything, anyone. And everyone turns a blind eye. Whatever. They don't care. That kind of lazy corruption, sexism, racism is what's *wrong* with this department. This country. But police reform will only happen from the inside. Not standing around writing op-eds in the *Times*."

Surprised by her vehemence, he jerked his head backwards. She was usually warm with her detectives, but cool and calculating about her politics.

"You know, Alex," she said, holding his gaze. "When I joined this department, we – well, Black officers – still got insulted at shift changes and at roll call, and we were stuck on foot posts, or as undercovers. They thought we were there to fill quotas. That's it. And if you were a woman, nevermind a Black woman, that made it a hell of a lot worse. Having to work twice as hard, and they thought you were half as good. Guys grabbing your ass. Bosses promising promotions if you'd sleep with them, and if you got a promotion for being good at your job, everyone thought you'd slept with the boss. And when Irma Lozada got killed in the line in '84, remember that? Everyone said, well, she was a woman, the perp overpowered her, maybe she shouldn't have been out on that post. They started wondering if any of us female officers should be doing the same jobs as men. Too weak, too soft. You think people said that about you and Eddie Trenemen when you were shot? About Ed Byrne? I'd just made sergeant, and I thought, they're never giving me a command post. Well, they did, but… When I made lieutenant and got promoted to C/O of the Seventeenth and then this squad… Jesus… The *shit* I had to deal with. Officers under *my* command who'd act like I was some kind of secretary. Men who thought they had a God-given right to not take orders from a woman. Every fucking right-wing rant about feminism, about affirmative action, and then some. I'd worked so hard to make lieutenant, but I'd wonder whether it was worth it. Every night, I'd lie awake in bed wondering that. It was people like Indelicata who liked it that way, who fought against the department changing, who thought women *should* stay as secretaries or matrons, like we couldn't be 'real police' and definitely couldn't be C/Os. When female officers work cases with him, he makes sexual comments in a creepy, demeaning way, or worse, like – calling it what it is – assault, putting his hands wherever the fuck he wants, like grabbing your thigh or your boob or just saying you have nice tits. And he acts like he's got some Goddamned privileged chauvinistic right to, and no one's gonna give a damn. And, well, no one does. They just give him Detective of the Month. I got a file full of complaints about him from the women in this squad *alone*, but you think Indelicata's bosses or my bosses or IA give a shit? I've told them, but they don't care. 'Boys will be boys,' they say."

Hadn't Alex heard stomach-turning rumors for years, whispered in precinct corridors or implied after a few beers, or noticed the way his female colleagues eyed Vito askance? Yes – but everyone knew that a cop was more likely to get a command discipline for being late rather than for telling a colleague that she had nice tits.

"Second thing," Gibson continued. "This department only ever gets better when someone steps up and says, this is wrong. Like Serpico. You got a chance to expose this piece of work for what he really is. You've known that since he railroaded those guys into murder raps and pinned you to that damned wall. No one's listening to me. No one's listening to any colleagues he's assaulted or harassed. No way in hell are they listening to civilians who've filed abuse of power lawsuits. There've been plenty. But right now, the US Attorney's listening to those wrongfully convicted defendants. That's sure as hell something. That's huge for police reform; huge for civil rights in this fucked up country." She tore his resignation letter into tiny strips and dropped the shredded paper. It floated anticlimactically into the trashcan beside her desk. "Alex, do not sink your career for this asshole. He ain't worth it. Now, where are you with those affidavits on the Lennon case? Al-Sanneh doesn't think she's emotionally disturbed."

Alex fluttered his eyelids, his brain stalling. He'd fired himself up for his dramatic exit from the NYPD, but Gibson sucked the air out, plummeting him gracelessly back into the work. Sniffing, he said, "I'm gonna read the case file again. I didn't think about it much last night."

"I'm sure you didn't."

"I guess most of the people we collar are disturbed in some way," he offered, because she'd ordered him to focus on the case and say something. "I mean, they committed a fucking murder."

"She kept the cover up story going for a while, until you put her in a corner," Gibson observed.

"Yes, she did."

As he opened her door, she stopped him with a hand on his arm. "You said you were in terrible pain for more than a month after that interrogation, and you *never* went to a doctor?"

He shrugged unthinkingly. "My side always hurts, and I couldn't be bothered bullshitting an excuse for why it had gotten worse. I'm used to dealing with it."

"Men." Hands on hips, she rolled her eyes. "Okay. Take care of yourself."

"Yes, ma'am."

Dazed and off-kilter, he returned to his cubicle and absently riffled through the Lennon binder. A year or so ago, a show had popped up on his television while he channel-surfed, a detective with bipolar or PTSD or something like that, and the guy bounced off walls, disobeying orders, shouting at his supervisors and partners, but the upside of it was that his illness made him a genius, the best detective in his department. Bullshit, Alex had thought. This illness didn't make him a better detective. It just made him feel like crap.

And here he was, calling himself depressed, saying he had post-traumatic stress disorder, but did he truly know what those conditions felt like? Not in the same way he knew what a bruised knee or the wound in his side felt like. When he was younger, it wasn't depression or PTSD; it was sorrow, fatigue, loneliness, which he first dealt with by drinking a lot, then later with work, AA meetings, swimming until he fell over from exhaustion. Was it easier in those days? He couldn't answer that. But he had an affidavit to write, so he read the Geberth quote for the millionth time, then he wrote his affidavit. As he'd always done.

Two days after the grand jury testimony, Alex and Ray held vigil on a darkened rooftop on East 108th Street that had a view into the apartment where Derek Brickl, Moreno's friend and 'business partner,' allegedly dealt cocaine, MDMA, and assorted synthetic narcotics. The detectives mounted scopes on the parapet, aimed at the windows of the place they were surveilling. During a cursory interview, Brickl had maintained that he was beyond drunk when Moreno was shot. Furthermore, he swore that he had absolutely no idea who would want Moreno dead. Alex had a feeling that this mope was the first in a long line of witnesses waiting to lie to him.

He squeezed his nose with a tissue. His sinuses stung, irritated by dust and smog encircling this rooftop. Bored, he whittled at an *NY Daily News* crossword while keeping one eye on the scope. Surveillance was rarely not boring. This fit the pattern. The target lounged like a stranded whale on his couch, watching TV on a screen covering most of the wall. The bodies of naked men and women flickered in the scopes. Porn. Slinging must be paying well if he could afford a giant flat-screen television.

"You wanted to *resign*?" Ray sputtered. He played with his smart phone but raised his eyes.

"Who told you that?"

"Cat."

"How'd she know?"

"How would she not know? Is the grand jury thing *that* bad?"

"I don't know." Alex crinkled his brows. No secrets in the Homicide squad, but had there ever been any? "They've got me over a barrel, and I don't know what I'm gonna do about it."

"What kind of barrel?"

"I don't wanna get into it. I said before, I don't want to put you in a position where you gotta protect me or perjure yourself."

"You told Gibson."

"Yeah. She ordered me to. You don't outrank me." A bleak smile played at his lips.

"She talked you out of resigning."

"Yeah, well, she basically told me to man up and tell them what they wanna know."

"Are you?"

"I don't know."

"You did something in the '90s. You should come out and say it."

"It's more like what I didn't do." Alex picked at his thumbnail. Ray had both high standards of ethics and chutzpah. Had it been him in that interrogation room all those years ago, he would have blown the whistle. Fuck Vito and his threats. But no one would ever suspect Ray of corruption or substance abuse anyway.

"Okay, if Vito did something, you should tell them."

"I dunno, Ray, I'm looking at my options with my lawyer."

"Does Hurley know?" A tint of jealousy shaded Ray's voice.

"Hurley doesn't know a thing." Alex cast his partner a sidelong eye-roll. Sometimes, it felt like Ray was a current girlfriend, James the ex, and the two were bizarrely covetous over him.

"Don't you tell him everything?"

"No, I don't." Ulcers gnawed through his stomach. He'd gotten himself scoped the other day. To his dismay, they'd found a small bleed. This again. But he was stressed, overusing ibuprofen for his wound, and not eating well. Cat had fetched him from the hospital because they wouldn't release him on his own after light anesthesia, and Ray had family things while James had been in Boston, collaring a perp.

"You sure you're alright?"

"No, you're giving me shit, and I've got enough shit going on." Alex peered through the scope, willing the skel in the apartment to do something more noteworthy than watch porn.

"Like a bleeding ulcer. Seriously, your medical history with these things isn't great. You need to be careful."

"Yeah." Alex irritably drew out the vowels, half-closing his eyes. While Cat had no discretion or filters, she wouldn't criticize anyone else for their poor lifestyle choices. That had been a relief. A whole car ride from Columbia Pres to West 87th with no one lecturing him. "Do you know a four-letter word for 'religious image?'"

"Uh, 'icon?'"

The word fit. Alex wrote it on the crossword, then he squinted through the viewfinder. The target smoked a fat spliff. Alex scribbled in his memo book. "What about 'garret?'" He spelled out the word. "Any idea what that means?"

"I think it's like an attic."

"Thanks—"

"You ever thought about cutting back on the amount of coffee you drink? It'll make your stomach more acidic, and you're like the worst coffee junkie I know. In a detective squad, which is saying something. No one needs six or seven cups a day."

"I think about a lotta things. Like applying for a wiretap warrant and bugging that guy's phones."

"Sure. Wouldn't be stupid. But I'm serious about the coffee thing."

"I get that. But I'm an addict. I'm either bingeing or cold turkey."

"You could try coming off it. It's not great for your gut or—"

"No."

Sighing, Ray rose to his feet and kicked some empty beer cans away. He stretched one leg forward, then the other, arching his back and rolling both his shoulders as he extended his arms. Yoga. Of course. "My back was getting stiff," he said, responding to Alex's doubtful stare.

"Who wrote *Walden?*" Alex asked. "High school English was way too long ago. Has an 'o' in the middle and a 'u' at the end. How many fucking words end in 'u'?"

"Thoreau," Ray answered.

Over the next two or three hours, Brickl smoked his body weight in weed. When he finished watching porn, he put on a movie comprising entirely of fiery car chases, but no one visited the apartment. Deep into overtime, the detectives bailed on their surveillance, packing the scopes away. If Brickl was dealing, he either didn't do it from this place, or he had no customers tonight. They could bug his phone, download his emails, or bring him in for the third time.

Ray gave Alex a lift to his apartment, commenting, "We're off, day after tomorrow. Thank God. What are you doing?"

"I have another meeting with DeSilva, then I'm gonna go to Staten Island and see Hurley."

"Why?"

"He said he wanted to meet up."

"About those '90s cases?"

"I'm fucked if I know, Ray. Maybe he just misses me."

He unlocked the door, the keys uncooperative in his cold hands. His heart stung with a sudden loneliness that cut him like a knife in the dark. Ray was driving back to his wife and three kids in Queens, and here he was, thirty years on the job, his body falling apart, and no one waiting for him after a late stake-out. The city crumbled and decayed, and no matter how many incompetents, dimwits, alcoholics, drug addicts, psychopaths, and good people driven to some terrible terminal anger he arrested and fed to the voracious maw of the criminal justice system, it demanded more, always more, and he gave it everything he had like the loyal servant he was. What had it given him? Alcoholism. Chronic injuries. Post-traumatic stress. A misbehaving GI tract. A federal investigation.

Chapter Thirty-Five

At 1900 hours, Alex clambered through the throng in the West 86th Street subway station, dizzy and achy with exhaustion after working an eight-by-four, with overtime, on the heels of the late-night surveillance. He navigated Broadway's four lanes, then Amsterdam's. When he glimpsed his reflection in shop windows, he flinched at the images of his pallid skin, greying hair, and craggy wrinkles under his eyes. He wasn't losing much hair, but it was greyer every day.

His iPhone beeped. A text from Sarah. *I saw a clip on the news about that case where the woman killed her kid. It showed you taking her somewhere in cuffs. That was a weird conversation we had in the hospital when you were there. I thought maybe we should spend some actual time together. I'm free tonight. But you're probably working.*

Baffled, Alex stared at the text, wracking his brain for the best response, or the least harmful, or the least stupid. On one hand, he wanted to lie down and not deal with anyone, not his colleagues, not his kid, not even the guy in the pretzel van. On the other hand, if he wrote that he wasn't feeling well or whatever, it would be another excuse in a lifetime of excuses she had never forgiven him for.

You can come over to mine tonight if you want, he typed. *I'm tired and not going out. Can cook something.*

Sarah replied, *Cool but I'll bring take-out. I'm vegetarian. Don't think you know how to cook vegetarian.*

He shoved open his front door, his hands tight to his body. Another vegetarian. It was catching, like an epidemic. How long had Sarah been vegetarian, should he know this already, and would she be pissed at him because he didn't?

If his ignorance of her dietary restrictions bothered her, she hid it surprisingly well when he let her into the apartment. She kissed him on the cheek, shocking him with genuine affection. "It's nice to see you, Dad. I haven't been to this place in ages." That made for a change – not leaping down his throat over some trivial misdemeanor. She had bought food at Kramer's, the kosher place on Broadway and West 84th, and she ate blintzes with onions and mashed potatoes, while he picked desultorily at brisket marinated in red wine sauce. Cramps rippled along his gut. Acid stung the back of his throat.

"What's wrong?" she asked, noticing.

He jabbed the brisket with his fork. If he lied outright to her, she would know. She was his kid, after all. Swallowing the brisket, he confessed that his ulcers played up. Stress at work with the high-profile case wasn't helping.

"Jesus, Dad. You know you've got problems with your stomach, you've had them for years, and you shouldn't let it get to the stage where—"

"Honey, I've been getting shit from Ray—"

"I'm not giving you shit. I'm saying I'm concerned."

"I'm fine, and you're plotzing." And she wondered why he avoided telling her things.

"If it's work causing you trouble, maybe you should think about retiring. Ellie thinks the job is too hard on you."

"If that's what Ellie thinks, she can always email or Skype me and tell me herself." Ellie had never said anything like that to him, but who knows what she talked about with Sarah.

"She knows you won't listen. Have you at least seen your doctor?"

"Yeah. I've got the prescription I need. Hypochondria-by-proxy runs in this family. Jesus." It had skipped a generation, from his mother to his daughter. On his fiftieth, his mother had sent him a 'happy birthday' e-mail, almost a thousand words, reminding him that his father had died of a heart attack, and he should get his heart checked out because his job and his lifestyle made him high risk, and she hoped he understood that. He did; he appreciated that genetics weren't in his favor, and he got his heart looked at once a year or so, but he found the patronizing e-mail maddening.

"It's not hypochondria when it's a real condition, Dad."

"Honey, we said we were gonna try to not fight, right?"

"Yeah. Right. What are they giving you for it? You're not on any kind of blood thinner, are you? Lots of guys your age are."

Instead of volleying a wiseass barb about *guys his age,* he grumbled, "No, I'm not. Here, this is what they have me on." He handed her the boxes.

"Okay. It's good you're not on anticoagulants." Sarah examined the meds. "That's the whole nine yards. They're not fucking around."

"No, they're not gonna fuck around."

"Are you still getting your liver function tested?"

"Yeah, I am and it's fine. So, what's with the kosher place? I thought you'd show up with a Chinese." Radically changing the subject, a time-honored tactic in interrogations, awkward meetings with supervisors, or conversations with his family.

"Oh, I'm trying to eat kosher now. Most vegetarian food is kosher anyway."

Alex raised both eyebrows. "You are? Since when?"

"Since I joined a synagogue. I'm trying to... I don't know... reconnect with our heritage and be more Jewish. The Union Temple of Brooklyn. It's a Reform congregation."

Alex couldn't hide the surprise on his face.

Sarah seemed unsurprised by his surprise. With uncharacteristic patience, she explained, "I thought it might help me, you know, figure myself out. It's a big part of who our family is. Our history. I know Mom sent us to Hebrew school, and we sometimes went to Temple, and I remember sitting shiva when grandad died, but we were too young to get it, and I know you didn't... and don't... bother, but like I said to you when you came to my apartment, I've been going to a therapist, and I wanted... I dunno... to like, connect with something deeper. I needed that... Like the traditions. The synagogue's really good, though. It's not just about going to Shabbat or showing up at service on Yom Kippur. They do seminars on what it means to be Jewish, on philosophy, on ethics. They do social action in the community. And they're really welcoming."

"Okay." He touched his front teeth with his tongue, at a loss for a response, but he suppressed his natural sarcasm. "Yeah, that's all... That sounds like a good thing."

"You don't get it." She was astute, like him.

"No, I'm never gonna personally get anything outta religion, and God knows I don't need to go to Temple to feel guilty, but it helps a lot of people." Sarah had always been chasing something, searching for self-actualization. With drugs. With nursing school. With a series of useless boyfriends. Why not Judaism?

"Did you know your great-grandfather?"

"What?"

"The Russian one. Did you know him?"

"Oh, not really. He died when I was two or three."

"Huh. I was talking about him to the rabbi. You know, how he had to flee Russia. I was curious about what you knew."

"Not a lot. My father said he didn't talk about Russia. Well, not really Russia. It was the Ukraine. But it was pretty fucking horrific. Like 2500 people died in the pogrom he escaped in Odessa."

"You know a little," she said.

He bared his teeth, furrowing his brows together. "I know bupkes. I Googled it once."

"What about your great-grandmother? Did she emigrate?"

"No, she was born here. She was called Sarah Spiegel. I think her family emigrated from Germany around the 1850s."

"What was great-grandad's name? Like his real name. Not the one we have."

"Mikhail Beskryostnov."

"Huh." She struggled through the train crash of consonants. "I guess he changed it so he could fit in."

"Yeah, he changed it 'cause he was afraid of anti-Semitism, and it sounded too foreign."

"Our name isn't Jewish at all."

"I think that was the point."

"Did he speak Yiddish?"

"Yiddish, Ukrainian, and Russian." Alex had a smattering of Yiddish words and no Ukrainian or Russian. Three languages, vanquished with three generations of assimilation.

"Do you know what he did, once he got to New York?"

"I think he worked in a sweatshop, like a lotta people. I honestly don't know that much. If you can stand a conversation with my mother, you should ask her. She knows a lot more than I do. Without resorting to Google."

"Yeah, I might." Sarah studied the grey-blue carpet, her eyes distant, as if lost in the Lower East Side's overcrowded streets at the dawn of the twentieth century. "I wonder if you still have relatives over there. Or in Germany."

"You know we have relatives in Germany. Dad's brother's family lives in Berlin."

"I know, but I mean, like from before your great-grandparents moved here. Have you ever tried looking?"

"I've never cared that much, to be honest."

"Oh." A pained look momentarily shadowed her features. "I might try one of those online things."

"Yeah, you should if you're interested. I'm sorry. I'm not feeling great. We were doing surveillance on a perp until 0300 hours last night, and I had to be in work at 0800." Sending her out after a short visit felt wrong, too abrupt, and pangs of self-reproach squeezed his heart. But tiredness superseded his hopes of staying semi-vertical or controlling the smartass.

To his surprise, she did not protest or guilt-trip him. Nor did she return to the conversation about his health and retirement. Instead, she gathered the take-out boxes and cleaned the dishes, which made him wonder who this young woman was and what she did with Sarah Boswell. Even more shocking, she gave him a tight hug as they stood in the doorway.

"Hope you feel better, Dad. Just don't be so damned stupid about your health."

That sounded more like the Sarah he knew.

Another kiss on the cheek, then she flitted through the door with cheerful assurances that she would see him sooner than a few months from now, which he didn't quite buy, but maybe she was trying to reshape her life and her relationship with him.

Chapter Thirty-Six

Early in the morning, Alex and Kima reviewed his testimony while the city held itself in its 0730 repose. The law office was bizarrely quiet, like an empty concert venue. No phones, faxes, or associates interrupted the meeting. This time, he enlightened her about his psychiatric diagnoses, showing her the scars on his left hand. It hadn't seemed like stuff she needed to know before the AUSA pointed his medical records at his head like a loaded firearm. Telling Kima felt like pulling the trigger himself. But she hadn't been a cop for a long time; someone who would see him as weak or doubt he could be reliable backup. It hardly fazed her. After all, she was a criminal defense attorney with clients who made him look as poised and unflappable as Barack Obama.

Her lips puckered while she absorbed his story. "Okay," she said after a moment. "Concealing your illness isn't in violation of any laws or regulations—"

"It makes me look too outta control or incompetent for the job," Alex countered, his voice quivering. "I coulda done anything. That's how it's gonna play to that grand jury. And Occupational Health don't know. If the department ever figures it out, I'll be killed by the bureaucracy, whether they send me to a rubber gun squad or not."

"You can talk about stigma and police culture all you want." Kima considered the window overlooking the park's mist-shrouded trees and meadows. After a moment, she moved her eyes to his face. "But what worries me is the fact that you concealed something, whatever the reasons. You concealed it to protect yourself. It's not fair or ethical, and it's definitely a dick move, and I can exclude it from evidence in trial court, but rules of evidence that affect a trial jury don't apply to them. Look, honestly, Alex, nothing's really changed since our last meeting. Your mental health stuff isn't the real issue. Not for the civil rights case. But you gotta seriously consider asking him for immunity. If he thinks it's in his interest, I can work out at a deal with him, for now, to postpone any further testimony until we fully consider our options. Like I said before, Indelicata's a high-profile target. He's made himself a celebrity. His face is everywhere, like he's gonna do a cameo on one of those reality shows...*"

"Has he?"

"Do I look like I watch reality shows? I don't know. But you *know* he deliberately set up Quixano and Serrachia and that other defendant you mentioned, and God knows who else to take those murder raps. He badly injured Quixano. Have you read the lawsuit? The guy suffered post-concussion syndrome for years. He injured *you*. *That's* how far he'll go. It's the right thing to do."

"You're saying you can get me outta testifying this week?"

"Yeah. So long as Sullivan thinks he can get something out of it. A pretty tenuous case against you for perjury, one that probably won't hold up to a motion to dismiss. He'll struggle to prove any of this was willful without your testimony. Or, if you make a deal, a stronger case against Indelicata for more egregious civil rights violations, witness tampering, obstruction. Trust me, he'll be interested."

"That makes me an unindicted co-conspirator?" He flexed a wearied eyebrow.

"Yeah, but it's better than being an indicted one. And you were under duress."

"Great." Alex didn't feel ready to flip on Vito, but he assured his lawyer that he would think about turning state's, if only to save himself from reappearing before the grand jury on Wednesday. Kicking the can down the road, but a lot of criminal justice was a can-kicking exercise.

He jumped on the next downtown C train and then boarded the bright orange ferry sailing from Whitehall. The boat unmoored itself, its diesel engines grinding. Alex spent the crossing sitting on the top deck with the wind tussling his hair. A vision played through his head: hurling himself over the railings, vanishing under the slate grey waves. It would solve his grand jury problems, but the MEs always told him that drowning in the East River was an unpleasant way to go, your body freezing but screaming for air as icy water filled your lungs. Tourists milled around near the railings, crowding one another for photos of Manhattan and the Statue of Liberty. They chattered in a dozen languages. The shimmering skyscrapers of glass and steel reared above the choppy water, hiding the city's grotesque, oozing underbelly from wide-eyed tourists on the top deck. They saw one city, but Alex knew another. He ran his tongue over his salty lips as he watched the flat shoreline of Staten Island draw closer.

The ferry lumbered into the docks. Alex followed the tourists over the footbridge, texting James, and then he found his old partner at South Beach, a vast strip of golden sand on the east side of the island. The beach curved towards the Verrazano Narrows Bridge, diaphanous cables and iridescent towers of steel and light slung between Arrochar on Staten Island and Fort Hamilton in Brooklyn. Once the longest suspension bridge in the world, until they built a longer one in England.

A salty sea breeze blew into their faces as seagulls swooped and shrieked overhead. They threaded around sunbathers scattered in the sand like a seal colony. Alex told James about Sarah's visit last night – her sudden uptake of Judaism and interest in his great-grandparents. He didn't tell him about the cutting.

"She's always been kind of a weird kid," James reflected. "Remember her goth phase?"

"Yeah, that was fun," Alex said, breathing in the brackish scents of seaweed and salt. "Her trying every-drug-known-to-man phase."

"I thought you said you scared her off heroin and crack."

"I thought I did. I hoped I did. But who knows? It's not like she'd come clean to me. She probably *tried* everything."

"Probably. But she's got her act together now."

"Sort of."

"Just like her Dad," James teased.

"Jesus." His eyes rolled backwards into his skull. "Everyone's on my fucking case."

"Anyway, I dated a woman who went to that congregation. They were pretty chill."

Alex scuffed his foot into the sand. "Oh. Who was it?"

"Julie, the ER doc."

"The one who dumped you 'cause you were double-dipping with that bartender?"

Emitting a short bark of laughter, James answered, "Yeah. Turns out, that was a fuckin' shit strategy."

"Who woulda thought, huh?"

"I was keeping my options open. Honestly, though, lots of people wanna dig into their family histories, like they can fill some hole in their lives if they know where they come from. My sister's been trying to contact every Hurley in County Leitrim. And there's more than you'd think."

"I didn't know she was into genealogy."

"She is now. Got into it when she went on vacation in Ireland last year and realized it's green and has lots of men with hot accents, and people aren't pissed off all the time."

"Unlike Boston or New York in every way. I guess it's better if Sarah's trying to figure out her shit by going to Temple or learning how to make borsht, instead of putting it all on me."

"For sure. Does she know you're back on ulcer meds?"

"Oh, she gave me shit about that. Said I'm not taking care of myself."

James scoffed, "She'd be right! Alex Boswell SOP."

"Don't you fucking start." Alex stopped walking and balanced on one foot. He poured a tablespoon of sand out of his right shoe.

"You got it under control now?"

"Yes," Alex said impatiently. "I'm on all the drugs." And foregoing the ibuprofen, so pain gripped his side like an angry pitbull.

"This middle-age thing sucks," James confessed. "You know, my doctor didn't like my cholesterol. Said I should do something, you know, like exercise. Or I'll be old and fat and dead."

"We're all gonna end up that way."

"Yeah, but I wanna put it off as long as possible. I've started jogging. At least I've got the beach here, so it's not like being a fuckin' hamster on a wheel in a gym."

Alex's laps in the pool were somewhat hamster-like. He found the repetition calming. "Ray thinks he'll live forever if he does enough yoga and gives up... I don't even fucking know what. And my kid's now a kosher vegetarian. It must be contagious."

"Last time I talked to 'Princess Ray,' he'd become vegan."

"He's off that now. I think he told me he was on this caveman diet thing. No grains or gluten, but I've given up on following his diet-of-the-week."

"No bread or pasta. That's fuckin' bleak, dude."

"Yeah, like how people ate before agriculture. He says it's meant to be healthier."

James guffawed, swerving around an old buoy, washed up and tangled in seaweed. "You know where it's really at? Cryogenics."

"Cryogenics?"

"Putting yourself on dry ice, like a frozen pizza, so they can bring you back to life in the future."

"They don't put pizzas on dry ice, James."

"I know, but it's like the idea of freezing the pizza. So, the pizza lasts forever, and then when you want it, you stick it in the oven for ten minutes."

"It's just you who thinks frozen pizzas last forever." Alex let a wave splash across his foot. "Most people actually throw them out after considerably less time than five or six years."

"Yeah, and I don't see why. I've never hadda problem." James giggled. "Just goes to show... Freezing keeps shit viable for way longer than anyone thinks."

"Yeah, right. People die of hypothermia when they jump into the fucking Hudson. After five minutes."

"There's a guy in some little mountain town in Colorado who's frozen himself, just waiting. They even have a holiday there to celebrate the fucker. 'Frozen Dead Guy Day.' Your sister's still in Colorado, isn't she? You should ask her about it."

"Sure."

"But dude, you gotta tell me, what the hell went down between you and Vito Indelicata?"

"What?" Acid sloshed against the ulcers, burning. Alex hadn't expected the conversation to leap from Frozen Dead Guy Day to his disastrous legal problems. How had Ray known? Sometimes, he wondered if his current partner and ex-partner conspired together.

"Gibson called me. She asked if I knew about something that happened when you interrogated Guillermo Quixano in '92. I said I didn't have a fuckin' clue 'cause I wasn't there. I barely remembered the case. Had to look it up. The vic was that guy who'd been decomposing in a basement."

"Medina," said Alex.

"Medina, yeah. At the time, I thought, no one's closing this motherfucker."

"I'd written it off by 1991."

"You and Vito collared the perp a couple weeks after the Heights riot." James swatted whisps of hair away from his eyes. "I'd been bottled in the head, so I paid zero attention. I had no fuckin' idea what was going on."

"Did Ray call you?" *About those '90s cases?* Alex couldn't chase Ray's comment out of his head. Ray speaking to James? Civilly? They couldn't stand one another! Ray thought James was a douchebag, while James thought Ray was so far up his own ass, he'd arrived at the small intestine. The worst part was that they both believed they knew the best way to handle Alex. As if he needed handling.

"Okay, yeah, he sent me an email," James growled, sounding annoyed. "Got his underwear in a twist about what you weren't telling him. He thought you'd told me, and I was like, no. I mean, something got fucked between you and Vito, but I sure as shit don't know what."

Alex studied the way the white edge of the sea raced up the glistening sand, but then withdrew into the ocean's oily mass, as if it didn't like what it saw.

"What the hell happened?" James pushed. "Why's the grand jury after you? *Everyone* knows Vito gets up to fuckin' sketchy shit. The guys who were that detective squad ain't gonna say jack against him. For the rest of us, it's all hearsay. But... you know something. Gibson said you did, you told her, and Espinosa's suspicious as hell. He's a twat, but he's a good detective."

By telling DeSilva and Gibson, Alex had released his secret. The hole where it cowered for years had opened like an exhumed grave. He picked up a rock, worn flat and smooth by waves and sand. He flicked his wrist and elbow, spinning it into the sea. It skipped lightly across the dark water, three or four leaps. He skimmed another rock, then another, as if the smooth motions of rock-skimming could help him process everything that happened and not telling his best friend any of it. But rocks just disappeared into the waves. Giving up skipping rocks, he sat on the sand and wrapped his arms around his knees. The sea breathed in his ears. Like a perp after a long interrogation, he told James everything: the ballistics analyst's lost report, Vito's fickle witnesses, and, finally, the hardest part, Quixano's interrogation. The heavy surf was battering his heart, whitecaps frothing with relief, anxiety, guilt. Because he was ratting on Vito. Because he should have told James years ago. Because he was telling James now. Part of him was horrified at what he was doing, but it felt as though he'd become two people, one trying to hold his tongue while the other felt relief at finally telling it all.

James blurted, "Holy fucking shit, why the fuck didn't you talk to me about *any* of this? He pulled evidence out of his ass to convict this poor son of a bitch because it was *convenient*. He threw you against a *wall*. He had the butt of his gun in your ribs? The *right* side! You must have been in agony. I can't even imagine it. Your side got worse around then. I came back to work after my concussion like a week later, and you were limping around, looking sore and totally fuckin' miserable, for months. People knew you'd taken a beating in the riot, so we all figured it messed with your wound. I can't believe you didn't tell *anyone*. Fuckin' hell, man."

"Quixano was indicted, convicted. What was I gonna say?"

"You used to look up to Vito like a puppy dog –"

"I didn't!"

"You did. Why the fuck do you think he liked working with you instead of anyone else in MNHS?"

"He worked with whoever caught the case."

"Well, yeah, but he brought you *in*. You were in his circle, man. No one else in the squad was."

"I didn't see it that way. And I really wasn't." Alex stared broodingly at the water, retracing contours of the validation he'd once felt when Vito took him under his wing. The memory was so distant and unreal that it felt like it had happened to someone else.

"It was that way. Then, I dunno, you got weird about him. You said you wouldn't work with him. *Everyone* thought you'd slept with that girl he was fucking. The cute one who wasn't his wife. I knew she wasn't your type, but just figured you realized he was a jackass, and you were being you, you know, a little bit nuts, but I was happy you'd stopped looking at him like he was fuckin' Columbo. You wanted to *be* Vito."

"Everyone wanted to be Vito," Alex sighed, his side aching.

"*I* didn't," James refuted. "I know everyone thought he was like this super-sleuth, like that guy in that movie, every movie, but I always thought he was a douchebag and fulla shit. He almost single-handedly started a riot that damned near got us killed. Remember that? 157th?"

"Yeah. I worked a case there a few years ago. Perp…or witness… we could never prove it either way… lived in an apartment next door to where that club used to be. I thought about it 'cause I was sitting there for a while, on surveillance. It's a barbeque joint now."

"Any good?"

"It's alright. Has good wings."

"Huh. Anyway, Vito's that guy… the guy who if he weren't so damn fat, he'd be blowing himself and putting the videos up on YouTube."

Alex pursed his salty lips and squinted his eyes. "What? Is that even physically possible?"

"Remember me telling you about investigating a murder related to a porn ring last year, like my first case after joining Queens Homicide? That took me down some weird fuckin' rabbit holes of the internet. You'd be amazed at what's physically possible."

"A super-sleuth giving himself a blow job. That's an image I won't get outta my head. But Vito's still a cop."

"Yeah…" James' blue eyes turned icy. "One who caused you as much pain as he could. He knew what he was doing."

411

"Doesn't matter. I can't testify against him."

"Believe me, you can."

"What happens when I do? I'm a whistleblower, a rat. No one in the department will trust me again."

James lifted his eyes towards the bulbous cumulous clouds hanging from the sky. "He's not the guy who skimmed a few bucks off the top of drug busts. Like, who cares, right? It's not even Knapp Commission shit. It's fuckin' worse. He injured you. Could have punctured your liver. Gibson's right. You should have seen a doctor. He put guys in prison on life sentences who didn't do the crime, and he damn well knew it. He *knew* it. It's not like this forensics crap, where it turns out bite mark analysis and all that is bullshit, but we believed it 'cause it was fuckin' science. That's an epic fuck-up, but it's not like there was any *intent* to railroad people. Who prosecuted Quixano's case?"

"Leon Mitchell and then Padraig Whelan." Mitchell, who had put Ernesto Serrachia in prison without questioning the evidence against him. The framers of the Constitution, Mitchell once said, could never have imagined the destruction drugs and violence would wreak on this city, living in a utopian world where there was no crack and no semi-automatic handguns.

James puffed out a breath. "Yeah. God, what fuckin' sleazebags."

"On the other hand, they didn't really believe in the exclusionary rule, so it made our lives easy."

"Mitchell went to work for Giuliani, didn't he?"

"Yeah," Alex brushed his old wound with his fingers, but just as fast, he let his hand drop, hopefully before James saw it. "That's why Whelan ended up as first chair on Quixano's case."

"Mitchell and Giuliani. A match made in heaven. Mitchell died of cancer, God rest his fuckin' slimy soul, but where's Whelan?"

"Moved to Ireland after all the mishegoss with screwing that journalist." Whelan was accused of ethics violations after sleeping with a reporter and, allegedly, telling her confidential information about cases. He fled the country before the New York State Bar Association disbarred him.

"Oh, yeah. What a prick. But seriously, Lex, you gotta testify."

"I took the Fifth."

"Fuck's sake." James stopped mid-stride. "Don't do that. When has a totally innocent person ever taken the Fifth? What do Gibson and your lawyer think you should do?"

Alex dug his finger into the corner of his right eye. "Ask for immunity and tell them everything."

"Well, there you go."

"I can't work if people don't trust me."

"You've been a homicide cop for like a million years. Just… grow a pair and stop being so fuckin' intimidated by Vito's juice. Okay, he got some medals, probably 'cause he gave out blow jobs to the right people, and he published a piece of shit book and went on TV, but he's not God."

"He thinks he is. That joke was going around the department for a while. 'What's the difference between God and Vito Indelicata? God doesn't think he's Detective Indelicata.'"

"So, what? His book still sucks. Just 'cause it made a bestseller list don't mean it's good. It just means people buy crap. I mean, people watch *The Apprentice* and shoot each other over a couple grams of cocaine. People are fuckin' stupid."

Alex scooped up a rock and flung it into the sea without skipping it. He raked his fingers through his hair. "I still look too nuts and unstable to be on the job in that book, and the US Attorney's got my medical records. That jury watches TV. They see people with PTSD on TV acting crazy and violent, getting flashbacks. And I'm a guy who carries a gun. Doesn't matter that I've only hurt myself. Doesn't matter that I can barely get off the floor when I'm ill. What are they gonna think?"

"Fuck the stigma. It's not indictable. Look, if you testify to that grand jury, you'll be saying what half the fuckin' NYPD knows anyway. Maybe they don't have the balls to say it, but they fuckin' know it."

"I'm not sure *I* have the balls."

"What do you gotta be immunized for anyway? Being assaulted isn't a felony."

"Lying about it sure is," Alex said roughly. "I perjured myself at that trial, James. The feds can prove that. They can say I deprived Quixano of his civil rights when I gave that bullshit testimony and never came forward while Quixano spent the last fifteen years in Attica."

"What testimony? I don't remember."

"Good. Means you can't perjure yourself to the grand jury if they call you back."

"Come on, Lex." James grabbed Alex's right shoulder.

At this point, he couldn't dig himself a much deeper hole. "They asked me on cross if I saw Vito beat up Quixano, and I said I didn't. I said I left the interrogation 'cause I was hurt in the riot and didn't feel well, and I don't know what happened after I left. I lied like a fucking rug. Quixano knows I was there. Vito knows I was there. The guys in his squad know I was there. There's probably a 'five somewhere, just waiting for some asshole to send an FOI request, that says I was there. But what the hell was I gonna say? There might've been some half-assed IA investigation, but Vito woulda made damned sure they found out about my drinking. He'd have flaked me with half a ki of coke, and *I* woulda lost the gold shield."

James drew in a thoughtful breath, letting sand and broken shells fall through his fingers. "Son of a bitch. No, you're right. I get you. I wish you'd told me, though."

"You woulda tried kicking the shit out of him. That's why I didn't."

A small, lopsided grin tugged at James' mouth. "Probably."

Alex felt like his brain was wrapped in membranous strings, and each contraction of his heart tightened the strings. "How many perps have we interrogated?" he said rhetorically. "We coulda got false confessions without beating them up, just being too damned good at it."

"Don't think about that. I did, you know, after the Central Park Five thing and those other ones, but then, well, it's a lotta fuckin' stress looking at every interrogation you ever did, so fuck that. Nothing we can do. Nothing. We did the best we could with the evidence we had. Anyway, you know how these negotiations with prosecutors work. Why's DeSilva so sure you'll get immunity? You got something other than Quixano and Serrachia?"

"Yeah, I do… There's more. There's shit the US Attorney and the *New York Times* don't know about. But I told DeSilva. She's as smart a legal strategist as anyone you'll meet. She'll sit on it 'till she thinks it's useful, but she knows." Alex marveled at James' philosophy of *fuck that,* forever James' easygoing attitude towards things that might bring on stress and heartache. James had never been a great giver of fucks. Consequently, very little made him depressed or sorry.

"What are you talking about?"

"I kept my mouth shut about Quixano, so Vito didn't think I'd ever rat him out. He had too much on me. And he had the juice to flake me. Probably without going near the shit himself. He had people. I think he had pals in the Dirty Thirty." Alex fell off his train of thoughts, watching half a dozen seagulls flapping and bickering over abandoned French fries. His stomach flipped one-eighty degrees. The gulls shrieked at one another.

"What's he done? I mean, what *else* has he done?" James joined him in staring at the gulls. One group squawked and circled above the birds who were hording the fries, divebombing and screaming.

Alex felt like he'd touched a powerline. His heart tripled its speed. Dammit, he regretted his candor. They climbed onto the fishing pier and wandered along the rickety wooden planks taking them out to sea. At the end of the pier, they halted. Grey sweeps of sea rushed up against the wooden legs supporting the structure above the water, and the detectives looked out at the container ships and oil tankers, hazy elongated forms marching across the horizon towards harbors and refineries in New Jersey. James sat down on the edge of the pier, his legs dangling, the shimmering water lapping below his feet, brownish-grey with a tinge of green when the sun caught it.

"You're not gonna leave me in suspense, Lex."

Alex fixed his gaze on the ships. He was holding a smooth, oval-shaped beach rock, and he massaged it around his palm, like the captain in *The Caine Mutiny.* "You remember the year I quit drinking?"

"Christ. That was a fucked up year. We were all drinking enough to sink one of those huge ships out there." James waved his hand at the tankers. "I mean, people joked about it...Saying Alex is the resident alcoholic, every squad has one... But no one thought of it as a serious thing until it was."

"Yeah. Least of all me."

"But who talked about that crap? I'd sit around with Marty and Bill, saying, 'well this fuckin' sucks,' but... it's like we couldn't even bring ourselves to be straight about it." Exhaling, James looked fleetingly saddened. Not typical of him. "Where's this going?"

"I was a mess. Then shit started hitting the fan with the McDonough case. You remember?"

"McDonough? Christ on a fuckin' bendy bus. It's not that."

Alex curled his lips into a troubled grimace. He flung his beach rock into the sea with enough force to wrench his shoulder. "Yeah, it's that."

Part 8

Chapter Thirty-Seven

December 1994

The mayoral election in 1993 was all about crime. Like the election four years beforehand, it came to a battle between David Dinkins and Rudy Giuliani, but this time Dinkins was weary, bloodied and beleaguered by a city reeling from recession, crack, violence, and the riots in Crown Heights and Washington Heights. Giuliani, an aggressive federal prosecutor, promised law and order. He promised to be "tough on crime," accusing Dinkins of being soft on crime, roaring in campaign speeches, "Entire neighborhoods have been turned over to drug gangs now."

New Yorkers were fed up with crime, tired of muggings on the subway, tent cities in vacant lots, and squeegee men at intersections; they were tired of the garbage and graffiti suppurating like infected sores on the city. The people who taped Giuliani signs on their windows didn't live in the most crack-ravaged neighborhoods, but they saw the rapacious headlines about crime, constant reminders of cases like the Central Park Jogger or Rabbi Liebowitz or Baby Hope or the riots in Manhattan and Brooklyn. The people who lived in those neighborhoods, on the other hand, felt too marginalized to have much hope or interest in the democratic process. For his part, Giuliani made it plain that he stood with the police department. The police unions backed him, and he showed up at a demonstration by police officers at City Hall in the fall of 1992 who were protesting the mayor's policies. The protest erupted into pandemonium; officers trampled the hoods of parked cars and barricaded City Hall. Cops believed that Giuliani was on their side, and other New Yorkers, nostalgic for the days when the city seemed less lawless, voted for him. He won.

Alex, like any homicide detective, was perfectly aware that murder rates had in fact been falling. 1993 had been comparatively quiet. Only 1,946 murders, an improvement over the 2,245 of 1990. Not that 1,946 was good – it just wasn't as bad. Alex found himself closing more cases, helped in part by science; advances in DNA identification, forensic entomology, mass spectrometry analysis of trace evidence, to name a few, but he also perceived that people on the war-torn blocks in Harlem and the Heights showed more alacrity in cooperating with him. People were sick of the violence. They didn't particularly like the police, either, but they could live with the cognitive dissonance of cooperating with a homicide investigation while despising the TNT units raiding their apartments and locking people away on long prison sentences for possessing a few grams of cocaine or weed. Not all of them and not all the time, because the inner-city was still the inner-city, but enough for Alex's clearance rate to creep upwards, past sixty percent. He hadn't been impressed by Dinkins' handling of the O'Keefe shooting or the riot in Washington Heights, but at the same time, he doubted that Giuliani possessed even a notional grasp – and even less compassion – for the conditions in New York's poorest neighborhoods. Still, everyone he knew voted for Giuliani, and he reluctantly did so as well, if only because Dinkins, however one might view his policies, was decimating the morale of the NYPD.

Giuliani and his Police Commissioner, Bill Bratton, roared into office like an Atlantic storm. They introduced everyone to Broken Windows, the theory that if minor crimes go unprosecuted, people will feel emboldened to commit more serious ones. They deployed hundreds of officers dedicated to enforcing 'quality of life' offenses, collaring graffiti artists, public urinators, the homeless, squeegee men. They brought in 'stop and frisk,' a controversial policy that allowed a cop to search anyone for drugs and guns if he or she had 'reasonable suspicion,' and no one was naïve enough to believe that the NYPD would be egalitarian or colorblind in its application. They shut down sex shops and peep shows in Times Square and everywhere else, including the one next to James' apartment, much to the detective's disappointment.

Then they introduced CompStat, a bureaucratic nightmare of paperwork which eroded some enthusiasm from rank-and-file police officers. It was a system for tracking crimes in every precinct, using statistics to pinpoint criminal hotspots where more police resources were needed, then targeting those areas with rapid deployment. Weekly CompStat meetings with precinct and squad commanders took place at

One Police Plaza, where a commander would get a public ass-kicking from borough chiefs if their precinct had a crime surge and they didn't seem to be doing anything about it. C/Os were anxious; no one wanted to be in the hot seat at 1PP, so they breathed down the necks of investigators and patrol.

Through policy changes and reshuffles, the justice system lumbered forward, its inertia slow but insuperable. During those final weeks of 1994, Guillermo Quixano went on trial for the 1990 murder of Jose Medina. The first Legal Aid lawyer had quit when Broken Windows flooded the system with defendants, precipitating a strike at Legal Aid, and then Quixano's new defense team filed continuance motions, delaying proceedings so they could bring themselves up to speed. Alex heard on the wire that the prosecutor had offered Quixano a plea of man one, but Quixano, insisting on his innocence, refused to accept it.

Alex was pretty sure that Padraig Whelan knew about the coerced confession. The ADA had a phrase for that sort of thing: "Good police work." At trial prep, Whelan told Alex, "Quixano got beat up when he was being held in the Tombs before his arraignment," in a tone giving Alex the firm impression that it was in his best interest to go along with the story. With the ADA and every other police officer on the case willing to say under oath that the confession was lawful, what could he do? In a city where a federal prosecutor had just won a mayoral election, most judges and jurors seemed likely to believe cops over a drug dealer.

Besides, he had to live with it, one way or another. Following any meeting with Whelan or pretrial hearings for Quixano's case, he numbed himself with whisky until the guilt and pain stopped gnawing through his insides. Those whisky bottles drained quickly, and occasionally, he worried about his alcohol consumption bolting out of control, like after the riot.

Even James perceived him drinking more, commenting one night, "Dude, you're hitting it a bit hard."

"It's fine," Alex said. Was it? If James noticed, he should probably cut back.

Quixano's trial opened. The prosecution's case-in-chief consisted of the accused's coerced confession, the doctored ballistics report, and Vito's eyewitnesses. Elizabeth Weltmayer told a muddled story and disintegrated on cross, confusing cases and defendants, while Luca Martinez, who had more crack in his head than brain cells, couldn't say how he ended up with the Colt. He'd stumbled across it somewhere. Or maybe someone had paid him to take it. It was two years ago, so how could anyone expect him to remember? He never convincingly tied the firearm to Quixano, either. The lab analyst sweated buckets and looked terrified, but he held up under cross.

When Alex took the stand, his direct examination was monotonous, a tedious recitation of his career, beginning with high school. It plodded through every SOP of death investigation. At first, he lied by omission, saying nothing that hinted at the conversation or drug deal between Vito and Weltmayer. He didn't breathe a word about the first ballistics report, the one contradicting the report admitted into evidence. The former document no longer existed. With a straight face, he testified that they'd found the Colt pistol in a stash house, under Martinez's direction. Yeah, he perjured himself, but the only complainants were his conscience and Quixano. Neither had the strength nor standing to object. A half-ton weight sunk into the pit of his stomach.

Cross-examination, however, would be testing. The defense lawyer asked him if he had assaulted the defendant, which he denied, not perjuring himself because he hadn't. Next, the attorney asked if Alex had seen Indelicata assault his client. That void of swirling emptiness reached towards him, and he felt his intestines snarling up like the Holland Tunnel with lane closures. The defense lawyer stared at him, his face composed, unreadable. Quixano slowly shifted his gaze upwards, from the floor to Alex. Sadness shrouded his face like a veil. Alex found himself holding in a breath. He let it go, his lungs heaving, and he said that he'd been injured in the riot – his back and his old gunshot wound hurting – so he left the interrogation room before Quixano confessed. As soon as the words flew out of his mouth, he felt both nauseous and relieved, an adventitious lightness twisting through his body. He'd dodged the question and only half-perjured himself – he did leave, and he'd been hurt. Those two statements were true.

Undaunted, the lawyer asked, "Were you aware that at some point, during the process of being arrested, booked, and arraigned, while my client was supposedly in your custody, he was injured? A fractured skull and broken ribs, to be precise."

"I was aware, but like I said, I left, so he wasn't in my custody the whole time." The sweat under his armpits soaked into his jacket. The wound in his side throbbed in time to his heart.

"You're saying you have no idea how he was injured?"

"I heard something about the Tombs, but I have no first-hand knowledge." How spectacularly would he tank a polygraph right now!

"Really? Well, I have my client, in a deposition in the civil suit which he's filed against the NYPD, saying that you witnessed Detective Indelicata violently assaulting him. Are you saying my client lied under oath?"

"I guess so."

"My client also said, under oath, that he asked for counsel the moment you placed him under arrest at LaGuardia Airport? Is that true?"

"No." Talons tightened their hold around his throat. He fixed his gaze on the scratched and chipped wooden doors on the opposite side of the courtroom.

"He stated, again under oath, that you and Detective Indelicata ignored said request for counsel and therefore interrogated him unlawfully. Is that true?"

"No."

"Or are you lying under oath?"

"Objection," piped in Whelan tonelessly, as if bored. "This is argumentative. Detective Boswell has already said more than once that the defendant did not request an attorney and was not in his custody when he was injured."

"Sustained," announced the judge.

The Legal Aid lawyer glowered at the judge, displeased; he knew the system had stonewalled his client, but he saw no path through it. The judge was uninterested in his arguments. He abandoned his cross there. Alex looked away from the lawyer's shrewd glare. The man was smart and streetwise, impeccably aware that whatever he said, the odds were hopelessly stacked against his client – getting an acquittal would be like moving a mountain.

Whelan bounced to his feet for the redirect. "Detective Boswell, defense counsel mentioned his client's litigation against the police department, wherein he alleged excessive force and due process violations. Are you aware of the outcome of that lawsuit?"

"It was dismissed as unfounded," Alex said flatly. He tasted something metallic, like adrenaline or blood.

"Thank you, Detective," the prosecutor said in a smarmy tone.

The judge dismissed him from the stand. He sensed Quixano's gaze boring into his flesh. Sorrow, disappointment, but not surprise. A white cop, or any cop, would uphold the thin blue line. Guilt rolled Alex's stomach under a nauseating wave, but he evaded eye contact with the defendant, beelining it for the door while staring at his feet. *The truth wouldn't help you anyway,* he thought as he glanced at Quixano over his shoulder. They could destroy Alex's credibility in a minute if they wanted.

A week later, the jury convicted Quixano despite the glaring weaknesses in the prosecution's case. A sign of the times, the skyrocketing collective fear of disorder that got Giuliani elected. Alex imagined the jury deliberations: the man was a drug dealer, part of the problem with the whole city; who has reasonable doubt? The foreman read out the verdict, and Quixano uttered no sound, only bowing his head, seemingly shrinking as he stood at the defense table, astute enough to know that a Latino man – especially a man involved in the narcotics trade – stood little chance against the criminal justice system, a colossal, voracious dragon eating everything in its path. Due process, the jury trial, and the defense lawyer, the only things standing between a defendant and the dragon, hadn't protected him. Court officers cuffed him and led him away, while his wife cried out to God in Spanish and then, with their three children, collapsed into sobbing spasms on the benches. Quixano cast an aggrieved look at Alex, his pain chiseled into his features.

The dragon will devour all of us, Alex thought. He had no power to stop it, no more than Quixano or a Legal Aid lawyer. Halfway through a bottle of Glenlivet, which he chugged after a four-by-twelve on New Year's Eve, he promised himself that he would work harder for the people of uptown Manhattan, for the victims who deserved more than the hollow facade of justice, a winking system going through the motions. No wonder the communities of the inner-cities resorted to their own extrajudicial justice. What had the state ever done for them, beyond proving over and over that it could not help anyone, no matter how poor or desperate, and that it had no interest in guilt or innocence, or life and death? One man alone could not counteract the arc of history that led to the state's apathy and the proliferation of drugs, poverty, and violence in the inner-cities, but dammit, he would push cases forward, with passion, determination, velocity. This work mattered, and it should be done with sedulity, even when the country and his police department showed cold indifference. He would be a throwback to detectives like Eddie Trenemen, who worked every single case until there was nothing left of it to work. He would abandon corner-cutting and shitcanning, cynically prioritizing clearance numbers and CompStat above the victims and justice itself. He would hunt for substantive evidence, beyond three-point fingerprint matches, tentative eyewit IDs, or inventive forensics. He would relinquish any lazy dependance on unreliable informants who will tell a detective anything. And he would keep his distance from Vito, a solar system of distance in that two square mile precinct. Since Quixano's interrogation two years ago, he'd been dodging any investigation associated with Vito, stretching as far as bribing colleagues to take them when he answered the phone on the wrong case. They wondered why, and rumors abounded, insinuating that Alex had slept with one of Vito's mistresses. But Alex preferred that story over the truth. The thought alone of working with Vito sent his blood pressure soaring and heart pounding.

On January 2nd, he typed out Vernon Geberth's "Remember, you work for God" epitaph and tacked it to his cubicle. Geberth's maudlin quote would keep his ass in line. Eddie had loved that quote and lived by it. Naturally, his colleagues assumed he'd posted it ironically, which made him like it even more.

As if openly defying Alex's promises to the Glenlivet, the work became unrelenting, and the squad politics felt insufferable. The detectives grew short-tempered with one another. No one had the energy for practical jokes. Minor misdemeanors, like leaving dishes in the squad room sink or hogging the photocopier, ballooned into class A felonies. Passive-aggressive memos circulated around the office. When investigations went to shit, they were quick to blame one another's personality flaws and investigative methods instead of the usual suspects – uniforms, precinct detectives, and ADAs. The city's drug problem showed no signs of abating, but Corcoran, stressed by CompStat, ramped up the pressure to raise clearance numbers. Nights out became prolonged back-biting bitch-fests; kvetching about supervisors, politicians, police unions, and anyone who wasn't in the pub that evening.

On a cold March afternoon with snow flurries teasing the city, Corcoran stormed into the station house after a CompStat meeting at 1PP. Everyone in the squad room buried their heads in paperwork. A couple detectives left the building. They knew homicide rates were dipping throughout the city, except for the 30th Precinct, where they had gone up. So far, the Three-Oh remained a murder hotspot, with twenty '95 homicides already, and it was only March. The detectives threw surreptitious glances at their boss' face and knew the CompStat meeting hadn't gone well, Corcoran and the Three-Oh commander taking the heat.

Pausing by Alex's desk, Corcoran demanded, "Boswell, in my office."

That tone never meant anything good. Warily, Alex snuck a swig from the whisky flask in his desk drawer, liquid strength against the flak coming his way. Still one of the younger investigators in the squad, he caught more than his share. Eight years of death investigation should shield him from the boss' moods. It hadn't yet.

His time right now could be spent on the case he had caught yesterday, a DV homicide where the vic had fled her abusive boyfriend, holing herself up in a women's shelter, only for the perp to stalk her to the shelter and ambush her with a Smith and Wesson Model 36 when she went out to buy food. Or it could be spent on the one he caught last week, a Bangladeshi taxi driver shaken down in a lot on West 110th Street and then shot. Forensics told him the tire tracks near the taxi belonged to a sports car, and witnesses reported seeing a black coupe – or maybe a blue one – leaving the scene. Or he could be following up the case he'd caught two weeks ago, an employee in a West Side hardware store who stabbed his boss after the manager fired him for stealing hard-earned drug money from said manager's side-hustle. The employee gave it up to Alex after an eight-hour interrogation, when Alex brought the guy around to the idea that if he admitted to fighting with his boss over the cash and the cocaine, and somehow the man accidentally ran into the knife, he wouldn't be charged with murder.

Alex had observed to James, "Thank God most perps are stupid."

Why did his boss want to read him the riot act? Because of a lousy CompStat meeting? He had put the hardware store case down. He had written an airtight arrest warrant affidavit for the DV case. His clearance rate crept towards the mid-sixties, the national average and fucking respectable for a detective who spent his career working cases in a city with some of the highest crime rates in the country.

The office door rattled closed. The noise had a chilling finality to it. Corcoran's face looked as gloomy as the dead eyes of the Irish revolutionaries on the wall behind him. "Boswell, I'm looking at all these overtime sheets, and I see you're putting in far more than just about everyone else. This gets expensive. What are you playing at here?"

"I'm trying to close cases, sir. And I am." His philosophy of working a case by hunting down everything in sight and grasping at every scrap of information meant that he worked a lot more overtime.

"Don't be smart, Detective," Corcoran snapped. "I can't be having people putting in this much overtime. It's not in my budget."

"I'm getting results, sir. You wanna lower murder rates here, you gotta show people you can solve murders."

"It isn't working. They are up in the Three-Oh."

Alex could also read CompStat reports. "And down everywhere else. Even the Three-Four."

Last year, the new Commissioner had split the Three-Four Precinct at 179th Street, making a new precinct, the 33rd, between 179th and 155th. Bratton suggested that more resources could be thrown at the roughest drug corners if the precincts covered smaller geographical areas. Matt Cohen had taken his sergeant's exam and left MNHS to command the new detective squad at the Three-Three. They had sent him off with the debauchery expected of the Homicide squad, a party where the last thing Alex remembered was moving a bathtub, found on the street, into Matt's apartment, then waking up on the floor of the Two-Five's disabled toilet. He'd been freezing, curled into a tight ball on cold tiles, unsure of how he'd traveled from SoHo to East Harlem.

"I *want* them cleared," Corcoran said. A red blush infused his pallid cheeks. "I understand. I don't need you to tell me why we need to do our jobs. Sure, I get what you're doing – I just don't have the budget for it. That's the issue, so it is. So, find a way to do it without all the extra overtime. And please, so God help me, clear some homicides in the Three-Oh."

Alex considered the irony. In a single breath, Corcoran told him to clear more cases and work less. A hot knife stabbed into his stomach. He resisted the instinct to double over. Stress. Or something he'd eaten. Grumbling a sullen, "Yes, sir," he sulked out of the office, then he bitched to James that the boss had hassled him about the overtime.

"You're doing way more than you used to, but man, you're getting shit done. Look at all the black next to your name on the board," James said. "He's got a stick up his ass from the CompStat meeting. Don't worry about it. He'll get over himself."

"We're all doing twice as much work now anyway," Alex complained. The Commissioner, in his unbridled enthusiasm for crime prevention strategies, had shrunk the budget and personnel of retroactive units like detective squads, and detectives who retired or transferred weren't being replaced.

At the start of the next day's tour, Alex, arriving late, shuddered at the somber atmosphere infecting the squad room. *Who died,* he thought, but kept it to himself. No one looked like they would laugh. The A team detectives and Brady, Keohane, Vasquez, and Ryan weren't insulting one another. The A team cleared out. Vasquez said he had to interview a witness and disappeared. Ryan took off for a meeting in the DA's office. No one teased Alex about being late and mildly hungover. He revisited a case file and notes he'd written a few days ago, working out a game plan for tracing a gun that Street Crime had confiscated from a teenager they'd collared on a narcotics warrant. The teenager hadn't committed this homicide, a 1993 cold case, but Alex had wheedled the kid into telling him that he'd bought the gun from a guy with one leg, with the street name of One Leg. Apparently, One Leg had found it lying in a gutter. *The fuck he did.* Alex tracked down One Leg's real name and his rap sheets. Closing a two-year old cold case – that would make him feel like he was worth his detective's shield.

Why wasn't he as lucky as James? When they showed up at the scene of a fatal stick-up job in the Three-Oh two weeks ago, James had eyeballed some skulking bystanders and liked the look of a white, wild-eyed crack addict. James made eye contact, and the crackhead flung his hands into the air, crying "Oh, my God, I'm sorry, I did it. I needed, *needed* twenty dollars." He threw a Colt Detective Special onto the road, then hurled himself at a surprised James' feet. "I know I have the right to remain silent, but I'll tell you everything." When interrogated, he said that he thought James had psychic powers. James was delighted.

"Why do they never confess to me when I *look* at them," Alex lamented.

"It's 'cause you don't have psychic powers," James chortled.

Corcoran disturbed his reverie with a curt, "Boswell, in my office, please."

I'm getting shit from all sides. Alex ground his fingertips into his aching forehead. He could do with psychic powers for reading his boss' mind, and he readied himself for the second 'come to Jesus' meeting of the week, or worse, a transfer order, or a command discipline for being chronically late, or maybe someone had complained about him or accused him of some malfeasance, and Internal Affairs or the Civilian Complaints Board had their eyes on him.

As Alex bumped the door shut with his elbow, Corcoran fiddled with a clicky pen, then said, "I'm sorry, Alex. I've been really hard on you, so I have. It's just that I've known some of the lads for a long time, when we were all in the One-Zero-Zero together, and then I formed this wee squad with them. I do treat some of the younger detectives differently."

Alex stared at his boss, dumbfounded. Only once in eight years had Corcoran called him by his first name – in the hospital, after he'd been shot. The man must be smoking crack that the TNT squads had confiscated from drug raids. "Huh?"

"What I'm saying is that I haven't been in the right frame of mind for this for a while. I've also got one kid in college and the other's about to finish high school, so that'll be two kids in college. So… I'm bringing you in here to tell you that I've been offered a chance at a promotion. Assistant Borough Chief of Detectives for Brooklyn. I'm needing a change, so I am, and the money will be useful. I've been talking to everyone individually, so rumors don't go too wild. You have another day before your next RDO?"

A brick had just clouted him in the head. Too stunned for words, Alex nodded.

"When you come back in, I won't be here anymore."

Alex digested this information. Unlike a lot of the guys, he had never been best friends with the man. You needed to be a member of the Emerald Society to join his inner circle. Still, Manhattan North Homicide was Corcoran's squad. He formed it. He guided it. He protected it from the whims of chiefs higher up the chain-of-command. He glued the squad together. Not having him there anymore felt surreal and worrying.

Clearing his throat, Alex said, "I'm sorry to hear that, sir."

"It will be better for you lads too," Corcoran said. "New blood."

"Do you know who they're reassigning here?"

"Sure. Lieutenant Jo Gibson."

"What's he like?"

Corcoran smiled, his blue eyes softening with amusement. "She. Joanna. I know her. She's a great cop. You'll be in good hands. She's from the 'hood', you know, the projects." He hesitated before the word 'hood,' as his speech had always been too proper, with the slight Irish lilt, to sound anything but weird when he used local African-American slang. "She'll know these neighborhoods better than I ever will, sure. I'm sure you will find that useful."

Alex blinked at him. Then it clicked. "Oh, you mean she's Black."

"Yes. And she's from the South Bronx."

"Okay, sir. Uh, congratulations on the promotion."

"Thank you, Alex."

As Alex unlatched the door, the lieutenant added, "Alex, don't worry about the overtime thing."

No wonder everyone looked so despondent, especially the old guard who'd been at Corcoran's side when he formed the squad in 1986. He also doubted that some of them, Rizzo, Brady and Keohane in particular, would take orders from a woman with any grace, even if she was the most competent commander in the NYPD. Well, it didn't bother him. This place could do with some new leadership. Inexplicably optimistic, he settled back down with One Leg's old case files, two robberies, one third-degree assault, and drug possession and loitering. There had to be something here.

Chapter Thirty-Eight

The day Liam Corcoran moved into a corner office at 1PP, Alex, on an RDO, ate lunch with Sarah at a deli called Gustavo's on West 78th and Broadway. It was their first time alone together in a year. Even though he tried reaching out, she held her resentment tight, doggedly arguing that he'd never given a damn about her. When he maintained that he did, she brought up his past offenses, like a prosecutor. A whole grove of olive branches couldn't make inroads.

She'd grown into a morose teenager. She had no interest in school, her grades climbing no higher than a C. She listened to grunge metal, which her mother hated, and she wore strictly black, which her mother also hated. Black eye-liner, black lipstick, black hair, black threadbare clothes with holes like Swiss cheese. She locked herself in her room for hours, blasting her music, or she disappeared with friends who went to raves and almost certainly took a lot of drugs. Catherine tore her hair out and tried to curb the rebellion, with horse riding lessons at Claremont and dance lessons at a Midtown studio, interspersed with being grounded. But Sarah wasn't like her sister, who listened to feminist singer-songwriters, got As, and won a full-ride scholarship at Mount Holyoke, a prestigious liberal arts school in Massachusetts. Catherine blamed Alex, at least his genetics. "Sarah's too much like you. Emotional and moody." A fair point. He tried telling Sarah that he understood; he struggled with his own dark moods. But she seemed indifferent, shrugging him off with finely honed teenage insouciance.

At least she showed up today, and no major crises hit the city and dragooned him into work. She wore a black Nirvana t-shirt, a black leather jacket, and black Doc Martins. They talked about the weather. They talked about her riding lessons and the incongruous riding school in an old tenement building on West 89th. They talked about OJ. "The LAPD fucked up but good," Alex said, then he explained how he would have run that investigation. Better. For the first time ever, she seemed marginally interested in his work. They talked about Clinton. Sarah said, "Why should we care who he's sleeping with? It makes him an asshole, but no one other than Hillary should care." Alex made assenting noises. Yes, he'd grown bored of hearing about where Clinton was putting his dick, and, to his surprise and delight, he'd found common ground with Sarah.

But he knew this truce was fleeting. After inhaling a lung-bursting breath, he swigged half his coffee and swallowed a big chunk of pastrami-on-rye. "You know, honey, your mother and I have some concerns about these parties you're going to." Catherine suspected that Sarah was taking Ecstasy and God knows what else at parties, and she had demanded that Alex, being a cop, deal with it. Although he feared further damage to their relationship, he'd promised to try. Thinking about his kid smoking crack or PCP or shooting dope scared the hell out of him.

Sarah folded her arms across her chest, glaring sourly at him through her blacked-out eyeliner.

"You gotta be careful about what you take," he continued. If only he could backtrack to the stress-free conversation about OJ, Clinton, and Claremont. "I hope you're staying away from crack. It fucks you up. It's not a party drug. It's really dangerous. Like it's fun once, then people get so addicted to it, they go nuts. They sell everything they own. They lose their homes. People are dying. They'll do anything to get a fix. It's awful, fucked up shit. I don't even wanna talk about the things I see. And heroin—"

"Jesus, Dad," she interrupted. "Do I look stupid? I'm not using crack or heroin."

"Okay," he breathed, feeling air whooshing from his lungs. "That's good. But some of that other stuff, like Ecstasy, Speed, MDMA, it's laced with all kinds of shit. Even rat poison. You have no idea. You don't know what's in it. And a lot of the people involved with selling it aren't good people. They're dealing worse drugs like heroin; they're running guns, trafficking prostitutes."

"Since when are you and Mom on the same side? You're saying that just 'cause you're a cop."

"I know it's true because I'm a cop."

"You assume I'm taking it. Is that what Mom told you? Aren't you supposed to be presumed innocent until proven guilty?"

"I'm just telling you to be careful."

"Okay," she snapped with a surly eye-roll. "Who are you? Nancy Reagan?"

"Just be mindful of what people are doling out at parties. I've worked cases where someone's ended up dead 'cause the E was laced with something."

"Whatever."

"Sarah, I need you to take this seriously." He breathed out again through tight lips, thinking, *this is going about as well as I thought it would.*

"I get it," she snarled.

"Good." He wondered if she really got it. Their brief camaraderie had vanished like early-morning fog. "How's school?"

"Sucks."

"There must be one class that doesn't suck."

"Nope."

She held to the one-word answers until he hailed a cab to chauffeur her back to Catherine's. If she was taking those drugs, or thinking about taking those drugs, she should know the risks. Godammit, he had done his best to explain it rationally, like she was an adult, instead of the hysterical 'all drugs are bad' talk her mother had in mind. It made no difference. She was still mad, and she twisted her head as she opened the taxi door to throw him a baleful glare.

Later, he found James, and they went on a bender with an unknowable number of beers and the Glenlivet. Alex woke up in the 42nd Street subway station to an ill-tempered Transit Police officer shoving him with his foot. Instinctively, he showed the Transit officer his shield.

The man grumbled, "Another drunk detective. Jesus Christ, they know how to pick 'em in the Detective Bureau."

Alex croaked out, "What time is it?"

"5am."

"Fuck's sake," Alex groaned as he clambered to his feet on legs that felt like wet spaghetti.

The Transit officer walked away, and Alex shuffled through the long, dingey tunnel to the 1 and 2 platform. The air grew sludgy. His head hurt as if a spike had lodged itself under his temples. Why had he passed out in the 42nd Street station? Where was James? He remembered nothing beyond drinking whisky with James and two other detectives in the Blackthorn. Who were those detectives? Their faces escaped his memory. And he'd rebuked Sarah for doing stupid and dangerous things? What a hypocrite.

A train screeched against the platform. People charged on board like the light brigade. Alex squished himself past a woman half-blocking the door with a four-foot tall pine tree. He hugged the pole inside the train, convinced that he would fall into the tree at the slightest rocking. Nausea surged upwards. *Don't do this to me, dammit,* he warned his stomach. Determined to not be the guy who pukes on the subway, he darted off the train at Columbus Circle, then vomited into a trash can. Commuters scurried past him, eyes ahead, until one guy stopped to offer him a bottle of Gatorade. With a squinty, pained smile, Alex thanked the man. Sugar. Fluids. Might help. He shivered as though he'd lost all his clothes in January. His teeth chattered. He was sweating and freezing, his body too hungover to regulate its own temperature. A roaring sound, an inbound uptown 2, split open his head. Any movement hurt, as if his joints scraped against a sharp rasp, but he boarded the train and survived the twenty-seven blocks without puking. When he got home, he showered, then slept it off for a few hours.

At roll call that afternoon, Lieutenant Joanna Gibson introduced herself. Alex held his palm against the bright pain in his head, kicking himself for going on a bender the night before meeting his new boss. *Way to make a great first impression.* Praying no one noticed, he crumbled an Alka-Seltzer into a plastic bottle of tonic water and guzzled it as quietly as possible.

The lieutenant was only 5'3, stocky, with a sturdy, self-assured manner, and she spoke in a drawling, South Bronx accent. She explained that she'd grown up in the Four-One Precinct, dubbed 'Fort Apache' because it was violent, almost lawless. The police department had seemed like one way to leave the Four-One, where too many young people were falling into the drug trade or drug addiction, so Jo Gibson went to the Academy when she turned eighteen. You had to be tough to survive the South Bronx, even tougher to be a Black woman joining the NYPD in the late 1970s. Her family told her she'd lost her mind. At times, she wondered that too, but she worked her ass off, rising through the ranks.

Three years ago, she'd made lieutenant and got her first precinct command, 'the Gold Coast,' the 17th Precinct. She liked the precinct squad and developed strong relationships with her detectives, but then the Chief of D's tapped her for the Manhattan North Homicide command. No self-respecting C/O would turn the opportunity down, so with a little reluctance, she left her post at the Seventeenth.

Alex overheard Brady muttering, "What's the fuckin' world coming to? Bet she got this job so someone at 1PP could tick a 'diversity' box."

As Brady bitched, Keohane nodded in sad agreement.

Alex chose – as he always did – to ignore them. He liked her, straight talking and scrappy, not afraid of a fight.

Each partner team then had a meeting with the new boss. Fearful that he looked as hanging as he felt, Alex asked his partner, "Do I look fucked?"

"Only a little," James teased. "Nothing a paper bag over your head wouldn't fix."

"Great. What happened last night? I don't remember a thing. I woke up in the 42nd Street subway station."

James smiled ruefully. "That's where you were."

"Where were you?"

"We met Maritza in the Blackthorn, remember? Then went to that club near Grand Central."

Maritza Bernal, a Mexican-American detective from the Two-Eight squad who James had been sleeping with on and off for the past year. Alex had tried pursuing her himself. A couple dates with drinks and dinner but no sex, and then in the women's bathroom of the Two-Eight station house, where he'd gone thinking he might get laid, Maritza had put both hands on his shoulders and said, "I like you, Alex, I really like you. You're kind and conscientious and you care about the work, more than a lot of cops. But you're too sad. I can't deal with that. You're just too sad." Afterwards, she started schtupping James. Alex forgave her, because she was right. In any case, he did not remember drinking with her last night or being in a club. Nightclubs jarred his nerves like a taser in the throat. He stayed out of them unless he was too drunk to remember that he hated them.

"Yeah, so we had sex in the cloakroom, you know, where they hang all the jackets…"

"How'd you get in there?"

"We're cops. We flashed tin and said we had to investigate something." James grinned at the memory. "Then we went to find you, and you were gone. I didn't think you were drunk enough to wander off. I wouldn't have left you if I'd known."

"I was wasted enough to go *into* a club," Alex said coldly.

"Sorry, man."

Alex expected James to have adventures like sex in a nightclub cloakroom. A jealous twinge shot through his heart. Just as swiftly, it faded, because it wasn't in his nature to be angry at James or Maritza. James wasn't sad – he was energetic, crude, and funny. "Don't worry about it," he said. "Look, the new boss beckons." She waved towards them as Marty and Bill exited her office. Marty and Bill didn't look like defendants who had just heard a guilty verdict, so that was a promising sign.

The C/O's office no longer contained the map of Ireland, the hurling paraphernalia, or the dead Irish revolutionaries. It looked like someone had detonated a bomb in an office supply store, with boxes, binders, notepads, and files scattered across all available surfaces. So far, the only personal touches were framed photos showing Gibson's family – two young sons and her husband – and an African mask hanging on the wall where the crucifix used to be. The obsidian eyes on the mask seemed to glow, reflecting the municipal fluorescent lights.

Smiling, Gibson shook both their hands. Her grip felt assuring and friendly. "Detectives Boswell and Hurley. Nice to meet you." She observed them glancing at the mask and added, "Corcoran plastered this office with Irish stuff. Just 'cause my ancestors didn't have a choice about coming here doesn't mean I can't do the same. But I was gonna go for less… like pub tchotchke."

Neither man felt like he should openly agree that a former C/O's office décor looked like pub tchotchke.

"Tell me what you're working on," she said.

They sat down and recapped their open cases. Gibson mostly listened, occasionally asking questions about why they did one thing or not done another, but she ostensibly agreed with their answers.

She didn't comment on Alex's prodigious overtime, nor did she ask James which part of Ireland his family came from and wax lyrical about County Leitrim. "We gotta be solving homicides," she said. "You know, where I was growing up in the South Bronx, no one thought the police cared enough to put any resources into arresting violent criminals there. It's Black, or Hispanic, it's poor. Lots of undocumented folks. So, people figured, they gotta take care of their own business – police ain't gonna do shit. I mean, they'll put people in prison for a few ounces of weed or coke or beat your ass if you look at them funny, but they're gonna do a half-assed murder investigation. People are dying, from homicide, from suicide, from addiction, and no one cares. And sexual assaults, DV cases, well, *nothing* is gonna happen." She scowled, but then recovered her composure. "I know we're under-resourced, but we have to put as much into it as we got. You gotta reach the families, the community, make sure they know we're working the case. They gotta know we're taking the violence seriously, and *we* care about the victims."

Alex leaned forward, listening. He crossed his legs and held his palm against his gunshot wound; he'd been too hungover to moisturize the scars. The skin felt hot and prickly, and his ribs ached.

"Alex, your clearance rate is sixty-six percent? James, you're around sixty-five?"

They both nodded, impressed. And she'd used their first names. She reminded Alex of his C/O in the One-Oh-Three squad, more uncompromising than steel when he needed to be, but easygoing and informal, just one of the boys. Well, or girls.

"That's good," Gibson went on. "National average is sixty-seven percent. It's lower in minority communities. A lot lower. We gotta keep pushing to be better than that. That's what I want to see from this squad. But not lazy. Not half-assed. I want good cases. Smart cases."

James twisted apart a paperclip. "Stop-and-frisk pisses people off. It's as popular as a prostitute at my grandmother's 80th."

"Depends on your grandmother," she deadpanned with a flickering smile.

"Very Boston Irish Catholic, ma'am," said James, suddenly the straight man. "But it doesn't get us cooperative witnesses."

"I get that. But like I said, we gotta show people we – the Homicide squad – wanna solve murders. And we're doing it for *them*, for the victims and communities. Nevermind stop-and-frisk. It's not a policy I personally agree with, but it is what it is. You guys are out in the field a lot? That's good. Even if it requires lots of overtime. Witnesses only cooperate when they trust us. When they believe we give a shit. I can't change the culture of this police department, but this squad can go out there and show that we care about the victims of violence."

It was like she echoed Alex's own thoughts. That was *his* philosophy, his approach to the violence. She would let him work as much overtime as he needed. She would back him when he had a flash of insight or gut instinct. She would trust him.

For a few minutes, the conversation sidetracked into schmoozing about mutual acquaintances, but then Gibson queried, "Oh, have you done a thirty-day canvass of Morningside Heights for that 110th Street case?"

"Not yet, ma'am," Alex replied.

"You should do it."

"Ten-four." Now seemed as good a time as any, and fresh air might cure this hangover. The new boss had given him his head. She'd ordered him to do the things he'd been doing since New Year. Buzzing like he'd shot a line of heroin, Alex grabbed a car and drove to West 110th. He scoured the Morningside Heights corners and apartment blocks for witnesses who saw a souped-up sports coupe or a taxi driver matching the vic's description.

Three hours into his unenlightening canvass, his portable crackled out his call number. Gibson ordered him to attend a shooting on West 153rd, now the new Three-Three's bailiwick. James had caught the case. So much for this canvass, but very few cases got the time they deserved. He jogged back to his car and raced uptown to 153rd, flipping on the lights and sirens to drill a path through motionless traffic. James was already there, interviewing the first officers, and so was Matt Cohen, now supervising the Three-Three detectives.

"Hey, Matt, you look good as a sergeant." Alex patted his belly. "Sitting around at a desk does wonders for your figure."

"Years of sleep deprivation and a shitty diet's done wonders for yours," Matt retorted.

They stood in sight of the DOA, a twenty-something Black male. Two thirds of his head had been blown away. He'd fallen against a hair salon window, and if you were being macabre, you might joke that someone had thrown a pizza at the glass. The precinct detective made the joke. Someone was always going to. A young CSU officer fainted, crumpling into his colleague's arms. The homicide detectives caught one another's eye, amused by people becoming unglued at Washington Heights mayhem.

Alex and James signed themselves into the scene, then crouched on their haunches over the victim. Pain, like a power drill, drove through Alex's stomach, muddling his investigative thought process. This kept happening. Indigestion? An ulcer? The hypochondriac voice in his mind could shut up. He had work to do, like photographing the blood spatter and tagging the 9mm shell casings on the ground. A semi-auto. Everyone had semi-autos now, the reason the department had mandated two years ago that all personnel replace their revolvers with 9mm semi-autos. He fished around the DOA's pockets and extracted a McDonald's employee ID card, a library card, eight dollars in cash, and a driver's license. Donovan King of 7278 Malcolm X Boulevard. East Harlem.

"How's your new boss?" inquired Matt. "I can't believe Corcoran's left. And a female C/O! Gosh, I remember Jean Allan joining the squad in '88, and that was like the most controversial thing in the world."

"World's changing," snorted James. "Still plenty of fuckin' dinosaurs, though, who are *fuming*."

"I bet Mikey's *pissed*," said Matt. "He calls female cops 'secretaries with guns.'"

"There are a few who aren't thrilled. They think taking orders from a woman is like getting their balls chopped off." Alex gently flexed the vic's left arm. It moved without any resistance. Rigor hadn't set in. "But I think she'll be good."

"I heard she was C/O of the 17th squad? That's not a tough gig."

"She was a sergeant in Bronx Narcotics before she got promoted to lieutenant." Alex related. "She's tough."

"She told Lex he could go nuts with overtime," laughed James. "She doesn't know yet what a bad idea that is!"

"She knows it means I clear cases," Alex said matter-of-factly.

James and Matt wanted to run the canvass together, for old time's sake. Anyway, Alex was hands-down the best interrogator in MNHS, so he volunteered to interview the witnesses corralled at the station house. That was almost truthful. He kept quiet about the scorching stomach cramps, and how he couldn't face running up and down stairs for hours.

Gibson met Alex at the Three-Three, saying she wanted hands-on experience with her detectives' work. He wanted to get a sense of her, so he was happy enough to have her at his side. Corcoran never got his hands dirty with day-to-day investigations. In eight years, Alex hadn't once seen him work a crime scene or interrogate a perp. Because he was both curious and outranked, he took a back seat, and Gibson's questioning skills had his respect after the first witness or two. She was a chameleon, fluidly shapeshifting; one moment she was a hardbitten police officer from the Bronx, then the next, she was a disappointed mother, or a consoling sister or friend. She saw the cracks in any witness' street-hardened persona and prised them open.

During a coffee break between witnesses, she commented, "You were shot in the line eight years ago. Took a bullet to your chest?"

"What? Yeah." Knocked off balance, he bit into his nails.

"Does it give you any trouble?"

"It hurts now and then, but nothing ibuprofen can't fix." He downplayed. It hurt to some degree all the time, and he could be petrified by eye-watering pain that lasted for days. He ate over-the-counter painkillers like potato chips. And he'd never told anyone about the nightmares or about his episodes of reliving it. He wasn't going to start with his new boss.

"Okay." She studied his face.

He dropped the eye contact. *Fuck, that was uncomfortable.* The shooting was reported in his personnel file, but she'd seen the things he was hiding. He was sure of it. Regardless, he had a case to work. They called the Gang Squad and then contacted King's friends and acquaintances, tracing his movements for his final twenty-four hours. He probably wasn't in a gang or selling drugs. No record, finished high school, took night classes at SUNY. He worked in the McDonald's on West 125th Street and sometimes drove trucks for a furniture company with an address on West 159th. His boss at McDonald's said he had been there all week, having finished a shift right before he got shot. His boss at the furniture company said he'd been on his way to work. Why would anyone work two jobs or subject themselves to the fast-food industry if they were slinging? Alex and Gibson kicked around the idea that King might have been killed because he got caught in the middle of someone else's turf war. Wrong place, wrong time. Unlucky, like Alex was.

The tour slid into overtime while Alex and Gibson interviewed King's friends and work colleagues, who seemed genuinely shocked and upset. They were wrapping that up when the desk sergeant called the detective squad room, pleading for someone to come down and get King's family out of his hair. Alex and Gibson fetched them. Mrs. King wept, trembling, convulsing, and the brothers raged, threatening retaliation. Unfortunately, they couldn't name the shooter, but they knew the crews who ran that corner. Only *those motherfuckers* would have shot someone so unashamedly, in broad daylight.

While the brothers fulminated about revenge, Alex blenched, sweating, his breathing shallow. Hot pain inside his gut hamstrung his thoughts. He *could* focus on this interview. Dammit, he was used to functioning through considerable amounts of pain. But this seemed different than his wound playing up.

"You want this to go on forever?" asked Gibson, looking from the brothers to the mother. "An endless feud, until everyone's dead. Is that where this ends?"

"Please, let us find the guys who did this and arrest them," Alex added. "If you have real information, like anything connecting your brother to those crews, you need to tell me."

"He didn't," wept the mother.

"We know," Gibson replied compassionately. "We know he was in school, holding down a couple jobs. But had he ever been involved, maybe like when he was a kid? All kids can do stupid things."

437

"No, Don was class, man," the older brother growled. "Just 'cause he's from Harlem doesn't mean he hung out with gangsters. Especially not Dominican ones."

"Well, he did have some friends when he was fourteen, and some of them have been arrested," Mrs. King sniveled. "But that was a long time ago—"

The younger brother interjected, "Since when does the NYPD give a shit? We ain't stupid. We know how it goes. In five minutes, it ain't gonna matter to *you* anymore."

"*I* give a shit," Alex said, lacing his fingers together on the table. "I'm the primary homicide detective on this case. You gotta trust me, even if I don't arrest anyone tomorrow, or the next day, I will make one. Please, let me do my job. Help me do my job. But you kill someone else, my job is arresting you. Where does that leave everyone? Fucking Attica. Is that where you wanna end up?"

Mrs. King wiped tears off her face and grasped her sons' hands. "Listen to the detective. Let the man work, okay?"

The brothers conceded. "Okay. But you better keep us in the loop, you hear."

"I hear you," responded Alex, his lips pursed and serious. God, he hoped he could put this case down. Only then could he give the family a tiny amount of closure. They swiftly exited the precinct, the mother weeping and the brothers shooting venomous glares over their shoulders. Alex released a strained exhalation, his shoulders slumping, then he wearily turned towards Gibson. She was staring into space, her mouth pressed into a thin line, too distracted by her own thoughts to catch the sweat beads on his forehead and the ashen color of his face.

She said, "Now we gotta hope those guys listen, or we got another homicide this week."

"Gotta hope we solve the motherfucking case." He rubbed his forehead with his sleeve. "I'll take another look at the gang angle. I mean, I've found that any skel desperate enough for a couple grams of crack will shoot someone in broad daylight, but maybe those guys were trying to tell us something."

A week later, Alex updated 'fives for the King case, writing that they were interviewing the dealers from that corner, but no one was talking. He left an answering machine message with the family, inflecting his voice with contrived optimism as he reassured them that he was working the case flat-out, making progress. Paperwork somewhat cornered, he escaped the office and recanvassed 110th. Yet again, he unearthed nothing. The taxi driver case spun out in the mud, another whodunit, and he felt thoroughly used up, disheartened. Two more cases with no physical evidence and streets full of witnesses who probably knew what happened but would never tell him. He drove back to East 119th. His muscles and joints burned as if fine grains of sand scraped at his tissues. For weeks, he'd been feeling somewhat unwell, but he hadn't gotten worse or better. A persistent virus? How long do they last?

A take-out coffee cup in hand, he carefully shouldered open the squad room door. *What the hell,* he mouthed, just about swallowing coffee before it dribbled down his chin. There was the entire B team, some A and C team detectives, and Gibson, all standing around his cubicle. Matt was there, parked at Alex's desk. Everyone wanted to catch up with Matt and give him shit.

"It's down," Gibson announced. "Donovan King is down."

"Huh?" Alex poured more coffee down his throat.

"A guy came in, a teacher at PS 004, and told me a kid in his class killed the man on 153rd," Matt explained, the squad listening like it was the case of the century. "He just walked into the station house and told me all about it. I guess this kid had been bragging to *everyone* at school. Little shit thought it made him a big man. Some other kid had some sense of responsibility and told the teacher. This teacher had all the details. So, we go pick up this seventeen-year old, and I talk him into waiving *Miranda,* and then we go 'round for like four hours, and he confessed to the whole thing."

Alex scratched the side of his head. "Why'd he do it?"

"He fucked up."

"I'll say."

"No, I mean, he thought King was a witness in a case against a buddy of his. He wasn't, but the perp had a description of some guy who kinda looked like King. Wanted to prove his loyalty."

"What'd you say the other week, Lex?" James commented. "Thank God perps are stupid?"

"Something like that." Alex replied. "Seventeen? What a fucking waste."

"Head to the bar after the tour? Drink the case down?" James asked everyone.

"Fuck, it's gonna get late," sighed Matt, his shoulders heaving. "I told Karen… It's been nice not having to give up my life anymore. Look at what it's done to you. Lex's desk is *worse* than a crime scene. I didn't even think that was possible."

James slung his arm around Matt's shoulders. "C'mon, Cohen."

"Marty's joining Club Divorce," Matt observed. "Case in point."

"Just one," urged James. "You miss us. We never see you anymore."

"It's never just one with you guys," said Matt. But he did in fact miss MNHS and acquiesced to going out for drinks with the old squad.

"I gotta talk to King's family, tell them it's down," Alex said, watching his boss and colleagues locate their jackets and keys. "I'll join you once I'm done with that." Though blind luck, he had kept his promise to Mrs. King. Being in service to that kind of larger-than-life suffering made him feel inconsequential yet somehow anointed, his twinging wound and his bellyache insignificant, dwindling against the hegemony of sorrow and loss.

Chapter Thirty-Nine

A deafening April deluge drummed against the station house roof as Alex reviewed a '94 case file, a DV homicide where the perp had shot his girlfriend and her lover. The oldest motive in the world, but it justified a break-up, not a 9mm. The perp was on trial, and Alex would be testifying next week.

Queasy and sluggish, he slogged through a murderous hangover. Last night, Corcoran had thrown a party celebrating his promotion, and everyone had gotten wrecked. Alex's memories were fractured: holding Rizzo's head in a toilet while he puked; James playing tunes on his pipes; Brady and Keohane singing a drunk, out of tune rendition of 'The Fields of Athenry'; Corcoran singing a slightly more in tune version of 'The Parting Glass'; and Alex waking up lying in the hallway of his own apartment, thankful that he wasn't in a subway station, a bush, or work.

The phone broke into his thoughts and his prep. Picking it up, he said flatly, "Detective Boswell, Manhattan North Homicide."

"Hello, Detective, this is Sergeant Conon at the Three-Four. There's been a shooting in J. Hood Wright Park. They want Homicide on the scene."

Three-Four Precinct. Shit. Alex asked, "Who's the catching detective?"

"Indelicata," responded the sergeant.

"Okay."

His body felt under attack; chemical weapons eroding every artery, heating his blood, seizing his guts. The intensity of it made him tremble. Far from Vito's orbit, Alex felt like he was a better detective. He could work cases in his quiet, industrious way, unimpeded by the blinding sun and sketchy ethics of the Vito Indelicata show. For almost three years, a blend of lucky shift rotas, dipping murder rates, and bribes had maintained a border zone, beyond the reach of Vito's magnetic field. Occasionally, he ran into Vito in the MNHS office or the Three-Four station house, and if he was unlucky enough to be stopped by the man, Vito inevitably prattled, "Hey, Lex! How's it going? We gotta grab a drink. Haven't seen you in fuckin' ages! I can't remember the last time we worked a case together."

Unfortunately, Alex could.

He kneaded his eyes and cheeks with both hands. Taking a deep breath, he stacked his case file into a passable order. *Don't look upset,* he counseled himself, then he stretched his legs and sauntered over to Marty and Bill's cubicles.

"Hey, I'm doing some trial prep." Nonchalant, he draped an elbow over the cubicle panels. "You wanna go pick up a shooting in the Three-Four?"

"No," said Bill, who looked as hanging as Alex felt. Darkened hollows had formed under his eyes. "We're all doing things too. You picked up the phone." That's how it worked. Everyone knew that.

Desperate, Alex stared beseechingly at his colleagues. He didn't care if they teased him into the next millennium. "Vito's the catching precinct detective. I can't work with him. Please, take this case."

"What the hell *is* up with you and Vito?" Marty asked. His eyes seemed brighter. How could he drink all that rum last night and not look like he'd died three days ago? "I mean, things have been a bit, uh, weird, with you two for a while. But you used to work with him all the time, like he was your other partner."

"What'd you fall out over?" Bill inquired. "You must have fallen out."

"Doesn't matter. I'll fucking deal. It's just that it'll be better if I don't. He likes you guys better than me. Come on, please take this case, and next time you're landed with one you don't want, a redball or whatever, I'll take it, okay?"

Bill and Marty looked at one another.

"How about we go to the Glendale tonight, and I'll buy all your rounds," Alex offered.

The deal was too sweet to turn down.

"Okay." Marty stood up and cocked his head towards Bill, who'd clipped his gun to his belt.

"You're a sucker for the sad lines around his eyes," Bill said.

"Maybe," laughed Marty. "But we *will* take you up on that, all of it, don't forget!"

"Cool, that's cool." Alex returned to his trial prep, but with one eye, he watched Bill and Marty shrugging their raincoats over their shoulders and striding out the door.

James chewed on the top of a pen. "What *is* your fuckin' deal with Vito? You'd rather have a shitty redball? The next cop shooting?"

"The way he does things gets to me. I can't keep my head straight."

"He's a fuckin' egomaniac, I hear that. But there's a lotta assholes out there. A large number of them are precinct detectives. Is your head ever straight?"

"Clearly not, but I can't deal with his bullshit."

"He's got fuck-tons of that. Any in particular?"

Afraid he'd said too much, Alex plucked at a bloody tag of skin on his thumb. "You know. Like his whole one-man detective show. Like he's the star of some Hollywood cop movie. I think he's got worse."

"Don't know if he's worse," James scoffed. "He's always been a douchebag."

"He hates *my* guts 'cause he was my rabbi for about five minutes, until I realized he was an asshole."

"I hear that. Your mistake was thinking he *wasn't* an asshole."

"I'm aware," Alex said somberly.

But he'd contained it; he'd passed the buck to Bill and Marty. No one had pressed him too hard to say why. If the wrinkles around his eyes softened Marty's heart, he would live with that. He took some notes about exigent circumstances: entering the perp's apartment without a warrant, the heart-pounding adrenaline when they'd cleared rooms, the plain sight search he had conducted.

When Bill and Marty returned to the squad room after working the shooting in J. Hood Wright Park, the four detectives piled into Bill's Lincoln. Bemoaning the leak in the footwell, Bill drove through the rain, down to the Glendale in Greenwich Village. Marty laughed at the leak, proclaiming that Japanese cars don't leak. Thunder grumbled. Lightning flipped its cosmic light switch. Overflowing drains flooded Broadway, and the car splashed through standing water. The passenger footwell, where Alex's feet were, turned into a puddle. Bill blew off parking regulations, parking on double yellow lines next to the pub, and they filed through the door.

Within minutes of starting his first beer, Alex felt sick, his guts burning as if he was drinking battery acid. So much for hair of the dog. But he'd promised Bill and Marty that he would buy them as many beers as they wanted. He gritted his teeth, fighting through it. *I'm just tired from Corcoran's party last night.* The party had been wild, and his digestive system had suffered heavy abuse. No wonder it was complaining. As he stood to buy another round, a surge of light-headedness sucked at his balance. He forced the muscles in his legs to work. Up to the bar, ordering the beer, somehow carrying drinks back to the table. Hopefully his colleagues were also tired and hungover. Refusing to look unwell, he slugged the second pint. He felt a stabbing sensation inside his stomach, like someone was in there with a knife. Static overpowered the Eagles on the PA and the voices in the bar. What bar? The oak tables and chairs were blurry, as if he had saltwater in his eyes, but he couldn't place them. Where was he? That bar in Ridgewood he used to frequent with Fred, Selvio, and the other guys in the One-Oh-Three squad. Every inch of wall space had pictures of Irish sea-cliffs, cartoon shamrocks, Guinness ads, and old horse harnesses. Tchotchke everywhere. The Foggy Dew. He remembered its name.

"Where's Fred?" He had to find Fred. The world crashed around him, his knees buckling, the floor rising to meet him.

Alex opened his eyes and saw a paneled white ceiling and bright fluorescent tube lights. IVs snaked out of his arms. A white board hung on the wall, with his name in red marker. Fuck, he was in a motherfucking hospital. His throat hurt. His stomach ached as if he'd been gored with a dull knife. Had he fallen or walked into a moving car and hurt himself? He fuzzily recalled buying a round in the Glendale. Waking up somewhere unexpected would count as a prosaic morning had he not woken up in a hospital. James slouched in the chair next to his bed with his chin on his chest, dozing. That wasn't good. If it wasn't serious, James wouldn't be here. They had taken his watch, so he had no inkling of the time, but the corridor outside the room was dark, the window blinds shut. Someone had taken his gun and shield too.

"James?" he said softly.

James' blue eyes flew open. He jerked upright. "Oh, thank fuck, you're awake."

"What time is it?"

"I dunno, like two am."

"What's going on? What hospital is this? What am I doing here?"

James looked like he'd been crying, his eyes puffed up, red-rimmed with a glassy film. He drew in a shuddery breath. "Beth Israel. It was fucked up, man."

"What was fucked up?"

"You finished a beer in the Glendale, then you looked really confused and started asking for Fred Symington, Nick Selvio, and a bunch of people we didn't know. You thought you were in some joint called the Foggy Dew. And then you collapsed on the floor. We thought, shit, we'd better get outta here, and when we dragged you outside, you started puking blood. We wondered if we should call a bus but thought, no, it would be faster to take you to the hospital in Bill's car. It was fuckin' horrific. We got to the hospital, and you kept vomiting, so the docs didn't even make you wait. Took you straight in. Shoved a nasogastric tube into you, pumped out like two liters of blood from your stomach. *Two fuckin' liters,* dude. Said you might've died if they didn't. They said they found bleeding ulcers. Like a blood vessel just went, had a massive fuckin' hemorrhage, but they thought you probably had them for a while. You've looked ill for a couple months. Can't believe you never said anything. Must've hurt like a bitch."

"Yeah," Alex muttered. "Wasn't great."

"If you're in that much pain, you should see a fuckin' doctor. Why didn't you? That was really fuckin' stupid."

"Thought it wasn't a big deal. Just indigestion or acid reflux or something."

"It's a big fuckin' deal. You coulda bled out if we hadn't brought you in. And they said…" James choked, losing the words.

"They said…" Alex prompted hoarsely.

"I dunno. Something about your liver. It was a lot of medical jargon. I wasn't really taking in everything they said."

"What's wrong with my liver? Am I fucked? Am I likely?" So, this could be it – dying of cirrhosis or bleeding out, nothing they could do for him. Even through the furry anesthetic threads clogging his brain, it struck him hard, a sharp and swift punch in the gut. Would his daughters come here to see him? Did he want them to?

James sniffed, swiping his nose with the heel of his hand. "I fuckin' hope not. They did some tests, said they gotta get the results to know what's going on and maybe do a biopsy. I shoulda said something about you drinking. I didn't know it was gonna get this bad. I mean, everyone drinks a lot, right?"

"What would you have said?" *I'm not done, dammit,* Alex thought, furious and scared. *I'm only thirty-eight. How are there hundreds of hard drinking cops in their sixties, but I'm this ill at thirty-eight?* Tears threatened to flood his eyes. He squeezed them shut.

"I don't fuckin' know," James said miserably. "You should go back to sleep, if you can. They said you should get as much rest as possible. They got you on Tramadol or something fun, so that should help."

Not as much as he hoped. Closing his eyes brought him to the backseat of a car with a gunshot wound in his belly, and Eddie Trenemen driving the car. He kept asking Eddie if he would tell Ellie and Sarah. Eddie said, "We'll see what happens." The car abruptly stopped because the George

445

Washington Bridge had burst into flames. Eddie acted unconcerned. "Damn, we'll just have to go another way," before abandoning the car and walking, *walking,* towards the Hudson.

Alex was half asleep when the gastroenterologist came in, the nightmare with Eddie so vivid that it took him a second to work out which nightmare was real. Probably the one in the hospital, with a diminutive Korean doctor called Ji Ah Seon arriving at 0700. As a man who dealt with death every day, he shouldn't fear it, but he couldn't say if he was relieved to see the doctor or petrified.

James' eyes were splotchy and swollen, and the shadow of a beard darkened his cheeks. He looked nauseated with worry. The doctor made him leave the room for the consultation. Blearily, he mumbled that he would find breakfast in the hospital cafeteria.

Once James had blundered out the door, Alex said, "You can be straight with me. Don't try to make it sound better than it is. Am I gonna die?"

Dr. Seon angled her head. "Not imminently, but you most certainly will if you don't quit drinking. Though it's anybody's guess whether a perforated ulcer or cirrhosis gets you first."

Oh well, he had asked for a straight answer.

"Right now, you've got mild alcoholic hepatitis," the doctor explained. "That means your liver is inflamed, starting to develop scar tissue, which we call fibroids. You've also developed some aggressive bleeding ulcers. A large blood vessel in your stomach hemorrhaged last night, which was why you lost consciousness. You lost a lot of blood. I'm not going to lie, that's pretty serious. Very." Here, she showed him pictures, the inside of his stomach riddled with bloody red and white craters like someone had fired a high-powered rifle at it.

He flicked his eyes to the side, the way jurors in a trial avoid looking at gory crime scene pictures.

"This didn't just develop overnight. Have you had stomach pain for a while?"

He nodded, prepared for the lecture on taking care of himself, like he would have heard from Ruann Harland, or his mother.

The doctor went on, "The good news is that you're conscious and lucid, and you look a lot better after twenty-four hours. Means your liver is still functioning, and the gastric bleed hasn't restarted. But we're going to keep you as an inpatient for at least the next five days. You need to be monitored for anemia and making sure the GI bleeding doesn't start again. I have to warn you, the symptoms of alcohol withdrawal can be dangerous in a small percentage of cases. They can include seizures, heart arrhythmias, hallucination, tremors. That also needs to be monitored."

Alex knew what the DTs were but thought of it as something that happened to other people. "What the... Why me? I know so many people who drink like fish."

"Ten to twenty percent of heavy drinkers develop liver disease and other complications. You have long-term pain from an old gunshot injury, yes?"

"Yeah." With this much luck, he would suffer the seizures and hallucinations too.

"Do you take painkillers for it? Like ibuprofen."

"Yeah."

"Taking lots of anti-inflammatory painkillers without any buffer will damage your stomach," the doctor warned. "Anyway, try to get some more sleep. And send your friend home. You need rest and so does he. We need to check your bloods again, for liver function and anemia. Are you okay with having your blood drawn?"

"Fine."

She squeezed his forearm with a tourniquet until the veins bulged, then she poked a needle into one, filling a syringe with blood. Nodding sagaciously at a nurse, she wrote a few notes, then she ambled out the door to her next patient.

Sleeping was laughable. The hospital room was roasting, and the air felt thick and torpid, like a subway station in July. Did the window open? They never did, or patients would jump out. A streetlight blasted through the hospital blinds on one side of the room. Fluorescent lights bombarded the windows on the other.

Clasping a pillow over his head, hiding from the light, he curled onto his side. How could his body bail on him like this before the age of forty? How do you survive as a teetotaler in the NYPD? Or anywhere? Whenever stress ratcheted up his blood pressure or his wound defeated over-the-counter painkillers (and apparently, they were also bad for him), he drank. What the hell was he supposed to do now? Only yesterday morning, he had thought himself in one country, the country of good health, and death had been in another country, and the two countries shared nothing. Last night, a bridge had formed between them, like those bullets eight years ago. But this time, his own body had pulled the trigger. He didn't understand this new country and didn't like it.

***

His heart woke him up. Palpitations, faster than any after swimming hard or chasing a perp. Sweat had saturated the hospital gown. His skin itched like he was having an allergic reaction. He clawed at his forearm. He ground his fingers into his side, then scratched at his thigh. *I'm having a heart attack.* He cast his eyes frantically around the room. There was James, reading a book. Hadn't the doctor told James to go home? "James," he hissed.

"You alright?"

"Get someone. Something's wrong."

James closed his book. He sat up straight. "What's wrong?"

"I dunno… Something with my heart. It doesn't feel right. You gotta get someone."

James' face whitened, and he shot through the door. Seconds later, he reappeared with a nurse in tow. James looked panic-stricken, while the nurse, pushing a cart of medication, looked composed and blasé. The nurse scanned the chart at the foot of the bed, listened to his chest, squashed his arm with the blood pressure cuff. A placating smile appeared on her face, and she grabbed a syringe from her cart.

"Alcohol withdrawal," she explained in a matter-of-fact tone, like this was a routine Saturday. For her, it must be. "But I'm gonna give you some Diazepam. I don't want this turning into seizures. Okay?"

Expertly, she slid the needle into the canula in his left forearm. The hit of benzos in his system knocked him into oblivion. As he lost awareness, he glimpsed James, head in his hands, crying. He had the drug-addled thought, *It's not that bad, is it?*

Four or five days passed, the first two or three barely remembered. As the Diazepam levels in his body waned, Alex appreciated the benefits of being a drug addict, the bliss of nothingness, so tanked on benzos he was comatose. Then he wouldn't have to deal with his life. He was here because of a personal failing; it wasn't a line of duty injury or a random medical malady. Drinking too much, or his body not resilient enough to withstand drinking as much as everyone else. A failure either way.

When his benzo levels attained equilibrium, between ennui and lucidity, he called his sisters. Ruth seemed disappointed but distant. Helen asked if she should jump on the next plane to New York. He preferred Ruth's reaction.

"Helen, please, no," he said. "Don't drop everything for this."

"You're gonna deal with this all by yourself?"

"No. James has hardly left the hospital," he sighed. "I'll figure it out. But please, don't tell Mom."

"Will you at least let her know you have an ulcer?"

"Are you kidding? She'd turn the bitching about my job up to eleven. She already hates it. I don't want her to know."

"Well, you have to go into rehab," she stated.

"That seems to be the consensus," he said mordantly.

"I'm not kidding, Al. You go to AA, I won't say anything to Mom."

"Swear to that?" Nothing had changed in thirty years. As kids, they'd often made deals with one another, clumsy childhood NDAs to not tell parents about one transgression or another.

"Yes," Helen answered. "Call me when you're out, or if you're going to be in longer."

And indeed, James hovered. If he wasn't working or sleeping, he was at Beth Israel. It got to the point where the nurses knew his first name, and one had his phone number. Once he'd reported that Alex was *compos mentis,* Bill, Marty, Sam, Jean, and a few others came by a couple times. Their visits distracted Alex from his sleepy boredom, although they left him feeling enchained, like an incarcerated prisoner, but with his health, rather than steel manacles, binding his wrists and ankles. Still, he'd expected his friends' visits. He didn't expect Gibson to suddenly appear in the doorway, a five-foot apparition draped in brightly-colored scarves. His heart convulsed in a little seizure. The boss, the last person he wanted to see while spaced out on benzos because he was an alcoholic with the DTs.

She seemed more troubled than judgmental, assuring him that he could take all the sick leave he needed, and then she explained, "I'm not putting you on limited duty or modified, and I'm not sending you to the Farm. I'm giving you a chance. But as soon as you're out of here, you gotta find an AA meeting or some kind of rehab and start dealing with this. It's not gonna be easy, I know it's not, so we gotta meet and stay on top of how you're feeling. You have to be honest with me about it. No bullshit. Okay?"

"Yes, ten-four," he said, surprised. He'd never honestly divulged any feelings to Corcoran, avoiding it even after the shooting. He had to be hardboiled and stoic. That was the job, wasn't it? Now he had orders. Ones that seemed alien, baffling. A C/O berating him for screwing up his life and his promising career seemed more perspicuous than one offering compassion and counseling. A gender thing? Some female C/Os were fiercer than most men. No point in overanalyzing the boss' mood or motives. Orders were orders.

The day before they discharged him, he gave James the apartment keys and told him to clear out the booze and make sure he cleared the squad room as well. Desk drawers, lockers, it all had to go. James was very un-James-like, nodding seriously instead of joking about a windfall of free alcohol. Alex wished he would go back to making inappropriate jokes – he preferred that James to serious James.

Equally as unsmiling and serious, Dr. Seon signed discharge papers, ordering him to avoid stress, ibuprofen, and spicy food while the ulcers healed. He could take small amounts Tylenol for his gunshot wound; nothing else. She cautioned that fibrosis could turn into cirrhosis long after you quit drinking, so he needed liver function tests every year, probably for the rest of his life. *Thirty-eight years old and more impaired organs*, he thought darkly. At this rate, he would be fit for the scrapyard by the time he was fifty, like James' piece of shit Mustang, where one part after another kept breaking, and it spent more time in the shop than out.

"This was the warning shot across the bow, Alex," Dr. Seon said. "You could have easily come in here several months or years from now, in a state where the outcomes of any treatment would be much worse. And now you've done the tough detox bit. So, you *have* to stay on the wagon, you hear?"

He heard. But the city felt bleak and hostile, a pitiless concrete wasteland. Even the subway seemed malevolent, cruelly tormenting him with advertisements for Bacardi and Coors on the strips above the windows. Overwhelmed, he cried silently on the uptown 1 train, blind to everyone around him. Usually, he semi-watched the people on the subway – his cop's instinct – but today, Bill Clinton and Rudy Giuliani could have boarded his car, and he wouldn't have noticed.

Chapter Forty

Because he'd made promises to James, his sister, his doctor, and his C/O, Alex located an Alcoholic Anonymous meeting in the basement of a Presbyterian church on West 33rd Street and Broadway, far enough from his neighborhood or any that he worked in to not include anyone he might encounter at his local shops or, he prayed, on the job. One in the Rockaways would be ideal but travelling to the far reaches of Brooklyn seemed as grueling as travelling to New Zealand.

West 33rd coursed around him, the traffic and people like fast whitewater. He stood on the curb, immobilized. His eyes froze onto the plain, wooden church door. An AA meeting was the last place he wanted to be, undoubtedly more torturous than the angriest CompStat meeting. It was in a church, no less. A terrible illness, driving a Lower East Side Jew into a church! He imagined AA as a combination of a religious cult, where you recite prayers and promise to devote your soul to God, and a summer camp, where you hold hands and sing *Kumbaya.*

Worse, the moment he walked through that door, he would be an alcoholic, a word he had never used to describe himself before. But he was one, wasn't he? He wasn't a guy who liked drinking; those guys could stop; they could hold themselves to one or two drinks. Alex couldn't remember the last time he had stopped at one or two or went anywhere without his whisky flask. How did anyone stop at one or two and not want more?

His heartbeat thundered, louder than the traffic, but he unlatched the door. Before him, an empty nave, with rows of pews like a courtroom and the austere wooden crucifix looming over a gloomy altar. The meeting was in the basement. He could turn around and leave. Then what? He ventured down the stairs. In the dim light inside the crypt, he saw about fourteen people on plastic folding chairs sitting in a circle. He'd seen cheerier meetings at 1PP. Everyone looked downtrodden, abused by life and now here, absolving themselves in this church basement of the hopeless and desperate. Alex instinctively grasped at his chest pocket.

451

But he only found a pen. His adrenaline spurted. His ulcer gave him a sharp bite. He grabbed a chair from the pile leaning against the wall and unfolded it on the edge of the circle. Two people – a white guy with a beard and flannel shirt, and a sallow woman with stringy blonde hair – shuffled to make room for him.

A tall, forty-something Black man with shoulder-length dreads and glasses welcomed everyone with unrestrained kindness. He spread his arms, as if embracing every miserable soul in the room, and he smiled, his eyes overflowing with compassion.

Alex shook like he'd come off a bender. He stopped breathing. He was sweating through his clothes.

The man pronounced, "I'm Will, for those who don't know me, and I'm an alcoholic." He read a prayer, then the twelve steps and twelve traditions of AA. Some of the attendees mumbled words along with him. Others sat in silence. There was a lot about God.

Alex wanted to be anywhere else. Rikers Island, for a start.

Afterwards, Will said, "Is there anyone new today? You are very welcome to introduce yourself. But it's not compulsory. If you're not ready, it doesn't matter. We will welcome you anyway."

Alex warily scanned the group. Their eyes flickered towards him, the only newcomer. But they pretended not to look. He could keep his mouth shut. They would forget his face if he drew no attention to himself. Most people, after all, were terrible eyewitnesses. For some reason he never could fathom, he murmured, "I'm Alex, and I'm an alcoholic." As soon as the words left his mouth, a dam ruptured inside his chest, and water coursed out of his eyes. What was this? A new reality controlled by an invisible illness; he had to reckon with it, survive it, and he didn't know what the hell to do with it.

The flannel-clad, bearded guy whispered, "I did the same thing."

"Hi, Alex," said everyone in the room, which was weird. Still, no one asked him any questions, a thing in the AA creed. You shared your story when you were ready, but no one would ask you or force you.

Will recited his story: he had worked in advertising. His father had been an alcoholic, but Will's descent started with Happy Hour drinks, lavish parties, buttering up clients with expensive Scotch, and it escalated as he found booze helpful for coping with the stress of the ad agency – especially, he added, being the token Black guy, under a mountain of pressure to prove himself – until he showed up at a client meeting too drunk to remember the pitch. He lost both his job and his Upper East Side apartment, he separated from his wife, and he crashed at his sister's place.

452

She told him to get his act together. He sobered up, embraced AA, reconciled with his wife, then returned to school for a master's in psychology instead of re-entering the cesspit of advertising. "I'm loving it," he concluded. "I love learning about people."

Several other people shared their stories with the group. Amanda, the woman with stringy hair, had found God, and He was showing her the way, although 'the way' seemed to involve more time off the wagon than on it, while Juan, a short, round Latino guy in his sixties, was trying to make amends with his children.

The meeting concluded with another prayer reading. *God won't stop you from drinking,* Alex thought with morose cynicism. Well, it would not stop him. He didn't belong here. Everyone dispersed, clumping into small groups. Alex evaded any eye contact. Head bowed, he folded his chair, then slunk towards the door, red-eyed, his sinuses throbbing. He prudently hugged the shadows. This was far too spiritual and bizarre for him, and he had no intentions of going back. There had to be another way.

A dark-skinned hand touched his arm. Startled, he stiffened his spine.

"Hey, it's great that you're here," Will said gently. "It's the first step."

"Yeah, well, I don't think it's really for me," Alex responded, wiping his sore eyes with his wrist.

"Why not?"

"I guess, I, uh, don't do religion."

Will offered a genial smile. "It's not really about that."

"Isn't it? There was a lot of it."

"A higher power, or God, or whatever can mean anything you want. Doesn't have to be a Judeo-Christian God. It's more like the universe…" Will paused for a moment. "More like accepting that you can't do this on your own, you know. People find it easier to think that there's something bigger in the universe helping them."

"Yeah. Right."

"You would think that. You're a cop, aren't you?"

"Yeah, how'd you know?" Alex furrowed his brows, thinking about that perp James collared who believed James had psychic powers.

Will's eyes dropped to the bulge at Alex's left hip, under his hoodie. "You're carrying. My uncle was a cop. You must see some stuff, huh? Anyway, these meetings are about hearing other people's stories. Helping each other. Your friends who aren't addicts, they've never been where you are. They won't understand the way someone who's totally been there will."

Alex had no wiseass rejoinder.

"You're in a pretty dark place right now... I can see it in your face. You're not even sure you *want* to be sober."

"I don't," Alex admitted. "I just have to."

"I hear you. I been there. But you know, Alex, you've gone so far down now, so far in, that you have nowhere else to go but through. Let us help you through."

Will's hand stayed planted on his bicep. Alex felt incapable of flight, spellbound by the man's powerful self-assurance.

"Look, man, give us a chance. Come back next week. Don't worry about all the God stuff... Here's my number." Will scribbled a Manhattan phone number on the back of a business card for a plumber. "If you find yourself stressed or overwhelmed, or about to walk into a bar, call me. I don't care what time it is. Okay?"

"Okay," Alex said doubtfully, but he slotted the card into his wallet. What was the last step they had recited this morning? Carrying the message to other alcoholics. No kidding, he did not *want* to be sober. He liked being drunk. He liked self-medicating. When he didn't feel well, he liked getting too wasted to care, and now he couldn't because he didn't like spending a week in the hospital, the DTs, bleeding ulcers, or liver biopsies. Fuck, more than anything he yearned for some whisky, the Glenlivet that wasn't in his apartment anymore. It felt like an ache in his bones.

He shoved his weight against the heavy church doors and surfaced into the bedazzling daylight and noise of Broadway. A fierce sun glinted off windows and concrete. Blinking out the light, he turned uptown towards Penn Station. Midtown traffic swept around him. Horns, sirens, and wheels roared in his ears. The close, spicy scent of city fumes infused his nostrils. He shouldered a path through the streets, crowded with locals, tourists, workers, all of New York, this teeming anthill. Yet Midtown seemed cleaner, despite the chaos. Rotting piles of garbage bags no longer barricaded sidewalks, the gutters largely free of plastic and cans, the walls repainted, the graffiti vanquished. Coffee shops, restaurants, cocktail bars, and a TGI Fridays occupied blocks where the brothels used to be. The theaters had routed the slingers. Flyers advertised *Rent, Les Misérables, Cabaret,* and *Death of a Salesman.* If New York itself could metamorphize from urban decay into a vivacious, modern city like Amsterdam or Berlin, then anything seemed possible.

Chapter Forty-One

Returning to work after only a few days seemed easier than vegetating in his apartment, bored, lonely, his mind imprinted with the locations of every bar and liquor store on the Upper West Side. His friends were all cops; their socializing meant going to bars or drinking at sporting events. Ellie lived three hours away, at school in Western Massachusetts, and when he phoned Catherine, looking for Sarah, his ex said dismissively, "You're thirty-eight, and now you're trying to sort your life out? Too little too late, Alex. Anyway, how long will this last? You always promise you're getting it together, and then you don't."

"Dammit, Catherine, I don't need this shit. Put her on the phone."

"She's out with friends."

"Tell her to call me when she gets back."

"I tell her to do lots of things, she doesn't do them. I think she's smoking weed and God knows what else. Heroin? LSD? I don't know what she's doing."

"She's not that stupid." He hoped not. "I've told her OD horror stories."

"Some of her friends are. Jesus, Alex. And when are you going to take some responsibility? She thinks you drink because of her, and you pushed them away, then you wonder why she's acting out?"

That hurt. "I'm ill. It's a fucking illness. When have you taken any responsibility? For all the times you've gone outta your way to keep them from me? Sometimes, I swear, you've learned my four-day shift pattern and worked out which ones I'm off, so you can make sure they're busy."

"Don't start accusing me of things I'm not doing," she said, her voice shrilly, then she hung up.

Swear words fizzled and died in his dry throat. He lay down on his side across the sofa cushions. Definitely better to go back to work. Although his stomach remained sore and sensitive, he didn't feel like he physically needed more time off than the week he'd spent in the hospital, and mentally, well, that was sort of a one-day-at-a-time thing, whether he was at work investigating murders or not, so he might as well be at work investigating murders.

However, his body disagreed. At every painful breath or aching joint, a scornful voice in his head sneered that he hadn't regained as much strength as he thought or wanted. He started that four-by-twelve feeling like he'd gone through the Washington Heights riot for the second time. Riding the subway was exhausting. Catching up with his paperwork was exhausting. Dealing with other cops, witnesses, lawyers, and lab techs was exhausting. And as he neared his desk after he'd been downtown at the lab, he saw a Miller Lite can sitting on top of it, like a trophy. It waited, beckoning. Swiftly he scanned the room. There, beside the photocopier, Keohane eyefucking him, his heavy hands over his mouth, convulsing in silent giggles.

"Cute." Alex picked up the beer and lobbed it as hard as he could at Keohane. The Irish detective ducked. The beer smashed into the floor, exploding into white foam that sprayed an office chair but missed the copy machine. *Fucking asshole deserved that*, Alex thought, holding his gut. Sniggers rippled across the squad room. Everyone thought Keohane had been deserving that for years.

Just then, Alex noticed a blackboard propped up against the wall, beside the file cabinets. Across the top, someone had written, *How long will Boswell stay on the wagon?* Below, they'd scrawled a table with the names of most detectives in the squad, along with a monetary value and an amount of time, ranging from two minutes to eight months. Only the Homicide squad, starting a betting pool over whether he would stay sober. What a bunch of fucking optimists as well. Because if you don't play, you'll be eaten alive, he wrote his own name on the board, wagering ten bucks that he would last for one year. His guts roiled at the thought. *How?* Nonetheless, he had to show his colleagues that he possessed a sense of humor.

But days crept past, each one demanding more of him as staying out of the bottle felt like swimming towards a shoreline that never moved closer. The blackboard taunted him with its lies. A year! He'd been delusional. The C team detective who said two minutes had been realistic. Alex immersed himself in his caseload, and when open ones didn't give him enough to do, he returned to a few cold cases, hopeful that the years had warmed up new leads. They hadn't, but it kept him out of the bars. When the other detectives departed for the ritual of post-tour drinks, he cowered in his cubicle, racking up overtime, or he fled to West 87th Street. Colleagues mercilessly teased him, prodding, "Come on, you're no fun anymore. Where is the Alex we know and love?" No way in hell did he have the willpower to sit in a bar with those guys, stuck with soft drinks while they got smashed. The only grace in his life came from the defendant in that DV trial, who plea bargained with the DA right after opening arguments, saving Alex from a court appearance.

Even Bill, Marty, and Jean, who could always find soothing words for families of murder victims, seemed at a loss. More distressingly, James was subdued, his razor wit blunted, although he denied it like a witness at a crime scene. Of course he was fine. His partner was an alcoholic who had almost bled to death internally, but he was fine. They both knew bullshit when it hit them in the face. But like real men in a militaristic organization, they sure as shit weren't going to talk about it. When the squad room repartee felt stiff and lost its rhythm, Alex longed to cry that nothing had changed, but everything had changed. They didn't get it. How could they? He felt as though every blood vessel in his heart had been cut from his body, but he couldn't articulate his pain. There were no words for it. Had he become a different person? Someone his friends didn't know. Someone *he* didn't know, either. The people at AA would get it, but he hadn't spoken at the meetings. Too difficult. He galvanized himself, anxiously running his hand along the plumber's card until the cardboard crumpled, and then he phoned Will.

They met in a Midtown coffee shop. It was the first of many shared cups of coffee, where Alex would neck straight expressos and Will would drink chai or flavored lattes.

"How am I gonna stay sober forever?" Alex asked between bites of a cinnamon roll. "What about Christmas? New Year? There's always a party, and people get wrecked."

"You're going to stay sober right now. Today," Will said. He drank a pumpkin-spiced latte.

Alex chewed on his last bite. "Today... sure... But tomorrow? I can't keep doing this. How am I gonna keep doing this? I'm gonna fuck it up one day. I know I am. There's no point in pretending I'm not."

"Hey, tomorrow there could be a nuclear apocalypse. Then we can drink, because who cares. But today, let's not. You can definitely get through today. You just said you could."

Will urged him to feel his pain, explore it, find meaning in it, not run from it. Hadn't drinking been a way of running? Yes, Alex conceded, but he didn't plan on 'exploring' it, either. He didn't know what the hell to do with it. Once, upset and pacing around his apartment, he phoned Ruann Harland, but he hung up when her answering machine responded.

Words dissolved in his throat. Talking to her wouldn't ease his grief for his old life, and he heard on the wire that she worked for the Department of Defense now and was engaged to a CIA agent she'd met on a counterterrorism task force after the World Trade Center bombing in '93.

Almost daily, he found fresh alcoholic beverages hiding around his desk or skulking on his chair. It took him seconds to ID the perps. Brady. Keohane. McCallister from the A team. Maybe Rizzo. He ground the enamel off his teeth while acting indifferent and hardboiled. Recovery slithered out of his grasp. If he broke, his colleagues would win that bet. And breaking seemed both inevitable and imminent. Every day at work, he saw addiction consuming people – the alcoholics and drug addicts chewed up by the criminal justice system, spat out and then devoured again. *They are no different than me*, he thought grimly. Unlike the people at AA, who seemed like they were from another planet when they espoused their weird stories of enlightenment. "We have power – we have made a *choice*, and we choose light," exhorted one as she handed out healing crystals.

What 'we?' He clenched the quartz crystal in his fist, reveling at the sharp edges digging into his flesh. Real pain, a distraction from the emotional pain skewering his heart. He gripped the rock harder. It could make his hand bleed, for all he cared. Well, he cared about his side hurting, and no ibuprofen or booze to dull the wound's steely edge. He cared when he spent several nights rolling on the floor in agony after getting overambitious with curries and a hot quesadilla. He cared about the pharmacy-full of pills he was taking for his ulcers. Every day, the drugs warned him about his lousy health, his lurking medical disasters. Sobriety was no more of a choice than a twenty-year prison sentence following a guilty plea.

Towards the end of a soggy four-by-twelve, Alex plodded into the office after working a homicide in Harlem. The vic was a nineteen-year old Black kid who'd been a CI for a Manhattan North Narcotics detective, and now he'd died for being a snitch. Alex wrung out his damp scarf and sank silently into his chair while his colleagues bantered about Marty's impending divorce. Divorce was like a rite of passage in this place, but his wit felt flat and tired. He had nothing funny or sarcastic to add. That kid could have been his CI. They all took those risks, informants and cops alike. This murder bothered him, even though he knew a good death investigator doesn't waste energy on theological questions about the nature of evil, or sociological questions about crime and poverty. No, he wonders if the wound came from a serrated blade, if the lividity pattern means the body was moved, or if the maggots are of any use at estimating time of death. A detective can only function if he's detached, clinical. Was he functioning? He doubted it. The city's murder rate might have flattened, but young people kept dying over the narcotics trade, and he felt sick about it.

Instinctively, he reached into his top drawer. His fingers brushed against a bottle. His heart skipped a beat, then flapped like a sparrow. Some asshole had hidden that there. Cutty Sark. Those cheap-ass pricks hadn't even bought something decent. But it was whiskey, and he was an alcoholic, no different than the skels he'd scraped off the street in his beat cop days after they'd downed lighter fluid. His fingers curled around the smooth glass. In a swift motion, he yanked it from the drawer, then he stared at the golden liquid inside. How easy it would be to have a little bit, just a mouthful! Just one swallow! Come on now, he told himself, there was no having 'a little bit.' His brain didn't work like that, or so they said in AA. He twisted off the cap. Spikey fumes of strong alcohol tickled his nasal passages. That impulse, even though the stuff tasted like drain cleaner. *Fuck it,* he thought. An image played in his head: James sitting next to him in the hospital room, tears streaking his pale blue eyes with blood. He shoved the bottle into the stacks of binders, then saw Keohane peering at him around the cubicle wall.

"Fuck you," Alex spat, springing to his feet. He stormed into the hallway. The door crashed shut behind him. He stood still, shuddering, leaning into the whitewashed breeze blocks, his colleague's snide giggling echoing in his head. Do you go back in or leave? There had to be a witness somewhere in the city who needed interviewing. At a loss, he slumped onto the metal stairs, burrowing his head into his arms.

The door squeaked. Thinking it was one of his douchebag colleagues, he whirled around, prepared to hurl expletives, but he swallowed the invective when he saw Gibson striding through the door.

She sat beside him on the stairs.

"What you're doing is tough, really tough," she said. "And those guys are jerks."

He'd promised her honesty. "I don't think I'm gonna be able to do this," he rasped in a soft voice. "I don't have the willpower, Lieu. I just don't have it."

"You do. I've seen the hardheadedness you bring to investigations."

"My head's a fucking mess. Every single day it takes everything I have to get out of bed. I don't have anything left for the job."

"You have enough. You got any leads on that kid on East 127th?"

"My CIs are scared and won't talk. They don't wanna be next. But Detective Spica had these kites he was working and told me who his targets were."

"Follow it up. The Narc detective gave you names, follow it up. Make that the one thing you focus on. Then the next thing, for that case or the next case. What is it?"

He shut his eyes and rested his head on his forearms again.

"The next thing, Alex."

"Gotta see if that one-legged dealer wants to talk, now he's looking at serious time for selling twenty ki, and we tracked him to the same cash deposit place as the vic."

"Good, then you do that. You're tireless, you're precise. That's how you do investigations. So, get your head in that. You follow me?"

"Yes, boss, I guess so."

She stood up and grabbed his elbow, so he had to get to his feet too.

"I have a lot of admiration for you," she said. "Addiction is a fucking shitshow to break. But you know you have to break it."

He felt like a man drowning in the sea, and Gibson had thrown him a life ring. If only he could swim to it. "How do you know?" he asked in a hoarse voice.

"My brother. Been in and outta rehab for years. Mostly out, to be honest, but I got more faith in you than my brother."

"Why's that?" Caustic laughter croaked inside his throat.

"My brother can barely hold a job down, and you can do this." Unfazed, Gibson pointed towards the squad room door.

"I honestly don't know."

They walked into the squad room, then Gibson reassuringly touched his shoulder blades before answering a phone call in her office. The Cutty Sark on Alex's desk had vanished, and James, who had been in court earlier, was writing a supplemental report and looking ready to murder someone. Brady, Keohane, and Rizzo had exited by the other door, while Marty and Bill had their heads submersed in a case file for a shooting they'd caught last week, a robbery suspect in a stolen car, shot by a detective, as if it was the most important case in New York. The atmosphere resonated with the leftover note of an argument.

"I read those shitbags the *riot* act," James seethed. His face was flushed. "Told them if I found one more fuckin' bottle of booze in this place, I'd take their testicles and shove them so far up their asses it would take the entire fuckin' Marine Search Team to find them again."

"Yeah," Alex said. "It's not gonna stop them."

"I fuckin' meant it. And they *know* I meant it. Never seen those pieces of shit so fuckin' scared."

"I'm sure." *Work the case*, like Gibson said. "Look, Detective Spica told me he collared a dealer called 'Lizard,' and his PC was based on information he had from his CI. This Lizard wasn't the only person he was gonna testify against. We gotta talk to him."

'Lizard,' really called Emerson Youssaf, was in custody at Rikers. Because the prison seemed easier to deal with than the tension in the office, James and Alex signed out a car, then drove to the island. As he stiffly pulled himself out of the passenger seat, Alex stared at the coiled razor wire guarding the walls. Physical pain and emotional pain intertwined like the barbed strands on the wire. His body could be impaled on those walls, bleeding out, strung up on the barbs forever.

James questioned the prisoner while Alex paid attention to his breathing. Every inhalation demanded effort, drawing on every scrap of conscious thought. Youssaf gave them two names, two guys in his crew who had always been punchy with their firearms, and James promised to meet with the ADA prosecuting his case after corroborating the statement.

Instead, some skel stabbed Youssaf to death in the prison. The Rikers authorities shrugged – these things happen. The perp had that murder added to the widening collection of felonies he was incarcerated for, but when Alex and James questioned him, searching for links to the gang that murdered the Narc informant, he refused to say a word. Then two Chicago Homicide detectives showed up at Rikers with a court order, offered some insincere apologies to Alex and James for undermining their case, and within a day, the perp was on a plane to Illinois. He was wanted for a murder in Cook County. At least he might get convicted in Chicago, but no one knew if Youssaf's murder was related to the murder of the informant, or down to nothing more than a prison altercation. It left the case like a broken-down car in the desert, red ink beside James' name on the whiteboard.

A few days after the Chicago PD's unexpected visit, Alex went out to dinner with Elana, now a sophomore majoring in biology. Fuck knows he wasn't in the mood for it, but this had been planned for a while, after his second AA meeting, where they'd talked about making amends to the people you hurt. He had nothing left in his tank, having depleted his sparse reserves comforting the informant's distraught parents after he'd broken the news that the case had run aground. It didn't matter – he could not flake out on his daughter. Part of making amends.

They chose an Italian restaurant on Broadway, two blocks from Alex's apartment. He made himself eat, one forkful at a time, while he listened to Ellie natter about her studies. The linguine simmered uneasily in his stomach. When would his GI system heal? Weeks? Months? Never? It was hard to feign listening with science he barely understood, and when he did, it had a lot to do with climate change and ocean ecosystems collapsing.

Suddenly, mid-monologue, Ellie faltered over sea level rises and asked, "Um, what's with you not drinking anymore? And Alcoholics Anonymous? You said on the phone you spent a week in the hospital. I just assumed it was something to do with your gunshot wound. You know, 'cause you've always had issues with that. But Mom said some things, like stomach ulcers... And going on about rehab. What the fuck."

He forced down a mouthful of pasta, off guard. From global catastrophes to personal ones. "Yeah, they've said I'm an alcoholic. I mean, I guess I am. Like I can't have just one glass of wine." His eyes shifted sideways, towards the people at the adjacent table having just one glass of wine. "There's no off switch in my head. It's like my own mind wants to kill me. And I gotta deal with it, 'cause my health isn't great right now. I'm sorry. I was pretty vague on the phone. Wanted to tell you in person. Shoulda figured your mother would say something first. I told her not to."

"Okay." She strung it into a three-syllable word. "Is that why you wanted to go out tonight?"

"Yeah."

"Okay," she repeated. "You were always kinda drinking. You always had bottles of whisky around. And you were always going out to bars with your work colleagues."

Had his drinking spun so out of control that everyone but himself noticed? That's how it usually works, they said in AA. Ellie twirled pasta around her fork. Her eyes darted worriedly between his face and her plate. Everything seemed to stop, even though it hadn't. People chattered loudly at the table four feet away, waiters rushed past, and opera wailed on the PA. That reality dematerialized, like his body was sinking fast into a nightmare. Handcuffed to an interrogation room table, confessing every failure in his life to his daughter. Had he handled this badly? Did anyone seriously expect him to handle it well? But Ellie seemed more shocked than pissed. He stared at an oil painting of a sunny Italian vineyard. He sucked down a long drink of diet coke, then he told her the whole story, sugar-coating nothing. As a sophomore, she should be old enough deal with that. After all, younger men and women had been drafted into war or joined the NYPD.

Ellie nodded, stabbing the fork into her pasta. "Wow, okay. I'm glad… I'm glad it took something. I mean, almost dying is bad…"

"Fairly bad."

"But now you know you have an… illness. And you can deal with it."

"Yeah, I guess so. I'd rather I didn't."

"I guess life does imitate art."

"What?" He sawed a meatball in half.

"Like every fictional cop, ever. The detective with a drink problem. I don't think it's possible to watch a cop show or read a police thriller without one."

"Yeah, well, stereotypes exist for a reason, huh?" As ever, deflecting with sarcasm. "But it's more shit than it looks on TV."

"And you're in rehab?"

"Yeah."

"What do they do at the rehab meetings?"

"Talk about what it's like. Strategies for getting through the day. Stuff like that."

"Huh. I thought AA was like a religious thing. Didn't you'd be into that."

"The religious stuff sometimes gets tedious. I don't really listen when they talk about it."

"But do the meetings help?"

"Yeah," he said in a soft voice. "They're like me. They get it."

Alex paid, and they left the restaurant, strolling at an unhurried pace towards West 87th. He hoped a gentle walk would help his digestion. Like any native New Yorkers, they crossed Broadway without waiting for the lights.

Dreamily, Ellie said, "You know, I have enough credits that I could graduate at the end of next year."

"As a junior?"

"Yeah. MHC is like living in a bubble. I think after three years I'll be ready to do something else."

"What's something else?"

"There's a PhD program in Australia I'm interested in. At the University of Queensland. I met the professor who runs the lab at a talk, and he said I could definitely get in and get funding. It's in molecular marine biology, looking at the resilience of coral reefs—"

"Australia?" He did a double take, whirling around to face her. Yeah, he'd dropped the bombshell of his alcoholism and his health problems, but he thought they had an enjoyable dinner, almost like a normal father and daughter, and now she wanted to go to Australia?

"Yes." She drew herself together, suddenly defensive.

"Is this about getting away from me?"

"Jesus, Dad. It's not about you. Maybe Mom's right when she says you think everything's about you. It's really interesting research, and Brisbane's meant to be a fun city. Getting out to the Great Barrier Reef is easier than going to Montauk. You can't exactly do research on the molecular structure of coral reefs in New York."

"Ellie, your mother has spent the last sixteen years telling you things about me that are totally crap, but it's her way of getting back at me—"

"Both of you are as bad as each other," she bristled. "Just using me and Sarah to have a proxy war against each other. Okay, and yeah, I want to move abroad and get away from all this family bullshit. Far away."

"I guess it won't make much difference. I hardly see you anyway." As soon as the words left his mouth, he regretted his foolish tongue.

"What's wrong with you and Mom? She was just as negative. Worse, even. Like Jewish mother guilt trip worse. Saying 'what have I done wrong? I try my best, and one of my daughters is a mess and the other wants to go to Australia.'"

"I'd just assume she'd blame me for all that."

"Dad, shut up. You know, I've basically got an offer to do a PhD at a really good research lab, and you guys don't even care. You only care about yourselves." She spun on her heel and sprinted up Amsterdam.

Without thinking, he ran after her, racing past the baffled faces of Upper West Siders, the tantalizing lights of bars, the glowing rows of streetlamps. Ellie had early speed, but Alex had the stamina from swimming and keeping himself fit enough to run down a slow perp. By 89th, she was spent, losing her speed. By 90th he caught up, but with no plan. He couldn't take her down like a perp. Breathing hard, he jogged alongside her, then seized her arm, forcing her to stop but with no clue how to deal with this, except he never failed to be amazed by how screwed up his family was. Who else would end up in a foot pursuit of their kid through the Upper West Side?

The city lights suddenly glimmered like fiery pinwheels. He heard himself gasping for breath. His emotions were also bolting away from him, first at his AA meetings, now on West 90th Street. "I'm trying so hard to get my act together," he wheezed as tears blinded him.

"Sorry, Dad. I'm sorry. It's just—" Ellie's voice shook with panic. Her father wasn't supposed to be crying. He was an NYPD detective, for Christ's sake.

"I'm trying so fucking hard. But everything, everyone, they've got to make it harder."

Bewildered, Ellie clasped his hand. "Uh, let's go back to the apartment, okay, Dad?"

Tears streaked streetlamps into bright white rain. A gentle breeze tussled the ginkgo trees. Someone walking three rat-sized dogs squeezed past. He groped for the keys while Ellie tightly grasped his elbow. They marched up the stairs, then Ellie darted into the kitchen to boil water and brew tea. Shaken by forceful sobs from deep inside his chest, Alex buckled onto the sofa, ordering himself to man up, to pull himself together, but he wandered through a tangled, confusing wood, with no clear path out. Sarah thinking he drank because of her, or his sister thinking it was the job, or some of his colleagues thinking he was being neurotic and overdramatic. It was laughable, this insistence on a reason, the amateur assumptions of people who could stop themselves at one pint of beer. He drank because he was sick, an alcoholic, like an asthmatic can't breathe because he has asthma. And he wasn't going to get better, the worst part. Every day would be like this – booze lit a candle inside him, and now it was dark.

"Dad?" Ellie walked into the living room carrying two cups of tea.

He snapped his eyes open. The tears wouldn't stop, and his nose was running. The spasms lit up his gunshot wound. He scrubbed at his tear-stained face with a sofa cushion.

"What's going on, Dad?"

I'm losing it, he thought. "I'm sorry," he wheezed. "I'm sorry for everything. I'm sorry for being too fucked up to be there for you girls when you were little. I'm sorry about my fucked up job. I'm sorry I preferred dealing with my shit with a bottle instead of spending time with you. I'm sorry I'm not saying the right things about you going to grad school in Australia."

She sat down beside him on the sofa, the cup vibrating in her hands. "It's okay," she whispered.

"It isn't. It never is. You're still pissed. Your sister is still very pissed. She won't even talk to me. Your mother said she thinks my drinking is her fault, but it's not. It's just this Goddamned disease."

"I'm not pissed at you. I'm not anymore." Tears shone on her cheeks. "Mom always said you cared more about the NYPD. She said that's why you weren't there. But she had it in for you. She didn't *want* us to like you. Sarah's just mad. Not just at you. At Mom too. At everyone. At the whole fucked up situation. And she's hanging out with these kids at school who do lots of drugs and get into dumb shit… I guess that's like a rebellion thing because it drives Mom crazy. Mom says she's like you – she says she's moody and depressed all the time, and that comes from you. Mom always compares her to me. Keeps reminding her of my scholarship, and Mount Holyoke, saying if she doesn't do well enough to get a full scholarship somewhere, she's gonna have to go to CCNY or SUNY. Like that's a bad thing. There's nothing wrong with those schools. I mean, *you* guys went to CCNY. Doesn't help that Mom makes such a big deal out of it and puts a lot of pressure on her."

"I wish Sarah would talk to me about this stuff. I don't care what school she goes to."

"Oh, she won't talk to anyone except for her loser friends. You know, when I tell my friends at MHC what you do, they think it's cool. They all watch *Law and Order* and they're like, wow, your dad is the real thing, a real NYPD homicide cop. Is it really like it is on TV? I say, well, I don't know, you were too busy solving murders to be much of a father and tell us, and you don't say a lot about work. But you've never, like, arrested a celebrity or a socialite. Have you?" She laughed a little.

"No," he snuffled through his tears.

Ellie smiled wryly. "Lennie Briscoe is an alcoholic. That's pretty accurate."

"Apparently." Gallows humor must be genetic.

"I tried to deal with it, with you not being around much, 'cause it must be a difficult job, like really awful sometimes, and Mom wouldn't let you be around even though you wanted to. I *know* you tried. I know Mom made it difficult. I know she would screen calls and delete your messages when she was in a mood. And she liked to take us upstate to see her family when your days off coincided with weekends. I just got used to thinking you weren't trying very hard."

"I coulda done better. When she went through phases of cutting me off from you, I just let her. I'd wait for her to be in a better mood. I shoulda fought it."

"Yeah, maybe. I dunno. But you know how stubborn she is. How she holds grudges. Maybe it was impossible."

"Could've gone to court and got a better custody arrangement."

"Maybe." Ellie shrugged doubtfully. "With your job and the affair and the way Mom spins stuff – I mean, she works in a freakin' PR company, so spinning is like her job – you really think a judge would have ruled in your favor?"

"Fuck knows. But I damn well shoulda given it a shot. I didn't fight." He cleared the gunk clogging his throat. "You can go to Australia. You should. You're right. You need to get away from all this. My bullshit shouldn't be your bullshit."

"I want to see other places. Mount Holyoke is still too close, and there's a lot of people there from New York. It's still the same mindset, you know. I don't want to end up like you and my mother. You guys think Connecticut is a foreign country. I want to get out, like really get out."

"You mean you don't need a passport to get past Westchester?" he joked weakly, wiping at his eyes with his palms.

"No. It's hard to believe, huh?"

"I know you wanna travel. It's great you can get into a good PhD program. And coral reefs – why not? It's what you wanna do."

She leaned against his shoulder. The shrieking white noise inside his head grew quiet. A moment of peace and silence but for the hum of traffic, distant sirens, the occasional creak in the old building's walls. Maybe this is what healing feels like, he marveled. Silence. Not the stillness bought on by having so much to drink you passed out, but silence emerging from a fleeting moment of grace, the feeling of crawling out from under the wreckage. Too bad he couldn't capture it, hold onto it forever; he knew the noise and turbulence would come back.

After a while, he asked, "When's your train back to Mass?"

"Tomorrow night," she replied, sounding wearied. "I'm seeing some friends in the city for lunch."

"Cool," he said. "You wanna stay here?"

"Does this sofa bed still work?"

"Probably."

"Are you working tomorrow?"

"The four-by-twelve."

Together, they wrestled the bed out of the sofa, and Alex pried it open with a spanner.

"Is this gonna collapse?" Ellie asked, while he crouched on his knees, wrapping duct tape around a joint on the legs that didn't lock anymore. "You can't fix everything with duct tape."

"No," he said with a faint smile. "But it'll fix this for tonight."

467

He threw some spare blankets and pillows onto the bed. As she arranged the bedding, he swallowed his meds. On his way into the bedroom, she squeezed him in another hug.

"I'm proud of you, Dad. I know you're trying to get it together."

The demons in his head would not stay in abeyance; he sensed them lurking, waiting, like fractures on old bridge pylons that couldn't be fixed with duct tape, either. But for now, he embraced her forgiveness as a small step closer to healing and repressed his sadness that she wanted to move to another country. If she did a PhD in Australia, he would do the right thing as her father and support that.

Chapter Forty-Two

"The department ain't the same," Brady stated as he sidled up next to Alex, crowding into his space.

Alex breathed in Brady's sickly cologne, and he tightened his lips and eyes into a vexed scowl.

"It's turning into a fat bureaucracy, and they're even hiring good little bureaucrats like Jo Gibson to run *this* squad. The fucking Homicide squad. She ain't real murder police. She's a box-ticker. It's this box-ticking bullshit. Affirmative action's gone too far. They promote someone totally unqualified. Oh, a Black woman? Give her one of the top squads in the Bureau. That'll make for some friendly *New York Times* op eds. What the fuck has she done? Run the Gold Coast squad? The East 40s? They probably gave her *that* 'cause it's a piss-easy precinct, so they could look good."

Alex sighed, and he wiggled earphones over his head, so he could listen to the tape from a wire and not listen to Brady's rant.

"Why the fuck didn't they give this command to O'Meara in the Eight-One? Now *he's* real police."

Alex didn't know O'Meara in the Eight-One. He opened the murder book for his case, jogging his memory of the cast list, then he reached for the 'play' button.

"And you know what, I'm glad I'm getting out," Brady sneered. "Detective work, real detective work, is dead. The last man, the last natural detective in this whole fucking department, is gonna be Vito Indelicata. Final drink with me and Sam, Alex? Next Thursday, the Blackthorn, after your four-by-twelve – gonna be a fucking great send-off. Like the old days. Stop by when you finish your tour. I know you say you've quit, but just this once, one drink. Gonna be our last chance, 'cause I'm moving to the North Carolina beach with my pension. This is my last day on the job."

"North Carolina sounds nice." *The middle of fucking Siberia would be better.* Alex wasn't even a little sorry to hear that the old hairbag was leaving. Still, the once dysfunctional but tight-knit squad felt like it had been dropped onto concrete, pieces scattering everywhere. Sam had transferred to Major Case to work white-collar crime and truck hijackings while several A and C team guys had retired, and Jean Allan had taken her sergeant's exam, afterwards transferring to the Six-Seven detective squad in Brooklyn.

"Lex, you gonna come?" Brady insisted, oblivious to the headphones.

Alex yanked the headphones backwards, so they fell around his neck. Eight years of working together in this place, and Brady only called him by his affectionate moniker when really drunk. *Now the asshole decides we're friends.* "I can't be in a bar, Mikey."

"Come down for one. One drink ain't gonna kill you."

"It will. I gotta get back to this tape."

As Alex straightened the headphones, Brady said, "Jesus, you don't have to be pissed at me. It wasn't me leaving those bottles of booze around. That was all Declan. He thought it would be funny."

Alex threw him the same look of bored skepticism that he had given to hundreds of suspects and witnesses, like he had heard these lies before. No question, Brady had been in on it with Keohane.

Muttering, "Sheesh," Brady skulked back to his desk.

With the headphones muffling the squad room, Alex listened to the tape, from a phone tap recording Mafia 'made men,' of interest to him due to the death of an uptown property developer who had, in an ill-fated stroke of civic duty, reported their shakedowns and money laundering to the police. Alex was working the case in conjunction with the FBI and the Manhattan DA's Racketeering Bureau, a multi-agency task force taking down the remnants of the 116th Street Crew, a longstanding offshoot of the Genovese family operating in East Harlem. Lowering his eyelids, he nibbled at his thumbnail, drifting through the rhythmic street slang, waiting, hoping for the gangsters to allude to the murder, to money laundering, or to slinging heroin. The conversation hadn't brought up any felonies when Gibson surfaced from her office, motioning for him to come in. He punched 'stop' on the tape player.

Was she after an update on the 116th Street Crew case? Unlikely, because they'd attended a task force meeting yesterday, and the tapes from the wiretap had only arrived this morning. His other cases? Doubtful. Like any good homicide supervisor, she let her detectives run their investigations on a loose rein. But once a week, they met about his health. Talking to the L-T about his medical problems and how he felt in himself made him feel ill-at-ease, more so than Corcoran's 'come to

Jesus' meetings. Yet those were her orders; she gave a shit, and that mattered. It was easier to stay on the path of self-destruction when you didn't notice or care who you took along for the ride. It was easier to die from alcohol destroying your internal organs if the deprivation was your own, not the deprivation of friends, family, colleagues. And it was far easier to meet with the lieutenant about it than be sent to the Farm, a rehab center upstate where cops went to dry out, and by all accounts, the place was run like a supermax prison.

Uneasily, he lowered himself into the chair and scratched at his side.

"Two months sober," said Gibson. "I'm really proud of you. How you doing?"

He considered this for a moment. Each day he didn't drink was, in fact, a day he didn't drink, and somehow those days had melted into months. A few colleagues still mocked him, although no one had hidden alcohol around his desk or locker since James blew up at Keohane. A biopsy of his liver late last week hadn't gone as well as he'd hoped. "I dunno," he finally replied. "They checked my liver again and don't think it's gonna get much better. They told me when I got sick the damage might be permanent."

"Okay, what are the ramifications of that? Obviously, it's working, or we wouldn't be having this conversation right now. No one with liver failure is up and walking around."

"There's scarring on it that's not gonna go away. I gotta take blood tests and get biopsies every year, 'cause it could deteriorate. They gotta keep an eye on it. But yeah, I mean, it works. A liver function test had me on the edge of the normal bell curve, but still, you know, functioning."

"That's good, isn't it?"

"Yeah, but it means I have to be careful, or more careful, with any medications I take, with diet, and I can never drink again. If I ever get Hep A off some bloody DOA, I'll probably get cirrhosis."

"I think you can learn to live with those things."

Emotions blocked his throat. "It's not like I have a choice."

"The alternative is definitely worse. Anyway, do you know of any police officer who's got Hep A off a vic?"

"Not personally, but I think I read something once."

"The risk is pretty low if you're not being stupid. Use gloves. How you holding up mentally, emotionally?"

That question shifted him towards a place inside his head he would rather not go. *Holding up? Are you really?* The place where he sometimes questioned whether his life was worth this amount of pain. He picked at torn skin on his thumb. "I'm... I dunno, it's like I'm thirty-eight, and my body's already fucked. As if I didn't already have enough chronic pain to deal with from the shooting."

"You learned to deal with your gunshot injuries," Gibson observed.

Alex exhaled sharply. "Yeah. By drinking."

"You just have stuff you have to manage. You basically had a life-changing injury eight years ago. Do you talk about it in your meetings?"

"Sometimes. Well, not me, specifically." He would rather cut off his hand than say a word about the shooting in a meeting. "My sponsor sounds like my ex-girlfriend – he talks a lot of New Age, spiritual bullshit. A lot about 'confronting trauma.' Lots of over-the-top self-affirmation stuff that makes you queasy sometimes. But he's a good guy. I guess he gives me a less fucked up way to look at things. He's not a cop."

"Another point of view can be helpful."

"They gave me this at the meeting last week." He dug his left hand into his pocket, fishing out an aluminum poker chip with gold-colored plaiting, inscribed with a circle inside a triangle on one side, and the AA 'serenity prayer' on the other.

"A two-month sobriety chip," said Gibson with a heartfelt smile. "That's fantastic."

"I survive another month, I get a green one," he said cynically.

"You'll get the green one. Your caseload okay?"

"Gives me something else to think about."

"Alright. If you don't feel well, you'll let me know."

"Yes, ma'am." If he woke up one day feeling well, *that* would be breaking news. He sank his molars into the back of his tongue. Would she ask him about the wiretap on those Mob guys or any other case? No, she was on the phone, but she trusted his investigative skills. More than she trusted his general life skills. As he jostled the headphones against his ears, he released a shuddering breath, stung by grief, by longing, pining for the days when he never talked about his health and his feelings to his boss, when he could go to parties and bars, when he could eat anything and not upset his stomach, when his liver could withstand abuse. Oh, well, that was one place, where he used to be, but he had crossed into another one, barely escaping with his life, and he had to live with it. He tried concentrating on the tape. A wiseguy complained about his mother-in-law. Alex half-closed his eyes, masking the squad room with his eyelashes. He rolled the sobriety chip around in his palm and felt his skin warming the thin aluminum. Two months, he'd survived two months on

472

this shitshow of a wagon, more than he ever thought possible when he'd walked out of Beth Israel. That was something.

The night Brady had his retirement party, a summer thunderstorm pounded against the city, casting a pall of sudden stillness over the length of Manhattan, where buildings and trees and cars seemed covered by a grey, muffling wet that missed nothing. In the last hour of the tour, Alex put off CompStat paperwork by writing a 'five summarizing today's 116th Street Crew wiretap that had no actionable intelligence. He typed at a slow pace, listening to the storm. The other detectives were chattering about taking a cab to the Blackthorn. Thoughts and feelings bounced like pinballs inside his skull, hitting one barrier, then another, disappearing before he knew what to do with them. He sweated up inside his jacket. His scar itched but hurt when he rubbed it. He rewrote a sentence half a dozen times. What did Will advise when he felt this way? Breathe in while counting to ten, then breathe out, like Charlotte once said when teaching him to meditate. Charlotte had called him an "alcoholic police detective." If he still had her number, he would call her, tell her she'd nailed it. *You were right all along.* She would only gloat a little, and she would have a new herbal concoction or meditation technique for him to try. He'd never liked Brady, but fuck, he wanted to go to the party, drink himself into oblivion, an iridescent world of smoky Scotch and golden lager lying beyond the grey drudgework of sobriety.

Bill and Marty were going, having known Brady since the early '80s. James wasn't. "I'm not showing my face at that asshole's party. Wanna lift back to yours? I got the car today." Alex gratefully accepted the offer, blaming the weather, although he wondered if James drove to the office today because he was worried that Alex would be tempted by the party at the Blackthorn.

Under the gloom of a racing, maddened sky, they splashed through the glistening pools of water, James slowing where floods were encroaching on entire streets. The windshield wipers on the Mustang groaned at every stroke. Crawling lines of headlights and taillights transformed the city into a slow-motion laser show. There were no parking spaces on West 87th, so James halted in front of the building, blocking the road.

He asked, "You alright? Want me to come up? I can find a fuckin' space."

Alex shook his head and worked his knuckles into his dried-out eyes. "Nah, not worth the hassle. It'll take you half an hour. I'm tired. I'm just gonna crash."

"Okay, see you tomorrow. If you're gonna do something stupid, call me first." The Mustang's V8 growled as it rolled away.

Alex took a deep breath and unlocked the door, feeling the air charged with the violence of imminent lightning, which suddenly broke across the Upper West Side in a deafening crack, as if the sky itself was breaking in three or four places. Only a few months ago, they would have gone on a post-tour drinking marathon, arriving at Brady's party wasted. Now James was being sober, serious, looking after him. He felt like his relationships with his colleagues had changed, the one with James most of all.

While lying in bed, he listened to rain battering his windows. He counted seconds between lightning flashing and thunder rattling the building. Rivulets of water coursed down the window panes. Even the air inside the apartment felt heavy with driving rain. The time between lightning and thunder expanded, wider and wider with each strike. After twenty or so seconds, it no longer seemed to matter.

A shock to his heart woke him up. An unremembered nightmare. He hadn't been aware that he'd fallen asleep. The storm had gone, and the sky outside was lightening into a pale dawn.

When he opened his window, he inhaled the sweet, earthy scent of rain rising through exhaust fumes and garbage. A delivery truck beeped somewhere. He rested his forearms on the windowsill and felt fresh air inside his lungs. Raindrops glinted in the transient light of the sun shining over granite townhouses across the street. The city seemed rejuvenated, refreshed, at least until the next body fell.

He showered, cleansing himself, then he shaved wearing a towel around his hips. His face didn't look as puffy as it once had, and his eyes were no longer bleary and red from too many banged up mornings. Still, crows' feet had plowed deeper furrows into the skin around his eyes. He scowled at a few grey hairs peppering his temples. The stress of the last two months on his face. But his belly looked flatter – if he squinted. The wound on his side was unchanged, a misshapen, red knot puckering out from his skin, and his ribs feeling stiff and sore.

By the time he left his apartment, the temperature was climbing towards the nineties. Mirages shivered in the June heat, like silver pools on the roads. He walked along West 87th, passing low-rises and townhouses with baroque balustrades, finely sculpted bay windows, and carved wooden doors. At Broadway, buildings of red bricks and glistening white limestone in the Renaissance revival flamboyance reared above the streets like ornate desert canyons. Alex tarried at the green railings guarding the West 86th Street subway station, watching commuters, winos, crackheads, the rich, the poor, the late, the confused, the lost, all racing in and out of the tunnel. *Who needs parties when you can ride the subway?* he asked himself as he boarded a train.

He scuttled into roll call as Gibson was making her daily announcements. Two months ago, he had slunk in late and hungover. Today, he was merely late. He sidled into a chair beside James, and his partner gave him a swift grin while his boss ignored his tardiness. Gibson stated that Declan Keohane had retired. Most of the detectives knew this, as the news had been broadcast on FINEST. No one was really astonished. They hadn't expected Keohane to stick around after Corcoran's departure. Bill reported that he had been offered a job working security in Trump Tower.

"Of course he did," Gibson drawled, bemused.

"Jesus fucking Christ," James muttered in Alex's ear.

"You're surprised?" Alex said. It made sense to him. "A man after Keohane's own heart."

"And he'll make a fuck ton of money. Bet Trump pays more than the NYPD."

"Probably, but it's still better than having him here." Alex never forgave Keohane for leaving erstwhile booze around his desk.

As soon as Gibson wrapped up roll call, Alex scooted into the bathroom to relieve his bladder. A dead fish rolled a glassy eye at him from the bottom of the urinal. You always knew when Bill had been on a fishing trip. Well, Bill could move it. When Alex returned to the squad room, he found that most of his colleagues had vanished. Bill and Marty had left to do something in the field with the Three-Two precinct cop shooting. The A team detectives had raced out for a DOA call. Gibson had taken off for a meeting at 1PP. The officers running the Wheel today had gone outside for a smoke. Only James remained, swearing floridly at CompStat and at the computer which had replaced his typewriter.

The phone trilled for attention. It might be the FBI asking about those Mobsters, or SAFIS with a fingerprint match, or the ballistics lab with results that Alex wished he had a week ago. It probably wasn't any of those. Alex reached for it. "Detective Boswell, Manhattan North Homicide."

"Hi, Detective, this is Sergeant Conon at the Three-Four. There's been a shooting in the 181st Street subway station on St. Nick Ave. Indelicata's there but they want Homicide forthwith."

"Ten-four," he said emotionlessly. Cinders burned inside his stomach. His long streak of avoiding Vito Indelicata had to break at some point. There was no one in the room to whom he could pass the buck. Besides, he knew it would be a redball, and no one would take it. Subways, like airplanes, make people feel trapped, vulnerable. Violent crime on the subway was far more alarming than crime above ground, and the media's hysteria was as inevitable and noxious as city smog.

"Shooting case," he said, not looking at James. "We gotta go to the 181st Street 1 train station."

"Shit," moaned James, knowing the implications of a subway shooting.

"I'll drive," Alex said in a gloomy tone.

Police tape cordoned off the whole block, from West 182nd to 180th, and the intersection at 182nd and St. Nick's had become a staging area, rammed with vans, cars, and personnel. The detectives signed themselves in and navigated through the overcrowded crime scene. It felt like a bar during the Superbowl. They brushed off a patrol captain, a CSU lieutenant, and a precinct detective. They wanted to see it with fresh eyes before someone told them what to do. A captain said that the Manhattan North Operations chief was on his way. *Fucking top brass*, Alex thought testily. Just what you want contaminating a crime scene. Someone who you couldn't tell to fuck off. Alex and James descended the stairs, scanning the steps for bodily fluids, shell casings, freshly torn clothing, cigarette butts, needles, or crack vials. All of which you might find on the subway anyway.

As the homicide detectives alighted on the platform, Vito bounced up to Alex, bubbling, "*Lex!* I heard a crazy rumor you're a teetotaler now. Tell me it ain't true!"

Alex threw him a stony look. "It's true."

"Aw, man. You're *kidding*!"

"No, I gotta dry out. I—"

"So, what are we gonna do to celebrate putting this case down? You were so much *fun* when you were drunk. It loosened you up. My God…those nights…You did some crazy shit. Absolutely crazy shit. A sober party? Like what's the fuckin' point?"

"I don't know, Vito," Alex retorted in a vexed tone. "But why don't you tell me what we've got." Jaw tensed, he wandered towards the cones and cops near the edge of the subway platform. You would think the worst social offense one could commit in the NYPD was not drinking alcohol. Well, probably, but it didn't alter Alex's reality or ameliorate his health issues, and he had to live with that.

"It's been so damn long since I've seen you," Vito slavered, oblivious to Alex's query. "Way too fuckin' long. Man, we were such a great team. We did great things together, solved some epic cases. Had some awesome times. Remember, when you first transferred to MNHS? We were like fuckin' brothers. I miss you."

It was like the violence of Quixano's interrogation had never happened. Vito, being Vito, probably shrugged it off, while it gnawed through Alex's heart like a parasitic worm.

That was three years ago. Forget it. Could he? Pangs drove into his breastbone, as if the memories wielded knives. Wiring himself into the present, he snapped on his gloves. The latex stung his skin. An officer was describing the victim as a twenty-one year old Black male. The vic himself wasn't there. He had been alive when the first officers arrived, and EMS had rushed him to Columbia Pres, but he'd arrested before they made it to the hospital. Neither the paramedics nor the ER staff could restart his heart. *Not a robbery*, Alex thought. Not a successful one anyway, because the vic's wallet had landed about ten feet to the right of the bloodstains. "This was found here?" he asked anyone in earshot. "No one's touched it?"

"No, Boswell," a patrolwoman said as she placed an evidence cone beside the wallet. "Well, we haven't."

He photographed it, then stood back while CSU stretched measuring tape between the wallet and the bloodstains, the stairs, the seating, and then they took their photos. The flashes dazzled his eyes.

"All yours," said the CSU sergeant.

He picked up the wallet. It contained thirty bucks, some loyalty cards for coffee shops in the Village, a credit card, and a driver's license and student card identifying him as Frankie McDonough, an NYU student with an address in Brooklyn Heights.

"Lex, you wanna go to the hospital?" asked Vito.

Alex didn't want to go near another hospital for the foreseeable future. "No. The crime scene's here. Not in the back of a bus, and it's not like he's gonna make a dying declaration if he's already dead. I hope every single person who was on this subway platform is being held, and the ambulance crew better be ready to give me a statement."

"Jesus," said Vito. "What's with the surly? Drinking Alex was way more chilled."

Alex inwardly flinched but shot him a glare filled with daggers. Turning his back to Vito, he squatted over the cones marking where the first officers had found McDonough. Had to be careful of blood now, but then, who wasn't? HIV, for one, would fuck up everyone, not just a guy with a permanently scarred liver. He squinted at the bloodied slugs. 9mm hollow points. Blood had smeared across the platform in a streak about five feet long and pooled into a wine-red lake. Vito's voice boomed in his ears, but this time aimed at a group of patrol officers. *Fuck Vito rattling some bullshit cop philosophy to those young uniforms.* Nevermind that the rookies seemed enthralled with the charismatic veteran. What did they know? What did anyone know? The muggy air inside the station was stultifying. Alex felt short of breath. His old wound ached terribly.

He pivoted to the subway tracks, eyeing the garbage strewn between the rails, but nothing looked fresh, although a detective was down there, picking it up. His gaze narrowed to the yellow paint delineating the platform's edge. Dark red splotches. He dropped to a squat for a closer look. Blood. Still congealing, like the blood from the vic. It wasn't much older or newer. The circular shape of the droplets indicated that the person had been standing or kneeling, and they must have covered the wound. No trails connected this blood to the pools of it twenty feet to his left or led anywhere else. Alex didn't see how it could be from the victim. From the perp? From someone else who got injured? Someone involved in the shooting? The trajectories worked. You could stand here, firing a gun, and hit somebody over there. He breathed fast, light in the gut. A couple years ago, New York courts had ruled that DNA evidence was admissible, and everyone thought it would transform criminal investigations. They said on a course Alex sat through at John Jay that scientists were working on techniques to develop DNA profiles from smaller and smaller samples. Not now, but in the foreseeable future, they might be able to ID people from traces of saliva left on a drinking glass, or a cigarette, or from skin cells on clothing. It was like fiction, the stuff investigators dreamt about – DNA identifications from nothing, one person out of millions.

This, however, was far better than nothing. Alex lay a six-inch ruler next to the blood for scale and snapped a couple pictures with his Kodak. He wrote himself notes, adding some squiggles and lines to his sketch. Then he called CSU over. For a minute or so, he watched two CSU detectives delicately swabbing the stains with cotton. After pacing out the distance between those droplets, the wallet, and the vic's location, he found the officers who'd responded to the call, two patrolmen from the Three-Four called Jenkins and Caro. Someone had called 911 on a pay phone, screaming about an active shooter in the subway station. Jenkins and Caro bravely ran into the station, expecting the worst. By then, the shooter had fled the scene, but the officers found Frankie McDonough bleeding on the platform, unconscious, but he had a weak pulse. Paramedics tried resuscitating and stabilizing McDonough while the officers sent out a frantic BOLO for every 1, 2, and 3 line station in the city. Alex reviewed the patrolmen's notes. Not an impressive amount of detail, but sufficient. He pushed his tongue against his teeth in concentration as he walked around the scene again: up the stairs, crossing over the tracks to the downtown platform, re-examining the concrete floors for more blood or stuff abandoned by someone in a hurry. Alongside CSU, he raided through every trash can above and below ground, on the off-chance that the perps had been stupid enough to dump incriminating evidence. When a young CSU officer asked if people were really that stupid, Alex quipped that he would rarely solve a case if they weren't.

Once he'd squeezed out every drop of evidence from the subway station, Alex drove to the Three-Four precinct house, crunching Rolaids between his teeth, swearing at Vito's mindboggling indolence towards crime scenes. Vito had ditched it hours ago. He would already be interviewing those eyewitnesses, or out doing whatever the hell he did on the streets.

It was the latter, thank God. But the witnesses were scared, tired, and still here, after giving brief statements to uniforms and other detectives from the Three-Four squad. Alex introduced himself as a homicide detective and apologized for the redundancy of it all. Last night's storm hadn't cooled the stuffy, overheated precinct house, but the A/C only worked in the squad rooms and commanders' offices. The sultry air in the interview rooms triggered a dull headache. He rolled his shirtsleeves up to his elbows, then unbuttoned his collar and loosened his tie. The eyewits looked tense and uncomfortable. Several were crying. Putting them at ease, Alex commiserated about the lousy A/C in the station house. They told him that one or two white males disembarked from the subway (one wit said one, the others said maybe two). Definitely white, because you notice when white guys get off at West 181st Street, especially when they have shaved heads. The shooter fired some rounds, two or three, but no one was sure. The witnesses dove for cover or scrambled for the exits. A homeless guy with a facial tic stated that he'd seen the perps leg it across the bridge to the downtown platform.

One or two white guys with shaved heads. Skinheads? Neo-Nazis? A hate crime? Oh, God, the city would implode. Alex called the Hate Crime Task Force. "I need records of any white supremacist groups operating in the city," he said to the detective on the phone. "Names, mugshots, rap sheets."

Of course, he could not overlook other motives, so he found McDonough's friend, waiting by himself in an interview room. Maybe the perps had been after the friend. Maybe McDonough had enemies. Maybe they had been after someone else on that platform, and McDonough got caught in the cross-fire. Maybe it was a case of mistaken identity, like Donovan King.

The friend, a skinny Afro-Latino twenty-year old called Sonny Vargas, huddled over the table with a blanket wrapped around his shoulders, as if unaware that it was almost ninety degrees. His features were sculpted into a frozen look of stunned terror. A gangbanger? Drug slinger? Alex's gut told him that neither was likely. Did he want a lawyer? Blankly, Vargas shook his head.

Alex eased himself into the seat beside the wit. He inhaled the guy's fear, pungent, metallic. "I'm Alex Boswell, with Homicide," he said softly. "I know it's been a Godawful day, and you've talked to lots of other people, but I swear, I'll be the last. I'm gonna tape this interview, okay?"

"Yeah," muttered Vargas, in too much shock to care.

Pursing his lips, Alex pressed the record button on his mini-voice recorder. Gibson had ordered her detectives to tape every conversation with key witnesses.

Speaking in a broad Dominican accent, Vargas said he was from Washington Heights, a classmate of Frankie's at NYU, and himself and Frankie were boyfriends. They'd been at a gig in the Village last night, then stayed at a friend's place afterwards. This morning, they had been returning to Sonny's apartment in the Heights. What gig? Who was the friend? A metal band. Vargas showed Alex the ticket stubs and related the friend's name, address, and number. Did anything unusual happen, at the gig or anywhere else? No. Not until a white guy with a shaved head got off the same train at 181st, but a different car, said something Sonny hadn't fully heard but it might have included the *n-word,* and then started firing a gun. Sonny hurled himself behind a trash can. When he crawled out from his hiding place, he saw that Frankie had been shot and the perp had vanished.

Alex shifted to the tough questions – did Sonny have any problems with anyone? Did Frankie? Were they involved in any illegal activities? Vargas wept. "God, no… no… I'm a history major… I *know* lots of stuff goes down in this neighborhood, but man, I've never been involved with it. Frankie, neither. He's not from the Heights. Me and my parents came over from the Dominican Republic in 1993. They've worked hard. They own a good business. They've never been involved in drugs, either. No one in my family's ever been arrested or had anything to do with the dealers."

"I run your name or Frankie's name through our computers, it'll say that?" Alex asked.

"Yes," moaned Vargas.

"The guy who shot at you, any chance you would know him?"

"No. Never seen him in my life. I don't know any white people who shave their heads."

"Did you get a good look at him?"

"No, no, I kinda glanced but didn't look, and then I just hid when the gun went off. I couldn't think."

"Any chance he could've followed you guys from somewhere else?"

"No," whimpered Vargas. "I think I'd notice a white skinhead on an uptown 1. My God, I shouldn't have hid. I'm such a coward. If I'd... I could have saved Frankie."

"Or you could be dead too."

"Would that be so bad?" Vargas asked wretchedly.

"Your family would think so," Alex replied in a gentle voice.

"What about Frankie's family? I could have jumped in front of those bullets."

Alex touched the witness' forearm. "I know that looks easy in movies, but when these things happen in real life, it's fast, scary, and you don't know how you're gonna react. Not even trained police officers know. They can't even jump in front of bullets. I was shot about eight years ago, and my partner was hurt a lot worse than I was, and I thought we were both gonna die. We almost did. I took a bullet to the chest, and it still gives me trouble. My partner was paralyzed." The wound twinged when he sniffed in a breath. "For years, I beat myself up, asked myself what I coulda done differently, but there really wasn't anything."

"You're a cop, though."

"Doesn't matter. I was scared shitless and badly hurt. It's not like Bruce Willis movies." Over the years, he'd found that he could cultivate rapport with witnesses who were themselves victims of shootings.

"I didn't know what to do," whimpered Vargas.

"Neither did I. Nobody does. I hear you, but the best thing you can do for Frankie is trying to remember whatever you can. Is there any chance you could recognize the shooter?"

"I don't know," gurgled the witness. "He was just a white guy with a shaved head."

"Just one?"

"I don't know. I saw one. But maybe there was another. I saw the gun pointing at us and panicked. That's all I could think about."

"Can you remember anything about his face?"

"No. I can't even see it. I can only see a gun."

"You definitely weren't coming up here to score drugs or prostitutes or anything like that?"

"No, man. We were going back to my parents' place. And just because we're gay doesn't mean we're sleeping around. That's such a shitty stereotype."

"Sorry. That's not what I was implying. I don't care what you're doing. I honestly don't. I'm Homicide. I just care who you're doing it with, and if they might be the sort of people who deal with their problems by shooting them."

"We weren't *doing* anything. I swear to God. Oh, Jesus." Vargas pawed his face, weeping. "You know, we stayed in the Village— we didn't come home after the gig last night because we thought the subway was too dangerous at two am. How crazy is that? We thought, eight am, people going to work, normal people going to work, this shouldn't happen."

"I know. It shouldn't. It's heartbreaking that it does. Your parents are in this precinct, right?"

"Yeah," muttered Vargas. "They're talking to another detective. The Irish guy with blue eyes. Said they never should have left the DR. And the police don't care about Black people getting shot. How much of your time is Frankie gonna get?"

"As much as I got." Alex weighted his voice with forceful sincerity. "You gotta believe me, I'm gonna work my ass off to collar these guys. I'm not gonna stop until I do, which I know sounds like a stupid cop cliché, but it's true. If you remember anything, you can call me at any time, okay? I'm sure my partner's done interviewing your parents by now. I'll get them, and someone from Victim's Services will meet you guys and talk about what we can do to help." The witness looked genuinely distressed, and Alex wanted a more extensive background check before questioning him further anyway.

"Well, the police in this country might be sorta racist, but at least they're not totally corrupt," commented Vargas in a thin voice as Alex opened the interview room door.

Sometimes. Alex was unsettled by his own intrusive thought. He wondered where Vito was and what he was doing. *Do you really want to know?* He felt depressed, run down, craving his whisky flask, but he consoled himself with coffee instead. Raising the specter of his shooting might help him connect with upset witnesses, yet it always left him feeling ill – hundreds of tiny black thorns piercing his brain and the wound rotting through his side.

Their investigation of Frankie and Sonny backed Sonny's story. Frankie studied theater at NYU, and he'd never been in trouble. Neither had Sonny, who was, as he said, a history major. He was also secretary of an LGBTQ advocacy society at the university. His parents were running a small but ostensibly successful clothing chain in the city. Frankie's father, Earl McDonough, was a major in the army, and his mother, Annette, worked in a real estate firm. Nonetheless, kids from the most stable families in the world can fly off the rails, but by all accounts, Frankie and Sonny hadn't. Their worst offenses were drinking and smoking weed at college parties. Alex chased that lead, not thrilled, but with a redball, you cover your butt and chase every weak-ass lead. He grabbed McDonough's weed dealer, a guy supplying half the NYU dorms with marijuana but had no connections with anyone around Washington Heights. A good detective recognizes when he's on the wrong foot, and Alex let that one go.

The ME autopsied Frankie the next day, and James journeyed downtown to observe. He came back to MNHS reporting that the cause of death had been two shots to the chest, which destroyed the lungs and caused uncontrollable hemorrhaging from the coronary artery. The ME surmised that the shooter had stood facing Frankie from no more than ten feet away. If Frankie hadn't been the target, he was the unluckiest guy in the world, taking two slugs to the chest at relatively close range while standing in the crossfire.

After speaking with the ME and James, Frankie's parents arrived at the MNHS offices. First, Gibson met with them, and they wept in her office. Once they'd patched themselves together, she introduced them to Alex, the primary homicide detective. Alex had taken an Omeprazole beforehand, but acid fizzled against his sensitive stomach lining. He gave his spiel, the one he had given hundreds of times, sorrowful, empathetic, but adroitly explaining that if Frankie had been up to anything or had any sketchy friends, he needed to know. Annette McDonough melted down into hysterical sobs, while Earl grasped both Alex's hands in his, begging, "Please, find these people. I don't know what else to do."

"We will," Alex promised.

"They were gonna get married," cried Annette. "Whenever they made gay marriage legal, the boys were gonna get married. How could he just be taken from us? From Sonny? How does this happen?"

"Keep us updated," urged Earl desperately.

"Of course."

Accompanied by the department's victim advocate, the distressed parents wobbled out the door. Alex slumped against the interview room sofa. His guts seethed, agitated. Coping with the anguish of victims' families never got easier, no matter how many years he did this job.

The media picked up that the police suspected a racially motivated attack, and it wasn't long before Rev. Jesse Jackson and other leaders of the African-American community were camping out at the Two-Five, the Three-Four, and holding vigils in the 181st Street subway station. Vito and James, who were better on camera than Alex, appeared on morning shows, soliciting the public for information. Headlines screamed about a rising tide of domestic terrorism. Look at Tim McVeigh. Look at the bombings of Black churches in Atlanta. Gibson stood like a one-woman blockade between the politicians, press, and her detectives. A Black C/O of the Homicide squad vaguely reassured Jackson and nervous politicians, but even with Gibson running interference, Alex lost countless nights of sleep. Every day, he felt hollowed out, his organs sucked dry by the strain on his frayed nerves and delicate digestive tract.

Some of his sanity and health was salvaged when eyewitnesses identified two individuals from the Hate Crime Task Force's collection of mugshots: Jesse Huska and Peter Norris, both with rap sheets, and their faces flagged by an undercover FBI agent attending white supremacist meetings in the city. A lead, thank God! Norris, twenty, had a record for drug possession, B and E, and third-degree assault, while Huska, only eighteen, had a sealed juvenile record. The riding ADA, Simon McNally, coaxed a judge into unsealing it.

"Oh, fuck," James said, reading the names and address on Huska's file. "There's a Detective Ronnie Huska who lives on Staten Island. He's in Queens Narcotics. You remember, he used to be on the Three-Four squad."

"Fuck." Alex hazily remembered Huska, a decidedly average detective. He had worked one or two cases with him. With pointless optimism, he asked, "How many Huskas do you think live on Staten Island?"

"Not fuckin' enough," James said glumly.

After asking around the department, they learned that Huska's son, Jesse, had been expelled from high school, convicted of third-degree assault for punching another kid, and allegedly, he had a crystal meth problem, but his father had convinced himself that he'd sealed the record forever.

Alex and James sat on their information, strategizing. How do you move forward without all hell breaking loose? It would, no matter what. Gibson looked waxen and sick to her stomach when they told her. But she ordered them to keep going. If hell broke loose, they would stamp out the fires. What else could they do?

A few days later, they got another break, a game-changing one – DNA from those bloodstains on the platform edge matched Pete Norris', and even better, Norris lacked the *cojones* for being a person-of-interest in a murder investigation. The detectives had brought the suspects in for cursory interviews, and they'd both denied being anywhere near Washington Heights but, having a limited appreciation for the investigative possibilities of DNA, they'd consented to cheek swabs. Alex sent the samples to the FBI lab. When the lab reported the DNA match, the detectives picked up Norris. He disintegrated within minutes once he'd heard the evidence against him.

"I didn't know Jesse had the gun or that he planned... planned anything." Norris writhed around in the chair. Tears trickled down his colorless face.

"How do we know it wasn't your idea, and now you're in a jam, so you're trying to pin it on him?" demanded James.

Desperation clouded Norris' eyes. "Because I'm still a Christian, and killing people is just wrong. The Bible says so. I wouldn't do something like that."

"Right, so why are you hanging out with white power groups? We know you are."

"I *was*," protested Norris. "I stopped going when they began talking about violence. I was only there because I was proud of being white. Aren't you proud of being white and Christian?"

"I'm Jewish," said Alex.

"Oh. But still, it doesn't mean I wanna kill anyone. Not Jews. Not Blacks. Not anyone."

The detectives caught one another's appalled eyeballs.

"What exactly did you think you were going to Washington Heights to do?" Alex cranked up the sarcasm.

"I don't know. I didn't know where we were going."

"It's an uptown 1 train. Where do you think it goes?"

"I just thought we were gonna score some meth off someone," Norris admitted. "I didn't know Jesse was carrying a gun."

"Really? You had no idea?"

"No, I swear to God. I didn't know he had it."

"Drug dealers are pretty dangerous people. You wouldn't carry one for protection, just in case?" Alex dangled the 'out.' "I mean, if someone wanted to rip you off, you gotta defend yourself."

"Yeah, but we had a trustworthy guy."

"A trustworthy meth dealer?"

Norris shrugged. "He's a good guy. What can I say?"

Sort of playing at 'bad cop,' James laughed abrasively. "If he was a 'good guy,' he'd be out feeding orphans in Somalia or finding a cure for fuckin' cancer, not slinging crystal meth in New York City."

Again, Norris shrugged.

"Well, for now let's say you're telling the truth." Alex wanted the guy's story, whatever it was. "When did you realize Jesse had a gun?"

"After we got off the train, you know, there were mostly Latinos in the station, but he pointed it at these two Black kids who were like, really well dressed, and said, 'those two...well... the n-word...are full of themselves,' and just *shot* them. Lots of people started running up the stairs or down the platform. I couldn't believe it. It was crazy. I totally panicked, I tried to get the gun off him, you know, grab it, but I couldn't. We fought, and he was like full of this *rage,* and I wasn't gonna get it."

"Were you injured?" Alex asked, thinking of those bloodstains with the DNA match.

"Yeah, I guess I cut my hand fighting with him. You know there was blood, but it all happened really fast, but like in slow motion. I mean, then we just *ran.*"

"Can I see the cut?"

Norris held out his hand, showing Alex and James two bloody band-aids stuck haphazardly over the palm. At the detectives' request, he peeled away the band-aids. It looked like he'd caught it on something and ripped off a quarter-sized chunk of skin.

"Do you know if anyone was hit?"

"One of the guys dived behind a trashcan. The other one fell down and was kinda sitting on the platform. Oh, God. I'd hoped Jesse'd missed him, or just grazed him, but obviously...shit, man."

"Where did you run?" said James.

486

"We ran onto a downtown 3 train, and I took it to Crown Heights. Somewhere, Jesse changed to a 1 and went to South Ferry, I guess. Back to Staten Island."

"Why did you go to Crown Heights?"

"I don't *know*," cried the perp. "It was as far as the subway got before they shut the line down."

Alex sighed, pulling the air from deep inside his lungs. A lead so close that he felt it tickling the hairs on the nape of his neck, but not proof beyond a reasonable doubt. The self-interested statement of an accomplice methhead would not win the love of a judge or jury, and it didn't entirely convince him, either. They needed corroboration.

Unfortunately, their luck had run out, and evidence wasn't forthcoming. Ronnie Huska had been on an eight-by-four at the time of the shooting. Huska's mother, sitting in her flowery '70s-décor living room, looking as fragile as old porcelain, told them in a quivering voice, "Jesse was here with me all day. Helping clean the house."

"You got anything to prove that?" said Alex.

She looked at him, her expression stone cold. "You'll just have to believe me, Detective."

Alex departed from the house, feeling a cool fluttering in his gut – he knew she was lying, but they couldn't give a cop's wife the third degree. Someone further up the chain-of-command or the police union would kick their asses from here to California. Where the Verrazano swept into Brooklyn, the Manhattan-bound BQE slowed into a parking lot, the traffic as stationary as their Goddamned case. Hopelessly bogged down in the four-lane jam, Alex channeled his innumerable frustrations into chewing a bleeding hole in his forefinger.

"Jesus, Lex, you're gonna lose all your fuckin' fingers," James grumbled.

"I gotta keep *some* bad habits," Alex argued. He dabbed at the blood with his other hand.

"This one?"

"What else have I got?" He lolled his shoulder against the door. They stopped beneath an overpass, stuck behind an eighteen-wheeler, and Alex gazed upwards at the bulging graffiti letters and psychedelic eyeballs etched high on the pylons. Someone with about six cans of spray paint had climbed up there. Or rappelled down from the overpass. That was ambition and chutzpah for you. Strangely, it seemed as though the eyeballs were watching him; he shivered, feeling like the air in his lungs had frozen solid.

Norris' statement was against his 'penal interest,' supported by the eyewitnesses, which meant it was credible enough for reasonable cause. In a second sworn statement, he said that they'd smoked up and 'planned capers' in Jesse's blue Camaro, because Norris' anti-drug housemate would call the cops, and Huska's father was obviously a Narcotics cop. A judge authorized a search warrant for Huska's car.

Warrant in hand, Alex and James parked at the diner in Staten Island where Jesse worked as a server. Officers had been tailing him, so they knew he hadn't skipped town. They had already interviewed his boss and colleagues. His boss described him as unassuming, while a fellow employee related a story about a Black customer coming into the diner, then waiting for a friend, and Huska had phoned the police, complaining that the customer was trespassing, 'looking shifty.'

The blue Camaro trundled into the parking lot, and then Huska clumsily backed it into a space, almost hitting the adjacent car. Alex and James jumped out of their Crown Vic and ran across the tarmac, flashing tin. Alex felt his ulcers scorching through his diaphragm. On some days, they hurt like a bitch, and on others, he could fleetingly forget he was unwell.

"We've got a warrant to search your car," he puffed through the pain. "Put your hands where I can see them."

Huska responded by spinning on his heel, then legging it towards the alley around the back of the strip mall. Taken by surprise, Alex, James, and the uniforms sprinted after him, a patrolman shouting into his radio that they were pursuing the perp on foot. No one had expected a cop's kid to be stupid enough to run. James caught up to Huska and dove to take him down. The perp swerved towards the building. Alex's heart seized. A knife blade, glinting in the sun. Huska swung it into James' left shoulder. James stumbled to his knees, then rolled, screaming, "Knife! The motherfucking fucktard has knife!"

Even more shocked, Alex and the patrol officers drew their firearms. The skinny white patrolman fired three shots but missed. Sense returned to Huska before someone emptied their clip. He flung the knife towards the dumpster as he flopped to his belly on the asphalt.

Alex's heart galloped. The gunshots echoed inside his eardrums. He couldn't hear anything else. Adrenaline flooded every artery. Staring at Huska down the black barrel of the Glock, he knew he could shoot him. Easily. He had threatened perps with guns more times than he could count, and while you're not supposed to point your gun at people unless you're prepared to shoot them, he never really was. This time, his finger quivered over the trigger, seconds away from blasting the motherfucker's head off with no regrets.

But Huska had relinquished his weapon and was sprawled face down. You can't shoot a man who has surrendered. You can, however, make his life hell. Using all his weight, Alex rammed his knee into the perp's spine and slapped the cuffs on him. He aggressively tossed him for more weapons and contraband. Upon not finding anything, he manhandled Huska towards a squad car, panting, "You're under arrest for assault on a police officer and obstructing government administration. We're still gonna search your fucking car." He rattled off the *Miranda* warning as they flung him into the back of the RMP.

"I wanna lawyer," whined Huska. "You know my Dad's a cop."

"Yeah, you're gonna need one, you piece of shit," Alex answered breathlessly, desperate to attend his injured partner. Someone else could book this shitbird. He whirled around to face a young officer, a Latina patrolwoman with her hair pulled into a tight bun. "You want this collar?"

"Sure, Detective." The patrolwoman was eager for collars. Low-grade felony arrests were more useful on her record than his.

Her squad car squealed into motion, towards the expressway, and Alex held his hand against his thudding heart, watching the car for a second, then he jogged over to his Crown Vic. James sat on the hood, legs outstretched, cradling his left arm. A thickset Asian patrolman called Hariri was examining the wound.

"You alright, James? You need a bus?" Alex gasped.

"It's just a flesh wound. It's nothing." Blood besmirched James' beige shirt and his dark blue jacket. "We gonna execute this warrant or what?"

"His car's not going anywhere. You sure?"

"I'm fine. It's not deep."

"It's deep enough," added Hariri. "You really should get stitches, man."

"I'm fine," repeated James. "I've seen worse."

"I'm sure you have. On dead people," said Hariri wryly. "You don't want it getting infected."

"Fuck, I almost shot that son of a bitch. *After* he was lying on the road." Alex sat beside James on the Ford, clutching his stomach with both hands. It burned like he'd swallowed lighter fluid and a match.

"An MOS's kid..." James' lips formed an 'o,' and he breathed out loudly. "Jesus, you'd spend the rest of your life dealing with the paperwork. That uniform who discharged his weapon sure will be. Is someone interviewing him?"

"Yes," said Hariri.

Alex panted, "I didn't fire when he pulled the damned knife—"

"Thank God for that," James cut in, grinning insolently. "You might've hit *me*. You're a terrible shot."

"—but I was so close to shooting him once he'd surrendered. Do you think my head's too fucked up to be out doing this?"

"I mean, he kinda stabbed me, so it woulda been a good shooting. No question. You wouldn't have been too jammed up, but it would be messy. It's not been an easy couple months, Lex. But you're doing okay."

"Who the fuck knows? Look." Alex raised his right hand, so James and Hariri saw it vibrating. Emotions swelled, erupted, and he balanced on the precipice of crying like he had at the AA meeting or on the street with Ellie. God, not here, not in front of cops.

"Well, you haven't shot anybody or started drinking again. That's okay, by my book."

Alex barked out a short, caustic laugh. "Mazel tov, huh."

"Yeah." James smiled through his pain. "Come on, take a breath, start digging through that car, and I'll supervise."

Alex, the patrol officers, and CSU ripped apart the car, gutting the footwells, the glove compartment, the underfloor panels, then unscrewing the seats. Alex removed the spare wheel from the trunk. There it was. The literal smoking gun. A Sig Sauer P225 underneath the spare tire. Suddenly feverish, he unloaded the magazine. 9mm hollow point bullets rolled onto his gloved hand. Like the ones that killed McDonough. A surging head rush, his heart racing, the high of a warrant getting you the thing you want, a case breaking. This one would promote him to second grade. He bagged the firearm, documenting how and where he'd found it. His hands were shaking so intolerably that he struggled to write things.

Leaving the clean-up of the search to CSU, they drove over the Verrazano, and Alex battled blood fizzing through his head as he traversed the BQE. *Concentrate on traffic!* Beside him, James clutched his shoulder while acting nonchalant and spitting out jokes, but his face was losing color. As they approached exit twenty-four, Alex edged the car into the right lane, flipping on the turn signal.

"What are you doing?" asked James. "We're still in the middle of fuckin' Brooklyn."

"Brooklyn-Methodist isn't far away. It has an ER."

"I told you, I'm fine. We gotta get this gun to Property. If we fuck around for six hours in an ER, the chain-of-custody's gonna be a shitshow."

"It's not."

"I'm not gonna die, Lex. Please, keep driving."

Reluctantly, Alex flicked off the indicator and stayed on the interstate until the Brooklyn Bridge. Thankful that parking gods were benevolent, he found a space across the street from Police Plaza. His partner seemed uncomfortable when he levered himself out of the Ford and limped past wide-eyed security personnel. But no one stopped him.

"I gotta fuck with this," James said tightly, side-stepping into a bathroom. "Then I'm gonna sit in the car. You can deal with the chain-of-custody shit, right?"

Alex leaned against the wall near the hand dryers, nodding, worried. But he brought the firearm to Property and rushed through the paperwork, obviously scatterbrained, because the Property Clerk, after scanning it, handed it back. "You forgot to sign here, Detective."

"Oh, yeah," he said, biting his lip, scribbling his signature. "What's the date?"

He dashed out of the building and flung open the car door. "Fuck," he breathed. The Crown Vic looked like a crime scene, with blood-soaked paper towels like red snowballs littering the footwell. Ignoring James' protests, Alex caned it the Fulton Street walk-in clinic, where they waited for two hours, and eventually, James received twelve stitches in his shoulder.

"It's a shit scar compared to yours," James laughed. "I said it wasn't a big deal. It was a glancing blow. Now I gotta deal with all the fuckin' line of duty paperwork. I was hoping to avoid that. Can you believe that kid? A fuckin' detective's kid." He gingerly shrugged on his shirt and buttoned it up. Crimson stains bloomed across the shoulder and chest.

"The kids from his school said he was violent and impulsive, and he was probably high. I didn't find any meth on him when I tossed him, but he'd probably been smoking it." Alex's hand fell to his ribs. His thoughts leapt to Eddie and Stella, settled in their Florida beach house. Eddie had mailed him a draft of a crime novel that he hadn't found the time to read. Last week, with Will at AA encouraging him to reach out to people, he'd written a letter to Eddie explaining everything that happened. Self-reproach tore through his heart as he handwrote that letter in his slovenly cursive – he had the job, a functioning spinal cord, and the entirety of his large intestine, while Eddie didn't have any of those things. But here he was, kvetching about a disease mostly in his head. He should read Eddie's damn novel.

He pushed knotted scar tissue over his tenth rib. It caused a sharp burst of pain, the rib shifting downwards. "James, you gotta change your shirt."

"I have one in the office."

They returned to the MNHS office, where James joked with people about the blood on his suit, and they found the long-awaited tox scan from McDonough, sitting on Alex's desk. Traces of weed and alcohol but not enough to matter. Vargas said they had been passing joints around and drank a few beers.

Word travelled the wire at light speed, and Gibson rocketed across the squad room. "Detective Hurley! What the hell are you doing here?"

"Working a case," James answered with an impish smirk, raising his eyes from the tox report.

"Yeah. You got bloodstains on your shirt and you're wounded. You should go home."

"We're on a roll," insisted James. "It's nothing. Lex told you, we found the gun."

"You found *a* gun," Gibson corrected. "The lab'll tell you if it's *the* gun. Look, you're investigating a cop's kid involved in what might be a hate crime. This is gonna be the biggest clusterfuck you've ever seen if it even goes a little bit wrong. You guys gotta be on it."

"We're on it like a rat up a kilt, boss," James replied.

Gibson raised both eyebrows, somewhere between amused and exasperated. "Is that what they do in Scotland for fun? At least your mouth works alright. But for God's sake, change your shirt."

James refused to let his wound slow him down; they burned through their overtime, sacrificing RDOs, working flat-out to track every lead and nail down every scrap of evidence. Their case languorously rolled forwards. The Sig Sauer was registered to Ronnie Huska. He'd bought it two years ago from a gun shop in New Jersey. While Alex regarded guns as a tool, an unfortunate and necessary part of the job and nothing more, some cops collected firearms like his mother collected tchotchke, and Ronnie was one of them. Since Jesse still lived with his parents, the detectives obtained a search warrant for their house, which included authorization to bring a K9 unit with a sniffer dog. They found two dozen handguns and rifles, most of which were antiques, but Ronnie had six modern weapons, unsecured, lying around like house plants. Anyone could grab one. They seized the two 9mm semi-autos.

"Lieutenant, are you authorized for this seizure?" Ronnie whined to Gibson, who was supervising the search. "Those are legal."

"We can seize anything pertaining to the homicide," she told him firmly. "McDonough was shot with a nine."

The detectives raided Jesse's room, unearthing white power magazines, porn, and a couple trashy spy novels. The dog barked at the mattress. They opened it, revealing baggies filled with glassy white rocks: crystal meth. *Means, motive, and opportunity*, thought Alex. And he was fucked up on a lot of meth.

The next day, Alex travelled downtown to 100 Centre Street to testify in a hearing for one of last year's cases, a crack-fueled domestic violence homicide going to trial. Protesters marched through Foley Square wielding signs demanding justice for Frankie McDonough. Eyes down, Alex circumnavigated the protests in the middle of the square, then he ran for the Criminal Courts Building. The heavy door swung shut behind him. The cops on security waved him around the metal detectors. Will from AA had counselled him to try breathing exercises in place of whisky. Inflate the entire lung. Think about the crime scene for the DV case. The furniture broken like they had a fight before it turned fatal. Crushed crack pipes on the floor. Blood splatter flecking every surface. The victim bathed in blood, sprawled across the floor of the East Harlem brownstone, stabbed eight times by her husband. Crime scenes were probably not what Will intended him to think about.

After his testimony, he wafted around 100 Centre Street. Those protesters marched outside, venting their rage at the justice system. Although they had no inkling that he was the primary on McDonough's case, he felt the unbearable weight of their discontent squishing his organs. Inside the courthouse, a parent berated his twenty-something child for getting arrested, again, then looked mortified when he realized that about a dozen people had overheard. Alex's mind free-associated to Sarah, with her rage at him, her rebellion against school and her mother, her sense that everyone thought of her as a disappointment compared to her sister. He should phone her. He should try harder to repair their relationship. She had been refusing to see him after his 'don't do drugs' talk, and, according to Ellie, she wasn't taking his sobriety seriously, the only thing she agreed with Catherine on these days. Catherine had phoned Alex last week, complaining that Sarah had snuck into a gig at CBGB, using a fake ID. She'd told her mother she was going to a study group.

"You talk to her," Catherine had said. "You're a cop."

As if that gave him insights on dealing with recalcitrant teenagers. "She doesn't listen to me. You've told her for years I'm worthless. Why the hell would she listen to me?"

"Well, Alex, she doesn't listen to *me*. Don't murderers listen to you?"

"When they're handcuffed to a table being interrogated for nine hours."

"Maybe you should try that with Sarah. Nothing else works."

He coughed, feeling like he had wool in his throat. "She doesn't talk to me. She believes every shitty thing you've ever said about me."

"Don't make this my fault. Just… talk to her." Exasperated, Catherine had hung up.

With this new cell phone, bought last month, he could call from the hallway of 100 Centre Street, or anywhere. No more waiting in a line for a courthouse payphone, overhearing all the complaining, the misery, the despair, the high stakes court-side drama. This time, he caught Sarah in a reasoning mood. She reluctantly agreed to see him on Thursday, four days from now. Perhaps his attempt to pull his life together would inspire her to do the same.

"Where do you wanna meet?" Alex asked.

"Not far from Mom's," she said curtly.

"East Village?" he suggested. "What about that steakhouse near Union Square? You know, the one we went to for Ellie's sixteenth birthday. I think it's called Union Station."

"Yeah, whatever. That's fine."

He made reservations for Thursday evening at the steakhouse. This time, he promised himself, he would not hassle her about her choices, not even about sneaking into CBGB with a fake driver's license. Kids did that. Hell, at least it was a music bar with a lot of history, which seemed more justifiable than a seedy dive of a nightclub. A couple years ago, he had used his juice as a detective to get seventeen-year old Ellie into the Bitter End for a gig. One of their secrets.

At the start of the eight-by-four on Tuesday, Simon McNally and a captain from TARU strolled through the squad room. Alex slugged down his coffee, then battled the overworked machine for another mug. Spitting and grinding, it complied. He tracked the two men as they wove around cubicles and walked into Gibson's office. McNally wore a bright blue Gore-Tex mountaineering jacket over his suit. The TARU captain wore a perfectly pressed uniform. They made an odd-looking couple. A surveillance operation, Alex thought. He returned to his desk, drinking the coffee impatiently. It burned his tongue and lips.

Gibson called him into the meeting, along with James and Bill. In a rush to caffeinate himself, he scalded his mouth and throat again, then he crossed the room.

"We've been talking to Pete Norris," McNally announced. "As part of an agreement with our office securing his cooperation, he has agreed to wear a wire and meet up with Jesse Huska, who's out on bail now, and see if he can't entice him into talking about McDonough."

Jesus. I wonder what they're giving him, Alex thought.

"You offer him free blow jobs for the rest of his life?" James, as ever, voicing the thought everyone had, but no one else had the chutzpah to say.

Unamused, McNally replied tersely, "There's an offer of man one on the table if he continues to cooperate with our investigation."

"Sweet," said James. "Sure beats murder one."

"TARU will set up the wire," Gibson explained. "You three are going in their surveillance van, on Thursday, at 2000 hours, to a location where Huska and Norris regularly meet. A vacant lot near a warehouse in the Meatpacking District."

Alex felt like he'd been kicked in the guts. "Thursday?"

"You'll get the overtime," said Gibson. "Is that a problem?" Her manner wasn't motherly or compassionate, like when they met about his health. Now she was stern, unbreakable, an NYPD commander who gave orders and expected prompt compliance.

Yes, he wanted to protest, but he knew that Gibson was in no mood to let the Homicide primary miss a critical operation. A joint op doesn't revolve around the knotty personal life of one detective. "No, ma'am, it's fine," he muttered.

Gibson and the TARU captain explained the op in more detail, but Alex absorbed nothing. In his head, he played different tactics, ways to phrase this dinner cancellation so it wouldn't sound like work was more important than spending time with his daughter, but he could not identify any, because work, this time, ultimately was.

As soon as Gibson sent him out of her office, he unfolded his cell phone and called Catherine's apartment. "Can you get Sarah?" he asked when Catherine answered. His pulse jetted like he'd overdosed on a speedball.

"Oh, you're not cancelling on her, are you?" she said.

"I tried, Catherine, but shit's hit the fan at work, and there's nothing I can do about it." How did she know? She must also be psychic.

"There never is. Everything is always beyond your control. You'd better tell her yourself."

Before he could defend himself, Sarah's voice snapped, "What?"

Then the truth, and nothing but the truth. "I'm sorry, sweetie. A work thing's come up, and I can't make it out on Thursday."

"You always choose work over me. I don't even care if you've quit drinking," she said bitterly. "You might as well start again. It obviously doesn't matter."

He winced, like he'd smashed his hand with a hot iron. "I don't. It's just bad timing. It's the case with the NYU student who was shot in the subway station. It's been in the news every day. James was even on TV. You know this is a big case."

"Except it always happens. And you always blame us, your boss, or the case, or Mom, or everyone. But you're so flakey."

"I can't *do* anything about this," he insisted.

"Yeah, right. You always say that."

"Sweetheart…"

"I don't want to see you. I don't want to ever see you." She hung up.

He dropped his phone onto a binder. The squad room sounds crackled like static on the radio, and her angry words stretched his soul until it was paper thin, on verge of ripping. He felt James' hand between his shoulder blades. James said something about the wire. Fuck this wire. Fuck the job. Fuck sobriety. His hand drifted towards the drawer where whisky once lived. But he'd asked James to get rid of it. He clenched his fingers into a tight fist, his hand twinging.

They could reschedule. Normal fathers and daughters could reschedule. He tried calling Sarah later that evening, then the next day, and the one after that, but it went to the answering machine every time, and she never phoned back. Along with her mother, she must be screening her calls, avoiding him. A classic Catherine move. She had probably told Sarah not to bother with him.

Inside the surveillance van on Thursday night, he felt shame like the whole Mississippi flooding, anger and loneliness redoubling inside him. He'd chosen this lifestyle. He could never make time for his own kid or put her ahead of the job. Why shouldn't she hate his guts? Acid bubbled inside his stomach. Trying to settle it, he attempted Will's breathing exercise, drawing in as much air as his damaged lungs allowed, until it hurt, then gradually breathing out. Elsewhere, James, Bill, and a TARU detective taped the wire to Pete's chest and gave him the spiel about the difference between a genuine confession and entrapment. The van door grumbled open, and a nervous Pete exited. Alex saw his face, dark and anxious, before the door slid shut.

"Sarah will chill out," Bill said. "She's a teenager. It's a tough age. My daughter hated me when she was that age."

"You weren't outta the picture for years."

"You've been trying to fix your relationship with your girls since I've known you," Bill replied. "Sounds like your ex is half the problem. I'm sure Sarah will realize that someday."

"My ex could manipulate you into believing the sky was green. I'd feel sick if I *knew* what she said about me to the girls."

"They don't tell you?" Bill asked.

"Hah," Alex snorted. "Sarah doesn't talk to me, and Ellie wouldn't, to spare my feelings." He focused on listening to the wire. Work could drive the thoughts of drinking away. Pete walking, clothes rustling, Pete's voice, Jesse's voice, chatter about scoring meth, how much meth cost, and some guy they knew whose meth lab blew up.

"Quit talking about fucking crystal," James muttered.

The conversation stuck with crystal meth for a while, and the detectives shriveled from boredom. Pete pivoted to politics, his dislike of the federal government and Bill Clinton in particular, as if that could bring Huska around to confessing to the murder. It didn't. Sounding wooden and suspicious as hell, Pete praised Randy Weaver, the white separatist who had an eleven-day stand-off with the FBI in Idaho. He suggested that the world was being secretly controlled by a cabal of twelve-foot lizards from space. Clinton was probably a lizard. Newt Gingrich was definitely a lizard.

"I think everyone already knew that," said James.

"Hey, that's unfair on lizards," countered Bill. "What did they ever do to you?"

When the lizards fell flat, Pete went for the direct approach, expressing anxiety about the investigation, saying he'd been seeing police cars following him. Huska dismissed it as paranoia (unlike the lizards). Whenever Pete tried to entice Huska into mentioning the murder, Huska acted evasive, disingenuous. The son of a bitch must suspect something. He wasn't stupid. They called Pete off. If he tried too hard, it would be inadmissible anyway, and Pete's acting abilities were limited. Huska had already proven that he was violent and unpredictable, and they didn't want their star witness ending up as a DOA because Huska suspected he had become an informant.

Pete re-entered the van, breathless and teary. "I tried, I tried. He just wouldn't. I really tried."

"Don't worry about it," said Bill.

"Lizards?" said Alex with an upraised eyebrow.

Puzzled, Pete squinted at him. "You're the police. You must know about the lizards."

"Yeah, I've met the mayor," James assured him, his voice weighted. "I got you."

Chapter Forty-Three

Reined in by his boss, McNally would not authorize an arrest warrant unless they had more than uncertain eyewitnesses and a meth-addled accomplice. They'd arrested people on far more tenuous evidence, but the District Attorney had his eye on the politics and the police unions.

"It's fucking shit," McNally grumbled. "Not fair. But it's just the game."

Intersections of demographics and politics were rarely fair or just. Neither was the work itself. Alex drove himself into a darkness that was more murk than black, working overtime exceeding hours in the day, at times wishing he could afford a few sick days, but he was terrified of showing any frailty. Some colleagues already doubted him. Vito and other precinct detectives taunted him about not drinking, laughing when he tiredly told them to fuck off. No, he had to act like a cop, stalwart and hardboiled, even though he felt so attenuated, so brittle, his disease devouring him like a worm eating holes in his guts, and a caseload well into double figures. Those other victims mattered. Maybe only to him and their families, but they mattered. In his head, he refused to make distinctions between the Frankie McDonoughs of the world and the crack-addicted homeless guys. But with the darkness came a tiredness, a weariness, and he never seemed to have quite the energy he needed to make the rounds of never-ending phone calls, interviews, warrant applications, surveilling, canvassing, analyzing LUGS, finances, lab reports, ME's reports. Still, the more he worked cases, the less time he had to think about drinking or worry about what to do with all the pain he couldn't wash away with alcohol anymore. Sobriety had left him stranded.

Long after an eight-by-four ended and the rest of the team had absconded to a bar, he hunched over his computer, typing out a 'five summarizing an interview with the sister of a dealer who'd ripped off a rival, and the rival had pumped him full of bullets. The ulcers hurt with a fierce heat. They were taking a long time to heal. His doctor said less coffee and less stress would help, but he couldn't escape either. Distracted from the 'five, he spent about twenty minutes procrastinating, drawing a flow diagram illustrating the differences between a SNAFU, a shitshow, and a clusterfuck, and how you identify which one you're in. He labelled the McDonough case on the diagram, halfway between shitshow and clusterfuck. That he taped to the white board, then he resumed staring at the computer. Pain lanced through his middle, mangling his attempts at writing, forming thoughts, or staying upright. The burning in his gut spread like a forest fire, consuming his whole body. Breathing shallowly through his mouth, he abandoned the 'five, then ate a Carafate. Thank God this place was empty tonight. Moving stiffly, he retreated to the interview room sofa and turned himself into a ball.

The phone rang, persistent, demanding. *Fuck off,* he thought. He'd only rested for about ten minutes. The drugs hadn't fully coated the inside of his stomach. Listlessly, he rolled off the sofa and trudged over to his desk. "Detective Boswell, Homicide."

"Hi, Alex, it's Cynthia at Ballistics." Cynthia Hardwick, a lab tech downtown.

He perked up. Good news? Had the bullets pulled from the 181st Street station matched any one of those firearms? The lab had a perpetual backlog. Ballistics results inevitably came in slower than he wanted.

"So, there's good news and bad news," Cynthia explained.

He felt his heart liquefying and sank forwards in his chair.

She continued, "The good news is that it shares some characteristics with firearm 2ABX7—"

"Sorry, which one is that again?"

There was a pause as she checked her paperwork. "The Sig Sauer found in the Chevy Camaro. Unfortunately, the bullets bounced around so much inside your vic that they're pretty battered, so it was never gonna be a brilliant match. I can't conclusively rule out every other 9mm weapon with similar barrel characteristics."

"If that's the good news, I can't fucking wait to hear the bad."

"Yeah, well, it took us a while to get the slugs. I know we had the firearms and the paperwork from you, but we didn't have the bullets collected from the train station and Property didn't, either. So, um, we started making calls and it turned out Detective Indelicata had them in his locker at the precinct."

"Oh, for fuck's sake," Alex groaned. What was wrong with that man? Chain-of-custody problems. That could be catastrophic. Any defense attorney with half a brain could argue that the slugs were of dubious evidentiary value because the police messed up chain-of-custody SOP. Then, nothing Vito did surprised him anymore. He grimly thanked Cynthia, who said the physical report should be with him tomorrow, then he called Vito. He swore he would bust his balls.

"Lex. Just the man I wanted to talk to," Vito said brightly.

"Why the fuck did you keep those slugs from the McDonough shooting in your locker for like a month?" Alex exploded. "Evidence SOP 101. Jesus Christ, Vito, what were you thinking?"

"Hey, don't worry about it. They were safe."

"You know that's gonna be excluded. Is chain-of-custody still a thing in your precinct? Unfortunately, it is everywhere else."

"Cool your jets. You at your office? I'm not far away. We'll talk about it in person." Alex heard the dialtone.

What a stupid mistake! Even rookie would know better. Livid, he took out his frustration on the phone, smashing it down. Ineptitude? Or something else? Vito was lots of things, but he wasn't inept. Alex couldn't deal with Vito's smug, puffed-up face or his overbearing ego, but if the precinct detective said that he was coming, the entire ESU would not stop him. The stress fed his ulcer. He swallowed more meds, but a chainsaw sliced through his diaphragm. Holding his stomach, he slid down from the chair, toppling onto his side, pulling his knees to his chest. This was moving beyond the shitshow, now approaching a super-nova of a clusterfuck.

Someone knocked, then the door squeaked. Shit. His hip and shoulder ground into the floor. He was curled up on his side under his desk, which wasn't professional or hardboiled, so he creakily disentangled his body from the scratchy carpet, limping for a step or two. But he met Vito at the door.

The precinct detective grinned like a Cheshire cat and enthused, "Lex, you're looking *great.*"

He was sweating and pale, and he'd been lying on the floor. Like hell he did.

"Come out for a drink," said Vito.

"You know I can't," Alex said.

"C'mon," pushed Vito. "Stay for like an hour. You been an Upper West Side Jew too long, pal. It's contagious, this organic, detox liberal fuzzy wuzzy crap."

"I have holes in my stomach. I almost died."

"Then have a soft drink. Whatever. It's cool. We need to talk but not here."

Had Alex felt stronger in himself, he might have told Vito to get the fuck out of his squad room. But Vito had immense gravitational force, like the sun. Unable to pull away from it, Alex followed him through the door, onto the landing between the MNHS office and the Two-Five detective squad room. His body protested, hurting as if he'd wrapped himself in strips of razor wire that stabbed into his sides and belly as he descended the metal stairs. *You need to get out of here! You need rest,* he argued with himself, slowing his pace. They passed through the Two-Five's main door, and the fortified steel thudded shut. The muggy evening air was so thick and velvety you could caress it. With a wide-mouthed grin, Vito firmly put a hand on Alex's elbow, directing him towards a grey Crown Vic. Alex tensed the muscles in his arm, but there was something strong and dangerous about Vito's grip. Opening the car door, Vito blathered about boxing, then his kid's high school football team. Alex found himself sitting in pools of his own sweat in the faux leather passenger seat.

Vito drove twenty blocks to an Irish bar called Finn MacCool's on East 96th and First. Both men exited the car, Vito grunting at someone he knew smoking outside the pub, then rushing into the building without chatting to his acquaintance. Alex felt the muscles and tendons in his knees melting, painfully giving way. He hadn't set foot in a bar since collapsing in the Glendale three months ago. Advertisements for alcohol decorated the walls, while shining bottles full of golden spirits stood in rows behind the bar. The taps glinted, glamorously silver under the lights. It would be so easy to have one beer, one would be all right, but if one was all right, why not two, or three, and by that point, who cares anymore? Oh, God, he should care— he'd been feeling the ulcers all day. He could feel them now, like he'd been impaled on something.

"I really can't be here," he whispered.

"You'll be fine. Hey, Ronnie!" Vito's attention was directed towards a man sitting wraithlike in a shadowy corner. He towed Alex over to the booth. "Lex, you remember Ronnie. He used to work out of the Three-Four."

And his Nazi son killed an innocent man and stabbed my partner, Alex thought intemperately, gazing into Ronnie Huska's eyes, and realizing nothing good could come out of this, on every possible level. He envisaged his flow diagram. Way beyond the shitshow, now squarely in the jurisdiction of the clusterfuck.

"Lex, just sit down. Listen for a bit. Relax." Vito fixed a disarming smiled on his face, and he almost shoved Alex into the leather booth.

"I've gotta go," Alex insisted, feeling a sharp twist in his gut.

"One minute, give us one minute," Vito said. "You're the only guy in Homicide I trust now. The only one. I need you to listen, okay?"

A chorus of sensible voices implored Alex to run – it sounded like Will from AA, Gibson, James – but something more formidable pinned him in the booth, facing the sad eyes of Ronnie Huska. Huska stared into his face as if he could reach Alex's soul and yank it out. Alex recoiled at the feeling.

"Boswell, you gotta listen," Huska begged. Tears glistened in his blue eyes. "I know you're gonna arrest Jesse for that murder. I know he hurt Hurley. I know. I can't… you gotta help me. If he's charged with murder, it's gonna *destroy* my wife, my marriage, my life."

"He destroyed another kid's life," Alex answered, his tone flat and cold. "His family. And your wife lied for him."

"I *know*," Huska said miserably. "I understand… but Jesse's a fuck up. He's totally fucked up. He doesn't think. That's why he knifed Hurley. He's taking meth. I mean, you obviously know that already. He's been fucked up since he was little and my wife and I, we didn't know what to do. We tried so many things. We couldn't even keep him in high school. He dropped out. Got expelled, really. He couldn't stay outta trouble. I don't know what to do with him. God, we tried. I don't know… He needs help, lots of help, not the rest of his life in prison."

"That's not up to me. My job is to find the perp and make the collar." Huska had a beer in front of him, golden like honeyed nectar, bubbling with a luscious, foamy head. Alex sucked in a labored breath and held his forehead with his right hand. Dealing with bullshit like this was much easier when he drank.

"You gotta do something. You're a good guy. A good cop. Vito says you are. We worked together on that De la Corte case in 1990. Remember? That Mexican girl."

"Yeah—"

"Did you ever find the perp?"

"No."

"You gotta help. I promise, I'll get Jesse help. I'll get him into psychiatric care. I'll find him a counsellor. Rehab. Maybe one of those 'hoods in the woods' programs. Something. If he's in prison after being convicted of a hate crime, they're gonna destroy him in there. They're gonna kill him. And now the death penalty's been reinstated here… It's a capital offense now." Huska choked and scrubbed his palms over tears raking his cheeks.

"That's what you tell the jury at the sentencing hearing."

"Lex, be reasonable. We're all cops here." Vito smiled at Alex with bemused affection, like Alex was the best man at his wedding, giving an awkward speech. He put his hand over Huska's. "Ron, we'll take care of it. We gotta look out for each other, no?"

His face bright red, Huska nodded. "Yeah, we do."

Alex's opposition to taking care of whatever Vito thought they should take care of drowned under a screaming cacophony. It howled at him, louder than his friends: give up, give in, have that drink. What would he gain if he rebuffed it? Another aluminum poker chip, a green one. He was an alcoholic. Why fight it? His diseased brain, indifferent to his health, craved one thing.

"We'll help him, yeah?" Vito said. "That's what we do."

What will you tell the people at AA? What will you tell Gibson and James, Marty and Bill? What will you tell Ellie and Sarah? He had weathered almost ninety days. Now he clung to an exposed knife-edge, a breath away from letting go, falling into oblivion. Forget the ulcers, forget the liver fibrosis, forget the torture of detox, bury these three months so deep, with rehab nothing more than an insignificant anomaly in a long, downward spiral. James and his daughters would get over it. People get over things. They cope. Did he believe that? Oh, fuck, the thing refused to be defeated by his will or his strength. He didn't have enough of either. It was there. It would take him.

"I gotta go," he said hoarsely.

Vito reached for his forearm. "Hey, Lex, we gonna make sure everything's square? You're my man for this. I trust you."

Alex squirmed free of the booth, then twisted on his heel, plunging for the exit. The sticky air outside hit him like he'd run headfirst into a damp, soft wall. Behind him, he heard Vito and Huska barging through the door. *Get lost,* he thought angrily, breaking into a run. He flew under red-hued sandstone low-rises, rusty fire escapes, pale grey walk-ups with balconies, and soaring, high-rise towers. The numbers on the streets fell. His heart and lungs strained against stodgy humidity. At East 86th, he cut across the city. The long blocks seemed longer than ever. His legs ached and his shoes scraped flesh from his feet. Second, then Third, then finally Park. Sobbing for breath, he staggered against the green railings of the East 86th Street subway station. No one was following him. The block was spinning. He tried anchoring his eyes to a Chase bank across the road, but he went down on his knees, almost passing out from the pain in his old wound. Feverish, he clawed at his tie, clumsily undoing the knot, then ripping open the top three buttons of his shirt. Several people asked if he was okay, offering to call an ambulance.

"I'm fine," he panted. "Just the heat."

Dizzy, he sat with his back against the railings, his chest heaving, wrestling down nausea until he could stand without fainting or vomiting. Blisters stung his feet as he unsteadily descended the stairs, searching his pockets for subway tokens. A 6 train shrieked into the station and opened its doors. He huddled over his thighs on the blue plastic bench inside the carriage. The train clattered to East 59th, where he connected with the N line. He'd run from a bar. He'd defeated it today. At the Times Square station, he pushed his way out of the N and hobbled aboard a 1, then he closed his eyes, only aware of the firestorm scorching through his side, his belly. It was a high-pitched shriek in his head, like he had tinnitus. He lost track of the train's progress until the conductor announced, "West 86th Street." His stop. He could have crossed the park on foot from East 86th and got here faster. The path through the park was well lit. For some reason, the magnitude of how badly he was functioning, he took three subways.

Chapter Forty-Four

Simon McNally played it cool, shrugging off the chain-of-custody debacle and bringing the case to a grand jury, which indicted Jesse Huska for first-degree murder. The old cliché cautioned that a prosecutor could persuade a grand jury to indict a ham sandwich, but on the day this grand jury returned a true bill, Alex found himself showered with congratulatory phone calls – Sonny Vargas and his family, Frankie's family, Giuliani himself, the NAACP, and every politician in New York City, from Senators to city councilors.

Alex sweated over Ronnie Huska and the slugs sitting in Vito's locker for weeks, but he only warned Simon about the slugs. He refused to think too hard about the meeting in that pub. It might have been nothing more sinister than Vito spouting bullshit, superficially reassuring his old squad buddy. *Like you really buy that,* a cynical voice in his head interposed. He quashed the voice. *What am I going to do anyway?*

"So long I can talk the judge into not caring, it's fine," McNally said confidently. His wiry hands were quiet, folded on his desk instead of reaching for his cigarettes. He really wasn't worried. "Juries understand science, sort of, and *Law and Order.* Mostly *Law and Order.* An expert tells them the bullet more or less matches the gun, they're happy. And I'm sure Indelicata can bullshit a valid-sounding reason that'll keep the judge happy. That guy could sell a bridge to anyone."

True, but Alex saw disaster everywhere. "I've seen judges exclude evidence like that, and don't bullshit me. If it gets past the judge, you know a good defense lawyer could convince the jury those slugs came from Mars."

"Yeah, don't worry, Alex, I got this." Simon leaned back in his chair with a smile and a confident gleam in his eye, like how he eyeballed that gas station wall before climbing it.

No more nights like that. Alex gulped down a reflux of acid and pain.

A couple weeks after the indictment, the defense surprised everyone, not bothering with excluding the slugs and instead, filing an omnibus motion to suppress, contending that the search of Huska's car was unlawful and therefore the court should suppress the Sig Sauer. That gun placed Huska at the scene, their only piece of physical evidence. At one of the thousand meetings with Hate Crimes detectives, Gibson, and ADAs about the case, James had said, "Well, like there's a fuckin' surprise. Huska might've turned his brain into oatmeal but his dad's a fuckin' detective. It doesn't take a genius to throw some clothes in the river or burn 'em."

Let them have at my warrant, Alex thought when he received the summons to testify in the hearing. An application he'd written himself: by the book, probable cause clearly and inarguably laid out, unassailable. Double-checking, he reread his affidavit. It looked kosher to him. The defense was filing spurious motions suppressing evidence he had handled correctly, rather than evidence Vito flagrantly hadn't. As ever, the man seemed made of material you could set on fire, launch into space, or sink to the depths of the ocean. Perturbed, Alex kneaded his chest and then swallowed his infuriation by eating an old Milky Way. It had been sitting in a drawer for months, maybe years, but those things would outlast cockroaches.

The next day, he journeyed downtown to meet with Simon, who paced around his office like the tigers in the Bronx Zoo. Stress bristled from his body. "They're going to fuck us. I know it." The lawyer chain-smoked one cigarette after another, and his office reeked like a dive bar. "I can feel it in my gut."

Alex knew many cops, but Simon was one of most brazen sons of bitches he'd ever worked with, a man who saw nothing crazy about climbing a sheer rock face thousands of feet above the ground, balanced on holds smaller than the bricks on a New York tenement. Alex's gaze wandered to a photo; Simon roped up to an airy ledge atop a thin rock spire.

"I wrote a by-the-book warrant application," Alex said incisively. "They got nothing."

"Well, yeah, I know. I reviewed it with you," Simon sputtered.

"You seen their witness list?"

"They're calling some of *our* eyewitnesses."

"Our eyewitnesses? Can I see the list?"

Simon dug out the paperwork for the motion, an affidavit-in-support and a witness list. The motion argued that the IDs had been suggestive, which meant that the search of Huska's car was unlawful, the fruit of the poisonous tree. So what? Every defense lawyer tried suppressing IDs. Every defense lawyer argued that your ID procedures were suggestive.

"This is all standard bullshit," Alex said. "The IDs were fine."

"He's calling our fucking witnesses, Alex," Simon growled, pointing to four names on the list. "If those wits suddenly can't remember what they saw, why the hell does the defense know that, and I don't? Or you don't. And why are they now defense witnesses?"

The meeting over, Simon lit another cigarette, and Alex buttoned up his jacket, fussing at his blue-striped tie until he slackened the knot. Simon stared past him, scowling out the window like a pissed off dragon with smoke puffing from his nostrils. Lower Manhattan offered no answers.

On the drive uptown, Midtown traffic ground to a prolonged halt. Alex idly listened for drama on the police radio, but his mind slowly revolved towards Finn MacCool's. What a wretched day – his ulcers acting up, his first foray into a bar after his hospitalization. *We gotta look out for each other. That's what we do.* His tongue felt raspy; he had no saliva in his mouth. Sweat seeped along his ribs, tickling his scar. Something rose inside him, like nausea, but more ominous, forcing its way through his body with power that left him breathless. *Fuck, fuck, fuck. Think like Vito.* Years ago, when he first joined MNHS, he'd used that as a mantra. How different things had been then! Vito's art, his juice, resided in his great ability to talk to people, to find a way under their skin.

Alex wriggled out of the traffic jam, squeezing around stationary cars until he raced along the sinuous curves of the West Side Highway. He parked near 174th and Amsterdam. One of the eyewitness lived in a brownstone overlooking the oaks and sycamores in Highbridge Park, a single mother called Eva Castillo, raising a son around the chaos of the crack epidemic but no criminal record herself. A detective's dream eyewitness. He held in a breath and knocked on her door.

"Detective Boswell," she said. "I didn't think you'd be coming by. I only talked to your friend, Detective Indelicata, last week. Would you like coffee?"

"Yeah." Spikes of pain jabbed into his bowels. He kept himself up-to-date on the 'fives written by every detective working the case, and none suggested that Vito had any recent contact with Castillo. "I'm just following up on a couple things. 'Cause there's a hearing coming up." He raked his tongue against his back teeth. Thinking, he massaged his face, as if he had a terrible headache. "I talked to Detective Indelicata yesterday, but I haven't… To be honest, I haven't been sleeping well, and

I can't remember what he said. Can you just remind me of your conversation?"

"You should see a doctor about not sleeping. It's not good for your health," she advised.

"I probably should."

She handed him a mug. "The other detective asked if I was sure I saw two men shoot those boys."

Alex dipped his head, sipping the coffee, in complete agreement with whatever Vito had told her. His eyes roved towards the small army of saints standing to attention on the window ledge. Below them, the trees in Highbridge Park were lightly tinted with red and gold hues.

"I says, well, it all happened so fast, and as soon as I heard the gunshots I lay on the ground. I thought I saw two men, but maybe it was one, it was so fast, and people were running. Detective Indelicata says if I wasn't sure, I should say one. He said, 'it's gotta be consistent. Everything's gotta be consistent.' Then he says, how sure are you about that photo thing you did? Where you picked the man from the photo. You know, everything was happening in seconds... He said, yeah, yeah, sometimes, your memory goes funny under stress. And I said, I'm sure it did, lord knows. I mean, that face, I'm not sure I could pick him out now. Lord knows..."

"Okay." Coffee splashed against his stomach lining, hurting. "When you testify, you'll say what?"

"I say... I saw one white man with a gun in the subway station. And I don't know... I don't know if I can remember his face. That's right, isn't it?"

No, no, no, he wanted to shout, Vito having done the defense attorney's job, confusing the hell out of the eyewit, but instead, he grunted, "Mmm."

"The detective said... if I don't say that...if I say something I'm not sure of... I can be charged with something called obstruction. I don't want no charges. I got a job, I got my boy, I can't be getting into trouble."

That's not what obstruction of justice was, but Alex saw in her eyes that Vito had shaken her to the core, and what could he say to change her mind? He would never be as convincing as Vito. He left her with some platitudes, then sprinted for the car. The tires squealed as he spun into a U-turn downtown. Another witness lived in Harlem, on 125th Street and St. Nick's, near the Apollo Theater.

No one answered when he pounded on her door. Rapping harder, he barked, "Police."

That got the attention of the neighbor, a slight Black woman wearing a turquoise hijab, who popped through the door across the hallway. "You looking for Ms. Wood?"

"Yeah," Alex said.

"You won't find her. She moved out a week ago."

Alex stared at her. Barbed wire twisted around his chest. "You sure?"

"Yeah. I helped her move a couple boxes."

"She say why?"

The Muslim woman responded with a blank shrug. "Just said it was time for a change."

"You know where she went?"

"Michigan."

"What city?"

"No idea."

"Did anyone come by before she left?"

"No idea. I work long hours."

"She leave you any kind of contact information or forwarding address, like for mail?"

"Nope."

"She seem upset? Scared?"

Another shrug. "Frazzled and stressed, but that's moving, isn't it?"

"If she comes back or contacts you, call me." Alex handed her his card. She wrinkled her lips at it. "Homicide? Jesus. She must be in trouble."

"No, she's not. I just need to speak to her about something she saw," he assured her.

"What is it?"

"I can't tell you. I'm sorry," he said.

Before the woman could ask more questions, he turned on his heel, jogging down four flights of stairs, drawing up frantic mental notes. Pull phone records; run an NCIC check; chase down the apartment's landlord; send a BOLO to the Michigan state troopers with details on her car. All of that assuming she had told her neighbor the truth, and no saying she had done that. His guts writhed with worry: she was in the wind. A fateful coincidence, or someone had spooked her into running. Goddammit.

He caned it back to the Heights, to the West 151st Street apartment rented by a witness who was unlikely to skip town, a low-level slinger called Ruben De Leon. De Leon's brother answered the door, gruffly snapping that Ruben had been collared by AntiCrime in a stop-and-frisk for possessing weed with intent to sell. Alex wished he could be surprised. Fatalistically, he flipped open his cell phone and hunched over the hood of his car, making calls to every acquaintance he had in AntiCrime, at last locating De Leon in Rikers. His AntiCrime acquaintance innocently reported that Vito had already spoken to De Leon about the Huska case. Alex gulped down two antacids, but they didn't settle his stomach. He closed his eyes and jammed his fingers into his throbbing eye sockets. Twenty minutes to Rikers if the Grand Central wasn't a mess. But the Grand Central was always a mess. He could walk away, forget his gut feelings, and pretend he didn't know anything. That was safer. That was what most people did.

Instead, he drove to the prison, where he slammed headlong into bureaucracy. Did he have the paperwork to meet with a prisoner? Had his supervisor signed off?

"This is urgent!" he shouted, the nausea heating his anger. "Relating to a murder case. People's lives could be at risk! You want me to tell your bosses and mine that you're obstructing a homicide investigation?"

After about twenty minutes, they gave in. He met De Leon in a conference room, only to find the witness suspicious and uncooperative, De Leon streetwise enough to know from the outset that Vito and Alex weren't in cahoots with one another. Alex interrogated him anyway; for two hours, he swung wildly from whispering to yelling, to rambling in baffling circles, building himself up, a towering figure of omnipotent authority, weaving a narrative that made him into God's own detective and anyone stupid enough to lie to him looked a thousand life sentences in the face. He flew at the witness with all his strength, thinking he should turn his back on the job now if the long months of sobriety and despair breaking his balls had diminished his skills in the interrogation room.

"Okay, Detective Indelicata came to me when I was still in the cage at the precinct." De Leon slouched over the table, the chains on his manacles rattling.

"Why?" demanded Alex, relieved. His health might be like a highway pile-up, but dammit, he still had his wits.

"He told me not to say."

"I'm telling you that you need to tell me. I'm done fucking around here."

"He said he could get me off."

"The drug charges?"

"Yeah."

"Outta the goodness of his heart?"

The witness squirmed like someone poured cold water over him. "If I say I only saw one white boy in the subway station when those Black boys were shot."

"One?"

"One."

"Not two?"

"Definitely not two."

"What else?"

"There's nothin' else."

Alex gave the prisoner a frozen stare, conveying the message that he knew the man was lying, and the only way out of this predicament was the truth.

"I was wrong about the photo array." De Leon played at the chain between his wrists. "That I said what the police...what you and the detective with black hair and blue eyes... wanted me to say. Telling you won't stop Detective Indelicata from getting my case dismissed, will it? My lawyer said this morning that the DA was gonna drop the charges. That's not gonna change, right?"

"It's like we talked about," Alex said in an icy tone. "You lie to me, you're looking at being sent upstate."

"It's the truth. I say, I didn't see no second white boy, the short one, I get out."

"Your previous statement is in the file. Did Detective Indelicata tell you what perjury was?"

"Only I know what I saw. That's what he said. He said he'd make sure it's alright. He said the statement don't matter."

The Rikers guards led the prisoner away. Tenderly, Alex stroked his throat, sore from two hours devoted to non-stop ranting. Prison doors clanged, thumping at his breastbone, and he flinched. He was in shock, but not as much shock as he would have been in years ago, before Quixano. It was easier now to accept that Vito was perfectly willing to throw justice, ethics, and any inconvenient legal precedent or fact out the window. How had Vito convinced an ADA to drop the charges? He probably had some dirt on him. Or, conversely, a hook. Dispirited and exhausted, Alex plodded through the prison hallways. On all sides, metal doors slammed, chains jangled, toilets flushed. No stillness in a prison. He advanced into the daylight, crossing underneath the sheer ramparts and razor wire, squinting at the sun in his eyes. As he started his car, he swore at Vito, at the witnesses, at cops helping out perps, flipping the system on its head.

The last eyewitness, Manuel Reyes, was a homeless guy with mental health problems and a crack habit. But without hesitation, he'd confidently ID'd the two perps from the photo array. Grinning jubilantly, he'd explained that he had a photographic memory. Reyes wasn't at the subway station, his regular haunt, nor was he at the homeless shelter run by a Baptist church on West 170th. The church volunteers directed Alex to a wooded area on 9th Avenue, overlooking the Harlem River. He parallel parked alongside the woods, guarded by a sagging, rusted six-foot chain-link fence. His palms sweated as he clambered over the fence, the chain swaying under his weight, adrenaline spiking his heart, but he swung his legs over the top and dropped down, landing in a crouch. The trees pressed in closely, like he'd jumped through a portal leading to a peaceful woodland. Was he still in New York? Yes – he inhaled the earthy scents of pine and urine, leaf litter and burning oil. Within five minutes, he stumbled upon half a dozen grimy, stone-faced homeless guys crowding around an oil drum.

Holding out his shield, he said, "I'm NYPD. I'm looking for Manuel Reyes. Has anyone seen him?"

The homeless guys muttered amongst themselves. One man demanded, "Why?" He had greasy, greying hair and clutched a scraggly, underweight Staffordshire terrier against his chest.

"I'm worried about him," Alex said truthfully. "He's a witness in a case."

"He in the Big House now," said the man with the dog.

Alex drew his eyebrows together. "Big House?"

"He means Bellevue," said one of his companions. "That's what he calls it."

"Bellevue? He's on the psych ward?"

The homeless guy nodded energetically. "Oh, yeah, he got picked up and taken away. He was runnin' down Broadway butt-ass naked. Police picked him up."

"Have any other police come here?"

"Yeah, always police around, tryin' to move us," the man growled, his tone dripping with derision. "Where we gonna go? The roach-infested homeless shelter? Where we'd be robbed blind?"

"I mean detectives," Alex said. "Ones not in uniforms."

"Like you?"

"Yeah."

"Nah. No one like you."

Alex thanked the homeless guys, who told him he could go through the hole in the fence further along, rather than risk breaking his neck climbing over it. The city lights emerged from the twilight gloom. Like a harried, overworked taxi driver, he drove downtown through more traffic jams, smacking his horn, losing his temper with every asshole blocking the box, then he parked under a 'no parking' sign at Bellevue. He flashed tin at every hospital employee he saw, searching for someone who would know what the hell happened to his witness. Eventually, he cornered a consultant psychiatrist, who swung him into an exam room, saying, "I'm sorry, Detective…"

"Boswell."

"Right. Well, I'm sorry, but I don't see Mr. Reyes testifying in your case any time soon. He's had a total psychotic break. Right now, he's refusing meds, and without a court order, we can't force him to take them. At the moment, he thinks he's both Jesus Christ and Mohammed, and the apocalypse is coming on Sunday. I don't see him being capable or competent to testify in court."

"Has he mentioned twelve-foot lizards?"

"Sorry?"

"Nevermind. Thanks, Doctor," Alex said in a tone implying anything but. You couldn't call a witness who was in the middle of a psychotic episode. *As useless as a jell-o dildo*, James would say. A toxic haze permeated every tissue in his body as he followed FDR uptown to the office. This time, he sat quietly in traffic as the toxins sucked the life from his road rage. This one was probably not Vito's fault, but Goddammit, the only eyewitness who Vito hadn't fucked with now thought he was the Messiah.

Mercifully, most of his colleagues were out. No one would ask why his face looked so white. He fell into his cubicle, elbows braced over the bloated case binder. His heart worked like a high-pressure pump, stretching the walls of his arteries. He curled his fingers around the phone, and with pained reluctance, he dialed Simon's office number.

"Yes?" barked the prosecutor. "This is Simon McNally," he added, remembering to be professional.

Alex told him that the eyewitnesses had all reneged or vanished, except for the one who thought he was Jesus.

"What the fuck? Has someone got to them?" Simon snarled. "You know witness tampering is a crime."

Yes, Alex yearned to scream, but his throat collapsed; accusing Vito of witness tampering would unleash a shitstorm, a vast explosion triggered by multi-agency investigations, and he would be at the epicenter. Like Frank Serpico or Robert Leuci. While those guys did the right thing, their careers afterwards had been blown up beyond recognition – until they wrote books and sold the movie rights. Vito would find a way to ruin Alex's career. His life would be picked apart like a carcass on the Serengeti, and he didn't think it would make a very good movie.

"I dunno…" He was sweating as if he'd run ten miles. "But we know why the defense is calling them."

"Who the fuck tipped off the defense lawyer?"

"They did. Approached him and said they weren't sure about the IDs."

"*Someone* put them up to that. You don't seriously think they did a one-eighty on those IDs off their own backs and then called Huska's lawyer to tell him?"

"I don't, but if someone scared the shit outta them, they're not gonna name names, are they?"

"Well, fuck," said Simon.

Alex shared his sentiments. On an impulse, he called the Three-Four detective squad room, unwisely resolving to chase down Vito and find out what the hell he was playing at, but the precinct detective had skipped town, away for a weekend in the Catskills. Son of a bitch. Screwing up his case, then drinking beer at some cabin in the woods.

Chapter Forty-Five

After a long eight-by-four where Alex worked five hours of overtime on cases he'd been neglecting, he concluded that he had done something unconscionable in a past life. And not only because he'd become a workaholic and given up on his social life, although he had. Ever since his hospitalization almost seven months ago, he hadn't slept with anyone, nor had he attended NYPD social events. How could he explain to any date that he was a recovering alcoholic, unable to share a bottle of wine over dinner or a beer after work? The biggest turn-off in the world, he feared. And how could he face a bunch of wasted cops giving him shit for being the only sober person in the room? He worked cases to exhaustion and jumped to answer the phone. His deteriorating emotional state seemed indubitable when he found himself cursing an OD victim last week. "Where is that fresh track, you motherfucker?" he asked the corpse. Was a murder, demanding hard work and long hours, too much to ask? They were in the stairwell of the Polo Grounds Towers, an impeccable location for being gunned down with a semi-automatic, and this son of a bitch had simply killed himself with heroin, sprawled on a landing with a blissful grin on his face and a syringe in his right hand.

"Where the fuck did you shoot your shit?" Alex demanded, squatting beside the DOA, squinting at the black lines like a road map along the man's veins. "Where is that fresh track? You realize I'm not gonna get even a minute of overtime for your junkie ass, hear me?"

The Housing cops heard him and looked at him in amazement. If one had fantasized about his career leading to a Homicide squad, he was probably reconsidering.

But what did ODs matter? Yeah, he could catch every homicide in New York and work each one until he was sick or sectioned, but it would never replace booze or sex or the drunken debauchery and camaraderie. Like the walking wounded, he stumbled through a battlefield, bleeding from every limb, every organ. His AA meetings and his dark blue six-month sobriety chip tugged him forward, one leaden foot at a time. He could surrender to his disease. He could saunter into a liquor store and buy as much whisky as he could afford. No armies really stood between him and Liquor Mart. Yet he trudged across this miserable swamp while the cravings and pain battered him like heavy artillery. Because surviving mattered to some people. He owed it to them. Mostly, he owed it to his daughters. Killing himself with booze before the age of forty seemed more hurtful than his twenty years of semi-absentee parenting. Ever since their fight about Australia, Ellie had been taking the train to New York regularly. Now and then, they went out to dinner at Upper West Side restaurants, and often, he finished work feeling as thin and friable as cracked glass on a derelict tenement, so they stayed in the apartment, watching movies.

Ellie worried over him, like she did eight years ago, after the shooting. "You really need to eat, Dad. You'll feel better."

"I'll try a couple pieces of toast." When his ulcers acted up, his stomach hurt, and his appetite withered. He could live on bread, yogurt, and candy bars.

"Okay, I'll make you some, but I've looked up your condition. Diet's important. So's exercise. If you keep something in your stomach, you'll feel better. Just not stuff that's hard to digest like candy bars and greasy take-out."

"Yeah," he said. Dense clouds loomed over the city. No light glinted off the granite facades of the Queen Anne townhouses. They looked as sunless and grey as he felt.

"You're doing really well. You'll be at seven months in like a week."

"Maybe I'll start a poker ring with all the chips I'm getting. I think the next one's copper."

"You talk shit about the chips," she chided mildly. "But I know you know it means a lot. Lots of people are super proud of you."

She stocked his kitchen with the stuff he should be eating – fresh produce from Whole Foods and bread from an artisan bakery on Columbus. Her visits pulled him through the black sludge in his head, the despair, the compulsions aching inside his bones, and he tried not to think about Australia. Talking her out of it would only drive a wedge between them. Thankfully, she had another year of college, if not two, so he suppressed it like an unlawful search, for now.

No, he reckoned he had committed a terrible offense in a past life because he received a phone call from a CI on that chilly, dark evening, passing on news that Peter Norris had been picked up in a Three-Four precinct drug bust. Norris apparently tried to sell meth to an undercover.

517

The CI, who recognized his face from the news, thought Alex might like to know. Alex felt his heart spasm like a butterfly. The suppression hearing was on the docket for tomorrow. What the fuck was Norris thinking, slinging meth with a homicide prosecution hanging over his head? An imminent court appearance! The sheer, uninhibited stupidity! Alex sucked in a hissing breath. Norris wasn't his first lowlife of a witness to get himself jammed up right before a court appearance, and he certainly wouldn't be his last. That stuff happened every day, but he'd heard about it from a CI, not Indelicata or someone else in the Three-Four. And that tripped every alarm in his head. The arresting officer's first or second phone call should have been to him.

"Why the fuck am I outta the loop?" he snapped at the CI, rhetorically, because the informant wouldn't know.

"Uh, I'm just telling you what I seen," the CI answered warily.

Norris' NYSIIS number wasn't showing up on Alex's computer. No one had processed him through Central. When did they collar him? The CI said Monday, two nights ago. So, he should have been booked and arraigned, but he wasn't in the system for any fresh charges. The CI relayed that plainclothes officers had busted Pete alongside a dozen other guys. A TNT operation. Fine, but Pete should have been arraigned by now. *You could stop*, Alex told himself. *Let it play out.* Like any self-destructive alcoholic, Alex didn't stop. He reached out to contacts in the DA's office and to cops who liaised with 100 Centre Street. It turned out that some of those perps had been arraigned at Night Court, but no one knew what happened to Pete.

Alex called Pete's housemate.

"More cops. You people arrested him on Monday."

"He hasn't been home since?"

"No, he's fuckin' arrested."

"He contact you, ask you to post bail or anything?"

"Haven't heard from him. Hope he can still pay the rent from prison."

As Alex dropped the phone into its cradle, it rang again. His contact in the Tombs said, "Hi, Boswell. That perp you're after definitely isn't here. There's no record of him being detained here this week."

"Ten-four," Alex said emotionlessly.

He dug his knuckles into his forehead. James and Marty were out interviewing Huska's white supremacist friends. Bill was somewhere, working another case. For a few seconds, Alex stroked his cell phone like a rosary. Leave a message for James? For Gibson? They *should* be alerted. He tasted stomach acid in the back of his throat, and he pressed his fist into his belly, as if he could flatten the queasy pain. The little flip phone stayed closed. He signed out a car and gunned it uptown to the Three-Four. Veins in his head felt engorged. His right foot was an anvil squashing the gas pedal.

Inside the precinct house, uniforms and detectives buzzed around an obstacle course of desks and boxes. Cops interviewed witnesses and complainants or shepherded cuffed perps across the squad room, all through a throbbing din – yelling, phones, fax machines, radios, doors, and heavy boots.

Oblivious to the mayhem, Alex cornered McGuinness, a patrol sergeant who worked with TNT units on the buy-and-busts. "Did you collar a perp called Pete Norris? White. Twenty. About six foot. I heard something, but there's no record of him ever going to the Tombs—"

The square-jawed Irish sergeant said, "Oh, yeah. That guy. He's still here. Indelicata wanted to talk to him about that big homicide case."

The taste of pennies flooded his mouth. "Indelicata's got him."

"Yes, Boswell."

This was worse than he'd imagined, or precisely the thing he'd feared. Were there completely innocent explanations for why Norris had been held here, neither booked nor arraigned? Not really. Alex swallowed some swear words. Allegations of corruption or witness tampering would fly like a brick, and it would be him, rather than Vito, falling like one. "Cool," he said, coughing. "They're in an interrogation room?"

"Yeah, room two," replied McGuinness.

Alex ran down the stairs into the precinct's murky lower levels. He almost collided with Vito, who emerged from the men's bathroom. The precinct detective held a Styrofoam cup full of water.

Vito's face broke into a beaming smile. "Lex, you must've got the news we busted Norris. I was gonna call you."

Alex felt every muscle in his body seizing. "Yeah, I heard. *When* were you gonna call me? What are you doing with him?"

"Hey, chill," said Vito, cupping Alex's left shoulder. "I was gettin' around to it, but it's been nuts here. I said I'd put this case down. It's down. I saved your ass from a clusterfuck as well."

"What the hell are you talking about?"

"C'mere." Vito tightened his grip on the shoulder and led him to the interrogation room.

Through the one-way, Alex saw Norris drooping over the table like his spine had turned to jell-o. His skin looked patchy, his cheek bruised, his eyes dull and sleepless. Alex braced his forearm against the glass, processing this. He tried to tune out the hot coals firing up in his stomach. Like the doorman of an Upper East Side high-rise, Vito opened the door, beckoning Alex in.

"Hi, Pete," Vito said to the prisoner. "Look, like I said, I brought you some water." He offered Norris the Styrofoam cup. "Why don't you tell Detective Boswell here what you told me."

Norris gratefully took the cup with shaky hands. His gaze slid downwards. Speaking quietly, he stammered, "I...I'm sorry, Detective Boswell." He fell silent again.

"Pete, we talked about this," Vito said patronizingly, hovering.

"I... I lied to you." Norris cast a sidelong glance at Alex but refused to make eye contact with him. "I told you... I told you Jesse shot those Black kids in the subway. But... but he didn't. It was me. I did it. I shot them. I took the gun from Jesse's house when we were hanging out, and I did it. Jesse wasn't even there. It was just me in the subway station." Tears tarnished his face. His eyes turned into glass. "I'm sorry... I'm sorry I lied."

Stunned, Alex stared wordlessly at the prisoner. Sweat broke out under his armpits. A fatal blow to the case against Huska. His own credibility and competency scrutinized. People would say Boswell wasn't up for the job anymore. It took Indelicata to wring a confession out of the real perp. "Why?" he breathed.

"Dunno," muttered Norris. "Just felt I had to—"

"Don't push it. Just matters that he did it, don't it?" Vito interrupted.

"You read him his rights, Vito?" Alex spun his body around, facing the precinct detective.

Smiling placatingly, Vito flapped a signed *Miranda* waiver in his face. "Totally. By the book. Just how you like it."

Did the waiver matter? Alex scanned it, knowing as well as any detective that you can manipulate anyone into believing it's in their interest to sign those things. "Outside," he said in a firm tone.

"Sure, man."

The detectives stepped into the corridor and gazed at Pete through the one-way. Pete, in a zombie-like stupor, picked apart the Styrofoam.

Alex asked, "How long have you been interrogating him for?"

"About eleven hours," replied Vito.

"Just you? What about your partners?"

"Does it matter?"

If IA ever investigated, yes. But he couldn't bring himself to say that. Instead, he sighed, "Eleven hours. Jesus Christ, Vito. Why's his face all fucked up? You do a corrective interview?"

"Well, gee, Lex, I guess he resisted arrest when the officers collared him on the buy-and-bust."

Alex knew that's what hadn't happened. "You'd have got him to confess to shooting Jimmy Hoffa if you wanted."

"I got you a confession. All wrapped up with a bow on it. And you wanna give me this shit again. *You* were about to let this guy walk with the mother of all deals."

"*I* was gonna put the real perp away," Alex fired back.

"Ronnie's a good cop. I have his back. I'd have thought you had mine. I'm disappointed to see you reacting this way." Vito put his hands on his hips.

"This will be excluded. It's coerced."

"It's damned good police work. Better than you were doing."

"Someone's gonna find out you let the real perp walk."

"You're so fucked up now you don't know what you're saying. Listen to yourself."

"This is crazy. You can't make Norris take the fall for this just 'cause Ronnie Huska used to be in your squad. Is that why you kept the slugs in your locker? Insurance? In case you couldn't talk the wits into changing their statements?" Alex squared his shoulders, as if he could make all 5'8 and one fifty or sixty pounds of himself fill the same space as the 6'4 precinct detective with a build like an overweight linebacker. Vito would not intimidate him this time. He was older, stronger, more certain of himself. *Just try digging your gun into my ribs again,* he snarled silently. Didn't Vito get it? Their victim wasn't some poor crackhead in a seedy alley whose untimely demise didn't even merit a two-sentence blurb in the *Post*. A cover up with this case risked igniting dynamite under the uptown streets.

Indifferent, Vito shrugged again. "I'm doin' my job."

"Your job is fucking over my case?"

"First of all, it ain't your case. I know Homicide thinks they're like the OGs on the block, but you're only an assistive squad, remember? It's still my case—"

Alex held up his hands. "Fine. Your case. Doesn't fucking matter whose case it is. It's Frankie McDonough's case. He's the one who's dead."

"Secondly," Vito continued, as if Alex hadn't said anything, "I'm doing the right thing by a cop, *and* still making sure Frankie McDonough gets the justice he deserves. Norris there, he'll get done for it, for sure. Everyone's happy. Ronnie Huska can get his kid the psychiatric help he needs, which trust me, he needs way more than prison, and the Blacks get what they want, 'cause a white guy gets put away for that kid's murder. He *was* going to those white supremacy meetings. As far as anyone's concerned, he's a fuckin' Nazi. You're not gonna deny that. Look… anyone asks, you tell 'em that when Norris was collared, he asked to see me. Right? He had something he wanted to say to me. You hear?"

Alex showed the whites of his eyes. "So Huska gets treated differently 'cause he's white, and his dad's a cop."

"No, just 'cause Ronnie's a good guy. He's helped me out a few times. I'd do the same for a Black or Latino cop, if it makes any difference to you."

"Right, so you gotta fuck around with my eyewits and gaslight this poor schmuck into taking the fall for him."

"Alex, cool it. You *know* you ain't gonna hurt me. You're just gonna hurt yourself. What's your game here?" His voice rising with each word, Vito lurched towards him, his hands in fists.

Vito *would* hurt him. Oh, he'd proven that beyond all reasonable doubt. If Alex was stupid enough to throw a punch, he would be levelled in a heartbeat, injured and bleeding on the floor. The precinct detective boxed for fun; he had a mean right hook and no fear of assault charges or any reprisal. Nothing had changed since the last time they'd argued outside of an interrogation room. Deflated, Alex stepped backwards with an aggrieved glare. His spirit and grit evaporated. Sparkling pain pulsed through his right side. What the hell was he doing? Standing in front of a train to stop it only got you squashed under the wheels. Would anyone else care that Vito had coerced a Neo-Nazi methhead into confessing? Norris had been at the scene, an accomplice with culpability anyway.

"Jesus Christ, man," Vito breathed. "I can't believe I gotta have this conversation with you. I told you before, you're the only guy I can trust in Homicide now. Brady and Keohane are gone. You got a woman boss. I thought you got it. You understood. You gotta stay with me on this. You gotta. What are you gonna do? You tell a crazy story that I told wits to change their testimony or beat a false confession outta Norris, no one's gonna believe that crap. That's what's crazy. You're an alcoholic; everyone knows your head's been all over the fuckin' place since you were in the hospital. You lucky you're not in a rubber gun squad, or on the Farm. Would it surprise *anyone* if you had other substance problems? Maybe they got worse since you been off the drink. Coke. Pills. Who knows what they could find, huh? Me, I'm a first grader with the Medal of Honor. You know I got the Medal of Honor, right?"

"I think I heard something about it," Alex said wanly. He sagged against the wall as if Vito had punched him in the gut. What douchebag in the NYPD brass had given him that?

"It's the right thing." Vito's tone became earnest, pacifying. "The people in your squad protected you when you were drinking on the job. You think they didn't know about you and your whisky flask? Worst kept fuckin' secret north a' 59th Street. I'm protecting my guys. I gotta do it. And Frankie McDonough still gets justice."

"Fuck you, Vito," Alex said, terse but hopeless. He wheeled around and marched up the stairs, feeling as if he had ten kilo weights attached to his feet.

He ignored Vito tailing him. "Hey, Lex, come on. Don't take it so personally."

Was there an impersonal way to take it?

Upstairs, Alex found the precinct detectives horsing around with tasing a watermelon. As if nothing unusual had happened, Vito leapt into the fray, firing the taser at the fruit. It exploded. Pink juice and slime caked the floor and an office chair. Alex ground his teeth against each other until his jaw ached. That watermelon could be his head, or his career. He stalked out the door, onto the hill of West 183rd. Wraiths of mist ran on a blustering wind, and a light, icy drizzle pelted the city.

Numbly, he twisted the key in the car, then rested his forehead against the steering wheel. The engine's vibrations thudded through his skull. He couldn't resist Vito's power, not in the past, and certainly not now, when his battle against alcoholism sapped his strength, leaving him on his knees. Why did he ever think he could? Sobriety was driving him to madness. His breaking mind rocked towards the work. Someone had to tell Simon McNally that Norris had confessed to the murder. Simon would be incandescent. The lawyer was irascible and temperamental, but he also cared. Alex touched the cell phone clipped to his belt, then jerked his hand away as if it stung him. He could not engage himself with legal morasses or the job anymore. Without thinking, he shoved the car into 'drive' and swung out onto Broadway.

The pain under his ribs burned hotter. *Focus on the road,* he told himself. Was this a heart attack? If so, he would lose consciousness in minutes, but he didn't, so probably not. Outside the car, neon signs flaunting beer speared into his head. *Give it a Goddamn break.* The car kept moving as if it had become sentient. It carried him beyond the bars, caught up in a river of traffic flowing through the entrance ramps curling from the Henry Hudson Parkway to I-95's flyover that swept across Washington Heights. He crawled along the Hamilton Bridge, eastbound. The river churned far below, the brown water sullen and dark, and then overpasses and concrete barriers shadowed the highway as I-95 skirted the demilitarized zones of the Bronx, the neighborhoods of austere, ragged tower blocks and crumbling low-rises. Just before the Throg's Neck Bridge, the interstate turned north. Alex stayed with it. He switched off the police radio and his cell phone. Soon he passed through Westchester, the suburbs of New Rochelle, White Plains, and Rye, and he glimpsed rectangular strip malls and featureless office buildings, a Lego city. At the edge of New York's urban sprawl, he crossed into Connecticut, and the interstate wove through the leafy, moneyed towns, with quaint stone buildings and spires of old churches poking above the skeletal foliage. Barren trees and concrete ramparts melded into a grey barrier along the highway.

Hours floated by, but he had slipped out of sync with time itself, reaching the post-industrial cities of Fairfield, Bridgeport, New Haven, each one appearing beside the interstate, then quickly disappearing as signs for the next urged him onwards. A labyrinth of entrance and exit ramps in the heart of New Haven split I-95 and I-91. I-91 – north, to Hartford, to the hills and forests of Western Massachusetts, to Ellie's school. *My God, not when I'm this fucked up*, he thought, and stayed with I-95, crossing the Quinnipiac River on a bridge with glistening pearlescent towers and thick white cables.

North of New Haven, the countryside along I-95 seemed idyllically pastoral, so dissimilar from the concrete spewing out of New York City. The interstate arced around rolling hills, through farmland and fields with cattle and horses grazing. A few towns later, it veered east, hugging the coast. Long Island Sound had become a flat, metallic sheet with whitecaps catching shards of light. Around New London, he looked over the crash barrier at the Atlantic, where dark sea flowed into sky. I-95 departed from the sea at the Rhode Island border, angling north, towards Providence. The greying light faded over farmland, and Alex crossed his second state line of the day, flying alongside fields and forests, indistinct, murky, speckled with sporadic lights. Around the outskirts of Providence, the lights clustered into galaxies as villages and towns merged together.

Near a place signposted for Norwood, he pulled into an interstate truck stop.

His legs and back creaked painfully as he clambered free of the Ford and arched his spine to stretch cramped muscles. He hobbled into the truck stop to pee. On his way out, he glanced at the buffet and the fast-food joints, but neither Burger King nor meat cooked into cardboard stirred his appetite. Wool clogged up his brain, his arteries. Moving sluggishly, he negotiated the parking lot and then slumped on the Ford's long, flat hood, watching the traffic. Vehicles ponderously hunted for parking spaces. Tired travelers perambulated through the automatic doors. A man in a Bob Marley hoodie bent over the engine of a battered Ford Bronco with its hood up, pouring water into its radiator. A woman wearing ice-stretched denim tried comforting a screaming child while her husband sat inside their Volvo, smoking. Everyone was on a journey to somewhere. No one wanted to be in a truck stop, but here they were. Here he was, shivering as the jagged fangs of a northerly wind pierced his clothes. He could follow I-95 forever, all the way to Maine. Hell, he could keep going north, to Canada. But what would that achieve, other than being on the Canadian border without a passport and with an NYPD Crown Vic he probably shouldn't have driven out of New York City in the first place. He couldn't run from the thing in his head. It followed him. It always had. He could drown it with alcohol; he could drive like a maniac for hundreds of miles; he could cry at AA meetings; he could work a hundred cases, and it was there, undeterred. A thousand tiny black spikes, burrowing into his nervous system.

His stiff muscles complained, but he ignored it and folded himself into the car. Slamming the door shut, sealing himself away from the world. He buried his face in his hands. His nose felt stuffed with acid that burned through his sinuses, dripping down his throat. Sniffing, he straightened his back and freed his sidearm from his holster. As if it was delicate, like an egg, he softly placed it on the dash. A Glock 17. He'd only carried it for a year and a half, the replacement for his .38 Ruger Service Six revolver. It was a dull, matte black, blockier and heavier than the Ruger. He picked up the gun. *Death is lighter than a feather.* Who had said that? He pulled the slide back, loading a round into the firing chamber, then he shoved the muzzle against the side of his forehead. A 9mm slug. Point blank. Well, he wouldn't feel much.

Adrenaline threw his heart into tachycardia. His hand seemed detached from his nervous system. It dropped from his head, racked the slide, and rammed the firearm into the holster. A torrent of wild nausea ensnared his guts, his stomach bucking, convulsing. He shoved open the door, then he knelt on the asphalt. But he hadn't eaten all day, so he spat out liquid and acid until the spasms petered out and his throat felt scraped and raw. Huddled on his knees beside the car, he saw his own body: a DOA in this truck stop parking lot, collapsed over the steering wheel, his skull and blood and brain splattered across the spotty blue-grey car upholstery. A Rhode Island detective would investigate it. They would run the plates, then wonder why an NYPD Crown Vic was here. They would ID his body from his driver's license and his NYPD card. A fellow officer, dead from suicide. *Fucking tragic*, they would say. Ellie's world would fall apart, like every anguished family he tried hopelessly to console at work. James had divulged that she'd met him at a Starbucks to tell him how worried she was about her father, and James promised her that he wouldn't let anything happen.

And he'd tried, at times imperfectly, but he stayed at Alex's side through the hell of sobriety, every day. Gibson, Marty, and Bill hadn't wavered, either, for that matter. Gibson acted wholly convinced that he could get better. Why did she believe that? Why did any of them believe that? His colleagues would risk their lives and careers to have his back, and Helen would be on the next flight to New York. They all deserved better than the misery death brings to the living. As a homicide detective, he recognized that pain; he saw it every day. *You can't do that to them.* His pulse pounded like his neighbor's hi-fi system. Yet his heart didn't feel like muscle and sinew, but gossamer strings and fragile glass, demolished into fragments.

Time no longer mattered as he impassively gazed at people and vehicles flowing through the truck stop. His empty stomach growled, but he felt too sick to eat. He blew his nose into a handful of tissues and dried his damp cheeks with his sleeve. Then he started the car. Tentatively, he backed it up, the way his father used to drive when his eyes started going. He couldn't spend the night in this damned truck stop. More like himself, he swung the Crown Vic around the parking lot, following the signs for I-95 South. On the entrance ramp, he pressed his foot to the gas, gaining speed, and he guided it into the stream of cars and trucks racing underneath the green sign with arrows pointing towards New York. The Ford swallowed the road. The highway glistened under an icy sheen of rain on asphalt. With traffic thinning, he pushed the car to eighty, ninety, the big 4.6 liter V8 part of his body now, stretching into a gallop, changing lanes, weaving around trucks at a thought, a breath, like he didn't have to touch the wheel anymore. The car read his mind. Near Port

Chester, he sailed across the New York-Connecticut border. I-95 must go on forever, Westchester and the Bronx broadening to the length of the whole United States. His watery eyes ached, like they were rotting into his skull, leaving him squinting at the road. But the concentration demanded by driving while exhausted distracted him from everything else.

Chapter Forty-Six

Startled by a weight on his hip, Alex shivered and sat upright. Several files, three empty soda cans, a stapler, and an unloaded gun clattered to the floor or tumbled onto the sofa. "You assholes," he muttered, annoyed at the detective squad pastime of piling crap on anyone who passed out in the squad room. Whoever woke the victim lost.

The detectives giggled. Marty said, "James, the CPL was a bit ambitious."

Alex sleepily threw a soda can at them. Last night, he had returned to the station house at 0300 and signed in the car. Hopefully no one would check its mileage counter. Halfway down the stairs in the 116th Street 6 station, he'd captiously recalled his discovery at the four-by-twelve two days beforehand: the MTA was doing night closures for maintenance. That made the journey home into a long, wet walk, an expensive cab ride, or waiting in the rain for night buses that may or may not show up. Tired beyond any measure, Alex withdrew to the office and crashed on the interview room sofa. He'd slept through the first hour of the eight-by-four.

"Fuck, man," said James. "We got court today and you look like shit. Why the hell did you sleep here?"

Court! The hearing. That had escaped his fractured mind. Oh, he hungered to spill everything: the truth about Vito, Huska, Norris, confess to driving to Rhode Island, to the irrationality of speed and flight. With the truth, he could release the pain pulverizing his insides. He imagined scaling the great wall of deceit he had erected after Quixano's interrogation, but then his mind flashed to Vito's threats, IA investigations, losing the job, losing everything. That sent him plummeting into the ground.

"I was working late, and they closed the 4, 5, 6 line after midnight."

"I hope you weren't drinking." James looked serious.

"No, I promise," Alex said earnestly. "I was tired and too cheap to get a cab home with the late-night surcharge. If you can even find one in East Harlem at three am." That part was completely true.

"You could have used the precinct dorm."

Alex breathed out sharply through his nose. "And been kept up all night by a bunch of guys farting and snoring like freight trains? This sofa's a hell of a lot more comfortable." The precinct dorms also contained illicit alcohol, and Alex knew where people hid it.

"I guess so." James chewed on his lip. "I left you like five messages on your cell phone. What's the point of fuckin' having that thing if you don't turn it on?"

"The battery died."

"The fuckin' *battery?* Why didn't you charge it? Jesus H. Christ. McNally's having a fuckin' stroke, man. Pete Norris confessed to the damn murder. Said he was the trigger man. Said Huska wasn't even fuckin' there. Can you believe it? The case is more fucked than a cheap whore."

Alex held his fingers against his sandy eyes. "Yeah, I know. That's why I didn't get a chance to charge my phone. I was at the Three-Four. I talked to him. That's what I was working on until 0300. Trying to verify his story or figure something out."

"Wait, what? Why didn't you tell me? Or Gibson?"

"Vito brought me in after the end of his four-by-twelve, and it was late, and what the fuck were you guys gonna do about it at one am anyway? She's got young kids, and you were out with that documentary filmmaker." His dexterity at lying on his feet, honed when he'd slept around on Catherine, felt as sharp and quick as ever.

"Fucking Vito. Of course he did. Son of a bitch." James' eyes shifted back and forth, as if he suspected something more.

"Maybe I shoulda called you," Alex admitted. "My brain wasn't working."

"Yeah, you shoulda. Filmmaker would've coped. Nevermind. What do you think?"

"I think Pete Norris isn't the sharpest tool in the shed. He's not gonna steal a gun from Jesse's father and then hide it in Jesse's spare wheel so he can pin it on Jesse. He's not that bright. But if someone got to him, scared the shit out of him… The guy has no balls. He'd change his story in a second."

"You think someone got to him? Any idea who?"

529

"No, I couldn't find anything," Alex lied. "Could be anybody, with Huska's father being a cop. Cops, criminals who owe a favor to Ronnie. Who knows." It hurt, like he rammed a knife into his own guts. No matter how many years he did this job, Vito, one of the most decorated detectives in the NYPD, would always possess the ability to screw him over.

"Well, fuck." James exhaled heavily. "You can't go to court looking like that."

"It's not that bad." Alex had removed his tie before sleeping. He rescued it from the floor, then retied it around his neck. "Is that better?"

"It doesn't fix the coffee stain on your shirt."

"Aw, shit." Now he remembered: buying coffee in a truck stop near New Haven so he could stay awake for the remainder of the journey, trying to drink it while driving, the plastic lid not being fully attached to the cup, the coffee dribbling onto his chest.

"You have a spare one here?"

"No."

"Here, take mine," said Marty as he shrugged off his sport coat and unbuttoned his shirt. "It's even *ironed*." It was common knowledge that Alex never ironed anything. Marty threw the shirt at Alex, who caught it, then stripped off himself.

Both detectives were bare-chested when Gibson wandered into the interview room. "Marty, I was wondering—What the *hell* is going on here?" She halted abruptly, her dark brown eyes saucers that flickered in a double take at Alex's scar. The size and viciousness of the wound seemed to take her aback.

"Lex spilled coffee on himself. He's using Marty's shirt, so he doesn't look like something we picked up off the street when he takes the stand today," James explained.

Gibson twitched both eyebrows. "Okay. Vasquez, come see me when you got clothes on."

"Dude, it looked like we were finishing up after having a threesome," James said, before he almost toppled over with laughter.

Alex pulled on Marty's shirt. It fit a little tight across the chest and long in the sleeves, but it looked more respectable than any clothes he had here, or at home for that matter, given Marty's taste for expensive, tailored shirts and ironing. Muttering, "I gotta take a leak," he scuttled into the bathroom. He shied away from the face in the mirror: the eyes creased and bloodshot, the cheeks gaunt but darkened by a shadowy stubble. The gunshot wound ached, letting him know how tired he was. Gibson had never seen it before. He wondered what she thought, or if she would say anything at their next meeting. Dammit, he would auction off a vital organ for ibuprofen, but his doctor had ordered him to avoid NSAIDs. Vigorously, he scrubbed his face with soap and cold water, but it didn't help him feel any livelier or look any better.

James drove them down to 100 Centre Street. He cross-examined Alex about his late-night misadventures with Norris and Vito. Why had James been cut out of something so important? *If only I could tell you the truth,* Alex thought, sickened by his lies. Eyelids half-lowered, he said that he'd questioned Norris, but only after Vito had interrogated him for eleven hours. Sure, Norris confessed, but he'd been dazed, stupefied, and Alex had trouble believing the confession.

"Jesus. Why the fuck did Vito interrogate him for eleven hours?"

"I guess Vito wanted to be thorough and see what he was playing at. Or who made him change his story."

"And?"

"And I dunno…" Alex trapped his tongue between his front teeth. "He wasn't gonna say."

"But eleven hours! He would've fuckin' said anything."

"I know."

James looked like he believed nothing, but he said, "What about you?"

"Me?"

"You seem fucked. More than usual. You slept in the motherfucking office."

"There's a 'usual?'" Alex tugged at the seatbelt cutting into his throat. "I'm just tired. I'm always tired, and my stomach's killing me. Side's not great today, either. I think this case has made my ulcers come back, and I don't have the energy anymore to deal with the bullshit."

James shot him a worried look. "Is there anything… I don't know… that would help?"

"Start drinking again?"

"Alex, I hope you're not seriously thinking of that. You've almost got to seven months."

Alex rested his head against the cool glass of the car window. Serious James. Serious James made him feel like a failure. As if the night sweats, the withdrawal, the stomach pain, and the daily temptations weren't enough. "I'm *always* thinking of that. That's what the fucking thing is."

"Yeah, I know. If there's something *else* that would help…"

"I could start smoking crack." Smartass answers covered up his anguish.

Without smiling or any smartass riposte of his own, James swerved onto Centre Street. He looked doleful, uncertain. That wasn't like James. None of it was. Alex felt guilt chewing at his flesh, like hungry rats; one rat for upsetting his partner, another for his wretched secrets.

Precisely as the detectives had foreseen, Simon's head was exploding. His hands worked feverishly at cigarettes he wasn't allowed to smoke inside 100 Centre Street. Like a captured wolf, he paced circuits around the witness prep room.

"Norris confessed? He confessed to Indelicata? He said Huska wasn't even *in* the subway station? Jesus Christ! How did this case *get* from an indictment to a dumpster fire? What the fuck is going on?"

Keeping his voice level, Alex said, "Yeah, we think someone got to him."

"I mean, you *don't* think he actually did it, and we're the ones who have fucked up?"

"No, I'm sure he was an accomplice. I still think Huska was the trigger man. I think Norris changed his story 'cause something scared the shit out of him."

Simon held out both palms in a gesture of despair. "I got that. You find a reason?"

"I spent all night looking and couldn't find anything."

"The police? Are there cops involved with this?" seethed Simon. He paused his pacing to stare fiercely at the detectives. "Like the witness tampering. Are there cops tampering with the fucking witnesses?"

"It's possible," Alex acknowledged, his tongue searching his mouth for a trace of saliva.

"What about Indelicata? Detective Huska used to be in his squad. Did *he* get to Norris? And the others? Is he scaring the crap out of my witnesses?"

"I don't know," Alex said with a straight face, but his insides squirmed. "Indelicata told me that Norris asked to see him after being collared in a buy-and-bust."

"Did he? Jesus. No one's gonna touch Indelicata," snarled Simon. "Not my boss, not anyone. But I know he plays fast and loose with IDs…"

Then the clerk interrupted his tirade, warning them that the hearing was starting in Part 86.

Before they entered the courtroom, Simon asked, "You'd swear an oath on your lives that *your* ID procedures weren't remotely suggestive?"

"They were not," Alex affirmed, keeping his voice steady and resolute.

"Fuckin' by the book," James added.

Zealously, Simon defended the warrant, arguing that whatever the witnesses said *now,* the investigating officers obtained the warrant in good faith given what the witnesses had said five months ago. Huska's defense attorney, Barry Docherty, insisted that the eyewitnesses were unreliable, tainted; they'd been coached, telling the detectives what they believed the police wanted to hear. Therefore, probable cause was not supported, because the police should not be allowed to profit from manipulating identifications.

Alex and James both testified, carefully explaining that between them, the witnesses had identified two perps. They'd ID'd Huska from a photo array. No, the detectives had not directed the witnesses in any way. They had followed the scrupulous procedures for eyewitness ID that they followed in every single case. They stressed that had no direct evidence of Norris, despite his confession, having access to or using the murder weapon. On cross, however, they conceded that Norris had spent time in Huska's house, and Ronnie Huska's firearms collection was unsecured, so Norris *might* have taken the gun. They also acknowledged that Jesse and Pete used drugs in the Camaro, which meant Pete had access to the car. That hurt.

Vito arrived in court a couple minutes late, festooned like a parrot in his magenta tie and yellow pinstripes. He made affable eye contact with Alex, as if the conversations in the pub and outside of the Three-Four's interrogation room hadn't happened. Sounding genuinely upset, Vito told a story about Norris' buy-and-bust arrest – how Norris had begged the arresting officer to let him see Detective Indelicata, and then he confessed to the shooting. The arresting officer testified next, corroborating Vito.

Alex stared at his bleeding fingers. He hadn't been conscious of picking at them, but fresh blood seeped out of wounds around his nails. What had Vito promised the A/O? A hook? A word in the ear of the Chief of D's? Beside him, James bounced in his seat, muttering under his breath, "Motherfucking son of a bitch."

And worse, Alex thought.

The defense called two of the eyewitnesses to the stand; Eva Castillo, followed by Ruben De Leon. Both asserted that the original affidavits were a mistake. They had been frightened and confused, but they had assuredly seen one shooter, and he wasn't Jesse Huska. They acted anxious but sincere, apologizing for the confusion. The detectives had told them there were two suspects, one of them short, wide-nosed, blue-eyed, cleanshaven, and you don't argue with the police, do you? As he listened, Alex gouged his bloody fingers into his temples and scratched at his hairline. Bullshit! He would never feed an eyewitness that much information. Docherty called Manuel Reyes' psychiatrist, who testified that Reyes suffered from schizophrenia and saw things that weren't there. Even if he wasn't too crazy to testify, he was unstable and suggestible.

After his testimony, Vito had parked himself in the second row of the gallery, straight across from the witness box. He stared intensely at each witness as they delivered their testimony. If that wasn't evidence of intimidation, Alex didn't know what was. When Simon started cross-examining the psychiatrist, Vito buttoned up his jacket, then swaggered out of the trial part. Alex felt his muscles aching with an urge to leap to his feet and run after him. They could have a cathartic confrontation outside the courtroom. But what would that achieve? Nothing. Vito would once again point out that he had the Medal of Honor, while Alex had substance abuse problems.

The judge ruled that the police had exploited an unlawfully conducted ID procedure, and he suppressed the gun. Between the waffling witnesses and the exclusion of the firearm, they had nothing linking Huska to the homicide, so the judge dismissed the indictment as well.

Court adjourned with a roaring, implosive silence in the gallery, rising to an enraged murmur, the sniffles and squawks of agony and anger, and the crowd, shepherded by court officers, dispersing to the hallway, the sound rising like a tidal wave, the clicks and whirrs of cameras, the dazzles from the flashes, the hungry reporters coming in a noisy rush. Alex leapt away from the journalists' microphones. His head pulsed. A hand thrust out and grasped his wrist, crushing the tendons, the pain immobilizing him. Annette McDonough had battled to the front lines amidst journalists and court officers. Her eyes were kaleidoscopes of pain. Her mouth worked soundlessly until words squeaked past her lips.

"How? How could this happen?"

Alex felt his blood overheating, like waking up with a hellish hangover. "I'm sorry... I'm so sorry. It's just the system... The way it happens..." His words were meaningless.

"The whole thing is racist, double-standard bullshit, and you know it."

It was. No doubt. More than she even realized. "We're not giving up. We'll get him, somehow."

She didn't look like she believed a word. Well, he didn't believe it himself. Gently flicking his arm unlocked her grip on his wrist. The crowd separated them. Reporters threw microphones into McDonough's face, cameras clicked, and her husband fought to reach her. Alex backed away, then he dodged two *New Yorker* journalists who were after him, personally. God no, he thought, fleeing into a bathroom. He locked himself in a stall and sat down on a lidded toilet, clutching his stomach, his ulcers resurrecting themselves past the medication. He heard shoes stomping against lino, the trickle of someone having a leak. He tried taking longer, deeper breaths, steadying his gut. *Do you really want to puke in a 100 Centre Street bathroom?* That would be a new low, even for him. Once he felt a bit less sick, he slipped through the stall door and leaned over the sinks, splashing icy water against his eyes, and he patted the back of his neck with a cold, soaked paper towel. He was unable to sort himself out. There was no more give in him, no more flex, but he had to find Simon and James and somehow fix this mess.

Evading erupting protests, more journalists, and the Manhattan DA's presser in Foley Square, he hotfooted it along the back route to the 100 Centre Street parking garage. His partner, the prosecutor, and Gibson waited beside the detectives' Crown Vic, Simon on a chain-smoking stress binge and James, who never smoked when sober, bumming a rage cigarette off the lawyer. The lieutenant wasn't smoking but she looked like she wanted to start.

"My God, this has become a fucking abortion," Simon spluttered. "What happened to those witnesses? I can't believe it. Two reneging. One's disappeared. The other's lost his fucking mind."

"You didn't lead them on in the IDs, did you?" asked Gibson. "If there's a Goddamned grain of truth—"

"No fuckin' way, boss," James snapped. "Come on. You know how many IDs we've done between us? Some cocksucker got those witnesses to spout more bullshit than you'd find at a dairy farm."

"*What* cocksucker?" Simon snarled. "What happened between them talking to you five months ago and talking to Indelicata a few weeks ago? Did someone threaten them?"

"I said... I don't know," Alex lied, feeling more waves of acid in his belly. "Shit happens. Witness intimidation is pretty much SOP for Heights slingers—"

"Well, do something. Do whatever you have to. I want this case back together. I want to find whoever fucked with those witnesses." Simon drew on the last embers of his cigarette, then he threw it violently at a trashcan. He lit another and stormed into the white light outside the parking garage.

"Start asking around, pull LUGS, see if you can find any evidence of someone contacting the witnesses," Gibson said.

A waste of time. Alex knew Vito had enough self-awareness to cover his tracks. Every so often, someone blew the whistle on corruption. "No, it's done. I did. It isn't gonna look good anyway if the wits flip-flop. Again. We gotta find some other way to put Huska at the crime scene. They'll admit that gun back into evidence if we can come at it another way."

"Check the phone records anyway," Gibson ordered. "Then start tracking his movements, his friends, find more evidence of all this Neo-Nazi crap. Just don't fuck around or fuck up. You want a warrant, every 't' on that affidavit has got to be crossed. And leave Indelicata out of it."

"Ten-four, ma'am." On all counts, especially the last. Earlier in the week, Alex had attended an appointment with Dr. Seon. She'd wondered why his blood pressure had rocketed and advised him that he would be better off with less stress. No shit.

Straightaway after leaving the bedlam in Foley Square, Alex and James retraced the investigation, first driving to the West 181st Street subway station. The shrine that the Heights community had created for Frankie still occupied a corner: stacked candles, crosses like scattered bones, statuettes of saints, a jumble of colorful flowers and striped Yankees jerseys, and as a center piece, a photo of Frankie wearing a cap and gown at his high school graduation. Even after five months, Heights residents indefatigably brought fresh offerings. Drawn to the shrine, Alex stood before the flowers and the crosses. He clasped his arms tightly over his belly. Frankie stared at him, his face accusatory, disappointed. *I'm sorry, Frankie,* he thought, allowing himself the rare luxury of wondering if the *Santeria* tradition, the construction of shrines with saints and candles, really let you commune with the dead. *I wish I was strong enough to do better, but I'm not. I'm barely keeping my head above water. You got unlucky, being killed by a police officer's kid. This police officer's kid. If it had been anyone else, I could help you, but I can't get this guy convicted. There's too much against me. I'm sorry.* Tears welled, scalding his eyeballs. He rubbed his cheek with his forearm.

"It's very sad about that boy," said a woman who was waiting for the subway, Latina, maybe fifty years old. She'd noticed Alex fixating on the shrine. "*Muy triste.*"

"Yeah," Alex agreed softly.

"*Demasiada violencia...*Too much violence in *esta ciudad,*" sighed the woman. "*Esta país.*"

"Yeah, too damn much."

He saw no forgiveness in Frankie's eyes. Only sadness. *I can get the accomplice. But if I tell anyone what happened, I'll probably lose my job, and dammit, I'm good at it. I stay, I have a lifetime of putting other people's murderers away. Is that enough? Can it ever be enough?* Oh, he was cracking, going mad. Had it come to this? Talking to a shrine? Looking for absolution from the dead?

He heard the metallic symphony, the rattling of wheels on the rails, the wounded howling of brakes. A subway screeched against the platform. It disgorged its passengers, then sighed, as if bored with its very existence.

James' voice dragged him back from his thoughts. "We ain't gonna find fuckin' *shit* here."

Alex wheeled away from the shrine. What would the crime scene tell them? They knew where the vic fell, where the perps stood, where they fought over the gun, where they made their getaway, but any admissible physical evidence was long gone.

"Fuck this," James said. "Let's go back to the office. Pull Huska's LUGS and try to find that missing wit. She's gotta have a credit card. And hell, if we sit over our phones, maybe someone will call us with a nice, friendly grounder. I bet that would cheer you up." He smiled cheerlessly and patted Alex between the shoulder blades. Then he headed for the stairs. Alex thought his partner's gait had lost its jaunty step.

Wading through splashy exhaustion, he followed James up the stairs to street level. Last night was a faster runner, catching up to him. Dazed, he shielded his face against daylight, but his eyes latched onto a dive bar across the road from the 181st Street station.

James saw him look. "Lex."

His chest rapidly rose and fell. That flash of self-destruction. It felt like fate that he should fail. His alcohol problems and Vito's Medal of Honor opened a credibility gap you could drive an MTA bendy bus through, but ultimately, none of that made a blind bit of difference – if you value your career, you don't rat. He might be a good enough detective to figure out why the witnesses perjured themselves about the ID, but for what? If he told the truth, his career, or his life, would run aground like the *Exxon Valdez*. To hell with it – he might as well trash his liver by heading forthwith into that bar, or he could pull the trigger next time he looked down the barrel of his gun.

James placed a hand on his lower back, steering him into the car. "Fuck this fucking case."

A grounder, a case that solved itself. Did he get those anymore?

Part 9

Chapter Forty-Seven

August 2010

Peter Norris never saw a jury. Frightened by New York's new death penalty statute, he plea bargained with McNally and got twenty-five years for second-degree murder. Ronnie Huska retired and moved to California, while Jesse served three years for the assault on James, then vanished once he'd finished his parole. In late 2005, ten years after Frankie McDonough's murder, Ronnie Huska perp-walked himself into the Manhattan North Homicide offices. Its premises were now on West 133rd and Broadway, a nondescript early-twentieth century low-rise instead of a fortified precinct house. Grasping Alex's scarred left hand, he confessed that his son had killed McDonough, and he'd covered it up. He said that he was a recovered addict too and now understood what he'd put Alex through when they met in that East Side bar in 1995. He said owning up to his mistakes and asking for forgiveness was a part of his recovery. He also revealed that he had a meeting with a *New York Times* reporter but wanted to tell Alex first. Alex had only just returned to full duty after his diagnoses. He wasn't in the mood to forgive anyone who had anything to do with that case. It had so nearly derailed him from his own recovery. But he wanted information. Where was Jesse? Ronnie had no idea. He'd become estranged from his son and didn't know where Jesse had gone after his release from prison.

They eventually extradited Jesse from Canada, and for the second time, a grand jury indicted him for first-degree murder. The case went to trial, this time with the Sig Sauer admitted as evidence because Ronnie admitted he knew Jesse had it, and he tearfully confessed that he'd advised Jesse to burn his blood-and-GSR spattered clothes. It meant the allegedly unlawful search of the car no longer mattered. The defense attorney tried creating reasonable doubt with Castillo and Reyes, the only eyewitnesses still in New York, but they had no idea what they'd seen eleven years ago. Even the dumbest jury gets that memory fades after a decade. Following a three-week trial, the jury found Jesse guilty and sentenced him to life. Unlike those other miscarriages of justice, Norris had been at the scene, still an accomplice, but a judge reviewing his case in light of Huska's conviction reduced his twenty-five year sentence to time served. Nine years was enough. He got out.

The media went bananas with the story – a devastated father foolhardily using his power as a cop to protect his son. Internal Affairs and the state attorney general's office doubted that one detective on his own could undermine an entire homicide case, so they investigated the Three-Four Precinct squad for corruption. Nothing ever came of it. No one really wanted to know, and only Norris implicated Vito, claiming that the detective had beaten him into a false confession, but Attica had turned him into a strung-out, incoherent mess. His accusations against Vito never gained any traction. Unsurprisingly, no one at the precinct talked, and Vito was too wily, too much of a master of the system itself to leave a trail.

This being America, everyone sued. The McDonoughs sued the NYPD. The Norrises sued the NYPD. Peter Norris himself didn't sue anyone because he'd renewed his relationship with Jesus, and Jesus, apparently, didn't think litigation had any place in his teachings. The NYPD settled with both families, while Norris moved to rural Kentucky and joined an evangelical sect.

During those proceedings, Alex prevaricated so much that he almost believed his own lies – to IAB, to the state AG, then to the civil litigators. The last ones deposed him, and he said under oath that he knew about the precinct detectives not handling the case particularly well, with the failure to adequately control chain-of-custody and so on, but he denied any personal knowledge of willful witness tampering or Vito's unconstitutional interrogation. For the last four years, he hadn't given it any further thought, not beyond the trepidation with which he treated any case with Vito and a random letter from Norris, sent last year, urging him to join his church. He'd promptly tossed it in the trash.

The case was like a boomerang. You throw it away, think you've seen the last of it, and the motherfucker comes back. On a broiling June afternoon, Alex compulsively chewed on his fingers as he sweated and paced below the front steps of the US Attorney's office on St. Andrews Plaza. Had James or Gibson convinced him in the end? Or had Kima

DeSilva, when she'd warned him that she couldn't fend off the federal prosecutors any longer.

On a long, solitary wander through Central Park, he had relived those cases from the '90s, turning them over in his mind, again and again. After Quixano, hadn't he vowed to work cases harder? To be more careful, more thorough? Hadn't he promised a bottle of Glenlivet that he would dedicate himself to pursuing justice rather than crime stats and clearance rates? Had he broken his promises by staying silent? The anti-snitch culture in the department, in any police department, cast a long, murky shadow, but he either faced an indictment or he faced the consequences of whistleblowing. His lawyer recommended the latter, and he *was* paying her a lot. The sinking sun's golden tendrils had caught the bronze wings of the Bethesda Fountain. As he watched shadows and light playing amongst the golden feathers, he thought about Quixano, Serrachia, and countless other defendants losing liberty, losing years of their lives. Could Alex have saved them fifteen years ago? He'd never tried. Instead, he'd sacrificed his soul and his health to the criminal justice system and, at times, to the institutional violence he'd tried to avoid seeing. But he *could* prove that it had the power to be a force for good, capable of dispensing justice. Prove to who? Himself? The federal grand jury? The *New York Times?* The people who thought the system was irreparably racist and corrupt? Or a *beth din,* a rabbinical panel of Talmudic scholars? Even as a lapsed Jew, he had nightmares about being tried by those rabbis. Every night, they waited for him. Lined up along a heavily ornamented dais like Supreme Court justices, power flowing from thick robes and brushy beards. *Were you truly seeking justice and righteousness*, they asked. *Or did you lose your way? Did ambition rule your heart? Did it cut out your eyes?* Oh, dear God, what could he say? He had no defense. He fell to his knees, weeping. Then he woke up, angry at himself for being so weak. Rabbis! Querying whether he was truly doing God's work! Since when did he care about rabbis, or God?

For three months, the rabbis interrogated his dreams. In the real world, the US Attorney had subpoenaed his medical history. Compulsion aside, the rabbis spoke a truth. There was only one road – telling those twenty-three citizens of New York secrets he'd buried for more than a decade. Only he couldn't stop thinking about that LAPD detective, Russell Poole, who'd derailed his otherwise illustrious career in Robbery-Homicide when he argued that the LAPD had covered up the murder of a famous rap artist because moonlighting cops might have been involved. It didn't go well for him. A nervous wreck, careening out of the police department, too tainted for any other law enforcement job.

"Hey, Alex." Kima appeared behind him, and he startled. "I'm so glad you came to this decision."

"That makes one of us." He smoothed over his jumpy anxiety.

"This code of silence isn't good. It doesn't make law enforcement better."

"You gotta trust the people who have your back," Alex countered. "And they gotta trust you."

"I get that. I've been on the streets. But how can citizens trust cops if they think the NYPD is as corrupt as the Mafia?"

"They usually talk when they're jammed up," he observed.

"So even *worse* than the Mafia. You're not protecting good police work, or good police."

"I know, but that's not the issue, is it?"

"Well, fundamentally, it is."

They waited in the lobby. Alex peeled skin from his fingers while Kima reviewed her briefs.

"You're doing the right thing." Kima smiled, rearranging her braids.

"I hope so." Some perps flipped because they had a spasm of integrity – the righteous thing to do – but most testified for the state because there was something in it for them. Like immunity.

A door squeaked, and then Sullivan beckoned them into his office.

"Ms. DeSilva tells me you're interested in a deal," he drawled in that slow, gloopy Southern accent. "What you got better be good, Detective. I've done her a huge favor, not calling you back to the grand jury for the last few months."

"Like we talked about, my client will tell you everything he knows, but he needs use immunity," Kima pronounced. She seemed taller, her shoulders squarer, her brown eyes steely. You would think twice about the choices that brought you here – before you fucked with her. She wore more rings than usual, and they flashed under the fluorescent lights. "He's got first-hand, detailed information that will assist in the prosecution of Detective Indelicata."

"The whole system has failed. Not just one man."

"Can't argue with that," Kima agreed. "But if you immunize Detective Boswell, you'll hear how this *one* man willfully played the system for his own ends, his own career and ego, and callously threw people's lives away. The system is only as good as the people in it."

"I've got evidence against Detective Boswell for his part in convicting Guillermo Quixano," Sullivan countered.

"You'd indict cops, good cops, who might have played a pretty indirect role in this, who could give you solid information, because the more indictments you hand out, the better it looks in the *Post*? What's next? A seat on the federal bench? You know, Victor, 'A citizen's safety lies in the prosecutor who approaches his task with humility.'"

"You don't need to quote Justice Jackson at me. I am doing my job. I'm making sure the police in this city do theirs. It would be nice if they did it right."

Alex felt like a racehorse on its last legs, its fate on tenterhooks at a kill pen auction.

"Detective Boswell has dedicated his life to this city, to public service." Kima spoke resolutely. "He was caught up in a police culture where whistleblowing can ruin an officer's career. You know what it's like. You're not that naïve. That's his worst transgression. And now he's prepared to come forward, to put his career on the line. You want the *whole* story about how the justice system failed these men? Detective Boswell will tell you more than you can imagine. All this hearsay you have about Detective Indelicata, my client can corroborate. He was *there*. You gotta prove *willfulness* if you want to sustain civil rights charges, and you'll struggle to do that without Detective Boswell's testimony." She tossed Alex a sidelong glance, her eyes inviting him to talk.

He coughed, feeling his Adam's apple contracting. Having worked with prosecutors for more years than he could count, he'd suspected that his information about Quixano and Serrachia might not gain him that holy grail of deals. The AUSA could make his case without him, and for any prosecutor, immunity was a trade-off: an immunized witness always had compromised credibility. Alex needed something else.

"You remember Frankie McDonough?" he asked.

Sullivan's thin mouth formed a slight frown.

"The Black NYU student shot by a Neo-Nazi thug in the 181st Street subway station," Alex supplied. "1995."

"Ah." Sullivan twirled a pen between his thumb and forefinger. "Yes... The guy who actually did it was only prosecuted a couple years ago because there was a cover up."

"I know about the cover up."

"The defendant's father was a cop, and he covered it up."

Alex licked his lips, his tongue dry, furry. His New York accent sounded coarse compared to the prosecutor's prep school Southern elocution. "Yeah, but not just the father. It was bigger."

"Didn't Internal Affairs and the state AG investigate the precinct?"

"Yeah, but no one talked." *Tawked.* For some reason, this guy made him self-conscious.

"Do you know who else covered it up? Indelicata?"

His gut did a barrel roll. "Give me immunity, Counselor, and I'll tell your grand jury."

Sullivan rocked backwards in his chair, his straw-colored brows furrowing. "Okay, Kima. I can offer him proffer letter immunity. King for a day."

"No, has to be letter immunity," Kima said firmly. "18 U.S.C. § 6003."

"Well, what's he going to tell me? Off the record. You know I need to peek under the hood."

Alex's heart jumped into double time. He felt hyper-aware of his breathing – it sounded far too loud.

Kima's mouth turned into slight smile, like she had a winning horse, then she brushed a few errant braids away from her shoulder. She opened her briefcase and handed Sullivan affidavits that Alex had written, which described his personal involvement in the cases and summarized his testimony. While the AUSA read, Alex laced his hands together over his belly, trying to save himself from feeling sick. But his hands would not stay still. He picked more holes in his fingers. Kima noticed, one eyebrow slowly rising. He'd never had much control over that tic.

"Huh," grunted Sullivan once he'd finished reading the affidavits.

"Detective Boswell is handing you this case on a platter," Kima said smoothly. "Federal civil rights under color of law. Obstruction of justice. Witness tampering. He can name a couple other officers and two former ADAs. Yours for the taking."

Sullivan rubbed his cheek, as though reflecting on his work, his life, why he'd given up a lucrative post teaching criminal law and the Federal Rules of Evidence at Duke University to work for the Civil Rights Division of the US Attorney's office. Those startling blue eyes seemed more thoughtful than hungry, briefly. He whistled out a breath, then said, "You understand, Detective, if you don't tell me the truth about absolutely everything, I will absolutely *nail* you for perjury."

"I understand," said Alex.

"I'll apply for a court order," drawled Sullivan.

"Thank you. This will make your case," Kima said.

"And save your client's butt while uprooting police corruption," the prosecutor replied drolly. "Your kind of case, Kima."

"Well," she responded knowingly.

Sullivan rose to his feet and shook both their hands. He opened the door for them with fluid graciousness.

"Thank you, sir," Kima said, shifting into a drawling Baltimore accent.

Alex felt his throat closing as he followed Kima down the broad staircase. His eyes watered, readjusting to the painful onslaught of sun glistening off bleached granite.

Kima was smiling triumphantly. "That went well, Alex. He knows he can't prove Indelicata willfully violated the civil rights of those men without your cooperation. Let's meet next week."

"What have I got myself into?" Alex asked.

"The right thing isn't always the easy thing." Her phone buzzed, and she glanced at it. "It's my kid. She's got an audition today. I gotta take this, but next week? I'll text you with a time."

"Yeah." He lost his voice, then cleared his throat. "Hope the audition goes well.

"Thanks, Alex. You'll be fine. Don't worry." She smiled, aiming for reassuring but falling short. The woman was playing roulette with his career, his life. *No, this isn't on her; this was always your game,* he admonished himself as he watched Kima jogging across Foley Square, simultaneously futzing with her phone. She was just playing the dice he'd thrown fifteen years ago. Playing them in her own way, maybe, but try finding a lawyer in this town who didn't have their own agenda.

He turned downtown on Centre Street. The Criminal Courts Building towered at his back, and the Federal Courthouse for the Southern District of New York reared skywards before him. If the architecture of those buildings represented the type of justice doled out inside them, you would choose the federal courthouse over the Criminal Courts, the former grandiose, with its magisterial Roman columns, its opulent cornicing and relief Latin inscriptions, and its statues of the Lady Justice, eternally presiding over the wide marble staircase. Alex clasped his head in both hands, scraping his scalp with the remnants of his nails. He'd thrown his dice. Over a cliff! Didn't matter how they landed because he was screwed either way. What idiotic thing had he agreed to? Immunity! For testifying against a cop. He was surely mad. James, Kima, and Gibson might be wrong – this might end his career, incinerate his status in the department to such an extent that it would take the Arson and Explosion Squad years to recover it. Or maybe he never would, like Russell Poole.

Chapter Forty-Eight

The federal government is like a long freight train. It takes a long time for it to crawl forward – around ten days in Alex's case. Sullivan applied to the Justice Department for authorization of immunity. After some Assistant Attorney General in DC ticked the box, Sullivan proceeded with an *ex parte* motion in court.

While waiting for the DOJ train to move, Alex attended a call-out to Columbia Pres: a Columbia freshman called Vicky Peretti, white, eighteen, and DOA in the ER from asphyxiation. The ER docs had found bruises and a head injury, and they'd called the police.

The Two-Eight precinct detectives had interviewed the distraught roommate, who'd accompanied the vic to the hospital. The roommate explained that Vicky had staggered into their dorm room after attending a frat party, but she had been asleep. She woke up when she heard Vicky coughing and thrashing, like she was having seizure. The roommate panicked and called 911.

While Ray and the precinct detectives canvassed the dorm, Alex attended the autopsy, where Andre Brown told him that cause of death was aspirating on her own vomit, but she had bruises and a concussion, most likely from a fall.

"I can say manner of death is an accident?" Alex asked, immediately wishing he hadn't sounded so hopeful. So unprofessional. As he watched the autopsy, he ground his molars until they hurt – he couldn't pick his fingers bloody in the examination room. His head was unraveling; he had a proverbial rope around his neck, and here was this white college kid who had died under suspicious circumstances, which meant the media and the brass would be all over his ass. He couldn't draw one breath without getting jumped on.

Brown frowned, lining up scalpels on a white cloth. "You don't clear this that easy. She's had recent intercourse, and it can't have been pleasant. There's bruising and injuries in the pelvic area, which I would say are *not* from a fall. I'm swabbing for DNA."

"Fuck." Alex squeezed his eyelids closed. His stomach dropped to the floor. Died under suspicious circumstances and *raped.* This was not the case he wanted right now. *Where's a drug murder or an OD when you need one?* "Sexual assault?"

"You know I can't really say without my crystal ball, but I can't rule it out."

DNA samples would go through CODIS, the FBI database, and the NYS DNA Databank, New York's database, which would match them with anyone who had been convicted of sex crimes or violent crimes. If the guy had no record, the DNA databases would be useless. Either way, he had to wait a couple weeks for all of that. He scampered through the glass doors. The sickly morgue taste fouled his throat and nasal passages at every breath, and he sipped in shallow gasps of air as he strode into the small square between the Bellevue Hospital complex and the NYU College of Nursing. A street van selling coffee was parked on the other side of First Avenue, near more Nursing School buildings. He drank three expressos, determinedly flushing the rancid taste of decomp from his throat. Jittery from his caffeine hit, he called Ray, who reported that Peretti had gone to a frat party that night with a freshman in her journalism class called Tony Miller.

After a quick comparison of notes, Alex drove uptown to Morningside Heights, rendezvousing with Rob Galeano, the catching precinct detective. Galeano was a short Italian, who had a thin, finely trimmed mustache and a slow, wearied approach to the work. *Meticulous,* people said, but Alex reckoned he was just lazy. The detectives convinced someone to let them into Tony Miller's dorm, and to their delight, the person-of-interest was doing homework in his room. Miller's eyes darted everywhere but the detectives' gazes, and he insisted that himself and Vicky had just been classmates, he'd been surprised to see her at the party, and he had no clue what happened at the end of the night.

Everyone lies. The first rule of death investigation.

"You know, Tony." Alex released a pained exhalation, as if Miller's dishonesty hurt him as much as the wound in his side. "My partner's already interviewed Vicky's roommate, who says you invited her to that party. We've talked to your cell phone company, and in a few weeks, they'll send us data... Every call you made, every text, everywhere you've been. If you called and texted Vicky, we're gonna find out."

"I thought you needed a warrant for that," said Miller shakily.

"We don't," said Galeano.

"Cell phone companies are a third party." Alex licked his lips, then pressed them into a stony grimace. "We don't need a warrant to access that stuff. Are we gonna find texts saying you guys were hanging out together? Going to the frat? Look, Tony... Either you cooperated, or you didn't – that's how this plays, and believe me, it's a lot easier if you cooperate. We're gonna find the evidence either way. So... You wanna start again?"

"Okay, we'd hung out a few times."

"Like dating? That's what her roommate said."

"I dunno. Maybe. We weren't like girlfriend and boyfriend, you know, but..."

"But? Were you sleeping with her?" Should he drop the bombshell of the ME's findings? No, he would wait until he needed to apply leverage.

"Yeah, a couple times."

"How was it?"

"Jeeze, that's a personal question." The witness reared back.

"It's my job."

"Um, yeah, it was fine."

"When did you last have sex?"

"I dunno... Like last week. This is really personal."

"Did you take her to the frat party?"

"I just mentioned it offhand to her, you know. She wasn't coming as like my *date*. I wasn't like responsible. I just said she could show up if she wanted." Sweat glistened on the witness' pale forehead. He would fail a polygraph in seconds.

"I think we gotta go to my office and talk there, okay?" Alex said. "Come on."

He feared Miller might ask for a lawyer or refuse to go, but the witness muttered, "I gotta email my sociology professor and say I'm missing class," and after sending an email, he placidly followed Alex and Galeano to the car. A bit of a douchebag, Alex thought, but deep inside, he must feel some guilt.

First, Alex let Miller stew with his own thoughts in the interrogation room. *Just making them think about where they are might soften them up.* He brewed more coffee and checked his email. NYPD admin stuff, irrelevant group spam, but then, a message flashed into his inbox: Carlos Medina, Jose Medina's brother. Alex's stomach somersaulted. Queasily, he clicked on the email. The man was out of prison and out of New York, working in construction somewhere in Pennsylvania. He was also pissed; his email ranting about how the NYPD had *never* cared about finding justice for his brother. They'd put some innocent Dominican guy away for it, then forgot about both men. Alex felt like his insides were decaying. Yes, he'd known there would be no justice for Jose Medina. His fingers burned with the truth, but given the ongoing federal investigation, writing self-incriminating emails would be both crazy and monumentally stupid. And Kima would kill him. Instead, he forwarded Medina a contact email for the Cold Case squad, which had ostensibly reopened the case after Quixano's exoneration last year. The chances of a clearance after twenty years were realistically zero, but sometimes, the stars align, and the wildest long-shot of long-shot cases gets closed. It's good to be good, homicide detectives said, but better to be lucky.

Alex felt spacey and wholly unlucky as he plodded down the stairs leading to the interrogation room. The frat case seemed like a distant problem that he wished wasn't his. Vito had extracted those false confessions from Serrachia, Norris, and Quixano, and his colleagues had made the Central Park Five falsely confess. How easy was it! He thought about what he would tell that grand jury. He thought about his considerable skills at manipulating whoever he'd detained in this room. What if he had been wrong about any case amongst those hundreds? What if he was wrong about this one? Oh, he definitely wasn't wrong about this one. But he'd lost his nerve. He should send in Ray or Cat. They would not hang themselves with the past. He breathed in, his ribcage expanding. The moment he stepped through that interrogation room door, he wasn't himself anymore, not Alex Boswell, with his questionable mental health, but an actor, a blank slate, whoever the perp needed him to be.

He felt himself going into a shaking rigor, and he touched his carotid. His pulse raced against his fingers. But he channeled his stress and his nerves into glaring at the witness. Miller visibly flinched. Putting on more of a grimace than a smile, Alex chatted amicably about the university, about the frat. He talked about what amounted to nothing, the intricacies of death investigation procedure or the CPL, occasionally hinting that he would get to something important, but he had to lay the groundwork with all this other stuff first.

"Should, uh, I have a lawyer?" Miller interrupted in a strangled voice.

"Do you need one? All I'm trying to do is figure out what happened to Vicky. You don't think it's better for Vicky, for her family, to just tell me? You get a lawyer, it takes a lot longer. Drags the whole damned thing out, and that's tough on her family. On you too. You must care about her. You know, I think this is weighing on you, Tony. Be honest, you're scared, right?"

"I guess."

"That's fine. You're not gonna get in trouble for being scared." Alex loosely folded his hands across his belly. "Was there a lot of alcohol at this party? I don't give a shit about underage drinking, but I'm just trying to get a picture here."

"Yeah, duh. It's a frat party."

"'Duh.'" There was the 'out.' "Okay, so you're drinking, you're fucked up. You know, you can make some really stupid decisions when you're that messed up. Shit can happen, and you're in a state, and you have no idea what's going on. That's what we call mitigating circumstances."

"Why do you think something happened?" asked Miller wildly.

"Because the Medical Examiner told me Vicky hit her head, and she might have been sexually assaulted."

"Oh, God." Miller covered his mouth with both hands.

"Once the DNA comes back from the lab, we can figure out who had sex with her. So, if they find your DNA, it's better if you've been straight with me about everything. It seems hard, but believe me, you'll feel a weight off your shoulders." How many times had he spouted this bullshit over the last two decades? Innocent or guilty, it was in no suspect's interest to confess, ever, yet Alex still sold it to people. Too easily, perhaps.

"Yeah, we'd slept together," Miller squawked. "I said, we'd hooked up. But not... I didn't that night. It was like before. And it won't just be me. I don't think it'll just be me."

"Are you saying you *know* she had sex with someone else?"

"The guys in the frat," cried the witness, rocking back and forth.

"The *guys* in the frat?" repeated Alex, emphasizing the plural.

"I didn't think it would all go so wrong. This is just so screwed up."

"It's okay. Just tell me what went wrong."

"I have to pee!" cried the witness.

Everyone gets a weak bladder during an interrogation. Galeano escorted Miller into the bathroom, and when he returned, Alex asked, "What happened at this party? You said something went wrong."

"Oh, God. It was like a thing... the new pledges – freshmen who wanted to get into the frat – had to bring girls to the party for the older guys, the seniors. Like these guys are on the rowing team, the football team, they've got serious currency. You want to get in the frat, you gotta get tight with those guys. They were taking girls upstairs to this room, one at a time. The girls seemed into it. Like they were having fun, like laughing and giggling. Like, I didn't think anyone was gonna be *raped*. I thought it was all consensual."

"How many guys were in this room?"

"I don't know. Some."

"You didn't spell it out that she was there to screw some frat boys?"

"Like, how would I do that? It's just kinda implied."

"Implied?" said Galeano dubiously.

"Yeah."

"You think Vicky got the implication?"

"I don't know."

"Do you know which room?" asked Alex.

"No… We weren't allowed upstairs. They kept calling it 'the rape attic' but like in a jokey way, but I don't know which one it was."

"'The rape attic?'" Alex couldn't roll his eyes far enough into his skull. "Jesus. Well, do you know what happened to Vicky?"

"She was *smashed*. I guess the alcohol hit her hard, you know. So, a couple of the guys had to half-carry her up the stairs. It's a lot of stairs, like thirty."

Alex ran his fingers through his hair, despairing of the callousness. What was wrong with people? He could ask himself that hundreds of times per day. "Let me get this straight. You saw that your girlfriend, or friend, was so wasted she could barely stand, and you let these boys drag her upstairs, knowing their intentions were to have sex with her?"

The witness gawped silently, then he squeaked, "I couldn't *stop* them. There were like five or six guys, like football guys. How was I gonna stop them?"

"Call the cops?" Galeano suggested.

"Yeah, right. I'd have been a pariah. And I thought it was all fine, like this is what the girls wanted," Miller sniffled.

"A gang bang while completely zotzed isn't what women want in my experience," Alex said. "But let's move on. They took Vicky upstairs. Then what?"

"I was drinking a lot, but yeah, she came back down the stairs. She looked really out of it. She kind of fell down a couple steps and hit the railing, which people thought was funny. But she looked like she was crying. She got up and just left the frat house. Didn't say anything. Didn't pay any attention to me."

"What did you do?"

Shrinking into the chair, Miller whimpered, "I did try to follow her. I tried. I'm not an asshole. But she was really upset and told me to get lost."

"Why was she upset?"

"Oh, God."

Alex spun a chair around and straddled it, placing himself so close that the witness could smell his deodorant. "Convince me you're not an asshole."

Miller spoke quickly, sounding out of breath. "Well, she was really hammered and not making much sense, but said she'd like passed out, but then she woke up and there was like a guy with his penis—like a guy having sex with her, and other guys standing around, and she tried calling for help but they held her down until the guy was, well, finished, and then they let her go, and she ran. Shouted all men could fuck off and didn't want me to walk her back to the dorm. Maybe I should have tried anyway, but I was pretty smashed too and just let her go. I swear, that's the last I saw her. Oh, God. That's the truth, okay?"

"Okay," Alex said.

Regrettably, Miller couldn't or wouldn't name the boys who had been upstairs or the friends of friends who'd asked them to bring girls to the party, but the case had grown legs. When Alex surfaced from the interrogation room, he found Ray, Cat, Marcus, Galeano's partner, and an assistant DA lined up beside the one-way. His colleagues smacked him between the shoulder blades and clinked coffee mugs. Dammit, he should feel elated. He'd broken a redball in less than twenty-four hours. But where those emotions should have been, he touched icy detachment, a cold fist gripping his heart. Nonetheless, he faked a smile for his colleagues, swigged the coffee, and then re-entered the room, where he made a tearful Miller sign a sworn statement.

Tingling pains shot along Alex's wrist, his tendons complaining. So far, he'd written search warrant affidavits and outlined a subpoena ordering the release of the frat's membership list. As he reached for his brace, the phone bleated. He jumped like he'd touched a hot wire, but his fatigue came through when he said, "Detective Boswell, Manhattan North Homicide."

"I need to talk to you about Lennon," Farah al-Sanneh told him curtly.

"Why?" Gemma Lennon had long since been indicted, and she should be in the limbo of pretrial legal skirmishes.

"Gemma Lennon's defense lawyer has withdrawn the 250.10 notice," Farah said.

"So, she's not using an EED defense." The obvious conclusion.

"No shit. She's basically saying she's not presenting any psychiatric evidence at all. We have her on video fulminating about angels and the devil. It was obvious to you, to me, that she would try an EED defense or a 40.15 defense."

"I guess Adams is changing her strategy." He should be as worried as the lawyer sounded. But he wasn't. "What do you want me to do about it? Doesn't seem like my circus."

"There have been stories about this federal grand jury and its investigation of alleged police misconduct almost every day for the last two weeks in the *Times,* the *Village Voice,* the *Washington Post,* even the fucking *Guardian.* Adams is talking to experts, psychologists who specialize in studying police interrogations. I'd say she's changing tactics. Because Lennon confessed to a police detective now enmeshed in false confessions and miscarriages of justice."

"Fuck," he exhaled without thinking.

"What does the defense know that I don't?"

"I'm going before the federal grand jury soon."

"I thought you already testified."

"I'm going back."

Farah digested this for a moment. "A second appearance? You've got a deal with the AUSA, don't you? You did something on those cases, and now you've got a deal. Immunity?"

"Yeah."

"What are you being immunized for?"

He tipped his head back. "Perjury, mainly."

"Fuck. Adams must know."

"How?"

"I don't know. There was a leak. There's always leaks. This place leaks like a sieve. And Adams used to work in this office. You think she doesn't have eyes and ears everywhere? You've got to tell me what you're going to tell that grand jury, in case Adams gets her hands on *any* of that information. If it's material to—"

"I can't," he interjected brusquely. "It's a grand jury."

Farah's voice sounded harder than the city pavement. "Only grand jurors, prosecutors, and court reporters are legally bound to secrecy. Witnesses can talk to whoever the hell they like. You're not under a gag order."

What would Kima advise? That seemed to be his mantra these days. "My lawyer thinks I should keep my mouth shut. I would need to consult with her."

"Right. Well, then I think you should do that." It seemed improbable that she'd once slept with him.

Lawyers on the left, more lawyers on the right, and he was the last domino, everything crashing into everything else, collapsing on top of him. The squad room was pitching and rolling. Oh, Christ, he felt ill, like he'd drank from the Hudson. He left his cubicle to crouch over a toilet in the men's room, fighting for air, trying not to vomit. He stayed there until the island of Manhattan stopped swaying.

Kima had said that the DOJ process was merely a formality – it was unlikely for the AG's office or a federal judge to refuse an assistant US Attorney's request for immunity. Her latest email surmised, *al-Sanneh has no legal basis at this point for compelling you to disclose anything. If she wants to discuss any matter pertaining to the civil rights case, it needs to be done through me.*

Neither statement reassured him. Which outcome would destroy his life? Receiving immunity, or not? The NYDA prosecutor compelling his testimony, or not? Whatever the outcome, waiting was agony, a knife doing twists in his gut, so he buried himself in work, engrossing himself with his open investigations.

Vicky Peretti's toxicology results came back – .15 BAC, which Alex expected, and rohypnol, which he found repulsive but not surprising. It changed the whole landscape of criminal liability. Someone who got themselves drunk was still legally responsible for their actions, which made proving Vicky's lack of consent damn near impossible. But if the perps had slipped roofies into the booze, that showed intent to get the victims so wasted they couldn't say no. It might even net him a criminally negligent homicide charge. The perps should have understood the risks of giving out roofies to the unwitting. That in itself was negligent, but then they failed to care for Vicky afterwards, and she died as a result of their failure to act.

As expected, the frat argued that it was under no obligation to cooperate without a warrant or a court order, but Tony Miller had grudgingly given them more names – other freshmen who'd attended the party. Armed with the tox scan results, Alex rewrote his warrant affidavit and phoned Rob Galeano. They would bring the witnesses into the Two-Eight for another round of interviews. He spent a couple hours crafting a press release with Gibson and the NYPD press office. Playing the media, hoping a carefully worded press release would encourage more victims to come forward. Vicky Peretti couldn't be the only one.

His iPhone cheeped, and he mistakenly looked at it: an email from Kima, announcing that Sullivan expected him to appear before the grand jury tomorrow.

Blood raced through his body, like a sluice had opened in his arteries. "Ray," he said urgently. "You gotta finish this press release and chase Verizon and the frat. I'm gonna be tied up with the grand jury."

"I'm proud of you." Ray slurped on a smoothie that was bright green, like summer grass in Central Park, the color no drink should ever be.

"Yeah, right. The L-T better keep me off Three-Four precinct cases. I can't imagine they'll have the same view. What the hell are you drinking?"

"Kale," said Ray. "It's got tons of stuff in it that's good for you. You should try it. It's great for your liver. Antioxidants, vitamin C—"

"Jesus," sighed Alex.

"No, you gotta go to church for that."

Alex lifted a bemused eyebrow at his partner. 'Princess Ray' was cracking smartass jokes, and he was worrying. *Is this how the world ends,* he wondered.

Chapter Forty-Nine

It felt like an ill-fated morning. Alex sliced open his cheek with his razor. The wound stung, and he spat out swear words. He sponged off the blood. You wouldn't think he'd stopped drinking in 1995. Some days, he felt like he'd stopped drinking yesterday, or last week, the pull to start again right there, breathing down his neck. That was the disease, though, wasn't it? You never stop being an alcoholic. Blood oozed along his cheek, and he held a wet washcloth against the cut. When the bleeding trailed off, he cleaned his face, then he raided his closet, selecting his best courtroom suit, dark grey with faint stripes, and he added an understated navy-blue tie.

The downtown 1 was rammed like a commuter factory farm, and he shoved his shoulder and ribs against a pole. Sweaty bodies squashed him on every side for the forty-minute subway ride. If hell truly existed, he thought, it must look a lot like an overcrowded New York subway. At the federal courthouse, he joined the line of people at security. Army guys hugging menacing rifles stood to attention near the doors and security gates. The security line shuffled forward, and Alex flashed his shield at the US Marshals, who seemed like ferrymen taking tortured souls over the Styx. He handed a Marshal his firearm before walking through the metal detector. With a slight smile, one law enforcement officer to another, the Marshal returned the gun. The world turns, no matter what, and federal courthouse security detail was the man's normal, boring day job. *Nothing here matters,* Alex thought as he holstered the firearm and proceeded towards the spiral staircase. *When I'm dead, no one will care about these cases.* But he scanned his phone for the grand jury room number, and his feet ignored his nihilism, steadily moving his body forwards.

As soon as he entered the grand jury room, those twenty-three jurors eyeballed him keenly. *Oh, an important witness,* their curious eyes seemed to shout. The clerk swore him in, speaking in a flattened monotone. Through a careful sequence of questions, Victor Sullivan alerted the jurors to Alex's use immunity, and Alex thought about Frank Serpico, who got a movie deal, and a hundred other retired detectives, who started second careers writing crime novels. Eddie Trenemen had published his novel – the tale of an NYPD detective uncovering an elaborate conspiracy involving the Mafia and the KGB. Alex found no comfort in that thought. If this trashed his career, neither Hollywood nor Random House would save him.

The jury, jaded after long months of testimony, pricked their ears when Alex dug up those secrets he'd buried – the baggie of crack stowed under the driver's seat of Vito's car, and then the gun wrapped in a plastic shopping bag. Had Alex come across *any* evidence conclusively connecting the Colt M199A to Quixano? No, he said. Nothing ever did. It wasn't traceable or registered to anyone. Its serial number had been filed off. Those jurors listened fixedly as he described Vito inveigling the lab analyst into altering his ballistics report. By the time he got to Quixano's interrogation, he had their rapt attention. Some looked aghast while others visibly cringed when he recounted the assault.

"Did you intervene when Detective Indelicata struck Mr. Quixano?" asked Sullivan.

Alex swallowed, forcing some saliva into his drying mouth. "I told him to stop. He threw me against a wall, said he'd end my career."

"Sorry? He threw *you* against a wall? Did Mr. Quixano see that?"

"No, we'd gone out to the viewing area." Alex lightly pressed his fingers into the soft muscle between his upper chest and shoulder, a few inches below his collarbone. "He pinned me with this pressure point. Then he shoved the butt of his gun under my ribs, on my right side, where everything was torn up by the shooting in '87. It's never healed that well. It's just this chronic pain thing I live with. So, I was in a *lot* of pain."

Every juror was staring at him, their mouths agape, their eyes widening.

"Would Detective Indelicata have known about your gunshot injuries?"

"Sure. The whole department knew. Well, *he* certainly knew. I'd told him I had trouble with it."

"And by pressure point, you mean somewhere that causes pain?"

"Yeah. We all learn how to disable suspects by hitting or restraining certain parts of the body. This one causes pain to the nerves all the way down your arms."

"And he knew that?"

"Yeah, all cops know that."

"Could he have 'ended your career,' as you put it?"

"Definitely. Everyone loved him. The Commissioner. The Chief of Detectives. The Manhattan Borough Chief. The police department doesn't treat any whistleblower very well, so who was gonna believe *me*? I was detective third grade. Indelicata was first. Quixano would have got convicted either way."

A juror, a thirty-something Black woman, raised her hand. Unlike trial jurors, grand jurors can directly question witnesses.

The juror asked, "What happens to whistleblowers?"

"You get transferred somewhere you don't wanna be. You get a post no one wants, like an obscure admin job. You can get harassed, bullied, even forced out of the police department. Stuff like that."

"Did he say what he would do to you?" asked the juror.

"Yeah."

"What was it?"

"He said he'd tell the bosses I was drinking on the job." Alex felt the words disintegrating in his throat. "A drunk detective in the Bronx accidentally shot his partner, and it was a whole scandal. We thought anyone caught drinking on the job after that was gonna be suspended or transferred back into uniform."

"Were you drinking?"

"Yeah, but I was a high functioning alcoholic. I had a flask I carried. I wasn't getting blind drunk, but I'd have some when I felt stressed. I mostly drank when off duty."

"A lot?"

"Yeah. Sometimes."

"And Detective Indelicata knew this? Like the flask?"

"Yeah." He wondered if any of these people had read Vito's book. He prayed they hadn't.

The juror didn't look impressed. "You're saying you let an innocent man do time for *that?*"

"Ma'am," said Sullivan. "You need to ask the witness a direct question."

"Was that his only threat?" rephrased the juror.

"Other than trying to break my ribs?" Alex shifted his weight forward, feeling his wound. "No. He said he would flake me. That's what we say when a cop plants evidence. He said they might find cocaine in my locker."

"Were you stealing drugs from crime scenes or Property?" inquired Sullivan.

"Absolutely not. Never."

"Were you using cocaine?"

"No."

"You say you have chronic pain. Have you ever resorted to illicit drugs as a result?"

"No," Alex snapped. His face had gone red. He inhaled, counting down to five seconds. The prosecutor was testing him. These questions might be accusatory, but a cross-examination would be far more harrowing. He couldn't lose his temper. "I just keep the pharmaceutical companies in business with legal ones."

"What about prescription meds?" queried a different juror, a sixty-year old white guy.

"No," Alex answered emphatically. *Jesus, he thinks I'm popping Oxycodone.* If only. "Over-the-counter ones. Nothing controlled."

"You're saying Detective Indelicata threatened to *plant* drugs on you, to frame you, in order to put you up for disciplinary action?" asked Sullivan.

"Yes. If I didn't keep my mouth shut about what happened in that interrogation."

"Could he have planted drugs?"

"Easily. He knows people. Someone would've done him a favor."

"You could have gone to Internal Affairs after he injured you, or if you thought he was going to plant drugs in your locker?" offered the juror.

"And make serious allegations against a colleague I could never prove? I didn't want to lose my job that badly. Like I said, he was first grade, and I was third. He had way more standing in the department than I did."

"To go back to that day... July 19th, 1992... What did you do after Detective Indelicata assaulted you?" pressed Sullivan.

"I just left. Went back to my office, did some paperwork, and caught another case that evening."

"Even though he'd injured you?"

Alex allowed himself a blasé shrug. "I'm used to dealing with pain."

"Do you know what, if anything, happened to Mr. Quixano?"

"I was working this other case. I assume Indelicata took him to Central Booking, but I have no idea."

"Do you remember what you said in 1994?" Sullivan asked.

"You have the trial transcripts, so you're gonna tell me," Alex quipped.

"Yes, Detective," the prosecutor responded dryly. He introduced Quixano's trial transcripts into evidence, then said, "At Mr. Quixano's trial, in December of 1994, defense counsel asked you if Detective Indelicata physically assaulted Mr. Quixano. You said, and I quote, 'I don't know. I left the interrogation room because I had injuries from the Washington Heights riot, and I wasn't feeling well.'"

"Yeah."

"You perjured yourself at the trial?"

Alex's heart tried breaking through his ribcage. He had federal immunity, and as far as New York criminal law was concerned, the statute of limitations on that had run out years ago. "Yeah, I did."

"Did anyone other than Detective Indelicata ask you to perjure yourself?"

"The prosecutor, Padraig Whelan, told me in trial prep to say that Quixano had gotten beat up in the Tombs – sorry, the Manhattan Detention Complex – while incarcerated before his arraignment, and that's why he was injured around the time of his arrest."

Sullivan's pale brows drew together. "The assistant district attorney told you to say Mr. Quixano was injured in jail?"

"Yeah."

"He presumably knew Mr. Quixano wasn't injured in jail?"

"I don't know, but the way he said it, I think he knew."

"You're speculating?"

"Why would he even bring up Quixano's injuries to me and tell me what to say in court if I didn't know the truth?" Alex sipped the water on the table beside the witness stand. It evaporated on his tongue.

"Do you know if Mr. Whelan was close to Detective Indelicata?"

"I don't know. They worked a lot of cases together."

"Did Detective Indelicata ever speak to you about Mr. Whelan?"

"He said he liked him. Called him 'good people.'"

"Did you think he was 'good people?'"

"Doesn't matter what I think. The New York Bar Association tried disbarring him for unethical behavior."

"Relating to Quixano's case?" asked the thirty-year old juror.

"No, for a totally different case. He slept with a journalist and told her stuff he shouldn't."

"Right," grunted Sullivan, who knew Whelan's disbarment wasn't relevant here. "Did you trust him?"

"No."

"Did Detective Indelicata say anything else about him?"

"Not that I can recall."

"Did he name anyone else who might have been involved in Mr. Quixano's or Mr. Serrachia's cases?"

"No."

"Are you sure?"

"He wasn't gonna tell me anything I didn't already know."

"But he trusted you to stay quiet?"

"Yeah." Alex rubbed his brow.

"Did you believe, at that time, that Mr. Quixano committed the crime he was tried for?"

"None of the evidence convinced me, but it convinced the jury." In a way, there was nothing remarkable about the case. Alex remembered how inevitable the conviction felt, in spite of the paucity of evidence. Vito's railroading aside, Quixano was another shit-out-of-luck Dominican guy from Washington Heights, devoured by the criminal justice system, digested and extruded.

The AUSA called for a short recess. A break, thank God. Alex trotted through the grandiose marble lobby and then ran into Foley Square, buying a coffee and a hot dog from a street van parked between the federal courthouse and 60 Centre Street, the civil court. Perfunctorily, he ate half the hot dog while sitting on the courthouse steps, but each bite of plasticky meat stirred up swells of nausea, and he couldn't finish it. His daughters and Ray all said he would feel better if he didn't eat this processed crap. Most likely. But he'd run out of time for finding anything healthy because the recess was almost over. He settled his belly with an antacid instead, then he traipsed morosely up the wide Romanesque stairs and crossed the security gates. When the US Marshal met Alex's eyes, the cheery smile slid off the man's face. Alex winced. *I must look like I'm going to a capital sentencing hearing.*

With an unctuous smirk, Sullivan welcomed him back. Sweat slicked his hands, and his shirt clung to his sides. His chest strained under rasping breaths as he answered more questions about denying Quixano counsel and police SOPs (yes, it is permissible to try talking a suspect out of a lawyer if they say something like, 'I *think* I want a lawyer,' but Quixano had plainly invoked his right to an attorney, and they plainly blew it off), before he walked the jury through the early stages of the McDonough investigation. At first, it had run as effortlessly as a *CSI* episode: identifying the suspects, the witnesses cooperating, finding the gun with a search warrant. But then the case unraveled when the defense filed their omnibus motion to suppress the IDs and the search.

"Why did you suspect that Detective Indelicata tampered with those eyewitnesses?" probed Sullivan.

"They were on the defense attorney's witness list. Even though they'd been prosecution witnesses. Something had gone wrong for them to suddenly become defense witnesses."

"But why did you suspect that it had anything to do with Detective Indelicata?"

"Ronnie Huska used to be in his squad, and after Quixano, I guess I wouldn't put anything past him."

"You saw him differently after Mr. Quixano's case?"

"Yeah."

"You had doubts about him?"

"Yeah."

"So, you inferred he might have done something to the witnesses?"

"Yeah, but I didn't have to infer."

"What do you mean?"

"Indelicata told me himself that he'd do whatever was necessary to protect Ronnie Huska's son, because we're cops, and we have each other's backs."

"When and where did he say this?"

"He brought me to a bar on East 96th. Can't remember the name, but it was Irish. It's a falafel place now."

"Why did you meet him in the bar?"

"I'd called him to follow up on that chain-of-custody problem I mentioned—"

"Just to clarify, that would be him leaving the bullets from McDonough's shooting in his locker instead of with the Property Clerk?"

"Yeah. He said he wanted to talk about it in person, and then he showed up at my office and took me to the bar. We met Ronnie Huska there, and he promised Huska he would protect his son from criminal charges."

"I know it was a while ago, but can you remember their exact words?"

"Kinda. Huska begged me to not arrest his son, and Indelicata said something like we're all cops, we have to look out for each other, and he'd take care of it."

"Did you know what he meant by that?"

"It meant he'd find a way to get the charges dropped."

"Did you say anything?"

"No." Alex tensed his muscles against tremors running along his limbs. "It was my first time in a bar since I quit drinking. It was… upsetting, so I guess I was dealing with that. And my stomach ulcers were playing up, so I was feeling lousy. I ran outta there and felt pretty sick."

"But did Detective Indelicata expressly state that he manipulated the witnesses into altering their testimony?"

"No. But after the defense filed the suppression motion, I spoke directly to two of the witnesses."

"Which two?"

"The ones who testified in the hearing. Ruben De Leon and Eva Castillo."

"When did you speak to the witnesses?"

"Oh, God." He furrowed his brows against his hazy memories. "Around the middle of August. I'm sorry. I can't remember the exact day."

"You didn't report your interviews in DD-5s or any paperwork?"

"No! I didn't want anyone to know about it."

"What did the witnesses tell you?"

"Ruben De Leon was in Rikers Island. He'd been picked up—arrested on a 220.06—I mean, criminal possession of narcotics. He said that Indelicata promised to get him off if he changed his testimony."

"Changed it to what?"

"If he said he hadn't seen Jesse Huska in the subway station."

"Was he sure he'd seen Mr. Huska before Detective Indelicata offered to let him walk?"

"Yeah."

"And you had personally witnessed him identify Mr. Huska?"

"Yeah, from a photo array. He picked him straight out."

"With no guidance from you?"

"Absolutely not."

"According to the hearing transcripts, he said that you and Detective Hurley 'pointed to a photo of Mr. Huska and nodded.'"

"We did no such thing."

"Could you have done it subconsciously?"

"No. I stand back and don't make any gestures or eye contact with the witness during an ID procedure."

"You're alleging that Mr. De Leon's testimony about the ID is fabricated?"

"Yes."

"Do you know the outcome of his narcotics case?"

"As far as I know, he walked."

"Okay. And you said you spoke to Ms. Castillo the same day. What did she tell you?"

"She said Indelicata spoke to her and confused her about what she saw in the subway station."

"Confused her? Can you explain?"

Alex swallowed more water and ran his fingers down his throat. His carotid was pulsing like it wanted to jump out of his neck. "She said she wasn't sure she could recognize the perpetrators' faces. She said he told her that if she testified about stuff she wasn't sure of, she could be charged with obstruction of justice. I mean, she couldn't really, but she was pretty scared."

"I have a transcript of her testimony from the suppression hearing." Sullivan opened his manila folder. "She said, 'The two detectives, Boswell and Hurley, they told me there were two men, and I needed to say two, and one was a short, white boy, cleanshaven with blue eyes. I can barely remember what I saw but I thought, they're the police. I gotta do what they say.' You're saying that is untrue?"

"Yeah. I'm saying, I would never lead on an eyewitness."

"What about Detective Hurley?"

"He wouldn't, either. He didn't."

"And you're now alleging that Vito Indelicata made Ms. Castillo and Mr. De Leon tell the court that you did in order to get the identification of Jesse Huska suppressed?"

"Yes."

"Did you have any further contact with Ronnie Huska in 1995?"

"No."

"When did you next have contact with him?"

"2005."

"What happened in 2005?"

"He showed up at the Manhattan North Homicide office and told me his son murdered Frankie McDonough, and he helped cover it up."

"Did he mention Detective Indelicata?"

"No."

"Did that surprise you?"

"Not at all. He would be loyal to Indelicata. He sure as hell wouldn't throw him under a bus."

"But he threw himself and his son 'under the bus?'"

"He'd become a stand-up guy."

"And during subsequent legal proceedings, did you, at any point, indicate that you knew of Detective Indelicata's involvement in the alleged 1995 cover up?"

"No." Alex curled his tongue against the metallic taste in his mouth.

"What did you say when you testified in Jesse Huska's 2006 trial, specifically regarding Mr. Norris' arrest and interrogation?"

"I said as far as I knew, Norris asked to speak with Detective Indelicata after he was arrested."

"What else?"

"I said I believed someone had pressured him into falsely confessing, but I didn't know who."

"Was that the truth?"

"No." He drank more water, but his throat and mouth felt hot and parched. "Indelicata told me to say that."

"Just to be absolutely clear, you perjured yourself in that trial because Detective Indelicata told you to?"

"Yes."

"Why?"

"Same as before. He'd physically hurt me, and he could get me jammed up in a million investigations and disciplinary actions."

"You were protecting yourself? Your career?"

"Yeah."

"Okay. Let's talk about that confession. You've explained how Mr. Norris had been cooperating with you. Now, how did you learn Mr. Norris was in the 34th Precinct station house?"

"A confidential informant told me he'd been arrested, and I saw on the computer that the arrest wasn't in the system. I had a hunch." Alex slugged the remaining water.

"Would it be a normal thing for a confidential informant to pass this kind of information on to you?"

"CIs pass on all sorts of crazy intel, but I would've expected the arresting officer or their supervisor to call me if they'd just collared a witness in my homicide case."

"And they didn't?"

"No one did."

"That concerned you?"

"Yeah."

"What happened when you got to the precinct?"

"I went down to the interrogation rooms and found them."

"You found them?" The prosecutor leaned over the lectern. "You mean you found Detective Indelicata interrogating Mr. Norris?"

"Yeah. Norris was injured. His face was bruised and cut up. I went in, and he apologized for lying to me, for saying Huska did it. He said he shot McDonough, and Huska wasn't there. He said he'd taken the murder weapon from Huska's house."

"Did you believe him?"

Alex studied his hands on the witness box. Veins and tendons rippled under the skin, while the scars on the left one twisted around his wrist, squiggling across the back of the hand. "No."

"Why not?"

"I'd been interrogating homicide suspects since 1987. My gut told me it was wrong. It didn't feel real. Indelicata told me he'd interrogated him for eleven hours. An aggressive, skillful interrogator can make anyone confess to just about anything in eleven hours."

"Would you describe Detective Indelicata as an aggressive, skillful interrogator?"

"Oh, yes."

"You've just said Mr. Norris had been injured? In the '06 trial transcript, yourself, along with several other police officers, attributed his injuries to resisting arrest in the buy-and-bust. Is that true?"

"No. I think he was beaten up after he was arrested."

"You think?"

"I wasn't there." Alex licked his flaking lips. "But Norris wasn't gonna resist arrest. I didn't think he would anyway. He was terrified of cops."

"Do you know if he was *Mirandized?*"

"Indelicata said he was. He had a waiver."

"Did you try to do anything about it?"

"Yeah." He wished his heart would slow down. "I told Indelicata to stop screwing around with my case."

"What did he say?"

"He said I should think of the squad. He said he had Ronnie Huska's back. He also said he would make my life hell if I did anything."

"You believed it?"

"Of course I did. And I knew he would without batting an eyelash. The Commissioner had given him the Medal of Honor while everyone knew I was an alcoholic with a mediocre clearance rate. I didn't have any fight in me. I was trying to get my act together and deal with some serious health problems."

"Were your health problems related to drinking?"

"Yeah."

"Did they involve any kind of cognitive impairment?"

Sharply, he shook his head. "No. It was all GI stuff. I had scarring on my liver and bleeding stomach ulcers."

"Were you sober during this investigation?"

Alex's heart thumped faster than before. "I got the two-month AA chip right before McDonough was shot."

"You hadn't been sober long. It must have been hard. Maybe you weren't very focused on work?"

"I was focused enough."

"Well, what did you do after the interrogation?"

No one knew about his mad flight to Rhode Island and disclosing it would splash his craziness indelibly across the grand jury transcript, making him look dangerously unreliable. Light perjury, immaterial to everything, wouldn't hurt. "I left the precinct. Went home. I didn't know what to do, but I was sure that I had no chance of saving Norris from a murder rap."

"Prior to this grand jury's investigation, did you disclose Detective Indelicata's statements or personal threats to anyone?"

"No."

"Not Lieutenant Gibson?"

"No."

"Not Detective Hurley?"

"No."

"What about Simon McNally, the lead assistant district attorney on the case? Could he have been aware of this witness intimidation or what you believed was a false confession?"

"God no. He was upset. He told us to investigate allegations of witness tampering, but for the reasons I said..." Alex wiped sweat from his hairline. "I couldn't say it was Indelicata."

"But he pled Mr. Norris out – second-degree murder."

"Norris was the only defendant who could be placed at the scene with the physical evidence we had."

"But both you and Mr. McNally believed his initial statement?"

"Enough for McNally to initially offer him a plea of first-degree manslaughter." Thank God Simon was in the Alps, Alex thought, and he hoped the lawyer was on some mountain and not reading American news. Simon, not known for his steady temperament, would blow a gasket once he learned that Alex had lied to him about what happened in 1995.

"Then why would Norris plea to the higher charge?" Sullivan argued. "If first-degree manslaughter was on the table."

"It wasn't on the table after Norris confessed to Indelicata. Norris was afraid of a death penalty case. McNally was afraid of not convicting anyone. Murder two was a compromise."

"Where is Mr. McNally now?" asked Sullivan. "Do you know?"

"Europe. Somewhere near Chamonix, last I heard."

The prosecutor pivoted to questions about James, Gibson, and other MNHS detectives. What did they know? They'd been in the dark, Alex stressed. With all his heart, he hoped the lawyer and the grand jury believed him, but if his friends and colleagues got subpoenas, they would survive. They hadn't *willfully* covered for Vito, or him. Sullivan smiled in that benign way of his and thanked Alex for his cooperation. Then it was over, like waking up after a nine-hour surgery. Alex retreated from the witness stand, feeling as if copious amounts of blood had drained from his body. He had turned state's evidence. A rat. Godammit, his emotions made no sense. Vito hadn't thought twice about destroying *his* career. Motherfucker probably hadn't lost any sleep over it.

Reporters flocked like pigeons, mobbing the hallways, the Roman steps, Foley Square. Alex sprinted for the City Hall subway station. The flashes of cameras burned his retinas. A searing pain sliced into his right side, and he staggered onto the escalator as it sank under his feet. Someone touched his elbow, a white man in a suit, an ADA called Reed Halman.

"Boswell?" said Halman. "You okay? This heat, man. I'm telling you, global warming is gonna make this city unlivable." He offered Alex a bottle of water, which he took appreciatively. Sure, heatstroke.

"Thanks," he breathed.

"No problem, Alex. Keep the water."

Alex poured half the bottle into his throat. He jogged down the escalator, squeezing sideways around people standing like boulders in the middle of it – didn't they have somewhere to be? Did he? Why did it matter if he caught the next train or the one six minutes from now? His sun-stabbed eyes adjusted to the artificial gloaming inside the subway station. Annoyed by the milling commuter herds, he limped to the far end of the platform. A 4 train screamed and sighed to a halt. Tailing the suited mob, he boarded it, losing himself in his dark reflection in the racing window. He was tired beyond fatigue, benumbed. Those memories tumbled through his head, and he marveled that he'd made it out of the bottle at all. God knows how when he'd floundered through death investigations with a black hole in his brain, sucking everything in. That first year of sobriety had been hell, but only in retrospect could he appreciate how ill he'd been. When you're in it, you're in it. You have no perspective, and it takes everything you have, and more, to make it through the day.

Then there was the night he fled down I-95; the night Vito coerced Pete Norris into a false confession; the first night he'd put his gun to his head. But he'd put the gun away. He'd turned his car around on that highway, wearily wheeling back into the thunder, tattered, beaten, alive. Sure, he might be a self-destructive alcoholic with a bottom-line objection to life in general, but beyond the darkest shadows, he saw glimmers of light. Besides, he didn't have the chutzpah for hiding out in Canada or for shooting himself, which left those glimmers as his only practical hope. He learned how to endure the thing he once anesthetized with lots of whisky. There were surprising days when he wasn't too depressed. The disease perseverated, an invisible companion at his side, but sometimes it stayed in the background. He could go to bars with other cops and drink sodas, although he usually avoided it. His MNHS colleagues ceased giving him flak about his sobriety, and even precinct detectives got bored of it. After a while, most people in MNHS who remembered him as the guy who got wasted every night were gone, and the detectives only knew him as the guy who used to drink but didn't anymore.

Part 10

Chapter Fifty

July 2006

The city steeped in steamy fumes, and Alex tinkered with a cabinet door. He'd never seen any reason to install a new kitchen when he could buy parts from the hardware store and fix this one. The door and its hinges were disassembled on the floor when his landline rang. Caller ID showed a Florida number. Stella Trenemen. Hearing her voice surprised him. It also poured cold dread through his veins. She hadn't phoned long-distance for the hell of it.

She'd last called him five years ago to offer condolences after Bill Ryan's death in the World Trade Center. At the time, his grief had felt cancerous, like the particles of toxic dust pervading Lower Manhattan. Sensibly, he'd irradiated it with denial. It felt as though he was always waiting for Bill to waltz through the door, smirking, like he'd played the most amazing prank. But there was Bill's name, imprinted on that long list of first responders who had died at Ground Zero. Late in 2003, Alex finally summoned the courage to go down there, to stand in the construction site beside the giant hole in the ground, to read the names on the temporary memorial. He listened to cranes and bulldozers, and he negotiated a reluctant truce with demons he'd smothered for two years. Along with most New York detectives, Alex had sorted through the WTC debris that had been removed to Fresh Kills, a landfill site on Staten Island, and like workers in a sickening assembly line, they'd searched the rubble for body parts which could be used to ID victims with DNA. To stave off losing his mind or drinking, he'd detached himself from the horrors in front of him, as he did at any crime scene. You couldn't deal with your emotions during the long, hellish days on Staten Island. Those body parts could be your friends, colleagues, the firefighters and cops – like Bill – who'd run into danger, and the civilians who couldn't get out. Back in '01, they didn't know how dangerous the debris was. They didn't know it caused cancer and other illnesses which would be killing their colleagues years later. A bright spark, a detective from Bronx Homicide who had a degree in chemistry, had given Alex an N95 mask. "I'd wear this if I was you." That man probably saved his life.

Two years later, he'd knelt amidst the scaffolding and wept, shuddering at grief he'd buried at Fresh Kills and denied himself at Bill's funeral. That had all the pomp and circumstance – the flyovers and the bagpipes and a Catholic church in Brooklyn packed with officers – but it didn't have to be for Bill. After all, Bill wasn't in the coffin. You could shut your eyes, pretend the rituals were for someone else. You could drink yourself blind at the wake afterwards – lots of people did – but James had herded Alex away from the wake, and they sat on the Rockaway beach on a day as clear as the morning of 9/11. The city felt different. It felt heavy, unsafe. It made you want to carry your sidearm all the time, even when off-duty, even when you knew it was useless against planes flying into buildings or bombs on the subway or anthrax in the mail. All the words had gone, used up by President Bush, Rudy Giuliani, the pundits and the priests, and the detectives couldn't talk shit or lob terrible jokes or do anything other than stare at the ocean, sharing sorrow, loss, and bewilderment. The silence was enough.

The day after the funeral, Stella had called from Florida, apologizing for their absence. Getting Eddie onto a plane was a mission, and like lots of people, she was wary of flying, or of being in New York. She said 9/11 had triggered one of Eddie's 'episodes,' where he wouldn't speak for days, or he would try calling 911 because he heard gunshots.

"Does he know about Bill?" Alex had asked numbly.

"Kind of," she sighed. "You know I told him. But he gets upset and says, 'No, Bill is fine. It's Alex who died. He died when we were shot. Don't tell me bullshit.'"

"He thinks I'm dead?"

"Sometimes. I'm taking him to the doctors next week for more tests. Maybe there's better medication they can put him on. I don't know."

Alex didn't know what to say. "Uh, I'm really sorry to hear that. He's gonna come out of it?"

"I hope so. He goes through these phases… Then he's lucid again, and it's fine. Or as fine as it ever is. The kids think he needs to be in a care home, but I think moving out of the house would be too hard on him."

A cord tightened around his guts. He had days when he felt like he was bleeding on that street. Sometimes, he heard the gunshots. What words or wisdom could he offer? At least Eddie never had to sift through rubble and body parts at Fresh Kills, breathing in the stench of incinerating flesh, jet fuel, and chemicals that made you feel ill for days, no matter how many crime scenes you had worked. But he couldn't say that. He reassured Stella that he was doing alright, considering the circumstances.

When Alex became unwell at the end of 2004, that conversation returned to him. He toyed with phoning Stella, disclosing his PTSD. Had anyone diagnosed Eddie? Did that help explain the 'episodes' she'd talked about when she'd called him after 9/11? According to Stella, they'd seen half the neurologists in Miami, but had Eddie ever seen a psychiatrist? No, Stella carried enough on her back. If Eddie had PTSD, dementia, and whatever else, Alex's mental health problems would only add needless weight.

Now he stood amidst screws and pieces of wood, listening to his whirring A/C and a driver on West 87th parallel parking by loudly revving their engine. He screwed a washer onto a bolt as Stella confirmed the sinking feeling in his belly. Eddie was in Miami University Hospital, his health failing.

"He needs to see you and Marty Vasquez," she said. "It might be your last chance. Please, can you come to Miami? I don't know how long he's got." Her voice sounded rough.

Alex opened his mouth to ask her about Eddie's medical details, but then he swallowed the jagged lump in his throat. "Okay. I'll get on a plane."

Immediately, he called Marty, and after a brief catch-up about work and mutual friends, they booked a flight to Florida together.

Two days later, Alex met Marty at the departures' terminal in LaGuardia. Marty looked old, hobbling with a cane because he needed a knee replacement. But he refused the little cart. Alex carried Marty's bags along with his own, walking at half his normal pace and waiting a lot as they shuffled through the security strip show, divesting themselves of shoes, belts, jackets, then they hiked to the gate.

The plane took off, New York vanishing below in the grey mists. Alex watched Marty awkwardly arranging himself in the squashed plane seat, and he stretched his own legs forward, as far as he could. It had been a while since he'd seen Marty. Bill's funeral, in fact. Five years had run away from him. The Dominican detective had retired in 1999, after the Amadou Diallo shooting, saying he could no longer work for a police department that was so dismissive of Black lives. Plainly, this wasn't news to anyone, but for Marty, Diallo had been both the final nail and another sad rerun of the same police violence shit. He'd 'switched sides,' from the point of view of some ex-colleagues, working for Washington Heights civil rights organizations that lobbied against aggressive policing as a policy response to racial and economic inequality. But Alex knew that was textbook Marty. The man loved the Heights community; he was on their side, and while police work made the relationship complicated at times, he'd never acted like an occupying soldier in a hostile country. It was his country, his people.

Alex also knew that Marty had cratered into a depression in 2001, when Bill died, because Marty had unexpectedly appeared on his stoop at 2300 hours, half a bottle of whisky in, wildly upset and wholly convinced that he could have stopped Bill from running into the towers if he'd been there.

"I don't think you could have," Alex had said, his voice gentle but certain.

During that flight, they didn't talk about 9/11, or Bill. It was easier to catch up on one another's lives and gossip about mutual acquaintances. Marty had a partner, who had two children from an ex-husband. He was moving to Ithaca next month. Yeah, it was freezing up there. The middle-of-nowhere. She didn't want to live in the city, but she had to stay in New York state.

"What? She's on parole?" teased Alex.

"Worse, she's a lawyer," Marty replied. "Can't be bothered taking the bar somewhere else. You seeing anyone?"

"I broke up with a woman called Becky a year and a half ago, but no one since," Alex said.

"Dating sucks at our age," Marty said solemnly. "You tried online?"

Alex snorted disdainfully. "I'm not *that* desperate." He hadn't tried anywhere. Since getting sick, he hadn't thought about sex or relationships. His emotional reservoir had run dry, and he had nothing left for dealing with other people's emotional drama. And every relationship contained deep reservoirs of that.

"Hey, internet dating isn't just for socially awkward losers these days. It's becoming pretty normal."

"I'll take your word for it."

Miami sprawled out below the wings, low-lying suburbs as far as they could see, and the jet banked, the horizon tilted, the airport lights ran out to one side, and with a juddering of engines, the plane dropped out of the sky. They had the sudden sight of the airport at ground level: a parked shuttle bus, a United Airlines 737 taxying to its gate, and with a thump, the plane's wheels touched the runway.

Once they'd navigated the maze of terminals in Miami-Dade Airport, they rented a car, Alex driving, following directions he'd printed from the internet. They passed countless strip malls and identical ranch-style houses with swimming pools and palm trees. The moist air swathed his body like a wet, woolen blanket. It stuck to the inside of his chest, like he breathed in damaged silk. *Why do so many New Yorkers move here?* His mother was one – she lived in Ft. Lauderdale. As if New York City in July wasn't miserable enough! Alex tried raising their spirits with lighthearted chat about all the New York Jews who retired to Florida. Marty forced an insouciant smile, observing that Alex was being chickenshit about the heat. Try visiting the Dominican Republic in the summer. Both men sensed that the banter barely concealed brittle emotions, like a half-assed attempt to cover a DOA with a sheet.

They met Stella at the beach house, a wooden structure perched on stilts, facing the Atlantic, and she greeted them with earnest hugs and cups of coffee and sandwiches. After they ate something, she drove them to the hospital, talking about the kids and grandkids. Their son, an engineer, still lived in Florida, while their daughter had moved to DC to work for the FDA. But Alex heard the strain in her voice. He chewed on his nails while sitting in the back seat of her Chevy Tahoe.

It was worse than she'd made it out to be. Eddie looked almost translucent, his skin like old brown paper. His breathing was painful to hear, the creases down the cheeks sunken, and a central line sprouted from his collarbone.

"Alex. Marty," he gasped. "How did you get here?"

"We flew here from New York," said Marty, his eyes flicking anxiously from Alex to Stella, as if he was afraid to look directly at Eddie.

"New York? That was a long time ago. How did you know I was here?"

"Stella told us." Alex made himself smile even though he had anguish in his eyes.

"She did? How?"

"She called me."

"Oh. You were shot too, Alex. I thought you'd been killed. Were you alright?" Eddie sounded so frightened, so afraid, and he held onto Alex's left hand.

"I was hurt but got better."

"You went back? To the NYPD?"

"Yeah. I'm still in Homicide."

"A detective?"

"Yes."

Eddie's gaze lowered to Alex's hand, clasped in his, and he turned it over, staring closely at it. "How did you hurt your hand? You never had these scars before."

"I put it through a window. Fighting with a perp," Alex lied, thinking for Eddie's sake, he should never hear the truth. He ignored Marty's quizzical look and hoped his ex-colleague wouldn't ask him about those scars.

"Huh. I didn't know about that," wheezed Eddie. "It's been a long time, hasn't it? But do you remember, the first thing to do at a crime scene? Control the space, preserve all the evidence. Don't just let anyone in. Don't let anyone touch anything."

"Yes, Eddie. That's right."

"And you know, the best detective to have on any case is Vito Indelicata. He's your man. He's like detectives used to be. He knows the streets. He knows the people. You don't forget that."

"Yeah, Eddie," Alex said, his voice level but catching in his throat. Those secrets were forever his to keep.

For about half an hour, Eddie rambled about MNHS, about the Three-Oh Precinct, about *Practical Homicide Investigation,* about people (some they knew; some they didn't), seemingly unaware that Alex had nearly twenty years in MNHS and Marty had retired, but Alex and Marty agreed with whatever he said. Marty made worried eye contact with Alex as Eddie grew more confused, agitated, and then started creakily singing spirituals from his childhood.

Stella moved towards his head. "I think you need to rest now, Eddie." She indicated with her eyes that Alex and Marty should make an exit.

"See you later, Eddie," Alex said.

"See you, man," said Marty.

Confused, Eddie blinked at them, as if they were two strange men who had entered his room for no fathomable reason.

In the corridor outside, Stella took both their hands. "Thank you for coming. I know it must be hard. I didn't even know how to tell you what he was really like. I mean, I told Alex a few years ago that he was struggling, that he got confused."

"I remember," Alex said in a husky voice. "It was like a month or two after 9/11."

"He improved, for a while. But then he got worse. I had to move him to a care home in '03. I couldn't take care of him myself anymore. There was only so much I could do."

Alex sank his front teeth into the inside of his lip. He hadn't known Eddie had moved into a home three years ago. That seemed like news he shouldn't have missed. He glanced at Marty. Did he know? The retired detective wore his interrogation-poker face.

"He's been going on and on about this stuff, but saying he wanted to talk to Marty, because I'm not a cop, and I won't understand," Stella continued. "He wanted to see Vito Indelicata too, but you know what he's like. He has like ten kids and fourteen grandkids and said he couldn't get the time to come down. And, well, Eddie keeps talking about Alex dying in the shooting and getting really worked up about it, and I say, you didn't, but when he's having a bad day, he doesn't believe me. Maybe he'll be calmer now that he's seen you."

"How you holding up?" asked Marty.

"It's been hard, to be honest, this last year. He's deteriorated so much. All these years with him in a wheelchair were hard enough, but now he doesn't know what's going on anymore or what's real. I'm exhausted." She straightened her spine, as if shouldering a heavy backpack. "Let's go back to the house. I've got a lot of food to make."

They spent the night at the Trenemens' house. Stella cooked a lobster bisque, laughing about practicing Southern dishes since moving to Miami. After dinner, they sat on the veranda overlooking the steely grey ocean and the white-tipped waves rolling across the beach. They conversed about life, politics, nothing of great import, and then Marty complained that his knee was bothering him and limped to his bedroom.

When he'd gone, Stella rose to her feet, turning and leaning against the railing. With her back to Alex, she said, "Eddie was broken after the shooting. His body, obviously, but his mind as well. He would never talk about it. Not once in the last nineteen years. It was like Vietnam. He never talked about that, either. I could see something was *wrong,* that he carried this terrible trauma, but he'd get angry if I brought it up. It was this masculine...construct." Her whole body shuddered under a humorless laugh. "God, I sound like an academic. It was all tied in to how he thought of being a man, being a cop, being a soldier. He couldn't *ever* talk about how he might be mentally or emotionally hurt. I tried to get him into counseling, but he'd say that he didn't 'believe in' psychiatry. Like it's some kind of religion. It was so damned frustrating... I think talking to someone professional, or talking to anyone, quite frankly, would have done him a world of good, but he didn't see it that way. If you..." She hesitated, as if she had to compose the sentence before she said it.

"I started counseling like a year and a half ago," Alex interceded. She was going to suggest that if he wasn't in therapy, he should be. "I got pretty unwell. My boss made me see a shrink. And she...the psychiatrist... diagnosed me with PTSD... I guess I've had flashbacks, panic attacks for years, but it got worse. I'm on a lot of Zoloft now." He exhaled from a place deep inside his chest. It hurt, but this thing *was* a part of him.

"Oh, that's a relief," said Stella. "Such a relief. Not that you're ill, but that you're actually dealing with it. Thank God for your boss. I'm glad some cops are realistic about mental health." She half-pivoted around to face him. "Can I ask what happened? I've never known. All I know is that two cops showed up at my class at Columbia *that* day, took me out into the hallway, and said you and Eddie had been shot. Can you talk about it?"

"Yeah, I practice it with my shrink," he answered with a tense smile. "You really want to know?"

"Yes," she said resolutely.

His memories vanished at the ER, but everything prior to that had always seemed crystal clear, like a horror movie inside his head. Hearing his heart thudding, he narrated the story, beginning with searching for a witness, ending with going into shock and losing consciousness.

"Thank you," Stella said when he'd finished.

Feeling wobbly, he plucked tabs of skin off his fingers and studied the sea, smashing and foaming against the beach.

"It must be triggering," she added. "I'm sorry. I thought it might help me understand Eddie better. It's too late to change his mind about therapy... Not that I think anyone could. But it really *is* a relief to know that you're being treated. I was worried."

"I'm managing it. The meds help. They take the edge off." Alex stood up and moved to her side at the railings. He thought she looked long past tired. Something in her eyes had gone, and when he hugged her on that veranda, she seemed to lean against him as if she had not rested for a long time.

The next day, Alex and Marty flew back to New York. For most of the flight, Marty read a Pablo Neruda novel, while Alex put on his reading glasses and wittered at the crossword in the Delta Airlines magazine.

Somewhere over Virginia, the flight attendants served refreshments, a distraction from Neruda and the crossword.

Sipping on a coke, Marty asked, "Did you know Eddie'd been in a home?"

"No," Alex said, raising his eyes over the rims of his glasses. "Did you?"

"No."

"We're shit friends."

"Yeah. But it's been almost twenty years since they were in New York." Marty wriggled his body, unable to find a comfortable arrangement for his long legs and arthritic knee.

"I've still got lots of pain from the wound. Never feels like it was twenty years ago."

"Man, I hear you. But it's not like Eddie and Stella moved to Long Beach. Florida's far. Fuck knows, you have a lot to cope with. Since this knee's got bad, I know what chronic pain is like. It's the pits. I don't know how you've managed for so long."

"I'm used to it. But it's not hard to send an email." He should send more emails to Stella. Or call her. During their conversation on the veranda, she had seemed tough, as tenacious as she'd always been, yet so lost, so alone. He hoped she had friends in Miami.

"It's easy to think you're gonna get around to it, but space it."

"Yeah." Alex shifted his hips towards the window, staring at the blue water and jagged green coastline. Chesapeake Bay, a jigsaw of land and sea streaked with roads and boat wakes. He groped blindly in the dark, faraway corners of his memory for what Eddie had been like before 190th Street. Smiling, upbeat and workmanlike in his approach to death and mayhem, energetic and fit enough to run the length of Manhattan. Those memories didn't last long, giving way to the nightmare. His wound pained him, stirred to life, and he held his hand against his side.

Part 11

Chapter Fifty-One

September 2010

The clock glowed, mocking sleeplessness with the time. 0134. Alex closed his eyes for a little while, then squinted at the clock again. 0138. Why did time creep so sluggishly at night, yet you never had enough of it during the day? One of those unsolvable conundrums. Unable to lie still, he abandoned his bed and furled himself into a ball on the sofa, watching TV. Late-night cable news. No breaking news, so they were replaying earlier stories. They talked about the wars in the Middle East, with pictures of Basra and Fallujah – smoky, bombed-out ruins in the desert's bronzed light. Soldiers wearing tan fatigues ran through a building. Dust obscured their faces. They moved lightly, as agile as cats, despite the rifles in their arms and the heavy packs on their backs.

The TV shifted from the warzone to the bright studio. The news anchor said, "Three days ago, Detective Alex Boswell from Manhattan North Homicide testified in front of the federal grand jury investigating the NYPD for civil rights violations in numerous miscarriages of justice."

Hearing his name, Alex sat up straighter. He flinched at the vision of himself on the TV: head lowered, scurrying down the wide courthouse stairs. Fuck, he looked overweight, washed-out, his eyes wrinkled and troubled. He hated seeing himself on television. The scene shifted again: Guillermo Quixano sitting on a red sofa in the studio, expressing eternal gratitude to the US Attorney for pursuing criminal charges against the detective who framed him. Quixano's face was wizened and craggy, riven with pockmarks and crevasses. A cane rested between his knees. Those needless years in Attica had not been kind to him.

The reporter asked, "Guillermo, do you know that Detective Alex Boswell from Manhattan North Homicide testified in front of the grand jury yesterday?"

"Yes," replied Quixano.

"You remember him, from your interrogation?"

"Yeah, for sure."

"How did you feel about that?"

"I don't know what he said, but I just hope he told the grand jury the truth. He knows the truth."

"It's true that you were a drug dealer in the early 1990s, right?"

"Yeah, I was," Quixano answered implacably. "But it's what everybody did. It was all around us. When you raised around it, it's normal. My whole life, I knew people who got locked up. But they did what they did. I thought, I'd go to trial, then I would go home."

"You have now filed suit against Detective Indelicata and the New York Police Department for false imprisonment and deprivation of substantive due process, so even if the grand jury declines to issue an indictment, you might receive some kind of compensation. But can it ever be enough?"

"Nothing will ever give me the last fifteen years back. Nothing. But I gotta take justice in whatever form I can, and at least I'll get something to give to my children. I owe them that. The state of New York owes them."

Alex lowered his eyelids until he couldn't see the TV. He was in that interrogation room. He was younger. So was Quixano, who didn't look like a man who'd suffered years of beatings. Quixano's body slammed into the cinderblocks, then fell to the floor like a ragdoll. Alex shouted at Vito, but his muscles froze, too paralyzed by shock and fear to do anything. Something hot pulsed under his ribs. A sudden pain, and he pressed his hand into his scars.

Quixano continued talking to the journalist, but Alex stopped listening. He punched the power button on the remote and wrapped himself in blankets as if he could cocoon himself away forever. Every cop in the city knew he'd turned on a colleague. Everyone else thought he should have done it years ago. Either way, a losing prospect.

Chapter Fifty-Two

Feeling listless and fuzzy, Alex slurped on his third cup of coffee. Before him, he'd splayed out the murder book for the Moreno case. It had bottomed out. No direct evidence linked Moreno's ex-girlfriend, his lodger, or his neighbor to his death. Still, there was no shortage of people with a motive. The 'business partner' told Joe Furness that Moreno had undercut everyone by selling 'burn bags,' baking soda instead of heroin or cocaine, an act of unrestrained capitalism guaranteed to make a man more enemies than he ever needed. Every junkie in East Harlem must have hated that asshole. But the case needed luck, a tip, the loose rock that became a landslide.

Where do you find that rock? He squished his stinging eyes with his thumb and forefinger. His grand jury appearance had only been two weeks ago, but it seemed like months had passed. *This* case hadn't budged in two weeks. And he felt like a boxer who'd lost too many rounds, but he was still in the ring, taking punches.

He didn't notice his cell phone ringing until Cat, on the other side of the cubicle, grumbled, "You gonna answer your phone?"

He saw Kima DeSilva's name on the screen.

"Hi, Kima," he said, holding the phone to his ear with his shoulder while scrolling through his email.

"They issued a true bill," the lawyer reported solemnly. "Indelicata was indicted."

At first, he couldn't speak. A million scalding minnows erupted through his arteries. Had he imagined them indicting someone? Yes – himself, hence testifying. But Vito had always been made of Teflon. If anyone wasn't going to be indicted, it would be him.

"What? Anyone else?" He switched windows from his email to the *New York Times* and *Daily News*. The papers weren't breaking the story, yet.

"So far, Padraig Whelan, who's still in Ireland so they're gonna have to extradite. Indelicata's boss in the '90s, Mickey Conon. Ronnie Huska.

And a detective who used to work in the Three-Four called Oliver Skegs. There could be others if any of those people start talking."

"I only gave him Indelicata, Whelan, and Huska."

"I know, but the grand jury's been empaneled for months. They've heard a lot of witnesses."

"What about other ranking officers? People above Conon?"

"Hah," Kima scoffed. "Plausible deniability. I bet you a million bucks someone knew, or just chose not to care, but they're gonna be sure Conon and Indelicata and those guys take the fall. Just the 'bad apples,' you know."

He did.

"The press'll have it in the next half minute. I thought you'd like a heads up."

"Yeah, thanks, Kima."

"You did good," she said.

"You still gonna say that when those wrongfully convicted defendants sue me," he asked dryly.

Unruffled, the lawyer answered, "They'll file suit against the NYPD. Deeper pockets, and they wouldn't even have a case if it wasn't for you. I gotta go, but we'll talk later."

He lowered the phone to the desk. His hand was shaking, and he clasped it with his other one. He thought about the cop in Queens who ended up on a psych ward after blowing the whistle on arrest quotas and fudged stats. That guy had approached *The Village Voice,* not a federal grand jury. *The Voice* published some damning articles, but no one got indicted. A cop could retire at forty-five with their full pension, and Alex was fifty-three, so he could leave the job whenever he wanted.

Multiple cell phones burst to life, like a rainforest dawn chorus of calls and notifications. Someone must have given Gibson a heads-up; she stepped out of her office, calling him in for a meeting.

"You alright?" she asked.

"Yes, ma'am."

"You put your ass on the line," she said.

"No shit," he admitted.

"They're gonna try to contain it. Spin it so it looks like it was just a couple bad actors and nothing to do with a department culture that prioritizes quotas above everything else, even when it results in miscarriages of justice. That's just the way it's gonna be. It's always the way. Always the 'bad apples,' but I never thought the grand jury would even indict, so..."

Alex wondered why everyone loved the apple metaphor for talking about dirty cops. "Won't stop them from making my life hell."

Gibson scribbled a circle on a notepad, testing a broken pen. She threw the pen into her trashcan. "It's bad optics if they transfer you now. Journalists would go nuts. It would be the most obvious cover up, ever. It makes a story about NYPD corruption into an even *bigger* story about NYPD corruption, and the US Attorney will be investigating the police department until 2020. The last thing the Commissioner wants is more federal oversight or a consent decree."

"They'll find a way." Wearied cynicism yoked his voice. "They could transfer *you*. I think I'd have to leave MNHS anyway. They find out I'm taking antidepressants, I'm done—"

"We'll see," she interrupted. "Give it time to blow over. You made any headway with Moreno?"

Alex sniffed, grinding his back teeth so loudly that his boss heard his tension. Did the Queens police officer have a pre-existing psych history? It would have made his involuntary commitment far easier. "Moreno was selling burn bags, but I don't know how we'll ever trace that lead. Find every disappointed junkie in Harlem."

"Good. Get on that," Gibson said coolly, as if the grand jury and the indictment had never crossed their paths.

Chapter Fifty-Three

Late, after the four-by-twelve, Alex plodded up his building's front steps and hunted around his pocket for his keys. As he untangled the front door key from the set, he felt a cool tingling along his spine: the sensation of someone watching him. He clenched his fingers around the keys, and his ears swiveled. A car engine idling on the road. He sharply looked over his shoulder. A dark-colored sedan. Sitting with its lights on and engine running. He squinted, making out New York plates. At that moment, two white males leapt out of the car, then strode purposefully towards number 127. Neither wore a uniform, but they carried themselves like police officers, moving with the confident swagger of men who believed they owned the streets. Alex felt his heart rapping out a staccato drumbeat. He had a vision – Frank Serpico, shot in the face after a botched drug raid, left for dead by his colleagues. He was alone. The two men were half his age. One held a tire iron. Either they had a flat and needed his help, or they had a weapon that wouldn't make noise or be traceable.

The men paused at the top of the stairs. Alex backed against the door, breathing fast, both hands balled into fists. He doubted that the men had a flat tire, but would they attack him, unprovoked? Hurt him just for the hell of it? They might! Bog standard witness intimidation. Part of his brain urged him to go for his gun. The other part froze his hand. The men hadn't done anything to justify use of deadly force. If he fired his weapon on an Upper West Side street, the slug could go through a window or a car.

"What's the difference between a Jew and a pizza?" sneered the taller man.

"Dunno," said his pal.

The tall man swung his tire iron. Reflexively, Alex jumped sideways, and his shoulder hit the building. The man missed, striking the railings with a heart-stopping clang. That justified deadly force! Alex reached for his gun, but the shorter man lunged towards him. Blazing fires of pain exploded in his right thigh. He let go of the firearm and collapsed onto his knees, his breath whooshing out of him as he struck the concrete. Pain wrenched whimpering noises from his throat. He held his leg with a cupped palm. It was wet, warm. Shocked, he looked at the leg. Blood spurted from his thigh. His dark grey trousers blackened as blood soaked through the fabric. The short man was holding a bloodied Stanley knife. *Fuck!* Alex swore, feeling cold, trying to think.

"A pizza doesn't scream when you put it in an oven," Tire Iron laughed.

"No one's got your back," Stanley Knife said. "No one."

Setting his jaw against the pain, Alex hooked an elbow around the railing, then heaved himself to his feet. He faced the men, panting through his mouth. *Go for the gun now!* His hand moved towards his hip. Leering, the tall man swung the tire iron at Alex's belly. Alex blocked it with his left arm. Something cracked, a lightning strike inside his forearm. It fell limply to his side, dead. He willed it to move, but the pain reared in a great flaming wall. White stars danced in front of his eyes. Warm liquid ran down from his leg, pooling inside his shoe. It squelched inside the sock. How much blood was he losing? Too much.

"Indelicata's a good man, a good cop," said the perp coldly. "He deserves better than you."

"I did the right thing, for once," Alex croaked, trying to bring strength to his voice. So, they were cops. Son of a bitch. He squeezed his shoulder blades together. White lights and dizziness thrashed his body like storm-driven waves. His right arm was braced against the railing, supporting his weight, and if he moved for his gun, he would fall over. His left arm hurt like someone had hacked it off with a sword, although he could see that it was still attached. He glared at his attackers as if he could burn them with his eyes. Stanley Knife had a mustache. Tire Iron had a rugged stubble. "You, on the other hand…" he wheezed. "You'll be writing Indelicata letters from your respective prisons."

Tire Iron's eyes gleamed with red-hot anger. He sprang towards Alex, shoving him backwards into the red brickwork. Calloused hands wrapped around his throat. Panicking, he clawed weakly at the hand. Those fingers were like stone, immovable, crushing the air and the life out of his body. A vat of hot oil poured through his arteries. The man's face hardened, and he squeezed harder. Alex's lungs screamed at the white-hot inferno inside his chest. It overrode every thought, every heartbeat.

"Calm down, man! You don't want a damned murder charge!" he distantly heard Stanley Knife shouting.

Now you say that? Words wheeled and disintegrated, confetti caught in a jet engine, whipped around, destroyed. A fleeting vision of his daughters, tears shining in their eyes. The faces of several ex-girlfriends, shaking their heads, like he had it coming. James and Ray, standing next to one another at a cemetery, heads bowed. Couldn't they find it in themselves to say horrible things one another, like they usually did? It didn't take long to kill someone this way. Cut off their airways, their carotid arteries, and you're talking minutes. That thought rang out like a cathedral bell, clear and loud. Then it vanished. Everything vanished: the agony in his lungs, the crashing panic, the red-faced man with searing hatred in his eyes.

Something warm and wet touched his face. It slobbered against his cheek. He groaned and coughed. The concrete slab was sticky from bloody pools. His body shifted sideways, but the left arm hung flaccidly from the shoulder. When he tried cradling it with his right hand, the pain knocked him backwards. His throat ached, and it hurt to breathe, but he *was* breathing.

Molly, his neighbor's golden cocker spaniel, shoved a wet doggy nose under his jaw. Weakly, he patted the dog with his functioning arm, then he tentatively eased his shoulders up against the railing. He'd been lying on his stoop, a foot from the door. His head swam like his brain had melted. Again, he tried flexing the left arm. The pain sent him spinning into a wheel of nausea.

"Good God, man. What happened? Are you alright? I've called an ambulance."

His neighbor, Davram Bari, the Pakistani-American high school teacher who lived on the second floor. Davram squatted beside his dog, one hand on Alex's shoulder, the other clutching a fleece jacket sodden with blood.

Alex tried to speak, but he coughed again.

The dog wagged her tail, her tongue lolling to the side of her mouth.

"Came out to walk Molly, and you were unconscious on the steps," Davram said. "There was no one here, and I don't think they stole anything. You still have your... uh... gun. And your keys and wallet. Your keys were on the ground. Your leg was bleeding a lot. I think I stopped the worst of it."

"How long?" His voice sounded hoarse, rasping across swollen vocal chords.

"Don't know... A minute or two?"

"Did you see anyone?"

The teacher nervously grunted, "No," then he lifted his head and scanned West 87th. "The city's been so safe…It's not what it was…I never thought of this neighborhood…"

"You're safe," Alex coughed.

"You've been *attacked*," Davram pointed out. "Right on our stoop. Doesn't seem very safe."

"It wasn't random. I know that for sure. It's *not* like the early '90s." Alex reached for the railings with his right hand, but dizziness, like a hammer, knocked him back to his knees.

Davram said, "You're hurt. I think you should wait for the ambulance."

Given he couldn't even stand, he probably should. And the bus was coming. Sirens wailed in the distance, drawing closer with each howl. Alex felt ice crystallizing inside his bones. His teeth chattered.

Davram observed, "You're shivering."

"I don't know if it's cold or shock or what." His words were sliding into one another. More blood was seeping out of his thigh, and Davram resumed holding the fleece against the wound.

"It's not that cold. If they don't get here soon, I'm going to have to cuddle you," the teacher said.

Paramedics and an RMP from the 24th Precinct arrived before that became necessary. They escorted Davram down the stairs, and the two uniforms, a white man and an Asian woman, interviewed both him and Alex. The cops seemed shaken, upset that a colleague had been attacked on their beat. *If only you knew.* But Alex couldn't bring himself to ID his assailants as police officers. Besides, he wasn't sure. They could have been perps who owed Vito a favor. When he said that one had his hands around his throat and he'd blacked out, those two officers failed miserably at concealing their worry. Their faces paled. EMS personnel secured him in the ambulance, administering gas and IV fluids as they bundled him uptown to Columbia Pres. The cold burrowed deeper into his insides. Hospital personnel asked him more questions. They repeated questions. Doctors tested his eyes, his reflexes. They x-rayed his arm and his chest, and then they put him through the CT scanner. They were talking about surgery. They said GA was risky because he had compromised airways, but the bones in his arm were shattered. If they didn't install plates and screws, he might lose some function. *Shattered?* Befogged with shock and painkillers, he heard himself demanding surgery.

Minutes or hours or days later – Alex couldn't say – he found himself very much alive and breathing in a private hospital room. They didn't house police officers on the communal wards. An ECG machine beeped. Pipes, buried deep within walls, groaned out low humming sounds. He wore a cast on his left arm, all the way from the hand to the shoulder, and the arm was firmly restrained in a blue sling. His brain felt clunky. But he sifted through hazy, broken shards, like he would search a ransacked apartment for evidence. His eyes lowered to the cast. Radius and humerus with multiple fractures near the elbow. That tire iron had broken the bones, then they'd shattered when he'd fallen on his arm after losing consciousness. A stab wound in his right thigh. They'd stitched the wound and pumped him full of antibiotics and Tetanus shots. It had missed the femoral. Bruised larynx and windpipe. The docs had loaded him up with anti-inflammatories, an attempt to reduce swelling which could block his throat. Carotid artery lesion. That sounded bad. Grade I, they'd said, which wasn't as bad as Grade II or III. They were giving him heparin, counteracting fatal blood clots. The doctors were holding him here for a few days. Making sure he didn't drop dead from a stroke or a blood clot in his lungs.

Alone in that hospital room, he began to shake, and he was laughing, or crying. His emotions felt like someone letting off all the fireworks at once. He'd been a stand-up guy. He'd testified before that grand jury. But the charges against Vito would be dismissed. Vito would play the system, like he always had. The indictment was like the US Attorney saying, *well, we tried, but the system is the system.* Alex's brain had been smelted into jellied pain. His blood had been siphoned out of his body, and then the body had been flung into a dark pit. Like smoke behind a closed door, guilt and stronger pain steamed through the cracks, filling the room. He felt sick to his stomach, resisting it at first, but then he retched into the trashcan beside the bed. He was weeping. Black flecks swirled across his vision. If he complained about the pain and nausea, maybe they would give him more Oxy, enough to hide his feelings deep inside a narcotic cloud.

"Dad?"

He blinked and made out a figure sitting rigidly upright at his bedside. A trim young woman wearing hospital scrubs. Her curly hair was gathered into a bun. She was dressed in a nursing uniform, but she wasn't the nurse who ran this ward. When he'd vomited, that nurse had rushed into the room and dispensed another round of pain meds. The heavy-duty ones, which disconnected his brain from his body, like someone cutting powerlines, but his vision seemed to be recovering. And his hearing. And his mind. Still, he felt groggy and queasy.

Sarah repeated, "Dad?" They must have called her. He didn't remember phoning anyone. "What the hell went down?" she said. "You had a reaction to the GA. You've been out of it all day."

"What reaction?"

"Severe nausea. It happens. But I meant before. What the fuck happened?"

"I was attacked in front of my apartment," he replied calmly, like he was complaining about a parking ticket. Why did he sound so calm? It must be the Oxy.

"Yes. Clearly. You didn't stab your own leg. By *who?*"

"Just two guys. I didn't know them."

"For *no reason?*"

He shrugged, as if he had no idea. Lying to his kid soured his stomach, but the truth had taken him to Columbia Pres.

"How are you this zen?" she demanded. "You didn't say anything to the cops who talked to you, either. Fuck's sake. You almost died."

"Not the first time. I've almost died before," he muttered. "If shit happens, it happens."

"What the hell is wrong with you? The feds should have had you in witness protection! They should have *done* something. And the men who hurt you—"

"I'm fatalistic," he said. "And it might not have anything to do with that."

"Oh, give me a break. I can't believe it was totally random, not with everything that's been happening. How much Oxy are you *on?*" Sarah sputtered.

"Some." She should have been a cop, he thought. Her bullshit-detection-system was as sensitive as any detective's.

"Is it possible for you to get out of New York?"

"Why?"

"These people are after you," she snapped. "They might come back!"

"Why? They've made their point." Then he hastily added, "If that's what it was about." *What was their point?* Discouraging him from testifying in any further proceedings against Vito. How would that work when or if this case made it to pretrial hearings or a trial? Godammit, he would have to skip town, but that was a future problem. He swallowed uneasily, and he kept his eyes fixed straight ahead.

"The hospital will hopefully discharge you in a few days. You had a mild carotid dissection. When you're out, you shouldn't do anything strenuous for a couple weeks. You'll be off work for a while anyway with that arm and the wound in your leg. You *could* leave the city. Doesn't Marty Vasquez have a place in Ithaca? You could go there."

Yeah, he mistily recalled the doctors warning him about the risks of raising his blood pressure, of pushing his heartrate too high. They said that he could give himself a stroke if he wasn't careful. He shivered and wiped his good hand against the white hospital gown. It felt like a web of thorns was spreading across his brain, making its way through his body, sprouting like rhododendrons inside every blood vessel.

"You know it's Yom Kippur next week. The first of October," said Sarah.

Alex startled. Suddenly, he felt more alert. *Yom Kippur?* How did that relate to the grand jury, his injuries, or Marty's house in Ithaca? "Uh, yeah." Like all Jewish holidays, it moved around, and he had never paid enough attention to the calendar to know it from one year to the next.

"I was wondering if you wanted to observe it with me. You know, come to the synagogue for at least one of the services, or maybe join me for the break-fast meal."

"What?"

"I think it would be nice if you joined me for Yom Kippur," Sarah repeated irritably. "It would be something we could do together that matters a lot to me."

Twenty-five hours of fasting and spending all day in prayer asking God to put you in the good books. Immediately, he imagined all sorts of things he would rather do. Get a catheter inserted. Have his prostate examined. Wasn't testifying before the federal grand jury atonement for the last two Goddamned decades? He had asked for forgiveness, in a way, immunity in exchange for the truth, and God couldn't grant you use immunity, only the Department of Justice. Taking a strained breath, he responded, "I haven't been to a synagogue since Dad's funeral. I'm on medication up to my eyeballs. And I don't think fasting would be good for my stomach. It feels full of acid if I don't eat."

"You don't have to fast. You'll be just out of this place. And you have a medical condition. I just think it would be nice, you know, 'cause it's an opportunity to put aside old grievances, to atone, to make a new start. Isn't that what we keep talking about? Making a new start?"

"Yeah. But you know I'm not observant."

"I know. But it's about the ritual, the history."

He scrubbed his stinging eyes and touched his throat again. It felt hot.

"It's the one thing…" Sarah glared at him. "It would be a way for us to come together. Look, the Union Temple's services won't be like the ones you went to as a kid. I'm sure. They're super chilled and free to everyone, even if you haven't been to a synagogue in years. They don't care. It's open to all Jews. Even non-observant ones. And the break-fast isn't like a formal meal or anything. It's just a big potluck at the synagogue."

"I'll think about it."

"That means you won't do it."

"No. It means I'll think about it."

"Maybe it would help you too, you know, finding wholeness, reflection, thinking about your life. Rabbi Saul is really good."

"That's what you think I need? *T'shuvah* instead of Zoloft." He instantly regretted the wiseass, his mouth running ahead of his brain.

"No, Dad. It's important to me. A thing I thought I could share with you, you know, that must mean *something* because you're still a Jew, even if you haven't been to a synagogue in twenty years. That's all."

"I said—"

"I'm trying, but you know what, do what you want."

"Honey—"

"Forget it."

"I told you, I'll think about it."

"No, you obviously don't want to."

"Sarah, knock off the passive-aggressive meshuggeneh shit. Maybe, okay?"

"Yeah." Her tone sounded flat, unconvinced.

He noticed his pulse, quick and heavy. A step upwards on the hill with Sarah, then slipping, tumbling right back to the bottom. He should man up and join her at the Yom Kippur services. Usually, he would turn to work as an excuse, but she was right – he wouldn't be at work for a while. He didn't know if he would go back to work, ever. *What?* He snapped at himself. Where did that come from? Like a strange voice in his head. Pain swelled in a molten wave inside the old gunshot wound. Yellow lights flashed before his eyes, and the room wobbled.

"Dad, you alright? Should I call a nurse?" Sarah asked.

"I'm okay," he said hoarsely. "Just really sore and tired." He should go to Yom Kippur services with her, or at least attend the damned potluck at her synagogue – like an AA meeting, but with more latkes.

"You need rest," she said. "Lots of rest."

When she'd gone, he limped into the bathroom. His leg hurt, but they hadn't told him he couldn't walk or attached him to a catheter. Clumsily, he operated doors, his gown, the toilet, all with one hand. He would have to work out new ways to do everything until he got this cast off. The overhead lights stung his eyes, the glare feeling ten times brighter than it actually was. He hazarded a sidelong glance at the mirror. The bruises on his throat looked identical to ones he'd seen on strangulation victims, the skin discolored by a patchwork of blues, yellows, dark purples. That man could have killed him. He cranked up the hot water tap as far as it would go, but it didn't pull the chills from his insides.

Yom Kippur! Had Sarah lost her mind? This Yom Kippur thing was plainly tied into the miscarriages of justice thing, Sarah's roundabout way of wanting to talk about it without really talking about it. Would she read stories, not just from New York, reporting on wrongful convictions being overturned? Did she wonder how many innocent people her father had put away? Did it cross her mind eight years ago, when the Central Park Five were exonerated? MNHS had been inescapably entangled in that mess. Would she understand that the 'voluntary' confession has always been a figment of legal imagination? No one in their right mind confesses to a detective without a little bit of coercion, and a lot more criminals would go free if the police couldn't interrogate anyone. The justices who wrote *Miranda* – or who dealt with its consequences – got that, thus 'reasonable deception' lived in the minefield of caselaw and statutes that had grown up around the Supreme Court decision. Society wanted two opposing things – offenders punished but rights upheld. Consequently, the courts had given the police leeway to bypass *Miranda,* with creativity only limited by their imaginations, so long as they paid it lip service. Like wanting sausage, but not wanting to know too much about how it's made. Defense lawyers would always accuse Alex of coercing confessions, and it went without saying that he exerted some coercion, but in that legal black box. Schrödinger's perp: when the box is shut, is the confession voluntary or involuntary? Is it even the truth?

When he imagined that conversation with Sarah, those words disintegrated, crumbling into dust somewhere between his brain and his tongue. He didn't see himself as very articulate on abstract matters of jurisprudence, or on any matter concerning Sarah.

The fluorescent lights stung his eyes, and he felt as though he was seeing the room under water. Dizzy, he tottered back to the bed, supporting himself with the wall and the wheelchair railings. A nurse meandered into his room, taking his blood pressure and noting his heart rate before drawing blood into a syringe. Should he tell her about his nausea and blurry vision? He buried his face in a pillow, which resolved the latter problem. Sarah had said it was a reaction to the GA. It should work itself out on its own.

Throughout his five or so days as inpatient, Ray, James, and Gibson hovered like moths who'd found a light. James raged, and if the perps had walked into the room, their tire iron and Stanley knife would have stood no chance against his bare fists. Gibson was mortified, mainly with herself, because she had assured him that nothing awful would happen and people would forget about it. She was also suspicious – she was too savvy a cop to be anything else. But unless Alex said – and he wasn't going to – that the men were connected to Indelicata, the Two-Four squad lieutenant seemed content with handling it like any random mugging. That guy had no intentions of stirring shit.

Today, the last day, Ray lingered in Alex's room, annoying him when he wanted peace and quiet. He paced around the place. He played at the blinds. He prodded at unused equipment. His dark Puerto Rican features were stormy, enraged, his eyes flashing.

"Don't you have anywhere to be?" Alex asked.

Ray dismissed the question. "Those perps *gotta* be associated with Indelicata. The hospital's letting you out tomorrow. You're not worried?"

"I'm not getting a presidential security detail, so there's no point in worrying." Spasms of sympathy shuddered through his body, each one for every single witness he'd threatened, begged, or manipulated into remembering something. Maybe they had good reasons not to.

"Police aren't the above the law, Alex. Your injuries aren't trivial. They need to be held responsible." Ray folded his arms over his chest.

"Responsible?" Alex laughed softly, but it sounded croaking and dry.

Ray eyeballed him, as if unsure of his sanity.

"So what if it's one of Indelicata's buddies?" Alex cackled. *Everyone* suspected it, although no one could prove it. "You find out who he is, arrest him, then the next guy's really pissed so *he* comes after me. What am I gonna do? Go into witness protection? A few people lose their jobs, maybe do some time, but there's a hundred more where they came from. I'll have to watch my back forever."

"You don't give up," Ray said mulishly. "Witnesses and informants take risks every day when they talk to *us*. But they suck it up and do it. You're right, we can't fight everything. But we take down one bad guy at a time. Like Frank Serpico."

"*Serpico,*" Alex snapped. "Fuck Serpico. If he hadn't written a book and gotten a movie out of it, where the hell would he be?"

"I don't know," Ray grumbled.

"He wouldn't be rich or famous. He'd be some guy working a bar job in North Dakota."

"But he told the truth. He made this police department *better.* He stood up for what was right. For truth and justice."

"You think anyone cares about truth and justice?" Alex growled. "Just...go. Get out of here."

"What?"

"I said, get out of here. Everyone's been here for the last four days, telling me what to do. Not just the past four days. My whole life. Do this. Get your act together. Everyone wants to squeeze something outta me. And I've given you all of it. I have nothing left, Ray, nothing. Fuck duty. Fuck accountability. My head's fucking exploding, and I want all of you to leave me alone."

Surprise shone through Ray's dark brown eyes. He moved towards the bed. "Alex, we're just—"

"Get *out,*" Alex shouted. Raising his voice fired up the pain in his throat.

"I think you need to talk to Dr. Gillard –"

"Get the fuck *out.*"

Ray stared at him with his mouth half-open.

"Please, leave me alone," Alex pled, tears leaking out of his eyes. Where the hell did those come from? What was wrong with him?

His partner's mouth worked soundlessly, as if his brain was trying out things to say, then rejecting them. Finally, he said, "Okay, Alex," in a tone suggesting that it was not 'okay.' But he withdrew, backing out the door and gently closing it.

Alex felt sickened by himself. Yelling at Ray had been out of line. But if one more person came in here and told him what to do, he would lose his temper at them too. Gibson had talked about him returning to work on limited duty in three or four weeks. Then Victor Sullivan had shown up, his slick manners discombobulating as he stuttered through an awkward apology – not taking threats to witness security seriously. He'd said that he could station US Marshals around Alex's apartment. Well, for a week or two, because federal budgets weren't unlimited. A security detail! To protect him from his own police department! He swiped at more tears.

Moaning softly at all his pain, his shoulder, his side, his leg – fuck, he could not identify a part of his body that *didn't* hurt – he rolled onto his left side. How hard would it be to OD on painkillers or go mad? One way or another, stay here longer. During previous hospital stays, he'd felt like a prisoner, desperate to be released. But getting out meant dealing with his life. He would rather stay here and avoid that, although it meant placating nursing staff who asked him about his bowel function. In the hospital, no one expects you to deal with anything.

Chapter Fifty-Four

Alex wore a scarf around his throat whenever he left his apartment. Today, he wore a white one. Scarves hid the bruises, the colors splashed across his neck like tie-dye. People would see that. They would wonder. His throat still hurt, but painkillers suppressed it to the point where he could swallow without tears.

Thankfully, a cold, wet rain pelted the city, justifying warm clothing. The scarf didn't look too absurd in Sarah's synagogue, where congregants sported scarves, suits and ties, flowing dresses, jeans and t-shirts, and baggy trousers and flappy shirts, like Charlotte Anderson had worn in the early '90s. *Charlotte!* Her face popped into his head. Freckled, with those wide blue eyes. He winced, the memory stinging. Sarah patted his arm, thinking he was struggling with his wounds. Jesus, he hadn't thought about Charlotte in years. If they'd stayed together, would his life be different? Would he have followed her down some alternative path? Living in a van? Smoking weed around campfires? He didn't know where she was. Not on Facebook. Yeah, he'd looked – who hasn't searched for their ex? For all he knew, she could be working in a corporate office somewhere. You shouldn't dwell too long on paths not taken.

Sarah held his good elbow as they advanced through the synagogue. The seating faced the ark, the large, ornate wooden cabinet at the front of the room decorated with a row of arches, Hebrew inscriptions, and the Star of David rising above gold-plated doors. She exchanged pleasantries and a few hugs, radiant with enthusiasm about the service and affection towards her congregation friends. Alex had never seen her so cheerful and warmhearted before. She introduced friends to her father. They greeted him with amiable smiles, shaking his right hand. No one asked him why he had his left arm in a sling. Outside of police precincts, people weren't that unashamedly nosy. No one would exclaim, "What the hell happened to *you?*" Civilians, even New Yorkers, were too polite. He returned their smiles and tried not to limp because he didn't want Sarah to see how sore he was.

"I'm so glad you're here," Sarah said into his ear. "This means so much to me."

Alex eked out another bleak smile. If sacrificing one day could repair one crack in their relationship, then he should try, for a change. Traditionally, you spend almost two days in the synagogue on Yom Kippur, but he would lose his mind if he subjected himself to that much self-flagellation. One day would probably break him, but Sarah seemed delighted that he'd made the effort. That should be worth it.

They squeezed into seats in the middle of the synagogue. The severe wooden chairs were meant to focus you on the service, rather than napping or daydreaming. His left shoulder ached, the muscles seizing under the sling. The upright wood at his back jammed into his spine and ribs, tweaking the old wound in his right side. Oh, well, you were meant to suffer during Yom Kippur. And he hadn't fasted like everyone else here.

"You alright?" Sarah whispered.

"Could do with a new body," he whispered back. "If I pray hard enough, will God help? Think he can exchange this for a new one?"

"Shhhh...Dad. You can't..." She scowled, disapproving of his glibness. "You've taken painkillers?"

"All the ones I'm allowed. They won't let me have any more of the fun drugs."

Sarah rolled her eyes at him, but the rabbi, draped in a heavily embroidered white cloak, had walked up to the bimah, the raised platform placed before the ark, used for Torah readings during services. All eyes of the congregation moved towards him, and conversation hushed.

"Return, return again, return to the land of your soul," he said in a sing-song voice. "Return to who you are. Return to what you are. Return to where you are born and reborn." He lowered his head towards his scrolls, now speaking in Hebrew, and members of the congregation who spoke the language answered the back-and-forth calls. Sarah murmured a few phrases. When had she learned Hebrew? Certainly not from Alex.

Switching to English, the rabbi said in a ringing voice, "For on this day of atonement shall be made for you; to cleanse you of all your sins; before the Lord you shall be cleansed."

Alex found himself setting his right hand against the stabbing pain in his ribcage, his eyelids falling until he lost sight of the short, bearded man in the white cloak raising his hands above the embroidered golden silk on the bimah.

***

He was walking east on West 190th Street. Why here, of all places? *You think you can fix it by coming back here?* A voice sneered, out of his sight. Behind him? Under those sun-bleached awnings? Before he could answer it, he started at splotches of bright red blood soaking into the sidewalk. Where was the DOA? The crime scene tape? The evidence cones? He looked at the blood again, then slid his gaze closer, towards his side. Fuck, he was bleeding! Blood poured from his wound, dripping down his leg. After all this time, the old scars had reopened. He left bloody footprints on the blackened pavement. But he could still walk, so he sped up his pace. Baffled by streets he should recognize, he turned south, nervously padding down an unfamiliar alley cluttered with Styrofoam, cans, and plastic bags. He moved lightly, warily, like he was being hunted. His foot found an old can, and it crunched, the metallic noise slashing open the eerie silence. He shuddered. Why do people in cities throw so much shit on the ground?

Like a sudden squall, dizziness roared into him. Auras brighter than the sun spiraled around beige low-rises. Choking on his own saliva, he leapt towards a little hollow formed by two dumpsters, and he sank to his knees beside an overturned shopping cart, surrounded by cigarette butts, glass bottles, and beer cans. Everything smelled faintly of urine. Knifing pain tarnished all thoughts. It consumed the alley, the dumpsters, the looming apartment blocks. He knelt against the shopping cart as if in desperate prayer to Safeway. His fingers curled around the metal cage. His mouth and the back of his throat tasted sour and rancid. But after a few minutes, he didn't feel like he was about to die anymore, although the blood had soaked through his shirt, his jacket, and warmed his thigh. He whisked dead leaves and gravel off his legs.

For some time, he wandered in a daze around Washington Heights. The hills felt steeper than usual, downright mountainous. He stopped halfway up the one on 183rd, out of breath, his legs aching. The back of his neck prickled. His heart fluttered in fast, erratic beats. The feeling inside his gut was as unpleasant and familiar as that acquaintance you never wanted to see again – the queasy dread he'd felt before the shooting, before the 1992 riot, or before the men attacked him on his stoop. The city became distorted, malevolent, and the wind reeked of decay. Alex spun around and sprinted as fast as he could along 183rd, heedless of his wounds. He ran until his lungs hurt, and his strength had burnt out. He was lost again, and he slowed his pace, confused. What street or alleyway *didn't* he know in uptown Manhattan? Surely, he'd walked every single one. Gunmetal clouds cast the city into a dismal gloom, a greyed-out twilight. He began walking with his head craned over his shoulder, one hand on his gun. Buildings faded into the deepening haze, and he couldn't see the neo-Gothic roofs and arches, the pre-Civil War columns, or the castellated towers that he'd known for twenty years. Shadows were moving, writhing out of gutters and cracks in the pavement, creeping towards him. Overtaken by panic, he scrambled down the hill, but the squirming shadows unfurled around him, and unseen fingers touched him, pulled at his limbs, trying to throw him against the concrete. His body twitched, and he fell, wanting to scream, but found no breath for screaming, no breath at all.

Sweat beaded on his forehead and trickled down his face. He held his scarf in a death grip, and he released it, stretching his aching fingers. Outside of his head, the congregation sang a Hebrew hymn. He didn't understand a word. Sarah's eyes were closed as she sang along with the cantor. For forty years, he'd never given a shit. Maybe he should have tried harder to be a better Jew. He didn't own a menorah or a single Shabbat candle. Grimacing, he tugged at the scarf again.

"Before a man is healed, he must acknowledge his illness," the rabbi said in English. "Before a person finds light, he must know his own darkness. Before a people is forgiven, it must confess its sins. We confess our sins and those of our fellow men, for we are responsible each for the other. Heal us, Lord, and lead us from darkness to light."

The cantor guided the congregation through another sing-song recitation of Hebrew hymns. Voices rose and fell with the cello and the piano. Sarah relinquished the harsh brittleness he'd always seen in her. The music carried it away. Rapturous, she smiled as she chanted the hymn, her shoulders relaxing, her whole body drawn towards the rabbi and the ark.

Alex rubbed the seized muscles in his left shoulder. Why was his hand shaking, his head light? The rabbi's words infected his brain, but they *shouldn't* mean anything to him. It was six-thousand year old propaganda, a religion like every religion he'd never believed in. Dammit, he was a street-toughened, cynical New York City detective. If he had a dollar for every perp he'd collared who claimed they'd found God, he would be living in the penthouse of the Eldorado. He'd viewed their conversions with derision. Spiritual absolution would not bring victims back to life. It would not erase decades of needless incarceration, either.

The rabbi chanted, "We have abused and betrayed. We are cruel. We have destroyed and embittered other people's lives. We were false to ourselves. We have gossiped about others and hated them. We have insulted and jeered. We have killed. We have lied. We have misled others and neglected them. We were obstinate. We have perverted and quarrelled. We have robbed and stolen. We have transgressed through unkindness. We have been both violent and weak. We have practiced extortion. We have yielded to our wrong desires, misplaced our zeal."

The congregation beat their fists into their chests at every sentence.

Alex's attention narrowed to the wound in his side, a hardened knot of pain under his ribs. His right hand rose to his chest, but he held it there, unmoving. Everything seemed faintly cloudy, as if seen through water. The inside of the synagogue rippled. He felt *himself* ripple. It happened again, like the synagogue and his own body had lost their substance, turning into a fog, with a high wind coming.

A fearsome, driving rain hurled into the glass, the drops beading, before losing cohesion and oozing downwards. A blanket of mist hung over the Financial District, and from his viewpoint on the fifteenth floor of One Hogan Place, Alex could just about identify the hazy outlines of the bridges and the taller skyscrapers – the Woolworth Building, 70 Pine Street, and 40 Wall Street. They didn't have any substance, ghost buildings rather than ones made of steel and concrete. Why here, of all places? The fallout of his testimony reverberated across every corner of his life, every case, every court appearance. It would follow him forever. Colleagues looked at him differently. Yesterday, Farah had emailed him to say she was accepting a 40.15 plea in the Gemma Lennon case – not guilty by reason of mental disease or defect. Because she didn't trust him on the stand? Because his credibility was shot? Or because the DA's forensic psychiatrist had evaluated Lennon and diagnosed her as too nuts to appreciate the nature and consequences of her actions? Farah hadn't included details. Her email had been terse, a two-sentence 'heads up.' He should email her. It wouldn't be too awkward if it only related to work. Changing her mind about the 40.15 defense might have nothing to do with him, but equally, it might have everything.

The mist outside grew denser, engulfing the bridges and the ghostly skyscrapers. Alex slouched towards the window, his shoulder pressing into the cold glass. There was nothing between his body and fifteen stories of air. He felt woozy, not knowing where the ground had gone. The window seemed too thin to hold his weight. And Farah wasn't here.

Actually, no one was. The Trial Bureau offices were chillingly silent, uninhabited but for himself and the fish in the office aquarium. He withdrew from the glass, spinning on his heel, hastening through a darkened office corridor, then he pounded the elevator buttons. *Hurry,* he thought at the elevator, working his mouth, trying to get a little moisture. *Why are you running,* he asked himself. *From who?* There was no one here! He didn't know, but he felt overwhelmed by relief when the elevator appeared. Once it delivered him to the ground floor, he raced through the unguarded security gates, fleeing the building on a crest of fear, then he ran along Centre Street until he saw the green railings of the nearest subway station, the Chambers Street J, Z line beneath the lurid classical façade of the Dinkins Municipal Building. Featureless, ashen fog curled around the building's Roman columns, so thick it looked like you could hold it. Although the street was deserted, Alex sensed forty stories of eyes watching him through the mist. He felt hunted. And a weird sense of déjà vu. *When did I feel like this before?* Sweat beaded on his forehead and tickled his sides. The hairs on his arms stood up. His lungs ached, and his breath whined in his dry throat, but he kept up his pace, staggering in a lurching gait down the stairs, into the city's bowels. The subway tunnels were desolate, at midday, as if they had been evacuated, but no FDNY or NYPD personnel had stopped him from going in. The only noises were his footsteps, his rasping breath, his racing pulse. Alarmed, he edged along the wall, sliding his shoulder and back along the smooth tiles. The main lights flickered, then died, leaving only emergency lighting and a faint sliver of daylight shining from above. He felt like he had smoke in his eyes.

Something moved in the darkness. Alex stumbled backwards and his shoulder blades struck a thick column. The shadows shifted shapelessly. Someone *had* followed him. He whipped his Glock out of its holster. Warm air brushed against his cheek, like a person breathing on him. But he hadn't heard any footsteps. A sharp blow across his side flung him against the wall, then a second blow cracked his arm and sent the gun flying. He heard it clatter across the platform but could not see where it had gone. Out of breath, he raised himself to his knees, ignoring the pain in his side as he pushed himself upright, but then he froze, hearing boots scuffling across the platform.

"Who wants me dead *today?*" he shouted into the silent subway station. He squinted through the gloom and saw the faint outline of a figure – a man, hunched pathetically, leaning on a cane. The man bent down, retrieving the Glock, then he aimed it at Alex's chest.

"You think you can get out of this by asking God for forgiveness?" The man's head turned to one side. "When so many lives have been wasted."

"What?" Alex panted. "Who the hell are you?"

"You think *they* won't realize you're crazy?" the man asked. "Someone's going to find out your secret. They could uncover all of it if they wanted." He raised the gun and pulled the trigger.

Alex screamed as the 9mm slug slammed into his chest.

"Dad? What's wrong? Are you okay?"

Alex fluttered his eyelids. He palmed his chest, clamping his damp shirt against his skin. Sweat, not blood. Sarah's hand was on his lower back. She looked worried.

"Jesus, Dad," she whispered. "You're soaking wet."

"I need some air." He'd sweated through his clothes. He clenched his jaw, then held out his right hand. It quivered like he'd been on an all-night bender for two nights. But he hadn't been shot. He wasn't bleeding out inside an abandoned subway station. He hadn't left the damned synagogue for the last three hours. Unsure, he rubbed his chest and right side, double-checking for fresh wounds.

"Let's go out for a bit," Sarah said, taking his good elbow in her hand.

The rabbi intoned a Hebrew prayer as they crept along the wall, Sarah mouthing *sorry, he's not feeling well* to a few people who eyed them curiously, and then they walked into a steady, relentless drizzle. Wind whipped along the Brooklyn streets. Sarah hesitated at the door, recoiling at the lashing rain, but Alex strode into the weather, uncaring, turning down the North Service Road and angling towards the withered trees in Prospect Park. A few stubborn leaves clung onto branches, but they were damp and shrivelled, the colors muted. He crossed Plaza Street, heading south, weaving through traffic lanes radiating around the park, then halting below the Triumphal arch guarding the plaza entrance. The Soldiers and Sailors Arch. Columbia and her four-horse chariot supervised the plaza from the top of the arch, and relief statues of Abraham Lincoln and Ulysses S. Grant, both on horseback, perched on the wings. Wheels hissed through standing water as vehicles careened around the roundabout.

Alex sank down on a square bollard in front of the arch. His gunshot wound felt alive, a wild, pulsing burn. The wind picked up, snapping at his hair and clothes, freezing his sweat. Faces pressed themselves against his brain. Hundreds of faces, names, case numbers. Some of them were guilty. Perhaps not all. *What if the forensics or witnesses were wrong?*

What if I was wrong? Hardening his heart, fortifying barricades around his soul, seemed like his best chance at surviving the violence on the street and the gross inequalities of the job, of the justice system, of the country itself. But he'd failed. After almost three decades, he'd failed. He'd tried alcohol. He'd tried exercise. He'd tried anti-depressants, and still, he could not stamp his feelings into oblivion. They pricked at him, making the smallest holes in his heart. Even the smallest hole would bleed out.

Whatever he did, people would continue killing each other over drugs, money, broken relationships, trivial disagreements, or blind rage.

Whatever he did, the system was far from infallible or trustworthy. Quixano, Norris, Serrachia, and the Central Park Five might be free, but how many other wrongfully convicted defendants languished in prison? How many more would? Could he trust himself ever again? Would anyone else? If the federal civil rights case went to trial, there would be discovery, and then he would testify in court. One day, his testimony would find daylight and cameras. He shivered. But people *should* bear witness to Vito's abuses of power. They should hear how Alex aided and abetted him. They should see that the whole damned justice system was as precarious as the ceiling in that Chinatown apartment he'd rented all those years ago.

What if he tried again? Tried to do it right. He'd tried after Quixano's conviction, and what good did that do?

Why? he asked himself. *Why are you still doing this?*

Another thought struck him like a punch to his aching throat: *They're going to find out I'm mentally ill no matter what I do now. It will be so easy for them to discredit me. Just like that cop in Queens. The man in the subway was right.*

"Dad, please, what's up?" said Sarah, a pleading note in her voice. She'd spoken before, but he hadn't heard her over the wind and his heartbeat. She huddled on the bollard, looking frozen and bedraggled. Her curls clung to one another in damp knots. "I know we fight a lot, and I've been unfair. I'm sorry. But you're really worrying me."

"I'm going to put my papers in," he said in a level voice, surprising himself.

"What?"

"I think I'm done," he breathed.

Sarah's face contorted with shock. "Dad! I know I've *said* you should retire, but are you sure? This seems so... out of nowhere. Isn't that something you should spend some time thinking about?"

"It doesn't make any difference," he said carefully. "*No one* walks away with their career intact after doing what I did. Don't know why I was stupid enough to think I would."

"What about Ray? Or Gibson? Do they know about this?" Sarah squeezed his right elbow.

He laughed, which disconcerted her. It would be months, with hours of rehab, before he could return to full duty. The break was too close to the elbow joint, making the arthritis inevitable. They didn't need to know, yet.

"You shouldn't make decisions like this on a whim," Sarah said, wiping rain off her face. "You're clearly upset. You should give it more thought."

Alex twisted his body around on the bollard. It dug into his thighs. Angrily, he jerked his arm free and sprang to his feet. Dizzy from the pain of sudden movement, he wavered above her, arms crossed like he was holding his guts in. "What do you want from me, Sarah?" he snapped. "You've been on my fucking case for five years about retiring. *Now* you're telling me to think about it?"

She sat up straight. "I just don't think you should do things impulsively after a traumatic experience."

"Impulsively?" he spat. "Jesus. I'm tired, Sarah. Fucking exhausted. My body's beat up. It hurts all the time. I can't remember the last time nothing hurt, but it must've been 1987. It's time to leave before they push me out, or someone puts me in another hospital. It's not like what your rabbi was saying in there. I can't ask God to forgive my sins, then it all gets waved away, like magic. I will pay the price. I have. With my health, my career. But at least I stayed outta federal prison."

"It doesn't seem like you've really processed this," Sarah sighed. "Any of it."

"Fuck processing. What does that even mean? I have to go." He felt ill, nausea surging like a standing wave. He wrestled it down, importuning his body to not be sick in view of his kid, or in the middle of Grand Army Plaza. Sarah was looking at him, her brown eyes starred with concern. His face must be as white as the granite arch.

"Dad," she protested. "What the hell is wrong with you?"

As she leapt upright from the bollard, he whirled towards the park, limping purposefully under the Roman arch, aiming for the 2,3 line station at the north end of the plaza. Sarah trotted after him.

"Dad! Let's go somewhere warm and dry and talk like adults."

"I need to clear my head."

"When has storming off *ever* achieved anything?" she yelled at his back. "You never want to deal with your problems. You just fucking run. You always run."

"I am dealing," he answered coldly. "Not in the way you want, maybe, but in the way I need to."

"What the fuck is that supposed mean?"

He didn't really know. "I'll call you later."

"What? In like five months?" she shouted, her voice crackling.

Maybe. That was his usual timeframe. Oh, he wished he could tell her that he loved her, or double back and return to the synagogue, like nothing had happened. When he tried to do the right thing for her, it ended up going wrong. But those waking nightmares from the services fogged up his head, and his heart pounded like it would break out of his chest. He'd been in therapy for long enough to suspect it had something to do with trauma, but if he disclosed unpredictable panic attacks and dissociative episodes to his shrink, or his kid, they would try talking him into a psych admission. *I would be an inpatient on a psych ward!* Nurses administering meds, doctors making notes of everything he did or said, his every movement controlled. It would scuttle any chance of working in law enforcement again. *Fuck that.* He had to fight this himself.

Favoring his right side, he downclimbed the subway stairs on the corner of Flatbush Street and Plaza Street. He bought a ginger ale from a vending machine inside the station. The tunnels were heated, but his clothes had become sodden, sticking to his skin, and the cold scoured through his bones. White tiles glistened under fluorescent tube lights. It was busy, New Yorkers scurrying in every direction with steely determination. To reassure himself that he wasn't hallucinating, he stroked the cool, white tiles and breathed in the fetid, dank subway scent. A silver 2 train shrieked, flying into the tunnel, then exhaling when it stopped. People squashed themselves into the train. Alex curled around his belly on an orange seat, sipping the ginger ale.

The subway lurched and rumbled towards Manhattan. An evangelical minister boarded at Wall Street, and he warned everyone in the carriage that the world would end in 2012. Some reputable source had issued a prophecy. Unimpressed subway commuters gazed at their phones, books, and newspapers. Alex stared at the splotchy yellow floor, splattered with mud and brown water. Apostles preaching to captive subway car audiences were commonplace, one of those New York things. But Alex listened to the sermon, thinking, a minister and a rabbi walk into a bar. Did they ever find a punchline? He raised one eye towards the preacher as the man declared that rivers of lava would spew from the gates of hell, the sun would fizzle out, and fires and floods would consume the planet. A lot like Alex's Skype conversations with Ellie about climate change. He should call Ellie. Undoubtedly, Sarah already had by now, to complain about him. The minister handed out leaflets promoting his church to disinterested passengers, then he disappeared at Park Place. Leaflets fluttered to the floor. The man sitting next to Alex folded one into an origami crane, Alex watching out of the corner of his eye, focusing intensely on every fold rather. But jagged shards of adrenaline impaled his veins. He rubbed his chest, where the man in the Chambers Street station had shot him. Like before, he found no blood nor injury. *It wasn't real,* he repeated to himself, pulling ragged breaths into his raw throat. *It feels like real pain. Like the wound in my side. I can't tell the difference.* If ratting on Vito to a federal grand jury wasn't a good enough reason to retire, then losing his mind should be. Raucous voices tore his attention away from the origami, his wound, and his sickness – two men standing near the end of the carriage, screaming at one another. If they started throwing punches, he would have to do something because he was still a cop. One, wearing a Hawaiian shirt, dashed through the door connecting to the next car. *Was that in my head?* Hard to tell on the subway. The conductor announced the next stop, West 72nd. That came after 66th, so the train was in the right place. Origami man exited at West 79th Street, leaving his crane on the seat. Alex picked it up. He had no idea why. Hell, he could learn how to make origami in retirement. That sent him to the clean edge of laughing and weeping again, like a madman.

Chapter Fifty-Five

Rain gave way to an unseasonably late heatwave. Heavy clouds smothered the city under a sodden wool blanket. The heat was oppressive, the air unmoving, gritty with pollution. The clouds bulged ominously, ready to explode into thunderstorms at any second, and Alex could almost believe in the end of the world. *The end of my world, anyway.* He was one stride away from plummeting over the edge. Without the job, an immeasurable void awaited. *What happens on the other side,* he asked. He couldn't see it, and the universe had no answers. All he knew was that it felt like an ending; a sad, anticlimactic one. His life fizzling out. *Himself* fizzling out. He'd organized his retirement papers. He was ignoring calls and texts from Gibson, Ray, James, and Cat. They were going to get suspicious – if they weren't already – so he should stop ducking their calls. Yet he needed a story. An excuse. A safer and less worrying reason than going mad. Something to stand between him and his illness, to protect his friends from the truth.

On a windless night, so still it felt like the weather died, his mind raced deliriously through stories, through pretexts, every one infused with suffocating sadness about the life he was leaving behind. Amidst the fuck ups, he had helped people. He'd walked with a purpose. He'd tried to quench the violence, one homicide case at a time. His chest felt tight. Then he heard his air conditioner spluttering. *Fuck,* he thought, too tired to leave the bed and fix it. The pleasant stream of cool air abruptly ceased. Why the hell hadn't he replaced that A/C years ago? And why was it eighty degrees at the beginning of October? Ellie was right – the ice caps were melting, and New York City was well on its way to being under water. When he shut his eyes, his brain played the TV news videos from New Orleans after Katrina. But New Orleans melted into New York, with people clinging helplessly to cars and debris as they floated down Broadway or Seventh Avenue.

Pain from his gunshot wound broke through his half-conscious dreams of flooded New Orleans-New York. Almost grateful, Alex heaved himself upright. First, he raided his emergency medication stash, buried inside the bowels of a cabinet, behind the cleaning products. Tramadol, leftovers from when he'd sliced open his wrist five years ago. Usually, he talked himself out of believing it lived there. He'd never trusted himself, rightly so, but he hadn't thrown out the meds, either. He casually unscrewed the cap – it had been easier when his left hand worked – and scowled at the tiny pill in his palm. Arguably, using old prescription narcotics as off-label sleeping pills wasn't wise or healthy. *Fuck it,* he said to the walls. That was before federal grand juries and men attacking him with Stanley knives and tire irons. He shoved the pill into his mouth, swallowing hard. Staying away from mind-altering substances no longer seemed so important. Yawning, he levered open his window, letting in the noise, and then he wriggled back under the sheets. But the open window offered no respite. The air outside was as stodgy as the air inside.

Still, the Tramadol lulled him into an overheated sleep, plagued with dreams so intense that he felt wide awake, shaking with adrenaline.

The apartment buzzer exploded, shattering the dreams. *Was that real?* He was never sure anymore. Disoriented, he looked at the time. 0300. What asshole was buzzing his door at 0300? Offhand, he had no idea who would do that. Not anymore. Twenty years ago, it might have been any of those reprobates in the Homicide squad, too drunk to get home from a nearby bar. The Homicide squad didn't really have reprobates anymore. The current generation of detectives weren't as wild as their predecessors in the '90s. For about five seconds, he wondered why, then he shucked his blankets aside and shuffled to the intercom. "Hello?"

"Lex, I gotta talk to you," panted Vito. His voice sounded husky with alcohol and emotion.

Fucking hell. Alex sagged against the wall, feeling his stomach writhing. *Is this real? Is Vito really at my door?* "Vito, what the hell are you doing here?" Should US Marshals have eyes on his apartment?

"We gotta talk."

"We can't. There's a criminal case. Too much legal crap. And your pals tried to kill me. Why do you think I'd want to talk to you?"

"'Legal crap.' Yeah, no fuckin' shit, man." It couldn't be a hallucination. His brain couldn't make Vito sound so much like Vito. "*I* didn't know what those guys were gonna do. They got my back, for sure, but they took it too far. Sorry—"

"*Sorry?* I have a broken arm. I blacked out—"

"*You* fuckin' ratted on me to the feds, you…" Vito ran out of breath, losing the words. "Everything's fucked up. Everything. My wife wants a divorce. She's kicked me out. My oldest kids aren't talking to me. I'm jammed up. I'm suspended. I'm indicted. What am I gonna do? What the fuck am I gonna do?"

"Your shit caught up to you," Alex said, his voice cold. "That's your problem. But US Attorney's pushing his luck with the statute of limitations thing."

"It don't matter," moaned Vito. "All that matters is that I was indicted. It don't fuckin' matter what happens next."

"You might weasel outta this. You've been weaseling out of jams your whole career."

"I ain't *weaseling* out of anything," Vito snarled, the intercom crackling. "*You* did the weaseling. You made the fuckin' deal with the feds—"

"You dragged me into your schemes, whether I wanted to be there or not."

"That's bunk, pal. *You* wanted that," Vito retorted. "You knew I was the best in the fuckin' business, and you wanted it."

Alex felt a roughened knot scratching at the inside of his throat. He let go of the intercom button, coughing. Then he pressed it again.

"No one's gonna let me investigate a case again," Vito continued in a breathless voice. "If I'm lucky and not in a fuckin' federal pen, I'm on modified assignment; I'm working parking lot security for the rest of my life, no matter what. Exiled at the impound near LaGuardia. They don't give a fuck whether it's dismissed or not. Point is, I make them look bad now. The anti-policing, liberal media's *won.* And they got to you. Can't fuckin' believe they got to you. Obama's Justice Department has it in for cops, man. Don't you get that? They used you. *We're* the bad guys, and those guys, those slingers, they're somehow the *victims.* What the fuck has happened to this country? Don't matter what the feds do or don't do or if I get convicted of these fuckin' civil rights violations. You remember what it was like, Alex? You did what you had to do. Fuck civil rights when the whole fuckin' city was a crack den."

"How long have you been drinking today?"

"All day. And last night. Ain't that your MO?"

Go to hell, Alex thought. "Go home. Sober up. If you really gotta talk, we can talk later, okay?" He had no intentions of talking to Vito, ever, and witnesses shouldn't meet with defendants during an ongoing criminal case. But he would spin any line that removed Vito from his stoop. "We can grab a coffee or something. Maybe when this is all over."

"A coffee," snorted Vito. "Jesus Christ, you've gone soft. You sound like an Upper West Side Jew."

The indictment hadn't changed Vito's casual anti-Semitism. "I've been an Upper West Side Jew for twenty years. We're not gonna do this at three in the morning."

"You were a good cop once, Lex," Vito said, sounding saddened. "Now I don't think I know you anymore."

Then silence. Alex jammed his finger against the button, saying, "Vito? Vito?" Silence. He ran to the window. The street below was quiet. He saw parked cars, a Prius taxi crawling down the road, a young woman in a short skirt and platform heels walking arm-in-arm with a young man in a plaid shirt and skinny jeans.

His mind ran on eight cylinders. He lay awake on his back, hands folded over his churning stomach, eyeballs glued to the ceiling. What was Vito doing here? Being wasted, obviously. What had he wanted? He was too drunk to know himself. What would he have done if Alex had let him in? Should Alex let him in? No, absolutely not. Vito lived in the Rockaways. The Upper West Side was a strange place for him to be at 3am. If his wife had thrown him out, he was probably sleeping in the Three-Four's dorm. Subways ran 24/7 in the city that never sleeps, and Vito had the same lackadaisical attitude about drunk driving that he had about due process and marriage fidelity.

The sharp report of a gunshot sliced open the stagnant night. It sent a shock into Alex's chest. An icy shiver blasted through his spine and limbs, shaking every muscle. He stopped breathing. When had he heard gunshots near his apartment? Never, in twenty years. It must be a car backfiring, or someone launching a firework. But dammit, it *sounded* like a gunshot. A cop ought to know the difference between a gunshot and a firework. Alex strained his ears, listening for more worrying noises, but the West Side chamber orchestra resumed: cars, distant sirens, planes. Had it been a real gunshot? God knows, he'd been hearing gunshots that weren't there for two decades. He pushed two fingers into his carotid. His pulse pumped along at an even pace. Not a panic attack, because his heart wasn't racing. He had no idea what it was. In his head or otherwise, it morphed his insomnia into an unruly, anxious beast. Desperate to sedate it, he swallowed another half-Tramadol, just 10mg more. A dangerous habit, this flirting with narcotics, but Vito Indelicata didn't buzz his door every night.

50mg of Tramadol travelling around his bloodstream lulled him into a blank, dreamless sleep. Somewhere, a live wire touched his heart, shocking him into consciousness. The buzzer screaming. *Again? Son of a bitch.* Was that real? It buzzed a second time. Vito returning? More of his sleazy acolytes at the door? The clock on the bedside table read 0500. Alex groggily listed into the hallway, holding himself upright with the wall, and he stabbed his finger into the intercom button. "What?"

"Sorry to wake you, Detective Boswell," said a female voice. She had a faint South Asian accent, and she sounded professional, serious, and slightly recognizable. "This is Detective Suryakantam Sherazi with the Night Watch. Can we come in?"

Alex's tongue felt woolly. He knew her. From some party? The friend of a friend? Someone who had been on one of those John Jay training courses for new DNA evidence protocols or using social media for criminal investigations? There weren't *that* many female Indian detectives in the department. He should recognize her. Confused, he mumbled, "Yeah, sure," as he buzzed her in. An itch on his thigh stung him, and he realized he was wearing boxers and nothing else, so he dashed into the bedroom, flinging on a t-shirt and sweatpants as fast as he could, one-handed. With gritted teeth, he buckled his sling around his shoulder. As much as he hated wearing it, the arm hurt less when supported by the thing. When he had one foot out the door, he whirled around mid-stride, seizing a bandana from the cluttered floor, then he tied it loosely around his neck. It stank of sweat. Better that than the Night Watch detective seeing the bruises.

If Night Watch had been called to a homicide, they would notify MNHS in the morning, when the eight-by-four started. That was the point of Night Watch. But they were here at 0500. The panic bubbled up from his gut, the acid rising into his throat. Sarah worked night shifts in the Roosevelt. Anything could have happened. The only reason Night Watch would bang on his door at 5am. To notify him. It didn't take much imagination to picture the worst things. He'd been a homicide detective for too long. And he'd shouted at her! He'd been irrationally angry. During Yom Kippur, of all times! So much for atonement. Why hadn't he called her afterwards? His heart sped up like it was on the last furlong of a race. Sweat glued his shirt to his sides and belly as he paced around the living room for the two minutes it took the Night Watch detective to climb the stairs. The longest two minutes of his life.

"Hi, Boswell," said Sherazi. She wore a black leather jacket and tight black jeans. Her gold shield dangled on a lanyard around her neck, gleaming in the stairwell's white lights. Yes, he knew her: Suri Sherazi. Cat Silver's girlfriend. She'd been a white shield with the Two-Four detective squad before her promotion to detective and transfer to Night Watch.

"What's going on?" Alex said, flattening out his voice.

"Vito Indelicata." Sherazi spoke in a clipped, nervous tone. "He was found DOA a couple blocks from here. West 88th and Broadway. A witness called 911 because they thought they heard a gunshot."

"Fuck." Alex went cold. His emotions flew all over the place, but he couldn't process information. It wasn't Sarah. Thank God it wasn't Sarah. He felt his rapid heartbeat slowing down.

"I knew you lived at this address," Sherazi went on. "You know, because of Cat. We were here for that party you had last year. I can't think of any other reason Indelicata would have come to this neighborhood from the Rockaways at this time of night. I mean, I can, like maybe he had a mistress or was moonlighting somewhere here or something, but, well, this was the first reason I came up with. I was wondering if you knew anything."

"Fuck," Alex repeated, barely registering the young detective's nervousness or her clear-headed intuition. "This is real, isn't it?"

"Yes," acknowledged Sherazi in a baffled tone. "What else would it be?"

"Indelicata came here," Alex said, breathlessly shooting ahead before Sherazi could follow up with more questions about his sense of reality. "He came here a couple hours ago and buzzed the door. He was wasted and wanted to talk. It was three am... I told him no. Fuck. Was it a stick-up job? What happened?"

"Don't know yet," Sherazi replied uneasily.

"Can I see the scene?"

It was against every protocol imaginable for the cops securing the scene to let witnesses look around, but Sherazi, being an inexperienced detective, awestruck by a Homicide veteran, uncomfortably abandoned both protocol and SOP. Alex knew that he should not do this, but he gave in to his morbid curiosity and shock.

"Don't tell Cat," he said.

"No, I won't."

"Or anyone. I'm not here."

"Ten-four." She knew they were blowing off protocol as well as he did.

They walked west, towards Broadway. Police car lights broadcast the scene, shooting off flares of dazzling red and blue strobe lights. A few cops he knew nodded at him, like he was meant to be here. No one challenged him. The sweatpants and the sling holding his arm should have been clues that he wasn't on duty. Unhindered, he ducked under the blue and white tape, but then wavered. Shit, this was stupid, impulsive, and if criminal charges ever came out of it, problematic. Did it occur to anyone else that he was balls-deep in conflicts-of-interest? He looked like a middle-aged, paunchy white guy with a broken arm, wearing navy blue sweatpants, a grey CBGB t-shirt, and a red bandana around his neck. He did not look like a homicide detective. If the Two-Four precinct squad wanted Homicide's assistance, they should bring in someone with no conflicts-of-interest, an A or C team detective, or one from a different Homicide squad altogether. Yet his feet took him forwards as if his body couldn't be bothered with his mind's objections.

Vito lay crumpled on his side, and a glistening lake of fresh blood pooled around his head. Alex's eyes immediately focused on the dark hole in his temple. Blood and tissue and white bony specks had splatted into a grotesque halo. Nausea belted through him in a spasmodic surge. *Oh, God, please no.* He screwed his eyes closed as he pled with his stomach to stay down.

"You alright?" asked Sherazi, seeing him hesitate and lose color.

"Yeah," he wheezed.

Fighting through his gastric upset, he squatted on his haunches, close to the body. Cloudy black powder burns formed a ring around Vito's wound. The shot had been at close range, the muzzle against his head. Sooty scuff marks marred the fingers of his right hand. Gunshot residue? An old, uncleaned gun might do that. No torn clothing, no dirt marks on his clothes, no scratches or bruises anywhere in plain sight. The firearm in question was probably the one adjacent to Vito's outstretched hand. An old Smith and Wesson 4506 from the early '90s. Blood and pale brain matter flecked both its dark barrel and Vito's white hand and forearm.

Sherazi saw him looking at the gun. "I don't think that's NYPD issued."

"Yeah, they woulda taken that off him when they suspended him," Alex said softly. "But Vito had a few of his own guns."

"Could that be one of them?"

"I think so." A hazy memory from long ago surfaced: Vito showing off a 4506 he'd recently purchased. They were in the Three-Four station house at 0100 hours, Vito waving the gun around, saying, *Look at this piece!* "It'll be registered to him." Firearm safety hadn't been Vito's forte, either.

"You sure? Would he keep an illegal firearm?"

"I don't know. Yeah, possibly." That unliftable weight pressed down onto Alex's breastbone. He wouldn't put it past Vito. If the man needed a drop piece, he wouldn't register it with the state of New York. "Who called it in?"

"Someone in number 1242 reported a gunshot to 911. But they hid with their family in a closet and didn't come out to look."

"That's the difference between Washington Heights and the Upper West Side," Alex quipped dryly. "In the Heights, everyone comes out to look."

"True. It was responding officers who found him."

"And the wit who made that call knew for sure it was a gunshot without seeing anything?"

"Said he'd been in Iraq." Sherazi fretted at the shield around her neck. She'd been an intelligence officer in Afghanistan before joining the NYPD. "If you know that sound, you know that sound."

Yes, it was unforgettable, unmistakable. Pain ignited in his right side, awakened by the memory, not helped by the awkward way he'd contorted his body to crouch over Vito; far enough away to not contaminate evidence (given he wore no PPE), but close enough to assess the wounds. "Gotcha. Any other wits?"

"Not yet. It's five in the morning in a quiet neighborhood. Did you hear anything?"

"Yeah, I heard a shot. I thought maybe I was hearing things... I sometimes..." Again, he stopped himself before he mentioned his illness. "I've been living here since 1990, and I've never heard shots fired in this neighborhood."

"Do you know what time?"

"Between three and five."

Nausea, shock, and an injudicious, strange trace of grief jostled for space in his head alongside the professionalism and emotional distance with which he approached DOAs. Instinctively, he worked the scene. Single close range shot to the head, probable GSR and blowback on the hands, no evidence of a fight. Vito had been trapped, his career in tatters, facing federal criminal proceedings, or a trial by internet if nothing else. What would Alex do under those circumstances? What would anyone do?

"What do you think?" asked Sherazi, restlessly rocking from one foot to the other.

"You can't say for sure at this stage," Alex replied in a low voice, stiffly rising to his feet, then moving back from Vito. How unfamiliar he looked in death. Small and frail, like the real Vito had disappeared as soon as the shot blasted through his head, replaced by a withered, pale replica that had lost Vito's essence. "But you'd better interview me. As a witness."

Sherazi squared her shoulders, reminded of her job: keeping the scene contained and interviewing witnesses when their memories were still fresh. Chastened, she fished out a memo book.

"He buzzed my door at three am, three-thirty, something like that," Alex recounted. "He was drunk off his ass. Wanted to talk to me. Said his life was falling apart. Said the indictment was my fault. I told him we'd talk later. I didn't let him in. I obviously can't talk to him because of, you know, the civil rights case. Then he said something like, 'You were a good cop once, Lex. Now I don't think I know you anymore,' and that was it."

"He left after saying that?"

"Yeah." Guilt cut into his bowels. If he'd let Vito into his apartment, would the man have killed himself? Not here and not tonight at any rate. On the other hand, Vito had been running around the city at 3am, drunk, with a loaded firearm. Why? As a death investigator, you have to ask yourself those questions. It squeezed the blood flowing into his heart until he felt weak and even queasier.

"And then you heard the shot?" Sherazi asked.

"No. Not immediately." The detective's questions pulled his attention away from that line of enquiry, thank God. "Maybe like half an hour, or an hour later. I tried to get back to sleep, so I'm really not sure. Look, I should go. I'm sorry, I'm a witness. I'm compromising your case. You don't wanna be in shit for mishandling a potential crime scene."

Sherazi gave him an imploring look. "Do you really think it's a crime scene?"

"No." Alex bared his teeth in a pained grimace. "Doubt it. But you gotta treat it like it is."

"Right. Yeah. Shit. I need to test your hands for GSR. Sorry. You know the routine. It's just you may have been the last person to see him—"

"I know," he interrupted, perfectly aware of the procedures they weren't really following. "Hand," he added. "The left one doesn't work."

"Oh, yeah. I see that. It's broken?"

"My forearm's held together with plates and screws. I couldn't grip anything if I wanted to."

Looking flustered, she grabbed some adhesive stubs from the evidence kit in her car. "When was the last time you were at the firing range?"

"I dunno. Like two months ago."

"You haven't fired or been near a weapon that's been fired in the last three-to-six hours?"

Lassitude rolled over him like a slow-moving tank. "I haven't changed brake pads on any cars, either."

"Yeah, you know all the questions." She nervously fumbled with the test kit.

He rested his flank against the car, holding his right arm out, and Sherazi dabbed the hand and forearm with the stubs. They pulled at his skin and hair.

"Sorry," she repeated as she secured the stubs in baggies. "I don't mean to treat you like a suspect."

"It's fine." God, he felt anemic and numb. He knew from his long years of being on the other side of this that the emotions, whatever they were, would come later.

Sherazi scribbled his cell number in her memo book, and then, after he'd restated that he should not be here, he turned his back on the scene, limping at a measured pace underneath crepuscular streetlights, passing the shadowed rows of 19th century townhouses with arches, cornicing, and balustrades looking chillingly Gothic in the pre-dawn haze. His legs didn't feel like they belonged to him. He lowered himself onto his stoop, chilled to his core even though the air was tepid and muggy. Birds were chirping, and morning commuters were already roaming the streets. The sky lightened to a smoky grey, a cloudy dawn, while the city lights melted into oncoming daylight. The night was ending, like so many other torturous nights that had dragged on forever, but just when he thought he might never see another morning, dawn streaked across the sky. Dawn even showed up when he'd put his gun to his head. Twice. The first time after Pete Norris' interrogation, and the second after a severe PTSD attack. His heart kicked at his chest, jumpy, erratic. Those feelings were as dangerous as his Glock: psychic pain more agonizing than any physical injury, his life unravelling, an irresistible hunger to not feel it anymore. But he'd never worked up the chutzpah to pull the trigger. Was that it? Were cowardice and guilt the only things that held him back from eating his gun? His shrink disagreed. Like a motivational poster in a corporate office, she always told him that courage lay in surmounting the pain. In treating the illness and living alongside it. In accepting that there was no such thing as straight or easy path when you've got a major mood disorder.

As if it heard his thoughts, his iPhone chirped with an email from Elana: she wrote that she might come to New York City as a visiting fellow, but first, he should fix his relationship with Sarah, which meant reaching out to her. Why hadn't he? She was upset about the Yom Kippur service. In Ellie's view, he should call Sarah *right now* and deal with that mess.

Damn her, didn't she understand that he was sick? Obviously not to its full extent. That was his fault – he hadn't told Sarah *why* he had a meltdown at the service. He couldn't unpack that baggage for himself, so he hadn't opened it for anyone, least of all his kids. Nevermind – he would deal with family later. He let the phone tumble onto his thigh without answering Ellie's email.

From the stoop, he saw the blinding red and blue squad car lights cavorting at the end of the block. At 0800 hours, the Two-Four detective squad would take control of the scene. They would bring in Homicide because a cop was dead. A suicide, most likely, but asses had to be well covered. The A team would investigate because they were on the eight-by-four catching cases. The media would lose their collective minds, Vito's life and death easily worth a made-for-TV movie or an HBO series. He would be bigger in death than he was in life. Yet the US Attorney had lost the man central to his conspiracy case, the poster boy for abuses of power, sleaze, corruption. Would the charges hold up against the others? In criminal court, who could say, but the wrongfully convicted men were still suing the NYPD, so they might get compensated, albeit without the visceral satisfaction of retributive justice.

Vito's suicide made sense in a way – his final act saving himself from taking responsibility, pretty much his MO for his whole career. There would be more questions for Alex: *Did you suspect Detective Indelicata was suicidal?* God, no, it had never occurred to him – Vito had too much hubris for that. Alex heard Vito's gruff Brooklyn accent sneering about his weak resolve when it came to doing the same thing. *What kind of man are you,* as if the precinct detective's voice susurrated through the traffic and the ginkgo trees. *Fuck off, Vito,* he thought, gagging on a lump inside his throat. Christ, he was speaking to dead people now. He curled forward over his thighs, which sent hot, biting pains through his side. It made it hard to think.

Inevitably, the investigation would close, the press would lose interest, and the police department would agonize over giving Vito an inspector's funeral, with its bagpipes, dress uniforms, and helicopter flyovers, or keeping it low-key. Alex would agonize over going or not. Doubled over on his stoop with his good arm around his knees, he felt like he'd gained second sight.

An inexplicable feeling of serenity – or perhaps shock and Tramadol – blanketed him as the sun ascended through the townhouses and the high-rise apartment buildings, the sandstone flushing burnished red, the New York heat boiling off the low clouds. The roiling nausea began to fade. The thorns inside his head stopped burrowing into his brain. His breathing grew steadier. He savored the peace on West 87th and within himself while he could. Undeniably shock, but he would take it. It wouldn't last very long.

Glossary of NYPD jargon and acronyms

AntiCrime – A plainclothes NYPD unit designed to catch crimes in progress.

BOLO – 'Be on the lookout for.' A broadcast issued to police officers with information about a wanted suspect or missing person or person of interest.

***Brady* material** – Exculpatory evidence that the state must turn over to the defendant under the US Supreme Court ruling *Brady v. Maryland.*

Bus – An ambulance.

CPL – Criminal Procedure Law.

CI – Confidential informant.

Collar – An arrest. It can be a verb – **to collar** someone – or a noun referring to the person who has been arrested.

Command discipline (C/D) – Disciplinary action imposed against an NYPD officer by their commanding officer. Penalties range from verbal warnings to forfeiture of up to ten days' vacation time, depending on the seriousness of the misconduct and the officer's disciplinary history and performance record.

CSU – Crime Scene Unit. NYPD detectives trained to gather evidence at a crime scene.

DCJS – Division of Criminal Justice Services. It has a variety of core functions but in the context of this book, it's mainly the database of criminal history records in New York state.

DD-5 – A complaint follow-up form used by detectives in an ongoing investigation, written whenever they do anything on a case. It's an in-house colloquialism that is somewhat anachronistic, as the original acronym, 'Detective Division Five,' has not existed for more than forty years. The current paperwork is an 'omniform complaint revision' and 'complaint follow-up informational,' but people still call them DD-5s or 'fives.

DEA – The Detective's Endowment Association, the union to which all NYPD detectives belong. Not to be confused with the Drug Enforcement Agency.

DOA – Dead on arrival, used as a noun, referring to a dead body, or an adjective, to describe someone dead by the time first responders arrive. "He is a DOA" versus "He is DOA."

Drop piece – A gun planted at a questionable police shooting to justify the officer's use of deadly force.

DV – Domestic violence.

ESU – Emergency Services Unit. The NYPD equivalent of the SWAT team.

FINEST – The teletype unit that links precincts and various departmental branches and communicates notable events, retirements, etc.

First officer – The first police officer to arrive at a crime scene.

Flake – To plant evidence on an innocent person.

Flashing tin – When a police officer identifies themselves by showing someone their badge.

Forthwith – NYPD jargon for 'do it immediately.'

Four-by-twelve/eight-by-four – Most NYPD detectives have a four-day shift pattern where they work two days from 1600 to midnight, two days from 0800 to 1600, and then they get two days off before the pattern starts again. A four-day period is called a **set,** and a single shift is called a **tour.**

Gold shield – The NYPD detective's badge. 'Getting one's gold shield' means making detective.

Grade – first/second/third – The rank of detective in the NYPD is bestowed purely on merit, not via any exam or other test (whereas cops take exams in order to be promoted to sergeant, lieutenant, captain). The three detective grades refer to the salary and general prestige the detective receives – with third grade being the lowest, the pay equivalent to police officer; second grade in the middle, the pay equivalent to a sergeant; and first grade the highest, the pay equivalent to a lieutenant. However, detectives of all grades still hold the same rank as police officer (unless they've passed the tests to become sergeants, etc.). Promotions to second and first grade are given on merit, at the discretion of the Commissioner. Grades, or even the gold shield itself, can be revoked due to misconduct.

Grounder – A case that's easy to solve.

Hairbag – A veteran cop who is bitter, burned out, and putting as little effort into the job as possible.

House Cat – A cop that never leaves the station house.

Juice – Slang for power and influence.

MDT – The in-car computer system.

Mope – Slang for perpetrator.

NCIC – National Crime Information Center. An electronic repository of crime data, accessible to every criminal justice agency in the United States. You can upload data in 21 files (or categories), which is then available to other federal and state law enforcement agencies.

Night Watch – A squad of NYPD detectives handling felonies between 0100 and 0800, when precinct and other specialized squads are off duty. At the start of the eight-by-four, they kick it to a precinct squad and/or to the appropriate unit.

NYSIIS – The criminal identification number you receive once you're arrested and in the system.

OLBS – Online Booking System. Records the offense, the arrest location, and other detailed information about the perpetrator.

Penal Law – The New York state criminal code. Describes elements of all felonies and misdemeanors.

Perp – Perpetrator

Precinct detective – A detective who works out of an NYPD precinct house, rather than with a specialized unit, and they investigate a wide range of crimes within their precinct's boundaries.

Rap sheet – Someone's criminal history.

RDO – Regular Day Off. NYPD acronym for days off work.

Redball – A high-profile case, one with lots of media attention.

RMP – Radio Mobile Patrol. The ubiquitous blue and white NYPD police cars.

SAFIS – The NYPD fingerprint database.

Shield – The NYPD badge.

Shitcan – To dismiss or bury or otherwise not do something, like paperwork, or investigating a case.

Skel – A derogatory term used to describe junkies and the homeless. William Safire states, "It is a shortening of skellum meaning a rascal or thief, akin to a skelder, 'to beg on the streets," first used in print by Ben Johnson in 1599, after the playwright got out of jail for killing a man in a duel.

Stick-up job – An armed robbery.

Staging area – An area outwith the crime scene, but cordoned off from the general public, for officials who will be conducting the investigation to convene and organize before entering the primary scene.

Supreme Court (New York County Supreme Court, Criminal Term) – The branch of the New York court system that adjudicates felony cases. Criminal Court adjudicates misdemeanors, and in Manhattan, both are located at 100 Centre Street, confusingly called the Criminal Courts Building. The NY Supreme Court is a court of general jurisdiction (the first court that hears a case), which isn't to be confused with the US Supreme Court or any other appellate court. For added complexity, Criminal Court handles arraignments for *all* incoming cases, including felonies. Transferring a case to Supreme Court requires a grand jury indictment, and then a second arraignment in front of a Supreme Court judge following indictment. The courts are divided into **parts,** which are units or divisions handling different stages or types of the criminal litigation process. **Part** is also used to refer to the physical courtroom where the legal proceeding occurs as well as the judge who hears it.

TARU – Technical Assistance Response Unit. They provide investigative technical equipment for wiretaps and other forms of surveillance and support all NYPD bureaus.

Ten codes – NYPD radio code, used to provide security for broadcast and speed up exchange of information.

Ten-four – Ten code for "I hear and will comply." Often used colloquially to mean "understood."

Ten-fifty-four – Ten code for an ambulance case.

Ten-thirteen – Ten code for an officer in distress and in need of immediate assistance.

The Tombs – Colloquial name for the Manhattan Detention Complex.

TNT – Tactical Narcotics Team. A drug enforcement program that flooded the streets with undercover officers, who would conduct buy-and-bust operations and arrest mostly low-level dealers.

UF-61 – A criminal complaint report.

Whodunit – A case that's difficult, if not impossible to solve.

Wire – Both NYPD slang for 'the grapevine' and shorthand for wiretap.

Printed in Great Britain
by Amazon